Path of a Guardian

Parts I & II

Saga Book I

Ramkus the Wanderer

By J. C. Anzarut

<u>Path of a Guardian</u>

There is no beginning, and there is no end. One journey, delicately balanced between life and death; but never an end. And so it begins, with no start, only an event. A time before, though, went something like this: a moth drawn along a beam of light, moving with another in the dance of movement, till one drops. It is replaced, and the dance continues; but forever along this beam of light the moth will travel. It is its nature, its dhamma, its attachment, its life, its journey; one with no beginning, and no end.

Awakened under the gaze of stars, the cry of the wind, willing the wanderer onward from his slumber. It was but a small meditation. The stars were moving, the sky floating as the electricity in the night air pulsed and buzzed. Up he rose, from his rocky perch, a path to a distant mountain lay straight in front. The path itself enclosed by a never-ending tree line, lit by a cyan light from a focussed moon. As large a path it was, the trees seeking fair distances from one another, grass and dirt. This was a familiar road, tread all too often. Nothing new on this ever-present path. The wanderer was once again ready. Ready for that great mystery of the next step. He knew he did not, could not, ever possess himself. A solitary movement of the cosmos, on its chaotic will; that is what all life was. What was next for him?

Seated at a table in a desert tea stop, overlooking the pale blue sky as it settled into dusk. The light changing from the blue to a stormy simmering orange; a warning of the heat that lay further inside this land. He watched the small fishing vessels, poised white top sails, caressing the sea; calmed, happy to end the day under the watchful eye of the sun.

The wanderer remembered, reminisced, felt a pang that tied him to a time before; a time that may not yet be even. Following this path of life as it took hold of him. He even felt an attachment to a woman whom he felt he knew in a different time, one that he felt familiar to, for visions he often had at times. Sometimes they were the same, and at other times different. In any case, he felt he had wandered hand in hand along life's mysterious paths, for a least a moment, with another.

In a villa, secure from the deluge of rain, the jungle steamed with a heaviness in the exotic heat. Crossed legged on the bamboo wood, the wanderer had a spark that ignited his mind. A vision of what may be, or already was. It enveloped his mind wholly, for it hit him as had often these visions done – with emotion. It was a reality, whether for this life or for another. How was he to know, he did what he felt - nay knew! - was his purpose, his journey. Nothing could prevent him from this, and it would only make him sick with unease to purposely stop. To stop, that was a true death; that was a true end. Death itself, he was ready for, for it did not mean the end to him; it was yet another journey. This was his life.

Paused on the beach, as calm waves lapped the shore. Lights from a coastal village, not too far from where he was positioned, helped direct his way. The twilight from the moon helped create a dream land for him, a land which he had moved through time and time again. He was pensive, for he was sure he felt an attraction for a woman, as he had done lifetimes before. Lifetimes he seemed to recollect, or thought he did. The same emotion aroused each time. To stay in this place, to leave the wandering life, it was to deny him own life, his own purpose. Could he, for a time, live and be merry, or was he to remain a drifting life force, doing his purpose for whatever it was that made sense to him. Would it affect his next life? What in fact would that entail, he wondered. He knew what it would be: he was a wanderer, through life, and through death; always wandering.

CONTENTS

Part I

The Awoken

Chapter I

He awoke in a field. The wind mercurially dancing with the trees in the surrounding forest, the long grass thrashing violently. It was a force to behold, one of life, one that filled him with existence. His chest rising, his senses creating a cacophony of feelings. Eyes open to the sky, a molten display of dark clouds rolling, thundering along; and as he raised himself slightly, he could see he was in a slanted field on a hill, and this chaotic force was withdrawing down towards an ocean that lay beyond the forest in front of his feet. He could see much from this vantage point, forests surrounded, left and right, front and behind. To his right, smoke, climbing to become one with the chaos above. It was coming from some chimney pyres in a small hamlet, well protected by the dense tree line. The little arena of buildings held no more than a handful of constructs. Sturdy and seemingly inviting, with the glow from embers in the hearths radiating through small glass pane windows.

The wind subsided abruptly, and the sight of the fires burning in the homes and buildings grew warmer and more inviting. He rose, mentally taking in the frame of his body, his length, his body's lines, its contours and sinews, along with his clothes. He wore a dark heavy shirt over hardy trousers, a greyish cloak, boots that were invariably sturdy. To his side was a large stick: a staff! Black with golden tipped ends, writing scrawled in the same gold coming down from the edges. He picked it up, not sure of his balance and movement, but he was adept, controlled: he was fit, and he could move. He found the staff to be light and manoeuvrable in his hands. He headed to the village, which began to feel as if it wanted to embrace him, shield him from the elements. The clouds started to menace and rage, twisting in torment, wanting to unleash a ferocious storm.

Getting closer to the village, he saw movement coming from a distinct building, a humble one with bluestone layering the bottom half of the exterior up to the windows which leaked embers of light.

The rest of the building was painted wood, up to the eaves. What really drew his attention, though, was that there were people! He saw their shadowed movements in the windows, sounds of debate, discussion, laughter. He judged it was the beginning of the evening, and the people were gathering to revel in their days' effort.

Approaching with neither caution nor care, he walked towards the door of the lively establishment where two men stood, smoking, laughing, drinking, and eyeing him with curiosity.

'And what might bring this stranger then?' asked one of the men warmly. He was rather rotund, red in the face, smiling from under a bucket hat and full of glee at his merry situation.

The other chimed in, his appearance was akin to his friends, save for his pudgy red nose, and his balding head being exposed. 'I ain't seen you before. You surely couldna' come from the forest? There be nothin' between here and the North for an 'undred miles!'

'No,' replied the man who had only just awoken from a field, acknowledging his existence for the first time. He had not considered where he was *coming from*, or *going to*, this world was completely new to him, and he to himself. *Who was he?* He stood for a moment, as the two men cautiously looked at each other, a little confused themselves but inebriated enough from their drink to feel they were to follow some etiquette and invite him into their little village inn.

As the man pondered these questions, he looked around the circular assembly of half dozen or so buildings which a road traced through the middle of. He took in the barks, the neighs, the clucks, the buzzing of insects, the chirping of swallows. *Who was he? Where was he?* He inhaled heavily and smelt the fresh air of the field, infused with the smoke of log fires. He exhaled.

'Where is this place?' he finally added.

The two were taken aback a little, as the delay in response had rendered them dumbfounded.

'This be our inn,' the man with the bucket hat answered, 'and this be the best inn for near an 'undred miles around!' The Awoken noted that the term *hundred miles around* seemed in regular use, and that it was likely these men had never journeyed far from this village.

'No, I meant this village, where are we?' the Awoken asked.

The pudgy nosed man replied, 'This be the village of Abergrass. We are of the most Northern point of Eastern plains of Elantra, err.' He scratched behind his ear and pointed, 'The seas of Pintos are East, and err, anything further up is almost constantly battered by the elements, no one would want go round there!' he exclaimed.

'What is Elantra?' came the next question from the stranger to these parts. The two men gave a puzzled look and a playful laugh to each other; the Awoken had pressed for information that seemed to show his odd predicament.

'Elantra be the whole of these lands, all that rests between the seas and mountains, all that man has set foot on… err, that we know of for certain,' the pudgy nosed man answered, surprising himself with his answer. He opened his eyes quite wide and then began squinting at his audience as if trying to draw some deep thoughts he once had on the topic from the fathoms of his consciousness. 'Elantra is the lands we live on,' he continued, but wasn't helping himself any further, he hadn't been required to explain such information before, and yet he felt he should know how to answer. He began looking to the ground and scratching behind his ear again, questioning himself now with a grunt.

The Awoken looked around at the trees, he knew them as pine: *How do I know that information, or that these buildings were made from old blue stone, and that the sign above the building reads "the more the welcome at Abergrass Inn!"?* He was able to make sense of the world, or at least particular details of it. He regarded the men with a little suspicion now: *Do they know anything about me? Could they be any help? Could the small bit of information they have stated be true?*

The man with the floppy bucket hat belched by accident and gave a little chuckle, consequently replying 'S'cuse me, I think I need 'nother - and some grub. Would you like to join us inside? It'll start rainin' soon, see it's beginnin' t' spit!'

The Awoken turned to peer inside; the embrace of the warm glow and the sounds of laughter from the crowd were too tempting to decline. 'Yes, thank you,' he replied.

He felt he belonged inside, not with the elements – or rather, against them.

The man with the bucket hat turned to his friend and gave a little wink and smile, the Awoken sensed it was in good humour, as he felt he could *read* this person. They stepped inside and were immediately greeted by the warmth of the numerous fireplaces that were about the place. Just inside the front door was a corridor that had a number of hooks with cloaks and hats resting upon them. The Awoken felt obliged to leave his cloak on the wall, as well as his staff resting next to it. The interior of the inn was of polished wood, with a low ceiling that added to a sense of cosiness and warmth.

The man with the bucket hat noted the staff the Awoken had brought to rest with a curious glance, exclaiming, 'That there be a beautiful piece of crafting, err, you got there. Must have cost you a pretty penny, eh?' He turned to the Awoken but did not get a response, nor a smile, only a small look of bemusement. The Awoken thought to himself: *Is it?* He had no idea, as he looked back at it himself.

The corridor ended with a stair case. Two doorways on either side opening into large rooms with roaring fires set in the fireplaces. Benches, tables, and seats were set for the patrons who were huddling around. There were cosy spots built next to the windows, where people were holding private conversations. The room on the left held its fireplace directly across from the large doorway; many books were set atop the mantle place above it. To the right of it was the bar and Innkeeper, moving about with the wait staff, tankards and plates clattering, acrobatically held so as to accommodate the localised movements of the crew. There was a massive fire behind the bar, with a number of meats being rested above it. The Awoken was shown to a seat by his newly made acquaintances.

'Fleureb! Three meads n' some meat n' bread please,' yelled the man in the bucket hat to the Innkeeper who was preoccupied directing his staff as to which tables certain meals and drinks were heading.

'Right with you, Rab!' the Innkeeper, a round balding man with an auburn moustache, yelled back without looking.

The Awoken realised the bucket hat man held as much interest in him as his other friend. That is, they were both looking as if they were about to tuck their chins into the chests and nod off.

The Awoken took in the room: it was decorated with numerous paintings of far off scenery, hung on the skerricks of wall space between the windows. It was a cheerful place, and it must have been able to hold the whole of the little village, along with some of the villagers from the surrounds. In fact, most of the village may well have been inside the inn at the time, for many men and women were already cajoling in the early hours of the evening, a few children were running about with dogs. A few people, however, looked out of place. Ruffians, about three of them in the dozen and a half people that were in the room. *Travellers? Merchants? Who knows,* the Awoken thought. They noticed his glare and left for the other room.

His eye pricked up as he noticed another man with an elegant manner. This man had well waxed, black-as-midnight moustache, and wore a large black brimmed hat over curly black hair, and a black suede suit to match. He was somewhat on the younger side of middle age, with cheerful brown eyes that seemed to exude a cheeky persona. On his lap rested a beautifully crafted wooden musical instrument with strings down its body.

The Awoken's attention was brought back to the table, as three tankards were brought around. As he stared at the polished metal that held the frothing amber liquid, he spied his reflection for the first time. Not very well, but it was the first conscious sense of being a *self* in this world that he had experienced; of being a *person* of this world. He looked up an about the mantel place where the books sat above the fire; a mirror was there. He got up from his seat as his friends were about to toast, and headed towards the vision that, in turn, walked towards him. He took in his reflection, *himself,* for the first time. Light brown/dark blonde shoulder length hair hung over staunch, powerful, broad shoulders, a sharp jawline, raised cheekbones, deep inquisitive blue eyes that held a determined gaze, a strong, prominent nose. He - as best he could judge – was actually a rather attractive man. A few of the patrons were looking at him over their tankards in amusement as he walked back. His acquaintances quietly took in this peculiar behaviour as the norm of a people in some far-off land they had never met until this stranger was invited to share their company.

The man in the black suede suit was well aware of this small trivial event, keeping a friendly set of eyes on the Awoken, under his broad, black brimmed hat.

The pudgy nosed man spoke in a friendly tone, 'I daresay, you look as if you hadn't seen yourself for a good year with the way you been behavin'.'

'Kerf, don't be insulting our new friend 'ere,' scolded Rab.

The Awoken felt he ought to explain his predicament, but he was overcome with a degree of hesitation. Too many questions lingered: *Who are these men for me to answer any questions to.* Laughter from the room on the other side of the corridor reverberated through the already loud room they were in.

Their food arrived.

'To our new friend,' Kerf cried suddenly, raising his tankard, Rab followed suit. The Awoken raised his, smashing them together with the others as seemed to be the custom.

The fermented fruity drink tasted both sweet and bitter on his tongue, rather delicious, especially for the first taste he had experienced. The others began breaking the bread and picking at the meat. The sensation in the Awoken's mouth when he bit into the juicy morsel of meat and sourdough bread was of pure delight, he was instantly gratified.

'What is this?' he asked.

'I s'pose it be beef,' Rab answered, looking squarely at the meat as if it held all the mysteries of life. He then looked to the Awoken and squinted, as if to intimate that a serious conversation was to take place. 'Without meanin' to be rude, what be your name, friend? This 'ere be Kerf, and I be Rab.'

Very much flummoxed, the Awoken realised he had no idea: *Who on earth am I?* Overcome by the hospitality that had already been shown, realising that his oddities were taking a toll on these men whom were seemingly enjoying their evening before he stumbled upon them, he thought it best to explain the short tale that was his existence – as best as to his knowledge.

'I do not know,' he said simply, 'you see, I don't really know what I am meant to know. I found myself lying in the field beside this village. I just woke up and walked here. I know nothing of before.' His eyes drew in, contemplating, not sure how to feel, for he only knew the emotions - or rather feelings - of being cold and warm.

The other two looked at each other in bemusement. The room they were in was starting to get darker and feel more confined. The glow of the fires and candles paraded around, creating silhouettes. His friends did not know what to say.

Rab started, looking down his nose, and then at the man who had risen seemingly anew, as if he were the gods work. 'I don't know what to make of it. Been in tha' field this morn, stretching me legs out before potterin' away at me work. Didna' see you then. Doubt I would have missed you either as I took a nice long stroll around and through. Great view at the top...' Rab slowed his speech, becoming lost in his thoughts before realising he was with company. 'But what I be meanin' to tell you is, I have not the answers for you, nor do I know what else to say!' he imparted.

In the corner of the inn's room, the man in black got up from his table, and strolled out into the corridor, all the while keeping an eye on the two local chaps and the Awoken. As soon as he had a quick look in the corridor, he about faced and came to the table of the three men.

'I am sorry to disturb you my dear fellows, but I could not help but watch and wonder if your friend here,' he placed a nicely manicured hand on the Awoken's shoulder, 'is one of those *men of the Guardian's Seat*? That order of, diplomats, if you will, that seem to descend from the heavens. Simply *appear* on earth without rhyme nor reason. Of no background, no ties, no lineage.' The man in black suede spoke with eloquence and moved with a grace and manner not befitting of a village tavern. He also seemingly held a greater knowledge of the world and its inhabitants than these villagers.

Rab and Kerf knew not what to say, as the inquisition - which was more of an introduction - seemed to give them some respite from what was becoming a very awkward evening on the drink.

'Were you listening to what I had said?' asked the Awoken in a casual tone. He felt no trepidation, nor any discomfort towards this well to do gentleman. *Why should I? Why should I feel anything at all? Who indeed am I myself? Do I need to be anyone? Did I need to be?* His mind raced around, delivering questions that spun round and round; questions he had no answer for. He was becoming anxious and annoyed at what he *should* know.

'Yes, I did eavesdrop I am afraid. I'm sorry if this has caused offence, but you... well, I have not seen *you* before, and I suspect you *are* of the travelling type - like myself. All these roads that throw many surprises and obstacles, not to mention people. The individuals whom travel them have a sense of others akin to themselves, at least this far up North. There is only one path this way after all! But I am digressing, not only did I eavesdrop, but I admired the staff you have left in the corridor... *a Guardian's staff.* I know a little about you, or rather your *brethren* - if you call them that in the Order. I have met one or two on the roads.'

The Awoken was somewhat shocked, but pleased and readying himself for what information may be forthcoming.

The well to do man with his large black hat caught the eye of the Innkeeper, winked, and continued. 'My name is Felipe, and I must excuse myself for a few minutes as it is time for my performance.' With a smile, Felipe strolled to a corner of the bar with bravado and poise, looking upon all those whom had been sitting inside.

Beaming a smile, he struck a bell by the bar to get everyone's attention, signalling that conversations should be ended or be

lowered as his performance was about to start. Patrons from the
room on the other side of the inn began to saunter in, whilst the
Awoken sat anxiously, having to wait for answers a little bit longer.
Rab and Kerf were through with their drinks, the Awoken felt he
should follow their lead. He did not enjoy the bitter aftertaste and
reached for the bread and meat to cleanse his palette. He swiftly
finished and looked to the other two who were beginning to open and
shut their eyes in a slow drawn out process, as if about to fall asleep.
They had also become sluggish in movement, but wore big dim
smiles on their red faces.

The crowd had all filtered in, now numbering about forty. Rain
began to patter outside. It was a very jovial scene, as everyone was
warmed by the cosy setting, with the rip-roaring fireplace combating
the heavy droplets on the windows and the ground outside. That
general surrender to a hard day's toils. The crowd were quickly
getting their tankards filled and grabbing snacks to nibble on before
Felipe was to play; he eyed them all with patience until they were
settled and prepared for him to take their attention.

'My dear friends,' he began with a powerful enchanting voice, 'I
wish to entreat you to some stories and music, brought from afar.
From distant, and not so distant times.' He began to play his six
stringed, wooden instrument. Plucking and strumming with his right
hand, whilst his left matched the tempo, placing fingers at certain
intervals on the frets of the skinny neck of the apparatus.

'He does play that guitar wonderfully, 'e does,' Kerf sighed,
mesmerised. It may have been that this performance was simply
something else to focus on other than a conversation he had little
more to add to, but it was evident that he, and Rab, were much more
relaxed listening to the show.

Felipe continued to play, sitting, with the guitar resting on his left leg
which was raised upon a stool he had placed at his front. It was
strapped from the bottom of the body to top of the neck, so could be
played whilst moving. However, Felipe looked intent on caressing
the instrument, as if a lover, instead of raising it from his embrace.

He suddenly broke into song: '*On the waters of our times once drifted two lovers. The maiden Elissandra, the other, Keilorudder.*' The Awoken listened intently, lost in the words, following the rhythm, the music, the sound of the instrument. They held a pure quality that asked no questions of him, did not require anything of him, only that he move his current state to a more blissful place. The music and performance continued, and the crowd – not only Rab and Kerf – were entranced, following the story and music. The Awoken turned his sight around the room, at all the different people, all the individuals. They knew things, they knew who they were. *Or do they?* He was lost in his questions of self and identity, whether it in fact meant anything. Then the idea of purpose came. He wondered what his *purpose* was. His eyes trailed back to Felipe, whom was positioned to his side. He realised Felipe was actually singing of this Keilorudder's purpose: to fight for his *love*, Elissandra; to move the waters of time; to chase her, to face her, to be with her. And nothing would stop him.

Love, thought the Awoken, he understood the word, but could not fathom it, could not appreciate it. However, he could feel that *pursuit*, to travel to the ends of the world for something. Internally he knew he had a purpose - the idea began to twist as if a knave in his gut, and angst was flaring up - he would follow this *purpose* to where he needed, to where it willed him. *What is this* purpose *though?* The internal angst grew, and all he could do to stop the inner turmoil that threatened him was turn and listen to the music. He calmed himself with the melody, following it once more, following Felipe's subtle movements of body and face. His fingers pranced along the fret board, and the Awoken was in awe of his ability. He wanted to be able to play like that, to save people from their thoughts, to move them. He recalled Felipe's brief words before taking to the stage, that he was of an *Order*? *How?* So many thoughts were running through his mind again, questions that could not be answered it seemed. He was able to speak, to read, to understand. He wore clothes, had a staff, a body; yet, no name.

Felipe finished up his performance to the arduous applause of the crowd. They yelled and whistled in appreciation of a job well done. The Innkeeper smiled, patting himself on the back for a good job by purely supplying the performer for his venue.

The crowd disbursed back to their original positions and rooms, whilst Felipe walked over to the Awoken and his company.

'Now, what was I to tell you? Oh, of who you are, of course!' He said with a cheeky grin.

Rab and Kerf were just as interested to hear what the bard had to tell as the Awoken was.

'You say you just *woke up* in the fields outside?' Felipe gave a wry smile. 'Then you know very little of whom you are, indeed what you are… I daresay you do not even know your own name?' He winked to Ramkus's look of astonishment as to how this man should know such things. 'You do have one, mind you, a name, for you require one to fit in with all people of this world. The earth from which you came commands this. Nay, not the earth, the cosmos! Your staff, it has a number of runes on it which are, well, either your staff's name, or yours. Not that you are bound to the staff, but it is something each Guardian starts off with… as the legend goes.'

Astounded by this information, the Awoken stared back for a brief moment, before raising himself from the table, and heading to the corridor to retrieve his staff. The shadows danced around, as he looked up and down the corridor in great anticipation for it, and the runes written thereupon…

The staff, it was no longer there!

The Awoken did a double check, re-tracing his movements in his mind. An anger surged through him as he gritted his teeth. He recollected the scene in the room he was just in, no one had handled it in there. He stomped towards the opening to the bar room on the other side of the corridor.

The Awoken immediately spotted the glowing golden ends as they dazzled, reflecting the light of candles. A group of five men, dressed in tawdry clothing, sat around a table in the corner, laughing and cursing, handing the staff around to one another to play around with.

They were the type that most people would dismiss immediately with disgust, the type no one would want to deal with, let alone meddle. The Awoken had not seen them at the performance. Naturally, they were not of the type of disposition to be interested in music and entertainment, finding no relaxation or use in it. Their only comfort was only in drinking and joking around with one another, for they lacked a temperance of the mind.

The Awoken approached the group. A voice in the back of his mind, nary but a feeling, an odd knowledge, urged not to attack. But there was also an anger, it had a voice too, and it whispered to him that he: *"Teach these arses who you are, what you are."*

'That staff,' the Awoken exclaimed in a low, foreboding voice that had strength and purpose in it, 'belongs to me.'

The men, who had been acting smugly, smiling to themselves with an air of arrogance, turned to him. One of the men snatched the staff from the table. He had short, stubbly reddened hair which was joined to his beard, a rugged, snarling face which matched his powerfully built frame that had been shaped through hard labour.

'Oo says it is theirs? You?' He started to smile with arrogance once more. 'And oo you be? This staff is ours, and ain't no one is taking it away from us!' The man began to clench his teeth, rocking his head from side to side as he rolled his shoulders.

'What on earth are you actually saying?' Felipe opined from behind to Awoken, 'I wouldn't bother trying to claim something that is clearly not yours, especially when you cannot make a claim to it due to your poor speech.'

The man grimaced, and his companions – who were all as hefty as he – got up at once, looking menacingly at the two *intruders*. The other patrons also got up, but rather to leave the room and out of the way should the tension escalate. Felipe was smiling happily, the Awoken was wondering what the hell had just happened. *Why would Felipe decide to prod these thugs?* He began to ready himself for a fight due to the damn bard's input.

'Give him back his staff, lest you wish to feel the wrath of a **Guardian!**' Felipe threatened.

'He ain't no Guardian,' protested the man, 'otherwise 'ed 'ave guardianed the staff!'

Felipe rolled his eyes, 'So you basically have admitted to taking an unguarded staff. Have a look at it, what kind of staff do you think you are admiring?'

Veins were beginning to develop along the thug's temple as he went red.

'Stop this!' the Innkeeper ran in. 'We'll not tolerate fighting in here. If fisticuffs is what you're looking for, do it outside, and never come back to this establishment!' He noticed Felipe standing among those in the tense argument.

'Monsieur Felipe, what is going on here? You're not part of this ruckus, are you?'

'No, my good man,' Felipe chuckled, patting him on the shoulder, 'at least not yet… My friend here has had his staff misplaced by these *gentlemen*. He was merely asking for it back.'

A number of the other patrons were gathering around the Innkeeper, locals wanting to make sure *one of their own*, one whom was of such an important and esteemed posting in the little village, was not harmed.

The leader of the troop looked at the Innkeeper. Then to Felipe. Then to the Awoken. He shrugged and threw the staff with force - and without looking - over to the Awoken. He then spat on the ground and grumbled under his breath, 'If we ever see you again, you'll be in for it.'

Felipe turned to the Awoken, smiling he patted him on the back turning him around towards the door. Rab and Kerf had been watching at the back of the group that had gathered, smiling drunkenly. The small assembly of villagers, ready to defend their beloved Innkeeper, started to file out.

The Innkeeper still stood there, 'Don't you start any trouble, Monsieur Felipe, this isn't one of those brawler's taverns, and I intend to keep it that way!' He looked to the Awoken, then stared back to Felipe to make his point, and walked out.

Felipe bowed after him before turning on his toes. 'Now let us see what the *Gods of the Cosmos* have ordained you to be known as,' he picked up the black staff with golden ends. The Awoken noticed the golden rune characters shining in the light: his name!

After a brief moment to build intrigue, Felipe studied the staff, then smiled to the Awoken… 'Ramkus!' he exclaimed with an air of fascination and a wide, gleeful smile. His eyes sharpened and focussed behind the newly named, 'Ramkus!'

A sensation, a feeling, sent the Guardian ducking and turning. Clenching his fist as his feet shifted in a circular motion to face what was behind him, he pivoted his hips.

He felt an arm touch the tips of his hair as it flew overhead, his own fist connected with someone's ribs. He pivoted his hips again, drawing his fist further into the body, breaking the bones, pushing through the torso. A voice of anger called to Ramkus: ***"Punish him more!"*** it cried!

The person whom he had hit keeled over on the ground, crying in agony. It was the brute from the table he had just had words with. He was panting and grunting as he moved on his knees. His band of men who had been behind him, expecting not to have to resort to any action themselves, looked at each other in bewilderment. Ramkus stood with his fists clenched at his sides, daring them for the next strike. The men picked up their comrade in haste, exiting outside under the eaves of the inn, cursing, not wanting to move out into the downpour of rain they were now faced with, but also not feeling very welcome back inside.

The Innkeeper quickly ran by and closed the door in their faces – the initial intention was not to let a draught in. Ramkus was in shock, his reflexes and actions had been so unexpected by all those around, himself included! How did he know how to move like that, to fight, to read a situation which could not be seen but felt. *And to react in such a way?*

Felipe was beaming with glee now. 'Ramkus, the legend, is born!' he cried. 'I am sure people here will be talking of this incident the rest of their lives,' he whispered mockingly, 'not much happens out this way…'

Ramkus could not understand why Felipe was so excited. He had just floored a man and broken his ribs, making him spit blood onto the ground – as well as his boot. He did not want to have caused such injuries, but that was his instinctive actions.

He felt foul.

'And so, my name is given with blood on my hands,' he said morosely.

Felipe chuckled and rolled his eyes, 'Don't be so melodramatic. There is much you need to be told. For one, you Guardians are ready born fighters, some of the best ever. You fight like warriors, not for gain, nor for game or sport, but because it is necessary to whom you are. Now, shall we sit and shall I explain the whole situation as it is – or as much as I know and can tell?'

Ramkus nodded and walked back in a small daze to the table they had been seated at. Eyes were all on him now, as the commotion had been witnessed by a few patrons and word had already spread around the inn. Rab and Kerf were even redder than before, drunk and merry, ready for an enchanting tale to be told by the bard; and to hold, in their own gaze, this somewhat heroic character of the story right here at *their table*, in *their inn*! Those whom had just been bested by this hero and fled outside – as per the chatter amongst the people – were supposedly a band of brigands. Not the worst type, though, for they had been permitted entry into Abergrass's little inn without any genuine hesitation, but were an awful nuisance to those who journeyed the highways between towns and villages.

The Innkeeper brought some ale to the table, 'I ain't seen anyone floor a man with one punch to the gut before, very light work you made of him.' The Innkeeper was – as most people in the hall – a little in awe. Ramkus thought to himself Felipe wasn't just joking, very little must actually happen in Abergrass: *This event does seem like it will be spoken of for quite some time.*

Felipe, whom had been holding Ramkus's staff, sat in patience with an air of grace and mystique.

26

He began once more after everyone appeared to have settled, 'Ramkus, as I said before, I know little of whom your people are, even less of yourself. You are what the people of Elantra call a Guardian. I am not sure if this is what your people call yourselves, but all Guardians begin their journeys in the same manner: "*The wind blows, and the breath of life fills you.*" At least that is what I have been told. You come from nothing, but are fully grown. You can speak, read and write, think, fight, feel. By feel, I mean you can *assess*, or *know*, the situations that surround you. At the very least, you can read them a lot better than many others; it is a trait of high intellect.'

Ramkus took in the information, but was unfulfilled. 'Yes, but what purpose do I serve? I still have little understanding of what I am meant to be or do, from what you have just said.'

'Ha, who really knows these things?' Felipe answered, laughing and looking at Kerf and Rab for some support in his philosophical quip. He got none, as the two were only absorbing what was being said, not ready to calculate that a response was required from them.

'You do have a purpose, as all people do,' Felipe continued, solemn now. 'Your people are seen as diplomats, intermediaries between kingdoms. You halt wars, adjudge and adjudicate situations and disputes; you are well respected for this, and it is in this manner I have met a few Guardians. You come from no lineage, you belong to no kingdom, so you are seen as impartial and neutral. Not to mention your instinctive fighting skills are well known, should the need arise.'

Ramkus was looking at the tankard he had not yet touched; the foam still sitting atop in a fluffy cloud that would not let anyone regard what was below. For one to do so, to delve deeper into the unknown, they would have to part what sat so perfectly above the drink. He was deep in thought, wondering about what he was being told, processing the information, this knowledge, wanting so many more answers. *How do I know what I am being told is the truth?* He could *read* the situation according to Felipe. He laughed a little as he thought this over, feeling that he was actually very fortunate to be in such good company, as if the Gods had predestined these first few vital moments of his existence in order to provide him with enough information that he required, or as far as he knew it.

'You call them *my people*, yet they are not of the same lineage or, of the same lands as each other?' he finally began to converse.

'Alright, Order, Guild, House, I don't know exactly what you call yourselves, only the idea of all being Guardians, and being of an Order. You're meant to be rather secretive, conservative. From legends that have been told, there is a central place for *your people*, a *Seat* as it is oft called, on a mountain somewhere far away from here. If anything, that is your purpose, to get there, to learn who you are,' Felipe answered as best he could.

'Assuming we all "awaken" in the same places, I should have found some of *my Order* waiting for me?' Ramkus mused.

'I cannot answer you that, Ramkus, as I said before, it has only been small pieces of information - nay, legends - that I have picked up on my travels. Those other Guardians I have met were not too forthcoming. The answers you seek are far from here. I daresay you are lucky enough that I was around to give you this much…' he said with a slight twitch of a smile to one side of his mouth.

Ramkus considered this for a moment, this *mission*, to seek out this mountain where his *people* were. It was a shame Felipe knew little more than this, but it was a start, and he was indeed lucky to have that much. He looked around the room at the people, and to the window that held only glimmers of life outdoors. In him stirred an urge, to move forward, to see what more was out there… **"NOW."** Was this not the normal assessment of what should be done? To make haste to his destination rather than sit in an inn and drink? He looked at Kerf and Rab, and at the crowd that was surrounding the table in an ad hoc circle so as to eavesdrop on the conversation. He was distinctly different from these people, it was apparent to him already.

'I do not know exactly where this place is,' Felipe continued, 'but it is most surely South of here, or maybe North… But definitely West…ish, I think. Out into the open world!' he frowned. 'To tell you the truth, I also would have thought there would be a better manner in which you people would summon or collect you, for there must be a certain education or schooling that I am guessing you go through to be cemented as a Guardian. You would have to go through some sort training, for look at you! No offence, but you do not seem to have any clue yourself as to whom or what you are. That is something we are taught from birth, really...'

Ramkus shrugged, 'Perhaps. Who knows, I can only believe what you are telling me. If anything, I do have an angst, to move, to hit the roads and see what is in this world I have arisen to. That place might as well be my destination. But the urge, to move forward, that is all I have to go on right now, none of this need of an education. I do admit I would like some things answered, though, but to see this world, that is what I desire for now.' He stated this resolutely, without emotion, letting the situation unfold for him.

Felipe bared his teeth in a wide brimmed smile. 'To wander, basically? Ah, I cannot blame you. It is what I do, travel, moving to and fro, seeing the world, drinking, admiring... It has been a little dull for *entertainment* here, though, so I shall be heading off soon. If you wish to wander these lands, you're more than welcome to join me to the next town, I shall be heading off tomorrow.'

Ramkus thought to himself, agreeing to the invitation. *A wanderer I shall be, I suppose*, he smiled to himself. There was a rush of excitement. It was as if he had been going through all the motions a man should, almost a *remembering* of who he was by pure feeling. There was a lull in the conversation in which both men took to their drink, eyeing each other in a friendly, but interpretative manner. Rab and Kerf were almost asleep.

'You two look like you'd better get back to your beds,' Felipe encouraged them to make a move. They both started nodding. They did not get up until Felipe - who also gestured to Ramkus to follow suit – got up. 'I bid you fine gentlemen a good evening,' Felipe said, bowing in an exaggerated movement.

Ramkus bowed his head to them also, and the two inebriated gents began bowing themselves, with Kerf beginning to hiccup. Once the two locals made their way out, Felipe handed Ramkus his staff that he had been holding the whole time.

'I daresay you haven't a place to stay this evening? No bother, you may bunk in my room.'

'Should I not get my own room?' Ramkus replied.

'Have you the money?' Felipe chuckled. 'The job does not pay too well in these small parts: food and board with a few coins if you're lucky. Which reminds me.' Felipe ushered Ramkus to stay, as he went and spoke to the Innkeeper, who pulled Felipe's guitar from behind the bar, and handed him a key. Ramkus was then led by Felipe up some stairs at the end of the corridor separating the two bar rooms, and up into an attic space with the key. There was a cot and some hay, which gave the impression the room was mostly for storage.

Felipe lit a candle. 'Yes, this is the bard's life, Ramkus. At least I get to see the world and be part of some defining moments in it.' He smiled to himself as he lay down on the cot and beckoned Ramkus to the hay. There was just enough for a makeshift bed.

'I have another performance in a bit, but I could not be bothered sitting any longer with those drunkards, having to perform for them and their dim-witted minds.' Felipe's mood became quite sinister and cynical, leaving Ramkus to wonder who this man was exactly. 'I prefer the courts,' Felipe continued, 'but, it's very rare to get that opportunity. And you must always keep moving, because of, well, *necessity*. I cannot wait to get to another capital where there are real people, and merchants' daughters. *You know what I mean?*' He laughed but realised quite soon after that his audience did not *know what he meant*. He considered this for a moment, that most things were still to unfold and be experienced by his new acquaintance...

But he already has those natural reflexes imprinted, not to mention the legendary *– as far as tales me be believed - fighting abilities. This could be very useful on the roads... Some extra protection never went astray.* He smiled inwardly.

The roads had been becoming more treacherous. Forced from the places they once inhabited: brigands, vagabonds, highwaymen, bandits, whatever they may be called, could not fight against an ever-expanding Empire which had enabled its people obtain control of others' lands. It's ever expanding influence and culture. Where else were the original inhabitants to go? How were they to fend for themselves if they did not want to suit up under the Empire's banner. He quickly recognised that his new *friend* would be a most useful ally on these roads. He knew that it would be easy to convince Ramkus, to befriend him, have him join him on the path.

And with a friend who is a Guardian, imagine the engagements a bard could be invited to, the diplomatic scenes, the stories, the women. He was getting a little carried away, not getting the exact calming of the mind he'd been after by coming up to the room. Still, he was well pleased to have a few moments respite from the crowds. It also gave Ramkus an opportunity to settle down for a bit too.

How would it feel to have become, *as he had?! To have awoken with no sense of identity, yet the tools necessary to live, nay, thrive in this world!* Felipe scratched his face as he stared at the ceiling. *Does the first impression count or is there an innate desire to be somewhere, to be someone, a duty*, he continued to wonder. He started to play his guitar a little without any direction or heed to what he was doing. He found it relaxing, a meditation at times when he had no need to play and entertain. He had always been deeply moved by music, and he could see Ramkus – who was grappling with his own thoughts – relaxing too.

He had not even considered that Ramkus was anything but a Guardian. He had just offered him the chance to accompany him, to travel into some rather dangerous terrain without even contemplation that he may not be all that he seemed… Felipe looked at Ramkus and decided that even if Ramkus was not a Guardian, the way he was tempted by music suggested he was not someone who – at the worst - would rob and beat him up once they hit the road - definitely not the type to take advantage of him. Even if he wasn't a Guardian, he was still welcome to join the bards travels for a time.

'The music Felipe, I cannot express how it seems to affect me.' Ramkus uttered out of the throes of his self-absorption.

A grin reached the edges of Felipe's mouth, 'Not many can. That is music my friend,' he chuckled. 'It is itself a mystery of life. Nay, it is life! A different form at least. I am pleased it affects you so. Happy and relaxed, I'm sure.'

'Would I be able to play?' Ramkus suddenly asked aloud.

Felipe had never actually been asked such a question by anyone whilst on his journey, and he presumed it was merely a hypothetical as to whether Ramkus actually could play. 'Of course you could. How *well*, though, is the real question.'

'Would you be able to teach me a little?' Ramkus asked.

Has this newly awoken, wandering soul decided to first thing he saw – lifestyle wise – was for him? It intrigued and beguiled Felipe, 'Yes, yes, of course.' Felipe's grin widened, he could see this working to his benefit. All those closed doors suddenly opening because of a *chance* find. 'But first, I must perform, and then I think it may be best to *hit the hay* for an early rise,' he winked.

They made their way down from the makeshift room and to the main tavern area again. Ramkus saw Kerf and Rab were still in the process of leaving, stumbling out the door, drunk and merry, arm in arm humming and smacking into the walls as they went out into the rain and off into the distance.

'Those two drunkards, lovely chaps, but there is not much talk in them,' the Innkeeper said behind Ramkus. 'Aye, they are pleasant, but try talking to em night in and out. They serve each other awright though.' He paused, 'I don't know if I actually thanked you for getting those louts out of here,' his manner became somewhat sombre. 'And, err, you ought to know they will probably remember the scuffle, although I wouldn't actually call it one at all. They will probably try and make an example of you... Just a word of warning to you, err, kind sir.'

Ramkus's eyes became intent and focussed, his face stone, gritting his teeth; he had already made enemies it seemed. 'Thank you, for the warning,' he said, tilting his head rigidly.

The Innkeeper backed away a little, unsure, timid of the stranger. 'I should also add,' the Innkeeper continued, 'those two chaps, err, Rab and Kerf, paid for your drinks and feed, for what it's worth. Kind of them, although I doubt they actually knew they were paying.'

'I shall thank them at some stage then, if I ever get to see them.' Ramkus answered a little curtly, unsure himself as to the uneasiness of the Innkeeper, but he continued to stand facing Ramkus, seemingly wanting to say something more. Ramkus kept his eyes on him, curiously.

'Monsieur Felipe said you might be a Guardian. Is that true?' he finally blurted out.

'I do not know. I don't seem to know anything, and I don't know if I should be angry about that, or as I actually do feel now: just as. No emotion, only racking my mind for answers to questions that seem to come from all angles,' Ramkus said, grinding his teeth now. The Innkeeper did not seem to think anything of it.

'Well, I'd like t' shake your hand anyway... We ain't seen a Guardian in these parts in a very, very long time... If at all! Some say they are Guardians, but they may just be bandits attempting to exert some authority. For you see, *your type* are legendary heroes in these 'ere parts.' The Innkeeper extended his hand and looked rather red faced and chuffed at the experience. Ramkus shook his hand questioningly.

'As I said, I don't know if I am. I don't even know what Guardians do.'

The bell sounded, and a performance was about to get underway again. The Innkeeper answered the *rhetorical* question, knowing he had only a few words he could say before having to return to the bar. 'You *fix* things, you stand in the middle of either side and make things right.' He was not sure he whether he was making sense, and quickly added, 'Diplomatically of course. At least that is what I can remember of you.' He looked to the bar, then back to Ramkus, and with a nod and smile, headed off to his duties.

Ramkus stood in the doorway as people wished to get past, so he moved just a little inside in order to get a view himself. Crossing his arms, resting his back against the wall, he tried to calm his mind for all the new questions that would be come to him. The fire radiated with heat, people were happy, content, silently consumed by the music being played. Silhouettes danced around the room, and rain fell lightly outside. He did not even know what he should be thinking now, what priority should overtake his consciousness. Perhaps he would find most of his answers at this *Seat* the Guardians were meant to be at. Even if he wasn't a Guardian, they would know something, *would they not?* Some insight into his strange origin; borne of nothing, arisen from the earth, awoken by the wind. The music began to overcome his troubled mind, calming him, relaxing his body. He let it take control, a seemingly natural reaction. It felt like an answer to his being.

Chapter II

Setting off on horseback, they made their way underneath the low glow of the stars, and the hum of the heavens. It was early morning, and there was little movement, save for a few carts in the streets. The smell of wet earth and the damp trees gave the air a heavy, pure taste. A few candles were lit inside bluestone cottages that were surrounded by serene small gardens. The homes were scattered down the road from the central part of the town where the Abergrass Inn stood. For about a mile it was a mixture of sparse woodland and fields. In one of the houses Ramkus saw the two affable chaps from last night mucking about with their window open, looking a little worse for wear. Ramkus raised his staff above his head in salutation, incidentally finding it a little difficult to ride with whilst in the saddle. Rab and Kerf looked out, pleased to see their acquaintance from night before, waving back with as much gusto as they could muster. Ramkus and Felipe moved along at a constant pace, whilst the sun decided to raise itself from slumber and provide light for the land.

Their path always seemed to be continuously travelling across the side of a hill, sloping down towards the direction of the sea, miles away. The road was only wide enough for two horses to travel side by side. It opened up onto a field and let loose the mysteries of what lay ahead. The path was to go down – as far as Ramkus could make out that it was indeed the same path – to sea level, then through a forest range. Further ahead, a good twenty miles off, he could make out a sizable town with a river flowing through it. Beyond this, hills, fields, lakes, forests, all making up a picturesque vista. The farthest his sight could discern was a mass of mountains, the peaks of which extended into the clouds which hung low in the sky as if it was descending. He could have peered further, had a morning mist of sorts not blocked the full range.

They had been lucky at the inn, for the Innkeeper wished to pay homage to one of the *legendary Guardian heroes* who had just blessed his inn, and had offered to sell Ramkus an old horse at a reasonably discounted price. Felipe, wanting to keep his ties with Ramkus, paid the sum for him. He also felt the kindness to buy Ramkus his breakfast and provisions for the road. *I will be compensated in the end,* he figured. *This will be my lucky break!* Felipe was - as he knew all too well in his wandering mind - sick of travelling through places like Abergrass. This last trip was an attempt to remember, to reinvigorate that adventuring spirit in him. It hadn't.

He found himself craving the luxuries of a court, not the scraps of a bed in an out of the way blimp on the map.

To stop him from following along those heavy thoughts of desire, he began to make idle chit chat, mostly to himself than to Ramkus. 'It really is an odd place that Abergrass. Seems to be where a lot of people whom don't quite *fit in* move, or those who are treated *differently* than others. Take for example those two you had been speaking to last night. The Innkeeper said that they live together – as evidenced before – neither wanting a wife. Content to live together and produce pottery and glassware, *apparently.*'

'What is wrong with a life like that?' Ramkus queried, finding himself coming naturally to the defence of the two. 'Why should people not do as they please? Enjoy their lives as they see fit?'

'It is frowned upon in these parts, or rather, not so much these parts but the further we move into the Empires territory. I meant no offence to them.' Felipe recognised the reproachfulness in Ramkus response, 'I was only making an observation. I cannot understand anyone who would want to live this far out from the luxuries and pleasures of society.'

'You are asking the wrong person,' Ramkus said soberly.

Their horses began the slow downward slope towards the forest. The long grass in the fields had dried out; it looked lifeless against the pink sky horizon that began to glow in sunlit picture. The clouds were lifting from the mountains in the distance, revealing a striking juxtaposition between the black rock and white snow. It shone vividly against the sky, becoming a breath-taking marker for the land. The lushness of the fields beyond, and the reflective glass dams that were dotted about the path ahead, gave an air of cleanliness, of calmness. As Felipe was hinting at, this area they had come from was rather a drab place, abusively beaten by the wind, drained by the elements, its colour was not as picturesque as what lay ahead. Still though, there was life there, stubborn and strong, resilient and continuing. Indeed, one may still say homely, but definitely not bustling with vibrancy and energy, such as what seemed to catch the eye on the path in front of them.

'I guess in time you will see. Abergrass really is one of the last bastions on the outer limits of our endurance. In winter, it is cut off from the rest of the world, impassable. I suppose one of the reasons nobody ventures there - nor the residents away from it - is that they are able to keep to themselves remarkably well. Nobody need bring supplies, as they can muster up anything they need. That being one reason there is no need to upgrade the roads to make it passable in the snow and frost.'

Ramkus, although listening, had nothing to add. He was in a better frame of mind than when he first started speaking. He had made up his mind that he needed to get to this mountain where his *people*, his *brethren*, were. That is, if he actually was a Guardian.

'Where is the *Guardians Mountain*, the *Seat of the Guardians* you spoke of last evening?' he asked Felipe. 'Can you point out the general direction?'

'Ah, it is over that mountain range, very far away. You'd best be sticking with me for a while before running off, otherwise you are likely to get lost or robbed.' Felipe thought he may be able to persuade Ramkus to stick with him for a *fair* while, at least until he did not need his presence to enter the ranks of a court, or something of that nature. *Just in case*, he thought, *Ramkus may choose to cut ties at some point because we aren't heading directly for that area.*

'I will be heading in that direction, so I can at least show you the way and give you some company, teach you some lessons of the world,' Felipe added.

Ramkus's interest was piqued. 'Yes, like teaching me how to play that guitar of yours,' he nodded to the instrument tied in cloth, around the back of the bard.

Felipe laughed, 'Of course my friend! In good time!'

They finally hit the first row of trees at the bottom of the hill that they had been travelling along. Ramkus looked back up, admiring what he had considered a hill was more akin to a small mountain, for it rose much higher than he realised. They entered the forest in which the trees stood quite sparsely apart, letting much light filter in. Although long tendrilled roots lay coiled and curled among the forest floor, the flora seemed very much alive, young and healthy, harmoniously comforting any who wandered into its inner sanctum. A deep rich smell of woodland filled their nostrils, made all the more powerful from the dampness of the evening before. The lashing of rain was now all but drying up in puddles on the dirt road.

'Where exactly are we headed at the moment?' Ramkus wondered aloud. He had been following Felipe's directions without really giving much thought as to where he was being led. He was becoming aware of his anxious *need* to get to the Seat of the Guardians. Although he had a desire to get there, he had only considered it would happen in due course. But now, he was becoming impatient in his anticipation.

'To Kerwood, a small town in the Sorbo forest, which is what we have just entered into. A nice little place, quaint. Still not many comforts though. The fish broth at the inn there is delicious and hearty. A river running through the town goes all the way out to the sea, allowing them to catch the best of the river, and the sea,' Felipe informed Ramkus, remembering the finer details of the town. 'They also have a very good stout that is brewed a little out of town.'

Ramkus nodded along. It sounded good enough to him, he knew no better. Frowning, as his staff hit some of the trees branches above, he adjusted it over his saddle which proved even less successful, as he almost knocked Felipe off his horse. Giving some thought as to how he may hold it over his back, he tried to do as Felipe had done with his guitar. He quickly decided against this, as it would become a little difficult to get off his back and into action immediately, should it be required for that sort of thing. He moved behind Felipe's horse, and held the staff balanced across the saddle. *At least for a bit to give my arms a rest,* he thought; not that they were that sore, but he was getting irritated by the constant hitting of things on the ground, and the branches that shot out from all directions onto the path. The staff itself was a little taller than him. He studied it, starting to admire its solid, intricate design. He wondered what its particular purpose for him was.

A heavy thud sounded all of a sudden: Felipe had fallen out of his saddle and hit the moist dirt path hard, head first. Ramkus's senses pricked up, something was coming at him from his left. He ducked and slid off his horse as a projectile flew over his back. The horses reared.

He jumped to Felipe who was lying face down.

Ramkus looked up and into the forest from where the projectile came from, but was met with the feeling of a cold blade on his right shoulder from behind him.

'Don't you dare move!'

Ramkus's eyes searched to his right; he saw that it was one of the group of men whom he had *upset* the evening before. He had one of the others standing alongside him, both smirking. They looked nothing but simple bandits whom had somehow been able to muster up some basic weaponry.

'Well what 'ave we got 'ere then? Ohh, it's that shit from last night! Fancy that.' A voice came from the forest, approaching the scene behind Ramkus. After rearing, the horses had remained steadfast and calm, not giving anymore care for the commotion. The remaining bandits from the previous night came out from the forest, walking past the horses, admiring the fact that the beasts had not run.

'You really screwed up last night. Should never have messed with me...' the voice continued. It was the man whom he had struck instinctively that came into his view. Ramkus looked at the others. Two were approaching holding large stones, threatening to throw them at Ramkus should he make a move. *They must have hit Felipe cleanly in his temple for him to have fallen so hard.* He felt no apprehension or fear at the situation; as with the evening before, he knew no fear - at least not yet – and could not truly anticipate the actions of these men.

'That staff of yours,' the leader picked it up from the ground next to Ramkus, grinning as he bent over, 'it's a nice one, ain't it.' He gave a guttural chortle, 'I think I'll keep it.' He paused, smiling through rotten teeth, 'And these horses. And that guitar on 'im.' The leader pointed at Felipe lying unconsciously. The man closest to Felipe bent over and took the guitar from the cloth strap.

Ramkus rose in protest and heard a loud thwack.

His knee gave way, pain shooting through his leg.

'Get down!' The leader yelled, spittle coming from his jowl. He reeled back after smashing Ramkus in the knee with the staff.

Ramkus began to feel an anger overwhelm him, he wanted to *punish* these men, to give them the pain he was now feeling: ***"Tenfold"***.

His eyes began to fill with rage as he bared his teeth. But still, he kept his head.

'Don't you ever mess with me, boy!' The leader raised the staff.

Ramkus knew what his action would be, but remained motionless as the staff came down on an angle.

He knew where it would impact; he knew he would not be able to withstand the strike.

But he took it, right across his temple…

As the white vibrations were releasing from his vision little by little, he saw the five bandits walk off down the path, laughing. Ramkus rolled onto his back, staring up at the sparse leaves holding to the branches, providing cover over the path. The pain in his left knee and the strike to his head started to overcome him. He lay motionless, on the cusp of passing out, as a voice in the distance reaches of his mind whispered: ***"Make the choice, make them pay!"***

XXX

He awoke to the sound of another groaning. He opened his eyes, finding himself facing the sky. The light had started to move past the middle of the day.

'Eugh,' the sounds continued, it was Felipe whom was letting out all the noise. 'My head, what on earth happened?! Where's my horse? Where is my coin purse?! Where is my **guitar?!** What the hell happened Ramkus?' He was wakening in a crazed and dangerous state.

'We were robbed by those bandits from last night. They knocked you out cold with a good throw of a rock to the head. And from the looks of it, you may need to clean it a bit. You're bleeding, or were, quite badly,' Ramkus said as he lifted himself to examine Felipe. He was delirious and experiencing blurred vision, as well as feeling quite nauseous. He tried to stand erect, but stumbled. His head was spinning and he had a very acute pain in his knee.

'You don't look too good either. Your face looks like it has taken a massive blow. What's wrong with your leg? You don't look like you can stand.' Felipe regarded Ramkus with concern, 'Must have been a pretty horrific fight if you're in that state, must have hurt them a bit as well?' he said matter-of-factly.

'I did not fight,' Ramkus answered tepidly.

'What?' Felipe was flummoxed. 'You didn't even hit them?' He stared at Ramkus in incongruity. 'What the hell, Ramkus?' He was becoming increasingly agitated. 'Why didn't you? That is what you're made for!' he scowled. 'Some use you are, if you can't even lift a finger,' he snapped before doubling over in pain. 'Why the hell did I even get you to come with me if you're not even going to fight!'

Ramkus held himself back, not able to get a word in to explain what happened, nor defend himself from the verbal barrage.

'You were the one who made presumptions as to who I am, or rather *what* I am. Do not lay the blame on me for this! You want me to show you some ability, what I am *made* for, when I have no idea about it myself?! How am I meant to do that? Is this the only reason you brought me along, simply looking to use me?' His head began to throb and feel heavy. He fell to the ground. He was in a rage, anguished by his inability to have done anything. It started to dissolve into a reluctance, a negative draining feeling, a depression. He coughed up some breakfast and spat some blood. He felt helpless, wanting to curl up and disintegrate into the earth, become nothing but the dirt he lay upon.

Felipe calmed down, realising that he could not have anticipated this event, and that this *Guardian* was not the super human he had initially hoped.

He sighed, 'At least they didn't take the water pouch,' he had this attached to his side, offering it to Ramkus who took it obligingly, but with a sharp look of bitterness. He drank a little, letting it rejuvenate and console him.

'I am sorry I don't know what I am doing. I'm sorry I have disappointed you with my inaction,' Ramkus said curtly, shoving the water pouch back.

'No, I am sorry,' Felipe replied, sighing. 'Let's just move on. Is your leg alright?'

'It's the knee, it is buckling a bit,' Ramkus checked for himself. Felipe pulled out a scarf and wrapped it hard as he could around the top and bottom of Ramkus's knee in an attempt to stop it from being unstable. 'That should hopefully brace it a little, how does it feel? Can you walk?'

'A little,' Ramkus moved a few steps grimacing. The knee began to loosen a little from the swelling that had formed. He managed to get up a decent pace.

After a short test of his ability to move, he was ready. 'Let's go,' he willed Felipe, who was still unsure of his companion being up and about and not resting further. Finally, he assented, and they plodded silently, further into the forest and down the path they had started earlier that morning, each in thought.

Afternoon light beamed through the tree branches, leaves filtered into different shades. It was a surprisingly open forest; it breathed, at times, that air of the sea as it rushed through. It was not a straight path by any stretch, and the sounds of rushing water indicated where early travellers must have redirected the road, to reach the creeks and pools of water. A few stone bridges, under which flowing rivers of clear water reflected the vibrancy of life that lived within it. Ramkus was feeling sore and sorry for himself. He was fighting conflicting emotions: half an enveloping anger; and half of despair. At other times he felt nothing, although it was more similar to consigning himself to the droll movement of life. Felipe had not uttered a word, he was slowly coming around to the fall of his burgeoning dreams. He knew nothing of this Ramkus, and had, as usual, allowed his excitement to get the better of him. He was also feeling stupid at the fact he ought to have known retribution would have been on the minds of those thugs from last night. They were not the usual hard type of bandit he had heard harrowing tales about, rather, they resembled a ragtag group of farmers fed up with the trials of farming life.

As the sun dropped increasingly further, Felipe's stomach began grumbling. He was now quite keen on the idea of finding somewhere to rest and warm up. A little clearing under a rocky outpost was not too far away: *From memory, it has some fruit trees growing about, and a pond where we can wash and tend to our wounds.*

Felipe made a motion to catch up to Ramkus, whose head hung as low as his thoughts. He had been leading the whole time. A quiet march, albeit, staggered and jaunty in part.

'Ramkus,' he said, not knowing how the *leader* would react, 'there is a clearing a little further on that we should make way for. May be worth also staying there for the evening as it will get dark soon.' Ramkus, coming out of his wavering trail of thoughts and emotions, looked at Felipe with an unreadable expression.

'Alright,' came the curt, direct response. He was starting to feel a little sickly and wouldn't mind seating himself down, sooner rather than later. His knee, although feeling quite loose, was still aching.

'It is not much further up. There is a little-known path that leads to it. Hopefully some of the apple trees still have some fruit left,' Felipe said with positivity.

The sound of food brought a sudden delight to the Guardian, whom had until then forgotten all about his other physical needs.

The path Felipe spoke of was indeed little-known and seldom used. There were markings on a boulder on the other side of the road from it, but the route was overgrown, and would only be seen by the keenest eye.

They made their way down the path to the clearing, a mass of large rocks were on the far side, offering a shallow cave for shelter where there was also the remnants of a fire place. On the left stood a small orchard of fruit trees: apples, pears, stone fruits, a dozen trees in total bearing a few of their delicious wares. It was enough for the two men to be contented with. Beyond the trees was the pond which appeared the natural conclusion of a small forest creek. A waterfall seemed to flow into it when there was rain, and its edges were surrounded by cliff face. The water stood as still as ice.

Felipe headed to the trees, picked up some fruit, throwing an apple to Ramkus whose mouth was agape at the serenely beautiful oasis in the Sorbo forest. 'Gather some sticks, Ramkus, we'll make a fire in that shelter,' he directed.

Ramkus followed the orders and started picking up tree branches whilst gobbling the apple. It was not as easy going as one would imagine, his leg was giving him great discomfort, grimacing every time he awkwardly bent down. Once the wood had been gathered, Felipe started smashing two rocks together, creating a spark.

'How did you know of this place?' Ramkus enquired. 'You seem very much at home here.'

'Ah, that is because I was not brought up to be a bard. No, fittingly enough I am of a lineage of what you would consider *forest dwellers*. These sorts of places are still very much home to me, as you have seemingly noticed. They offer proper respite from the world, which was their intended purpose,' Felipe explained with an air of levity.

'You mean they are man-made for travellers and those wishing to get away?' Ramus asked with interest.

Laughing a little, Felipe answered Ramkus: 'No, not *man*-made, probably made by the first inhabitants of these lands a long, *long* time ago. And what these inhabitants were is always up for debate, or even if they ever were here - as some may lead you to believe. According to legends, they were mythical *people*. So yes actually, I correct myself, they are, in a sense, *man-made*.' He got up and breathed heavily, 'Look at how pristine this place is, the row of fruit trees, the pond; the place is protected from the elements, a true shelter.' He stood and breathed in the cool serenity before continuing. 'My family had always accustomed themselves to these types of lands. Maybe we actually *are* descendants of these true first people and it *is* in our blood. But who knows,' he mused to himself in a romanticised daydream. There was truth in what he was touching on, but he didn't want to openly admit it. 'Anyway, we can lick our wounds for the night.'

Ramkus noted how the air of cynicism had lifted from Felipe. He was much happier than he himself was. A good time to get to understand this companion.

'So, how did you come to be a bard then?' Ramkus continued his questioning.

'My family used to tend to the trees, the ones best suited for use in making musical instruments. Although we were not the luthiers, we knew enough of them in the towns that surrounded us. I remember the day we were shown what our wood had created. I was able to play the instrument that I had sourced the wood for. The feel, the sound, the guitar, it *possessed* me,' Felipe said as if reliving a dream. He stared into the growing flames of the fire as he sat back down, 'We forest dwellers are still very musical, but it is not for us to end up as bards. I guess I was different, I needed to travel. I felt so constricted not being able to see what was out there out in the grand, wide world. My *supposed* role in the scheme of it all was to follow my family trade, tend to the trees, source the wood. But that was not good enough for me.' He looked calmly about the picturesque scene, sitting as perfectly as a statue, before coming to lie on his side, enveloped in the embers of their small campfire. He suddenly jerked back up, 'I should tend to this cut of mine. You should probably check yourself over too.'

He got up and jauntily, and made his way to the pond.

Ramkus stared into the fire, thinking upon the little poetic life that his travelling companion had left behind. He sounded so very different out here, as if there was something that had been taken off his shoulders. Earlier today he was all for the *luxuries of life*; now, he was gratified in a small clearing that offered a freshness of perspective. *Perhaps the rock had knocked his brain about a little, he actually feels at home.*

Unfortunately, unbeknownst to Ramkus, this type of mood would not last long.

Felipe came sauntering back. Ramkus thought he still looked a little out of sorts.

'Not too bad a cut, mostly bruising. Water is nice and cool, go try it. Could even bathe in it if you wished,' Felipe suggested.

With a shrug, the Guardian ambled down in the deepening blue, evening light. He trudged through the flavoursome smelling orchard which looked vibrant and colourful, and out onto the water's edge. He could see his reflection in it, and considered it may be a good thing to at least wade around in the crispness of the pool, icing the knee in the process. It was feeling rather stiff and worn. As he did this, he felt he might as well take Felipe's advice and bathe properly. He cast off his clothes and looked at his reflection, his body, for the first time. He was broadly built in the shoulders, lean, sinewy muscles, he carried no real weight around the stomach, but bore a heavy built, hairy chest. He deemed himself to be athletic in build: a warrior's build. He walked into the centre of the pool and dropped himself in, feeling contented by its cool enveloping waters which traced over the body he had just exposed. His muscles relaxed, unwound, and so did his mind. Despair and anger were leaving him, and he was satisfied, floating in the healing waters that seemed to lift him up to the velvet tapestry above.

He returned from his refreshing swim to the makeshift camp feeling pacified and healed. He handed Felipe the scarf he had wrapped around his knee, insisting it was not required further. Sitting, looking into the flames that had flared up, they watched the sun get lower and leave them with the twilight of the night. Felipe threw some more wood on the pyre that was steadily building, letting the flames rise sharply, flickering and crackling. He then sat passively in the still, statute form he had been in before.

He began to speak in meditative tones: 'I have met many souls and seen many things on my travels, Ramkus. I have always tried to have the best of times on the road, only seldom did I have ill-fated situations arise, but I still painted them with colourful hues.' He paused, looking to Ramkus, 'I have also been fortunate to have spoken with those that put reason to all the madness of the world. In fact, I learnt the most from these types, along with techniques to combat the worst of days,' he stared deeply into the eyes of Ramkus, and smiled. 'One thing I have learned, a way I have always dealt with frustrations and the loss of fortunes, is to meditate.'

Ramkus studied him, he did not know what he was getting at.

'Meditation releases the mind, let's all the dust settle down. Best of all, you tend to find a voice that gives direction when you require an answer. It is always there, it only needs you to let *it* come to the fore of your mind, past all the misguided thoughts and worries.' He sighed, 'This is the best advice I can give you for the situation we are in: to find one's way.'

'You feel we should meditate then,' Ramkus stated flatly.

'If you insist,' Felipe joked. 'Now, sit as still as possible, let your mind wander, keep a steady breath.'

Ramkus obliged his fellow traveller, following his example, sitting cross-legged, hands resting. He continued to study Felipe, making sure he was in the same position and not mocking him, before he became calm and still himself.

His mind floated in a dark embrace. Questions flowed to the forefront of his mind, and then back. His identity, what was it, a constraint on his consciousness, on his actions? Where was he to go, only forwards, to this distant land? Did he feel he has the strength and want of effort to do this? What was the purpose of it all? Emotions flared, from anguish and angst, to despair, anger, frustration, and finally a contentedness to remain in this darkness of thought, the void. He did not care if any revelation came. The flight he felt, as if being held by no body, was liberating; but he also felt, at the very fringes, a rage that burned, needing to be settled. For what though? To go back to his body, to his dilemma, his life, *and stay? Then a voice came to him, from the back of his mind. Menacing and powerful, direct and authoritative; it was part of him.* **"Choose!"** *it said,* **"Choose your devil!"**

He opened his eyes, not able to make out the meaning of what he had heard. Only half an hour had passed, and Felipe was still enjoying those scenes of darkness. He decided to leave him to his own devices and climb the rock outpost that sheltered them, and see if he could spot Kerwood from the vantage point. The rock face had enough porous sections to allow him a good grip, even with the temperature dropping and a coldness enveloping the surface. Small insects buzzed in the background, little other life stirred at this time. As he climbed up into the darkened light, he saw a glimmer, a glow, coming from a little further down the forest highway.

It was a fire…!

He tried to squint and make out any figures that may be lurking, wondering if it was the *darn bandits* that had accosted him. He felt despair when he remembered the events, the feeling of sinking into the ground and giving up. But this depression was being combated by an anger, an overwhelming sense of a need for retribution.

"Choose!" the voice had said. He contemplated what he ought to do,

scratching his chin as he thought through his two options: leave the bandits be; or get Felipe's and his belongings back.

He decided on the latter.

Clambering down from the top vantage point, he made enough noise to disturb Felipe. He was already up and about, waiting for him.

'You seem to be pleased with the view' Felipe said.

'I saw a fire a little further up the path, I think it would be worth a look, may be those that robbed us,' Ramkus replied hurriedly, with obvious excitement. 'Quick, let's go now!'

Felipe hesitated, 'What for? What if it is them and they see us, they'll give us another beating, or better yet, kill us!' he said.

'I doubt they will be able to do that, this time *we* have the element of surprise!' Ramkus argued.

Felipe stared pensively at his companion, 'And then what? We see them, with our possessions in hand, get upset, and walk away?'

'Ha! I thought you were certain of my abilities as a *Guardian*,' Ramkus answered back mockingly. 'Well, I feel I could teach them a lesson, and should in fact! Would be a *kind* gesture…' A glint of madness was creeping into Ramkus's eyes, an aggressive spirit seemed to have arisen in him.

'Calm yourself, Ramkus, you're obviously excited and want to exact some revenge, but you do not know your capabilities, or strength. You're wounded as well!' Felipe pleaded.

Ramkus squinted, he did not realise how carried away he was getting, or how his actions - his want of action - spoke clearly of inflicting a painful revenge. *Is this who I am?* He calmed himself, but was still keen on having a peek at the camp up the forest highway.

'We may be able to sneak in and retrieve our things without anyone noticing. Don't you need your guitar back, bard?' Ramkus pressed.

Felipe was pensive once more, Ramkus had hit a chord – figuratively – with the entertainer.

'Yes, I do,' he said calmly with a gleam of agitation, 'but I can always get another one without risking my head!' He scratched his wounded temple, not sure if he intended the pun.

'How will you be able to afford one? You make your money from having a guitar in the first place, it is your instrument, your tool, what you base your entire persona on,' Ramkus continued along this point.

He was right, Felipe knew that people in these lands were less inclined to pay for a performance of poetry than music. They were a simpler folk in these parts, and music was the only thing an outsider could really offer that they would pay justly for. It was either trying to get his guitar back, or manual labour till he could buy another guitar. The problem with that was there were no luthiers or stores which would sell him such a fine tool of trade for tens of miles.

'Fine, we'll have a look. But only a look. And no sudden heroic actions! We will just see what is there, and then discuss what we may do...' Felipe consented.

Ramkus smiled and gave a slow tilted nod, his eyes were full of a strange knowledge, a passion reserved for those that dance a mad dance unto themselves. They started back up the over grown path and on towards the light in the forest.

The light of the moon and stars was covered by a mass of clouds; it was dark in these forests, but not as cold as it had been the night before. Two embers from the fire burst upward into nothingness, the rest of the flares were concentrated and still. The raucous behaviour of the bandits was adding more to the atmosphere than the forest's chorus of noises. The horses were tied a little further away from the campfire, which was only some way off the highway to begin with, between some trees in a makeshift clearing. Belching and farting, swearing and revelling, they were the only cares for these callous men. One was snoring loudly, sleeping with his back to the fire. The others were joyously bantering. The disgusting smell of a hard liquor was pervading the scents of the forest. They were handing around a demijohn of something similar to turpentine, laughing as they took swigs of the dastardly gross drink. Although Ramkus and Felipe had entered from the same direction, Felipe had spotted his guitar as soon as they were within a decent spying range and had made his way off towards it at the back of the campfire. Two of the men were sitting beside a tree, handing it between themselves for a strum. Their singing and playing was awful to the ear, but it was one more thing to keep the laughs going. The leader, whose back was to the path, threw a stick at the one who was sleeping as he began to snore a little too loudly.

'What a stupid shit, can't 'old 'imself up after some drink, can 'e,' the leader laughed.

'Reminds me, I gotta take a shit myself,' another one whom was sitting next to the leader said. Lucky for the two adventurers, he meandered off into another direction away from where they were positioned outside the campsite. Ramkus spotted his staff lying on the ground. He dared not move. Felipe, however, was creeping in too close.

Suddenly, a large cracking sound shot out.

A branch had snapped under Felipe's foot. He looked towards Ramkus and gave a look of indignation.

'The 'ell?!' the leader stood up and turned around.

Ramkus immediately ran at him as the other two got up; the sleeping one rolled over onto his other side.

Although drunk, the leader threw an accurate punch at the figure darting towards him.

Ramkus weaved under and gave him a punch to the ribs with his left hand, right where he had the night before, then followed with a hook to the temple with his right, twisting his hips and following through. The leader was down.

Ramkus saw the one who had been playing the guitar, lunge at him. The other was facing off against Felipe, who was throwing punches with his wrists up facing him, head titled back. It would have been rather comical to encounter; however, it was infuriating for a drunken bandit who couldn't make out what was going on.

The bandit who had gone off into the bushes was quickly and quietly returning in order to reach for a sword.

The one coming at Ramkus did not count on Ramkus getting in so close, so quickly. He was right in his face before he realised. Ramkus threw a right circular elbow to his face. Reaching over the bandit's shoulder, he grabbed him and thrust his right knee into his hunched over body, twice pounding the bandit in the sternum. The poor fellow was seeing stars and had lost his breath. Ramkus followed through with an almighty push, drawing power from the ground and directing it into the man's sternum once more.

The bandit was propelled backward, straight into the path of the one Felipe was facing off with. The only thing that stopped the man flying backwards was the sudden jolt as he sandwiched his accomplice – whom Felipe was able to strike in the face one more time – against a tree. The force of the impact gave an almighty thud which cracked a branch above the two off the tree and on to them, covering them from sight.

Felipe gave himself a smile, wiped his hands and dusted himself off, before placing his hands on his hips and thrusting out his chest out with bravado.

The one whom had gone off into the bushes now rushed onto the scene, holding the sword he ahd retrieved at the ready. Ramkus picked up his staff, beginning to rotate it, spinning it around in his hands, behind his back, above his head. He was on the other side of the fire as he moved, forcing Felipe to jump back and out of his way. His cloak was following the motion, as if part of a dance ritual, making Ramkus look like some demonic creature through the flames. The bandit watched him as he circled the fire in step. He was looking into the eyes of a beast that belied a great satisfaction from what was to be his demise.

Embers began to spray out in the direction of the trembling bandit, as the motion and spinning of the staff's movements created a fan for the fire. Ramkus jumped through the flames and smacked the sword out from the bandit's hands. The man, in shock, ran into the bushes, pulling his falling trousers up as he ran. He'd forgotten to do them up properly after coming back to camp.

Felipe threw a stick at the exposed bottom as the bandit fled, 'Serves you right, you lout!' he yelled after him.

Ramkus was grimacing, the jump through the flames had not been a good idea, he had reinjured his dingy knee on the landing. He at least had a staff to lean on now.

He hobbled over to Felipe who was still acting the hero, when he felt his ankle get entangled and trapped. He looked down, into the eyes of the leader who had his dirty paws gripped on Ramkus.

'Ya shit!' he coughed.

'Do you never learn?' Ramkus replied, as a voice of anger in the back of his mind said: *"Choose!"*. This anger was immediately followed by a fall, a fall into a depression: *Why does my life have to be as such?* His gaze went cold, mind clear, before he crushed the staff onto the leader's ribs and looked away.

The leader let out a 'Ooh' sound, crying in pain once more.

'Get your stuff, Felipe, and let's go,' Ramkus commanded.

Felipe, full of glee, picked up his guitar, holding it up to Ramkus, showing he had indeed retrieved his prized instrument. He then saw to his coin purse, which was attached to the leader. This was a little more difficult to retrieve, as the leader was still rolling around in agony. He wrenched it from the man and gave a quick kick to the leader's ribs as a farewell gesture.

'Ooh!' The leader cried again.

Ramkus had already released the horses and taken the reins, as Felipe, gave his guitar a strum, nodded, attaching it to the side of his horse.

'Oh, they have bloody dirtied it! Grubby mongrels!' Felipe cried in disgust.

Ramkus, trying not to hobble, gave a faint smile to Felipe, before wincing as he led the horses away from the fire.

'At least there seems to be a little bit more coin in the purse, though,' Felipe weighed it in his hands. 'All's well that ends well, eh Ramkus?' he laughed. The glow of the fire and its warmth was becoming lesser and lesser, as they made their way onto the forest highway. The clouds were beginning to part, allowing a glistening show of stars, as if to reveal all the truths of the night.

'Should we go back to the clearing?' Felipe asked.

'No,' Ramkus said in a deep, wise voice: 'We go forwards, always forwards, my friend.' He was surprised with his own response, but did not show it. The feeling of despair hit him, then one of anger, and a voice in the back of his head called out: ***"Choose your devil!"***. He sighed, and pressed forward, trying to forget his emotions.

They wandered under the starlight and moonshine. The clouds had completely moved on now, showing no remnants of being there. The bluish tinged twilight beamed through the sparse leaves as if spears from the heavens, onto the path, giving a comforting sight to the travellers. They knew not of their next predicament, nor did they care, they were happy now just to have their things back.

Back at the campfire there were pains and groans. The leader was "oohing", rolling as much as he could. The two under the tree branch were rocking to get from under the branch, and each other… The runaway was hiding a hundred yards away, shitting himself. And the sleeping one rolled onto his other side, snoring peacefully as he did so.

Chapter III

The forest opened once more, with neatly placed rocks starting to line the sides of the road.

'You are an odd one,' Ramkus remarked to Felipe, 'I could have sworn, for how relaxed you were in that clearing, that calm nature of yours was all wiped away by your excitement and bravado as soon as you hit that bandit's campfire.'

Felipe smiled, then sighed to himself. He knew he was an erratic person, but the last day had presented one of the more incredible events of his past few years, decade even. He had not felt so alive in years!

Dawn was providing an orange glow from the East. It was shining over the whole of the sky, lighting up the hovering snow sitting atop the mountain peaks far off on the horizon. Sounds of man and animal toiling, of water splashing, and all other small hubbub resonated from places not too far away.

Kerwood: they had arrived a little after daybreak. The town was split down the middle by a canal. Modest, but well-built two-storey buildings stood along either side, overlooking the rushing waters. Many small docks stretching down along the central focal point, where fish were being piled onto platforms that lay along the canal. It held that certain aroma fresh fish markets contain.

'This is a major hub for fish supplies for many of the neighbouring towns,' Felipe mused, watching Ramkus observe the scene.

It seemed to Ramkus to be the only thing in this town, and the smell, although not unpleasant, was not exactly the thing one wants hitting their nose first thing in the morning. He jumped off his horse, and began walking. A sharp pain shot through his left from his knee: *It has been immobile for too long*, he thought.

'I think we should try to find a physician for our wounds,' Ramkus said in a pained voice.

'Not a bad idea, but I do not know if there is one in this town. I have only ever really enjoyed the inn. Sound sleep and hot food may do us some good too, don't you think?' Felipe responded, following suit and jumping off his horse. He led Ramkus to one of the grander structures, a signboard standing out the front of its eaves declaring the "Kerwood Inn" in fancy scripture and colourful patterns.

The place smelt of tobacco, and underneath that, fish. Dimly lit, smoky, but still holding warmth from the night before.
'Monsieur Felipe!' A voice cried out, 'You are back so soon? I wouldn't have expected you for a few more days at the very least!' The voice was of a man wearing glasses, thick moustache, balding with bits of grey hair, rotund; the typical type of person who seemed to run these establishments: the Innkeeper.
'Ah well, I couldn't keep away from my *favourite* inn for too long,' answered Felipe with a wink and grandiose bow. 'Now listen my good man, we didn't fare too well on our journey here. Attacked by some riotous thugs we were, is there a physician nearby that would be able to see to our injuries?' He patted the Innkeeper on the shoulder in a friendly manner.
'I am sorry to hear that Monsieur,' the Innkeeper said with some concern, 'but yes, yes there is one physician about. However, he and his daughter live on one the beaches out at sea. Quickest way for you to get there would be to travel by one of our fishing boats going out that way.' He paused to study them and guffawed, 'The doctor is a slightly odd fellow, believes in salt air as a remedy for most things. Doesn't like dealing with people too much. Odd for a doctor.'
'Thank you, Innkeep,' Felipe nodded, 'and before I forget, would we be able to get some of your fine food?'
The Innkeeper nodded obligingly, eyeing Felipe's new companion for the first time properly.
'This is my understudy,' Felipe grabbed Ramkus by the shoulder, bearing all his teeth with a smile. 'He will be staying with me.'

'Well, Monsieur Felipe,' he studied his face, placing his hands on his hips, presiding to be a critic. 'Is he up to performance standard? If not, he will need to pay. Double tenancy and all.'

Felipe lost the smile. 'How contemptible of you Innkeep,' he quipped, 'but fine. We do need a room with two beds.' He looked to his *understudy*, 'Lest you wish not to pay Ramkus, and sleep on hay again?'

Ramkus shrugged, but knew full well he did not entirely enjoy the *quaintness* of the Abergrass attic too much.

'We only have beds, no hay, so he must pay or perform,' the Innkeeper reaffirmed his position.

Felipe gave a reproachful look, 'Even for one room?' he grumbled but did not go further. 'Fine, we shall see that he does then.'

With that, Felipe sat down at one of the large tables, Ramkus following, and soon they were presented with some bread and the fish broth Felipe had spoken so highly of. To Ramkus's surprise, for a soup that must have been the leftovers of the day before, it was still very good. The warmth reached some of the tired muscles that were frozen and aching. They finished quickly and went into the room that had been prepared for them. Ramkus thought to himself that the Innkeeper could have been the brother of the Abergrass Innkeeper, for they were identical in build and appearance, save for this one wearing glasses and having greying hair – or what was left of it. They lay down in the humble wooden abode and dozed off on the thoughts of all that had happened in the past day, letting it play through their minds one last time before sleep arrived.

The sounds of the day had begun to creep into the room. Market stalls, the steady murmur of people, birds chirping, the sound of carts, barrels, crates, and boxes, all keeping their persistent steady echo. The sun was raising itself up, peeking through the window before crawling along to meet two beds on either side of the small room that the two adventurers inhabited. They were gently breathing in the safety of the confined space.

The inn had stood for well over a hundred years, greeting many weary travellers. It held the smells of joyful evenings, of comfort away from the elements, all tucked away inside its wooden frames. It was a large building, housing many rooms for travellers and wanderers; those who did not wish to sleep out at sea for another night, coming up the river to settle on steady ground and serene surround. It took up almost a fifth of the space for buildings that were joined along this side of the river. The rest were stores and homes, all of which identical except for their paintwork. All were two storeys, although some distinguished themselves with flower pots outside their second-floor windows. It would have been an absolute picture of beauty if it wasn't merely considered a fishing village. The canal that ran through Kerwood was man made, coming along from a bend in the main river. It went through the town, splitting off into two channels towards the end: one returning back to the bending river; the other running through to neighbouring villages, which in turn ran onward to more villages in the lands that abounded. The river system went deep into these lands, they were its veins, the water was the lifeblood which carried vital supplies to the people throughout. This was a distinctive feature of these surrounds. Another pronounced, but not essentially notable design for these parts was that it had two sets of roads to travel through: the original forest path; and the efficient "commercial" route.

The original roads through the forests and open plains did indeed meander off course at times, heading towards spots where the waterways often ended in dams. Travellers would find plentiful fruit trees and water, they would survive well on their way should they follow these oft forgotten trails. The negative aspect to this path was that it did twist and wind. Then again, it made for a very scenic journey as a consequence. These facts alone led many to believe they were plotted out by the original inhabitants, the forest dwellers - long before man in his current form had arrived, in any case. This was an event which had caused the other straight, direct road to be created for quick travel for merchants, or which an *army* could march down. It allowed for greater precision in timing for journeys, effectively a more efficient way to travel. They were not pretty to say the least, but in time, it became the one most people used. The twisting and winding forest paths were therefore travelled seldom, seen only as paths for forest strolls or tracks to certain natural marvels, not a highway anymore. In this way the patchwork of the forests, the land, had been built in the natural rhythm of man's development and control, dictated by the needs and desires of inhabitants which wished to conquer the elements, and each other.

As Ramkus dozed off, he pictured the sight of mounds like huge anthills. Hills covered in trees which sprawled out as if they were rippling water. A fog surrounded them in the depression, and he took flight from this view, to mountains covered in a silky snow and ice. Perfect and crystalline in their gleam. Diving over the mountains, beaches emerged, where azure seas melted into the yellow and white sands. These gave way to the vivid greens of tropical forests where dots of colour from exotic flowers and fruits blossomed. Farther over these forests, it became a red sand desert. Rugged at first, then slight rises and dips in the dunes, providing a calming red, inland sea against the blue sky. Unearthly and exquisite, it matched the tapestry of the mountains. The wind picked up white wisps of granulates, crashing them into the great walls of a city in the midst of the massive expanse of arid earth. The sky had turned a blood red and maroon, then time shifted and it became cyan. This desert city looked as if it was built from nothing, somehow placed by the heavens: brick, marble, and rustic, set upon the earth. He could not fathom what he saw, he could not read it. Whether these places existed or not, or were of a time before or after – he could not decipher. It was not of his position to do so. The seed of a desire to see what lay out there in this world of tranquillity, of beauty, of movement, of spirit, had been cast. Deep within his troubled and toiled mind, some peace was found. A

connection with the dream world, one where emotions tied
to his thoughts and imagination. In his deep sleep, the
world was open to him.

He awoke with pain in his knee, but a clear mind. Getting up and feeling a mess, he looked out the window at the hustle and bustle, that calculated movement of the human endeavour. It was not too late, but he knew he was in need of some attentive care, and soon. Felipe was still dozing.

He thought of what an erratic man that Felipe was, his mood change bordered on ludicrous. He wondered if it was always an act and whether he would ever see the *real* Felipe. *Perhaps it is an act in the face of adversity, a way to face his demons. All must suffer their weight on the path, many with knowledge and thoughts they can only accept when it is necessary...* Ramkus considered he may be being a tad harsh of Felipe, it had been a tough day yesterday, and for all the troubles that it had presented, the calmness and surrender in that clearing had seemed to purge them of the negative mental constraints their beating and loss of their possessions had caused. *Yes, we retrieved them, but the ill effects of such situations can linger on one's mind. Why am I thinking like this?* Ramkus began to rouse himself from the odd thoughts. *What do I expect of myself. To be a straightforward being?* He could not claim to be that by any means; he had, after all, only came into being a few days previous. He was, for all intents and purposes, starting to feel a sense of self, an identity, a stream of consciousness that was unto himself. The way he fought that night with his staff, it was so natural, so enjoyable. He looked out the window at the people: *What would they think of me? Why should I care what anybody thinks?*

Felipe stirred, waking with a grunt. 'Ah, you are up already,' he said.
'I woke in a bit of pain. I'm really going to need to see that doctor soon,' Ramkus grumbled.

'Well, I don't feel like spending too much time here anyway, even if my head is starting to feel a little bit better. Let us see what this physician's place is like. Would be nice to dip my feet in the sea,' Felipe said joyfully.

They were still tired and sore, in definite need of some care as their mental states became fragmented and simplistic. Ramkus headed for the door with Felipe in tow, simply following their cues to get to a place which would offer some comfort to their ailments.

As they arrived into the main hall, Ramkus took in the sight properly. A tall roof which bore sturdy timber structuring, darkened and holding smoke from the fire used for cooking the food below. There were a few women cleaning the floors and tables, others were moving about, tending to the kitchen, the Innkeeper was busily cleaning glasses.

After enquiring as to the best route to the doctor's beach hut, they were retold to take the river passage as before. It unfortunately seemed to be the only possible route, for they had hoped there would be another way so as not to risk any nausea, however, they accepted this was the mode of travel for these parts. They could hire one of the boats that had already come downstream for the day to deliver cargo and was traveling back out again. This was the manner in which many people did their business, waiting on the tides to bring cargo or people up or down the river system.

After brief enquiries, the two were able to enlist the services of a "taxi" vessel to help take them out. It was the smallest taxi operating, and could easily have sat eight men. Felipe brought his guitar, Ramkus his staff, and they lay back and let the taxi driver take off from his mooring, pushing it out under the bridge, past the buildings, and into the bend of the river.

The gentle lull of the rocking boat, the interspersed rays of light that warmed the body, the green leaves tossing in the calm winds, all brought Ramkus back to his dreams. Little wrens chirped and flew about on the banks of the river and the semi submerged log snags, offering a small change of sound.

The sails fluttered about in the wind, as the boat hit a greater vein of water. A few boats passed by in the expanse of the now bigger river, joining from other water routes. The river was fifty yards across, the tree branches parting for the all-encompassing blue sky. Soft clouds rolled on, and off Ramkus wandered again into his thoughts, something that were his, were him.

There was a darkness, as if light was not blocked out but consumed, claimed by the blackness. He lay on the ground: a cold floor, dark, feeling of rock, which he steadily raised himself from. There was a sound in the corner, something scurrying about. A damp light hung over an area that appeared to be the corner of this arena. Nothing but darkness pervaded the room, for even as the light hit the floor, no reflection bounced off. The light seemed to be absorbed by the bleakness. All that could be seen was glazing flesh, a sickened body, cowering in the corner, keeping to itself, whimpering. Ramkus dared not take his eyes away, nor move from his spot. But suddenly, his eyes were drawn to a spot, twenty yards ahead of him.
A skull, the bald skull of a man.
A hand ran over it. The skin was pale in the light, as if it had not seen day before, as if it did not belong of any earthly place he knew. The hand wiped down on the heads apex. Eyes shot up, red with heavily dilated black pupils. The eyes consumed Ramkus, as if about to devour him.
"Choose!"
The eyes roared in anger!

He awoke with a jolt, rocking the boat.
'Easy now,' Felipe called out, 'we're almost there.'
The rivers shore was now a coastal shrub, far different from the forest scene they had left in. The river was now opening up into a vast mouth, joining with the sea, doubling from the size before,

smashing into the tidal waves. The salt air hit his lungs, and he relaxed again.

The boat settled itself with a crunch, firmly imbedding into the sandy shore just before it opened completely to the open sea. The roar from the waves gave the impetus to move quickly rather than admire the setting. It was a refreshing scene, as the blistering sea air smacked the wanderers about their faces with a cold shock. They set off in the direction the boat driver had directed, to a large beach hut half a mile down the shore. Struggling to get much traction in the sand - as well as finding it a difficult walk due to his knee - Ramkus took to a sand ledge which held itself together with overgrown sand grass. The late vestiges of sun bathed them with a rich warmth. Waves crashed in as sea birds squawked in flight, diving into the waters far out from land, seeking food. They agreed to themselves that this was a medicine in itself.

Upon making it to the hut, they were greeted by a girl who appeared to be in her late teens, not overly distinctive features, but she held an attractive air about her.

'Greetings,' Felipe beamed with a wide grin, his eyes opening to a large gaze. He was once again full of animation.

'Greetings,' Ramkus added, bowing his head and smiling.

The flamboyant Felipe began to make his whole body move when talking, making grand, articulated gestures. 'My friend and I have come a fair way to see the physician whom we heard was around these parts. Although, obviously, that is not the only attraction around here,' Felipe said, eyes gleaming.

The girl giggled and started to blush. 'Greetings to you too, you must be after my father then. He shouldn't be too long. He has just gone for a walk to the well. Please, sit. Would you like some tea?' She asked in a manner that appeared rehearsed.

'Certainly,' Ramkus interjected, trying to stop the charade of his companion. He gave Felipe a warning shot with a reproachful look, 'That would be much appreciated,' he finished.

They were shown to a wooden table that sat behind the hut. It was set upon a little patch of grass, protected by from the winds by some coastal trees.

'Why is your father so far outside of the town?' Ramkus enquired. 'It was quite a trek getting here. Should he not want to live in a community where it is more comfortable, especially with a daughter to look after. I assume you live here with him?'

The girl nodded.

'Yes, don't you wish to live in a nice town or city?' Felipe added with curiosity.

The girl smiled, 'I do, but my father wishes to remain here, and for me to be with him… to protect me,' she said with a hint of sadness. 'But the reason he is here is, well, a lot of sailors and fisherman crash on the shores all year round. When they are rescued and brought to dry land, they are in such an exhausted state that they are in no position to be taken to town. They would not make such a journey, suffering from shock of the shipwrecks and near drowning. This is the best place to help them. It means we can assist as many people as we can.' She was very casual in her answer, although there appeared a bit of dejection with the way she answered, a state that intimated she had to continually convince herself that this was what she really wanted. Felipe, the astute people person he was, picked up on this.

'So you do wish to be in a town, do you? Meeting people, enjoying life, enjoying music? I doubt you get much of that around here?' He pulled his guitar from around his back.

'Oh no, not at all! We may get an old sea shanty from a recorder or harmonica, played by one of the sailors every so often, but not anything else,' she answered pleasantly.

Her eyes were alight at the sight of Felipe producing the fine instrument, resting it on his lap, readying to play. Before he could begin, a crunch of branches sounded, and a middle-aged man wearing spectacles walked out of the thicket behind the little group. He looked weathered by the elements, fairly lean, carrying two buckets of water.

'Ah, visitors!' the man spoke with delight. 'Very good to have some people come by, been a while since we had anyone cross paths with us.'

The two wanderers rose and bowed their heads respectfully.

'What brings you to these parts?' he continued.

The two looked at each other. 'We seek some medical attention. We were set upon by some thugs yesterday, and are still feeling the effects,' Ramkus replied in a candid manner. 'Have we come to the right place?'

The man nodded, smiling. 'Well, yes, you have. Let's go inside and see what ails you.'

The physician introduced himself as Yazin as they entered his "office". It was a room that was separated from the main dwelling of the hut via a sturdy wall and door. Felipe wished to be looked at first, which unfortunately started with Yazin cutting a few of Felipe's curly black locks - much to Felipe's protests - to get a look at the wound on his temple. The remedy: a few days of ointment, after cleaning the wound, and bandaging around the head to stop any infection from setting in. Felipe was most insulted by this, fearing he would look the fool, until Ramkus suggested tilting his hat over the side to covered the blemish on his being. He tried it out in the mirror, pouting as he did it. The girl took an interest in this narcissistic show, clapping as Felipe entertained her with a regal bow. He was careful not to seem too enthused.

Ramkus was diagnosed with concussion due to the almighty whack he had received to the head from his own staff, but it was his knee that he really wanted Yazin to attend to.

'It is in a very bad way,' Yazin remarked, 'I doubt you will be able to travel in such a state for a while, until it heals itself somewhat. Quite a bit of strain on the ligaments. One can only hope that there hasn't been any bone damage. I can make a concoction that will relieve some of the swelling, and possibly help with any bone damage too. I'll have to collect a few ingredients. In the meantime, put this on, it'll give it some support,' he said as he searched through his chest of drawers, coming out with a leather brace specifically crafted to support the knee. 'You're in a bit of luck that I have these certain appendages. Sailors tend to require such things from time to time.'

Ramkus fitted it on, tweaking it a little with the straps at the back. 'Thank you,' he said in a reflective manner.

'Pleasure, now I shall step out for a bit to get those ingredients, I won't be too long.' Yazin made to leave.

'I'll join you, give you some company,' Ramkus said, trying to get away from the ridiculous Monsieur Felipe for a brief moment. He needed some time away from the irascible bard who was now focussing all his attention on the girl.

The weathered doctor smiled happily, and led Ramkus outside and down a path from the hut which traced the outline of the beach. It was mostly protected by the coastal shrub from the erosion of the sands and heavy gusts of sea mist. The beach ran for miles, and little else could be seen in the distance as the lands were enveloped by sea mist. The greying clouds above had spoilt the azure blue that they had set off under. The wind blew with strength, picking up sea water from over the waves, spitting it onto the two men in meek droplets. Sea birds started gliding ashore, making noise as if to warn each other of an impending weather change.

Ramkus and Yazin talked of the sights, the beach, the sailors, and those small places dotted around. About half a mile away from the hut they stopped. The movement of the sea, the sound of the waters crunching into the sand, the constant movement; Ramkus felt a great urge to go into the water and made comment of such. Yazin believed it actually would be beneficial. So, without hesitation, Ramkus, left his clothes at the beach, and ran into the cold waters.

He felt the calming, soothing, freezing composition of the sea for the first time. It was meditative. Time stopped, there was nothing other than the movement of the currents, the flows of the waves bobbing him up and down. The darkness of the rich, blue depths, all consuming. He looked below to what seemed an unfathomable well of the cosmos. *What secrets does the sea hold?* He was in that moment, free from the small existence he had lived so far; had endured; had enjoyed. All that was melded into this one point. He floated without constraint; without will; without care. All was lifted, all was as it should be. He was content once more: *he* was no more.

Making his way back onto the beach through the heaving rush of the crashing waves, he applied the leather brace. It resembled somewhat a forearm guard an archer would wear: two pieces of leather stretched to fit over a knee, and a hole where the knee cap could fit through. It ran up his thigh a few inches above the joint, and a few inches below, able to be tied on both sides with string to compress the two pieces of leather, but also allow for flexibility.

He dressed into his other attire and waited for Yazin who was meandering back to the spot from his foraging.

'You seem to have enjoyed yourself,' Yazin said, coming back holding a few herbs and strange items that looked to have been washed up onto the shore. It looked like shellfish shells.

'Indeed. As good as new, much rejuvenated,' Ramkus replied with a grin.

Yazin stared out to sea like a forlorn, solitary figure. 'Some people are born to fight the waves, stirring in them a wholesomeness, an activity that brings life to them.' He let out a cough and came around to himself. 'What am I speaking of... Hah, the ramblings of an old man! It has been a very long time since I have really spoken properly to anyone, other than Tilda. My mind does wander. Let me know if I am becoming a little, err, *eccentric* for you. I doubt I can recognise it in myself anymore.'

'Ha! No, you're fine, I am all ears to the *ramblings* of another,' Ramkus said with a happy wink.

They started along the path back to the hut, as Yazin continued to speak, 'I have basically become a recluse. Ever since my wife was killed.' The pleasant mood dropped as quickly as the wind change the weather.

'Killed?! How did that happen?! I am very sorry to hear it.'
Ramkus was beside himself, not knowing how to respond, not
knowing how familiar he should be about asking questions.

'The Empire,' Yazin stated grimly. He stopped as tears welled in his
eyes. 'They killed her. They do what they want to those who don't
believe in their dogma. The bastards.'

'No reason at all?' Ramkus asked, with an incredulous look.

Yazin looked at Ramkus for a few moments. Ramkus noticed a
flicker in his eyes, a tension in his demeanour seemed to follow. He
felt, somehow, he had met the two sides of Yazin after knowing him
for only a brief time.

'Aye, they had their reason.' Yazin sunk his head low, 'A long time
ago I lived with my wife and Tilda in a town a bit further up the river
from Kerwood. I, as physician, doctor, surgeon, medic, have taken
an oath to help all those that require such skills in the medical way;
never able to refuse assisting one in need. Of course, I am still
allowed to make a little money from it on the way. But that is my
essence, that is what I feel and know is my work; the purpose of my
life in this world. It is not for me to judge others, only to tend to
them, no matter who they are or what they represent.' Yazin took a
deep breath before letting go. 'One night I was called urgently to the
aid of two men in the town. One was an Officer of the Empire, who
was known as a violent man. The other, the son of the pharmacist.
Of course, I had a good relationship with the pharmacist and knew
his family. His son was a good lad, and it never made any sense at
the time as to how he had had seemingly become embroiled in a
violent fight with the Officer. The Officer was clearly drunk though.

'In any case, I was called to help the Officer, not the boy, as they
both lay on the ground with puncture wounds from whatever they
had found to stab at each other. The Officer was howling in pain, not
too bad off, but the boy was close to death! What could I do but help
the one I felt was in greatest need of my help, the little I could give.
It was not a judgement call on whom I was fonder of, only who
needed my attention the most!'

Yazin's eyes pleaded for moral support, his body stooped, 'I had the boy taken to my home so I would be best equipped and able to help him as I could. Then... then...' he began shaking, visibly distressed. 'They burst into my home, up to the second floor where I was operating on the lad. My wife, she was helping me, holding a lantern. They, they raced up the stairs for the perpetrator whom had "attacked" the Officer. As they tried to pick him up from the bed, my wife, she tried to cover him, defend him from the intruders. But one of these "soldiers" grabbed her and thrust her to the glass door that led to our little balcony... She smashed through it and went over the balustrade, falling on the pavement a floor below.'

Yazin paused, his face bleak, drained of emotion. 'She was dead. Dead because I helped this poor boy. I don't know who the soldier was, but there was no inquest into the death. No, all that happened was that I had black mark placed against my name for helping the boy, and a dark depression, a riven, throughout my whole being. The boy was carried off and died not soon after whilst imprisoned without any medical care. He could have at least been saved had I been able to tend to him. It was the least that could have been done. But I was too distraught anyway. My world, my life, it had been shattered. My work was the destroyer of my love. *I* had killed her with the choice *I* had made. I suffered dreadfully the next few weeks. Tilda was only an infant. I cannot remember how she was looked after, but I can only imagine the generosity of neighbours when I was so complacent and lost to the world. I had to get out of that claustrophobic place, I had to leave. I travelled around with Tilda in tow for a number of months, until we came to settle by the sea. I basked in the sunshine, bathed in the waters, and felt the world we had left disappear from view. I was at some peace.' He remained silent, looking out to the waters. 'I find my place fighting these currents every day. It helps me forget the past, focus on the moment.'

A gentle breeze of sea air rocked the shrubs from side to side.

'I am sorry,' Ramkus said calmly.

'No, it's fine, I just can't help but feel anger for the Empire. The way they treated us commoners, with utter disregard, as if we are nothing.' Yazin clenched his jaw tight.

They remained silent until Ramkus, not knowing how to proceed, started up again, 'Do you know what happened to the Officer?'

Yazin frowned morbidly and shrugged, 'He survived. Probably still drinking at one of the taverns in the town. But I do not blame him, I cannot blame anyone, it is not for me to judge. If I did, I would find no peace on this earth. To my eyes, though, there is no justice in the world, only those who live and die.'

The brief pause between them did not lift until Ramkus queried further: 'Did you find out how the fight started?'

'Ha, apparently the boy had taken a liking to the Officer's daughter. Although they were both of age, the Officer did not approve of anyone not in the Empire's ranks, and so he died for such an indiscretion.' A look of despair crept onto Yazin's face, 'This is not a pretty world my friend, not everyone is of a kind disposition. A dogged intent to fight, kill, and control rests on many a heart. But what are people meant to do against those with such a nature, fall to their knees and grovel? Despair at such an existence?' He shook his head, 'No we stand, we stand up to those and we live by another code which seeks the fairness for all people. A code for those who do not judge, who wish for peace and good times. Many do, but the numbers, they seem to be dwindling in recent times. The Empire keeps growing, as are the number of Officers and the reach of the Empire's rule of law. That warmongering culture, spreading farther and farther...'

Ramkus pondered this predicament. *What is my role to play in this: supposedly a facilitator between the different people who inhabit this world, these lands? To help people, is that my role; my job; my nature? What is a Guardian? Why do I feel no overwhelming instinct or nature then, only a sense to live each moment as it comes. To walk the paths, to wander them.* As far as he knew, he had no home; lest everywhere on the face of the earth be his home, and how best to see it all than wander it, as he did his thoughts. He pitied the

physician and his tale, and of his daughter, Tilda, whom was
enduring out here in the isolation as well. Not an easy existence,
being beaten by the forces every day, literally facing them as the sea
breathed life, howling at them at other times.

It was beginning to grow dark and clouds started to roll with
foreboding tides, displaying waves of grey, white, and black. He
hoped the taxi boat that dropped them off would soon be coming
back in from its fishing haul and going back upstream to Kerwood.
Rain looked inevitable.

'You may stay with us tonight, if you wish,' Yazin offered, catching
Ramkus in his deep thoughts.

'Thank you, but I am not sure we will be able to as Felipe is to play
at the Kerwood Inn for his - and perhaps my – board,' Ramkus
replied.

'Ah, well, it would be a pleasure to have you stay in my care, if you
do wish to reconsider,' he inclined.

Ramkus, listening to the winds and rain, with night coming, began to
think it may indeed be the best option.

'Well, we shall see what Felipe has to say,' he reconsidered.

'Ah, yes. You do know, it is very easy to talk to you my friend.
Very easy to open up. Has anyone told you that before?' Yazin
asked.

Ramkus smiled courteously, wondering if that was perhaps the way
of the Guardian: to listen.

As they entered the hut, Ramkus regarded the small dwelling in finer
detail. A nice pot of stew was boiling on the fire stove, the crackling
flames within the solid fireplace in the wall permeating just the right
amount of heat. There was a table in the middle, and a wall with a
door that separated the medical office from the rest of the house. On
this wall hung medical equipment: scalpels, needles, glass jars,
medicines, herbs. The other side of the main room had two beds,
side by side, partitioned by a small wall that only reached head
height, enough to give the father and daughter some privacy. All

well and good, until a certain situation arose which froze Ramkus and Yazin to their spots: Felipe and Tilda were in bed, together...

'**Tilda!**' cried Yazin. He started breathing heavily, reeling from what he was seeing.

Felipe jumped up and grabbed his clothes from a chair.

'Sorry, we were just,' he stammered.

'**Get out!**' Yazin yelled, eyes protruding, veins becoming prevalent along his temple, as his body turned red. Rage was setting in. 'Get Out! Get Out! Get Out!!' he yelled.

Felipe ran right by the two outside.

He then ran back in to get his guitar, and out as fast as possible again. Ramkus sensed this was some sort of thrill for Felipe, all in good humour...

The girl was cowering in the sheets of the bed.

'Yazin,' Ramkus began, 'I...'

'Out!' Yazin screeched, his finger pointing to the door, face burning with rage like the hearth of a fire.

Standing, mouth agape, Ramkus didn't press the issue. As he exited, standing at the door outside, he turned to speak, to at least apologise for that damn fool he had been journeying along with, and to thank him. He didn't get the chance, as Yazin came to the door, and slammed it shut.

Wind rushed passed him as it did. He, stood with the door in his face, staring; he was flummoxed by the whole series of events. After a few moments, he turned to the *idiot* Felipe.

'I cannot believe you would do that, she was just a girl! He was helping us!' Ramkus growled.

Felipe, who had seemingly gotten over the whole affair already, responded, 'Come now, she was almost twenty, her father holds her against her will. She was a damsel in distress, wanting to be free, wanting to do what *she* wants. I was showing her a good time, a sensual one that the she would rarely get - and I doubt she ever has!'

'Do not try and justify yourself to me by deceiving yourself of some facts. We were here to see that poor man, to seek out his help, not

offend him and take advantage of the situation!' h continued to
berate Felipe.

'How was that taking advantage of the situation? You think she only
fancied me because she had been offered very little with what passes
by? She instigated the affair as much as I. It was *I* who was being
courted when you went out, not *her*. I tend to attract girls like that,
no matter where or when. Whether I myself choose to allow them
the opportunity is another matter! For if it *was* up to me - and I
wanted to - I could *charm any woman; any place, any time,*' Felipe
stated with an arrogant smirk. 'But all that aside, I am talking to a
Guardian. What do you know of the *dance of lovers.*'

'You are incorrigible, you think so damn highly of yourself and
forget all others who are affected by your actions!' Ramkus seethed.

'You mean, *you*?' Felipe said accusingly. 'Hmm, perhaps you
wanted her for yourself!'

'Don't be so utterly ridiculous. You now sound as if you are the
victim!' Ramkus scowled.

They stared at each other for a while. Ramkus with repugnance,
Felipe with hubris.

'You really ought to put your pants on,' Ramkus said, calming the air
between them. 'It's not the best look.'

'Yes, sorry' Felipe replied, calming down.

Ramkus looked away, 'Leave some of those coins for the man'

'Why!?' Felipe said in an agitated tone.

'Because he did, after all, tend to our ailments. He also gave me this
leather knee brace. Leave him some coin, Felipe,' Ramkus turned
back, frowning at the bard. Felipe finally realised it was a fairly
serious matter for Ramkus, and gave in to the Guardian's demand,
tossing some money to Ramkus who placed it at the foot of the door.
The clouds started to cackle, just as Felipe had adjusted his guitar on
his back. Sensing it was about to storm heavily, Felipe threw his
cloak over himself and his precious cargo.

'Let's hope we can get back quickly,' Ramkus said forebodingly,
knowing it may end up a tough ask.

They set off towards the mouth of the river.

The rain did hit quick and hard, and it did not look to have an end in sight as it rolled in heavy droves from the sea. There appeared to be a few fishing vessels a fair way out, as the duo scoured the sea for any life to wave down once they had made it to the river's edge. The few boats they spotted did not seem to be leaving their spots.

'We will have wait,' Ramkus shook his head. 'Let's at least go into the forest for a little protection.'

Heeding the suggestion, they found some shelter amongst the larger trees in the forest. There was ample cover to provide a dry area, enough to allow Felipe to pull out his guitar as they sat down.

'You know, people have died for lesser offences than what you have done,' Ramkus remarked whilst watching the tide coming in.

'Oh, leave it be, I was only having a bit of fun, she was too. How else are we meant to live? *What is life without enjoyment?* In fact, what is the point of life other than *to* enjoy it? Yes, we toil in our troubles, but, **the enjoyment of life is paramount!**' He looked out to the river, a faint smile crept on his face as he played a few notes, Ramkus remained silent and stern.

He turned towards Ramkus with a questioning look after a few moments had passed, 'How would *you* know what people have died for, especially for *offences* like that? Pth!' He stared off at the river once more, waiting, watching attentively for a boat. The heavy droplets made the water look as if it had dishes dancing and moving on top. Coastal scrub bushes moved hither to and fro with the strong gusts, never enough to threaten their foundations, though.

'Fine, whatever you believe,' Ramkus said. A sudden shot of despair crept along his train of thought. *What is the point of life; what is the point of my existence?* He had merely stood to attention, doing what he was made for - *If I was* made… *How indeed did I come to be!? I just was, I just awoke.* There was no before, at least he had no recollection of anything before. *And now? What am I to do now? Follow this Guardian path I have heard only skerricks of information about, having to abide by it once I meet this* Order. *And that is*

74

assuming I am a Guardian after all. Will I have some enjoyment in life after that?

He felt sick, as if all the pressures of reality were hitting him at once. He wished to sink into the ground and abandon this existence in which he knew so little of what he was; already this world seemed unjust to those who deserved to be heralded and prized. What type of world had he awoken to? What type of person was he to be? The despair overwhelmed him as he stared off into the ground. He had nothing, he was nothing, he had no freedom of choice. *Or do I?* For the first time he considered that maybe he was not bound to some duty, to some life as a Guardian - even if he did not know for sure he was one. He lifted his head and looked to the river, rain rolled down from his hair, as a deep rich smell of damp earth hit his olfactory sense.

What stops me from having fun and enjoyment? Maybe Guardians are allowed to live a happy existence. If not, I do not have to be one! He had the whole world at his feet. He may not have anything, but that meant he was bound to nothing; not to any people, not to any place. He could wander to all far reaches, tasting all that life offered. There was no point in the grovelling. He could *be*, and therefore he could *live*. He looked over to Felipe, who was playing absent-mindedly on his guitar.

'Why not give me a lesson now?' Ramkus asked.

Felipe turned his head, wearing a surprised grin. He responded: 'But of course, not a bad idea at all!'

In this first lesson, Ramkus found an instinctive rhythm for the music, he had an ear for the notes. In fact, it surprised Felipe a little that someone could have so much a natural talent from the very start. As Ramkus played, a small appreciation, a love for the music, came over him, ever so slightly building into a genuine adoration and love. It was akin to the relaxation of a meditation. It almost enveloped him completely, calmed him. It became like his swim in the sea with how it affected his mind; with its void of feeling and sight, this pervasion of the ears and mind. He was once again content, over the small malaise, back to a peaceful and harmonious existence. The incident before: forgotten.

As this was taking shape, a boat started to drift into view up the river towards them.

'Oh shit!' Felipe cried, 'We're going to miss that boat!'

The boat jutted along, closer and closer, Felipe jumped up and yelled, 'Can we get a ride, kind sirs?'

It was a little unfortunate that it was actually two old women. They took offence at Felipe's mistake and turned their cheeks in repudiation.

'Sorry, my ladies. Please?' he tried again.

They decidedly did not look to the river's edge, as Felipe and Ramkus chased them along the muddy river bank for a short distance.

'Ladies, please!' Felipe yelled. Speaking to Ramkus as they ran, 'We will just have to jump in the boat, they won't have any say in it that way!'

'If you say so. If you think this is the *path to enjoyment,*' Ramkus chided.

Felipe, with guitar in hand; Ramkus, with his staff and feeling quite stable on foot with his knee braced up, continued running along the bank, looking for a clear spot to make the jump. Ramkus was a lot quicker and jumped straight into the boat where there was a space for seating, landing with the grace of a cat. The two ladies were stunned, and immediately steered the boat to the centre of the river as Felipe jumped. He missed the seating space he was aiming for, and fell into a day's worth of catch. It smelt putrid, and as Ramkus began to laugh at his misfortune, Felipe was given a great whack with a paddle. The old women had taken up arms!

Ramkus was laughing until he himself was hit on the side and flattened out.

'You bastards!' The women cried out, 'We will not be taken by you!'

Ramkus could not stop laughing, even when being given the beating, wondering if Felipe still thought he could *charm any woman; any place, any time.*

Chapter IV

After the initial paddle beating, the trip was not too unpleasant. Felipe had, in his infinite wisdom – and to stop being hit by the women's paddles - explained he would pay for the voyage, in fact he offered three times the amount as the first trip they'd taken out to sea. The old women had accepted – reluctantly – to stop beating him for such a sum.

The wind blew with strength, and the boat sailed along the river at pace, for they were in luck with the tide coming in also. It had turned out, as another piece of luck would have it, the reason the women did not travel in the centre of the expansive mouth of the river, was so to have a little shelter from the winds and rain; they would not have cared to come in and help two passengers looking for travel, even if they weren't insulted to begin with. Had the weather lifted, Ramkus and Felipe may have indeed had to have waited long into the night. Probably a good thing for Felipe, as Ramkus was still seething, brooding over the poor behaviour Felipe had exhibited, in his opinion. The leaves blew in all directions, as the branches waved about. The rain was only spitting by the time they had hit one of the many river arteries, stopping altogether once the river started to twist and bend through the forest. An orange and yellow skyline was exposed on the horizon, and the clouds appeared to have lifted from their position, creating a scene of space and serenity that was very unlike the compressed and dark setting it had only been half an hour before. They were still drenched in any case, so they made their way into the man-made canal of Kerwood, smelling of fish. Felipe was as gracious as ever, bickering to the old ladies that they had manipulated the situation for the poor travellers, getting such an absurd amount of payment by forcing them accept outlandish fees under duress. He finished by saying the two women ought to be reprimanded for their *river-way robbery*.

But they had made it back to Kerwood, and were at least feeling comforted by the thought of some warm food and drink in front of the massive fireplace of the inn. Felipe even went so far as to insist they have a bath in the bathing rooms found in the basement to warm up their bones… and get rid of the smell. All necessary in order to get into *prime performance mode*, naturally.

Huge wooden barrels that could easily hold half a dozen men - if they were used for the purposes of transporting people - were found in the *bathing room*. Ramkus counted four of them, each with a small ladder to get inside. Although there was water in them already, it was cold and uninviting. Large kettles on stoves were being boiled to the side of the room, positioned on hooks which allowed the kettles spouts to be poured onto small aqueducts connecting to the bathing barrels, filling them with the piping hot water to heat them. Two girls were operating and filling the kettles apparatus, making light work of what would be far too heavy for even two men to lift manually without the marvellous manoeuvring system. Felipe and Ramkus got into the baths after tossing their cloaks aside and wrapping towels around themselves. The girls were giggling, eyeing the two of them. Ramkus blushed, feeling he was the true target of their gaze.

'Come on girls, fill up the tub!' Felipe yelled with his back to them. There was a plank inside the edges about halfway up the barrel for the men to sit. The placed the towels over the side as the girls became more attentive to their task, dismissing their playful smiles as they focussed on letting the kettles pour down the aqueducts. Steam shot out as they poured, and the water raced down into the tub, piercing the cold waters, letting vapours rise above the barrel. The hot water began combining with the cold, becoming lukewarm, then warm, then hot. This took a good few minutes, as the steam and vapours created a heavy fog of damp hot air that warmed the lungs. Ramkus raised his head back, enjoying the warmth, arms resting back on the barrel's sides. Sighing deeply and contentedly, he took in the scene of the bathing room: it was quite well lit by candles, and the last vestiges of light were shining through the small windows that popped up at the top of the walls just above ground level - not to mention fire of the stoves burned with illumination. Felipe began to go on a monologue about bathing rooms and bathing houses, stating that this was one of the larger bathing rooms he had found for a town this size. Ramkus supposed that it was probably because most of the people of Kerwood smelt of fish a large proportion of the time. Not all of them would have their own baths, or their houses were too far away, making it a necessity to have a good one in town. *But then, why would it bother the people if they were so used to the smell? Maybe it is simply used to warm people up*, Ramkus mused.

'Ohh, the luxuries! The pleasures of life! You see why I speak so highly of this type of lifestyle? Utter relaxation! The Empire built a great many bath houses for their armies. They demand places that are under their dominion to have bath houses for their troops, should they ever visit such places.' Felipe informed Ramkus.

Mystery solved, thought Ramkus, smiling to himself in contemplation. 'I did not think this was part of the Empire, these forests?' He quizzed Felipe.

'No, these parts have always been part of the Empire, they have always been compliant. The people: they are simple, they live and do what they are told. It may not have the trimmings of the Empire, but they have always been seen to be part of it, obeying all requests. To be fair, I don't think that it really bothers their lives much,' Felipe explained.

The girls started giggling again, eyeing Ramkus, making him blush. 'The pleasures of life, Ramkus. Why should you not enjoy them also.' Felipe gave a wink after turning around and having a look at the two kettle bearers

Why should I not, Ramkus considered. *What stops him from enjoying the luxuries of life?* He found himself desiring the affections of the two girls. It gave him a little bit of pride; *But why do people not always enjoy the pleasures? Is it that it is unhealthy?* He summed it up as all people playing a part in the grand scheme, work-wise; not everyone can enjoy pleasures all the time, or ever for some. *But why should people not enjoy as much of these pleasures outside of work as the can?* It was odd that his mindset was already implying a need for duty, one which would not allow him to *enjoy the pleasures*.

Felipe started up again, 'Do you ever - not to sound rude – feel a need?' He laughed after recognising who and what he was speaking to.

'What do you mean?'

'A need. A desire, I don't know how else to speak about it to someone that has basically only begun their voyage through life. A *carnal* need.'

Ramkus was unsure. He felt no *carnal* needs.

'I am talking about, *with women...*' Felipe added.

Ramkus was still unsure that he - as far as he could tell – did have any *carnal* needs. Did he find these girls attractive? *Somewhat.* Did he have a need that could be taken care of by them? He could not say, and he felt the answer would lean towards "no" in any case.

'They say Guardians do not enjoy the pleasures of life, at least not all pleasures,' Felipe continued, as he was sure he had confused the mind of this newly awoken. 'I was just curious to see if you were like, well, other men.' He paused, intoxicated with the steam, 'I haven't heard of a female Guardian either, come to think of it. They all seem to be men.'

'I cannot answer these questions, or even add to your knowledge,' Ramkus said matter-of-factly. He was becoming a little agitated with the topic that plagued his thoughts with questions already. 'All I can say is, I do not feel this *carnal need,* as you put it.' He went silent, off into his thoughts. Maybe it was something that had to be *done* before he knew his desire or need. There was much that played on his mind, but he let it all seep from his consciousness as another shot of hot water hit the cooling tub. Steam was rising, and he was content once more; relaxing in this luxurious barrel. Felipe turned around and made some gestures with his hand. One of the girls brought over some soaps and scent. The scent was dropped into the barrel, as Felipe handed one of the soaps to Ramkus, and the other he used on himself. The girl was staring doe-eyed at Ramkus the whole time, he returned a friendly smile, trying not to become embarrassed and flustered. She was a fairly plain girl, probably in her mid-twenties; she looked quite strong and sturdy, as if the work in the inn had adapted her body to various rigorous activities. Ramkus was not outwardly desiring of her.

'Perhaps, most probably, you have not seen someone to your liking yet,' Felipe said, he was reading Ramkus and pressing the issue.

'Why do you care so much, Felipe? Are you trying to excuse your actions with the poor doctor's daughter, Tilda? Is it that you wish for me to follow in your pursuit so as to make you feel less guilty?' He knew it would not be the same situation though, and that there would be no guilt involved as they were not being brought into someone's house with trust and kindness in the same manner.

Felipe scoffed, 'No! But I do wish for you to understand, and I don't think you can! It is one of the reasons to live! Yet there are some that dismiss it, as if it is repulsive! They are prudes, and I do not wish for you to turn out to be one. Guardians tend to be as such.'

'Is that from experience?' Ramkus quickly rebutted.

'In a sense, yes, but let's stop fighting, I just came to relax before tonight,' Felipe evaded.

Ramkus did not say anything, he started to consider why anyone should have to move at all, to live. It was merely instinct for him to get up from the field he awoke in. No desire, just instinct.

The steam continued to rise from the bath, and the new scent with it. Ramkus relaxed and soaked it all in.

XXX

They entered the great hall of the tavern, Felipe with an exaggerated, joyful smile. Night had fallen, and the hall was filling with patrons: mostly local sorts, but a few individuals that did not fit the picture entirely. One was a hooded stranger, smoking a pipe in the corner. He looked menacing and was eyeing Felipe and Ramkus as soon as they entered. It was obvious he was not a friendly sort, as the *locals* - as far as Ramkus could tell - were keeping their measure from this man. They were spouting their general banter in close knit groups, every so often giving a good shout over to other locals with much volume. There were either seated on the large bench tables or standing, seeming to take no notice of Ramkus or Felipe, all consumed in the tales of the day; of the fish caught, and the weather. 'Very boring talk,' Felipe said with a hint of indignation. 'No great thoughts have ever sprung from this tavern.'

Ramkus was once again feeling an animosity towards Felipe and his disingenuous attitude towards people who simply lived life in different circumstances. They made their way to the bar and ordered some of the famous fish broth and local fresh bread from the extensive menu that consisted of: fish broth and bread. This time at least the broth was fresh, with produce caught that day. They were also treated to some of the dark ale from the local brewer up the river; the Innkeeper was quite proud of it, as he was one of the only establishments to have it on offer. Finding a spot near the fire, they settled amidst other tables packed with townsfolk and the people from the surrounding farms. The two observed the atmosphere and scene.

Wooden floor boards that, although had been scrubbed time and time again, held no gleam, lifeless and seeming to contain dust that had now become solid. The upper rafters of the hall were filling with touches of smoke from the fireplace, and tobacco smoke from those in the building who were cradling beautiful, exquisite hand-crafted pipes; *Must be their favourite possessions', to put so much thought and care into them*, thought Ramkus. At the corner of the wall, meeting the bar area, a little dais for speeches and performances. Men, women, of all ages were entering the place, constantly pouring in, filling it quite quickly. The two ate in silence. Ramkus looking over the people spotted a pretty girl. Red haired, high full cheeks, button nose, fairly buxom, green eyes. She caught his gaze and smiled at him. He quickly faced his broth, feeling pangs of embarrassment. Felipe, the ever-keen observer, noted Ramkus's sudden reaction, having a look behind himself to calculate the reason.

He smiled on one side of his mouth, nodding, 'Not bad, maybe she *is* your type, maybe she will be the one to break you from you - *noble* behaviour. The pleasures of life my friend. Why should we not enjoy ourselves in the little time we have on this mortal coil?' The smile grew across his face.

Ramkus looked back at the girl who was talking to her group of friends, probably all in their early twenties. She was also keeping a small check on him as well, smiling when she met his eyes. This *eyeing* built to the stage where they were holding the gaze of each other, her whilst she was in conversation with her friends, him whilst sipping on his broth.

The broth held a bit more of a bite than in the morning, and the ale was actually delightful; Ramkus could have ended up guzzling a great deal of it without realising, had his attention not drifted towards a man standing by the huge log fire on the wall, staring into it, lost in thought. He seemed glum, lost and wayward, having the look of a soldier to him.

Although Ramkus and Felipe's clothes had nearly dried from the day's rain, there were still cold patches that needed heating up and steaming out. Finishing their meal, Felipe made his way back to their room to prepare for the night, leaving Ramkus to move to the fire and warm out his clothing completely. As he approached the spot next to the glum man. He looked possessed by the fire, leaning his hand atop it as if he had opened a great scroll and was reading its contents. The man, in his daze, turned to Ramkus. He had a beard of a few week's growth and seemed a little grubby, but still held an air of order reserved for those who demanded respect – although in this case, he hadn't demanded it, for he was still in a mood of despair.

Feeling for the man, Ramkus thought he should hear of what troubled him. He knew not why he cared, perhaps curious of life's mysteries that are wrapped up in each individual; or perhaps listening to all trapped, deep dark stories, the world would somehow open up to him. *Maybe it is in the nature of a Guardian.*

'I hope you don't mind me standing here,' Ramkus began in an earnest manner, thinking this the politest way to begin any dialogue with a point or question in mind. 'I couldn't help but notice that you staring into the fire, lost in thought, and did not know if you would be annoyed to have someone encroach upon your space.' He was speaking a little too over the top, berating himself inwardly.

'Is it obvious? Hell, I bet it is,' the man spoke in a strong voice; a soldier's voice. He looked like one with his posture and stance. 'Please, enjoy the fire, there is enough space for both of us. I did not realise I was turning people away.' He looked around the room at the locals; they kept to themselves and their chatter. This man who had now joined him was definitely not of their ilk. 'You're not a soldier, are you?' Asked the man.

He had a well-trimmed head of blonde hair, sharp features with heavily imbedded battle scars; his eyes were intent and questioning, but not of an aggressive nature.

Ramkus, a little taken aback, replied, 'No, never, I am…' his voice trailed on as he searched for a description of himself, 'a wanderer.' *Yes*, he thought, *the perfect description without giving much away of myself.*

The blonde-haired man scrutinised him, 'You are aligned with a certain region, people, kingdom?' The man realised the potency of his questions. It was vexed and unnecessary, showed he was fearful of someone.

'No, not at all. I am aligned to no one… Are you?' It seemed a little careless to ask in such a way, but was spoken with such innocence that the man seemed to want to confide in him. Ramkus thought that this intimacy where people spoke freely and trusted in him, may also be some sort of trait that he, as a Guardian, possessed. *For Guardians must* – as he saw it – *have to have some ability to be trusted by others of all regions, people, and kingdoms.* He mused on it only a second, as the man gave him a trustful smile, and relaxed his shoulders.

'I *used* to be,' he began with resignation, 'I used to be aligned with people. My people. Under the order of the Empire.' He shook his head, 'I used to be a soldier in the Empire's forces, fight with them, travel with them, conquer with them. I *was* one of them. Asking no questions, being trusted within the rank and file, treated as one would expect to be treated. I had served for a very long time,' his voice trailed off as he gazed downward.

He appeared as if in his early thirties to Ramkus - who was surprised he even had an idea of *age*.

'I had served long enough to see how the Empire has changed, becoming a beast that continually needs to be fed, to devour. Uncontrollable and without an end in sight. To grow, to control, to the extent that innocence will - if seen to stand in the way - be eradicated.'

Ramkus squinted trying to read the man.

'I cannot support what the Empire stands for now, it is not what it once was. It has become barbaric, cynical, fearful of itself, turning in on itself. Maybe it is *I* who have changed. However, and it always has been like this. I have only had the blinkers of my vision lifted.'

The manner in which he spoke did not afford Ramkus to fully follow or comprehend. He did not know if the blonde-haired man was speaking of the Empire itself, the army; or part of the army he was with.

'So, you are no longer aligned to what you feel is unjustifiable? You now stand on your own?' Ramkus finally responded after a moments silence.

'Yes,' the deserter replied with a weak laugh.

'Let us drink to that.' They lifted their tankards.

After a brief pause, Ramkus continued, 'Was there a campaign that changed your mind?'

The deserter stared for a while at the fire, 'Yes. Well, it in no way could be called a campaign. No, it was merely an exercise of control and might. Of destruction. I used to be in charge of an outpost, close to the Sunden Mountain Range, far from here. We had a good rampart that ran smoothly enough and was set up to keep in check the mountain people, as well as forest dwellers nearby. They both lived in their small cities or towns around the area. As you know, very hard to *move on*, and distrustful of the Empire. I don't blame them, I believe they were here for a lot longer than we ever were, but have adapted and become more human. We actually lived in a rather harmonious setting, and were gaining the trust of these people, bartering with them, living side by side. *Almost.* We had cultivated a bridge for our cultures to appreciate and accept each other: the mountain folk, the forest dwellers, and the Empire's people.' He sighed and bent his head down before bringing it back up to continue.

'The orders from the Capital were not to create such a *bond*, however. No, the orders were to make the people *assimilate*, to control them, for fear of… well, an uprising, even though these people held no abilities to start such a rebellion.' The man clenched his jaw and brought a fist down upon the fire's mantlepiece.

'I did not follow those orders, I had other reasons amongst the feeling we were creating something special. Everyone felt that. Over time, however, the Capital *felt* that we had been given enough time to exact control, and that it had not been done to a sufficient extent. They sent out the *Burbar Regiment*.' He turned to Ramkus with a disgusted look. 'You have heard of them?'

Ramkus shook his head, intent on letting the man vent his obvious anger.

'No, well, I'll tell you who they are. They are a murderous group of thugs who wish for nothing but blood. Their leader came with an iron fist, taking the helm of the outpost immediately after arriving, forcing us to pick up arms and put an end to the Mountain and Forest peoples of the region. See, they did not think to assimilate, they only wanted to see the rush of blood over the terrain. They started out, heading into the mountains, butchering the people who ran, shackling those that had asked for mercy. Many of our troops who were ourselves forced to ride with the Burbars were sickened by the acts. Desecrating, pilfering, massacring and binding their friends in chains.' He breathed heavily. As he looked forlornly into the flames. 'But they did not break ranks, for this was the will of the Empire. I could not commit such acts, though… I could not succumb to being involved in such atrocities. I was able to warn the people of the Forest, and in doing so, hopefully saved *some* of them.'

The deserter was silent for a long time, Ramkus did not know if he should say anything or not.

'And so, you are here,' Ramkus said, grasping for something to break the silence.

'And so, I am here.' His eyes were reddened with rage and sadness. 'Here. Alone. A fugitive... I can only imagine that I am to be made an example of. How often does one of the Empire's own show such a disregard for orders or for the will of the rulers, breaking from the chain of command.' He shook his head showing a damaged spirit, a fighting one that had been battered and was in danger of being lost in the dark loneliness of his ruminations. 'I should have fled over the mountains and on into the desert, to some other kingdom. Maybe they wouldn't treat me poorly. But the Empires reach, its influence... its stretching to the most isolated of bastions. I have been here for a few days.' He stopped, looking about the hall, 'I am expecting they will show.'

The man seemed to take pride from letting his story flow, committing himself to a cause which he could justify to the world. His eyes glistened an inner strength and resolve that he had done his part in sharing the story.

Ramkus eyed the people, the lively action of the scene, waving to and fro in the light of the candles and fire. His view rested back on the pretty red-haired girl he had been exchanging glances with before. He'd forgotten all about her. She gave him a little smile from a distance. More of the locals had taken to smoking their pipes, creating a hazy atmosphere with the powerful smell of tobacco. The smoke that was lifting to the ceiling rafters was descending as if a fog. In the corner, the dark hooded stranger still stood with his back to the wall, head down, but giving the sense he was keeping an eye on Ramkus and his new acquaintance, looking pent up and ready to pounce.

'You do not wish to fight?' Ramkus asked, turning his attention back to this deserter. 'I would think that one in the corner may be sent after you. He has been watching us for a while, as if readying himself.'

The deserter looked to the man in the corner and scoffed,' I highly doubt he is. He is not the type the Empire would employ. Not of the *culture* or *look* the Empire is trying to create.'

'Are you sure? He may be a spy, incognito?' Ramkus pressed.

The deserter scoffed again, 'No, he doesn't have the qualities of the Empire.'

Ramkus felt the deserter re-lifted with an air of arrogance when talking of the Empire in such terms. Something ingrained, as if he took pride that the Empire were his enemy above all: a worthy adversary he knew all too well. Ramkus began to muse on the hypocrisy that this man's indoctrination into the Empire's belief in *types* of people being so well founded in him had seemingly created a division from his initial outlook - *And this was what he was meant to be running away from!* He smiled to himself, finding it funny that he should muse on such things when he knew so little about the world, himself, and life.

The man grabbed two drinks from a bar girl whom walked by with a tray of tankards, returning some coin and a faint smile.

'Good stuff this ale, and the food. Could be my last meal,' the deserter said in macabrely. 'It is a beautiful neck of the woods - pardon the pun – at least it has not been destroyed by growth, still has a rustic charm.' The mood began to lift with these comments as hushes descended upon the patrons.

Felipe started to make a grand entrance from the direction of the rooms. The crowd were gathering and turning their heads. The deserter's curiosity picked up as he glanced around the hall, and then to Felipe who was about to take the dais. Felipe started with a small soft guitar song which allowed the patrons to get their drinks and finish off conversations before the main act.

The man nodded to himself and said in a humble tone 'Thank you for listening, everyone else here keeps to themselves.'

Ramkus inclined his head, 'A pleasure.'

'I would like to hear of yourself, if I may be so permitted,' the deserter said.

Ramkus, thinking to himself, gave a little chuckle. As much as he did not know *himself*, he did have a few tales to tell of already. 'Me? Well, I...'

The music became louder as Felipe began his performance in earnest. Most of the crowd were in place and eager to listen to some musical tales. The deserter and Ramkus rested their tankards upon the top of fire place.

'This is the story of the sea god,' Felipe sent the crowd in a rapturous applause with an obvious favourite for a fishing village.

And upon these water's lie,
One who may cast the die.
Of He whom chance and fate,
Can of himself set the date.
For mere mortals let it be known,
The path best to be blown.

The song continued, evoking images of the stormy waters that Ramkus had entered during the day. The place where the sky met the sea, shrouded in mist, along with the lengths of the beach. The roaring crash of waves, wanting to crush the sand underneath, only to be drawn back into its own recesses. It calmed Ramkus, listening to the romanticised story of the sea and its great god, Tolmu, who had chosen a mortal warrior to fight for him and his claim to the land, to the world. The warrior helped make rivers for Tolmu to travel further into this land. He fought tree and earth spirits, conquering the territories for his master, until he met a girl whom made him put his spear aside. She was of the great earth: the mountains; and she was spreading their earthen claim to the lower reaches. Tilling the world, making it picturesque and inhabitable. The warrior gave up his duties, leaving Tolmu for the girl. Tolmu was angry, rage-filled! He wished for retribution against this wayward warrior he had entrusted. He put his powers to work, creating a massive storm. Though the two were seemingly out of harm's way, high on a mountain, the storm from the sea rose and brought down great volumes of rain upon the land, creating havoc for the earth and forests. A great mudslide occurred, and the girl was washed down into a ravine which filled with water and lifted her away to one of the great rivers that the warrior had helped make. He cried out to her, and to Tolmu, but neither answered. When all seemed lost, a great crack appeared in the earth, and a voice came to him. It was the earth, the mountains, that spoke to him. It told him to once again pick up his spear, create rivers that would flow to them and not to sea. And so, he went to task, working as hard as he could. The mountain supplied their own water, which rushed from its peak to the newly formed passages. Eventually, the mountain's rivers met and linked with the rivers of the sea god. The sea god was unaware of this linkage of waters, and the mountain spirits were able to use this to their advantage, grabbing the girl, dragging her up river and back towards them inland. Tolmu finally noticed his folly of not keeping watch of the mountain spirits at his back. As he raged at his mishap, he gained strength and speed, racing up the channels, overtaking the rivers flow upstream, he reached the girl and pulled her back to sea again. The warrior was able to dive in and save the girl whilst the water was inland... However, unfortunately, she had drowned, and so he buried her in the earthen cracks created by the mountains. With tears of sadness, rage, and anger, he dove back into the river, fighting back at Tolmu, all the way to the sea. The mountain's waters rushed with him, giving him backing and strength, till he reached the sea, where the mountain could offer help no more. Tolmu raged back, pushing him up the river, towards the mountains, until the mountains gathered their own strength and helped propel him back to the sea until they lost strength once more. And to this day, the fight continues back and forth, waters rushing up and down the rivers, from mountain to sea, sea to mountain.

The crowd adored the tale, singing along word for word. It deeply resonated with them. Felipe was about to begin his next song, when a loud crack came from the entrance of the inn. The door had been smashed open, and five men in red tunics covered by leather vests and bracers of armour, came in. The deserter that Ramkus had been speaking to seemed to be in disgust, turning his back, looking to the fire. The five men made their way over and surrounded him, pushing Ramkus aside.

The crowd was silent.

'Solento, you piece of filth,' one of the five said: an older man who was adorned with a heavier leather that was of a finer etching, indicating he was the leader of the group. 'You thought you could escape us?'

For what it was worth, the deserter – Solento - put on a face of resilience, 'No, I knew you'd come, I just wanted to taste some freedom, something I have never had before!' He gave a look of contempt as he stared them down. 'Five of you to take me?

The leader cocked his head, 'Don't think it a compliment! You are under arrest for desertion, you will likely die for that!'

'Die? I was already dead. You are following orders, judging them to be ultimately for the right cause. You judge me without realising the Empire has deserted its fundamental humanity!'

'Oh, you cocky brat,' the old leader slapped Solento with unexpected force. 'Too well learned, or perhaps you were brainwashed by that *forest whore*?'

Solento's eyes fixed on the leader, he kicked him, but missed as two had whom congregated to his sides, grabbed his arms. The leader, and the two other idle soldiers, started to punch him till he fell to the ground, whence the leader proceeded to kick him. Ramkus jumped in and threw the leader away. As he grabbed another, the leader stabled himself and cried, 'Stop! Who dares touch an *Officer of the Empire*?'

Ramkus punched the man he grabbed to the ground, ready to pounce at the Officer. The Officer drew a sword and pointed it at Ramkus's throat. Ramkus did not flinch; this upset the Officer as his threat was not taken seriously. He turned the sword to its flat side and smacked Ramkus in the side of the head. Unfortunately, it was the same side that had been bruised and given Ramkus concussion. Ramkus instantly felt queasy, stumbling back.

The Officer spat to the side, as he kept his sword traced on Ramkus, leading him away from Solento.

'You dare provoke us? You dare challenge us?! Who do you think you are?!' The Officer's eyes were full of rage. Solento was pulled to his feet.

The Officer snarled, 'Do you know that this man fled the Empire, all because of a forest girl? He disobeyed orders and brought about the deaths of two neighbouring peoples, the "native" peoples? Had he followed orders, he would not have so much blood on his hands. But no, now he has to answer for himself... For how he let a forest wench distract him from doing what was right to save *her own* people.' The Officer began to smile cockily, facing Solento who was bloodied and bruised. He was only able to stand due to two men holding him up. 'She died at my hands Solento, and you know what that entailed...' The Officer laughed callously.

Solento's eyes bulged as if ready to kill, but one of the men who was not holding him punched him in the groin. Ramkus felt sick at the sight of the repulsive torture, as blood dripped from a new gash sustained from the fresh smack to his head.

'If I was not in such a good mood, I would have you taken with him,' the Officer warned Ramkus. He signalling towards, 'Take him boys.'

The soldiers bound Solento up and dragged him out the entrance of the inn by rope. The Officer was still watching Ramkus. 'Hope we meet again. I think it would be more pleasurable for me,' he said. 'I will teach you a few lessons in what it means to *mess* with the Empire.' He smiled and walked through the parting crowd, not even giving the people a glance. Ramkus was left standing, felling ill, regretting that he had not done all he could have.

Is a Guardian not meant to help in these situations? Could I have done anymore? He looked at the silent crowd. They looked on in anguish, with heads bowed like naughty children.

The silence was pulsating, and only broken by Felipe, who cried, 'Now for my next song!' Ramkus looked to him, as he returned a friendly wink. Felipe was saving him from the crowds focus, and the hassle of any further situations.

The crowd turned to Felipe on the dais, and Ramkus took his cue, retrieving his tankard from the top of fire place, and sitting down at a table to steady and calm himself. He looked around: the whole crowd's attention was back on Felipe, smiling. The mood had lifted. Except for one patron: the hooded stranger who had been resting with his back to the corner. He was now standing, smiling at Ramkus. His dark hood covering most of his features. His dark clothing concealed any weapons he may have had on him, even his size was a mystery.

He continued to stare for a few moments longer, smiling menacingly, then left the tavern.

If only I had had my staff with me! he thought. But he did not, and he also did not dare chase after the soldiers, or the hooded stranger. He fell back into depression. His ears ringing, his sight blurred, head throbbing. *What is the point of such an existence? To continually be subjected to punishment, to pain? For what gain? Why continue on if it only means even more of this torture? It makes no sense to be placed in a world where no gains, no enjoyment, nor satisfaction comes without pain that ends up being the stronger, greater, ruling factor in the balance.*

He looked into his earthenware tankard, taking in the workmanship; it was all he could do to stop sinking further into an irretrievably deflated state. The tankard was handmade, not delicate, purely for the consumption of beverages and not for looks or decoration. Produced in a hurried state, for establishments which were supposedly at the *ends of the world*, and did not require finer craftsmanship. For a simpler folk whom had simpler lives; where such a tankard would fit into the whole myriad of simple sights, sounds, tastes, smells. In fact, this cup spoke deeply of Kerwood, its perfunctory use had gone a long way in its main task: bringing ale to the lips through the hands of so many. It was indeed a beautiful tankard in its own simple way. So much could be said about it. Ramkus soon realised he was completely absorbed by this simple token, this item.

He suddenly heard a crack and something spill. One of the rowdy locals had dropped and smashed his tankard.

And so ends one tale, as all do: with death. His depression came back, but only for a fleeting second as he looked to the crowd. His sight was beginning to lift from its blurry state; the ringing in his ears was subsiding, and his throbbing head was not as prevalent to his thoughts. Clapping started, and he realised Felipe must have finished his song, requesting a short break. He was glad Felipe had allowed him the opportunity to gather himself, and had seemingly instigated him to do so. It was now very dark outside, and the candles were all blazing with light across the hall. The fire emanated great heat and light, becoming the only true beacon of life in the town. Sparks came from the relighting of tobacco pipes, and the scent of the smoke overtook that of the resident fish smell.

'I must say, trouble seems to find you everywhere,' Felipe jested as he sat down next to Ramkus. 'As much as you did what you probably felt was right, I do not think you can really pit yourself against soldiers of the Empire.' He pulled off his hat and placed it on the table, showing a mass of black hair that ended with curls. 'To take on one soldier is to take on the Empire… Do you want to do that? They are easily provoked, and steadfast in their opinion of people. They are all of one wit and will, backing each other, whomever requires backing. Which means, my dear friend, they will seek revenge if one of their own has gotten themselves in some bother. You don't want that sort of enemy following you wherever you go. And they are *everywhere*! At least as far as I have travelled.'

Ramkus shrugged dismissively, letting his eye wander around the rooms once more. He became bitter and morbid at the prospect of enraging the Empire. As he was about to face Felipe, his eyes met the pretty red haired girl again, giving an instinctual smile. His embarrassment had worn off with his beating apparently. He turned to Felipe, shaking his head 'So what do we live for Felipe, when we have so much misfortune and pain. I have only been awake for two days, and look at all that I have already seen, experienced. There is so much pain and suffering, there is no justice, there is no complete, happy state... lest you become a simple person, living a simple life.' Felipe regarded him with an intense curiosity, 'Perhaps that is what you want with life, Ramkus. The *simple life*, one with *simple pleasures* in abundance. Sure, there will be hardships and a toiling for those moments, but the life is much more constant, and the pleasures are therefore *in constancy*. I do not think that this is what you *are* though. I think you have something else you will find instead. I do believe you *are* a Guardian,' he squinted his eyes and paused, 'but you are also different from *them*, you are already thinking differently than they.' He paused once more, and smiled to himself, 'Yes this world lacks justice. The laws of the many kingdoms form mere foundations to keep those people in ruling position's power safe and unthreatened. Life is not all that bad if you abide by those laws. Honestly, I have not had many exciting experiences for such a long time. It has been, interesting, different. Do not feel bad for what you cannot change. I assure you, things are not always as bad as you have experienced. So, pick yourself from this bleak attitude; life is worth living!'

Ramkus lifted his head, realising that he did not have the full array of life's experiences so far. He looked at the red haired girl again and smiled, then looked to Felipe.

'Thank you. It is not easy to know how to react in this world, especially when your first experiences are so mixed, the stories full of sadness,' he exclaimed with resolve.

'You must not focus on such things, you need to move on. Live the moment!' Felipe said with explosiveness.

'You know, Felipe, you do surprise me quite often... already! A mix of wisdom comes from you.' Ramkus smiled, as his eyes trailed off to the red haired girl again.

'I have experienced much Ramkus, I am not so young as I may appear. I have learnt a lot, and from many different people. Maybe you should try meditate again. Or...' Felipe's voice trailed off as he suddenly caught on to what Ramkus kept looking at it. He had a look himself at the pretty green eyed, red haired girl once more, whom was keeping abreast of Ramkus's attentiveness. 'Or maybe you should enjoy the pleasure of life my friend,' he smiled, giving a wink. 'Just don't give her your *love*...'

Ramkus frowned a little, whilst Felipe jumped up from the table, winked again, and then to the red-haired girl, before making his way back to the dais.

Ramkus watched her now, as she broke away from her group. Feeling a bit embarrassed, he looked into his tankard for some friendly advice on what to do as the music started again, with the revelling crowd following suit. He looked up as the girl stood by his side.

Smiling at him, arms behind her back, 'May I sit with you?' She asked in a pretty, innocent voice.

He felt blood rush to his head, as his face turned hot and flummoxed. He hoped it was the heat of the fire.

'Of course,' he replied in a weak voice, 'it would be my pleasure,' he coughed up in a stronger volume, blushing as he used the word pleasure.

She sat down with grace, and a bit of playfulness. She wore a light blue skirt with a white blouse: very much keeping with the fashion of the Kerwood people.

'For what it is worth, I think you were quite brave to stand up to those men.'

Her eyes were beaming, Ramkus was enraptured and forgot to reply for a few moments. 'Thank you,' he finally coughed up, 'I am not sure whether anyone else thinks as such, though.' He was now fixated on this girl, falling into her big green eyes. 'What is your name? He asked softly.

'Clara. And yours?' she replied.

'Ramkus. I dare say, you are the prettiest thing I have seen in this life,' he could not help but blush, feeling absurd at his forwardness. She in turn also blushed, looking down, biting her lip. She grabbed his hand.

'You are not from here, are you? Where are you from?' She enquired with animation.

'I, I am not sure, I started in Abergrass, but…' He was feeling a deep attraction to this girl and was not able to think straight. He wanted to be close to her, to hold her.

'Abergrass?' She laughed, 'you are not too much a stranger then!' He gave her a hefty smile, 'And you? You are from here?'

'Yes, well, on a farm outside of Kerwood. I work at the mill. It makes most of the flour for this region. You must come see it!'

'Is it your farm?'

'No, my parents, it has been the family's farm for eons.'

She did not espouse too much learnedness to Ramkus: she was but a simple farming girl, but that mattered little to him, for she held a warmth unto herself, a beacon to him - especially considering the state he was in. She had dragged him out of the deep ravine, showering him with an affection that made him feel joyous.

The crowd became more raucous, as their thirst desired quenching of not only alcohol, but the music and stories Felipe was imparting. He was becoming more enlivened himself, jumping about. He gave a wink to Ramkus.

'Would you like to go somewhere a bit quieter?' Clara asked.

'We can go to my room if you'd like?' Ramkus answered happily. She smiled, 'Lead the way,' she said, biting her lip, still holding his hand.

As he led her to the room, she came close to him, caressing his arm, slowly raising it to his pectoral. Ramkus was breathing heavily, more infatuated with the girl than he thought possible. He turned to her as they reached the room, grabbing her body, pressing himself against her, leaning forward. His lips moved close to hers, hovering above, breathing intensely through his nose. She bit her top lip, pressed against the wall, closing her eyes, turning her head so as not to allow the kiss so quickly. But he waited, his breath gently blowing on her. She faced him once more and wrapped her arms around his neck, and leant in to kiss. Ramkus felt electricity ignite him, purpose. He *was* of purpose! His despair was destroyed. Her lips were calculated, forcing their way over his.

He lifted his head, looking down at her. He finally opened the door to her side, letting her lead him in. They lay on the small bed, her on him, kissing, bodies pressed against each other. She started to pull off his top, as he hers. He kicked off his boots, as she did, and all the remainder came off with ease as they held each other in a total embrace of bodies: moving, mingling, enjoying the pleasures.

XXX

They lay for a while, enjoying the heat resonating off each other, pleased and satisfied at the world. The bed, however - built for only one person - made the closeness even more noticeable, as repositioning themselves gave little respite. Her head, resting on his chest, rising and falling.

So this is one of the pleasures then, Ramkus thought, reenergised and feeling none of the effects of the night. Her breathing was gentle, small, gliding over his chest. The candle to their side flickered, as their shadows played on the wall.

'I've never seen a man like you before,' she mused, grabbing his lean muscles. 'You're like a soldier, but feel for people. They don't, they only do their job.'

Ramkus did not reply, he was too content to spoil the moment.

She continued, 'We don't get many travellers here, you see. The only outsiders are the soldiers. Rumours tell of a special sacred place they protect, somewhere they hold their forces, deep in the forests far from here. They come, do what they please here, and leave. All the rest of the travellers are from towns, trading on the water of the rivers. None are very worldly. I was lucky, I can read and write, as well as count. My parents taught me.' She looked at him for approval. He gave a faint smile over his chest. She lay her head down and started again. 'The mill is at a beautiful glade, lots of open space. The sun rise is amazing in the morning, and the sunset the other way, over the mountains in the evening is spectacular! You will love it...'

Ramkus's contentment suddenly dropped, as he became suspicious of her predetermined plans.

'You will get to meet my parents, and sisters, and brother. He is to take over the running of the mill but will need someone else who's strong to help,' she continued.

He was getting rather anxious now, not enjoying the sweaty body that was dragging him away without his approval. Another's intentions for him, stifling his small little life of freedom so far.

'It is late,' he said abruptly, 'we should sleep.'

He made a movement for the sheets and blanket, wrapping them over himself and Clara. He hoped she had not picked up his sudden petrified state. He slept staring at the ceiling, wondering how to get out of this situation. Hopefully Felipe could help; but he was still playing in the main hall as far as Ramkus could tell. He could hear banter carrying from that way, as well as from out on the street people left the premises. He could not to pick himself up and move. He was sickened that he had somehow influenced this girl's ideas and fancies. He felt trapped: *I did not mean for this!* He waited for Felipe, trying to calm himself down.

Finally, he fell asleep from the exhaustion of the last few days.

Chapter V

A fog was hanging over the rivers canal and laying low in the streets either side of the town. It partially cleared as early morning rays of sunlight filtered through from a yellow and orange sunrise. It began peeking over the whole fishing town in a gentle crawl. A rooster crowed as cats ran back to homes with a quiet patter of steps after their nightly meetings. A lame dog decided to give a bark and howl, and the first carts rolled in for the morning, carrying either barrels to the fishing ships, or goods to sell in town that day.

Felipe briskly made his way back to the inn whilst whistling. He was seriously hoping the doors would be open, and remnants of the fire still ablaze. He didn't dare dream the room would be free to venture to, for he knew what *that* type of dreaming often led to: bitter disappointment. 'I bet the Innkeeper will also stay true to his word, making me pay for *his* bed...' he grumbled to himself.

He saw the sign of the Kerwood Inn, hanging just in sight of the morning sun. He also spied - though his dreary eyes took time to adjust - standing at ease before it, three of what he could only guess were soldiers of the Empire. *The ones from last night.* As he strained his eyes, he also saw that there were two others on horseback. He stopped walking at pace, and went much slower, *thinking*.

The soldiers did not take too much notice of him, and in any case, he did not have anything to fear from them for the night before, *Do I?* He was merely the entertainer for the evening, *Wasn't I?* It was not the first time he couldn't remember all of what happened from a previous night of merriment. His footsteps crunched on the ground. The officiating soldier whom had his back to the approaching Monsieur Felipe, turned, poised, ready to attack.

'Ah, it is the bard!' He smiled devilishly, 'I suppose you were out, barding, *if you know what I mean.*' He gave a twisted wink at Felipe, twice. 'Say no more.'

'Ahh, oh? Yes, yes of course.' Felipe said in a confused state, noting that there was only a barbaric joviality to the words of the soldier. 'You know how it is,' he tried smiling. 'But a bard must also rest, so, if you'll excuse me...'

The soldiers moved to let him head towards the door, but before entering, curiosity got the better of him.

'There will be no morning show for a good couple of hours,' he said, 'so what brings you here at this hour? Certainly not the fish broth, although delicious, it can get a little bland.'

The soldiers looked at each other, then to the officer. He squinted his eyes, keeping them firmly on Felipe, scrutinising him from head to toe. Felipe considered he must look rather ridiculous and tired after not getting any sleep.

The Officer spoke, drawing out his words, 'The man last night. He needs to be taught not to meddle in things that do not involve him. Do you agree, Monsieur bard?'

'But naturally, the Empire ought to educate all those unfortunate not to have been brought up in such a well-ordered lifestyle,' he replied in slightly mocking tone, forgetting that these men were actually capable of teaching him a lesson. The soldiers gazed at him, piercing right through his bravado. 'Of course, sir, of course. He needs some sense beaten into him,' he nodded. 'I bid you adieu, good sirs.' He quickly turned his back and hurried inside.

I must warn Ramkus, he thought, *but I might end up getting involved, and that would start a chain of misfortune where anybody who is seen to be helping could end up being involved - and so on and so on. Meaning more will be punished! Such is the way of these soldiers.* He laughed at his thoughts, and then burped. He was clearly quite drunk still. He shook himself and made his mind to go warn Ramkus. *I wonder what they would do to him*, he paused, *probably kill him.* His thoughts stopped, because that was actually a possibility. He braced his mind and became serious once more.

A knock came at the door, startling Ramkus from his light slumber. He was still holding Clara whom was sleeping soundly upon his hairy chest. He was happy laying there, listening to the sounds of the waters of the canal and the other odd noises of the early morning, finally free from the thoughts spurred on from Clara's desire to have him *forever*. The knock came again, louder.

Felipe burst in.

'Ramkus!' he stopped and looked. 'Oh... *she is a pretty girl...*' he said, admiring Clara a bit too much for Ramkus's liking. Ramkus pulled the sheets further up.

Ramkus sensed something was amiss from the sudden entrance. He pulled Clara off him and covered her up. She was still enveloped in her dreams, mouthing faint words with indeterminable sounds, moving her curvy body at short intervals. Ramkus threw on his undergarments, knee brace, and trousers, as quickly as he could, then gave Felipe a little slap to wake him from his fixated trance on Clara. 'Oh, ah, sorry, umm, what was I going to say?' he shook himself from his state. 'Oh yes, those soldiers from last night are outside, wanting to fight you, maybe even take you away. They will probably wait until there is a little more activity in the streets to make an example of you. Probably sentence you to some heavy punishment,' Felipe said in an unemotional, matter of fact tone. He was obviously still sleep deprived.

Ramkus stared at him, incredulously. He blinked and began to process exactly what Felipe had just said.

'Well, maybe it was good you did not come back last night, although,' he moved closer and pressed to Felipe's ear, whispering, 'I am sort of in a situation with this one. I don't want to *have* her, but she seems to think I have chosen to be *with* her. You know, as in *partner* with her.'

Felipe stared at him, he began to laugh heavily, 'Don't be such a such a sentimental fool. She isn't holding you back, emotional blackmail is all part of the game!'

'How am I to tell her that I won't be seeing her again?'

'Do you really expect her to be that infatuated with you? Oh Ramkus, my boy, you have a long way to go. You must not think so highly of yourself. That is for *me* to do.' He paused, 'Of *myself*, I mean, not of you.' He gave a perplexed look, trying to consider exactly what he was saying. He looked back at Clara, then to the window, then to the door.

Ramkus, getting the drift of Felipe's searching looks, prioritised the danger of an impending arrest and or beating due to last night's other activities. 'Felipe, do you know if there is a back door?' He did not dare venture to the window which looked over the main street.

'Were all five there?' He thought to himself that he may be able to take on two of them.

'All five, two on horseback.'

Ramkus let out a deep breath. 'Back door?' He repeated his first question.

'I believe so, which should lead to the stables. I think it is behind the bar.'

Ramkus peered at Clara, then made his way to his clothes, changing quickly. 'I guess this is a good enough excuse to run.' He kissed Clara on the forehead and smiled. Turning Felipe, he grabbed his staff and made his way to the corridor, 'Let's go then.'

Felipe began to chortle, 'You certainly make life interesting, Ramkus.'

'It seems to be all the good I can do at the moment,' he replied with resignation, readying himself for his next move.

'You're also a sickly romantic,' exclaimed Felipe as he belched, realising he needed to depart quickly himself.

They moved to the main hall. There was no one but the Innkeeper, dozing in the corner. To Ramkus's amazement, he seemingly never left the hall since the night before. They saw the door that headed out the back of the premises into the stables, and charged towards it. Felipe stopped just before it, collecting his valuable guitar which had been kindly kept behind the bar. They quickly made their way outside, onto the gravel and straight into the stables, rushing to place the saddles on their horses. They ventured as quietly as possible out the one alley way that led to and from the stables behind the Inn.

'Quietly, quietly,' Ramkus urged Felipe, 'We may be able to evade them and sneak onto the path at the bottom of the town.'

Felipe nodded drunkenly as they rode out onto the street. Luckily the soldiers on horseback had their backs to them as they exited. Carts and horses were travelling by, ready for the day, making it easier to lose themselves with the morning crowd. They strode out in full view, calmly heading down to the end of the town that flowed downstream to the sea.

'Ramkus?!' a girl cried out. Clara was hanging outside the window looking for him.

'Ramkus wait! Don't leave me!' she cried as she spotted him. The soldiers turned to the direction she was looking.

Felipe shifted his head, Ramkus stared at him, eyes with a steely gaze.

'Ride!' he commanded, and they took off in haste towards the road they had come into town in the first place, following it in the same direction that had brought them from Abergrass.

They heard the shouts of soldiers behind them, and sounds of heavy hooves on gravel shortly after. The path twisted and wound its way over crescents and hills, it could barely fit one horse at times. As much as Ramkus wanted to believe they could outrun the riders behind, they kept on their tails, not letting up the chase. *There are only two of them*, he reminded himself. *I should be able to take on two*, he thought, not out of arrogance, but pure belief. They pressed against their horse's manes, Felipe was feeling the worse for wear. They raced along the well-worn road, jostling with the greenery, the droning morning mist relishing the chase.

'Is there not a place we may hide in wait, Felipe?' Ramkus shouted. Felipe did not respond right away, whether trying not to pass out or vomit, or racking his mind on the question.

'Yes, I know a spot,' he yelled back. 'A little further on.'

The shouts of anger and mere pretension of the soldiers rang with the cacophony of hooves. Birds who were pecking at food on the ground were flapping frantically to get away from the impending cavalcade of disturbance.

'Up ahead,' Felipe panted, almost doubling over.

They stopped abruptly at a seemingly flat area, densely lined with trees and shrubs. A small path that many would not notice led off to the left. They jumped off their horses and followed the path quickly, for a rider could not make it through the overgrowth on horseback. Roots were breaching the earth, whilst branches hung above like a ceiling. They hid behind a large tree after leading their horses a little further off the path.

'Do you feel like a fight, Felipe?!' Ramkus howled.

The look on Ramkus's face frightened Felipe: it was the look of someone taking joy from this whole charade.

'Don't worry, they are both mine,' Ramkus continued in a matter-of-fact way, as if he had found some inner strength and knowledge that enlightened him to his capability of *handling situations*.

Felipe eyed him curiously, not saying a word, then turned his gaze to the path. He could hear them swearing and cursing the track they were travailing. The trees that hit them and the surroundings they were so unfamiliar with upset by them greatly. *This is why they made their own roads*, Felipe thought, *as if to attack the forests, the environment they did not know and did not feel part of.* Felipe despised such behaviour; deep within him, he knew he was a forest dweller – even if long removed from the forest - and for all that was destroyed he took to heart, all that beauty was lost. Yelling aroused him from his thoughts.

'They went through here! See, their trails ended, and they headed into the forest!'

Whether the soldiers yelled this as a forewarning of the impending bashing they were about to unleash, or whether they were clearly delusional about having to contend with someone ready to fight for their freedom, they certainly made their own movements known. They had dismounted and were starting to stalk the forest ahead. Felipe could see the tiny movements from the bushes and branches. Small robins, who had resettled after the earlier disturbance, took flight once more. There was a glistening every now and again, as unsheathed weapons reflected small slivers of sunlight from the rising morning sun. He looked at Ramkus: he was pensive, ready to pounce, akin to a cat waiting for its prey to get into range.

One of the soldiers suddenly fell down, his foot caught on a grounded root, the other turned his head. Ramkus shot out.

He flew at them with his cloak gliding after him, aiming his staff out under the still standing soldiers leg. Before the man could face him, his legs had been taken from under him, as the staff came up with one end high above him. Ramkus jumped up, coming down hard on the torso of the soldier with the staff, completely winding him.

The other soldier had scrambled to his feet and jabbed with his sword. Ramkus jumped back as the man started to swing at him. Ramkus deflected the shots, the staff rang out as if a blacksmith was hammering on an anvil. Thrusting back with his own weight, Ramkus angled the sword off to his side, rushing behind the soldier, carrying through his staff sideways at an angle, knocking the soldier in the stomach. In the same motion, he turned, grabbing the soldier from behind, bringing his staff up to the soldier's throat from behind, choking him.

Gasping for air, Ramkus let go as soon as the soldier had passed out. The other soldier was up again, keeling over. Ramkus smacked the sword from his hand and delivered a strong thrust to the man's stomach. He let out a gasp of air, falling down, winded and hurt.

Felipe was very impressed, 'I knew you'd prove to be a good fighter!' He exclaimed, coming from his hiding spot in the shrubs. Ramkus was too preoccupied. He grabbed the horses reigns as he spoke: 'They'll come for us down this way, we should go back to town and head for the path at the top of the town to evade them, if we can.'

Felipe could not care less which path they took. He followed the orders, but was of the mind that there still was a chance that the Empires men in town would be out on the street, waiting for the prize to be brought back.

As if Ramkus had read his thoughts, he nodded, 'They could not possibly have been so arrogant as to think only two of them would be able to capture us. They must have sent more down this path, so we can lose them by doubling around.'

'I'm sure, you could take on any of the others we meet anyway. But do not doubt the arrogance of these soldiers. They don't deal with much trouble out these ways, they are the complacent ones and *will* attack without being ordered,' Felipe added.

They started to trot down the path back to Kerwood, both coming down from the chase in their own way. Felipe was all smiles once more, whilst Ramkus was focussed on listening for any sounds that may warn of the soldiers approaching, especially around tight corners. They had sent the two riders' horses off rider-less, in the other direction, so it would be a while until those soldiers made it back into town. *This may have been a foolish idea*, Ramkus pondered, *what if people further up come upon these horses, and question what happened?* He rued his decision making.

'So how was last night?' Felipe was glancing with enquiry.

Ramkus stopped his pondering and considered the question. 'The *pleasure*?' Ramkus took a deep breath, pausing, trying to make sense of his emotions. 'It came at a cost,' he said with calculation.

'What do you mean?' Felipe probed.

'I hardly got to speak to her before we were… *embraced*.' Pausing again, he summarised it all in his mind before continuing. 'She thinks I have chosen her as my spouse, wants me to go to her farm and work at the mill. I felt so trapped by the thought, Felipe. I was stuck in that room with no escape as she fell asleep on me. I did not dare disturb her. I did not want to harm her in any way.'

'Ha! You fool! This is how girls in these far reaches think they can ensnare men. There is not much around, you are a rarity for them. Something they wish to hold onto as you offer more than the other local lads. She knew you would not stay, but it was worth her while making the effort. Yes, she likes you, but she cannot have you. You cannot give yourself to anybody, unless it is… well… *that one you are meant for*. At least that is how it will be described by the poets. Enjoy the pleasures with them - they do too – it is just more natural for them to feel any man they are with could be the person they should be with permanently. Unfortunately, in my case, I am probably not the best person to speak to. I don't believe in *love*, only in enjoying oneself. Maybe if you find someone who allows you to enjoy yourself to the greatest degree, that is the person you are meant to choose.'

Ramkus weighed Felipe's advice for a few moments. 'I could not face a life living around here, it is not me. It is not what I am meant for. It is not my *life*. I feel that, *I know that*.'

Felipe smiled, 'The simple life is certainly not for a Guardian. In fact, I don't think I have heard of a Guardian ever being allowed a choice to live such a life. To give up what they are for a life of their own choosing.'

'So, you're saying I did not even have a choice to begin with?' Ramkus shot back, careful not to let his emotions cloud the situation.

Felipe looked at him. 'No, I think *you* are different from them - your *brethren* - which is itself, odd. The Guardians I have met were all stoic, draconian in their manner. They never *were* for the pleasure of life, never fully for the attractions and beauty of existence. They were almost devoid of a human element – something you *do* have.'

'So, I may not be a Guardian after all?' Ramkus said with an air of sullenness.

Felipe considered the question, 'There is too much pointing to *you* being one. Though, I guess you can only ask *those* questions of those who are Guardians.'

'Are there many?' Ramkus was trying his luck, pushing Felipe for desperate answers he knew could not be answered absolutely.

'I do not know, from what I have heard though, it is only a handful. Anyway, let us stop talking of this as it will only play upon your mind further. We have more pressing issues at hand.' Felipe turned his attention to the road.

'I think someone *else* will be playing upon my mind, more so…' Ramkus said under his breath, looking defeated.

'Ramkus,' Felipe said, bearing a huge grin, 'she was your first, there are plenty more out there who will try and play upon your mind. Enjoy life, enjoy the moments you spend, enjoy the embraces, but do not feel guilty for having a good time. What else is there to it? What else could the point of life be?'

Ramkus sighed, resigning himself to the task at hand, letting the conversation and his thoughts end on that topic.

They reached the southern entrance back into Kerwood, reading their surroundings. It was unfortunate that their was only one bridge in town at this end, which meant their path had to be the one that went straight past the Kerwood Inn. As they continued to ride out onto the main road of the town, the soldiers were nowhere to be seen. The place was bustling with the workers in the canal, and the shops and market stores on the street. They rode very slowly.

'Is there any other road up to the top end of town, Felipe?' Ramkus asked anxiously.

Felipe shook his head.

Moving at a canter, passing by carts selling vegetables, bread, fish, meats, cheese. The smells reminded the two they had not eaten since last night. They were beginning to get peckish.

As they passed the inn, the Innkeeper came barrelling out, shouting at them. 'You owe me for last night, for two people!' He blocked their horses' path.

Felipe and Ramkus were mortified, looking around, trying not to draw any more attention to themselves.

'What do you meant two people, it was only for one, and we are sorry we forgot to pay,' Felipe replied quickly and curtly, trying to calm the situation as soon as possible.

'And what about the girl? Three people to that room!'

Ramkus was getting impatient, Felipe scrounged around for the few coins he had left to get the pedant Innkeeper out of his face.

'You're going to have to pay your own way from now on, Ramkus,' he grumbled to Ramkus, who was half listening. Something felt wrong. He looked around behind himself and Felipe, five soldiers were walking up to them, poised. As he turned the other way, another five were coming around. They brandished spears and swords. *How on earth did they sneak up on us*, he thought. Some appeared to be dripping with water, sodden from hiding in the canal. 'Trying to run away from us, are we?' The Officer barged out of the inn with a plate of breakfast. He set it down and wiped around his mouth, still chewing with it open. He rested his hand on the hilt of his sword. 'You really don't want to take your punishment, do you? Well, it will be much more severe now, you have tried to escape a questioning for a serious crime committed here last night. So now you will be arrested.'

Ramkus was snarling with one side of his mouth lifting. 'What the hell are you talking about!' As much as he was raging inside, he was trying to calm his mind and consider his options.

'Yes, what happened last night?' Felipe chimed in with a diplomatic tone.

'Quiet bard! You are now an accomplice! A girl was savagely beaten last night, she gave us a full statement of the attack, as well as the perpetrators,' the Officer said with indignation.

Felipe and Ramkus looked at each other. They were in no mood to fight, and the soldiers were in no mood either, shivering after hiding in the cold waters. It seemed a little rash to have them in such a hiding spot. Then again, this Officer didn't seem to care about anything but himself. It was he who was complacent and arrogant, whereas these "underlings" seemed like poor, young men, enlisted in the Empire under duress.

They started to walk in on them, slowly.

'What do we do,' Felipe whispered, they have bribed some girl to claim we beat her no less. A typical trick they employ. They are the law here, they will take us to one of their district capitols, where we will be judged as guilty with only the girl's statement being used as evidence!' He looked morbid and sickened, stressing his point through his teeth.

Ramkus gritted his own teeth. 'More likely they'll just give us a beating whilst under arrest here,' he replied. 'Lucky they don't yet know what we did to those other soldiers...' Ramkus grimaced, 'Shit.'

111

'What do you mean *we*? You were the one who gave those soldiers a hiding!' Felipe yelled incredulously, flailing his arms, disregarding the secretive speech he had instigated.

'What is this about soldiers?' The Officer spoke. 'What did you do **them**!'

The Empire's men who were surrounding them became somewhat pensive upon these words, steeling their weapons, closing in on Felipe and Ramkus. Ramkus shook his head, giving Felipe a daggered gaze. He became tense. The air of aggression was rising. Ramkus was starting to breathe heavily, a voice in his head was crying out savagely to draw his staff and take them all on. This subsided as calmness and reasoning took over. *There are eleven of them, how can I compete with that many? Surrounded, each with a different weapon to attack from either close or long range.* He had no idea if he was capable of defending himself on horseback and whether he may have only just been lucky with the two in the forest.

'What did you do to **my men**?! Speak!' the Officer spoke in a drawn-out manner. His eyes becoming bloodshot, the other soldiers closed even tighter.

'I am tired of these two, kill them, now!' the officer ordered his men. The soldiers were ready to lunge, until they heard a heavy clatter of horse shoes and a neigh coming from the alley way that led behind the Inn. A horse with rider ran out, bowling over two of the soldiers in front of Ramkus and Felipe, the others jumped out of the way. 'Ride!' the rider screamed at Ramkus and Felipe: it was Clara. She rode through the cleared path she had created in front of them, whom without hesitation, spurred their horses to follow. Dodging carts and townsfolk who raised their fists in road rage anger, they headed to the top of the town, not looking back. The path rose a little on an incline, creating a vantage point view over the town and its surrounding areas – which were predominantly forest. The soldiers were still running after them when Ramkus peered back, but the three rode on without delay, heading to the top, almost steering into some wagons, quickly changing direction at the last second to avoid catastrophe.

The road out of town was wide and accommodating, and they were soon racing with forest on either side, and a clear path in front - save for some wagons and farmers with wheelbarrows carrying their stock in and out of town. Homesteads on the fringes of the forest path were a blue as they hurtled along. These sights became sparse, as the riders travelled, slowing down once the immediate threat diminished. Clara had been in front the whole time and had only now turned around to look at the two. Her face was bruised, her eye black. Ramkus felt his stomach turn, an anger surged through him. He rode up beside her as they slowed to a canter.

'What happened, Clara? What did they do to you?!' Ramkus asked, holding back his temper.

She averted his gaze, looking down. She spoke slowly, holding back from showing any emotion, 'They wanted to use me as a false victim of an assault... an assault by you two. All so they would have a legitimate reason to arrest you.' She was stoic in her speech, but tears began to well. 'They said it had to look real to the townsfolk, and that there would be more bruises if I said anything against them.' Tears rolled as she wiped her eyes.

'I am so sorry Clara, why would they do it to you?' Ramkus said, his concern only placated his building torrent of rage that an innocent should be involved. He stopped himself on this realisation that she had been embroiled in the whole wicked fiasco by accident. Because she was with him last, and the townsfolk knew this. Had she never drawn his attention to herself... Ramkus began to feel guilty for *pursuing the pleasure*. This sunk him into a despair, realising that so much had to be given for a few moments of enjoyment. What was the point of it all. Perhaps the simple way of life was better. To not draw attention to oneself and enjoy the simplest delights of life without pressing for anything more.

'I am truly sorry Clara,' Ramkus repeated, 'I did not think you would become involved.'

'How can you be sorry, you didn't do anything wrong. It's those bloody arrogant soldiers. They ride into town, acting as if they own the place.' She had stopped her crying. 'They treat us like dirt. I am glad we have given them some grief and damaged their pride!' She smiled through her red, watery eyes, sniffling.

'I think there may be a bit more than damage to their pride now,' Felipe added, as he hedged forward to join the two in their private conversation. 'Ramkus gave two of the soldiers a *lesson in manners* before we ended up in that trap...'

Clara continued to smile at this news, then a concerned look crossed her face. 'I should have known you weren't any normal person, Ramkus. There is a presence you carry that says you don't live a normal life. I can feel that.'

Ramkus smiled at her, knowing full well she understood he could not be entrapped in a simple life.

'I would love a life of adventure,' she dreamed, suggestively glancing at the two.

'I don't think it would be right for you, girl.' Felipe stated gently. 'Ramkus here is a *Guardian*. He has no idea what his life will entail. But no doubt, it will be one fraught with fights and dangers.'

'Did you not see what I just did? I was bound by my hands by those oafs. I broke free though, and was able to get to my horse and barrel over those men and help you two.' She pulled her head back proudly, 'I can live such a life!'

Felipe gave a chuckle, 'Perhaps you can my dear, but you must also travel very far. Very, very far. Will you be capable of that?'

'Anything would be better than this boring life!' She exclaimed.

Ramkus listened to her desires, happy to not be in the limelight.

The right side of the path was looking less dense, as it opened up to green pastures as far as the three could see. With rolling hills, windmills dotted about, crops, pastures, and farmsteads: it was farming land. The streams and dams glistened with the ever-rising sun, and sounds of cows from distant fields were heard. It was a beautiful sight to Ramkus, but something all too familiar to Clara. Ramkus spoke again, 'Thank you for helping us back there. You really saved us.'

The beaming smile Clara gave showed an evident satisfaction in her exploits, an approval of her abilities. Ramkus did not want her to follow him, but he also did not want to hurt her by suggesting she was better not to follow the *adventuring life* so soon after praising her. He thought of how absurd it was to think of the adventuring life, when he had only enjoyed a few days of it so far. So much had happened already, so many people met, so much activity; and he still had so many questions of himself. At least he felt he was acquiring some sense of what he was capable of, what he liked, where he wanted to go. He smiled, realising the despair he felt before had once again lifted, and the pleasure was worth enduring the pains and trials. He seemed to carry different selves that came about at different times: *Is this normal?*

'My family house is this way.' Clara said matter-of-factly, leading the way through some smaller paths that led into the fields from the main road. The two others followed obediently.

'At least you will get to see my house and the mill, Ramkus.'

They entered Clara's family home; it was the quintessential setup for the region: a large fire place at one end, an anteroom on the other end which housed a kitchen, more rooms at the rear, a large table in the centre of the main room with a massive wooden with benches, softened over time from many family meals. 'No one is around at this hour,' Clara explained, 'as they are all out working. I will likely be scolded for coming back so late, *without a care for any of the others labours.*'

She was not beholden to this life, not held back from pursuing a different profession, but it was hard to break free from the *normal* life of people in the community of which she grew up. They were farmers, and for generations they had been on this land, sewing their seeds. Her full name was Clara Miller, to give context as to how far back the family held and ran the mill, it was literally who they were. Ramkus had not even considered the use of second names until he heard this.

The kitchen in the anteroom was large and smelt of sweet flavours. They sat down as she prepared something of a ploughman's meal for them: cheese, cold meats, bread, pickled items. She offered them cold water in glass cups which she was proud to have obtained, as they were items that had been *brought from faraway lands*.

She was showing motivation towards the travelling lifestyle again. The two said nothing as they all ate and drank. She spoke of her family, and how they were all quite well educated compared to some of those that lived around on the neighbouring lands and villages. They enjoyed books that they came by via travelling salesmen, amassing a fair amount in a small home library. She became dreamlike, describing how she would love to visit places where there were proper bookstores. She dreamed of leaving, it was clear, but she – without realising – was bound to this land; to her lifestyle, to her family. The two adventurers let her dream, they themselves were content to listen and relax before the inevitable departure.

'We need to be off.' Felipe said after a pause in the daydreams of the girl.

'Oh!' Clara said, shocked back to reality. Her eyes doe like, pleading already without saying a word. 'Please can I come? Have I not told you enough of how I dream to venture from here?'

'Clara,' Ramkus said in a comforting tone, trying to let her dream as long as was right, 'this is your life, here. What would your family think?'

She became stubborn in her manner.

'You may never be able to see them again. Don't you think you may miss them?' Felipe said, 'It is not as beautiful out there as you may imagine. In the last three day's we have been beaten up in fights, chased, robbed. We are somewhat showing the effects of our pains only now!'

Ramkus remembered his knee with this comment, noting that it was indeed starting to hurt a little. Felipe continued, 'It is not the life for you, at least not the way we travel. Maybe one day you will be able to, but the road we are on now is a dangerous one. Who knows if we will be chased by more of the Empire's soldiers. You are best to stay here, lay low, until your own injuries heal.'

Clara turned her head to that comment, forgetting her dismal start to the morning. She started to weep, after resigning herself to staying. She looked to Ramkus with longing eyes, a last-ditch attempt. She may not be able to travel, but she may still be able to have convince her new-found attraction to stay. He looked at her with a small heartfelt frown.

She sighed, getting up from the table and gathering some items from the kitchen, the other two picked up and headed outside, getting on their horses, readying to leave.

Clara came out after a few moments and handed some victuals to the two of them.

'Will we meet again, Ramkus?' she said sadly.

He smiled thoughtfully, 'I do not know, Clara. I hope so.'

Clara looked away at the at the road the two were to travel, wishing, hoping, one day to follow.

'Please take care of yourself, try to stay away from the town for a while, keep as far away from those soldiers.' Ramkus added.

'They should leave soon enough, they arrested that poor man last night. That's all they do here, come arrest people and then leave. You were unlucky they were there last night.' Clara said

Felipe smiled as if about to perform, 'Trouble seems to find *this* one everywhere.'

Clara smiled at this, looking at Ramkus.

'Take care, I hope to hear of your adventures one day!' She said.

'Thank you, Clara,' Ramkus replied, as they made their way off, 'for everything.'

They nodded to her, turning their steeds towards their path, ready for the next part of their journey. Felipe in good spirits, as his intoxication and subsequent hangover had lifted; Ramkus struggling to process what on earth had just happened in the last few hours.

Chapter VI

Ramkus flicked a twig to his side that he had been bending and breaking. Felipe had his hat over his face, lazing on a little hillock that overlooked the road and trees on the other side. The sun bore a heat that went straight through their clothes. It was energising, reassuring that they were free to enjoy themselves. The cleared grasslands spread far behind them, sparsely planted fruit trees and sheds scattered about, most only visible as specks in the distance. Ramkus was still in contemplation. He was already feeling a separation from Clara, a girl he had only really just met, but he had shared an intimate moment. The air of melancholy could be felt by Felipe. He had tried to let it pass, but was in need of consoling – as well as breaking so as not to get on his own nerves.

'Let her go from your mind,' He said, 'it would never have worked out, you were not meant to be with her.'

'How do you know that!' Ramkus snapped, 'How do you know that I was not meant to live that life?'

'Have you forgotten how trapped you felt by it all? What you are experiencing will come to pass,' Felipe replied.

'She risked her life for us,' Ramkus protested.

'Yes, she held her nerve well, and she got herself into trouble by doing so. Remember, it was her that alerted the soldiers to our planned escape in the beginning,' Felipe said plainly.

'I was talking about when she charged the soldiers on horseback. Now they will go looking for her,' Ramkus would not let it go.

'They could not care less, that would be too much effort. They don't care that much for what happens out this way, only for a bit of fun.' Felipe bit his lip back.

'They were after that Solento man, though. They must have been tracing his tracks, they'll do it to her.' Ramkus was disputing for no other reason other than to dispute.

'That is bullshit!' Felipe scoffed, taking his black, wide-brimmed, suede hat off his face, straightening up. 'That man wanted to be

found. Had he really wanted to flee he would not have been in a
territory that is under the control of the Empire.'

'Why would he not want to flee?' enquired Ramkus in confusion.
'Who knows: wouldn't know what to do with himself anywhere
else?' Felipe stood up and stretched his back, starting to have little
doubts peck at his mind, along with a fear that those soldiers would
be travelling this path with the man Solento that Ramkus had
mentioned. 'In any case, time we kept moving. The next town is a
few days away. The only way we will stop you from being so
besotted is finding you another girl. Clara was your first after all, the
emotions you are feeling are like that for your first.' He got on his
horse, chest stuck out, as if an authority on the topic at hand. There
are plenty more girls for you to meet, Ramkus. There is never *the
one*, it does not exist.'

Ramkus eyed him. Somewhere in his chest, beyond his aching bones
and muscles, in his essence, he knew this was not completely true.
He was adamant, but yet did not speak of it nor register it for longer
than a moment. But in that moment, he knew he would die thinking,
feeling otherwise.

'Hurry up,' Felipe said, urging Ramkus of the importance of every
minute, even if he was the one who required a good half hour nap
after eating lunch.

'You have to admit, she was a good girl though, Felipe. She even
thought to give us some supplies.'

'Yes, yes. She was very sweet, kind hearted, and brave. And a
looker! I will give you all that. But **forget** about her!' Felipe went
to his horse as Ramkus hurried after him.

The chirping of robins at the edges of the woodland was the only
sign of life for many miles. They rode through the scenic
countryside; it did not appear to change in any significance in the
miles ahead. The path was straight, gently rising in parts, falling in
others. To the right, the ever-stretching farm lands; to the left, the
forest, thick with vegetation. There was the odd tree on the right, not
much else.

'It is very boring out here. Very simple,' Felipe mused - a tendency of his that crept in every now and again. He would also whistle and hum at times. He did not dare to play his guitar in the saddle, and when Ramkus asked why, he explained that he had once been fined in a city for not having his hands on the reigns, not to mention also losing a guitar or two after falling from his horse when trying to impress fair maidens in such a manner. This was due to the horse suddenly whinnying *after being spooked*, he inferred. Ramkus joked that it may have been the horse's way of telling him to focus, Felipe looked at him with daggers in his eyes, scolding him that he should never say such things about a bard, especially if he wanted to learn the trade. The embarrassment was still evident.

The afternoon sun was starting to give way, and the birds were squawking furiously at the pending evening.
'Are there any of those resting spots or clearings around here, Felipe?' Ramkus asked with optimism.
'No, not on these main roads, one of the only downsides. These roads were built for mobilising large armies quickly, if necessary. We will probably hit the end of these farmlands by night fall, though. We should probably look to break camp before then, sleep out under the stars.'
There was a cracking of something coming from the forest. The two wanderers turned, slowing their horses. The sound was constant, as the vegetation seemed to be getting severely smashed. It broke the calm serenity of the scene.
"*Mooo*" A cow suddenly emerged, bashing through the foliage.
'What in the hell?' Felipe cried, 'Stupid critter must have gotten lost.'
Ramkus watched the cow, giving a chuckle. He released the firm grip that he had had on his staff, lowering it from a striking position.
'Must have gotten bored of the *simple life!*' Felipe joked.
'Ha,' Ramkus said, acknowledging the dreadful joke, but too weary to pull Felipe up on it. He was also rather tired of this stretch of land, and was happy for something out of the ordinary to happen.

They kept moving, drawing along.

'I am starting to understand what you mean now,' Ramkus started up, 'about this type of living. If it is like this path - beautiful as it may be - I am not made for it.'

'There you go, you see what I…' Felipe stopped talking, 'Why is that cow following us still?'

'Probably has nothing better to do,' Ramkus answered.

Felipe stared at it for a while, before opening his eyes with a startling realisation, 'The cow is possessed! It is either trying to warn us or kill us!'

Ramkus actually laughed this time, looking back into the deep black eyes following him. 'Wait, so it could either be warning us, or trying to kill us. Should we wait to find out if it is either be a good cow, or an evil one?' He was starting to think of how they may have some fun at the cow's expense.

The cow kept pace with the two.

'I don't like the look on its face. It screams for our souls!' Felipe cried.

Ramkus was unsure if he was being facetious. He turned to Felipe and stared with confusion, 'What do you mean by our souls?'

Felipe was bemused by the question, but proudly stuck out his chest, once again an authority on the topic. 'A soul: it's your essence, your being. It is the eternal part of you, the flare that burns through your body, only to be released upon death.'

Felipe's horse suddenly jolted, dashing ahead with Felipe still in the saddle. 'That bloody cow has bitten my horse!' Felipe growled. Luckily it was only the tail, but it was enough to annoy the horse.

'Get away, you monstrous heathen!' Felipe, turned around to the cow, 'Shoo!'

The cow stood motionless whilst Felipe jumped off his horse and ran at the cow to scare it. It jumped away and started down the path it had come.

'Insolent demon. Begone!' Felipe cried, making some sort of warding gesture with his hands before climbing back on his horse.

'Yes, so souls,' he started back on the previous topic, 'it is what

makes you whole, what makes your body come to life.' He was
perturbed by the lack of eloquence with which he would usually
muster on the topic, but he was preoccupied by the odd occasion.
'That cow, it has a corrupted soul.'
'So, the soul can be influenced? It can also be both good and evil?'
Ramkus probed.
'I would say so, it is what defines a person internally. Why some are
bad, and some good.'
"Moo!" The cow had returned.
'What did I tell you, damn cow!' Felipe cried in anguish.
A voice cried out, 'Aye, what are you doing with Bessy? You're
trying to steal my cow!' A rail thin man with a large floppy hat
came out of the bushes. 'I ought to tell the authorities on you!'
The two men stopped, looking at this man in utter confusion.
'The cow only wishes to eat the horse's tails, please rid us of it if you
would, lest *we* tell the authorities on *you!* For… for… trespass to our
persons!' Felipe was getting carried away.
'I think not, you thieving pilgrims! You were trying to steal Bessy!
Ohh my poor Bessy….Give me some coin or I'll tell the authorities,'
the man said in a matter-of-fact way, as if rehearsed on many an
occasion.
'Where on earth are these authorities that you speak of? We are in
the middle of nowhere!' Felipe was peeved by the accusation.
'Settle down,' Ramkus insisted.
'The authority be just over yonder,' The man stated. 'You wish to
risk it?'
'Bull shit!' cried Felipe in an outburst of indignation.
'Yes, I doubt that too,' Ramkus started to chime in. 'And judging
from the way you speak, you have practiced your lines. You're just
trying to swindle whomever comes through, by claiming they were
trying to steal this cow. In fact, I wonder if it is even yours!'
The man showed surprise. 'It is mine, look, black spot on the right
inner rear leg.'

The men - intrigued - got off their horses to confirm for themselves the black spot that no one would have really looked at unless they owned the cow.

'Alright, it is yours,' uttered Ramkus, 'but you are a swindler. You have trained the damn cow to chase after horse's tails!' Ramkus was getting angry. 'Further, you prey on people whom do not know the area, claiming the "authority" is around here. It is just an opportunity for you to trick whomever is unfamiliar with these paths. It is a ludicrous ploy!' He moved forward, domineering over the man who cowered away.

'Alright, alright, I admit it, although it was meant to steal items from horses, not eat their tails. Bessy is a failure.' He lowered his head is sadness.

'Has this ever worked before?' Felipe asked, curious, and a little impressed with the whole plan.

'Aye... Not, it, no...' The rail thin man was shaking his head in shame. Ramkus was in disgust. He got back on his horse.

'You should not be preying on poor travellers. The time spent training Bessy could have been spent milking her instead.' He started off again, past the man, not looking at him.

'Full points for creativity,' declared Felipe.

The two rode on, exchanging a quick glance at each other when out of distance, then having a good chuckle.

'The excitement never ends!' Felipe quipped.

They made camp a little way off from the entry into a dense forest beyond the grasslands. Feasting on the supplies given by Clara and looking into the campfire they'd made, they were happy with their situation, with their story. The night sky was clear, a dark blue with a sprinkling of stars, the moon was almost full, beaming light on the farming lands. Felipe pulled out his guitar, remembering the lessons he had promised.

The sounds carried off far into the fields and the forest, all the way into the night sky, with nothing else but beetles and bugs to combat the acoustics. The soft crunching of the small fire seemed to accompany and wave its way into the melody. It was conducive to the mood and created a scene as if it was the forest for which they played.

'Why did you wish to join up with me, Felipe?' Ramkus started after some moments of peace. 'Truly for the reasons you had said after we were robbed outside of Abergrass?' The mood was calm, Felipe thought back, and answered in the same peaceful manner he had found himself in whist in the sacred, secretive rest stop on the way to Kerwood.

'Because it is no fun travelling alone. This path, it can be very, very lonely. There are only a few instances where you have some human contact on a personal level. And aside from that, to travel with others – wayward strangers - is not easy. You don't know if the person you are travelling with will up and go in another direction at any point, nor if they are trustworthy to begin with.' He tossed a small rock onto the fire and webbed his hands. '*You*, I trusted you immediately, and I knew – or guessed – as to what you were. You make for an easy companion. At least for as far as we can go together.' He paused, now it was his time to question his companion. 'Why did you trust to travel with me?'

Ramkus leaning on the guitar, considered his own motives. 'I think it was purely because you said you were going the way I should go. I never had any reaction against it. I had nothing, not even a cause or a course to travel until you told me I did, and I suppose it is where I am to aim. I would have thought, though, that these Guardians would have sent one of their own to explain everything to me and guide me to that *Guardian's Mountain* that the *Guardian Seat* is atop of.'

Felipe picked up the gist of the conversation, 'I am not sure what procedure they do have, or whether they even know if a Guardian has *awoken*. Do not feel that there is a certain arrangement in how things are meant to be, many paths lead to the same spot.'

Ramkus looked deep into the fire.

Felipe continued, 'You will face choices in life, paths, junctures; you will be forced to choose. There may not be any reason to pick one choice over the other, maybe it will be made simply on which way the wind is blowing.'

Ramkus smiled at Felipe's imagery.

They heard a "moo" along the road.

'Oh, don't tell me the swindlers back for more trickery! Probably wants to feed the cow on our horses again,' Felipe said bemusedly, shaking his head and frowning.

The rail thin man was walking up the grass hillock with his cow following behind.

'What do you want!?' Yelled Felipe. 'You'd better not be coming to beg from us.'

'Just to sit next to the fire with some travellers.' The rail thin man approached them, as they sat comfortably. 'There ain't no crime in that is there?' he shrugged.

Felipe looked at him suspiciously, then to Ramkus.

'Please, sit,' Ramkus said, beckoning to the ground.

'And don't try and trick us... Keep that cow away from the horses!' Felipe cried, pointing to Bessy as she moved towards their mounts.

'Aw right, aw right. Bessy!' He called the cow over. To their surprise, it obliged.

'Well don't ask us for anything else. You can keep warm by the fire, but that is it!' Felipe added.

They sat in silence for a few minutes, watching the fire.

'Would you be able to spare some food?' The rail thin man asked, breaking the silence without much care.

'Oh! Here we go!' Felipe showing his agitation, carried on in this way.

'Felipe, stop being a prick.' Ramkus turned to the man, 'Sure, here.' He handed him some bread and cheese.

'Thank ye, thanking ye kindly,' he replied with a grin. He ate the food slowly, not swallowing, enjoying the rhythmic motion of simply chewing.

'Ain't many travellers like you around these days. Usually just farmers, merchants, soldiers. No one of interest comes this way.' The two adventurers did not speak.

'Where are you headed?'

'None of your concern,' Felipe said curtly, Ramkus looked at him and rolled his eyes. Felipe begrudgingly changed his tune. 'We are just travelling - wandering more like it – anywhere we please, anywhere the road takes us.'

'Although,' Ramkus started up, 'speaking for myself, I am aiming to get to a far-off mountain, where the Guardians are meant to be. Heard of it?' He asked, hoping for any small nugget of information.

'Nay. Can't say that I 'ave. Is it some religious temple or something?'

'No, at least I don't think it to be religious?' Ramkus gave a querying look to Felipe, who shrugged his shoulders in response.

'To tell you the truth, Ramkus, I don't really know if it is a religious thing or not. I know the people in Abergrass knew what you were, but Abergrass is a…peculiar village. They are on the edge of the world by choice, a lot of them have come from places far and wide. Well educated a number of them. You'd be hard pressed to find any others that know what you are.'

'Well it was only really the Innkeeper there that knew what I was, not sure anyone else did.'

Felipe gave a curious smile. 'Don't be too surprised by this, but people do put on fronts to protect their interests.'

Ramkus narrowed his gaze, mulling on this, 'Like you perhaps, Monsieur Felipe?'

'Ha! Abergrass? Where those weirdos are?' The rail thin man piped up, 'Ain't much there but those who want to be left alone. Unhappy with living in other towns, regions, kingdoms. A few other places like that, far off.'

'There must have been a reason to have them founded in those spots though, surely?' Ramkus considered the idea of small hamlets, popping up on the fringes of societies, and the purposes they served for the inhabitants.

'You mean the exact positions? Perhaps,' Felipe began to think upon this as well, the reasons why these out of the way towns stood to exist, thriving on such a small number of people. He did not get a chance to fathom why some people enjoy solitude.

A sharp neigh shattered the solemnity, as one of the horses whinnied. 'Your damn cow has bitten my horse again!' Felipe growled, jumping to his feet. 'Shoo! Shoo! You demon spawn!'

'Now don't do that!' The man jumped up and gave chase after his frightened, prized heifer. She'd gotten off quite far into the night, and the rail thin man could not be bothered chasing too far. 'She'll be back' he said, not too perturbed.

Felipe came stomping back from calming the horses, 'That cow should be taken to an abattoir!'

'Oh don't say that, she's my only companion.'

'Why is that?' Ramkus interjected from curiosity.

'Well, the community sort of fell apart once the Empire started outlawing the temples we used to 'ave. I used to be a Minister, and although I was probably seen to be unpopular, the community still had to respect me. Then one day, religion was outlawed 'ere. Got too many people "questionin'" *existence* and *authority*. Y'know.'

'I always thought such religions were outdated anyway, and nobody believed in such faith.' Felipe stated in a calm demeanour.

'Aye, that is also true, but some did, and there were community gatherings as well. There is no reason to outlaw and berate others religious views, when they are tryin' to do good, to tie a community together. No reason to attack what may seem *outdated*.' The rail thin ex-Minister was evidently quite upset. 'So now, cause that temple was repossessed, I am left with nothin' – save for Bessy.' He started to sob.

'There, there,' Ramkus said

'I don't fall for those types of tricks, Minister,' Felipe said flatly. The sobbing stopped, 'Worth a try,' the man said, whilst Ramkus was left with a frown. 'True story though. He looked around, trying to see if he could spot his cow coming back to the small camp. 'I'd best be off then to find where she has gotten to. I thank ye for the bread and cheese, as well as the warmth.' He stood up and started off in the direction Bessy had run.

'Safe travels,' Ramkus called out to the departing ex-Minister. 'By the way, what was your temple and religion about? What was it called?'

'We mostly prayed for good harvests. People would make sacrifices to Goddess, for her protection and healthy crops,' the ex-Minister said loudly as he stopped and dusted himself off.

'Who is this Goddess they made their sacrifices to?' Felipe queried, with a yell noting the question was not fully answered.

'Bessy the cow.' And with that, the rail thin ex-Minister turned, and walked off into the night air.

Felipe gave a heavy chuckle. 'Once a swindler, always a swindler.'

Heathen cow, thought Ramkus.

They made off into the forest-proper the morning after, leaving the fertile farming lands behind as the farming side of the path met the trees, spreading across as if a fence line. They were in good spirits, ready for whatever situation may arise. The path twisted a little through the trees, it was not as dense as they had predicted before entering. There were streams that flowed through parts, with small sand banks and gentle creeks populated by fish, seamlessly gliding in the one position. The path rose and settled at a plateau after a while. The track was well maintained. The whole way was seemingly cut with militaristic precision when it came to its width. They stopped at times, Ramkus using every opportunity to practice the guitar, Felipe watching the forest, listening to the sounds, at peace, even if he did not want to admit to it. Moving at a constant pace, they pushed forward.

'So why do they call you a Monsieur?'

'I guess I prefer the title,' Felipe answered, 'it sounds a little bit more fancy, a good thing for a bard.'

'Ah, so not a forest dweller thing?' Ramkus asked.

'No.' Felipe laughed, 'No, there are no real titles with the forest dwellers. Apart from the ones who head the villages.'

'When were you last there, back where you came from?' Ramkus continued.

'My supposed home? My birth place?' Felipe gave it some thought as the wind blew gently across the tree branches. 'I couldn't tell you Ramkus, it has been many, many years since I was back there. I have seen so much in that time. You must remember that the forests - to the forest dwellers - is more of a home to some and less to others. I guess it is a generational thing, or even something that comes with your lineage. I did not have this *pre-forest dwellers* blood like others, so I guess it was bred out of me.'

Ramkus nodded, 'And the mountain dwellers?'

'Mountain *folk,* being the right nomenclature' Felipe corrected with an air of intellect, but knowing full well he makes the mistake on occasion. 'The same situation I believe, but who is to say that all communities are like that. Some forest dwellers', and some mountain folk communities have preferred not to make much contact with the rest of the world. They let the kingdoms concern themselves, whilst they live their lives free from the politics.'

'That didn't exactly help the people of the *Sunden Mountain Range* – I think Solento called it that – as the Empire wanted to control them,' Ramkus stated.

'Yes, it happens, for reasons like resources, labour, or land. But the Empire is more aggressive in such pursuits than the other kingdoms,' Felipe replied.

'How many other kingdoms are there?' Ramkus asked.

'Oh, countless, it is a big world Ramkus, Elantra is only a continent. Perhaps your *wise Guardian brethren* would be able to answer you. All you need to know at the moment is that the Empire controls this region. Over the mountain pass though, it is a whole different story, a whole region of different groups, not one kingdom. A few warring cities unfortunately, even where the cultures and people of each of these groups is fairly similar to each other. War, battles, all the bloody time, still breaking out in spite of it. And why you may ask? Because men are so damn fickle and make issues out of nothing, purely to keep themselves preoccupied from their own thoughts.

They are never content with what they have, and believe conquests are the only way to make themselves happy. That simple life you just passed? Well, as you even said, as good as it may be, it is not right for some of us, and good luck to anyone that it can suffice! No, some of us need to experience all life has to offer. Some fight for more, whereas others wander to its farthest reaches; just to see; just to know.' He paused from speaking, breathing in deeply. 'To a seldom few still, this world is just not enough.' His face could not be discerned.

They continued on.

They reached a peak which shared a glimpse of the massive scale of the journey to the next town. Felipe pointed out an orange looking structure, way off into the distance. This was their next stop: Refton. They meandered downward, seldom passing a wagon or cart. There was a brief civility of pleasantries with the few merchants and farmers, often mentioning their wares just in case a sale could be made. The formalities of conversation were otherwise formulaic, and the two spent a little time deliberating with these people on the higher platitudes of their thoughts for the day.

'Clara won't be found by those soldiers, will she?' Ramkus, who had been quietly mulling on the thought, blurted out.

'Ramkus, please! Forget her! Once we get to the next town we are going to find you another girl f, so you can see that she is not worth thinking of!' Felipe guffawed.

'I just want to know she will be alright...'

'Yes, she will be!' Felipe was once again at his impatient best. Ramkus was silent.

'I am sorry Ramkus, it has been a long time since I have travelled with another. I also forget that you have not had the proper education, or, experiences in life yet.' Felipe looked ahead, thinking to himself. He turned to Ramkus with a gleeful smile. 'I will take it upon myself to give you these lessons. You are, after all, learning the ways of the bard. Ha! Think of it, a Guardian bard! Oh, that would be very interesting, solving diplomatic and legal problems with songs and music, letting the true meaning of the words of the bard ring out and change the world! I love it!' Felipe's mood picked up considerably, as did the pace of their travel.

Ramkus shrugged his shoulders, such a fate was fine for him, as he knew nothing else so far.

They arrived at a small, well-used campsite under the forest canopy. It was a clearing between the trees, with a few pits showing remnants of recently burnt out fires. A large, red painted shepherds hut that sat atop massive yellow wheels had been parked a few yards away from one of the allotted fire spots. A large, burly man with a thick, black beard sat next to the fire spot, its flames flaring. At the sight of the two wanderers, he stood up and gave a jovial smile.

'Ahoy! Welcome fellow travellers.'

The two gave appreciative nods.

'Good day. You do not mind us sharing the fire?' Felipe exchanged.

'Of course not, make yourselves at home, it is not ours to own.'

'Thank you,' Ramkus replied. He followed Felipe's lead and led the horses to a small creek for watering, which held small patches of thick grass for food at its edges. They spied a girl cleaning and washing in the stream, but said nothing.

Seating themselves back at the fire, they pulled out their victuals.

'Would you like some cold meats?' The Burly man asked, 'I'll exchange for some of that cheese?'

They agreed, delighted to have some meat for the first time in a few days. Something of new flavour. The girl came back from the stream.

'Ah, let me introduce my wife, Revla. Oh, and I forgot, I am Hodgerise,' he introduced himself, as Revla gave a small smile, saying nothing.

'Well met Revla, Hodgerise. I am Felipe, and this is Ramkus. Where are you two headed?'

The couple looked at each other.

'Wherever the roads let's us. I mean takes us.' Hodgerise said, as Revla went into their wagon. There was a sound of clattering inside, Hodgerise ignored it, 'Yourselves?' He asked.

'Refton.' Ramkus replied, curious as to why the woman was making such commotion in the wagon. He exchanged glances with Felipe, who said nothing. 'So what do you do Hodgerise?'

'Ah?' Hodgerise was twiddling his thumbs, 'I, um, well I used to be a butcher, salted meats being my specialty.'

'No wonder the sausage was so delicious!' exclaimed Felipe. 'What is it?' He regretted the question and its possible implications as soon as he said it, but to his surprise, Hodgerise responded plainly.

'Pig, cow, horse… just kidding! Well, at least not in these parts. Many spices and herbs. It is a recipe I shan't reveal. But I am not sure when I'll get to make any more.' He stopped talking, quickly following the abrupt silence, asking, 'What about you two?'

'I am a bard.' Felipe announced with an air of pomp, 'And this is my apprentice.'

'Well I am also considered a Guardian,' Ramkus added.

'Ah, one of those people that live up on the mountains?'

'Ah, no; not one of the mountain folk per se,' Felipe interjected. 'They are, though, the types that come down from a certain mountain to solve diplomatic and legal impasses.'

'So, they are *special* mountain folk?' Hodgerise asked with interest.

'No, they are not mountain folk, they live on a mountain – I am not even sure it is right to say that even.'

'But surely that means they dwell there?' Hodgerise asked innocently, obviously confused.

Felipe shook his head, 'They are different. Have you never heard of a Guardian?'

'No, not really.'

'Where are you from Hodgerise?' Ramkus asked, redirecting the exchange before it became too heated.

'From Muolton, far West along the Sunden Range.'

Felipe grimaced.

There was a clatter in the wagon again, Hodgerise got up and entered the residence.

'What is he hiding in there?' Ramkus turned to Felipe and whispered.

'To tell you the truth, I thought it may have been a person he was turning into minced meat. He is acting rather suspiciously,' Felipe replied, keeping an eye on the wagon door.

'And you heard that he was from under the Sunden Ranges: the place Solento was around?'

'Yes, but that is a massive stretch of mountain terrain, it could be very far away.'

The clatter ended and Hodgerise and his Revla came out of their abode, looking a tad off colour.

Ramkus did not know if he should say anything. 'Is everything alright?' He finally asked.

'Yes, sorry, just ah…' Hodgerise was thinking of some way to answer, 'domestic dispute… with the cat.'

'Yes, the cat,' Revla followed Hodgerise in answering, trying to smile.

'Cats meat…' Felipe whispered to Ramkus jokingly.

Ramkus tried not to smile, asking a question to forget the comment. 'Have you seen any others on the roads?'

'Ah yes, there are a few people out on the roads at these times. Travel is easy at the moment, it is not cold. Many wandering about. Not so much on this path though. Is there much down that way?' Hodgerise enquired.

Ramkus looked at Felipe before answering, 'Not much, not much at all. Almost the end of the world that way. The simple life.' He realised they were not even sure of where these people were headed.

The door of the wagon busted open, and an old decrepit lady with a cat on her shoulder came bundling out in an erratic fashion.

'Blurgh, grr, busy blue rain flew!' She was talking gibberish.

'Damnit! Get back inside!' Hodgerise growled.

The old woman's eyes fell upon Ramkus and widened as she straightened up. She rushed at Ramkus with demonic pace until she was at his ear.

'You will die by your own blood!' She drawled out.

Her gaze was an utter void, sending shivers down Ramkus's back as he bent over, shying away from this terrifying ghoul. He realised he was clutching his staff, perching backwards, petrified of the old, worn out creature.

Hodgerise grabbed her as Revla apologised, 'Sorry, I am so sorry' she said, as they both rushed the old lady back into the wagon. The cat which had come out with the old lady was nonchalantly licking itself, waiting for its chance to get back inside. It was a while that it had to wait, as the three spent some time in there. Ramkus and Felipe couldn't quite come to terms with what had just occurred, staring at each other, sitting firmly upright, stunned.

Hodgerise and Revla returned meekly.

'A million pardons, we are so sorry,' Revla said.

'Who was that? Felipe asked in a guarded tone, still in shock himself at how the lady had seemed to be possessed.

'That is my mother,' Revla said, as Hodgerise looked around like a little child who had done wrong. 'I am so sorry, she has seemed to have gone mad, people say she is predicting peoples' fortunes, as if she is an oracle. Are you alright?'

'Ye, yes,' Ramkus brought himself to answer. *Die by my own blood*, he mulled.

'Did she say anything to you Ramkus?' Hodgerise enquired, 'I thought she may have whispered something in your ear.'

'No, nothing.' Ramkus straightened up even further.

'We are very sorry for that,' Hodgerise continued, Revla was continuing to look pale. 'You see, she was not always like this, but a few years ago she was kicked by a horse in an accident. Ever since she has been speaking gibberish, intermingled with "prophecy". It was fine, until a few people actually came to consult her. Paying customers! We looked after her in the shop we had, upstairs where she couldn't hurt anyone. That was until the Empire moved in and banned all "occult and religious behaviour". Of course, the definition of what an occult or religious was, was up the them, and they deemed mother the head of a cult. She was to be sentenced to death, so we fled. Well, it was only when the Burbar Regiment came through our town that we did so – who knows what for. I am really very sorry, I hope she didn't frighten you! We need to move somewhere where there is no one who will bother her, nor us. As you can see.' Hodgerise was bleating with sorrowful eyes.

'A massive sacrifice,' Felipe scrutinised the two wayward refugees, showing concern for them. 'If it is any solace, you should be fine further out from here. The Empire rarely touches these lands.'

'Thank you, kind sir,' Hodgerise said, as he began to wrap his big arms around Revla and console her. 'I hope that is the case. Here, have some more meats as an apology.' He went to the wagon and foraged for some cold, salted cuts.

The two adventurers accepted the foods gratefully.

'We may sleep a little out that way tonight, purely for... *musical reasons*,' Ramkus said, feeling he may have insulted Hodgerise had he not validated it otherwise. But he was still shaking a tad and wanted to get away from the wagon.

'It is understandable,' Hodgerise said, knowingly.

A good half hour passed before Ramkus and Felipe excused themselves and made camp in another spot a fair number of yards away from the wagon.

'Did she not say anything to you, Ramkus?' Felipe began his inquiry. Ramkus breathed in heavily, 'She said: *"You will die by your own blood."*'

'Oh...' Felipe frowned, 'Fair enough I suppose.'

Ramkus was unsure of what to make of it. For the first time, he was aware of his mortality, that he Would one day die, and it could be somehow related to his blood – or at least the "fortune reading" was what was playing on his mind. *What exactly does that mean?* He was restless as he wrapped his cloak around him, trying to fall asleep. His eyes rested on the sky between the leaves, as if only glimpses of the true nature of his reality could be seen behind this veil of nature. The infinite was in shadows, whilst reality was within grasp. *What happens upon death*, he thought. He rolled about till he found a comfortable position, calming himself, feeling the hard earth beneath him. Solidity, certainty, life, existence. He preferred this, it calmed him, rather than the endless night now, falling into a void where the infinitesimal expanded beyond comprehension, and he was but a mere fragment; not a self, but of the whole, looking at its own never-ending self. *Die by my own blood*, he thought, finally falling asleep with a little chuckle, realising there was nothing to fear, nay **knowing** there was no such fear. The knowledge of the secrets of existence dawned on him, dancing in his mind before being lost forever again upon the moment of sleep.

They woke early and left Hodgerise and Revla's little family wagon undisturbed. The air was crisp, and the morning light penetrated through the leaves. They did not speak until they had their first break by a creek. Ramkus contemplated the *fortune telling* from last night, as Felipe bit into some cold sausage meat.

'Do you think she actually gets her "prophecies" right?' He asked Felipe.

Felipe took a moment to collect his thoughts and remember the events of yesterday, 'Well, hard to say really, they are usually for time far into the future. I doubt she really was a prophesier, just a crazy old cat lady.'

'You did not think it odd how she moved and acted when she came at me? She was like some sort of animal,' Ramkus persisted.

'Like a banshee, perhaps? Ha! No, I think they were having us on.' Felipe laughed it off.

'You're just saying that to rationalise the situation, as well as make out you weren't a little frightened by the whole ordeal. You saw how Hodgerise gave us the meat as an apology,' Ramkus expostulated.

'Probably just to shut us up so we didn't blab to anyone about his *cat meat*!' Felipe joked.

'Well, if it is cat meat, you certainly are partial to it…'

Felipe gave a chuckle, 'I do not know exactly what happened last night, it was out of the blue, that old woman attacking. There was no apprehensive, atmospheric air to the meeting. No need to worry ourselves any further. Unless the meat is poisoned because they wanted to rob us…' Felipe smiled off into his musings of some elaborate ploy to rob unsuspecting journeymen.

'You're incorrigible Felipe, you are too flippant with your thoughts.'

Felipe laughed, 'that was a joke Ramkus. Anyway, let's get going again.'

They climbed back into their saddles.

'If anything, it is proving that a lot of things seem to happen around you, Ramkus. I'm starting to enjoy this whole ordeal. Who knows what is in store for you next!' Felipe said excitedly.

At least I know how it ends, Ramkus thought.

The path, although straighter than the trail from Abergrass to Kerwood, twisted amongst hills, rose others, and descended too. The trees differed little, the leaves bristled with the wind above the two, flittering their green life filled bodies with a dance that others caught onto. A few streams ran through the paths, some with bridges built over them, nothing big enough to be considered a river. The path was calm, and little other than the birds, streams, and dancing leaves could be heard. It was peaceful as if it was a garden that had been well maintained. The two took the trek rather leisurely, Felipe explaining that this was the best way to live: not to have a care in the world. They did not meet another soul that day.

The next day began the same, except the two started in better spirits than the previous morning. Ramkus was thinking less and less of Clara, or of the prophecy. He was focussed on trying to understand the world, the universe, and even the cosmos. How was it that he came to exist, could he have existed before? Felipe gave indefinite answers, saying it was for the philosophers to debate; the here and now is what was important. Ramkus expected such questions had plagued Felipe at some point in his life, with no suitable answers discovered. He did mention he had travelled to a land where he had been indoctrinated into a philosophy which spoke of being enlightened in the *here and now*, and the reason for his meditations – which he had neglected due to having his travelling companion pulling him into unexpected adventures – was a way of tranquillising the mind into a state which could accept the *here and now*. He spoke fondly of this land and its people, very different from other regions or kingdoms. A lot of respect for the finer details of existence, and pursuit of arts for art's sake. A very beautiful culture, he explained, not turbulent like the rest of the world seemingly was. He mentioned names of regions and kingdoms, of places he had been. Ramkus could not take it all in, but had the sense he would visit most of the spots at some point in his own travels.

They camped at the top of a hill, one of the major rises in the forest, upon a cleft which had a gargantuan rock mound resting upon it. They could see over the forest from this position, even to the light of their destination: Refton. It was seemingly massive from what Ramkus could gather. There was a pond a little further down from their perch, where they led the horses for the night before returning to the cave-like shelter beneath the solid, well-place, rock-mound. It looked like it had been cut out over time by other wayfarers, providing shelter from the elements. There was evidence of a recent camp fire, signifying its continued use.

They set themselves down and started to tend to making their own little heat source. The cave like shelter held a view looking over the forests. A bit further away from it the hill began to slope in a steep drop. The path was alongside this slope, downwards for the last portion of the trip to the town.

'We'll probably get to Refton after midday tomorrow,' said Felipe, assessing the distance.

'Looks like a massive town!' declared Ramkus with enthusiasm.

'Massive, heh! Well, I guess from what you have seen, one of the major port towns of the Empire in this region. They have quite a presence there.'

'Is it safe for us then?'

'It will be, there is at least some semblance of order. I doubt that patrol from Kerwood would have overtaken us at any point. Also, it would be shameful to claim they were beaten up by a bard's apprentice, as well as admit as to why they were after you in the first place. That would only get them into trouble with the higher ups. We'll be fine. Their presence is felt quite differently than from those other outlier places. They are on the edge there, whereas they sit in the lap of luxury in their own towns. Happy, content, I daresay jovial. A good audience for you to try your performance skills. Now, let's continue our lessons. Play!'

As Ramkus and Felipe continued with their performance practice, an old man began to walk up the path. The two watched as he approached. A long wispy white beard, bald top, deep eyes that looked hardened and keen. He wore a robe of thick brown cotton, and stood with a cane, resolute and outwardly pleasant.

'Peace, friends.' He greeted them as he entered the little shelter. 'May an old man enjoy the fire too?'

'Of course, well met friend,' replied Ramkus. 'Please, rest yourself.' He felt it only appropriate to treat this old man with the utmost respect, for there was something that hinted to the great depths of this man. He had an air about him, peaceful underlying contentment of the everyday, and this was felt by the two. For Ramkus, this man held some hidden power.

'Would you like some food?' Ramkus added whilst Felipe produced their dwindling supplies.

'We shall be heading to Refton tomorrow, so shall be in a good position food wise. Take as much as you please,' Felipe said.

'Thank you, friends,' the old man seated himself down in a cross-legged position and started to eat some of the victuals presented to him with a bow of the head in thank you. He bore a smile that spoke of compassion, yet something that worked behind the veil of the human experience.

'What brings you to these parts?' Ramkus asked, a little intrigued by this character.

'Ah, I'm on a pilgrimage.'

'Where to?' Ramkus continued.

'Nowhere important,' the old man chuckled, 'it is essentially to see the worlds wonders and its people. To see the beginnings of chaos, the dawns of new eras.' His eyes rested on Ramkus, still of their friendly demeanour.

'Well, pilgrim, what news do you have for us from Refton, or the rest of the world?' Felipe said nonchalantly.

'War still rages in some corners, conquests for territories. The good die whilst the evil survive… The usual story of existence; and we strive on. We must remain positive that it will change though, that the balance is shifted. I know it will.' He chewed his bread, cheese, and salami slowly, smiling as he did, in delight and gratefulness.

'There is no news from Refton, other than it is fairly busy from what I saw. Not my sort of scene. I prefer to be out in nature, with the few who can enlighten me.' He nodded to the two who smiled in reply.

'Do you not feel unsafe then?' Ramkus, curious as to the moribund answer upon the state of affairs in the world, queried further.

'No,' came the reply, 'the world sees nothing to gain from an old man, such as myself.' He looked out onto the forest below the cleft. The light was sinking back to earth, as the stars decided to shine through the dusk blanket. It was a deep blue sky this evening, and clouds covered the moons light. They sat in silence, save for the fire's playful noises. A sense of peace and calmness shrouded them. The world had stopped spinning in order that they could enjoy the magnificence of the moment.

'That is a nice staff you have there,' the old man praised. 'I dare say it looks like an Enforcer's piece.'

'Enforcer?' Ramkus repeated, bemused.

'Enforcer of peace, guardian, spiritual warrior, all names for those that make their presence known on the people and the lands. All in the name of peace. You look like you are not even initiated in *your* Order yet; what you are.' His gaze fell on Ramkus with such authority.

'Very good guess, pilgrim,' Felipe interrupted. 'Do you know much of these people, this Order?'

'Only that they are a force to be reckoned with – as if nature wills for the people itself! And a reason why the world is not in total conflict. They – you,' he nodded at Ramkus, 'hold the balance; control the balance…' He did not finish – that is, if he did have anything more to say, in any case.

'The hell!' grunted Felipe, the old man turned and jumped to the back wall. A stranger was standing, facing them, brandishing two swords. His forearms wrapped in leather, his face covered.

'Arrgh!' he yelled, jumping towards Ramkus.

Ramkus jumped to the side – thanks to his quick reflexes – and missed being hit as the blades came swinging down. His staff was lying on the ground, just in range for him to leap onto the ground, grab it, and get into a defensive position without thinking. His reflexes once again came to the rescue, as he parried and deflected the next assault. The assailant was slashing at Ramkus, hitting the staff with force that would have hacked off a limb.

Ramkus jumped around the fire, making sure not to get trapped, their shadows appeared as if a performance. Felipe and the old man retreated as far away as possible. The assailant lunged again but was deflected as Ramkus pirouetted and swung his staff back, missing as the assailant dodged and weaved.

The deadly foe lunged again and again, as Ramkus kept moving backwards, around and around, spinning his staff, looking for an opportunity to counter attack.

I have seen this man before, thought Ramkus. His eyes widened, *The Kerwood Inn: he was the man in the corner!* Ramkus did not have much time to ponder the thought, as the deadly stranger started to ramp up his attack, now slashing and jabbing at Ramkus with ferocity. Ramkus could only move backward and deflect. The speed and intensity was incredible, and Ramkus was only barely able to defend himself with natural reflexes.

'What do you want!' Ramkus cried out at his foe. He did not answer. He lunged again, but this time, Ramkus got just enough of an edge on the sword to make the weapon reverberate, opening the stranger up for Ramkus to shoulder him out of the shelter and onto the path. Ramkus jumped atop his foe, falling upon him with an elbow into his shoulder and torso. The stranger let out a scream as he kicked Ramkus off. They held their weapons tightly, the stranger on his feet, circling with Ramkus. Both were ready to pounce. But the stranger pulled back and laughed.

'Good, good.' The stranger said in a distinctly foreign accent. Ramkus could detect a menacing smile, but still could not see the face of the man. All of a sudden, the man jumped to the side of the road, down the slope, vanishing.

Ramus was panting as Felipe and the old man went to gather him. He was in a state of shock, and it took him a while before he thought to make sure he was all intact, still watching the spot where the stranger had leapt down, just in case.

'What. The. Hell!?' Felipe said in disbelief, shocked himself.

'Are you alright, my boy?' the old pilgrim asked Ramkus. He did not answer and was led away by the arms of the two. He soon came to his senses as he was sat next to the fire.

'That was the man from the Kerwood Inn, Felipe.'

'I don't remember him?' Felipe said with a frown.

'I had asked Solento if he was some part of the Empire. He said they did not have such types,' Ramkus said in a shocked state.

'You are right about that, boy,' replied the pilgrim, 'I do not see anything that speaks of the Empire in that man. He is from somewhere entirely different and far; of where I do not know. One thing is for sure, though, you are being watched by someone, or some peoples.'

Ramkus looked up at him, he had been sitting still, but watching the road outside the humble rock shelter. The pilgrim showed a compassionate care in his eyes.

'We may need to keep a watch tonight,' Ramkus replied without emotion.

They went silent, whilst the clouds passed by the moon, and a breeze gently swept by the forest below.

'The man wasn't trying to kill me.' Ramkus mused after a while. 'I think he was testing me.' He turned his body to face the others when none answered. 'He said: *"Good, good."*' He stopped and looked down into the deep fathoms of the fire. 'He wouldn't have been a Guardian, would he?'

'No,' both replied in unison. The old pilgrim spoke first.

'Guardians are not like that.'

'He's right, they firstly don't have weapons like that. They also don't attack others like he did. He was something completely different. Why would a Guardian want to attack another Guardian? It just goes against what you are meant to stand for, from what I gather: peace.'

The old pilgrim eyed Felipe for a while. 'Are you alright?' He turned to Ramkus.

'Yes, yes, I am fine,' he shuddered. 'I just don't know what to expect anymore. So many *unexpected* events. So many people wanting to attack me. I have done nothing. Is this what the life of a Guardian is like? To be continually fighting?' he said as if drained of his will.

'All life is a struggle,' the pilgrim said in a sage tone. 'Some struggle more than others.'

'What is the point of struggling through life then?' His despair was once more evident.

They were silent for a time.

'Life is as it is,' the pilgrim picked up his attempts to reassure Ramkus, 'I do not know the other struggles you have had, but they are part of existence and should not be allowed to affect you in such a manner. One must keep a balance in life, between the positive and negative; the light and the dark. It is in everything. It is the nature of things.' He stared deeply into Ramkus, 'You have a long way to go, but know that it is always better to move forward than to stay stagnant. Always forward, never back.'

Ramkus nodded, calming down. He looked towards the distant lights of Refton, wondering what tomorrow would bring. The glow in the distance gleamed under the cloud cover which was just letting the

143

moon peak over onto the forest. He could see the reflection of the sea now, as stars were twinkling upon it as if the town lay on the brink of the cosmos. *It would have been a beautiful evening*, he thought to himself, *had life not continually made things so interesting.*

He stretched out his leg and realised the brace was loose. He moved it around to see if it was broken, which it was not. His knee was in a little pain, however.

He shook his head and gave a chuckle. 'Least he could have done was give me his name,' he joked to his companions. They gave weak but comforting smiles. There was a fear in their eyes. They were still very wary themselves and their own safety. They sat in silence once more, and let the night move on.

Ramkus had been awarded the second watch, the old man the last. Ramkus was not sure the old pilgrim would be able to do anything other than wake the other two. He felt the danger had passed though, but still appreciated the fact the other two were willing to keep watch during the night. He settled down against the wall, staring into the last recesses of the fire. Its coals still cindering. He closed his eyes.

A voice was laughing. He was in a dark, cold, stone prison.
*"**Choose your devil**", came a voice from the front, someone sitting in metallic throne. Its anger, its violent intent, was palpable in the air.*
A whimper came from the corner, a flash skin in the sparse streams of light.
*"**Choose one. What is it to be? Make yourself! Make yourself mighty. Powerful. A leader!**" The voice directed. The eyes shot out from in front. Ramkus had the urge to lash out at whatever, whoever, it was. But why, what was the purpose? Better to grovel in this world, as there is only trial after trial, turmoil after turmoil.*
The voice laughed at him, maniacally. The eyes looking as if to stab without remorse. Water was dripping somewhere.

144

*"**It is not in you to choose anything other than me!**" The voice continued as light cascaded down a staring face, teeth baring a murderous smile. "**There is no other choice for you!**"*

What did this person want?

The scurrying on the ground to the side continued, the creature kept stirring and whimpering. Ramkus stiffened his back. The despair he felt waned, giving way to his own feelings of anger.

*"**Choose your devil, make yourself!**" The voice laughed, as it pounced at him, knocking him backwards and into an abyss. He saw nothing, but felt a fall into the nothingness of everything. No feeling, as if an implosion of himself, and then an expansion into all the space that could fill the chasm of his descent. He was lost in an infinitesimal space he felt he knew, where there was not a thing; and he did not fear it. This void, it pierced his psyche, and he knew the nascent seed of intent of the cosmos had been planted. Nay! It was always there, it had simply taken root.*

He hit the ground hard.

He awoke with a fright. Dawn was beginning to breach, the old man, true to his word that he would take his turn, was seated, watching just outside the rock shelter. He turned as he heard Ramkus's sluggish movements and heavy steps. He smiled.

'Did you sleep well, lad?'

Ramkus, shaking off some weariness, approached the man, standing to his side, looking out. 'I am not sure,' Ramkus uttered, blinking. 'Odd dreams.'

'Ah,' the man said thoughtfully. 'Such dreams hold great meaning.'

'It is one that seems to be so real. A voice that keeps beckoning to make a choice.' He paused, remembering the feeling of falling, 'And then utter darkness, nothingness.'

'The void,' the pilgrim stated. 'A dangerous place to find oneself,' his voice became stern, as he eyed Ramkus from the corner of his sight. He rested his chin upon his cane. He smiled as Ramkus turned to him with the look of a seeker.

'What can you tell me of it?' Ramkus asked, now fully turned to face the old man.

'That you will have to find out for yourself!' He grinned, 'That is also part of life, its mysteries: nobody holds the answers for you alone. Your path is for *you* to lead. To take control of. To make choices for. Will you sink to your knees, or press forward with conviction, might, and power?'

Ramkus gave a querying gaze, wondering if this pilgrim somehow knew of his intimate situation.

'But that is your choice, and you live however you choose. I am sure you will be given a path to follow with your *Guardians*, but it will be for you to choose it.'

Ramkus sighed heavily. Felipe could be heard muttering to himself in his sleep.

'So much for a simple path, obstacles seem to fly out at every corner,' Ramkus said as he stared off into the distance. 'I am not even sure of what I am meant to be doing, or where I am meant to be heading.'

'How many can truly say they know? Hmm?' The pilgrim stretched his arms out, 'And at least you have obstacles, they make life *interesting*.'

Ramkus smiled faintly, nodding gratefully to the old man for his words of kindness and understanding. How much wisdom and guidance would really be gained remained to be seen. He moved back to his spot in the shelter and dozed off again to thoughts of Clara.

Birds were chirping not too long before daybreak, as the sun hung low but was already heating the land. The trees seemed to revel in the light, with small critters darting about, looking for an early morning feed. Light beamed off the distant ocean, heralding Refton as the prized and gloried gem of conquest for the day. The three ate their victuals, the two adventurers once again sharing with the old man. They were in good spirits for what the day would bring, and far from the odd events of last night. Ramkus and Felipe gave the rest of their food to the old pilgrim, saddling their horses before jumping on.

'Life should be enjoyed, my lad. Everything can be enjoyed if it is seen in such a way. If I was to give you a piece of advice, it would be to choose that path above all else,' the pilgrim imparted on Ramkus.

They were motionless for a little while.

'Take care, pilgrim!' Felipe took off his black, wide brimmed hat. Ramkus looked to the old man who still held a powerful presence about him. 'Perhaps we will meet you again. Until then, travel well.' He nodded.

'Perhaps we will. I wish you well on your path, too.' The pilgrim turned his back and departed.

Ramkus and Felipe turned their horses to the path ahead, making their way down the road cut into the slope, happy to have met such a nice person on their travels.

'We didn't even ask his name!' Felipe said incredulously.

'I don't think we were meant to,' answered Ramkus.

Chapter VII

Refton was visible from miles away, as the hill they walked ascended to clear vantage points of the town and its surrounds. Laying on a bay, a wide river ran through two sloping sides that descended into it like a small valley, splitting the town as it met the sea where long docks extended into the waters. It was similar to Kerwood in this respect. A two story, three-foot thick, orange wall surrounded the boundary of Refton, with sentries guarding the innards and exterior of the large settlement. Large shipping vessels lined the docks at the river's mouth, and small fishing vessels were moored outside them. The sea sparkled with radiance; it was a fine day by any account. There was a hubbub from market stalls and people moving about the streets. The buildings all joined, painted in red, ochre, orange, yellow. Children were running around, soldiers (in the Empire's attire) and townsfolk muttering at their incessant play. There was a joviality, a movement to this town.

The two wanderers had entered the large gate, standing a bit taller than the wall it connected. They were greeted with nods of acceptable entry from the guards at the gate, and not a second thought.

Through the streets they meandered, until they came to a large open piazza, with building on all sides, one with a large balcony.

'We will probably end up at this place, but I'd prefer we try somewhere else first,' Felipe gave a wink to Ramkus.

Ramkus admired the balconied building for a moment: it had rose vines growing around it, looking well maintained. *A rose amongst the prickles*, he thought.

They led their horses through the winding streets, listening to the vendors sell their "fine", "authentic", and "best quality" goods, as well as "cure all" medicines.

'Hungry?' Felipe asked. It was rather a suggestion than a question, as he went over to a street stall and purchased some fried meat that was wrapped in a thin bread for both of them.

They continued walking: past elderly men sitting outdoors, arguing
and debating; women sweeping their front porches; younger women
staring down from the second storey windows at either their children
or men. Walking out to where the river dissected the town, Ramkus
looked at massive grates that were on either end of the river through
the town: one under the sentry wall at the outskirts of town; the other
under the last of the bridges crossing the town before the docks.

'They're to stop people going through willy nilly,' Felipe said
plainly after noticing Ramkus's absorption in the constructs.

'Ah,' Ramkus replied before asking, 'Where is this place we are
heading to, Felipe?'

'On the other side of town, just over there,' Felipe pointed to a
seemingly rowdy establishment. 'If you really want to have a good
time, that is the place to go. It is also a great place for beginner
bards.' Felipe laughed as Ramkus had a shot of ambivalence to the
whole guitar experience surging through his body.

'Come on, if you can impress that crowd, you can impress anyone.
They should forgive you any mistakes, they're usually heavily
drinking by noon,' Felipe gave Ramkus a wink as they moved down
to one of the main bridges over the river.

They looked out to the illuminated, glimmering waters of the sea,
feeling the warmth of the sun embracing their faces, hands, and later
sink into their attire. A light sea spray was providing the olfactory
senses a clearing sensation. As much activity as there was in the
town, there was peace to be had here. They settled their horses
outside the establishment. Ramkus noticed the sign posts in small
letters reading "Soldiers Saloon", and the rickety old signboard
above read "Sea Soldiers Spit".

'Lovely' remarked Ramkus with a frown.

'I know, it is very charming,' Felipe replied with a sideways nod and
smile.

They entered through swinging grated partitions into a smaller hall
than that of Kerwood. It was very lively, with many "off duty"
soldiers of the Empire clinking mugs, tearing apart meat roasts,
slapping the servant girls' behinds, who would in turn be throwing

winks about. There was musty salt smell to the place, and the men who were not soldiers littered small pockets of the salon, throwing snarls and angry glances.

'Right so, let's see what crowd we have here,' Felipe said. 'It is always important to know what kind of crowd you are dealing with.'

'Looks pretty mixed I'd say,' Ramkus remarked thoughtfully, 'although it appears the *clientele* are all of the male gender...'

'Very good' replied Felipe, not sensing the sarcasm in Ramkus's voice. 'So, the best type of songs are usually the hearty melodic ones, where the *male* crowd can get involved.'

Ramkus felt the despair again. Having to perform at such an early stage in his learning seemed unfair, cruel, twisted. He wished to get out as soon as possible. All he wanted to do was learn the instrument for himself, not perform for others.

'I'll go talk to the innkeeper, you never know, they may pay extremely well!' Felipe stated with a smile, Ramkus detected a sarcasm in what Felipe had said, but tried not let it get the better of him.

As Felipe went off in search of the owner, Ramkus looked more astutely at the crowd. The soldiers were easily identifiable in their red army attire and leather tabards. It seemed to Ramkus that the regular infantry were looked after a tad bit better than the simple country enlistments, with a little extra leather afforded where it counted. A number of corpulent, older *soldiers* - most probably officers close to retirement - were perched with their men, cajoling the younger to do certain acts that would *get* them in better stead for promotions. Those hanging around the sides of the hall seemed to be *wiry* ghoulish types, wearing sleeveless shirts, fairly mangy. These pockets of people seemed odd, not talking to each other, all set in positions, the same distance from each other and the soldiers. Ramkus thought that they didn't look the type to speak. The carolling of the soldiers continued as Felipe returned.

'You're on!' He said with glee. 'You can start now, here,' Felipe thrust the guitar into Ramkus's hands, grabbing his staff off him.

'But, I, who,' Ramkus stuttered, not expecting to have the whole ordeal thrown at him so quickly. His mind folded, clearly distraught. Felipe looked him in the eye, placing a hand on his shoulder, 'You never know when you'll get another shot, Ramkus.'

Ramkus frowned, but resolved himself to get through it, moving over to the corner of the hall reserved for bards. He shook his head as he saw a heavy streak of urine in the corner. *Let's give them hell*, a voice at the back of his head said. 'I wish it did not stink so bad,' he muttered to himself.

He took his position, no one at the tables seemed to notice. Those hanging around the edges of the saloon eyed him, scowling, spitting, sneering. He strummed the guitar, and began to sing:

Upon a galley ship,
A man was given the whip.

He thought a sailing tune may be effective. No real reaction came, apart from the people at the walls - as if trying not to look at each other - shot quick glances about. Ramkus pressed on, louder....

The man he gave the lip,
And for that he was given a rip.

A few had started to take notice. He kept going, now almost screaming, adlibbing.

And now if you don't sip,
I'll smash you in the hip!

One of the older generals took interest in the bard's performance. 'Shut up you lot!' he growled. 'We have some entertainment!' He must have been rather high ranking, for everyone obeyed.

Ramkus smiled, continuing his guitar work, singing the tunes. Soon all the soldiers began to become involved, singing along. *A good choice*, Ramkus thought, as he had them all clinking the drinks, moving to and fro, smiling and bellowing. They all appeared red-faced.

He took huge delight in the scene, the orchestration of this merry crowd. It felt good to be able to do this and it lifted him from the earlier depths of despair and hopelessness felt when he was propelled to take the stage. He was now elated, until he looked at one of the men standing on the edges of the saloon who was unsheathing a blade. The others around the room followed suit - around ten in all - their metal sparkling in the sparse rays of sunlight draping through the coloured windows. He dropped the guitar immediately and screamed, 'They're attacking!'

He raced at the closest of these wiry men whom had the look of murderous intent. Not all the soldiers noticed what was happening, but a few did, and they alerted the others to defend themselves, quickly throwing their tankards at the attackers.

In the blink of an eye, the whole scene had changed from a revelling romp, to an all-out brawl. Blood was being spilt as the drunk soldiers struggled against the deft movements of the assailants. Ramkus himself had been able to surprise the closest attacker, ramming him with his shoulder to the wall, cracking him in half against the windowsill. The assailant came to though, as Ramkus gave him a quick jab, ducking under the swing of the man's blade. He moved around the man and grabbed him by the neck, forcing his head down to meet his knee. He was out.

Ramkus then moved to the next attacker who was forcing his blade into the soldiers, having already chopped one of them. Ramkus tackled him from the side, knocking into another attacker. All three were on the ground.

By this time, many of the soldiers who had not been initially hurt, were on their feet, brawling, brandishing their weapons, fighting. It was all out chaos!

Felipe was standing at the door, petrified, not knowing how to react to the frenzy. Frozen in his spot, he watched as Ramkus deftly threw himself into the fray of battle; he knew he'd be fine. He then looked at his guitar which was at the end of the room and in danger of being trampled on! Bodies were flying, blood was flashing here and there, bone crunching hits were reverberating around the hall. He had to get his guitar out of the fracas as soon as possible, but how was he to get it out of this melee unscathed?

Men were being thrown to the ground, ineffective at enforcing their dominance as soldiers in these close quarter combat situations. The attackers were being forced back, pelted with uncoordinated drunken punches from the soldiers which were just as effective when they hit their comrades. It was drunken fighting at its best.

Ramkus had one of the two attackers he'd taken to the ground in a choke hold. Once this one was knocked out, he noticed how the soldiers had immediately taken to the other, giving him a good beating and protecting Ramkus in the process from being attacked as he focussed all his attention on the one he had choked out. He raised himself from the ground, watching the remaining attackers being overwhelmed, beaten, and bashed. Two attackers had made it out the door where Felipe had been standing. *Had been standing!* Ramkus felt a sudden pang of panic that his friend had been carried off. He looked around in search; Felipe was behind the bar with the Innkeeper, crouching down, holding his guitar. The commotion was dying down, a lot of heavy panting replaced the sounds of hard hits and grunts. There were a dozen odd soldiers on the ground, less than half of them were bearing deep cuts, the rest concussion from the blows of the attackers... or their own men. The remaining attackers who had not escaped were being tied up with metal chains. Only two seemed to be conscious, eyes moving around under heavily beaten up faces, spitting blood. Ramkus realised his own heavy breathing, his heart was pounding, his hands tense and ready to either deflect or punch a surprise attacker. He controlled his breathing, his heart, and his muscles; closing his eyes, he relieved his mind of the situation.

One of the larger, older soldiers, came over to him.

'You did real well, my lad. Not only did you see what was happening and warn us in time, you knocked out a couple of em'!' The man said.

'Who were they?' Ramkus replied in an exhausted voice.

'Bandits, pirates, brigands. Doesn't really matter, they were good for nothings that wanted to spill the Empire's blood. For what? To feed their anger I suppose – that they could not join our ranks and be one of us. Or maybe they were just wrong in the head. Either way, we showed them we are not to be messed with!' He patted Ramkus on the back in a jovial manner.

'The way you are speaking, you seriously do not care for their motivations? Seems to me you have seen this type of thing before,' Ramkus asked, bemused.

'Indeed, we do, all the time, lots of little attacks by people of all types, and for all reasons. Luckily there is no central command directing these sorts of attacks. An organised assault by such miscreants all banded together could end up being devastating. As long as we have only small skirmishes to deal with, we are fine. Come to think of it, we haven't had a proper war for a very long time – at least on this front – I don't know how well we would go in a real battle as it has been so long. Probably would smash whomever, still. I do miss a good battle!' The man was clearly pleased to spin a good yarn and was about to get lost reminiscing on his warmongering days, but caught himself as Ramkus doubled over, catching his breath. 'In any case, thank you for helping us. We may have shed a lot more of our own blood, had you not been so wary. You're a pretty good fighter, you know, and you don't perform too bad either.' Ramkus, not really knowing what to reply, said: 'Ah, thanks? You too…'

The man looked at him and gave a large chuckle, patting Ramkus on the back. He actually towered over all the men, which Ramkus did not realise until he had straightened himself up.

'I ought to report what has happened. Thank you once again, maybe I will be able to see your performance properly another time,' the man paused, 'or maybe you should consider joining our ranks instead. Either way.' He nodded, and strut off proudly. As he was about to exit the swinging partition, he turned his head. 'Is this yours?' He looked back and pointed to a staff that was resting beside the doors: Ramkus's staff.

'It is,' Ramkus yelled back, above the sounds of panting, groans, and laughter.

The man gave it a good look. 'Very nice.' He turned back to the door, raised a hand in goodbye, and went out into the sunlight and fresh air.

'Ramkus!' Felipe shouted upon spotting him. He raced over from behind his hiding place. 'Are you alright?' the Master Bard asked, looking him over. 'Of course you are!'

'I see you got your guitar in one piece,' Ramkus replied with a hint of sarcasm, still breathing heavily.

Yes, I suppose I was a little preoccupied with my *livelihood* than my *accompaniment*. But you know I would have been useless, and you were always going to come out the better.'

Ramkus frowned, 'You never know Felipe. All my actions seem to be reactionary, impulsive; I don't think about them. I don't like getting into fights. Worse thing is, I was starting to enjoy performing for that rowdy bunch, and then it turned into a massive brawl before I even finished the first song.'

'Ahh. You'll you get another chance.'

The soldiers were busying themselves with how next to proceed, clamouring about how the town authorities should be by soon. Some began to vomit after all the excitement, and drinking.

'Let's step outside for a bit,' Felipe said after watching a soldier dry retch. He turned back to Ramkus with a face of morbidity.

Ramkus grabbed his staff as they sauntered out into the daylit, busy streets. People were still going about their daily routines.

They rested up against the posts they'd tied the horses.

'That place was starting to make me feel sick,' Felipe said.

'You're not going to be ill are you?' Ramkus replied with a wry smile.

'Don't be ridiculous, it is just I can only stay in such establishments for a certain period of time, especially when I know there are other places that are palaces compared to here, and where we are welcome!'

'Well then, should we not be entreated to this little palace of yours, or should we wait for the town authorities to show up?' Ramkus started to think of what the authorities coming might entail: waiting around, raising suspicions - exactly what he did not want. 'In fact, let's move from this place. Not much more to be said or done. Happy with that, Felipe?'

Felipe bowed, 'After you then my young bard. To the palace and away from the squalor!'

Making their way back through the busy streets, a different air hung over the whole picture of the once serene town: one of caution. They did not know who's suspicions they may have raised. There were two attackers whom had escaped after all, and they would easily recognise these two minstrels. There was also the potential to be dragged into the whole debacle by the Empire, or the town authorities. Ramkus had assumed it was an Empirical town, and that all the services were controlled by the Empires strings in any case. He didn't want to draw any attention to himself after escaping Kerwood; he tried to forget about that incident, lest it come back to bite him. Felipe had allayed the original fear, but it kept sneaking back into his thoughts from time to time.

Men were starting to come in off ships with crates and barrels along the side of the river, crossing back and forth between the two sides of the town. It was just as lively as before, with people selling all sorts of wares, spruiking the quality of the products, the materials which they were made of, or the names of the places from which they originated. Ramkus had calmed himself reasonably well after a while, taking it all in, still wary of the surroundings, but content that he was able to handle himself both as a fighter and a bard. He also looked forward to settling down in a room at the place Felipe had been praising. *Any place with rose vines growing along the balcony must be very nice*, he considered.

Felipe had begun to whistle, sticking out his chest and walking proudly with confidence. Ramkus surmised that Felipe was only trying to calm his own nerves. He'd put himself in danger, purely for his guitar, although he had come out the better, and for that, he was pleased. Ramkus started to think that they had not quite understood the gravity of what could have occurred. Had the attackers been able to get one second more advantage, there could have been a greatly different outcome in what may have transpired: many more slashes taken, more bloodshed, more death; perhaps even his own. He stopped this train of thought as two eyes stared at him on a low hung balcony: a cat. It stared intently and curiously at this man. Ramkus stared back, locking his eyes with the feline beast, continuing the contest over his shoulder as they passed it by.

'Cast your eyes on one of my favourite spots,' Felipe yelled back at Ramkus, breaking the competition.

They once more stood in front of the picturesque Inn. Ramkus had a much greater respect for it after the Sea Soldiers Spit saloon. They led their horses to a stable behind the establishment, and went back to the front entrance, walking through its wide doorway. It was quite grand inside, beautiful, with a heavy orange glow filling the main hall. Perfumes of many types - a lot with hints of exotic fruits - wafted in this main area. It had a balcony area above the bar, small round tables, murals and paintings of natural settings adorning the sides. A large, heavy rose etched framed painting of a pristine lake hung above the fire place situated on the left wall, presenting itself as the showcase piece. Another massive landing to the right where the staircase lay, connecting to the floor above the bar. Candles were hung up high, almost to the second level, all lit, and the source of the orange glow. There was – as with the saloon – many individuals already enjoying themselves in the early hours of the afternoon. Ramkus did note that not everyone was drinking alcoholic beverages, and the crowd was evenly balanced between men and women, a number playing cards.

'Many merchants and their wives, and *daughters,* come here,' Felipe said, 'they are the types who really appreciate fine music. The best of these, though, *the ones who really appreciate the finer things in life*, are the lady merchants. They are always up for a good time,' Felipe winked at Ramkus, beaming a very pleasant smile.

'I can only guess what you have on your mind once more, Felipe,' Ramkus said sternly.

Felipe continued to smile, 'Let's see what type of room we can muster.'

'Hopefully two,' Ramkus quickly replied.

Felipe gave him a sideways look, nodding in agreement.

They moved to the bar and attracted the hotelier's attention. Ramkus rested his back against the bar and looked more closely at the setting. Perhaps a wary reaction to the whole attack before; he wanted to pre-empt any such event, should it happen again. It was actually very obvious that such a thing would happen, now that he thought about it: *Anyone in their right mind would see that the positioning of those men, and the* feel *of their intent, would sense something was off.* It was not so easy to read the situation here: a lot of men and women, dressed in fine clothing of various fabrics and colours, sitting down talking, playing cards, eating a range of foods daintily. Many attractive girls who must have been the daughters of merchants that Felipe had specifically mentioned. His spirits suddenly lifted. He also noted there was no cloaked man like the one in Kerwood, either. 'What can I do for you, gentlemen?' The Hotelier finally wandered over. A tall man, with a black beard, looking rather powerful, but also well mannered. 'Ah, it is *you* Monsieur Felipe! I almost didn't recognise you with that facial hair. Must have been a long journey for you to come here in such a state.' He looked Ramkus up and down with friendly but judgemental eyes. 'And you also travel with a companion I see. Not that I have anything against that *sort of thing.*'

Felipe looked at him; first quizzically, and then perturbed. 'This is my apprentice,' he said in a scolding tone, 'and I would like TWO rooms!'

'No need to take offence, Monsieur,' the Hotelier said defensively, 'I was under the impression you did not take on apprentices, and… Anyway, I assume you mean you will both want board for performing.' The Hotelier's manner became calmed in an attempt to diffuse the offence caused.

'Yes, and coin,' Felipe replied curtly.

'Well, that usually depends on how many patrons you are able to draw through the doors, and we already have a bard here this evening.'

'What!? *Who?*' Felipe growled.

'Not sure of their name, a lutenist from one of the islands.'

'A lutenist?' Felipe scoffed, 'So you will deny us from staying and performing due to some lutenist?'

'I did not say that, Monsieur Felipe, I merely wished to point out that we already have entertainment for the evening. Should people be brought in, we would have to pay them their fair share. Besides, there are two of you. I have not heard your apprentice's ability before, it would be double the coin count for the both of you. Not that I distrust your judgement in your apprentice's skills.' The Hotelier opened his palms, 'If you wish, I will let you both play, but you will be competing with the lutenist. I will warn you now though, that it is unlikely that you will get much coin, as it is only right for the first act to have first rights to any additional purse thanks to patronage due to entertainment.'

Felipe thought for a second. He looked at Ramkus and smiled wryly. 'Compete with the lutenist, you say. Well, I dare say it will be us who bring them all in tonight!'

'Compete? Did I give that impression? Well, in any case, if you bring in more customers, you will be compensated appropriately… so long as none of the *riff raff* are brought in.' He lowered his chin and eyed them. They both nodded their understanding before he continued. 'I will allow you two rooms, but please clean yourselves up before tonight.' The Hotelier rubbed his face, raising his eyes. The two wayward adventurers unconsciously followed suit, rubbing their own faces. The Innkeeper then raised his nostrils and sniffed, making a face before walking off to a cabinet further down the bar. Felipe turned to Ramkus and whispered, 'I had completely forgotten, we have been on the road for a fair few days.' He sniffed Ramkus who gave a reproachful look. 'Don't you worry, we will be in a better state later this evening.' He turned to the Hotelier who was coming back. 'Ah, Innkeep, thank you!' The Hotelier had the hint of a snarl for a moment at the mention of the incorrect title, as he returned with two sets of keys. Felipe looked at the Hotelier/Innkeeper, placing the back of his hand to his nostril, leaning away from Ramkus. He gave a disgusted sniff at his friend's scent and pointed with his thumb indicating that it was time to take off and freshen up. The Hotelier nodded his assent with a frown.

Walking up the stairs to the guest rooms, they mulled the situation. 'A lutenist!' Felipe cried with indignation. 'Absolutely no match for us!'

'You do realise that we only have one guitar, don't you?' Ramkus said, trying to temper Felipe's outburst of passion.

'Ha, all the better. You play the guitar whilst *I play the room*! We shall make sure the lutenist rethinks competing against us!' Felipe was beaming as he concocted his strategy.

'I don't think he even realises he has *competition*. He had no idea we were coming, he has a right to a living as a bard also,' Ramkus reminded Felipe.

'Semantics!' Felipe said dismissively, waving his hand.

They reached the top of the stairs, the balcony had a number of small round tables and chairs atop the bar area, whilst the rooms for lodging were opposite these, continuing along a corridor to the right.

'What room are you?' Felipe asked, inspecting Ramkus's key tag.

'The other side of the floor. Oh well.'

'What is yours?' Ramkus enquired.

'On the balcony, yours is down the corridor. You wouldn't mind swapping, would you? Means I won't have to deal with too much sound at night from outside of the room,' Felipe asked without candour.

'Fine by me,' Ramkus replied, not really considering what difference it may make.

'Actually, it may serve me better,' Felipe said, coming to a smile as he thought over his choice.

Ramkus ignored him, then thought aloud: 'What did the Innkeeper mean by cleaning ourselves up? Our facial hair?'

'Ha, yes. I haven't allowed myself to be seen with this much stubble for a long while. We'll be fine, we will just go to the barbers – at least this town has one!'

After inspecting their rooms and placing some belongings aside, they made their way out into the little piazza in front of the Hotel.

Ramkus finally got a good look at it in all splendour: The Rose Hotel it was called, *very apt.*

'Wait till you settle down in that bed tonight, my dear Ramkus. Not only will it bring the grandest sleep because of our travelling, but the beds are truly a return to civilisation!' Felipe said in an enthused state.

'Already thinking about sleep, are we? I thought we had a competition to do battle in,' Ramkus replied with a smirk.

Felipe frowned, 'You know what I meant, one of the pleasures of life. A simple one for me: to have a comfortable bed.'

They walked down a path across from the hotel and onto a main thoroughfare, passing many stores selling all sort of gizmos and gadgets, knick-knackery, pots & pans.

'This is it, feast your eyes on a barber shop!' Exclaimed Felipe, enjoying the role he played in introducing Ramkus to everything new.

'You are overdoing it, you know?' replied Ramkus sardonically. 'It looks merely like a barber shop.'

They stood in the front of a window where a few chairs could be seen. Men with blades lathered patrons faces before running the sharp *tool of trade* across the white foam, scraping off hair with great efficiency - and even less blood. Felipe sauntered in, as if he loved playing the continual role of some mock life. Ramkus bet that this was the only time Felipe faced a sharp weapon. Remembering the *blades* drawn earlier, Ramkus was very cautious of the surroundings, checking the scene, sensing the place out, but came to the conclusion that no one posed any threatening presence.

'Welcome, sirs,' a man with a curly moustache said, 'Just a shave?'
He wore something of a leather apron over a white shirt. No blood
stains could be detected – a good sign.

'Indeed, for the two of us' Felipe replied.

'Very well,' the man said, 'shaves for the two companions.'

'He is my apprentice!' Felipe exploded defensively. The man looked
at him quizzically.

'I think you're reading into what people are saying a little too much,
Felipe' Ramkus whispered, elbowing him in the ribs.

Felipe looked at him over his shoulder, nodding with a little grunt. 'I
have my reasons,' he said under his breath.

Ramkus began to wonder what these reasons may be.

Seated in chairs on either side of a man whom was in the process of
have his hair tweaked, looking into the mirror. The man looked like
he was inspecting his nose hairs, all whilst the barber tending him
was trying to get him to sit still.

There was more cutting, lathering, laughter, conversation being
carried out on all sides.

*'Supposed to be a good tomato crop this year.' 'I hear the saloon
ain't likely to last another month.' 'Did you see how he performed on
the field in his last outing?' 'The problem with the Druings is their
stubbornness.'*

All types of banter filled the room, the hum was lively, warm, and
friendly. Ramkus was content, resting back as his barber lathered the
stubble that was near a beard and becoming unbearably itchy and
warm.

'So, what do you with yourself, sir?' the barber attending Ramkus
asked.

'I'm a... bard apprentice,' he quickly answered.

'Oh, very nice indeed. Get to see the world, enjoy some fine food,
experience different cultures, meet a few girls, heh heh. A very nice
life you have chosen for yourself.'

Ramkus smiled, *I have met great fortune in joining with Felipe*, he
thought, *a lot of fun has happened... and pain.* His smile became
neutral, but he pondered upon what the bard life may hold. From the

stories and songs Felipe had told, there was a vast wide world out there, much to see and experience; to live.

'Thank you,' Ramkus finally imparted to the barber. Realising he needed to fill in the void of conversation, he added: 'I kind of fell into it. I didn't exactly choose it.'

'But you chose to follow it, I assume? So you did have a say in it. Although some men are born into fateful situations, they must still pick their virtues. Believe that came from the writer, Runtillo.'

'I guess I did have a choice; you're right.' He smiled once more, as he thought of his choice to follow Felipe's advice and enjoy the pleasures of life; something – as he understood – he would not do whether by choice or nature, as a *normal* Guardian. And there would be many women tonight! His eyes traced along the ceiling, as his chin lifted.

'I should have asked,' the barber said, 'whether you would have liked any particular facial style: mutton chops; moustache; goatees are very popular with the bards; chin beard? Just as we are on the topic, may as well make the choice as to how you would like to appear.'

Ramkus lay on the question for a moment, but had no idea what would actually suit him. This required the opinion of his "mentor", as the matter was essentially what would suit a bard. *Sometime we have to make our own choices*, a voice from within spoke. He took this advice, and went with his gut choice instead of asking.

'Mutton chops, please,' he said after some deliberation. Not knowing what they were, he just thought it sounded interesting enough. *Sometimes it is good to take a stab in the dark*, he agreed with himself.

'Right you are my lad.' The barber took his blade and made a swift cut along Ramkus's face, cutting through the lather and facial hair to the skin. It was a smooth, clinical cut, the cold blade he was expecting was fairly warm, due to its sharpening. The barber continued as Ramkus casually took in the ceiling and the perimeter of his vision, sure not to make any movements during the delicate procedure. He heard Felipe laughing away as he had his stubble removed. The chorus was becoming more audible.

'I hear that one of the kings is looking for entertainers. Not sure why around here, their kingdom is miles away,' one of the barbers said, talking with Felipe.

'Most have heard I was about!' Felipe said earnestly, then chuckled. *Mundane banter*, Ramkus considered, but he still listened with intent.

'I wouldn't mind,' continued Felipe, 'working in a royal court. I have been travelling for so very long, where else is there for a bard to settle down – in comfort – than a royal court. One is always treated to the finest things, always able to hear the most interesting news first, the politico. The appreciation for the craft is also second to none. Yes, I would say the court life is where I wish to head. Stay in such a life for a few years, earn some considerable money, then retire.'

'Sounds like you have it figured out!' Ramkus's barber was now wading into Felipe's conversation. 'But why could you not just stay in a nice town with a few taverns?'

'Because I would become bored, feel underappreciated, wear out my welcome probably. Royal courts are the pinnacle of bard hierarchy, and I wish to make a permanent spot for myself at one,' Felipe said loudly back.

'To each their own,' Ramkus's barber said, returning his attention to his customer. 'And you should now have a look at yourself,' he said to Ramkus. The barber held out a handheld mirror to Ramkus. He admired the sideburns - the "mutton chops" – even if it did look at little odd, he did not have to keep them for too long.

'What do you think Felipe? Ramkus yelled out.

Felipe – and the man in the middle of the two – turned, scrutinising Ramkus's new cut with his eyes, nodding sideways after his intense stare, and frowned. 'To each their own, I suppose.'

'Ha, jealous!' Ramkus said with a touch of glee. This was fun to him, changing his appearance. 'Thank you, Mr barber. He has all the money, he is the master bard after all.'

'Ah, well we shall wait for him then. Take it you don't have such dreams of grandeur as your master?' The barber replied, biding some time - Felipe was actually taking an extraordinary amount of time, making sure his little facial hair was in order; neat; trimmed; organised.

'To tell you the truth,' Ramkus stated as he looked down, 'I have never actually thought about what I want to do. Other than I have to get to a certain spot in the world. So far, life has been one ride.'

'Ah, *that destination.* no one wants to get there too quickly,' the barber put his hand on Ramkus's shoulder. Ramkus looked reproachfully at him, not comprehending what the barber was meaning. 'Don't rush there, do not let it consume you. The great Runtillo spoke of man and his need to get to one spot. Just be happy, lad.'

Ramkus gave a very puzzled look. Maybe the fancy cut was going to his heads; he seemed to be in his own little world. *Maybe my dream is to get to this one* spot... Ramkus pursued this thought; *what an horrific idea, to be in only one spot day in day out.*

No, it was not for him, movement, going forward, travel, it was steadily but surely becoming part of him. It is what he had done from the beginning. He could not let one destination be his *destination*; it was a mere step on the way to somewhere else. He smiled as he remembered, from what he had gathered, that Guardians did seem to travel. Still, he knew nothing of their way of life. Perhaps it was only a rarity to travel, and there must be those who stayed at the top of this *Guardian's Mountain* all the time as caretakers. He had choice though: he didn't have to be a Guardian if he didn't want to be. *Do I?* He could choose to be a bard. How would these Guardians know he even existed? They never *came* for him or heard of him. Unless that man in the night - who fought him in the cave on the small peak – was one of them. Lost in his thought, he didn't realise Felipe had gotten from his chair, happily whistling.

'Time to go for a drink, I say,' Felipe gave a wink. Ramkus broke from his thoughts, nodding resolutely.

Out through the ochre, orange, and dark pink painted walls of the streets, and onto a main thoroughfare with store fronts; a few stalls were opening up with food to sell to hunger-stricken afternoon customers. This was annoying the store proprietors behind the stalls, whose shop front displays were being hidden to the odd passer-by. Harsh words were being exchanged.

Ramkus watched the verbal barrages. 'Should we break up this quarrel?' He asked Felipe, feeling a need to step in and calm the situation.

Felipe looked at him in indignation, 'No! Why do *we* need to get involved? It is not for us to calm the situation. I daresay this is actual the normal scene here, and if we *were* to get involved, it would only lead to us incurring some fiery vitriolic blasting. No, it is back to the hotel for us, we need to prepare for tonight, and also have some fun.'

'You mean, enjoy the pleasures?' Ramkus followed along.

'I mean we enjoy the pleasures, or at least try to,' Felipe confirmed. Walking back through the streets to the communal square in front of the hotel, small sparrows chirped overhead; some flew down into the open space to collect crumbs that an old man was scattering for them. There was an overload of orange light, as the sun began to settle and create an overhanging orange sky that peaked above the ochre terracotta rooves of some of the town's buildings, coupling with the orange, yellow, pink and ochre walls. The green leaves of small trees on balconies dashed the haze, as if daggers that piercing though the overwhelming orange atmosphere. There was a smell to this late afternoon in Refton, of food that had risen from the pantries, kitchens, and ovens of the households, seeping through cracks in the buildings and streets, giving it an older, traditional scent of homeliness. The piazza also had some street vendors opening up, although these people were not finding quarrels, rather, they were replaced by actual customers.

'We won't eat any of that stuff,' Felipe stated, 'the food at the hotel is actually rather good for being considerably far on the outskirts. Keeps the merchants and dignitaries happy, I guess.'

Ramkus was interested to see what *rather good* entailed, as he was
starting to feel quite hungry from the scents in the streets.

Felipe stopped and turned to Ramkus, 'Let's see what those mutton
chops actually look like.' He turned Ramkus to face him, patting him
down. 'It shall pass, I suppose. They aren't really necessary
though… for a bard, that is.'

'I only wanted to try something out, make my own choice,' Ramkus
protested.

'Indeed, you did, and you will learn from it,' Felipe said with
authority.

Ramkus shook his head.

'I only say this to you,' Felipe conceded, 'because tonight we are
going to have to work as a team, and I need you to be presentable.
You may only have to play guitar - with me doing the rest – but still,
you must *work*, and help *me work* the crowd. *Your* energy, *your*
looks, will help me beat this other bard enough that they wished
they'd never got in our way!'

'I still don't see how you can be so angry with someone we have
never met. Someone whom came before us to this hotel. Someone
that has had no idea about us even existing. Someone who is in the
same profession as us as bards, and may actually be a good person!'

'Trust me, no bards are good. Only us,' Felipe said pretentiously.
Ramkus rolled his eyes. He wanted to see and speak to this bard, see
what he had to say about the world and barding life. In fact, it
seemed he wanted to see this bard simply to compare him to Felipe.

'I don't know why you have to be so defensive, Ramkus,' Felipe
went on. 'It is a dog eat dog world, I need you to back me up, as I
back you up. Understand?'

'You mean how you back me up in fights?' Ramkus chided.

'No, how I have put up with your company, paid for you, educated
you. I may not be a fighter, but I have still given of myself - and my
money - to you. We are a team now.' Felipe was being serious for
once.

Ramkus knew he was right. 'You have helped me a lot,' he
conceded, 'but most of all you have taught me what to do and what

not to do in these lands. You are right, we are a team now. Let's *give them hell* tonight!'

Felipe winked, 'We shall, we shall indeed!'

XXX

After practicing in their rooms for a few hours, and attending to the orchestration of how they were to present that evening, the pair strolled down the stairs of the hotel and took a table near the bar. The place was buzzing with all sorts of characters. Colours, perfumes, and fashions were all paraded about. It seemed that there were more women than men, and many of these women were young and attractive. According to Felipe, these were the daughters of merchants, and looking for suitors.

'Let us continue our education,' Felipe gave a wry smile. 'Let's see what we have here.' He looked around the room, not so much to look as to survey the surrounds, but as if he was taking in the sights and sounds: the buzz. A bar maid walked over, fairly pretty, but not what Felipe had in mind it seemed. He dismissed her with haste and without consideration after ordering two meads.

'Ramkus, go speak to that girl,' he hid his fingers as he pointed in the direction of a rather straight-laced girl. Very presentable, thin, stately, wearing a deep green velvet dress, brown hair that was tied back with a hair piece. 'She looks like she may want a bit of fun.' Ramkus eyed Felipe and gave a frown. He got up and approached the girl whom was standing on her own, seemingly waiting for someone who may be taking their time to arrive - she did not seem in a rush. He strode up, admiring her green dress that went all the way to the ground, a white kerchief covered her neck. He smiled as her gaze fell upon him; she returned a look of bemusement.

'Hello' - he came out swinging, brazenly.

She gave a curious look before replying slowly: 'Hello.'

Ramkus soon realised he was not sure how else to follow up in this conversation. It had been a lot different with Clara, she had basically *hit* on him.

'Ah, nice place this is,' he said, fidgeting with his hands.

'It is,' she replied as if waiting for him to actually make a proper advance to ease into a conversation.

A question! He thought, *I need a question. That should break the silence.* He quickly came to his senses, 'Where are you from?' he asked timidly.

'From the city of Trucce, in the Vicce kingdom,' She replied smoothly.

'Ah, really?' He raised his eyebrows.

'Yes, do you know it?' She became a little livelier.

'No, I can't say that I do.'

'Oh' she replied, looking away.

This was going wonderfully…

'I'm a bard's apprentice,' he said, trying to save the already dire conversation.

'Is that so?' she said, feigning some interest, 'What instrument?

'The guitar.'

'I see'

There was silence again in this excruciating exchange, he wanted to sucker punch himself in the stomach, it'd be *much more* bearable.

'Well, see you,' he said, hurrying back like a coward to Felipe and the mead that had been brought in his absence. He grabbed the tankard and threw its contents down his throat.

'Easy now, what happened?' Felipe asked with curiosity, a little wary of his friend's sudden alcoholic tendency.

'It was awful,' Ramkus said, he felt himself fall into a slight despair again, wanting to hide under the table, or better yet, actually go to his hotel room. 'I am going back upstairs,' he said.

'No you don't! A bit shy? Had a bad situation? And you want to run away already… That is not your style my friend, nor what a bard does either! The show goes on, no matter what. Now tell me, what happened.'

Ramkus explained the dull conversation and his lack *in the art* of conversing.

'Ah, I see, I daresay you need to be taught *everything*; right from the start.' Felipe frowned, 'Well, firstly, conversation: you need to be interesting; have questions to ask; comments to make; stories to tell. As long as you are smiling, confident, and able to carry the whole conversation without coming off as brash and arrogant, you are in a good position to break through to the more natural conversation. Simple?'

'Sounds too easy, coming from you,' Ramkus said, still feeling the dejection.

'Right, watch,' Felipe got up and moved to a table with some younger women on it; they appeared to be occupied with their card game. But as Ramkus watched this odd first exchange from a stranger entering into a situation that he had not been invited to, he noted the smooth attitude of Felipe; his continuous smile; his engagement with the women. He was there for a good five minutes as Ramkus watched from the sides. Felipe looked to Ramkus and waved him over to the table. Ramkus obliged. He sat down at a spare seat on the card table, in between two of the three girls Felipe had ben chatting to.

'Here he is, my apprentice, Ramkus!' Felipe said with glee, 'We shall be pulling at your heartstrings tonight!'

'Hello, Ramkus,' one of the girls said.

They were a little older to be daughters of merchants, *perhaps they are the merchants themselves*, Ramkus surmised.

She continued, 'I'm Corinth, this is Exelda, and this is Mrill.'

'Well met,' Ramkus responded, Felipe looked at him, and laughed.

'He is in need of a little coaching on how to speak to such beautiful women as yourselves,' Felipe said. The girls - or rather, women - giggled.

Mrill turned to Ramkus as Felipe started speaking to Corinth and Exelda.

'A bard's apprentice then, are we?' Mrill didn't seem as refined as expected.

'Yes, at least for now, we shall see how I do when I get on stage!' he said, a little too enthusiastically.

'You haven't performed before?' she asked curiously.

'Actually, I did, this morning, but that became a little bit rowdy and nothing really came of it.' He laughed to himself.

'Ah, this morning? Here? I don't remember anything really happening today in here,' she said, confused.

'No, at another… *establishment*. In any case, we shall be performing tonight, in fact, we will be *competing* with another bard,' Ramkus stated.

'Really?' Mrill clasped her hands, 'That *will* be fascinating. I wish you luck.'

Ramkus took in her green eyes, black hair held back in the same fashion as the other women. She wore a purple dress that went up to her neck, with sleeves only half way down her shoulder.

'Thank you,' he said. 'So what brings you to Refton?

'Trade,' she smiled, 'I trade in spices. This is one of the farthest parts I usually come to, but it is one of the most beautiful. The forest that surrounds Refton's edges are quite exquisite – if you know the spots to venture.' She smiled.

'So you like to go for walks outside the town's perimeters?' he asked.

'I do, but it is mostly from travelling through them that I get to see what there is on display, I cannot stray too far from the town itself, I am a merchant after all...' she said forlornly.

Travel, thought Ramkus, *perhaps I could be a merchant if I wanted.*

'Do you enjoy walks in the forests?' She asked, 'I can only imagine the thrill to be a bard - or *apprentice* - wandering down roads, besides gentle river beds, playing, composing new songs, taking in the splendour.'

'No,' Ramkus said sadly, 'I have only really travelled through them, not been able to take strolls.' He did not want to let on too much about his rather new existence in the world.

'I shall have to take you to one of my favourite spots some time.' She said, smiling at him.

'I'd like that,' his response was courteous, but formal. He kept thinking how he did not want to lead her on. He looked across to

Felipe, who was being fed some grapes by the other women as they laughed.

'Delicious!' He exclaimed catching Ramkus's look. 'You must excuse me though, Ramkus and I need to prepare for tonight. Don't we, Ramkus?' Felipe gazed around with happy eyes.

'Yes. It was lovely to meet you,' Ramkus said cordially to the women, nodding to Mrill last.

'Remember the walk, Ramkus.' Mrill replied, Ramkus bowed slightly, as the they left the table.

Felipe took him gently by the arm and led him to another table, catching the bar maids eye and asking for two more meads.

'How was that for you, Ramkus? Did you see how easy it was after you broke through into a natural conversation?'

Ramkus nodded.

'I dragged you away because, well, it makes it better for me. I mean us, *hypothetically*, as they start wanting us more. Also, I noticed Mrill actually did take a liking to you. Unlike Clara – who seems to have *made the moves* on you – you have to be the one making moves. You know what that entails?'

Ramkus shook his head, picking up the mead that had been placed in front of them. He was getting his confidence back after it had been burnt by his first naïve attempt.

'Well, you have to be playful, Ramkus. That means moving in closer, joking around, touching the girl gently. Everyone likes to be shown warmth from another person, just like how animals like being petted, people do too.'

Felipe started to demonstrate such taps and gently gestures on Ramkus.

'I thought you didn't want to be seen like that, Felipe,' Ramkus joked, indicating to his being "petted".

Felipe became stern, 'I don't. I was only showing you!' He clenched his teeth. 'Anyway, there it is.'

Remembering Felipe had said he had his reasons for having issues with such things; he let it be. He was still quite intrigued with Felipe's ability to get on with people so easily when he wanted;

putting on his show face. *He does need to be on his best behaviour after all*, he thought, *for he is a bard.*

'We have our show soon, let's get something to eat, then prepare,' Felipe said, scratching his eyebrows and putting on a smile.

He really is a showman, Ramkus thought, *I wonder what else he is hiding.*

They moved upstairs and onto the balcony overlooking the hall; it allowed a good vantage of the stage, and easy access to Felipe's room. Spiced pheasant and side of seasonal vegetables was brought up to them. Ramkus was delighted with the aromatic smell and exotic flavours of the spices, as well as the little nuts and dried fruits that decorated the meal. For all he knew, the food he had eaten so far had never been seasoned, even with salt.

'To tonight,' Felipe clinked his tankard with Ramkus's. 'To showing this audience who the real bard is!' Felipe was getting himself worked up again.

'Have you ever had to compete with another bard before?' Ramkus asked when he wasn't enjoying a mouthful of succulent meat with varied vegetables.

'Well, I have actually, although it wasn't this type of arrangement,' he paused. 'Not that I like to boast, but I competed in the Eredin Bard Festival, making it to the finals five times, winning it twice!' He began to sink into some pleasant thoughts as he lent back in his chair.

'What's that?' Ramkus asked after the indefinite pause had lingered and led him to whet his intrigue.

'What's *that*!? Oh, I forgot your predicament.' Felipe smiled mockingly, 'Well, it is the grandest bard festival in Elantra, held every two years, the best bards from all over the globe come to a town named Eredin, in the Reelo Kingdom, Sort of a central land mass in Elantra. Very, *very* pretty place. Well known for inspiring great prose and poems, as well as playing host to many bards all year round. Hence why the festival is held there. A great venue, if I do say so. A sort of home for our craft, where we all feel welcome and

rejuvenated upon staying for a time. In any case, every two years, bards from all over the globe feel the calling to go to this festival, mostly to meet other bards, artisans, or great craftsmen; all exchanging stories, drinks, poems and song. And those whom are considered the very elite of our profession are asked to compete in the Eredin Bard Competition, the main attraction of the festival.'
Felipe puffed out his chest at this. 'So, as you can see Ramkus, you are in very good company when it comes to bards.'
'Was this a long time ago?' Ramkus asked. His intrigue had been piqued, for it was the first time he had spoken to Felipe of his career "accomplishments".
However, Felipe did not know if Ramkus was being facetious or not. 'Are you saying I am not up to scratch, Ramkus? I would hold your tongue, it is an awful offence to say a bard has lost his ability…'
'No, it was a legitimate question.' Ramkus went on the defence, 'Stop being so touchy, remember, I'm the one that ends up in fights, not you.'
'Sure. It's just that I,' Felipe's voice twirled off, 'I am actually quite old, Ramkus,' his voice broke a tad, suggesting this "bard duel" was getting to him. 'I just look quite young. Thanks to my forest dwellers blood, I suppose, we don't age as quickly as others. So, to answer your question, yes, it was a long while ago. I haven't been in many, many years. I was hoping I would have been able to become a court bard some time ago. Seems you have to be in the favour of high-ranking officials for that to happen - go figure - like most things it, seems.'
'So you really would jump at the chance to be a court bard?' Ramkus pressed him.
'Of course! It has been my dream for a very long time.' Felipe's enthusiasm came straight back.
Ramkus mulled this over for a few moments. 'How do you know you would enjoy it?'
Felipe pounced at the question, 'I just do, I just know…' he stopped, thinking. 'But you are right, perhaps I just need to live the dream.'

There was a little excitement brewing from below, as one of the sides of the hall was being cleared of patrons, chairs, tables. A dais was brought from the kitchen area and placed down.

'Ah, now, let us see who we are up against,' Felipe said. His eyes narrowed as he smiled sardonically.

They watched below as the crowd gathered beneath. Someone hushed the crowd in anticipation as they instantly became a captive audience. The Hotelier came out, strutting onto the dais.

'Ladies and gentlemen,' he implored, 'have we a treat for you tonight! Not one, but **two** acts!'

He waited for applause - a mere polite round of clapping.

'Without much further ado, I present to you, Sigil!'

More polite clapping, as a young girl walked onto the stage.

'A girl?!' Felipe cried, 'We are competing with a *girl?*' He was rather bemused. A sly smile came across his face, as he focussed his attention on the girl bard named Sigil.

She wore a blue velvet vest over a white flowing blouse, blue velvet pants, a small blue cap with a feather attached. Platinum blonde curls fell down to her slender shoulders. She was only very slightly - as far as Ramkus could judge - not very tall, but she came across with poise and grace, and a dash of playfulness. She must have been in her early twenties Ramkus guessed, with her sharp features; nose, cheeks, chin. *Very beautiful*, he thought.

'We have this in the bag,' Felipe slapped Ramkus on the shoulder. 'Just you watch,' his eyes widened.

Sigil bowed to the audience, with her light brown lute strapped to her shoulder. Silence fell, and she began playing.

She sang of lands, far away. Of islands and the people that inhabited them, their trials and tribulations with nature. She sang of fairy tales, of the beauty that lays hidden from this world now. She was enthralling, and Ramkus was transfixed on her. Felipe was scoffing at times, rolling his eyes. Ramkus paid him no heed. He was getting tired of Felipe's juvenile behaviour, and decided he would not let it affect his enjoyment of this show.

The audience gave a polite applause, as Sigil finished her set.

'Now, dear patrons,' the Hotelier opened as he came back onto the dais, 'we shall have the next act before a break and second performance.'

Felipe jumped up and quickly grabbed the guitar from his room, passing it to Ramkus.

'Let's show them what it is to be a real bard!' He told Ramkus, looking as if he had a hint of madness to him. 'Play me a song!'

The Hotelier spotted the two above the balcony, 'Ladies and gentlemen, our next act, Monsieur Felipe, and his *apprentice*!'

Polite applause as the crowd turned to the balcony where the hotel owner was gesturing to the pair.

Ramkus began to strum, as Felipe danced in front of him, down the stairs - Ramkus following behind. Felipe was moving between the audience's women, charming them, singing, twirling about, hands held behind his back when he was not making large gesticulations. He sang of the beauty of the world, the women whom were found throughout, and of love. He made his way around many of the tables, trying to engage as many of the people as he could - Ramkus felt they were doing laps of the place. Luckily the hall was well laid out, not too full so as to be able to move through the crowds with ease. The patrons were transfixed on this moving minstrel, this playful spirit who seemed not of this world - no one gave much heed to Ramkus. Finally arriving to the dais, most of the women had closed in on the bard, eager to hang on every word.

Before this song was to finish, Felipe spied Sigil sitting at a small table on the wall to the side of the stage. He moved in as he had with the other women, trying to make her swoon; but his eyes held a different intent, one that did not speak of love, but of domination. Ramkus was feeling a touch of sickness at Felipe's intention to *best* the poor bard girl. He manoeuvred himself to that side of the stage that Sigil sat in order that he could stop the behaviour making him feel he ought to *teach* Felipe a lesson. *What an odd feeling*, he knew that he was once again able to detect emotions that were being flung about, and Felipe's were not of the kindly type. Sigil, he guessed, was feeling intimidated, threatened - even if she did not show it.

Strumming away, he smiled at her. Her eyes hid on the floor, but
sensing his presence, let them rise to greet his with a shy smile.
Felipe was pacing about on the other side of the dais, as he finished
up in a bowing position. There was rapturous applause. Ramkus
knew it was all for the devilish Felipe, not he; but he did not care, he
was fulfilling a promise, a job, that kept him fed and gave him a nice
bed for the night. He could only hope he did not become like Felipe
in terms of feeding an ego, which meant crushing others. Felipe
thrust his arm out to Ramkus to begin the next song.

He was finding it quite enjoyable, playing the guitar as
accompanying music to the main attraction; it kept him out of the
spot light, but gave him the thrill of playing for an audience. He
looked across all the faces, their enthusiasm, their pleased gazes for
the performance they'd been privileged to attend. Even the men
seemed quite engaged with this act; it gave them a bit of
entertainment that they usually were not provided with.

After a few more songs, it was time to finish up for a break. Felipe
was perspiring, but the audience were on their feet for him, throwing
roses at his feet, the hotel owner was in utter delight at the sales
behind the bar and patronage. People seemed to be selecting the
expensive wines; they of course complemented the fine
performances. Felipe was beaming, saying 'Thank you, thank you'.

'Calm down people, calm down,' the Hotelier came back on the
stage, beaming. 'There will be, as I previously said, second
performances by both acts in a short while. Let's give them a break,
and give you the time to grab some more refreshments at the bar!'
Patrons heeded his words and streamed to the counter for more
drinks.

'Looks like you may be right about that extra coin,' the Hotelier
whispered into Felipe's ear, patting him on the shoulder with a quick
smile.

Felipe turned to Ramkus, but his vision was attracted to the
opposition: Sigil. He made his way towards her.

'And you, *my dear*,' Felipe said charmingly, but with a touch of
madness, 'I shall teach you what it is to be a bard!' He took her hand

and kissed it. She jerked back, turning her face to hide. Ramkus was incredibly agitated by the display, and let it be known by his presence; *Felipe has no right to act in such a manner*. But Felipe continued anyway, moving closer to Sigil, caressing her shoulder. 'Felipe, **do not touch her**,' Ramkus said in a low, firm, authoritarian voice. He felt a strength, a wild instinct readying him for a fight. This was unlike how he had fought other fights, there was an anger, and a sense that he wanted to inflict pain on whomever he could. A sneer came across his face, slowly turning into a nasty smile.

'Felipe, backed away from her,' he gritted through his teeth, as if daring Felipe to see what would happen if he did not obey.

Felipe faced him incredulously, shock and terror shooting through him as if some monster had been unleashed. Felipe reacted by slapping his hands, raising an eyebrow, and walking to the bar.

What had I become just then? Ramkus thought to himself, *what had just overcome me?* The smile he felt across his face, it was not his. He had seen it before, he knew what it looked like, even if he hadn't seen his own reflection. He closed his eyes, and let out a deep breath before approaching Sigil whom was still sitting at the little table on the wall. Her face was turned away from the onlookers, a tear ran down her cheek. Ramkus stood for a moment, feeling sorrow for the poor girl who was alone and being ridiculed without just cause. He looked at her with a deep affection, that he wanted to make her feel as spritely as when she walked onto the stage, bring her spirit back from wherever Felipe had scattered it off to.

'You sang beautifully,' he said softly. She turned to him, showing her reddened eyes.

'Thank you,' she gulped, staring at him for a while without expression. 'I am sorry I am like this, I should be used to the subjective behaviour of men. I am, after all, on show, on the stage.' She breathed in heavily through her nose, pulling herself together.

'No. I am sorry. And no, you should not be subjected to that type of behaviour. I... I really don't know what to say other than *he* should never have acted like that towards you.' He watched this girl: confident and yet so fragile in this confusing, restrictive world.

She smiled faintly, 'You are sweet. Please, sit with me.'

Ramkus smiled back, pulling a chair. The place was humming an orange glow from the candlelight; many faces, talking, murmuring in the background. All on show themselves, all on stage, all busy in their own little worlds; laughing, drinking, enjoying their existence. Apart from this incident with the irreverent and offensive Monsieur Felipe, the place felt warm and happy. Ramkus spotted Felipe, amongst a throng of people, talking to all those around as if this was his private party. He turned back to Sigil whom had cheered up somewhat, drinking some concoction that had the smell of sweet fruits and honey.

'He is not usually like that. He has been a little crazy ever since he heard we were not the only bards in town,' Ramkus apologised.

Sigil smiled, 'Don't apologise for him, he was like most are: domineering.'

Ramkus was flummoxed by this statement, reading between the lines that this was not the first time Sigil had been subjected to such treatment. 'Why should they feel the right? You have the right to live doing what you do, without men moving around you, feeling they can get close to you, touch you.' He shook his head.

Sigil was bemused and wary, 'You are not from around these parts, are you?' She stared at him, 'To tell you the truth, I am not either.'

'The life of a bard, eh. To travel, wind in your face, enjoying the sights of the world.' He mused happily of the little, but significant, existence he had been privy to. 'My name is Ramkus,' he had forgotten the hotel owner had introduced the acts, but not *his* name...

'Mine is Sigilund, Sigil for short,' she answered. Her eyes began to shine, reflecting the light. 'Thank you,' she said, as one of the bard maids placed a candle on the table. He noticed her light blue eyes as they shimmered. The tears were still present around them, albeit, drying up. She stared at him with curiosity, enveloping him in her gaze, reading him, reading *into* him. At least, she was trying as best as she could to do so. He could play this game too, but thought against it. She did not need more men staring intensely back at her, even if it was in a different vein. He could tell all he needed to: she was alone, travelling this world - whether by choice, or the force of fate - she was battling to keep her head above the waters in these subjective, oppressive societies, and she was winning! *At least, so far.*

'You're, different,' her voice became quite delicate, like thin glass that could shatter. She shook herself from her trance, 'Sorry, I mean, I am quite good at reading people, it is a trait of some of my people: to see the side of a person that is unblemished by the sun, but has become darkened by desires.

He gave a wry smile, 'The essence of a person?'

'Yes,' she gulped, 'the essence. You, you're... there is something that is not of this world in you. You are unlike any normal person. I can't exactly put my finger on it.'

He was becoming unnerved by this delicate little thing. She had started off so strong in her entrance on stage, but now, was all exposed, as a mysterious flower that was opening itself to judgement. Whether she was able to read him or was judging him on his actions, he could not tell, but he was not in the mood to continue this scrutiny. It was like being on the stage. Maybe one day he would feel comfortable, maybe even become an exhibitionist like Monsieur Felipe, but not tonight.

'Tell me of where you are from,' he asked her, leaning an elbow on the table, head resting on his palm.

She gave a delighted smile, to think and talk upon something she loved. Her curls starting bobbing, as her eyes lost the last strands of redness and now smiled along with her lips. *She was back!* He thought - *whomever she actually was.*

'I am from the Isles of Montreyer, you know where they are?'

He shook his head.

'Oh,' she replied with surprise, 'they are to the East of here, North East to be precise. A whole different world. My people - although *I* do not appear to do them justice – are warriors. Not only do they love to fight themselves and neighbouring islands or mainlanders, they feel it the greatest honour to die in battle. Sailing massive warships around, they raid other lands, merchants, whomever they please.'

'They have not come here en masse?'

'No,' she giggled with a sniffle, 'my people don't necessarily like the warmer climates,' she sighed. 'And their brutish fighting ways are not as prevalent as they once were; many are merely farmers, toiling the lands.'

'What of your family?' Ramkus lowered his arm along the table.

'I was the youngest of seven, the smallest also. The runt of the family. I had to fight all the others for every scrap I got. And I am not much of a fighter as you may guess,' she shrugged and smiled, 'but I found my way with music. My grandfather used to play for the village on occasions. He taught me. And my grandmother taught me to look into people.' She turned her head to the side, showing a glimpse of resignation. She turned back; the light of the candle shifted on the angles of her features, sharply accentuating them.

'And I saw into some of my people,' she sighed deeply. 'I have been travelling for a few months now, arriving here yesterday.'

'Where else have you played,' he asked wistfully.

'All the islands we stopped at. I played on the ship that brought me here. A very nice transport ship, luckily, full of merchants. Some of them being women which made the voyage easier. As you can imagine, it isn't easy being a female bard… especially on a long sea voyage.' She tilted her head towards the direction of the bar where Felipe was still show-boating.

'I am sorry we had to compete, I know you did nothing to bring it upon yourself,' he began to apologise again.

'It's fine,' she butted in, 'we all have to eat, don't we? Besides, this is a lesson. Who is he, anyway?'

'He is Monsieur Felipe, a friend, Although I doubt his character and intention sometimes. He has helped me.'

'Helped you? How?' She asked, intrigued by him once more.

'Made me his apprentice, let me travel with him.' He wanted to take the focus away from himself, 'Felipe is a Maestro. He has won the

Eredin Bard Festival twice!' He was hopeful the significance of this little bit of information would not be lost on her.

'No wonder he has he crowd eating out of his hand. Only the **best** compete in that competition, let alone win it!' She shook her head, 'You'd have to be channelling some inner demon.'

Ramkus gave a low chuckle. 'So, have you enjoyed this bard life so far?'

She paused, thinking over her answer. 'It is not exactly what I expected from it, then again, it is everything I expected. My experience has been limited, so perhaps now that I am on the mainland it will be different. I get to experience the proper travelling life that I had imagined. And there is so much to learn!'

'There is indeed,' Ramkus nodded with a warm smile.

'Ladies and Gentlemen!' The Hotelier cried out across the hall. A hush fell over the crowd. Sigilund grabbed a glass of water that had been sitting on the table, throwing it back down her throat, giving a hiccup as she stood, clasping her fingers to her mouth.

'We will go in reverse order now. Monsieur Felipe!' The Hotelier had seemingly forgotten about Ramkus. Felipe beamed from the bar, looking towards Ramkus instigating him to start the performance once more. Ramkus obliged, and so it began again.

Noticing she was somewhat pleased by the change in order, beaming slightly under the knowledge she could now gather herself, Ramkus whispered to Sigilund, 'Perhaps you are lucky, you can finish up strong.'

She hiccupped again in answer, giving a charming smile thereafter. The procession was as before: Felipe in his outrageous manner, threatening to take off his clothes for the ladies; Ramkus following, playing along happily, thinking of nothing more than the music. It enveloped him, infused him with a spirit, an energy. He was imbued with something that was above this existence. He was content, often looking to Sigilund with a warm expression. She looked at no one else but him.

As they proceeded through their second set, there began a small battle at the entrance. Many soldiers - ones whom seemed to be of a

high stature and rank - were taking residence in the Rose Hotel for
the night. There started to become a little pushing and shoving;
Felipe took no notice, till the soldiers began to seat themselves in
close proximity to the dais, whistling to each other, talking loudly,
calling for drinks. The other patrons were not amused, and a few
choice words were exchanged between the soldiers and these
patrons. The bickering started to play out quite audibly, threatening
the performance. Felipe was losing his audience, and he himself
became quite enraged. Soon the volume of the new entrants became
louder than the performance, and many of the merchants were now in
heated argument with the soldiers. All of a sudden, a punch,
somewhere - maybe multiple ones – were thrown, as people began to
hushing each other. A fight had broken out, and a few of the male
merchants were thrown outside as the soldiers took over. The crowd
who had been there from the start of the evening, started to take their
leave. Soldiers started jeering Felipe, and his *forward* performance,
laughing at him, throwing scraps of food from the tables, left-overs
from those whom had been forcibly removed. He did his best, and
Ramkus could do nothing to lessen this fall from grace for Felipe.
He pressed on though, to his credit. Ramkus knew that had he not
been so provocative to begin with, had he known the audience would
change, he would have performed quite differently, instilling more of
the music his *new* audience would like. He left to the sound of
applause - that his show had ended.

The crowd was still in its deplorable state. Fights looking to break
out

Felipe moved himself off to the side of the stage nearest the bar,
Ramkus following suit. *Poor Sigil*, he thought, *at least I can keep an
eye on her, If anyone should act untoward...*

'Ahem! I present Sigil.' The Hotelier bellowed, as if he was
presenting nobody of any importance. A deep disgust for this owner
welled up in Ramkus, but he looked over at Sigilund, happy, free,
charming, smiling to her crowd. As she started, a metal tankard of
ale was thrust into Ramkus's chest, the hand that held it was Felipe's.
'Drink!' he ordered, not too pleased with how things had turned out.

The soldiers were happily laughing and singing along to Sigilund, she had finished her first song strong, even if with a little luck of being able to prepare for this certain crowd - these men did look rather lecherous, worse than Felipe. Ramkus felt a hand on his shoulder, Felipe pulled him away to be at the bar.

'I cannot believe our *putrid* luck,' Felipe scowled. 'Why the hell did these soldiers come here? I doubt we will see any of that extra money now.' He bit his lip bitterly, beginning to sulk on the bar. 'And you! Trying to stop me from...'

'Being an asshole,' Ramkus finished.

Felipe continued to bite his lips, shaking his head. He looked to his side: soldiers were congregating along the bar.

'Why are they here?' Felipe continued to question at a whisper. 'I don't understand how the hotel's patronage could change so suddenly. This hasn't happened before. It would have been fine! Had I known and prepared!'

'Fookin' 'ow much?!' One of the *charming* Empirical soldiers at Felipe's side yelled to the barman.

'I don't think this is a regular haunt for most of them,' Ramkus chimed in, agreeing with Felipe's sentiments. Felipe raised his eyes to the heavens with reproachful exasperation from the display he had just witnessed.

'Fookin' rip aff!' the soldier said, begrudgingly throwing his money on the counter. 'What are you lookin' at,' the bald-headed thug of a man grunted at the two bards.

'To tell you the truth, my dear man,' Felipe went into character again, mocking the thuggish soldier, 'I was wondering what an awfully fine young man as yourself was doing in an establishment like this?'

The music was still cheery, people were still jovial, drinking beer, no need to begin a fight now the soldiers had the place to themselves effectively.

'Usual joints shut. Some big fight 'appened. Marshalls investigating the place.'

'Ah, thank you, my friend,' Felipe smiled courteously, then turned towards Ramkus. 'That brawl today, at the Sea Soldiers Spit saloon, no doubt!' He shook his head, 'Those indecent bandits have ruined tonight. I ought to have killed them when I had the chance!' Felipe added, hitting the bench top with his fist.

Ramkus raised his eyebrow, 'You? Kill them? I am pretty sure you would have run away without ever thinking of ever helping me.'

'Semantics,' Felipe waved his hand nonchalantly.

The Hotelier came over to the two travellers. 'Meet me on the balcony outside, overlooking the square in a few minutes.' He smiled softly, but with a hint of anger: his nostrils seemed to be flaring.

Ramkus and Felipe shrugged to themselves as the bald soldier wandered away. They stalked up the stairs in the direction of their room, and onto the top level which connected around front with the adorned rose balcony. Ramkus kept glaring at Sigilund, making sure she was alright. She was focussed on her crowd and did not look up as Ramkus walked across the second level of the hotel.

The balcony smelt of the heavy scent of roses. Very fresh, utterly delightful compared to the smells the soldiers brought with them.

'He seems very angry,' Ramkus said.

'I don't like what our chances are for getting paid at all now. We may be kicked out with the way he was raging,' Felipe grumbled. They stood, looking out at the shadows the light inside which cast onto the square below. The Hotelier came out furiously; the crowd had really sent him into a fit.

'Bloody soldiers!' He shook his head, 'Can't believe they decided to come here tonight. Why does it have to happen *tonight*, of all nights!? All they drink are the cheap drinks, I am making no money off them. They stay for that Sigil girl, playing *their* type of songs. I make no money with that type of stuff, in fact I am losing money because they have chased off the proper clientele that were brought in initially *by you*, Monsieur Felipe.' *He actually appears to be deferring to Felipe*, Ramkus thought, utterly bemused by the change of manner.

Felipe, whom had been listening intently, reacted with sympathy. 'I know, it is such a shame, but this is what happens with some *particular* bards. They attract the wrong crowd,' he replied.

'Good for *you*, bad for *her*. She has screwed up tonight, I mustn't pay her any special fee for such a debacle. It is all yours Monsieur Felipe,' the Hotelier said, producing a small coin purse which seemed to be on the heavy side. 'I added a bit more than I should have, sort of as a gesture of goodwill; that you may stay another night… Please?'

The powers had certainly shifted, 'I'll think about it,' Felipe said with a smile.

The Hotelier bowed, and sauntered off to the ruckus, 'Never should have hired the riff raff!' he scowled as he left.

'You sly rat, Felipe. Blaming that poor girl for tonight's crowd troubles,' Ramkus growled.

'What else was I meant to say? That it was our fault? Because you got into a bar fight which got their drinking spot closed down?' Felipe chortled.

'Don't blame me for what happened!' Ramkus's blood was beginning to boil once more.

'I'm not, but *he* may have, and then both us and Sigil may not have been paid. Better someone than none at all. Anyway, here,' Felipe picked out around half of the coins from newly provided coin purse, and placed them into his own pouch, throwing the remainder to Ramkus. 'You earnt it, even if you didn't play by my rules. You at least made it easy for me to perform.' He began nodding to himself upon recollection.

Ramkus frowned, 'Don't you think Sigil deserves it?'

'With *my* performance?! Are you serious?'

Ramkus did agree, he had never seen anyone perform like that before. But then again, he hadn't really seen anyone else but Felipe perform until tonight. He still felt bad about how mistreated Sigilund had been.

'Look, if you feel so bad, give her your share. See, simple!' Felipe said, then looked out onto the street, and back to Ramkus. 'And if I may take my guitar back, please?'

Ramkus, realising he still had the guitar slung on his back, handed it to its rightful owner.

'I think tonight may be a good night to be outside, creating some sonnets. Don't think the place will get too quiet till much later. I'll see you tomorrow morning,' Felipe said with a smile. And with that, he walked off brusquely with a step in his stride, back into the noise, playing off some of the dejection he had received from the latter crowd.

What an odd turn of events, Ramkus thought to himself. He looked out for a moment longer, before going back inside himself. He stood at the top of the upper level balcony, overlooking the hall. He watched the raucous behaviour of the soldiers: their cheering, their drinking, their revelling way. And he watched Sigilund, playing so softly, sweetly, above all that degradation in front of her, as if in her own little world.

It suddenly occurred to him that this was the first time since Kerwood, that he was alone. Even then, though, it did not take too long to meet another to share some time with. So no, the last true time he was alone was when he was enveloped in the deep waters near Yazin, the doctors cottage on the beach. It was not too late, and he was not feeling overly tired. As Felipe had suggested, the night would probably be quite long for the hotel itself. At least Felipe had things in mind he could do, but what of himself? He decided to have a walk around Refton, see its sights at night. It did not seem overly dangerous - even if it was a town the Empire had *influence* over. Better to be under their noses than in their line of sight. He wasn't even sure if they were still searching for him, after the events of his departure at Kerwood. In any case, he needn't take his staff from his room, lest it raise suspicion. He may as well leave the coin purse in his room as well, just in case.

He exited onto the well-lit pavement outside the hotel and wondered where he should head off to: *the water, to the water*; was his guiding thought. It seemed to have become a bastion for peaceful thoughts for him, wherever there were pools of water, of coolness, ever since that swim he took.

He bided his time, walking the dully lit streets. The lights from houses were nothing compared to the hotel, but he was still helped by the glow of the moon in assuring his steady footing. The clouds played with the moon, dancing in front, letting its beam dim every so often, only to come back in a magnificent glow. A white cat jumped down from a balcony in front of Ramkus, purring. He gave it a scratch behind its ear, *first time I have been able to pet an animal, something Felipe had not realised about me when speaking of how to woo women. Many things I have not done.* He started to speak aloud to the cat, which kept purring monotonously, much more audibly than before. 'I have to go now, maybe I will give you a pet again later,' he said, beginning his walk once more. The cat followed for a bit, but left after it became too much effort to keep up. The sounds of the hotel had continued down the street, but were soon forgotten, swallowed by the night and his steady walk between the tight walls of the buildings that lined the street. No other action about, in stark contrast from the day; no street vendors, no customers, no people moving to and fro, only the single person walking quickly off somewhere for the night.

He finally made it onto the main artery of the town. The massive grates making the water sound as if it were a waterfall by smashing against the metal. He walked towards the mouth of the river, as the moon peeked over a cloud that had its edges shine through as a mix of its own colour and that of the twilight the moon projected upon it. There were sounds in the ocean, of men moving cargo on ships, and waves tapping against the wooden vessels. The sweet smell of the sea, that salty aroma, became stronger as he walked by benches positioned for the views of the river. Small candles flickering, metal signatures readable as their colours stuck out from the wooden boards they were printed on.

It was still warm, *warm enough to swim, perhaps*. He made his way to the edge of the town, meeting the sea: a massive stone wall stood to greet the waters, should they ever rise up in revolt against Refton. It connected to the wall that circled the whole of the town, with steps leading up onto it. Ramkus decided that if it were prohibited for anyone but the Empire to rise to such a vantage point overlooking the sea and Refton's inhabitants, then it would have guarded it better. He was right, finding a bench at the top where the townsfolk could look out at the great rolling expanse. He did not take up the seats offer though, standing transfixed, peering out at the water; the ever-moving waves; the constant flow. It was refreshing for him to see, and it took him away from his thoughts, back to a content state, happy to just watch the white specks of sea froth lit by the moon's glow. It was otherwise a clear night from the sparse clouds that moved at the moons level; much could be seen all around. Many large ships were moored on either side of the river's mouth. Transport ships, merchant ships, all docked to wooden- ramps that came from the shore. There was a small bit of beach down below the wall, but it was insignificant, bearing little sand. A boardwalk against the stone wall stretched for a fair distance along the bay on both sides, off which the wooden ramps extended. He focussed back on the waves, his breathing slowing. He sat on the bench, still locked on what was in front, only what was in front. Happy for this change to just sit. He closed his eyes, and began to meditate without even realising.

Eyes looked up at him in the stone dungeon. Better lit than before. The creature of human flesh was still cowering, but not making any movements. It was calm. The other savage was still in front; a steely gaze lay upon Ramkus.
"You're coming to the right decision," *the voice of this demon of a man declared. White teeth shone sparks of delirium; a smile readying as if to gnash into him. The shadow of the room still rapt the man in mystery, save for the strong features that seldom were hit with the light.*

189

Ramkus guessed who he was seeing, whom he was speaking to. He would still question him, though.

'Who are you?' Ramkus finally spoke in a determined voice.

"Ha! You already know the answer! I am your friend; your only friend," *It spoke back.*

Ramkus smiled, he felt no threat now. 'I daresay that will not prove to be the case,' he answered.

"And why would you say that?" *The voice of the man roared back, his body pressed forward in his throne. He was wearing thick set of black leather on his shoulders, with spikes adorning it. His face still hidden from complete view. The human animal stirred in the corner; its feeble legs showing as it shivered and moaned.*

Ramkus smiled back, baring his teeth now. 'I just know,' his eyes widened, as if he himself wanted to pull this man from the depths of darkness, the depths of the void.

*The man sat back in his throne, back in his shadows. **"We shall see."***

'I thought I may find you here,' a sweet voice said behind Ramkus, a voice that could only belong to that pretty apparition he had been admiring on the stage.

He smiled as he turned.

'Sigilund,' he said with tenderness, 'how did you finish up? Those soldiers were adoring your performance.'

'I wish that's *all* they adored,' she replied meekly, sitting down beside him. Her curls were glistening in the twilight, her features pierced the night. 'It didn't end too well, it became quite rowdy in fact, and it wasn't even the soldiers. The hotel owner - that pig – blamed me for them powering in and replacing the usual crowd. He was such an arse.' She paused, catching herself. 'I had to get out of there. I saw you leave, so decided to see what you were up to.'

He glanced at her, 'Well, I am not up to much, as you can see.' He breathed in the sea breeze and leant back, resting an arm on the wooden bench seat, 'Just admiring the night, the waves. To tell you the truth, I wouldn't know where to go, usually I would have stayed at the hotel or Inn that I had performed at.'

'But not tonight,' she interjected quietly.

'No. Not tonight. And for obvious reasons.' He looked at her again, 'Like you, I am new to this world,' he smiled to himself at his words, 'Trying to figure it out, trying to understand my place.'

'Yes,' she peered down, 'I am new to this, all I can do is follow my dreams, follow the life I have always wanted. At least I thought I wanted,' she sighed. 'It is such a beautiful sight over there. I feel I am looking at my past, though.'

'How so?' he inquired.

'That is the direction of where I have come. My future is elsewhere.' She started to sound a little saddened by this musing, but Ramkus thought it best not to pry, especially as Felipe had already upset her this evening.

'You'll get there,' he said. Detecting this scene was only going to provide Sigilund with memories she did not need at this time, he invited her to walk along the wall, as far as was permitted to the public. She took him up on the offer, and they began to slowly meander along in a peaceful silence, looking over the town from their vantage point. The terracotta rooves, the dimming lights scattered about. Mounds of trees and hills lay beyond this sign of civilisation, a reminder that the world had not been conquered – yet - and the very life blood that ran through this town still spread throughout the world - or at least the little-known world that Ramkus knew. Darkness began to spread as the moon hid itself. A chill from the night took flight on the winds of the small bay.

'*Brr*, I am starting to get cold. I didn't think I would need my jacket,' Sigilund said.

'I didn't either, seems the weather can change at will here. Shall we go back now?'

Sigilund mulled the question over, 'Ok, hopefully they have been able to calm the soldiers by now.'

They walked back to the steps, along the river, and up the dimly lit streets - meeting the cat for another pet – before standing back in front of the Rose Hotel. It had quietened a little, but was still reasonably busy when they wandered in. They looked at the Hotelier behind the bar whilst making their way up the stairs.

He turned his head with indifference, unimpressed at the sight of Sigilund, but ended up having to yell at a soldier who was picking his nose and wiping it on the bar indignantly. It looked to make the Hotelier quite sick and fuming.

'My room is over here,' Sigilund said with a touch of hesitation. 'Mine is along the balcony,' Replied Ramkus. An awkward silence flooded their departure. Struggling to break it, Ramkus searched a fitting way to continue the conversation he remembered Felipe's remark: 'I daresay it will be a lot quieter in yours.' He remonstrated himself mentally for how that may be interpreted, *You fool, Ramkus!*

The silence continued as Sigilund seemed to become a little emotional. 'Good night, Sigil, and perhaps I shall see you in the morning.'

'Good night, Ramkus… Thank you,' she said meekly.

'For what?'

'You've treated me nicer than any other person has in a long time.' She seemed – to Ramkus - to hold herself back from crying.

He smiled, 'It is a pleasure, and you have been a joy to watch… perform. Sleep well.'

She returned the smile and made her way to her room. He walked down the internal corridor, and into his room. Taking off his top clothing and boots, wearing only trousers, he fell onto the comfortable bed. *What an exhaustingly long day.* He stared at the ceiling. His body began to sink into the mattress, as he naturally stretched his body all out, relaxing the muscles, feeling bruises, scars, and welts that abounded all over. How many fights had he been in? It seemed like every day. He was lucky not to have had any serious knocks at the Sea Soldiers Spit. He began to fully relax and sink into his dreaming thoughts, coming back to questions at the back of his mind of what he saw when he mediated, whom he met there.

A knock came at the door, shocking him from his near slumber state. The knocking came again, softly. He rose and opened the door. It was Sigilund. He looked at her a tad bemused, before slowly realising the first thing to do as she stood there, unsure of herself.

'Sigil, come in,' he said with warmth. She smiled as she entered the room. She was wearing only her blouse and trousers, no fine regalia, no boots.

'Sorry,' she said, 'I just… couldn't be alone tonight.' She stood in the middle of the room, staring at Ramkus with deep set emotion. She leant to one side, locking her elbow with the other arm.

'Please, sit,' Ramkus motioned to the bed, looking at her curiously. She followed his suggestion and sat. 'Would you like me to fetch some water or anything?' He really had no idea what to do, or if he could help in any way.

'No,' she replied, softly. He sat down beside her. 'I'm sorry,' she said in a soft voice, staring into space.

'Don't be.'

'I know this may be odd, but may I sleep with you tonight?' She asked. Ramkus looked at her confused. 'I don't mean like that, I just mean share the bed,' she said hurriedly to excuse what must have appeared quite a forward proposition as Ramkus's facial expression was bewildered. *It was from your careless insinuations from before!*

'Yes, of course,' he said, looking around trying to act nonchalantly. 'Ah, okay.'

She let out a weak sniffle as she lay down on one side of the bed. Luckily it was a lot larger than previous beds Ramkus had boarded in. He lay down next to her; her slender little body not taking up much room. Still, he made sure there was enough room for both, even giving her a little more space to be sure. Sigilund pulled off her trousers. Her blouse was a lot longer than a normal one, acting as a night shirt as it dropped to her knees. She pulled the covers up, and turned to him on her side. He was on his back as he turned his head.

'I just don't want to sleep alone tonight, Ramkus. I have been alone for so long.' Her eyes began to well. He held out his arm as she came in and rested her head on his muscular, hairy chest. He embraced her, and she let out a soft whimper. 'I left my whole family, all my friends, my village. *To be treated the same as I was treated before?*' she continued to whimper in a sad reflective tone.

'What do you mean?' Ramkus replied.

'Life was hard for me in the village I came from. Where I come from, women are still treated as cattle. I was…' she broke down.

'It's alright, you are not there now,' Ramkus tried to console her.

'No, it's not alright, not for what I did,' she cried.

He held her tightly, trying to warm her with his body heat.

'Nor was the contest' she finally said, sniffling. 'One of the other island men, a warrior, came to the island. He asked my family for me as his wife. My family said no, so he challenged us to a contest. He was huge. My father was a big man, but was nothing compared to this towering giant.'

'What's a contest?' Ramkus asked.

She stopped sniffling a little, 'A contest for my people is a duel, it is the way justice is dealt out, even if it is unfair to those whom are not built of might. My father would've never stood a chance…'

'And so, you ran away?'

She was silent for a while, stopping her sniffling, and closed her eyes. 'Yes, I ran away, so there would be no point for the contest to take place.' She nestled her head and shoulder into

Ramkus further. 'Do you know how it feels to have no one,
Ramkus, to be completely alone in this world?
Such an odd question, he thought, for he had come into being
with no one around, *alone*. He had met people, had been
everywhere he knew with Felipe, but he knew, deep down, that
would not last. Yes, he was alone, but he did not know what it
felt like because he had never known anything else.
'No,' he replied, 'I don't know how it feels.'
'It is as if the world is looking to close in on you at any given
second. As if everyone is out to stick barbs into you, get what
they can from you.' She started to cry again. 'That's why I just
needed to be with someone who was just the complete opposite
tonight. To remember what the world can feel like.'
'Come now, it does not have to feel like that,' he said. 'It will
get better, once you've understood it a bit more.'
'I hope so,' she said, stopping her tears. 'I *am* feeling a lot
better actually.' She moved her head around, taking in the room
as she opened her eyes fully. There was a dim glow of a candle
on the drawer, next to his newly acquired coin purse. Her eyes
searched the room, finally resting on Ramkus's staff against the
wall in the corner.
That's beautiful,' she said. Ramkus looked up at where she was
looking.
'Oh, yes,' he replied without emotion.
'I bet it cost a fair bit,' she went on.
'I'm not sure,' he replied.
Her eyes looked up at him from his chest. 'Well then, I am sure
there is a story behind it.'
'There probably is, but I am yet to know it.' He did not want to
get into *his* story of the world.
She searched his face, curious as to his cryptic replies, why he
seemed to be dodging such innocent questions. She finally
rested her head again. 'Tell me of yourself, Ramkus.'
He paused for a second. *How to answer such a pertinent
question*? 'I don't really know, Sigilund,' he said, 'I am not sure

who I am; what I am.' He resigned himself to having to tell his story. 'I just awoke one day in a field, and have been travelling down this path not knowing where it will lead. I was told I was a *Guardian*, and that I need to head to where other Guardians are supposed to live.' He spoke softly, slowly, purposefully. '*Guardian*' Sigilund murmured, mouthing the word in a half waken state.

Ramkus was in a heightened state of thought, barely noticing her little *contribution* to his soliloquy. 'I am purely running on what I have been told: that I am heading somewhere where I will be taught the answers to my questions, where I will find out the role I am to play. I am not even sure I want that, or the answers to my questions.' He watched the flickering light die out on the ceiling. 'I seem to have been given a choice - that of being a bard - but I feel I am destined for a different life. It is what I have been told by others. Everywhere I go, I mean something to someone, whether it be good or bad. Just last night, I was *randomly* attacked by someone who wanted to test me. For what reason, I do not know. So, to tell you of myself, I really don't know what to say. I just am. Just wandering forward. Always forward. A wanderer.' He stared at the ceiling as he let out a sigh. *A wanderer or a Guardian, or a bard, or whatever I choose*! He looked down to the girl in his arm, the slightly little thing nestled up against him. She was deep in sleep, breathing gently. He let out another sigh, and kissed her on the forehead. Holding her tightly, hoping to embrace her the whole night, but daring not to get too close for the embarrassment of his nether region. He did not want to let her down in her moment of weakness; her moment of need of need. He closed his eyes.

When he awoke the next morning, she was gone.
As was the coin purse.

Chapter VIII

'What do you mean she took all your money?' Felipe was incensed, eyes wide open, mouth aghast as he leant on the outdoor table, waiting for Ramkus's answer.

'It was not there in the morning, nor was she. I would have offered it to her anyway, had I remembered or even had the opportunity. *The poor girl.*' Ramkus answered, looking around at the street, feeling a deep pang of regret that he did not get the opportunity to say goodbye, nor offer any other help to Sigilund.

'Poor girl? She played you, you idiot!' Felipe cried, arms flaying about in uproar.

'I don't think so. In fact I cannot even fathom that to be the case,' he replied, not taking any regard to Felipe's agitated state.

'So, she slept with you, *but you didn't do anything?* You just confused her? Sounds like she played you, my friend.' Felipe leant back in his chair, taking a sip of fruity midday drink served at the small tavern they had stopped at a few miles outside of Refton. 'If I was in your position I would have had a bit of pain down there… possibly the whole night,' Felipe gave a wry smile, but stopped at the thought of how his companion had been so foolish.

Ramkus blushed and turned away, 'Yeah… that was a little, *trying.* Anyway, I did what I felt was the right thing and gave her some kindness. Didn't seem that *your* antics last night helped much either. It really affected her.'

Felipe rolled his eyes, 'It was all part of the show… And she was rather attractive.'

'You're incorrigible. And old. Please don't do that entrance again, we may end up meeting her at another venue. She is - after all - a bard. Travelling the one road that we are too, probably.'

'True,' Felipe said, as a plate of cheese, bread, tomato, and olives was delivered by the serving girl. 'Thank you,' Felipe said with a smile, as he watched the girl walk back in to the tavern from behind, deep in thought, making mouth movements like a fish. 'Sorry, what was I saying? Oh, well, soon the road does actually split. Many forks leading to the different areas where this kingdom has developed its own towns and villages – or cemented their rule over through coercive means. I guess they then all lead to the central city of this region in some fashion. Not the prettiest of cities, mind you. In any case, we are not headed there. We will re-join the highway out of this Empires realm.'

The two began to eat their midday meal. They had been travelling since very early; Felipe did not want to spend much more time at the hotel: he was not feeling the best after being essentially booed off stage by the soldiers. The soldiers may end up there again tonight, he had reasoned with Ramkus, not worth the money to have his character shot down again, even if he could change the act to suit the rowdy crowd. That would simply annoy the hotel owner. No, the best thing - Felipe had said - was to get back on their way.

For most of the mornings travel, the highway had led South through the forest, deep and heavy with vegetation. Not much light shone through the leaf canopy. The day was well underway when they had made their way to a small, flat glade, where a few buildings stood on either side of the highway. One being a tavern with a nice outdoor area. Felipe explained that these sorts of "mini towns" were dotted outside villages in case people forgot to purchase items for their trips, or realised they might need something additional. They were also a good place to have a cooked meal, especially if travellers had left early to beat the traffic that sometimes arose. Felipe called them "Convenience Villages", or "Conville's" for short.

The sun had risen into the blue depths of the sky, showering them with warmth. Felipe breathed in heavily after finishing his meal, leaning back in his chair and put his feet on one of the free chairs.

'So, which way are we headed?' Ramkus asked, curious as to the directions and roads of the world.

'Ah, well, I was thinking we stick between the two main mountains to the South-South West of here, instead of venturing along the Sea completely. I don't think there is a path that way in any case. So, heading South West, we should hit the ranges saddle and march across that, leading to the beautiful fields of Fritiland. That is a true bard's paradise, much inspiration can be found there. That path leads past some mountain folks villages, so we shan't be out of touch of civilisation for too long. They are a nice change from the common rabble we have been around for a while. Good hearty meals, drink, and heavy tales come in abundance with those folk. Also, one of the major cities for the Empire is, hmm, I am guessing almost directly West or a little North West from here, in the centre of between sea and mountain range. Many of the Empires armies are held up there, ready to go out and exert their control. It was not always the Empire's, they just seemed to wrest political control from the natives, either by way of economic influence, or, well, force. But it has seldom come to that, most of the people in these regions - this kingdom - are Empirically inclined, so to speak. Such a simple culture that carries itself along without much care for anything else.' Felipe stopped talking, picking a rose from a rose bush to his side. He smiled at it, becoming lost for a second before putting it in his black, wide brimmed hat's ribbon sash that flowed around it.

'So South, basically,' Ramkus said, looking in the direction he believed was due South. Not much could be seen, at least not above the buildings and trees.

'Do you remember the massive mountain we saw a few days ago, from our trek outside Abergrass?' Felipe picked up in a pleasant mood. 'That is one of these mountains. We had a remarkably clear day then. There is sometimes a haze that tends to come from the West, from the main city. Smelting offshoot rises into the atmosphere without us realising – and also, sometimes, the sea mist comes far across into the forests as well. It is somewhat of a peninsula that we are curving around, if you hadn't noticed the way we had been tracking. For some reason it does not tend to occur in hotter months, though.'

'Smelting...' Ramkus said, not knowing the word.

'Making arms: weapons and shields. One of the reasons it is not the prettiest city. Well, it's actually outside of the main city area; massive furnaces, working day and night. An economic juggernaut of an operation. Those arms are shipped down the rivers, out to places like Refton, then shipped off to other lands for sale; likely to be used *against* the Empire in some fashion,' Felipe laughed. 'One of the great ironies of life, that which you provide can come back to cut you.'

Ramkus wasn't really listening; he was thinking about Sigilund and what had become of her. He wanted to find her, hoping he would stumble upon her along the path.

'Do you think they may have seen Sigil here?' Ramkus asked.

'Oh, let her be, Ramkus! Listen, if she had indeed *not* played you - as you continue to protest - there must have been another reason she left abruptly,' Felipe answered. 'At least you have forgotten Clara,' he added as a snide remark. Ramkus frowned upon the mention of her.

'I know, but...' Ramkus began to rebut.

'Ramkus, I dare say - once again - you are love stricken by a pretty girl!' Felipe interjected, leaving Ramkus to simply frown. 'Anyway, let's get back on our way. Are you able to *pay this time*? Oh... That's right, *Sigil took all your money...*' Felipe mocked, 'I am kidding, my friend. She'll be alright, a fair bit of money she has to look after herself with now, as long as she doesn't run into...' He didn't want to finish.

'As long as what?' Ramkus asked.

'Nothing, my friend,' Felipe smiled, looking at Ramkus's staff resting against the back wall of the tavern. He nodded to himself, acknowledging something in his mind. Turning back to Ramkus, 'So, shall we?' They both got up, settled the bill.

'Is there anything we need whilst we are here?' Ramkus asked as they walked out to their horses, saddled just outside the Tavern.

'No, and besides, the prices they charge here are exorbitant compared to proper towns. Massive mark ups for such a "convenience",' Felipe grumbled.

'Wouldn't that mean they are prime targets for bandits?' Ramkus asked.

'Yes, now that you say it. And these roads are… Well, there are a lot of soldiers about, so it would not seem the best option to the bandits, necessarily. They would dare not risk it.' Felipe brushed off the concern.

'Lot of merchants travelling the roads as well, they would have to keep the roads pretty secure, I'm guessing,' Ramkus added.

'Merchants tend to travel with hired guards,' Felipe stated.

'Ah,' Ramkus said, his eyes widened, 'Sigil!'

'She'll be alright,' Felipe said, noticing Ramkus's heightened emotions. 'Sheesh, calm down! I am sure she is smart enough to look after herself. In any case, just think of us now, and keep an eye out!'

Ramkus was not pleased with this development, but there was little he could do. It was not as if he had done anything wrong. 'Everyone makes their own decisions in this world, just like which path to take at a fork in the road,' Felipe tried to console Ramus's heated passion. 'Look, we may catch up to her or see her in the next village, it is not too far away. A two-day journey.'

It took a second for Ramkus to come to any thought. 'You're right, she chose to go off alone.' He sighed, 'All I can do is hope she is alright.'

As he said this, a group of soldiers on horseback trotted down the thoroughfare, around a dozen he counted.

'And as I said, there are a lot of soldiers on the road at the moment,' Felipe stated once more, nodding in the group's

direction. 'Actually, it has been a fair few we have passed.' He
followed the soldiers with his eyes, 'Strange…'

'What do you mean strange?' Ramkus asked.

'Oh, nothing, just getting a sense that there is something big or
somebody important around, somewhere in the region.
Heightened security measures with this many soldiers about.
Anyway, let us go forth!' Felipe gestured with full extension of
his arm in the direction they were headed.

They jumped on their horses and set off down the road, back
into the dense forest. Ramkus pressed forward with pace.

'Don't be in such a rush, my friend,' Felipe shouted as Ramkus
went a little too far ahead. 'Remember what I said about
keeping your eyes about you. I do get a strange feeling around
here.'

They entered under a wooden archway, marking the boundary of
the Conville's village glade, and into the deep forest. It was a
lot thicker than the previous ones, overgrown in most parts. The
sense knocked Ramkus right away; it felt dark, miserable,
heavy, and dead. The trees looked grey, a lack of pure moisture,
leaves withered.

'We should be fine on the Empire's highway?' asked Ramkus
with a tad bit of trepidation from the sudden assault of sensation
regarding the change aspect.

'I'm not sure.' Felipe was looking back around continuously.
'Ramkus, I generally don't advise to keep at a slow pace, but it
might be wise. Something isn't right in here.'

Even Felipe feels the ill in the forest. 'We can't see the sun, that
is all.' Ramkus kept moving forward with steadfast
determination, steeling himself. He set a pace that was tempting
that which they feared and could not see. The path – oddly for
an Empire's path – wound around small hills, best described as
mogotes, although they were well concealed. A darkness set in;
the air was heavy. Ramkus deciding the pursuit would be futile
with all things being considered, let up on his pace. He began to
urgently sense something was not right now too.

'Did we take a wrong turn at some point?' Ramkus whispered just audibly enough for Felipe to hear, knowing full well there had been no other paths to take.

It seemed like it was late evening in the forest; tree branches appeared to fight each other, forcing themselves back from grabbing whatever they could prize off the path; roots fell on top of each other in trying to get at the open space of the cleared ground. The road was dark, the canopy now a blue. The sound of their horse's hooves echoed the as sole marker of life in this stagnant wood.

'I do not believe so,' Felipe finally answered, 'although, I am not sure.' His voice was tepid, teeth clattering a slightly. 'Just keep an eye out. I'm sure this will be the worst part of it. I think we are just in a bit of a gulch which has overgrown.'

They pressed on, slowly, cautiously, ears pricked and eyes scanning. A bird fluttered in a tree, giving the two a fright. A running brook could be heard, but not seen, as they moved further into this cavernous, old tree riddled path. There was no greenery on this road, only hardened, gnarled roots and branches that had grown into jagged spears.

Ramkus began to study the ground, he couldn't read if there had been many wagons, horses, or travellers through here - or at all. It started to become somewhat of a boggy mud. His senses tweaked.

'Felipe, I think we may be in a bit of a trap here...' He whispered with alertness.

'What do you mean?' Felipe's focus was as keen as it had ever been, teasing out any revelation as to their predicament.

'The ground is perfect to ensnare riders,' Ramkus explained, 'the trees won't allow anyone to head around as its too narrow.'

'What do you propose we do?' Felipe said in a tone that relinquished all authority to Ramkus.

'I'm not sure.' Ramkus thought for a second, 'Keep going, perhaps we were not the first to come through here. Not the first to fall into such a trap, today.'

They kept moving through the boggy mud, horses breathing heavy, even they were alert to the situation.

'Stop!' ordered Ramkus, Felipe obeyed, watching Ramkus grip his staff with both hands and quietly dismount.

'Hold the reins.' Ramkus left his horse with Felipe, and continued on the ground, moving along the tree line.

Felipe watched with baited breath. The path itself did not meander out of sight too much. But who knew what really lay in front, as there seemed to be a fog descending about fifty yards ahead of their vision. Ramkus went up about halfway; crouching, listening. Sweat began to expand into small bulbous beads on Felipe's forehead. His muscles began to twitch as he tried to prepare himself for anything that may come out.

Ramkus returned, slowly.

'What did you see?' squeaked Felipe.

'More like what I heard. There are definitely people on the path. I can't tell a soldier from a bandit, though. They all sound the same. Many voices, however.'

Felipe gritted his teeth, 'What do we do? Go around them?'

Ramkus scanned the trees. They looked too dense and closed together, limiting any retreat from the path as there was no chance of leading a horse though them at all. He looked down the path, and smiled.

'We charge through,' he said, with a nasty smile.

Felipe - although not one to *truly* scare easily - turned white. His body began to shake uncontrollably.

'Settle down, Felipe. The people are just talking, they will not be ready for anybody charging them. They are in the same situation as us. In fact, we have the upper hand as we know they are there, whereas they do not know about us.'

Ramkus's eyes shone with brilliant belief. Felipe felt inspired, he believed in Ramkus's idea – even if it was a fool's belief in order to stop his fear from overcoming him…

'Alright,' Felipe began to shirk his head, as if going into a berserk state, 'let's do it Ramkus!' It was the mad performer from the night before once again taking control!

Ramkus bared his teeth, nodding with a pensive knowledge, prepared for action.

He jumped on his horse.

'Felipe, ready?' he asked in a commanding voice.

Felipe nodded.

'As far as you can, keep to either side of the tree line, it is the firmest ground along the path.'

Felipe nodded again. Ramkus looked to him, then the path. He gritted his teeth and bared the snarl of one ready to turn into an animal.

He nodded back, and gave his horse a kick; Felipe followed suit.

"Good choice", the voice from the back of his mind howled, as Ramkus pressed close to his horse.

They thundered quickly along, quiet except for the heavy trampling of their horses' hooves. The tree branches were scratching and biting; Felipe swore, cursing to cut them all off. The mist felt like it was fighting against their efforts, letting a darkness enshroud them. Forward, forward, and further forward they galloped. *Surely we must have to meet these voices along the road soon*, Ramkus thought. Nothing. They kept riding at a breakneck speed, with the hooves splashing dirty muck as they kept as close to the sides of the forest highway as possible. The whole climate had cooled considerably, and Felipe felt his perspiration become a thicker globule of clammy water. Onward they pressed.

They had gone perhaps five hundred yards into the bowls of the forsaken forest: still nothing. Ramkus stared, his face perplexed as he led them to a gentle canter. He looked around, still pensive. No sound or light was cutting through the mist, and the trees moved with an eerie menace.

'Something just does not make sense. I could have sworn I heard where those voice were. I could sense their presence. Now, nothing.'

Felipe looked around cautiously, unsure what to make of it all. 'Well, we weren't attacked, that is a good thing. Let's keep going forward, till we get out of this cavernous forest. It is starting to make me feel sick. Claustrophobic place it is.'

'How much farther?' Ramkus asked.

'I… I cannot remember, Ramkus.' Felipe sounded bereft of thought, seemingly fallen into a haze of confusion, as if the forest was afflicting his mind.

'What do you mean? You have trekked the path when you came from this direction?!'

They trotted side by side as closely as the path allowed. Ramkus was waiting for the master bard's answer, one that would be a typically *bardish* one.

'Well, I didn't. I mean, I did come this path, but…'

'Yes?!' Ramus waited with bated breath.

'I was in a carriage… With a lady merchant… My horse was led by the guards we came with…' he muttered.

'Were you not aware of how long it took? Did you not look out the window?' Ramkus pressed him further.

'We were. I was…. Preoccupied by the lady.' Felipe could not conjure up any witty response, so the truth sufficed.

'Preoccupied?' Ramkus asked. Felipe grinned with raised eyebrows. Ramkus rolled his eyes and let out a deep sigh of frustration, 'You're incorrigible. Some help you are on these roads. I really do suppose *I* was just brought along for protection,' he joked macabrely.

Felipe coughed, taken aback that the topic was raised again. A moment passed in which Felipe did not continue to respond.

'Really?' Ramkus shook his head, feeling lied to. He didn't expect Felipe to go back what he had said previously to allay his fears, that he was more than a bodyguard, rather a travelling companion.

'Only initially,' Felipe remonstrated, 'but now we *are* a partnership!'

Ramkus bit his lip. *Am I really in a partnership, or purely protection*, he pondered, feeling manipulated. He weighed it up against the fact he would not have come so far had it not been for the help of Felipe.

'Circumstances change,' Felipe continued.

'True,' Ramkus replied curtly, he knew not what to think. All he knew is that he was leading this small "partnership" now, in a world he had no idea about. *Maybe Felipe is manipulating me for other ends.* His head was swimming in this enclosed forest; he was struggling for breath as the place seemed to close in on them further. *Why did I bring up that topic again?* He wanted to yell at Felipe, let out a rage that was welling up. His muscles were contracting, his teeth grinding, he wanted to get out of here. He started pressing forward again.

Why is he so against finding Sigil? Perhaps he is jealous of how she spurred him and yet opened herself to me. In fact, he did seem to want *Sigil last night!*

'So, tell me the real reason you did not want to rush off after Sigil? Jealous?' Ramkus grunted at Felipe. His eyes were bloodshot.

'Of course not!' Felipe cried in protest, 'Where did that come from? Why would you insinuate that?!' His blood pressure started to increase now too. Overcome with the same affliction as Ramkus, the claustrophobic sensation, wanting to lash out and escape for air. 'Why would you dare question me?! *The Great Maestro Felipe*? Such contempt!' Felipe sneered, one side of his upper lip lifting.

Ramkus's breath started to get much heavier, his muscles tensed ready to snap. 'You want her. You hurt her, for having the *audacity* to challenge you, even when she had not even known. You are a real shit, aren't you!' Ramkus's eyes were popping out of the sockets.

'I should give you good smack, fucking Guardian my arse, you haven't the temperament! After all I have given you, you turn on *me*?' Felipe rebutted.

The mention of Guardian, of what Ramkus was meant to be, was a punch that left him mentally winded. He calmed himself. *Why is my blood boiling?* He shook his head. 'I am sorry Felipe, I am losing my mind in here. This path is making me feel sick.'

Their horses kept moving, watching.

'I should think so. Turn on *me,* will you?' Felipe said with an air of indignation.

Ramkus let it slide, mostly because he wanted to, but partially because a group of six bandits on horseback had suddenly found their way out onto the path in front of them, two came up from the rear.

Felipe's mouth dropped. The bandits clothing ranged from leathers, chain mail, and fur.

The two "partners" stopped as soon as they saw these men.

'Looks like we have two more to add to the collection today, boys,' said a heavily armour cladded, dirt ridden brute with a spear. His dark eyes and many facial scars belied a belief in any emotional side he may have ever had.

The other men laughed, but it seemed part of an act, as if they had heard it all before.

Add to today's collection? Does this mean?! A horrified look came over Ramkus's face.

'Frightened, are we?' The brute questioned, holding his spear out in front of Ramkus, lengthening it along the horse so it would go straight through Ramkus in a quick thrust.

Ramkus studied the area quickly, eyes darting over the path. It had opened up at its sides, enough for a band of merry men to lie in wait for anything that may come past.

"Fight them", the dark voice in his mind said, *"Fight them, show them who they dare deal with!"* Another emotion came over him, one that dropped his confidence, sunk him into the

shadows, wanting to cower from them. He kept searching for an alternative approach.

'Off,' the heavily scar-faced man said, gesturing with his spear. The other bandits held out their weapons, a few with swords, an axe, and a club. Felipe looked to Ramkus who stood firm, weighing up his options.

"Fight them!", the voice screamed in Ramkus's mind, as a blood-rush began to fill him. But the alternative emotions from before rose from the depths again, combating his rampant decisiveness. He gritted his teeth, judging the feelings coming over him: to give in, and not fight; or to take matters into his own hands. These feelings - as far as he could tell - were not part of his nature. Even with the aggressive voice in his head, he was beginning to realise exactly what he was, who he was. He clasped his staff, and heard something coming from afar.

'You!' yelled a voice along the path. Hooves smashing the boggy, drenched terrain echoed in the background, along with the voice.

The man with the spear tilted his head, 'Shit, run boys!' The horsemen in front turned their horses around. The one with the spear had his horse whinny. The two from behind were about to smash through Ramkus and Felipe, but the adventures quickly and reactively, arranged their horses to the sides of the path so as not to get in the bandit's way. Ramkus and Felipe looked at each other with confused glares. The sound seemed to have been carried from much further down the path than they'd realised. Abruptly, however, an orderly squad of a dozen Empirical soldiers on horsemen ran along the highway. They came to a stop when they reached the small clearing-like spot that the bandits had used as their trap, as if knowing full well beforehand where this little area was.

One of the soldiers dismounted, 'You two, off,' he commanded of Felipe and Ramkus. The Empirical horsemen had made a small circle. The two obliged the command, feeling they weren't actually being threatened this time, merely questioned.

They walked into the middle of the orderly circle, the soldier who was barking orders took off his helmet, studying them as they approached. He took particular interest in scrutinising Ramkus's staff. He seemed - to Ramkus - to exhibit a simplistic but reliable character, not of the drunken debaucherous types from last night or in Kerwood. His armoured tabard was of the thickset leather he'd seen yet, and had intricate etchings covered with gold trimmings. Ramkus assumed he must be a rather senior ranking officer to wear such fine regalia. Although not beaming with compassion, he was not offensive or confrontational.

'I believe we just saved your hides. That bandit troop could be heard a mile away. This is one of their typical spots to wreak mischief,' the senior soldier spoke.

'Who are you?' Felipe blurted out with a lack of consideration.

'We are one of the several Kings Guard. Currently we are keeping these paths clear, as there has been a noted rise of banditry in the area,' the man said, avoiding the fact he was asked the question as an individual.

Kings Guard, must be very senior. A bit odd that they would be given such a lacklustre job.

'Ah,' Felipe said, 'I daresay we should thank you, then.'

Ramkus was somewhat annoyed at the suggestion they could not have saved themselves. He realised the arrogance in such thoughts, and decided he should remain quiet, maintaining his suspicion.

'You are welcome. You two?'

'Two what?' Felipe asked, perplexed.

'I meant, what are you two's professions. From the looks of you, you are bards?' The man gave a faint grin.

'Yes, we are, too,' Felipe said.

'Two bards, right,' the man was getting a little frustrated, as if there was some point he wished to come to. He strained his closed mouth, moving his tongue around to get something out from under his gums. He spat, 'I wouldn't mind having two bards travel with us, we like such entertainment.' He moved his hands to his hips, as he looked at his squad whom all nodded in agreement.

'Yes,' they replied without enthusiasm, as if ordered to agree.

'It would be enjoyable to be accompanied with two bards.'

The head of the Kings Guard looked back at Ramkus and Felipe, 'See.'

Ramkus got the strange sense this was quite premeditated. The question of joining them was not an option at all, nor a suggestion. He felt ambivalent at the idea of travelling – for however long – with these men. He put this down this feeling to his general overall mood, not to mention his initial interactions with the common type Empirical soldiers, hoping that his first apprehensive thoughts were wrong. He began to ponder why an Empire had a "Kings" Guard and not an "Emperor's" Guard.

'We would enjoy this immensely, always better to travel in bigger groups,' Felipe accepted without hesitation. 'My name is Felipe, and this is Ramkus, my apprentice.'

Felipe stuck out his hand to shake the Kings Guard Officer's. The man took it in a stately manner.

'Poncho,' the man said, he then struck out his hand to Ramkus. Ramkus glared at him for a second, not sure of whom he was placing his trust in, what the next *manipulation* would be. He took the hand officiously, nodding, not showing a smile.

Poncho stared deeply at him in return, then his staff, giving a hint of a smile.

'Right, let us be off quickly then. It would be good to make the first campsite before nightfall,' Poncho said.

'Wait, how far is that? I don't remember any campsites last time I came through this forest – or at least there being *in* this forest,' Felipe said.

'Well you were *preoccupied* at the time,' Ramkus said with a dash of vitriol.

Poncho looked at them, guffawing. 'A good few miles we will need to go. You shouldn't find the pace too overwhelming, though.'

Ramkus shrugged, this was the only path, and it had been chosen for him.

Felipe got onto his horse happily, no longer feeling threatened by bandits or his travelling companion whom appeared to be having a bout of ill thoughts.

As Ramkus began mounting his horse, the voice came to him again *"Fight them"*. Ramkus smiled, chuckling to himself at the depths of madness where such thoughts arose.

The voice had begun to sound sane.

The path continued an upward climb, although it was difficult to tell due to the manner in which the path wrapped around. The enclosed nature of the soulless scene felt like a kiln, dusty and choking, it allowed no vision outwardly, which in turn meant nothing could see inwardly, either. Cut off from the reality that abounded elsewhere, the alien landscape tore at the mind's visions of the lush world they knew. As the lifeless branches of the trees subsided, the path opened up, and the trees became less tightly knit. A wild fire had been though the overgrowth, leaving blackened and charred remains. It appeared to have been quite recent, as no green aftergrowth had come to take up residence in the old, dead forest's stead. However, that may also have been because nothing green and fertile grew in the bowls of this forsaken, oppressive inner sanctum. The earth was littered with a charcoal ash plume. Light seeped through, but even it seemed to shine with a timid weakness. They travelled along silently: Ramkus at the head with Poncho; Felipe somewhere towards the back, not sure of himself and whether he should try and make conversation.

The burnt forest still hid the nature of mogotes, their steepness allowing nothing to get in or out. The path, making its way between these mounds, continued to show little life lay between this place, only the scarred blackened stumps and dead soil. Ramkus - trying not to let any negative thoughts re-enter his consciousness - was vigilant of all that was around, even if it was very little. He drew upon some source within himself, intending to surmise any of the true intentions these soldiers had. They seemed to be stone walls, devoid of all but their orders and ability to carry them out. Their eyes were set upon the path, alert to all that could arise. The scorched forest finally gave way to a woodland that was rotting. Fungus growing all over on dead limbs, roots that had let go of their steadfast integrity. The smell was pungent, wet, not like the smoking remains before. Still, as before, the horrendous hills did not let any path in between them, save for this sole, burdensome one. The decay was tormenting Ramkus. He yearned to get out, into the open, away from this crumbled, crowded place: it was either angry, destroyed, or dying. It was unnatural, as if it was some *powerful force's* wicked playground, where all that was imbued with malice was let loose to play. *At least there are no beasts in this place... at least none that are known of.* They could only be imagined as creations of nightmares. Finally, though, after this march through the tormented forests, the travelling troop of Empirical soldiers and bards came to a crest between two large hills, rising for a few hundred yards, before opening up to show the lie of the land ahead. A large, open terrain of green forests, rivers and brooks shimmering under the setting sun. A lake or two could be seen close by, and many, many miles away, the ridge of the two mountains Felipe had spoken of days before, their glacial tips contrasted by the blue sky. Ramkus breathed in the sight of sanity. The sea, although almost out of sight by the rise of the hill to the side, was still there as a powerful marker of stability. They had moved quite far inland, whilst the coast had curled quite far around from Refton. Ramkus knew where he was to head now: between these two massive monoliths. Their ridges acted as divisions between the lands. There was no visible area that was flat, not even near the sea.

'I agree, it is good to see the sights of the living world again,' Poncho said, noticing the relaxation in Ramkus. The two took in the sight whilst the cavalcade of men came to ease their torment. 'Never the less, we must press on.'

According to Ramkus's senses, the squad had picked up in mood too. Their strong will giving way to peaceful thoughts, ones natural to men with no pressures.

'Freedom!' Felipe yelled at the rear, hands to the heavens. The soldiers looked at him with questioning glances. 'Oh, come on, we are free of that awful forest, lighten up, lads!' He smiled, as they turned and moved.

Felipe was able to make some conversation at the rear, the soldiers often answering his questions and queries. Either that, or replying curtly in a manner which suggested he hold his tongue. Ramkus continued to walk in silence, aware Poncho, although not wanting to make conversation, was feeling the need to ease the thick air of tension that still abounded between them. 'So this was your first time to the Erevon Realm?' Poncho asked, his horses hooves filling the void his question had left. The light of the sun was once again giving way to a darker light under the sparse tree canopy. At least the sky could be seen in this *lighter* forest they wandered through. It was considerably open and sparse in direct contrast to the oppressive death stained one from before. Ramkus wished to forget that place as soon as possible.

'Erevon?' Ramkus replied, quickly realising his response would lead to more questions. 'No, this is my first time.'

'You and your companion did not get here along that awful path before, though? He would have said so when questioned previously, would he not?'

Ramkus stared at him, 'I didn't realise this was an inquisition,' he said coldly.

Poncho, recognising how he was coming across in appearance, and deciding how he *wished* to come across, pulled back. 'I am sorry, I meant no offence. I am merely curious.'

'Well then, no, we came by ship, from the islands of Montreyer,' Ramkus lied, knowing that it was a reasonable answer.

'Ah. And how were they?' Ponchos said unemotionally.

'Fine. Just fine,' Ramkus replied coolly. 'Have you been?'

'Ha! No, never travelled across the Pintos Sea by ship before. Too much work required in these regions for the Empire to allow the time.'

'Ah,' Ramkus replied, preferring to take the opportunity to stay silent.

'Where are you from then?' Poncho asked suddenly after a brief pause, his eyes narrowing ever so slightly.

Ramkus had to think quickly, 'Eredin, where the bard's festival is held. Hence why I am following the path that I would not dare stray from, for I am under the guidance of Monsieur Felipe: two-time winner of the festival!'

'Oh,' Poncho replied, 'yet you carry a staff and not an instrument. Or is it a flute?'

Ramkus stayed silent, seething at this soldier. *What does he want from me? What does he know of me?*

The last vestiges of light were still visible as they made their way onto a glade. A copse of trees in the middle, and a running brook to its side. In the middle of the copse was the remnants of campfires. How long it had been since it had been used as a site, one could not tell, as the copse had cultivated such a convenient area to protect travellers from the elements. In fact, it seemed too conventional. *Perhaps the forest people had* groomed *the place.*

The troop made camp, drinking from the stream that ran beside the copse, filling canteens and eating their victuals. Ramkus and Felipe were very much involved in the scene. Felipe, playing away at the guitar, Ramkus taking over and giving relief from time to time: singing and playing to prove the point that he could do so when Felipe required a short break.

'Well, well, you do play well, Ramkus. Even if you do not have an instrument yourself,' Poncho said.

Ramkus laughed it off nonchalantly, still guessing at the nature of Poncho's intentions and seemingly tepid jabs at his abilities as a bard. *Maybe he has guessed who I am, Poncho is of the Kings Guard after all, he may have dealt with Guardians before. But why does he have so much fun chiding me so?*

The fire in the centre was a brilliant glow, with its red and yellow flames dancing to the bards' performance, and moving the men to hearty sighs as they were relieved of their duty and tried to rest. The air was still warm, no need to wrap up in one's cloak. They did not stay up too late, as the day had been long. Ramkus, grabbed Felipe for a "quick chat". He felt he had to state the reason to satisfy the questioning glances of the soldiers as he wandered off by the brook.

'I do not trust these men, Felipe,' Ramkus said in hushed tones, knowing he had to make his point quickly, lest there be some odd sentiments and change in manner towards the two bards for moving away from the group. They were being kept a close eye on – at least that was Ramkus's suspicion. The fire in the middle of the copse showered light only on those inside, beaming as a beacon intermittently to the outside world. The running stream was the only sound that could be heard away from the light roar of the flames. The night was calm. The sky a deep, rich blue. The moonlight faint.

'Oh, why must you always worry, Ramkus. Is that what you must always think? They are *fine*. Better than *you* have been…' Felipe stared off into the distance. 'Now, let's get back to the fire.' He turned to go, but was jerked back to face Ramkus.

'Let me finish my thoughts,' Ramkus said intently, emphasising his wish to say his piece.

'You can finish them on your own, can you not?' Felipe walked off back to his spot at the camp.

Ramkus was aware he had not spoken to Felipe since he had been so very aggressive and cutting in the oppressive forest before the bandit encounter. He had almost wanted to come to blows with him. He sighed, dropping his head, realising his folly, as well as Felipe's for not having more faith in him. Still, he was ashamed, owing Felipe an apology, even if he felt he had been manipulated by the master bard initially -and faintly knowingly. He walked back to the camp, back to his own spot, sitting cross legged. He rubbed his face, subconsciously noting how the mutton chops were beginning to irritate his skin.

The soldiers were mirthfully talking to Felipe; to Ramkus, not so much, apart from Poncho. Trying to be friendly, Poncho sat cross legged next to Ramkus, his stubble glowing with the light. He eyes determined, his face still full of duty, even when speaking in the calmer ambience.

'My father used to take me camping in these sorts of spots. Making a camp near a flowing stream. We used to sit on the bank and fish, pan frying anything we caught almost straight away. Nothing better than fresh fish cooked straight on the pan. Well, save that it be in good company. Familial company being the best.' Poncho looked at Ramkus.

Ramkus could not tell what thoughts this man had, his attention was drawn to a glow from Poncho's right wrist. A bracelet, heavy, ornate, almost seeming to be branded on his wrist, with no room to move up or down his arm, no detachable lock. *Did he grow into it?*

'What is that bracelet you have there?' Ramkus said admiringly, 'It looks as if it was part of your arm.'

'Ha! Well, it almost is!' Poncho looked at his wrist, showing Ramkus. 'It is the Kings Guard bracelet or band. In the Empire, people of stature are presented with these bracelets. There are different bands according to the different stature, position, allegiance, family, or even realm that one is in. This is one of the mid-rank ones. Barons, dukes, kings, queens, they all have different ones on their wrists, embroidered with various jewels sometimes, or insignias to show which house of the Empire they belong to.' Poncho smiled reflectively.

'It looks like it cannot be taken off,' Ramkus said, keeping his attention on it.

'Well, it can't be. Once bound to the Empire, it remains a mark of who you are. There is no real way to take it off without harming yourself. You'd scar yourself in the process. Not that I have seen that happen with these Empire bands, but I have with marriage ones…' Poncho explained.

'Marriage bands?' Ramkus Blurted out.

'Yes, the same principle. On the left wrist – right for a woman. The couple will have matching bracelets to signify their commitment to each other, that they are bound to each other, for life,' Poncho went on. 'But, that is not always the case, and some would prefer to cut off their arm than spend another minute with the one they are *bound to*, sometimes.'

Ramkus looked at Poncho with bewilderment.

'Hah! I jest boy, the bracelets can be taken off as I said, but it does scar, and only an Empirical blacksmith or jeweller knows the secret procedure in which that can be done. They have a special device which burns the metal off, leaving only a small mark.' He chuckled, 'It's why some men choose only *light* marriage bracelets.'

'How do they get it on?' Ramkus asked.

'A cast is mad around your arm: a thin one of some leather and silk I think – I can't remember exactly if that is it, to tell you the truth, I was too drunk in celebration at the time. Might have been ointments applied as well. Some circular device is placed on the arm, with the metal inside, and let to cool over the leather and silk - the materials disintegrating it in the process. But before it touches the skin, it cools so as not to harm the wrist, and ends up essentially skin tight.' Poncho showed that it had hardly any space to move, only the smallest of space in between

the bracelet and the skin that allowed it to move up and down
only slightly. 'The worst to wear must be Royal Counts
bracelets. They are, but naturally, hefty ornate pieces. Luckily
those Counts don't need to move around much,' he gave
Ramkus a wink. 'A good life, otherwise.'
*Why is he suddenly so friendly to me? Maybe the slight mention
of the Empire, and its customs?*
'I see you have a no wife then,' Ramkus said, 'or partner.'
Poncho gave a quizzical look, 'Partner?'
'Well, man, if that is who you wish to be bound to.'
A deep breath was inhaled by Poncho. He spoke deeply and in a
controlled manner, his soldierly demeanour angered: 'I am not
that way inclined. No man in the Empire is. To even think if it
is a crime.' He looked away.
Ramkus did not know how to follow up, other than probe what
he thought was a choice that should not offend. He thought of
Kerf and Rab in Abergrass, the first people he met who appeared
to be in a relationship, happily living together. He remembered
Felipe comments the morning that they passed the old chums'
cottage. Happy with each other, doing no harm to others.
'Why is it a crime?' Ramkus dared ask. He felt he wanted to
stand up for what ought not be deemed criminal. A strong sense
of morality and justice came over him; unlike that power from
the deep dark reaches within him, something more in tune with
order, of necessity, his essence beating true.
'Excuse me?' Poncho guffawed savagely, 'Why is it a crime?!
It is unnatural!' He shouted, unable to hold himself back,
shaking as he had to calm himself down. He obviously did not
want to break some duty to uphold the Empire's values, but his
own beliefs and what he felt the Empire may wish him to do –
smiting Ramkus for his insolence being one of them. However,
he was at least able to hold himself in restraint from snapping.
Ramkus himself felt a strong sense of duty, to protect, rise
within him, even if it was only a verbal argument. An electric
surge went through his limbs, his body. He became steadfast,

his mind clear. Whatever was happening to him, he knew he held some force inside that strained to be unleashed. *Is this some strength the Guardians are able to draw from? When there is some order that needed to be spread across this plane; is this how the Guardians do it?*

He was still sitting cross legged, but mighty in his stature now. Poncho was still agitated, but even his skin pricked up at the power emanating from Ramkus, the electricity in the air. The fire was weakening.

Poncho's men watched the two journeymen - they had been ever since Poncho almost began shouting.

The trees were amplifying the dark blue night sky's calmness on the copse's edge. All still clear, calm.

Poncho shook back from what was a threatening encroachment on Ramkus. And that is where they left it. Ramkus could see Felipe from across the fire on the other side: wide eyed, pensive, observing. He relaxed and started talking to some of the other soldiers.

Ramkus breathed in that sweet air, deeply. He breathed out, with all the tension that he held, all the power he had drawn upon, dissipating. He was starting to realise *what* he was.

They arose early the next day. Little was spoken, at least in Ramkus's direction. The soldiers were quick to break camp, washing and eating swiftly. Felipe was still in his rather chipper mood from the night before, laughing with the soldiers as they made their way back onto the path. Ramkus watched Poncho who did not to wish to make eye contact with him. He seemed to be lost in his thoughts, Ramkus surmised. *Perhaps thinking over his Empire's laws*, he hoped. He himself was still riding on a high from last night, realising he held a calm strength, a deep power he could draw upon if need be; if in want. He looked at the blue sky, dotted with a few wispy white clouds. The sun's morning warmth enlivened the energy of the land.

He tried to bask in it as much as he could, letting it fill him with warmth and vigour before they entered the forest on the other side of the glade and back into a cool shade. They moved along the path; a sparse forest with movement from critters here and there. A deer often caught in the corner of one's eye at times, only to vanish when the head turned. It was pleasant and refreshing, nothing like the torturous path of the day previous. This reflected in the troops' demeanour, breaking through their brick wall attitude. There were smiles, just not from Poncho.

A few miles into the forest, a fork in the road became apparent. Ramkus wished to grab Felipe and make to move onto the road that led to higher ground, leaving the soldiers behind. But he did not know which one to take, and was merely hopeful that it was the one that would lead to the mountain pass, and that the soldiers would not be bothered to follow.

As they came closer, a notice board sharing advertisements for particular wares was seen, often stating the word "best" for whatever article being spruiked. *It couldn't all be the best swords in town if there are three advertisements saying the same thing. False and misleading.* More importantly, there were sign posts: one that stood pointing to the right reading Relton, *not too inventive with names around here.* The other signpost to the left side simply read "Private". The squad stopped here for a rest – at least that was the impression Ramkus got from them, they never stated such.

'I wonder how many have travelled to "Private", not realising it wasn't a place!' Felipe could be heard laughing. 'Well, I guess only some have the privilege to be able read.'

'They should be able to understand the red cross underneath it,' Poncho said to Felipe, unimpressed with the poor attempt at a joke.

'What if it was a blind man, stumbling his way through the forest?' Ramkus quizzed Poncho.

Poncho shook his head at this, 'Why would a blind man be wandering the path unaccompanied?' he responded gruffly.

'Why not?' Felipe rebutted quickly, moving up to the company at the front, winking at Ramkus. Ramkus hoped this was conciliatory.

Poncho stood there, looking at the two, clenching his jaw, waiting, as if he was trying to hold something back. Felipe and Ramkus stared at him.

He finally spoke, 'This is our way, I would like it if you joined us.'

'Ah, we cannot I am afraid, our way lies along the other path,' Felipe said. 'To Relton'.

Poncho moved his lips around, 'We will pay you two handsomely for your entertainment,' he seemed to be hiding a snarl.

'We are in a bit of a rush,' Ramkus said, 'but thank you for the offer.'

'Wait, Ramkus, from memory, Relton is a few days away.' Felipe sniffed - not one to turn his nose up at good coin. He looked at Poncho, 'What is down this path? How long does it take to get there?'

'Do not press me for such information!' Poncho stopped, his men gathering around the two bards. The bards stood wide eyed, not understanding the meaning of this sudden change in manner, but suspicious none the less.

'I'm sorry,' Poncho said, 'It is a... secret. It would take a day to get there.'

Ramkus frowned, he could see that this was not the best option for them. He wanted a quick escape from this Kings Guard squad.

Still, as if it couldn't be helped, Felipe pressed Poncho for more information. 'A secret huh? But lots of coin for our efforts?' he grinned.

'Alright,' Poncho said, 'it is the Summer Palace of the Ronato Family, one of the royal families. It is a secret from common folk. The Summer Castle sits atop it'

Felipe's eyes widened; Ramkus was unchanged.

'Ah, no wonder the Kings Guard is out here!' Ramkus said, 'still, I think we best be on our own way,' he made to leave.

Poncho was holding himself back from uttering some command, 'I would *advise* you came with us,' he slurred through gritted teeth.

'Yes, Ramkus. The royal family should be in residence too!' Felipe said, overjoyed at the prospect. 'Now I know why the region looks so much nicer in Summer, no pollution from the Capital!'

'I don't think we should, Felipe,' Ramus said, keeping his eyes on Poncho.

'Ramkus, come on,' Felipe said dismissively, as if his friend was letting him down.

'No, Felipe, I *don't* think we should,' Ramkus said sternly.

Felipe frowned, 'Perhaps this is where we say our goodbye then. A bit abrupt, but it was bound to happen. You are on your way to bigger and better things. I, finally, am off to a royal court!'

'I would advise you,' Poncho interjected in the exchange, 'to come with us,' he responded, staring at Ramkus. There was a definite threat in his eyes, directed solely at Ramkus, as he completely disregarded Felipe's enthusiasm.

'Come on, Ramkus, just for a day. You could make some money and make off on your journey on a better footing. Perhaps even get your own guitar! Either way, this is the path I am taking,' Felipe gestured down the left "Private" path with a smile.

The other soldiers stood ominously, at the ready, but in a *relaxed* state.

Ramkus felt hopeless, that great energy from the night before, depleted. He had sunken back to fighting with that grovelling mental state, helpless. He gave in to his friend's pleas.

'Okay, I will join you, but only for a day, then we may have a proper farewell – should you impress the court so much that they hire you full time,' Ramkus said to sound as if he did not register the threat.

Felipe's eyes were alight, 'Good lad!' He patted Ramkus on the back.

Poncho bore the semblance of a smile, as if a weight had been lifted from him. 'Good,' he simply stated.

They moved off after a few moments, Ramkus stood still, letting the soldiers go on. A few eyes were on him until he finally followed the troop, feeling weak, sunken. The arrogance and strength he had known was gone as well. He was becoming that creature from the depths that scurried along the floor, cowering. This angered him, and he shook his head. 'Never again,' he said to himself, 'I am better off alone from now on.' He knew this path would of no be good to him, but he would go along with it and learn that these little feelings are what design one's destiny. *One should never override what they feel, only ever follow it.* He already knew this, but still, he went against his instincts, deciding this would be the last time he was forced to make a decision through manipulation and duress.

After this, he knew he would be alone.

Chapter IX

The castle was gradually creeping out of the forest's depths. Its
spires reaching into the sky, as if attempting to conquer it. The
company rode slowly down a criss-crossing path, the steep hill
creating a great vantage point over the evening mist that had
begun descending below them. The trees, a hundred yards tall,
kept their grandeur when looked at individually; but when the
castle – which was built upon a rock bluff standing high above,
even without the castle upon it – was in clear view, it gave such
a stark contrast against the trees that they completely failed to
inspire any contemplation.

They descended into the large ravine that surrounded the rocky
bluff with flat, forest land, steady on the path. It seemed as if
there was an ominous hum in the forest, as if the land was
commanded by the will of those whom tended to it. But who
was its master? Was it these men who have staked claim,
placing their massive construct atop to send a foreboding gesture
that they could – and would – conquer what they pleased? The
walls of the main keep stretched into what seemed the cosmos
from the view point below. The squad did not stop, moving
through the forest till they came to a twenty-foot gate wooden
gate, connected to a stone wall.

'Well, well, look who's decided to join us at this late hour. The
Captain of the Kings Guard himself,' a chubby man who looked
red in the face said through the grated door.

'Let us in. Quick,' Poncho said with annoyance.

'Who's that you got there?' the man replied.

'None of your business, you drunken buffoon. I said quick!'
Poncho sneered at the man, visibly angry.

'Now, now. No need to be rude,' the man blundered off to the
lever controlling the gate. 'I was just curious.'

Poncho remained quiet until the gate was high enough to get in.
They moved quickly inside without word. Poncho acted quite

regally, with his head held high. There were still a number of
trees behind the stone wall, looking as if it was part of a well-
maintained garden. The wall itself appeared to go all the way
around the bluff – or at least as far as one could see.

As they continued along a few hundred yards into the flat
surround, the trees ended, and green, luscious grassland spread
all the way to what must have been a beach, as the ocean could
be seen and heard far off.

So much for travelling inland toward the mountain pass.

The bluff was sandstone upon closer inspection, and rose up as
if it had shot straight from the earth, hundreds of yards tall, and
hundreds of yards in circumference. Before it, the lawns joined
to brick cloisters built in a square shape around an army training
ground. One side held a brick building, and, not too far from it,
a stable. There was an evening lull to the whole place; candles
were being lit, as well as large torches that stood in the ground
along the paths. The fog they had descended into – and through
- did not touch this inner tended area past the thick forest; it was
as if the essence of the forest was being kept at bay, and the
forest was desperately crying out to reconnect with this clearing,
only for it to be met with silence.

They dismounted as attending soldiers took their horses' reins.
Poncho then lead Ramkus and Felipe to a small rise which a
large set of steps heading into the massive rock bluff, atop which
sat the well-founded castle. The steps led to a large entrance
that had been cut straight into the bluff, showing how it had been
hollowed in part. They entered the foreboding rock face.
Surprisingly, inside, it was indeed adorned as if it was the castle
itself. Dark - as one could imagine without any normal light -
but as well-lit as it could be, considering, for those venturing
inside could still find their way. A large set of stairs moved up
the innards, then around the edges once it hit the back wall, and
then again through the innards once that length had been traced.
This continued a number of times before rising to the top where
the castle they had seen perched high into the sky from the

treeline sat. Poncho moved without taking in the sight, walking with an air of expectance. They climbed up, and up, and up. Ramkus felt they had become prisoners in this blackened, sandstone construct. Soon, as they rose the many steps, they hit corridors that traced around the edges that allowing people to peer outside the bluff through small holes and into the surrounds below. Laughter and music began to come into focus, as they finally reached what was the surface. Out through a last set of doors, and out into a brick square. Brick buildings lined either side, holding balconies. In front of them: the massive spread of stairs that rose to the main keep.

The laughter and revelry was coming from one of the buildings on the side. The sky night had descended, and people were "off-duty".

'Ha! Those fools have started without me,' Poncho chuckled. 'Come, this way.' He eyed the two; the rest of his squad seemed to relax and smile.

As they walked to the building to the right, Ramkus took in the sights of the constructions: there were shops and lodgings standing before the main hall in a town, with space for the masses to watch those of importance when they stood mightily above all others, upon the steps of the castle. These buildings failed significantly in comparison to that which was the "main keep", or as it probably was, the castle. He caught a small glimpse of the view through alley between the buildings. It looked over the sides of the top of the bluff. He realised how far they must have risen about the forest.

The building Poncho had led them to was a great mess hall. Many soldiers, ones who bore less of the oafish resemblance than their counterparts in the villages and towns Ramkus had visited – one may even say they were handsome. Still, their love of drink and revelry were apparent, as was their manner in singing, laughing, and eating. It was a full house of about eighty odd bodies.

'Men!' Poncho yelled, 'You started without me?!'

'We didn't think you'd be back so soon,' one yelled back from the long wooden tables, 'nor that you'd complete your mission outright!'

The soldiers were drinking on two large tables that stretched the building. It was fairly well lit, candles on the tables as well as the pillars holding the floor above up. Some of the men were playing a flute cheerfully.

Poncho peered around, then his gleeful appearance took a turn. 'Why are so many of you up here at this moment?' he asked aggressively. 'Have we not got a troop on watch?'

'It is our night off,' another yelled back, 'it was meant to be your lots turn.'

A look of disgust and anger came over Poncho's face. 'You morons!' he sneered. 'Who the hell told you that you could take the night off if I was not here? Which imbecile was in control whilst I was not around?' His face turn red.

'Djuayne,' one said, as the place became quieter. A sense of dread, the sense that punishment was about to be dealt out. Ramkus and Felipe stood silent, observing.

'Djuayne...' Poncho said, drawing out the name, '*the ever popular Djuayne.*' He breathed out heavily to calm himself. 'And where, pray, is Sergeant Djuayne?'

'In the main hall of the castle, they have a ball on tonight,' One of the men answered.

'They always have balls on...' Poncho huffed. 'Right, I will have a *talk* with Djuayne. I would suggest one of the squads gets out there on guard duty – I don't care who - before I get back, or I will serve out some hefty punishment!' Poncho paused, 'And someone get me a drink. A hard one. Now!'

An earthenware cup of some alcohol and a pouring jug were brought out by a servant who appeared to be a novice soldier. Poncho sculled it, poured some more from the jug, and handed it to Ramkus and Felipe. Felipe declined with a small wave of the hand and courteous smile; Ramkus sniffed it. An awful smell:

strong, like some chemical he did not think he could stomach. He tried it still, and coughed; it burned his throat. Poncho took the cup back, and finished the rest.

They wound their way through the throng of soldiers, back outside. Poncho told his squad they could retire for the night; he would show the "guests" to their accommodation, and to where else they might be "required".
'I thought you *definitely* needed entertainers,' Felipe said with hope.
'We do,' Poncho said curtly, not really bothering to come up with an adequate response as to the pretences of them coming along.
Felipe shrugged, he was still excited to have his half chance to shine and become a court bard. He had not let Ramkus in on this intention, but it was easily read upon his face. Ramkus knew whatever false reason they were brought here on, Felipe would still make the most of it.
They approached the steps which spread out lazily in front of the main keep like ripples. Ramkus looked to the view on the right where no buildings obstructed the sight: far away, the two mountains stood. The white tops still gleaming from a low-lying light that came from behind them. The lower ridges spread all the way to what he guessed must have been the ocean, and further beyond sight. *A clean line through the land of Elantra.* No wonder Ramkus had to seek the saddle, the lowest point he could see; the only point that seemed possible to cross. Green forest stretched out in front of these two monsters of the landscape, as if a blanket for them to be revered in front of. A massive undulating river snaked through the forest, as seen by the large swathes of tree-less portions of forest which it cut through; for the forest was dense, and nothing of the ground could be seen. What lay further out to the right, away from the mountains, was anyone's guess. Anything could be hiding within it. But Ramkus knew that this must be where one of the

Empires production centres must be the Capital – at least he could recall being told so. The low pink sunset was dying away under the heavy, deep blue of the night sky. The stars began coming out. They were so close they felt atop this bluff, that one felt they could reach them. The mountains stood still. Deadly calm. Far away.

Entering the massive arched doorway of the main keep, and were greeted by two guards in full armour on either side. Merriment was heard throughout, as servants rushed about. There was another set of stairs to a mezzanine which they stepped up, and into the chaos of what must have been the main hall. It was a room that was lit as brightly as if it were directly in sunshine; silken cloths covered the walls, various large statues – mostly of heroic looking men – stood along the walls where the cloth did not run. The walls and pillars were a fashioned yellow sandstone which great detail had gone into designing, creating an experience of warmth. The roof was three storeys high, held up by the massive circular pillars of sandstone. Impressively dressed men and women were talking and drinking with goblets in hand, expressing great exuberance; some even smoking various pipes or cigars. A band was playing in the corner, a calming ambient music that did not overpower the conversations. There was food laid out on tables to the sides, a buffet of exotic meats, fruits, cheeses, cakes, and canapes; servants were picking these up as well and darting around offering the delicacies to the guests. The food looked as if it had been hardly touched.

A few glances were paid in the direction of the three new entrants. They walked the marbled floors, not knowing whom may have been a merchant, a duke, diplomat, or what not. Ramkus looked at the wrists as if that may give a clue. It did to some degree, but he could not make out too many as long shirts of fine silks were worn, covering the arms all the way to the hands of many the men and women.

Poncho led them around, looking out for someone. 'Ah,' he said, 'Djuayne, that shit.' His eyes rested on a man who was looking as if he were annoying one of the women with his presence. He was tall, over six foot seven, muscular – as he wore only a short tunic under his leather breastplate, showing off his gargantuan, chiselled build – long brown hair that looked well maintained, green piercing eyes. He wore a decorated soldier's outfit, and held a ceremonial short sword to his side. He stood with confidence over this girl whom was not impressed. He reeked of arrogance from yards away.

'Djuayne!' Poncho called out, as he walked over to the man with the accompanying bards.

The giant Djuayne looked up – or rather, down – a large smile coming across his face. 'Poncho, what a pleasure to see you dear *comrade*,' he responded mockingly in a booming voice.

'What is the meaning of you not putting any guards on duty?' Poncho shot straight back.

Ramkus stopped listening to the conversation as he looked at the girl Djuayne had been brushed off by. She was observing him with inquisitive eyes. He looked to his side; Felipe had already run off to entertain the guests with his bravado. When he looked back, the girl had already approached him, standing right in front. She clasped his hand and led him away from the quarrelling soldiers.

She wore a tight, light blue dress, held lithely about her shoulders by straps, revealing her arms and sides, as well as much of her back and top of her chest. She was tall, half a head shorter than Ramkus, long blonde dazzling hair, grey blue eyes. She looked as if she knew how to fight. Not necessarily a petite girl, but slim and fit.

'My father said I should find a man with a long staff,' she spoke with a delicate but affirmative voice.

Ramkus smiled, half about to laugh. 'Did he, now?' He held his staff out, lowering his eyebrows.

She laughed with good humour. 'Indeed... my name is Sophia.'

'Ramkus,' he divulged, quite taken aback by the girl. She locked her arm around his with a gentle touch, electrifying Ramkus's intrigue.

'Let's go talk somewhere else, I can't stand these soldiers,' she said with an air of indignation.

They walked a little away in a graceful state of movement, as if a dance. 'In fact, I am sick of military talk,' she added after a pause. 'You are not a soldier though, are you?' she asked as if a plead.

'No, not at all. I am a… bard.' He rethought whether that was actually a positive occupation of some worth to the type of girl found at a castle banquet. She laughed at his answer in any case. 'Well then, *bard*, you must have come far to get here?' she chided. She gave a quick glance at his mutton chops and winced.

'From Refton,' he replied.

'Refton,' she mused. 'Are you hungry? I know it is not fathomable to actually eat at a ball, but I haven't been able to eat much today. My father has been very busy *lecturing* me.' She rolled her eyes and smiled.

'To tell you the truth, I am rather famished,' Ramkus answered, his eyes intent, staring into hers.

They walked toward the buffet. Ramkus admired the smells and the aesthetics of the exotic dishes. A lot of seafood was on offer.

'Oh, I love oysters,' Sophia said, as she slipped one from its shell into her mouth without hesitation. She looked at Ramkus as if beckoning him to follow suit. He picked one up, let the morsel of strange meat fall on his tongue before letting it flow down his gullet.

'Yes, very good,' he choked.

She smiled deeply, 'I take it you are not accustomed to such foods?' She asked, raising her eyebrows.

'To tell you the truth, I have not been able to try much in my lifetime.' He took another oyster to prove he was not afraid, this time chewing it in his mouth.

'How about some caviar?' Sophia said, dropping a silver spoon into a matching large silver bowl, adorned with simple gems. The contents of this bowl were of a fine, spherical, black bead. Sophia placed the black substance on a cracker, then came towards Ramkus, placing it in front of his mouth. He squirmed, and then got the hint, opening his moth for this next "delicacy". She nimbly placed it on his tongue, slowly, delicately; her scent was of berries, strawberries, cherries, and apple. It hung on his olfactory sense a lot longer than the salty, but delectable, caviar. Understanding this game now, he searched the table for something for her. *Bananas? No, too much, plus, too forward. Some of the meats? Probably not appropriate either.* He stuck with "condiments on crackers", going for some camembert.

'Nice choice, I do like my cheeses,' she said, as he came close to her, placing the food in front of her mouth this time. Her tongue met the edge of the cracker as she devoured it whole with the ends of his fingers, pulling her head back suggestively. She began – and struggled – to chew the cheese and crackers in a flirtatious manner. Her scent was still intoxicating him.

'They didn't tell me you were so handsome,' she whispered.

'Who didn't?' Ramkus asked, taken aback and perplexed. She giggled, and then looked behind him with concern.

A hand came down upon Ramkus's shoulder, forcing him to turn around.

'What do you think you are up to, *bard*?' A voice boomed a good head taller. Ramkus looked up: Djuayne, the man reeking of pretension.

Ramkus stared at him, 'Whatever I am doing is of no concern to you,' he roared back.

'Oh it damn well is a concern to me!' Djuayne yelled.

The hall fell silent, as they became the centre of attention: all the eyes of the fifty odd guests fell upon them, waiting for the next move. Even the band had stopped playing.

'Back off, Djuayne. You could really live to regret it.' Poncho had suddenly come into the picture, wedging between the two.

'Quite right, you do not want to mess with me,' Ramkus said arrogantly, a sneer across his face.

Djuayne bared his teeth like a wolf,' Oh, is that so?'

'Oh, you idiot,' Poncho growled at Djuayne.

'Why don't we have a little duel then? Tomorrow,' Djuayne glared at Ramkus, paying no heed to Poncho's words.

Not knowing what he had gotten himself into, Ramkus nodded, baring a nasty smile, 'You're on.'

Poncho shook his head and grabbed Ramkus by the arm, leading him away; Ramkus still smiling with an aggressive intent over his shoulder at the threat. His eyes met Sophia's as he was ushered through the crowd that had gathered. Sophia's expression was that of sadness and worry. He started coming to his senses. They passed Felipe who was happily engaged with two ladies, arms around their waists.

'Come,' Poncho ordered.

'I bid you adieu, ladies,' Felipe said, as he chased after the two.

They went up another level outside of the main hall before Poncho spoke.

'You are going to get your arse whooped, you moron,' Poncho stated plainly.

'I don't know about that, I am not too bad a fighter when it comes to it,' Ramkus replied, but he was now unsure of himself, timid and averting eye contact.

'It's quite true, the odds will be quite good as you're an unknown, I would put my money on you,' Felipe said reassuringly.

Ramkus was feeling a little forlorn. The reaction stemmed from his intense desire to prove a point that he needn't have bothered to. He had never intentionally sought a fight, they had just sort of happened.

'This can be your room for the night. Guards!' Poncho yelled to some men who were standing at the end of the corridor. 'Mind these two. Make sure that they are not disturbed...' he told them as they approached closer. 'And you two, if you need anything, just ask. I may also come fetch you in a little while.' Poncho gave a quick nod to the two guards who were wearing metal soldiering regalia, and now standing either side of the door to the two bards chambers.

Felipe grinned as he opened the door. It was a simple room: a writing desk, two single beds, a lounge, a bowl on a marble platform. Large windows looked out onto the forest from which they had come, high above the world.

'Not bad, but I think we can do better,' said Felipe. 'I shall ask the guards for an upgrade.'

'You do realise we are effectively prisoners here,' Ramkus said, making sure the door was closed. This was first opportunity he had to speak to Felipe alone.

'That may be the case, but we are also in a castle. I for one am going to make the most of it.'

'Don't you realise...' Ramkus had lost Felipe's interest as he opened the door.

'Kind sirs, would we by any chance be able to get two separate rooms, and ones that are a bit more befitting of our stature?' The guards looked at each other and grunted. 'Bards, aren't you? Of stature?' one replied.

'I am no ordinary bard my learned friend, I am a two-time winner of the Eredin Bard Festival! I should think verse written of me – and by me - should have flown through the taverns.'

'Ha! Whatever you say,' the other said, as they both turned back to their original positions.

Felipe shook his head, closed the door, and sighed. 'Maybe not then... they had no idea who they were talking to.'

Ramkus decided not to keep Felipe's ego in check, it wouldn't help. 'Felipe, I really am not too pleased being here, I think it wise to get out as soon as we can.'

Without a pause for comment, a knock came at the door.

'Yes?' Felipe said.

'Kind Sirs, I have been ordered to bring you some dinner,' a voice came back.

Felipe's mood picked up; Ramkus's sank low.

'Well then, come in!' Felipe cried with joy.

A portly fellow jostled in with a wheeled tray. Two plates hidden under silverware domes were presented to them. The portly chap left the tray, bowing as he exited, shutting the door behind him.

'Now what have we got here?' Felipe said with intrigue, inspecting his reflection on the silverware domes before entertaining his curiosity.

Ramkus looked out the window at the waving forest top under the blanket of a darkening sky. It was lit low under the moon which had made an early entrance. Clouds hung low, and in the areas where the large river flowed, fog could be felt sinking into the riven. It was becoming cool.

'Oh, how divine! Perillo Bugs!' Two halves of a crayfish were lying on their shells, showing the fine meat - and lots of it.

'These are fantastic, lots of meat, unlike lobsters and crabs. Easy to pull out as well.' A salad to the side, and a few slices of bread and cheese accompanied the meal.

'Felipe, I should be out there, I should be heading towards my goal,' Ramkus replied despondently.

'Ha! My lad, it is not the goal that is important, it is the journey. Now, eat up!' Felipe gestured to the food with his arms upturned, as if it was *his* gift to give.

'As long as the journey does not completely side track one from the goal, I might agree,' Ramkus frowned wistfully.

'Oh poppycock, who is to say that.' Felipe pointed to the direction of where Ramkus wished he was meant to be heading towards. 'That - your actual goal - you may well find you don't like it. Enjoy what you have here, *now*.' Felipe's focus went back to the meal.

'Well I certainly don't like being in this place. If you haven't noticed, we haven't had the best experiences with the Empire so far.' He looked now at Felipe, whom was feasting away with glee.

Deciding it would be best to get a full meal in, and not only a bit of caviar and oysters, he joined him reluctantly. Felipe had used the desk chair, bringing it to the wheeled trolley, Ramkus stood, as there were no other seats, save for the lounge.

'Someone will get fired for that,' Felipe said with a mouthful of bug, 'I'll let them know we need another chair. That is, if they keep us here.'

'I guess. We shall see,' Ramkus responded without excitement.

'Oh, chin up, we are in a castle, one of the Ronato family's finest properties, I'm sure. And - from what I gather - they are in residence! A lot of people of importance in that hall. You know, the Ronato's are one of the big three royal families? Actually, no you wouldn't... They are, in fact probably the most powerful of the three. Always seeking expansion.' Felipe spoke like a nobleman, as if he knew the gossip.

'Then what do they want with us as entertainers? Don't you think it was a little suspect the manner in which we were brought here?' Ramkus probed this insipid *nobleman's* knowledge, trying to persuade him to see the other sides perspective.

Felipe pondered the question. 'To tell you the truth, I am trying to make the best out of the situation. And you aren't helping, and haven't been in recent times...' he scolded, reminding Ramkus of the earlier dispute between them that had still not been resolved.

Ramkus looked at Felipe with regret. 'I am sorry about how I got so heated in that forest; sorry for almost biting your head off... It was as if something was taking over me, or coming *out*

of me. I am sorry, I should have been more, controlled.' He
resolved his apology with a faint smile, showing the sincerity.
Felipe smiled, 'It's alright. Whatever happens, we will remain
friends. Understand?'
'Indeed,' Ramkus nodded broadening his smile.

The two finished their meals and tried to leave the room. As
suspected, the guards did not let them wander about too far. The
boundaries were essentially down the corridor, and to the privy.
After a wait, Poncho entered again.
'Stand,' he commanded.
'Ah, we are not your soldiers nor prisoners,' Felipe smiled
reverently.
Poncho stood without any appeal to common courtesy.
The two rose and came towards him. 'No chance we could get a
better room, or two separate ones?' Felipe asked half-jokingly.
Once again, Poncho merely stared at Felipe.
'You are to remain here till tomorrow,' Poncho stated.
'And then we get to entertain some princely chap and make
some coin, right?' Felipe said, keeping up the act, having a bit of
fun at the expense of Poncho's stiff resoluteness.
Poncho rolled his lips, 'Something like that.'
'And what of the fight?' Ramkus quickly asked.
Poncho shrugged, looked at the two, and left the room. Felipe's
gaze fell upon the door, still not fully comprehending the
situation they were in.
'Ha, not prisoners,' Ramkus gritted his teeth, 'my arse…' He
scanned the room, 'Perhaps we can escape?'
Felipe almost laughed at the concern, as well as the possibility
of scaling the walls outside at such a height. 'Ah, leave it, you
never know what may be happening. May simply be seeing
what we are like before offering us some work. Mind you, he is
a soldier, he has no real idea as to proper protocol with guests.
It is who he is.'

Ramkus grunted, falling on his bed. It was rather comfortable, similar to the one in Refton. He stared at the ochre ceiling.
'Let's wait till tomorrow then,' Felipe said, also relaxing onto his bed.

In a room above theirs, two pairs of eyes were watching.
'Is this the one from Kerwood?' A voice of slithering malevolence asked, staring into a mirror, which – through a series of pipes, holes, mirror contraptions - reflected a mirror image of the scene that was occurring in the two journeymen's room below.
'Yes,' muttered another voice. It was the sound of a beaten man, battered and bruised in his struggle to even stay conscious.
'Good. Very good. We may well end all the suffering tonight,' the slithering voice replied, 'but that would mean we won't get to have all that fun.'
The eyes of the battered man averted looking at the mirror, pleading for an end to the misery of his existence. He had known it would end badly once he left the Empire's ranks, but he did not expect this.
'Guards, I have no use of this filth anymore,' the slithering voice hissed to two other men who stood behind. They grabbed the tortured soul and dragged his almost lifeless corpse away.
The slithering voice's merciless eyes watched the one named Ramkus in the mirror, muttering to himself sardonically. 'Well, well. What *do* we have here.'
Another man entered this "viewing" room.
'Ah, welcome Sergeant,' the slithering voice said.
'Silque,' the Sergeant responded. A powerful voice that was heard from above: the sergeant was tall.
'Is he whom you saw?' Silque asked.
The Sergeant squinted at the mirror, 'Yes, that is him. Hmm, he even has that other chap. Wondered what he was doing. Yep, and there is that staff, as I said,' he replied.

'Yes, yes, I see. Thank you, Sergeant. Thank you for…
bringing this man to our *attention*.'

'You should have seen who else's attention he had in the hall
tonight!' the Sergeant growled. 'I don't think he can do
anything *but* draw attention to himself.' He paused from his
distasteful thought. 'Is that all you called for?'

'Yes, yes. Thank you, Sergeant,' Silque did not look at the man.
He rubbed his sweaty hands together. 'Yes, I heard he had
already drawn *attention*,' he muttered, before backing away
from the reflection of the man in question. 'What shall we do to
you, what shall we do…' he muttered to himself.

The door of the room made only the faintest sound as it closed
behind him.

Chapter X

They were summoned early in the morn by a lowly porter, being
led to a waiting room where fruits, toast, eggs, cold meats,
cheeses, sweet pastries, juices, tea and coffee were on offer.
'Half an hour, he said. You know what that means?' Felipe said,
his voice echoing in this superb chamber where four guards,
replete with armour, stood at the sides of the entrance and exit,
unmoving. Only Ramkus and Felipe stirred.
'It means double that. Ooh, Ramkus, I am *excited*!' Felipe
continued in an excited manner, true to his word. His guitar
slung around his back.
'You do realise he said you did not need to take your guitar.
And you do know what that means?' Ramkus responded
mockingly, the contempt was difficult to conceal across his face.
Felipe did not seem to be listening; he was too busy filling his
plate from the buffet that had been laid out, humming to himself.
Ramkus shook his head, 'It means that we are not having a
meeting with the King, with regard to our musical credentials…'
He grabbed a banana and unravelled it. 'Don't eat too much,
Felipe,' Felipe looked up at that.
'I do not intend to, I just wish to *try* everything,' he stated.
'How thoughtful,' Ramkus replied. He was in a foul mood. *I
should **not** be here!* he thought, gritting his teeth.
'Well, basically everything will be thrown out after breakfast,
anyway. Yes, it is wasteful, but it will happen regardless,'
Felipe said nonchalantly, carrying on his humming.
Ramkus stood at the window overlooking the land below. The
mountain pass that he sought to cross, so far off in the distance.
'I hope it is quick, and then we can take our leave. Get out of
here as soon possible,' Ramkus started up again, yearning to hit
the road, and get out from under the Empire's eye. The light
blue sky leaked inside, the sun beaming down; he wished he
could have been basking in it, care free.

'As I keep trying to tell you, let things be. Don't be in so much of a rush,' Felipe said, more focussed on chewing one of the pastries, making groaning noises of pleasure. 'This is divine, you must try it!'

Ramkus glared at him with derision, leaning on his staff which he had brought without thought, as if it were simply part of him. He had made a mental note of trying to take each situation in his stride, but it did not feel right. Everything in his body told him he ought not be here. He did not mind waiting in other places, neutral places, nor being in a rush to get to his destination; but this place did not sit well with him.

Minutes passed, and on the half hour mark – whilst Felipe was still scoffing down pastries, getting sugar all over himself – the porter returned from what must have been the path to the royal court.

'Kind Sirs, if you would follow me, the King will see you now.'

Ramkus became very unsettled, knowing that something had befallen his fate; decisions made, all so he would end up here against his will. Felipe on the other hand was in the most joyous of spirits, wishing to make the most of his situation. This was his golden chance - his only chance - to become what he had desired for such a long time: a Court Bard; his dream.

They followed the porter through another small antechamber adorned with artwork, and were ushered into the royal court room.

It was a large hall, with beams supporting the delicate arched roof, well-lit with windows on either side of the grand chamber. The ground, was of a chequered marble and seemed at odds with the ochre colours, as if it were trying to oppose it, outshine it. In the centre, up a number of steps, a throne of fine artistry was set, layered with gold leaf and red upholstery. There, where all eyes would be drawn, sat the King. He could not be missed, as his crown of a simple gold shone with a bright intensity. His fingers held a number of intricate rings; his wrists were embraced by glorious bracelets. He wore a red cloth, similar to the Empirical soldiers, but it was a deeper, finer fabric, with an engraved leather vest with jewels on its edges. A cloak of fur finished off his kingly attire. He did not seem too stern a face; a white trimmed beard, long whitening hair; grey blue eyes. His arms rested upon the thrones arm rests which had the faces of lions cut upon the ends of them. Ramkus noticed that there was a light that shone on the King in order to make him stand out from all those that stood around. It also appeared to hide some gaunt looking advisor in the shadows behind the throne.

He noted Poncho and Djuayne standing below the steps the throne was on, off to the Kings side. On a landing area to the Kings right, another pudgy man, who stood across from Poncho and Djuayne, and appeared to be joined by a face that Ramkus had seen before: the tall soldier who had seen him fight – and even congratulated his efforts - at the Sea Soldiers Spit saloon in Refton! Before Ramkus could gather his thoughts, he looked to the Kings left, and was even more taken aback. There stood the most elegant, beautiful, regal girl he had ever seen. *Sophia!?* She was dressed in a fitted aqua dress showing off her fit features, and was peppered with a light touch of makeup that accentuated her faultless beauty. Ramkus was mentally stunted, focussing all his attention on Sophia whom gave him a modest smile. Before Ramkus could react to Sophia, the pudgy man made an announcement.

'His reverence, King Irving the fifth of the Ronato Family, of the Empire of Elantra.' He took a breath. 'You may kiss his feet,' the pudgy man ended.

Ramkus gave a bemused look, whilst Felipe made a move for the feet.

'Ha! Do not bother yourselves,' the King interjected in a high-spirited tone, 'it is an ancient custom done away with, except that the announcers do not listen and have a desire to continue to announce such silly things. You may bow instead.'

Ramkus bowed sharply, Felipe prostrated himself on the ground.

'Stop making a fool of yourself,' Ramkus whispered at the side of his mouth.

The King seemed not to care too much, he looked at Ramkus, then to his staff, admiring it; wondering about it. Ramkus's eyes met Sophia again, giving a slight smile. The King noticed.

'It is my pleasure to welcome you here… *Bards*. I hope you will find yourself at home,' the King started again. 'All amenities are at your disposal.' He stopped as the gaunt looking man by his side spoke to the him in whispers. The King nodded to his words.

'Thank you, my Lord,' Felipe said after this statement.

'Thank you,' Ramkus followed suit.

'Now, it was promised you'd be able to provide us with some entertainment tonight. We still look very much forward to this, as it is also a very important celebration for us. The great hero Procto has his night celebrated this evening, we would appreciate any songs relating to him,' the King said suggestively.

Felipe nodded, as Ramkus looked to him to see if he accounted to knowing any such songs. 'It would be a pleasure, your majesty,' Felipe replied.

'There is also some other entertainment we need to take care of today, my liege,' Djuayne butted in. 'It is only fitting that it be on Procto's celebrated day!' He beamed with vigour.

The King looked at him quizzically, as did Sophia, then to Ramkus anxiously.

'Yes, my liege, this gentleman here, is to fight me today,' Djuayne said, moving towards Ramkus leisurely. 'His name is Ramkus, and the other is known as Monsieur Felipe. As you are well aware, once a challenge has been made, it must be carried through with, lest there be a *heavy* punishment dealt. For it is an insult to our customs, otherwise.'

The King did not look too pleased to hear of this arrangement. The gaunt looking man looked a little fazed, but regathered himself, lowering himself to the King's ear, whispering. The King still looked concerned.

'I see, Djuayne,' the King nodded his head thoughtfully. 'Do you know who Djuayne is, Ramkus?' The King asked concernedly.

Ramkus shook his head, 'No, I do not.'

The King sighed, pausing for a moment. 'Djuayne is a Captain of the King's Guard, and more generally a Sergeant of the Empire's army. He was born into a noble family, and has therefore been provided with the very best education that one can have. And that includes, in its majority, vast training in weapons and combat.' The King paused again, 'Not only has Djuayne here been provided such excellent training from birth, he also excelled at it, to the level where he is now our champion and considered one of the great weapon masters of the known world. Even for a person of natural ability,' The King paused again, unsure of himself, wondering whether he was saying too much. He started again, 'Even if you are person of natural ability, and someone who has been well trained… you stand no chance against Djuayne. He is known throughout Elantra as one of the best swordsmen… ever.' Djuayne was smiling at this, pleased with his King's words. 'In essence, Ramkus, I am afraid to say, you have picked a fight with someone who will deal out a lot more than you can handle. And, as is our custom, one cannot back down from an organised duel.'

Ramkus was now unsteady. *Why does this have to happen to me, and why does the King care?*

'But do not worry,' the gaunt man spoke; his voice hissed, as he raised himself to stand beside the King, 'this is not a fight to the death. Djuayne will fight with a wooden sword, and you with your… *staff.*' The man smiled unsettlingly, regarding Ramkus's attachment.

As much as the voice rattled his nerves, the resonance from the gaunt man's chide began to give rise to a bit of relief. It was merely a duel, and, not one to the death. He looked to Sophia whom was anxiously biting her lip.

'What is wrong with you girl?' the King said as he looked upon her.

'Nothing, father,' Sophia replied.

So, she is a Princess!? Ramkus was astonished. And she seemed to be a very pleasant one at that. He watched as the King gave her knowing a wink.

'Well, it shall be a fitting celebration for Procto. I will see to it that my servants provide you with what you require. And as for tonight, well I suspect it may only be Monsieur Felipe who will be performing. None the less, you will both be paid well for helping with the entertainment. Hopefully we can speak on more casual grounds, but court protocol and custom still seems to override me every time, hence the manner of this meeting.' The King smiled, 'Until then,' he nodded.

Felipe and Ramkus bowed – Felipe a lot lower than a man of any self-respect would.

'I shall see you on the steps of the palace for our *celebration*,' Djuayne said. 'A few hours after lunch, means you'll at least get *some* treatment from your beating before the proper festive occasion.' He smiled with a sneer, pretentiously.

Ramkus stared at him, then looked to the princess before picking the prostrating Felipe off the ground to leave.

Poncho, Djuayne, and the short pudgy announcer had all left the royal court without saying a word, whilst the large Refton soldier gave a few solid nods to in the direction of the throne before he exited last. The gaunt, slithering advisor remained by the King, along with Sophia.

'So, he is the one, eh?' the King said to no one in particular, then looked at Sophia. 'I see you have taken a liking to him.' His emotions were hard to read, Sophia blushed.

'Your majesty, may we have a little talk in private,' the advisor's hissing voice whispered.

The King hesitated, 'Sophia, would you please leave us?' His
voice was soft but stern, and his face held a smile of ease.
'Yes, father,' Sophia replied, as she gave a quizzical glance at
the advisor, before returning the smile to her father, curtsying,
and leaving.
'What is it you wish to speak of, Silque? Of that *Guardian* no
less. You really think he could be of use to us?' the King
questioned.
'I do, sire. He is young, very young,' Silque answered without
hesitation. 'An impressionable age. From our accounts, he has
not even made it to the Guardian's Seat yet. He has no idea of
himself by our reckoning,'
'How do you suppose that? I must admit, I am not familiar with
how Guardians become such.' The King shone a furtive glance
as he clenched his lion carved arm rests. A feeling came over
him, ill at speaking of something he did not know.
'They awaken, your majesty. I have studied such ancient
accounts in my time. They themselves are an ancient force, a
political one, as you would have been versed in your history
lessons, long ago,' he recognised how that could be interpreted,
and rushed on before a response. 'Although, not as common as
they once were – and not holding as much political clout as they
once did - they still all hold innate *abilities*.'
'And by such abilities you mean, physically?' the King's eyes
queried.
'Yes, your majesty, but they also wield a great force of
character: people listen; people follow their orders. It is almost
speaks to a sixth sense, to accept what we are told by some
mystical beings as they know what is the *righteous* path. But
they are still men.' Silque was moving in a melodic manner,
pacing to and fro in front of the King as he spoke, using his jaws
sparingly.
The King was silent for a time, tensing his hand in his palm, his
elbows stretched on the lion etched arm rests. He tapped a
finger on his closed mouth. 'So, what makes you think we can

bring one into our ranks and fight for us? If they have such *sixth sense* abilities, they should know not to be *coerced*, to be free from any allegiances. Correct?' He paused to make a point. 'I have not heard of a Guardian *turning* or becoming sub-servient.'

'That is true, your majesty,' Silque came to stand before the King, his face directly in front of him. 'But we must be the first to try. Imagine having a Guardian on our side! The force we would have at our command!' Silque's shallow eyes started to beam with an intoxication, a hunger for power.

'Well, we shall see how physically well adept he is a little later, I suppose. Still, how do we turn him? How do we make him ours?' The King mused.

Silque pulled back into his natural restrained manner, 'As discussed previously, I think the small seed has been *planted*; and the taste of intrigue has enlivened your daughter already...' Although he may be seen to speak out of turn, Silque knew his way around the King. This "small seed" had been planted in anticipation, just in case.

'I think she may indeed,' the King replied curtly. 'I guess it would be better than Djuayne, he is a contemplable brute sometimes,' he chuckled. 'Still, it is her choice. Better not to have any say in the matter.'

'Subtle hints do not go astray, sire.' Silque smiled almost mockingly.

'No, indeed, as we have just seen. However, it is all well and good for one side to be interested, but Guardians do not marry, they do not have children - from what seems to be the folklore surrounding them,' the King said in protesting tones.

'True, your majesty, but he *has been seen with women*. He may have had a different experience than others, or perhaps once they get to their *keep*, they change their ways... He did look as if he was interested - from what I could gather. As for children, if they have not been known to be with women in the first instance, who knows...'

The King nodded, 'We shall see Silque, we shall see.'

'You should see him, Giselda,' Sophia declared admiringly as she set herself for the next bout, her wooden sword in hand, training gear on.

'But what is he *like* as a person? You did speak to him for a few moments?' A short cropped brown-haired girl called back from the other side of the training platform. She held herself with great poise, positioning for the next round. Her small, fit frame ready for the blows to be dealt upon her – and to deal herself – as she bared her teeth. She may have actually been scary, if not for her gentle features which belied a strain of the first peoples. Sophia was the first to move, with cat like finesse and grace, charging Giselda, battering down with her wooden sword, her blows deflected, as Giselda counterattacked at Sophia's abdomen. Sophia pirouetted, tapping Giselda on the shoulder. Giselda jumped sideways, crouched, and assailed back at Sophia, her sword was deflected downwards and held by Sophia's sword, locked. Neither budging, the smaller Giselda would usually have lost easily, but Sophia's mind was elsewhere.

'I did,' Sophia said, as she relaxed, signalling the end of the day's training - a sweat had been broken. Giselda let go and followed Sophia over to the servants who were offering towels and refreshments.

'He did not really say much, I think he may have been unsure of himself in the banquet hall. I don't know where he has come from, or his post. Neither Silque nor father will tell me, but he carried a presence, that's for sure.' Sophia's eyes started to rise as she reminisced on all she knew. 'In any case, he does not carry the air of arrogance that Djuayne does,' she sighed.

'Djuayne is going to hurt him, isn't he…' Giselda said. Sophia did not answer as they entered the baths.

It was an indoor pool of heated water. They - save for the servants - were the only ones there. Stripping, they got into the water quickly. Warm waters enveloped their silken bodies without so much as a splash.

'Is there anything we can do?' Giselda asked with hesitation, bobbing in the water.

'I doubt it. I just hope it is not too much of a beating to make him leave the castle as quickly as possible.'

'You never know, Sophia, he may end up unable to physically leave after the fight,' Giselda's voice held the hint of a suggestion.

Sophia let herself sink under the misty ripples before re-emerging back to the resting perch that Giselda now sat on.

'I just wish I did not have to be in this position where it is pressed upon me to be married so early. I hate being a princess, sometimes.'

'Oh, hush,' Giselda wiped Sophia's hair out of her face, cupping her head. She smiled with one side of her mouth, 'At least your father has allowed you to have some choice. Many others would not.'

'Of such a select few though!...' She blushed, 'But this particular one is very handsome, the type I would have had desired the attention of, in any case...'

'Are you going to be able to speak to him before the duel?' Giselda said.

'I'm not sure, I doubt it. What should I say, anyway?' Sophia grabbed Giselda's hands. 'Maybe I could give him a kiss for good luck!'

'Oh, Sophia, does that not seem too keen? Let him chase *you* for a bit. You are the princess after all! Get him to serenade you. From what I hear, he can actually play the guitar quite well, he is not only posing as a bard.'

'You should see the actual bard, he is such a stereotype!' Sophia threw back her head with a laugh.

'I heard he was a great lover,' Giselda blushed. 'He is actually quite famous...'

Sophia gave a furtive glance. 'Says who?' she giggled as
Giselda blushed deeper. 'Oh, I wish I had travelled, like you!'
'It is not all fun and games, much safer being the friend of a
princess,' Giselda winked.

The two had done away with "servant girl" and "master" titles
long before, as a friendship had blossomed through the years.
Giselda was around ten years older than Sophia, but acted just as
young as her at times.

The steam continued to rise in the baths, the massive columns
around the pool held droplets of condensation on their rough
stone surfaces. The girls were perspiring, far more than when
they were training.

'If you do want to see him before the fight,' Giselda started
again, 'you must start getting ready, now. I don't think we will
have much time to get ready before the lunch.'

Sophia rolled her eyes, '*Another* banquet for *another* hero. It's
as if the heroes have become the Gods with the way we treat
them,' she raised her eyes at Giselda. 'But I suppose we must
do what we must do, especially if you want to attract Monsieur
Felipe the bard's attention.'

Giselda blushed, 'I don't think it will be necessary, he'll
probably be looking for someone younger these day's…' she
said forlornly. 'Anyway, let's get going.' She got up quickly,
heading towards the servants for a towel, leaving Sophia to mull
on the few words spoken on the topic of Giselda's younger days.

Silque quietly and determinedly walked the hallways of the
castle. He held great hope that he would - at some stage - bump
into Djuayne. Silque's movements were like that of a serpent,
his head moving at his neck with a slow, muscular motion that
was rhythmic to the rest of his body. He looked up and down
the hallway connections, till he saw his intended target walking
boldly. Djuayne was waving his arms about in an expressive
manner, talking with a booming, jovial voice. He was with
Poncho who seemed to be in his own thoughts. Silque followed

up to them at speed; he looked as if he was gliding across the floor with his cloak covering the ground without a jerk in its movement. The two did not hear his approach.

'Captain Djuayne, Captain Poncho.' He purposely knew to use the Captain titles, as it was more ceremonial and prestigious to be a Captain of the Kings Guard than a high-ranking empirical Sergeant - and better sounding.

The two Captains of the Kings Guard jumped with a fright; the expressions on their faces when they turned held contempt and annoyance at being taken by surprise. When they realised who it was though, Djuayne beamed his confident, buoyant smile, whilst Poncho merely nodded and remained in a passive, neutral state.

'I hope I did not startle you,' Silque started.

'Not at all, we were just talking about you…' Djuayne replied in a friendly voice.

'Oh, is that so? And what, pray, were you saying?' Silque asked, bemused.

'Nothing much, just how you are a wise counsel for the King,' Djuayne said after realising the folly of even stating Silque was a topic of conversation.

'Thank you,' Silque nodded. Poncho remained quiet.

'Are your preparations for the fight going well?'

Poncho watched the exchange, wondering what the reason for this whole conversation, or even why Silque had sought him out to hunt down this Ramkus chap, only for him to end up in a duel with Djuayne.

'Of course I am. He does not stand a chance,' Djuayne answered.

'Yes, yes. But you see Djuayne,' Silque looked at Poncho, pausing.

An awkward moment passed. Poncho took note from the others expressions that he was not wanted.

Offering no cordial exchange or excuse - in fact, being quite pleased that he could leave – he broke the silence. 'I shall take my leave,' he said. He bowed slightly before wandering off down the hall in a military march.

Silque waited till he was out of earshot. 'You see Djuayne, you are not fighting an ordinary man,' he continued.

'How is that?' Djuayne pricked his ears and examined Silque's expression.

'He is a *Guardian*, Djuayne. You know what that is, hmm? Good. He holds natural ability which I doubt he even realises. I would hate for him to take you by surprise at some opportune moment.' Silque's voice was melodically lulling Djuayne to listen attentively.

'Does he have any weaknesses?' Djuayne was beginning to - for the first time – question whether he may break a sweat.

'We had reports from a bartender, in some backwater town's inn, that he had hobbled in and requested a physician to look at some wounds. The bartender noted specifically that he struggled to walk, looking to be a knee injury.'

'I don't suppose you know which one?'

Silque shook his head, 'May I add, Djuayne, Ramkus is a guest of the King's. It would not be befitting of you to beat him *too* badly. Perhaps a *knock* that shows who is the supreme fighter, enough to put him in bed for a day or so, *with injuries*.' Silque's eye began to twitch, 'Do you understand Djuayne?'

'You want me to incapacitate him. Easy,' Djuayne said, matter-of-factly.

'Well, yes. We don't want him, ah… leaving us too soon.'

Djuayne glanced at Silque, before looking down. 'I wouldn't mind seeing him get the hell out of here. He is attracting too much *attention*,' Djuayne gritted, looking away again.

Silque smiled, 'The Empire would do well for your best efforts, Djuayne. I'm sure you will have a fine bout, even if a quick one.'

Djuayne looked down on Silque, straightened himself up, and bowed. Silque gave a crooked nod, his nose protruding as if a bird could be perched on it. He walked on in his sly movement, leaving Djuayne to contemplate how much he wanted to hurt this Ramkus; this Guardian; this man who showed him up last night.

'I don't know how to prepare myself!' Ramkus cried to Felipe, the situation was becoming quite dire.

'Well don't look at me, practice prodding a wall or something. Do some fancy staff movements,' Felipe suggested, pacing the room. 'I wouldn't worry too much right now, anyway, the fight is in another few hours. Maybe we should take a swim in the pools? Since we *are* allowed a little bit of freedom now.'

Ramkus's head was in his hands, looking at his feet, sitting on the bed in anguish. 'Felipe, what the hell is going on?! How did I end up in some special "hero tribute duel"? And for the Empire?' He looked to the widow, 'I should be on the road. I have so many questions that are starting to swirl in my head. Where am I from; where am I going; who or what am I.'

'You think you are the only one? Ha! That is every persons' conundrum, you're not *that* special.' Felipe folded his arms as he stopped pacing, 'Well, actually, you probably are *that* special, as a Guardian, so to speak. But that is not to say any person is not entitled to question their own existence. Now stop thinking along such lines, and start preparing yourself. The door guards have put the odds on you at fifteen to one. I have bet a good deal of my gold on that.' He grimaced, 'So you'd damn well better pull through, lest I end up having to stay here and make up for such a loss.' Felipe withdrew from his lecture and drifted off into his thoughts.

'Just ask if they require a bard, it's all you've ever wanted. I am just holding you back,' Ramkus replied tersely.

Felipe did not answer. He was now looking out the window at the lush forest of fertile green juxtaposed by the deep blue sky and the white capped mountains that reflected the radiance of the midday sun. He was happy to look at it, observe it, but not to be within it; for Felipe had to fend for himself in such places.

He sighed as he sat on his bed. 'You may be right Ramkus. You may be damn well right.'

Ramkus looked up from his feet.

'I don't wish to hold *you* up,' Felipe continued. 'I most probably will do if we stay on the same path. Your way lies far through those mountains,' he gestured to the unobservable path through them. 'I do hope, though, that I have taught you enough to get by.' His mood was now that of melancholy.

'What are you saying, Felipe?' Ramkus asked, perplexed at the sudden change in the atmosphere.

'I am saying goodbyes. No doubt you will want to get the hell out of here as soon as this *duel* is over. You'll probably have to do it quickly, very quickly I am guessing: no goodbyes.' He looked at Ramkus with admiration, 'Isn't that so?' The suddenness of their parting was dawning on Ramkus.

'Do you really wish to stay here, Felipe? You do not really know what these people here are like. We have only been shown what they have wished for us to see. This is also the Summer Palace, not their main abode.'

'All the better then!' Felipe replied. 'Their main residence is supposed to be in a magnificent city; lots of life, lots of trouble to make. I just can't keep going along the road, Ramkus.' He smiled, 'I have to make them understand they cannot be without me, firstly.'

The wind blew through the large windows, blowing the light silk curtains away from their position besides the walls. The scent of the sea came through: the smell of salt; of life; of perpetual movement. It relaxed Ramkus, who took it as a sign that he must press on, like the waves that keep rolling in on the beach; one after the other; changing but never stopping.

'This better not be some fight to the death,' Ramkus remarked with a hint of jest. 'I guess I'll do it, then I am out. But not before a proper goodbye!'

'Ha! That's the spirit!' Felipe patted Ramkus on the back. 'Now, let's go down to the "arena".'

They met a small delegation of *duel organisers* outside the castle, as a number of people were beginning to make their way down the stairs in the hollow rock structure.

'I thought the fight was meant to be up here?' Ramkus said to a member of a delegation who had approached him. This man was dressed in a white gown with a long gold cloth around his neck which dangled down his gown. He began to busy himself in front of Ramkus, bringing a box of items with him. It seemed he was making quite a bit of a fuss, just so he could be taken notice of by the rest of the delegation who nodded in approval and left the man to his devices.

'*Duel, up here*?' the man finally answered. 'There is to be only fighting on the proper earth, nothing that is hollow or may be deemed defiled may hold any fighting,' he responded in a monotone, preaching voice. 'This is to honour Procto! He who fought on foreign lands…. *On **solid earth***. Only ceremonial procedures occur up here upon this Rock.'

Ramkus looked at Felipe who shrugged.

'Now you will be anointed duellist,' the man suddenly threw some dust from his hand at Ramkus, who sneezed profusely and was blinded by the abruptness. The man then took a vial of scented water and poured it on Ramkus.

'What on earth!?' Ramkus cried out, trying to regain his vision. Felipe smelt the scent with appreciation.

'You are now cleansed for the duel,' the gowned man declared as if a weight had been lifted.

'Can I be cleansed?' Felipe said, 'I want to honour Procto too.'

'The cleansing is only for those who are able to show the honour in an appropriate and rightful celebration,' the gowned man said.

'Why would you want to get yourself dirty anyway, Felipe?' Ramkus said, as he observed some white and brown flecks on his shoulders. He sniffed himself: the water had some citrus scent to it. 'Hmm,' he commented in appreciation.

'Now, if you'll follow me,' the gowned man finished.

'So, Procto is a big deal with this Ronato part of the Empire?'
Felipe started up again before they began their saunter down
from the castle through the hollow rock. This caused the man to
stop and answer.

'He was the greatest we ever had, and he was of *our* kingdom in
the Empire,' came the reply.

'Felipe, ask your questions as we walk,' Ramkus interjected.
It seemed they were going to be some of the last of the people
down to the stairs, as everyone had been rushing before them in
anticipation.

'I am afraid I cannot do that,' the gowned man said with a waft
of piousness.

'Do what?' Ramkus asked.

'Walk and talk. One must only do one action at a time, lest one
not give their full attention,' the man said as if a lesson.

'*Never whistle whilst your pissing,*' Felipe hummed to himself.

'Right… whatever you say,' Ramkus said to the gowned man.
He was getting fed up with the wait, it was excruciating. He was
itching to get down, fight, then leave. 'So, the duel is outside
this rocky outcrop, is it?'

'Yes, it is on the Lawns of Bequeathment…' the man said
before Ramkus cut him off.

'Good. Felipe, you can continue your talk. I'll catch you later.'

'Ramkus, wait. I'll ask my questions later, don't run off without
us,' Felipe said as he grabbed Ramkus's arm and whispered in
his ear. 'I need to learn all I can to impress these people.'

'Ha!' Ramkus paused for a moment, and smiled as if a wind of
confidence had reached him. 'You need no help, Felipe. You
can impress any person you put your mind too, so long as you
hold no malice in it. You are *the* bard,' he said with genuine
affection.

Felipe was quite taken aback by his words, expecting some
rebuke for being selfish. 'Thank you, Ramkus,' he said,
confused by the sudden warmth. Ramkus had seemingly
dispelled his anxiousness. *Perhaps it was the items that the man*

had dispensed upon him, Felipe thought, for Ramkus had started to glow with pride.

'Now, will we get going? I wouldn't mind at least one person on my side down there,' Ramkus said decidedly.

Felipe now understood the change: this was a man who was about to be discharged of his burden, a man who was about to be free – *or maybe it still is the stuff that man threw upon him.*

'I'm on your side, as has been requested,' the gowned man said, as the other two were appreciating the reliability of their friendship.

They turned and looked at him queerly. 'What exactly are you?' Felipe asked, bemused by the interruption from this stranger who had now become his friends ally.

'I am a priest of the Empire, of the Ronato sect. My name is Harold.'

Ramkus looked at the man in confusion, 'Ah, right. And who requested you to *back* me up?'

'The Princess.'

Ramkus's face twisted into a smile, he gave a chuckle and blushed, nodding to himself. 'Right. Well, let's get down there!' He could not wait to get this over and done with. His air of melancholy was lifting, his retreat was in sight.

Although Harold was unable to walk and talk at the same time, he was quite quick on his feet, leading his small delegation of Ramkus and Felipe down the stairs. This time they were taken around the inside walls of the cavernous rock, where small portholes showed views of the bay, the mountains, and the forests which were all on the outskirts of the Summer Palace area. They wound their way up and down, continuing around onto expansive balconies with sandstone columns that gave even more impressively wonderous views; much nicer than purely following the interior staircase. The closer they got to the bottom, the more they realised the whole of the castles personnel and guests must have descended to the outside lawns for the "festivities". Ramkus was wary not to ask a question, lest Harold stop and give a lecture - the question and answer sessions were mostly on the part of Felipe who conducted himself as an inquisitor – he wanted to get the whole duel over and done with; he needed to focus and required as much of his concentration on what was before him as possible.

Felipe was humming to himself the same tunes being played by the bands down below. The sounds of frivolity and merriment, of festivity, were getting louder and louder, as the delegation finally made their way out onto the verandah that looked upon the lawns and soldiers' training facilities to the left of it. The sight had changed completely since the evening before. The mist had lifted and tents were adorning the grass. The whole of the grounds was now visible, with a large galley ship not too far in the background, docked in the small bay that the massive rock mountain stood watching. There was a magnificent garden of flowers to the right of the lawns that the two had not noticed when entering the night before. All in all, it appeared stately, fit for a King.

The magnitude of colours on all fronts was in stark contrast to the atmosphere for the "duel": a fight to honour some fallen war hero. The blues, purples, yellows, reds, turquoises, whites, and golds, all made for a cheerful scene. The "field of battle" was centred in front of the verandah's balcony, so as to allow a clear view of the square path of lawn: fifty yards by fifty yards, clear markings for the actual centre of the ground were coloured, with a white circle on the ground in the centre of the field.

People were moving about. Tents held tables where guests were seated in positions providing decent views of the arena. They were a raucous crowd, with many drinks, foods, silver and golden dining ware being laid out before them. Most of the guests were merchants, royals, and soldiers. The servants were making themselves scarcely seen, but still ensuring cups were flowing. There were almost three hundred souls in the whole vicinity.

Ramkus looked straight in front of the verandah where a single tent, much bigger than the rest, was set. It was perched on some wooden scaffolding to give it height and superiority.

'The Royal tent,' Harold said monotonously. 'Our tent is over there,' he pointed to a small tent at the edge of the others, one that did not have its opening directly facing the arena, but directly towards the Royal tent.

There were only a few items in it: some wine, water, wooden seats, a table, a few pieces of bread.

'It is unwholesome to fight on a stomach of much more than the bare necessities,' Harold lectured.

Felipe was pacing in the corner, wishing he had brought his guitar. Ramkus had his instrument, though: his staff; and he was unsure as to the whether it would be allowed, or what his opponent would be fighting with, either. They tent on the other side – most probably Djuayne's tent – was closed from viewing.

'This is a very honourable thing to be involved with,' Harold kept up his attempts to raise the morale. Ramkus was quiet, contemplating in a reserved manner, obviously anxious at what he was to face.

'You'll be fine,' Felipe chimed in, trying to encourage him, feeling sickly himself from his own anxiety.

'Is it the first one to submit, Harold?' Ramkus asked without looking up.

Harold looked perplexed by the question, 'Well, not exactly, it's more like first one to go down.'

'You mean: this is a fight to the death?!' Ramkus was starting to be overcome by the occasion. Felipe looked aghast.

'No, no,' Harold chuckled. 'First one to be knocked out.'

Felipe had stopped his pacing with his arms crossed, and looked to his friend, imagining him to be a rookie soldier about to face his first planned battle. 'Don't worry, Ramkus, you'll be fine,' he repeated without noticing himself. He turned away and frowned to himself.

Where the hell is that internal fire I had with the bandits, or even with the Empire's soldiers who chased us from Kerwood, Ramkus thought. He held his head in his hands. Suddenly the curtain parted. He looked up, seeing a radiant smile beaming down on him: Sophia. He quickly pulled as much of himself together as he could to greet this angelic face. Sophia was joined by another girl behind her: brown, short cropped hair, smaller in stature than Sophia, of a sweet persuasion, but outshone by the immaculate beauty that stood right in front of him.

'I hope we are not intruding,' Sophia said with girlish charm. Ramkus smiled and was about to say *not at all*, but it was Felipe who got the first words in.

'No, Princess, your presence brings blessings of good fortune,' he bowed emphatically. He was once again on his best behaviour. Harold regarded him with curiosity, as if bowing in such a way was an odd practice. Sophia herself was taken aback, but her eyes rested on Ramkus.

'Indeed, a good luck charm you are… Princess,' Ramkus said, eventually, not knowing how *familiar* he could be with the royal. 'Thank you for providing the services of Harold to us.'

'Oh, of course. It would be unjust and cruel not to provide a priest for one of these *honorary tribute fights*,' she quipped like a disapproving teacher may have. 'I am sorry I was unable to get more of an entourage for you. I would be in your camp,' she blushed, 'but it is **not allowed**,' she finished sternly. 'As per some ancient customs we are constantly reminded of.'

Harold looked like he wished to leave, as Felipe began eyeing the girl behind Sophia with interest.

'And who, pray, is this gem?' Felipe grabbed the hand of Giselda. She blushed, but looked deeply into his eyes with a touch of sadness.'

'This is Giselda,' Sophia said.

'Pleased to meet you, *again*, Monsieur Felipe…' Giselda said
reproachfully. Felipe went red and shut his mouth, running
through his memory of when the two may have met before.
There was an awkward silence in the tent that was only
dampened in its volume by the hubbub outside.

'So,' Sophia broke the silence, 'we only desired to wish you
good luck.' She walked towards Ramkus, leant over and
whispered in his ear: 'And to tell you that we will be rooting *for
you*,' she kissed him on the forehead regally, smiled at him
within breathing space, and left.

Looking back as she walked with Giselda in tow, who was
giving an odd, unnerving look to Felipe. Ramkus rose and
watched as they left. Felipe looked into nothingness, whilst
Harold was keeping to himself. Ramkus wondered, in a
romantic daze, if her last words were flowing on from the
playfulness of his conversation the evening before. He woke
himself from such contemplations, realising he had a fight - or
rather a *duel* - to jump into.

'Harold,' he said as he sat down on his stool again, 'can you tell
me what the rules of the duel are? Am I fighting with my staff
against Djuayne, and he a sword that is *blunt*?.. In other words,
my *real question* is: **how do make sure we don't kill each
other?!**' Ramkus's face was of deep concern, as if it had only
occurred to him what the fight may entail.

'Your opponent – Captain of the Kings Guard, Sergeant
Djuayne Antagno - will most likely be fighting with a sword, a
wooden one,' his monotone voice droned on. 'It is each
fighters' choice what they wish to fight with. Djuayne is a
master of many weapons, but the sword is his favoured one. He
will likely choose the long sword, to combat your length with
the staff. That is, if you choose the staff.' Ramkus looked at
Felipe, who was still looking into the ether. Ramkus shrugged,
'I know only the guitar, otherwise.'

Harold did not know if this was a joke, pausing for a moment
before continuing. 'So, you will fight with a staff; and he, a

wooden long sword, most likely.' Harold looked at Ramkus with concern, 'I must warn you that it is said he has attained the legendary status of sword master for the long sword. Whether it is true that there are such masters is still of some conjecture, but he is well known by the Empire as our best swordsman.'

'But it will definitely be made of *wood* for this duel?'

'Well, there is no rule. It *would* be cruel otherwise,' Harold laughed at his use of the word "would", leaving Ramkus confused.

'Sorry, yes, I would be surprised if he fought with anything else, especially when he wants to hurt you. But the sword will not be sharp, so there is unlikely to be a fatality.'

'Great. *Unlikely*, you say,' Ramkus looked away for a moment, then returned a suspicious gaze upon Harold. 'How do you know so much about these fights or duels?' he asked.

'It is imperative of Empirical priests to know about all warfare, our ways are steeped in duels and war like ceremonies. Mind you, we give tributes to war heroes and war gods, therefore it is a natural part of our faith and practice,' Harold answered.

'Sounds like war and conquest permeates everything here,' Ramkus mused.

Harold shrugged, smiling with understanding.

The smell of cinders began to waft into their tent.

'So, the idea is for one of us to knock the other out. That is it? There is no point system, no arena boundary?' Ramkus pressed for confirmation.

'That is the aim, to knock the other out. There is no out of bounds, but you are unlikely to wander too far from the centre of the ground. It has been prepared with markings for the gods and heroes to watch from above,' Harold said.

The scent started to take Ramkus's curiosity, 'What is that smell?' He asked, getting up to open the tent flap and look out. He took in the pomp and ceremony from the tents that surrounded the arena, watching as ashes were being spread over the white markings of the arena's "core".

'They are throwing ashes on the ground to mark the destruction of Proctor's enemies. Probably rabbit ashes, anything that burrows and lives in the earth,' Harold stated as he stood next to Ramkus.

Ramkus was once again overtaken by the multitude of vibrant colours; the inside of the tent had been rather dark - as were his thoughts. He much preferred being out in the sunlight. Looking across to Djuayne's tent, a large group of people were buzzing about it. He regarded the King's tent; the Royal guests were deep in cheerful conversation, drinking, eating, awaiting the main event. Sophia was seated there, standing out from the rest, piercing through all the other objects in Ramkus's sight. She was speaking animatedly with Giselda.

Resigning himself to the obstacle at hand, he turned and looked back into his tent. Felipe was now drinking some wine with his feet up, resting on the bench.

'What do you mean *those who burrow*, Harold?' Ramkus queried.

'Those who lived *within* the earth, such as those who built *into* the Rock – as we call it - that our castle sits upon,' Harold gestured to the bluff standing before them, letting his hand rise until it was pointing to the magnificent castle standing atop. 'Which is why we can only do it on the solid ground, something we can truly *trust* in.'

'The first people, you mean,' Felipe said without any care. 'He means the forest dwellers, the mountain folk; those who "burrow".'

Harold nodded, 'Yes. The first people. Hiding in their hovels, their holes. Not fighting on the solid earth where it is an even ground. Cowering from where those who are righteously in the favour of the Gods will win what is rightfully theirs. The strong shall live.' Harold was resolute in his summation, a hint of charge in his monotone voice: a charge of pride.

'He means that the Empire takes exception to anyone that does not fight *fair* and *even* battles. Those that hide away from

264

conflict. The Empire believes that conquest is the point of life, hence why they are so *soldierly*, so militarily focussed… *Hence why so much of this land Elantra is taken by them*,' Felipe said with the air of depression, touched by a deep thought from long ago.

'Ah, yes, this is true,' Harold continued. 'Conquest is life, if we one day face a stronger force, so be it, that is the way of the world: one side verse the other. We train and fight to remain strong, which is why your opponent is deemed one of the most dangerous fighters by anyone's standards; because *our* standards are so high.'

'Then why do you have so many drunkards and soldiers who are inadequate?' Ramkus asked reproachfully. 'The lands of Elantra, the farms we have travelled through, they are littered with them.

'They are not pure born Empirical soldiers usually; and we have not had a good war to put everything in order. Minds begin to teeter when you don't have to be a tight knit unit with a single focus,' Harold was acting as the voice of reason.

'And you believe all this, Harold?' Felipe asked in a perturbed voice.

Harold, whom had been quite friendly to them so far, was hurt at the accusation; that his beliefs should be considered merely beliefs and not truths. But he was getting on their nerves, and his *Empirical dogma* needed rebutting.

'It is what is it,' he replied curtly.

Ramkus studied Felipe, whom was once again in a little fit. He reminded himself that this priest was in *his* corner, so calmed himself, putting his energised state down to the impending ceremony.

'Excuse him Harold, we have not met the best examples of the Empires men when journeying here…' Ramkus felt sorry for the priest, realising he should probably be feeling sorry for himself instead. *After the explanation of Djuayne being an elite fighter, or* soldier, *I really messed up.*

A gong sounded.

'It is time, Ramkus,' Harold said in his monotone voice, he was attempting to look priestly, as if he was someone who could offer Ramkus some solace. Ramus breathed deeply; Felipe got to his feet, placing a hand on Ramkus's shoulder. 'Good luck, my friend,' he said, trying to muster a smile.

'Right,' Ramkus nodded, taking in one little inhale more. 'Let us begin this *duel*.' He exhaled

They proceeded out the tent with heads held high, Harold leading the small procession; the crowd began to quieten. He trailed along to the front of the King's tent; the members of Royal entourage – including Sophia and Giselda – sat in respectful silence. Ramkus looked to the other side; the masses were still hanging around Djuayne's tent. There was a raucous cheer, as the tall, powerful figure of a man draped in fine leathers, strode boldly out. He was a head taller than anyone, and cast his gaze down upon Ramkus as soon as he spotted him. His followers patted him as he moved through the crowd – without any ecumenical assistance – to his spot.

'Ha, no priest,' Harold commented.

'Is that unusual?' Ramkus asked.

'Highly; very presumptuous, if anything,' Harold replied.

'Of what?' Ramkus pressed.

'Victory.'

Djuayne's shadow crept across the grass, to the front of the King's tent. His consumed, arrogant gaze did not leave Ramkus until he arrived at his position, turning to the King, bowing, turning again to stride to the centre of the makeshift arena. Ramkus watched, maintaining a cool air.

'May you fight divinely,' Harold said, 'time for you to meet one who will probably be revered as a hero himself one day.'

'Uh, thanks,' Ramkus said with a grimace, turning to Felipe, looking for some sort of helpful advice.

'Break a leg,' Felipe said. 'One of his, preferably.'

Ramkus gave a little chuckle at what seemed the inappropriateness of the occasion, but was apt as well. He bowed to the King, taking a deep breath he moved to the centre circle, eyes fixed on his opponent. The fire that he had met before; that unbridled rage and arrogance of the man known as Djuayne Antagno, gave Ramkus chills. Would his skills with the staff be good enough to match a... he looked at Djuayne's weapon: a long Weapon of sorts, but **not wooden!** It was black, of a sort of metal, and Djuayne handled it as if it were mere stick.

'Now you will get your lesson, you idiotic pissant.' Djuayne said with a sneer.

Ramkus studied him as they settled in the white marked centre, poised with their weapons. The gong sounded, and the crowd erupted in a chorus of bloodthirsty cheers.

Djuayne came out heavily, strongly, ferociously; flailing the massive, metallic weapon - and on the first hit, Ramkus found out that it was indeed an imitation long sword.

His strikes were met with the quick, deft parries of Ramkus's staff, who was being edged back all the while. His reactions were the only thing saving him from being hit, as the strength and speed borne by Djuayne would overcome even the most grizzled veteran.

Djuayne changed the strikes power generation from his hands to his hips, deploying more extreme strikes; Ramkus deflected, and spun around to the side of Djuayne.

He did not expect Djuayne's leg to be able to kick at head height, let alone with the heel of the boot from the opposite side of Ramkus. It came from behind in an impressive gymnastic movement!

Ramkus caught the kick on the cheek, his eyes going a little white in vision and wavering – *what am I in this for*?

He was knocked from his balance.

Djuayne used the momentum of his kick, spinning himself around. His sword spinning with his body, smashing Ramkus in the ribs; hard.

The wind was knocked out of him. He was at least glad that the long sword did not have a sharp edge, it was more like that of a large, heavy, baton. Had it been a proper sword, he would have had his stomach sliced open. He was hurting, on his knees, as Djuayne's actions were met with raptured applause.

Ramkus was next met with a crush against his skull; Djuayne's fist knocking him down to the ground.

Down, but not out.

He rolled onto his back as he watched the mountainous man come after him with rage filled eyes. His sword raised to be brought down upon Ramkus's life. Ramkus steeled himself, gripping his staff as the sword came down. He used the staff's momentum to swing himself out of the way, collecting Djuayne's ankles at the same time.

Djuayne let out a cry filled with bestial anger.

Ramkus, up now, spinning his staff, began his attack by bringing his staff down on Djuayne's shoulders; then following with the reverse side against Djuayne's hip; followed by a snap to the stomach.

Djuayne leapt back to defend from further strikes. He shook his head, glaring and baring his teeth; his eyes bloodshot, enraged by the challenge.

Ramkus was out of breath, trying to control his movements, but he had very little time.

The angered behemoth that was barely a man, came back with a vengeance. Djuayne sensed a bewilderment in the crowd that such a man as he should, perhaps, lose.

This spurred him into a fit of laughter, as he burst with haste into an electrified, frenzied attack. Ramkus moved back, and back, and back, deflecting the onslaught. He had to do something, he was parrying left and right, dodging strikes from above, strikes to his stomach. *This man is a demon!*

Scrapes and bruises were being picked up by each fighter, but they were insignificant in slowing the immense pace set between them.

Ramkus had to stop Djuayne before he allowed him an opportunity to do another spurious hit.

Too late, Djuayne feigned a downward attack, moving in, close to Ramkus, kneeing him in the ribs. Ramkus's head came down, and he was met by an uppercut from Djuayne's off hand, then a strike from the sword hand to his temple.

He lurched back, barely aware that his staggered movements had luckily moved him out of the way of a downward strike from Djuayne's sword.

He was brought to his senses, getting in close to Djuayne himself this time, deflecting a strike as his kicked Djuayne in the hip; then spinning, allowed his staff to collect Djuayne's mid-section.

The staff followed, wrapped around Djuayne as Ramkus grabbed the other end and struck into Djuayne with his knee.

Djuayne gave out a yelp, throwing his arm out, hitting Ramkus in the head and away from him.

He lent down over his feet eyes agape at the insult. Ramkus could have attacked him from behind in that instant, but could not bring himself to do it. Instead, he moved to Djuayne's side, getting ready to kick him.

As his foot came in, Djuayne grabbed it, lunging at Ramkus, collecting his whole body and smashing him into the ground with a massive thud.

The earth rolled as Djuayne threw an elbow to the head of the struggling Ramkus.

He came in with another elbow, as Ramkus rolled from under the huge mass that had fallen upon him in the throw. He attempted to get an elbow hit on Djuayne himself, following it with a punch which appeared more effective due to Djuayne's reach.

He had a ringing in his ears, and felt little - other than a sickly, hurling sense. His desperate punches connected with Djuayne's face, bloodying his nose; he jumped back off Ramkus, grabbing for his sword, retrieving it whilst in the pits of disgust at this *Guardian* daring to draw blood from him.

Ramkus, for all that he could do, got to his feet, hunching over, holding his staff, attempting to ready himself once more. The agony of the pain was beginning to numb, but his muscles and bones would not move freely. He could not hear the crowd anymore, it was silent apart from a small ringing.

Djuayne's next rage driven assault began again, but this time - as he feigned another attack from on top – he jumped to Ramkus side, and kicked Ramkus's left knee with his heel.

The knee crumpled as Djuayne looked to bring his sword down on Ramkus's side, but instead, he feigned and smashed the sword into Ramkus's knee again.

It gave way completely, with Ramkus ending up on the ground, writhing in agony.

He looked up into eyes of hatred; the bludgeoning sword came next. And that was all he remembered.

The crowd was silent for a long moment, but the cheers that eventually rang out were deafening. The victor, the unbeatable Djuayne Antagno, had conquered a Guardian! Sophia looked away, overcome by helplessness for the gallant Ramkus; feeling far greater desires for him all at once. Giselda comforted her as best she could, careful not to draw attention to themselves. It did not matter though, the crowd – and Royal Court - was on the field, celebrating their champion. The King on his feet, applauding; Silque was rubbing his hands together with a dreadful smile growing across his face. Felipe and Harold were tending to the limp body of the Guardian, shooing away the crowd that had a total disregard for the man lying there. The only one who was watching the two men attempting to carry

Ramkus to safety, was the one who had bested him. *This is not the end*, Djuayne hoped.

Chapter XI

Ramkus opened his eyes; they rolled from the back of his head. There was an odd noise from wherever he was, or from whomever was there. He was confused and in a state of ignorance to his predicament. His eyes focussed on the crowd moving about him. Faces all looking down upon him as they spoke, yelled, cried – he couldn't tell. The roof was of an ochre colour, and he was lying down staring straight at it: that much he knew. He closed his eyes, the body started to wake itself, however, he could barely move it. Opening his eyes again, focussing on what he could. A face on his left he recognised: Harold. He gestured to another face he knew: Felipe. He smiled and spoke some words Ramkus could not make out. There was a look of agony, of fear. A man to his right with spectacles and a clean white garb lent down and gave Ramkus a hard slap. 'Wake up!' the man said.

'No need to rattle his brain any further!' Felipe yelled across Ramkus's body at this man.

'Are you a surgeon, *dear bard*?' the man shot back. 'No, didn't think so. I know what I'm doing.'

As much as this man looked like a butcher to Ramkus, he felt a confident arrogance permeating from him. The steadfastness in his treatment of his battered body: he was trustworthy… This was a hope from Ramkus, more than anything else. "Let him be bandaged up and rested", he wished the man would say.

'Now, now, *Guardian*, think back, if you can, to a fight you may have had, yes? Yes, well, it looks like your knee has been quite damaged up. Very horrific, never seen anything like it, so best thing I can do is operate.'

'No surgery needed, let me just cut it off. I'm sure he'd prefer that.' a nasty voice, full of hubris and gloating, yelled from somewhere near the foot of the – *table?* Ramkus queried to himself as to what exactly he was lying upon. No, it was more rather a large type of rock; *hard as the battered peak of a mountain* – his head was swimming. Djuayne walked up to the foot of this slab of rock, twirling Ramkus's staff around, smiling – nay, beaming – he pulled out a knife from his back and came close to Ramkus's knee. Eyes closed shut, full of hate, of rage, of power, of arrogance; how dare he be challenged by this *Guardian*. Ramkus squirmed as best he could, but his muscles would not allow it.

He looked to his companions on his left; they had moved away in fear. But not too quickly, as Djuayne, the monstrosity of a man, a gargantuan mass of power, came at them with the look of madness.

'Get away from him you brute!' a feminine voice cried out, a voice that seemed hurt: Sophia. She came at Djuayne from the foot of the rock bed also.

Djuayne looked to threaten her, moving in to give her a slap. She stood with determination, to meet whatever fate; but a poniard was unsheathed silently, aimed at the bowel of this bully.

'You touch her, and you will be killed,' Giselda said in a low, cold voice.

'What is going on here? Djuayne?!' A voice of authority. Djuayne looked with trained, tamed eyes; but his body was ready to unleash. He moved away as Ramkus caught a glimpse of the King, followed by Poncho and Silque in tow.

'Don't do anything stupid,' Poncho, said as he lifted his sword two inches out of its sheath; his point being made.

Djuayne moved without care, past Giselda's poniard. He walked up to Poncho, raising his arms after sliding the knife back into its spot at the back of his belt. He left without a word. Ramkus had strained his whole body to see these events - still not enough to make much sense of it all. Sophia started panting; Harold and Felipe looked at each other; the surgeon cracked his hands in Ramkus's face without any bedside manner.

Ramkus's eyes rested on Sophia, as he drifted into a slumber.

Silque smiled: the Guardian was falling into his devious plans.

*He had not dreamed when knocked out, merely woke up in agony. This subsided, and he was in a restless flight; a blindness had enveloped him, a fire shone in the distance. He walked; no, did he? Was he swimming in these murky depths? A voice of maddened reason hummed his own ambition to him: of vengeance, revenge for something that had happened. But what had happened; where was he. He approached the fire, or did it approach him in this night? - If it was a night. He was alone, was he not? The fire had a warmth, a voice: "**I am your only friend**". It was a voice he knew, had been with him since the dawn of time, the day when everything came into existence. Reality was his! A face appeared behind the orange glow, it was on fire! No; it was simply a flame in the void, in the riven of time and space. The clink of the cosmos was little more than this heat, this energy. "**Follow me!**" the voice said, the face: bold, of power, of cunning, of energy, of sadistic intent. "**I will lead!**" it said, laughing maniacally. Ramkus wanted to reply, but he had not the thought of what to say. Moving towards the fire, facing this demon within. "**You will succumb, there is no choice.**"*
Choice? I am being given a choice? I make my own choices! The suggestion otherwise angered him. His devil continued to laugh as he lunged through the flame to meet him.

He awoke in a cold sweat. Sheets, soft sheets, covered his body. He could still barely move his muscles, sitting up after great strain. A breeze was drifting through a large window, the wind picking up the thin curtains in its force, gliding across his well shaven face – *no more mutton chops*. The moon shone through a cloudless velvet, navy sky. The sounds of the night were the only embrace of another's existence. He looked down at his legs, lifting the sheets as best he could to reveal the shattered limbs. He could barely feel them. The moons glow revealed his left leg heavily wrapped in a cast. A canister was attached to the leg through a small hole in the wrapping, right into the knee. He could not feel the leg at all, but he realised the bandage as still being flexible, rather than a proper cast. *How do I even have the knowledge of what a cast is?* The thoughts wandered, he was beginning to fade again, especially as he became privy to some of the excessive bleeding his leg had made within the sheets. He leant back, knowing answers to his questions were well out of his grasp. He felt he had made an horrendous mistake: that whatever journey he was on, he had messed it up. Would he even get to where he was meant to be? He couldn't even move now, how was he going to get away? Where on earth was he? He began to pant, looking around at the calm, serene surrounding. A water jug was within his grasping distance. He grabbed it, deciding to drink, to calm himself. It did so, and his eyes became leaden again, drifting back into a restless sleep. Until he heard the words: "Hush, hush", and the soft embrace of another human's touch, one of love, one of compassion and caring. One that lead him away from his struggles, his muddled dreams, his cold chills; off to a light rest where he felt nothing but the tender touch of sweet existence.

'You're awake!' a friendly bard-like voice sang out as Ramkus opened his eyes. He took in a gaily moving figure. 'Although, I think you may have wet the bed. You stink of urine.' It was – but naturally - Felipe.

His vision came to. He was in the same room from the night before, although sunlight was piercing heavily through the windows. Ramkus felt its rays, he also felt the sheets. They *were* wet… but from sweat, he deduced. He tried to sit up, Felipe assisted him by bringing some pillows to place behind his back. He grabbed the jug of water and poured Ramkus a glass.

'You look awful. Slept poorly I imagine,' Felipe said without concern.

Ramkus could not be bothered thinking of a witty retort, 'I guess so.' He tried to move his leg around, his good one at least.

'You were out for three days! And not a good slumber, mind you.' Felipe's gaze became sympathetic.

Ramkus looked at him. If he really wanted to, he could have made a questioning look, but it was too much effort for now. 'Three days?' he croaked instead, giving Felipe his empty glass of water to refill.

'Three days... you looked like you were in a fever. Tossing and turning as best you could. Sweating - the cold clammy type. The only time you calmed down was when I played a ballad... well, not really, that seemed to agitate you a little, as if you wanted to get up and play with me. At least that's how I took it. Truth be told, the times you were at peace were when a certain admirer of yours was here, holding you. I have never seen a girl do that for a man she hardly knew, whose sweat looked sickly.'

Ramkus blinked a few times, 'Sophia,' he murmured, the warmth of her embrace coming back to him. He remembered another warmth, one in a deep darkness, and a voice there. 'Sophia was here?' He asked Felipe after a time; Felipe was busy admiring the view.

'Oh, yes, came quite often. Seems the King has also taken a liking to you too. He has been asking for updates on your progress,' Felipe replied nonchalantly.

A knock came at the door, opening. A man in a white cloak walked in. 'Ah, you are back with the living.' It was the surgeon. 'How do we feel?'

Ramkus rubbed his eyes, 'Awful,' he wasn't sure he liked this surgeon or not – he was still questioning whether the procedure done on his immobile leg was really necessary.

'Ah, well, this may make it a bit worse... But it is only going to make you feel better,' the surgeon replied.

Ramkus's energy seemed to regather itself – weakly – he gave the surgeon a reproachful look. The surgeon did not notice: he was busying himself with his work. Lifting the sheets where the dark blood had clotted for days, protecting the wound.

'Here, place this in your mouth,' the surgeon ordered, placing a small piece of wood in Ramkus's mouth. 'Should be quick. Would have done it a few days ago, but we need you to be awake so your body didn't go into shock.'

Ramkus felt a sudden pulsating, squirming feeling through his knee, as if a tendon was being wrenched out of it. The seconds of this pain slowed in relative time; this odd conjecture of a twisted, sickly feeling continued; it was almost unbearable. Felipe watched on.

'It's out. The blood-pump. Used to relieve the internal bleeding.' The surgeon showed him the canister where blood had drained into from the tube that had just been pulled through his knee, left within the operation site since the operation.

Ramkus's stomach churned, he felt like throwing up, but there was only water in his stomach, and that was being released through his pores. The whole feeling of the tube being dragged through the tender knee continued as a phantom feeling. The muscles and nerves still squirmed.

'Now, let us see about the wrapping,' the surgeon drew out his words slowly, precisely, in the same methodical process as he undid the actual wrappings that were keeping Ramkus knee in a firm position. In doing so, the leg moved about, stretching in places that healing had begun: odd, painful, suggestions of crippling effects that were dormant before, now awoken.

'Looks like you have quite a superior healing quality about you. It is much better than expected,' the surgeon said as he focussed on the knee. Felipe was wide eyed, trying not to look, but his curiosity failed him.

'Lucky you have that staff, should be very useful to walk around with.' The surgeon looked to the corner on Ramkus's side: there stood his sturdy Guardian's staff.

Purpose came back to Ramkus upon seeing it; a renewed sense of his desire: to become what he was meant to be. This was to be a lesson, an obstacle to overcome. The pain was momentary, his journey lay ahead.

'How long till I will be able to get back on the road?' Ramkus asked.

The surgeon ogled him behind his spectacles, 'Hasty, are we? I shall not let you leave for a few weeks. You need to regain flexibility, build strength. Maybe a few months in fact.'

Ramkus eyes widened; a steely determination to get better *much sooner*, came over him. An anger at his circumstances started to build. It rose towards his opponent: Djuayne; and then he remembered he was in this situation at Felipe's behest to visit to the Summer Palace in the first place. His eyes, full of fire, rested on Felipe who understood straight away he was being blamed for the delay. He returned a guilty expression. The surgeon looked between the two, aware of a tension that had suddenly arisen.

'And with that, I will take my leave. I will see you again, soon.' The surgeon scuttled off, closing the door as Ramkus – blood pulsing, making him feel faint but psychotic – was about to unleash a torrent of abuse toward Felipe. But the door opened again, and a bright smiling face entered.

'Ramkus! You're awake!' Sophia ran to his side, studying him for a while, almost forgetting her stately position. Still, she bent down and hugged him. Her face then came in front of him, as her long blonde hair shielded the view of the room he may have had – save that he could not take his eyes off her in any case. She pulled back… Giselda had entered the room, quietly, looking at Ramkus before her eyes met Felipe. Felipe became like stone.

Although Ramkus digested this odd predicament between Felipe and Giselda, he did not process it.

'I am so happy you are awake. Finally! You slept horribly. How are you feeling?' Sophia asked with concern.

'A lot better now, thank you.' Ramkus's mood lifted, no longer full of anger.

'The surgeon said it may be quite a while before you get your strength back. You are in a fortuitous position by being here, as we have the most advanced of surgical procedures as well as all sorts of training facilities that can assist in your recovery. I can help you as well, of course,' Sophia blurted out, blushing in the process. She regained her composure, realising he obsession with a man she had only briefly met a few days ago was coming on a little thick. She was letting her guard down, but she could not help it, she wanted to.

'Thank you,' Ramkus smiled, 'it would be good to have a guide around the castle. Especially if I am unable to get back on the road for a fair while. The quicker the better, though.'

His words seemed to cut through some dream, an illusion of sorts. Reality hit Sophia, and she retreated into herself, presenting the girl of the night of the banquet again. More reserved and intelligent in her stature.

'Very well,' she said. 'We shall see how quickly we can get you back on the road.' The suggestion that this was some sort of a game came out on the wisp of her words; a sentiment that Ramkus knew would present challenges for him. But he was not in the mood to overthink things. He was tired, and hungry.

The door opened again, causing everyone to turn. Whom should enter, but the taunting adversary, chewing on a piece of meat, he held the protruding bone as if it were a weapon.

'Oh, good to see you awake, Ramkus,' Djuayne taunted as he approached the small crowd.

'Djuayne, why are you here?' Giselda said. 'Can't you see he needs rest, not some nasty, aggressive brute whom has already beaten him?'

Djuayne stared at her with repugnance. 'I could ask the same of any of you. I should especially like to ask that question of the Princess.' His head lurched as his body followed in the direction of the Sophia. His massive figure threatening the air of the whole room. The energy that was felt was an off-putting stimulus; agitated by the contempt this man still held for Ramkus. He bent his head in a crooked manner, coming closer to Ramkus, sitting on the bed.

'How's the knee?' He asked smugly, resting his hand on it, leaning closer to Ramkus, chewing on the meat he held in front of his face.

Pain shot through the joint; areas that did not want to be touched - let alone resting on a bed – felt compressed as if in a vice; fire bubbling underneath the skin, in the muscles. Agony came about in his face, but he strengthened, resolving himself to show his power and control; breathing heavily, his face reddened. Djuayne was coming in too close; the pain was becoming too much, Ramkus snapped and struck out in an attempt for relief. A strike that hit Djuayne flat on the nose. He fell backwards, off Ramkus's knee, giving some respite to the pain. Djuayne - surprised, and shaken from the indignation – got up and threw the bone of meat at Ramkus, hitting him in the already faint and sore head. Djuayne readied to pounce on the bed-ridden man, but a sword was held at his throat.

'Get out,' Giselda commanded, holding her poniard at him. Djuayne, knowing he had pushed his luck, stood up slowly, glaring at Giselda. Arrogantly shrugging after a few moments, he walked away, stopping before the door, he turned. 'Princess, I would seriously suggest you reconsider your choice in such lowly *hand maidens*… as well as your, *allegiances*.' He strutted out the door, slamming it shut.

Ramkus felt his hand, facial makeup was on it.

Sophia saw him scanning the powder. 'Hah, you did get him quite good in the bout. He has bruising and cuts on his face from some of the hits. He is keeping it hidden as best he can.'

'I think you have made him even angrier than he need be,' Giselda trailed off in her own thoughts.

Felipe was shaking his head, his eyes reddening, 'I am sorry Ramkus. I did not know this would happen.'

Everyone turned to the man whom had been a gargoyle before
then.

Ramkus, faint in his head, but still hanging on before the
weakness and weariness took him, nodded softly. 'It is fine
Felipe. But could you please get me something to eat, I am
really hungry.'

XXX

It was decided the best course of action for Ramkus to get back
on his feet would be essentially that: get him on his feet. After
Giselda and Sophia took their leave, Felipe escorted Ramkus –
after being provided with a pair of wooden crutches – to a small
dining hall close to the main kitchen. The King had ordered the
two wanderers be given free rein over the palace, and that they
be provided with anything they requested. Ramkus thought little
of it; he was in a rather deranged state. It was also the first
opportunity he had spent any significant time in a single place.
He was - in what could easily be considered – the lap of the
Gods, with all food and all comforts he could want at his
disposal – save that he was seemingly incapacitated and
suffering from a malaise of troubling thoughts. He put that aside
for the moment, as there was no escape from this palatial life…
for now.

Felipe on the other hand was feeling a deep guilt for what he
now recognised were his selfish actions. Every knock, every hit
that Ramkus had taken on that small battlefield, he had also felt.
He was, for the first time in a very long time, reconsidering his
life choices. This was brought on not only from Ramkus's
predicament, but also from a little seed his forefathers had lain.
He *was* one of the first people; although he did not wish to
recognise himself as such very often. Though, seeing one of his
kinsman - as a subservient handmaiden no less - one whom he
had relations with long ago; it overwhelmed him. It was a kick
in the stomach he was not expecting. To see, to feel his

heritage, his people, succumbing to forces that had always been so bitter in their conquests. Forces that treated his people with contempt and held a lack of respect for these lands and his people's role within it. He needed to know *she* was doing this out of choice, not fear.

The chef was on standby for the two, Felipe had requested a small feast worth of food, for the *man who had stood up to a giant*. Fish, crayfish, meats, vegetables, followed by fruits and cheeses, were brought into the private dining hall. The table could seat a dozen or so. It had an old oak scent, with a draped table cloth adorned with candles, jugs of wine which were silver and embroidered. No natural light came in, but a breeze from the kitchen was felt every time the door was opened. On the wall fine art was hung, mostly of natural settings, otherwise of Empirical soldiers in heroic poses. It did not make an impression on either of the adventurers, as Ramkus gorged on food for the first time in three days, and Felipe was deep in his thoughts. The chef was pleased to bring out his delicious works for the them, one of the only opportunities that he had to take any recognition for his handy work. Small conversation was made with him, as he took a liking to the ferocious appetite of Ramkus, and the charming sounds of the master Bard.

When Ramkus felt himself content, he rested back in his chair. His poorly leg begin kept off the ground by a tuffet underneath the table which he rested his good right leg on also. He felt a natural state of energy start to burn through, and his memory of the vicious hits started to come back to him; the sound of the crowd; the feel of his staff connecting with his opponent's blunt, metallic weapon in his powerful strikes.

'What was Djuayne using as a weapon?' Ramkus suddenly asked. 'He was meant to be using a wooden sword, wasn't he?' Felipe looked up at the face of Ramkus: *a man searching his thoughts rather than dealing with them,* Felipe considered to himself. He envied this, but it brought now a little joy that his friend wasn't suffering. 'He was, I think - or at least that is what we anticipated. According to that Harold fellow, it was a *blunt* object that was to be used. One that could not kill.'

'What the hell was he using then, a longsword that was blunt?'

'It looked like it. To tell you the truth, I did not actually see it. Everyone was focussed on the way in which you two dealt damaging blows and defended with lightning speed. It was all a blur.'

'I wish it were a blur, I can remember every hit now,' Ramkus began playing with the flame of on one of the table candles.

'I'm really sorry, Ramkus. I did not mean to put you in this situation,' Felipe leant towards the Guardian.

'Ha, don't worry Felipe. At least not now, wait until I have regained my senses. I still can't believe that kick Djuayne did: behind himself, head height, with his heel! That was not natural,' Ramkus stated in disbelief.

'Most of the movements did not seem possible. I am amazed you lasted so long. It really says something of your natural ability as a Guardian. You haven't even been trained!'

Ramkus continued to stare into the candle and the faint smoke that lifted from it. *'Guardian,'* Ramkus said to himself without emotion. He rummaged through the memories he had of the days before; his dreams; his inner demon who claimed he was his only friend.

He reminisced of the night and its velvet warmth whilst he lay awake from the sordid dreams, thirsty, confused. Of the next long slumber, and the soft voice that sang to him to come back to, back to her.

He turned to Felipe who was looking at the high ceiling that was in a pressed arch with an inverted spire dropping from the top. The whole of it was the colour and texture of limestone.

'Were you often in my room? I mean, I awoke and you were there. That was not pure coincidence, was it.'

Felipe frowned. 'Indeed, I felt obliged to. Actually, a few people had visited you. I made sure none of that Djuayne type. Sophia was a regular as I have said, sometimes with or without

Giselda…' Felipe paused for a second. 'Harold visited a few times for some sort of "blessings": it consisted of throwing some water on you and smoking out the place. The surgeon came, obviously. Actually, Poncho visited once, that was funny. I don't think he expected anyone else in there, not that he was going to hurt you or anything. I think he was pleased you gave Djuayne a few good hits,' he stopped.

'That was all?'

'Yes, that is all that I saw. You expected more? Or you think someone else came?'

'I just get the sense, someone may have. Just a feeling. Anyway, what is next?'

'I was told there are some chambers you can use to get you strength back. In the meantime, we enjoy ourselves,' Felipe shrugged.

Ramkus nodded, 'I see,' he replied. He looked around the "small" dining hall, scrutinising its features. 'It has been an odd adventure so far. Still a long way to go as well.'

Felipe nodded, guarding himself from any queries as to his plan. They were not forthcoming. He knew Ramkus could sense his trepidation, and being of the friendly sort - to him at least – he would not press further. Not yet, anyway.

'I guess I could teach you a few moves when I am able to start moving a little bit better, or rather, am able to stand unassisted,' Ramkus jested.

Felipe smiled, 'I think it is more the time for *you* to be trained as a bard. In fact, this is the best opportunity yet!'

They finished up, thanking the chef for their meal. He had asked them to come by any time, and they certainly delighted in such a request. Felipe led the way – assisting with an arm when required - through the corridors and cloisters that were mostly on the outside of the construct, allowing sublime light in, as well as views of the moving forests that abounded from the Rock. It seemed all their views were of this side of the castle, none of the sea itself. That was until Felipe - after what seemed like a long

walk to the crippled Guardian as he hobbled on his crutches –
took him to a rooftop garden. Trees in massive pots were placed
around the edges, and a huge oak tree growing within the
middle, which under its branches maintained a well curated area
of grass.

'What a sight, eh?' Felipe said. 'Now this is where
performances from bards should take place!'

Seats were spread amongst the potted trees and grass strip that
lay down the centre, up to the oak. The sun was at its midday
peak, a clear sky, only a few specks of cloud. Ramkus was in
awe of the garden. He was also surprised that no one else was
about.

'Where is everyone?' he asked.

'That I am not sure. I have seen scarcely another soul up here,
maybe it is actually a sacred spot for them?' Felipe chuckled,
'Then again, how much is sacred to *these* folk. Fighting and
conquest, not much else.'

'Yet they are able to make beautiful gardens like this,' Ramkus
gestured with his hand, carrying it out to a view of the other side
of the castle which he had not seen: the sea. He took a breath
and hobbled over to take it in. The glistening form of the waves,
rolling, crashing; the smell of salty water. The sea continued on
into eternity, reflecting the sunlight as a vast plane to be
wandered. In there was a freedom that he had felt once. One
that now felt an age ago. Out there lay something he wished to
see. One day, when he was given the chance to wander this
world, he would see those islands. *Islands, like the isles of
Montreyer: the ones of Sigilund's home.* Thoughts of the poor
girl flooded back to him. She was probably long gone now, who
knows where. He stayed standing, searching the ocean afar.
Looking down to see a few massive ships docked at the small
harbour that the grass of the gardens below connected to. He
looked back behind to Felipe, his gaze immediately falling upon
the two mountains and the ridge to where he was meant to go.

He was torn between the two sights. Where he knew he *must* go, and the other that he *wanted* to.

'Beautiful sight, isn't it,' Felipe said.

'It is. *Much to explore*,' he replied softly. He looked at his knee, 'But not for now.'

'You'll get there soon enough, Ramkus. Do not rush off to the ends of the world too quickly. Life is a lot larger than that.' He gave Ramkus a wink, and smiled.

Ramkus returned it, but held the curious notion that Felipe was withholding some age-old wisdom that one can only learn for themselves. He scrutinised the sea again, then the mountains and the forests that moved and extended their reach below. He may have lost the fight, but he was not defeated.

He could never be defeated.

Chapter XII

Time moved slowly in these halls. The two men made the best of the situation, with the many festive events being held to mark the end of the height of the summer contributing to their enjoyable stay. Although guests came and went, the two were undisturbed, roaming the chambers laid bare of anyone - save for servants and guardsmen whom they grew accustomed to seeing, almost forgetting such their presence. Food was plentiful and they were left to come and go as they pleased from the castle to the gardens… that is, if Ramkus dared put himself in the position of climbing down the innards of the Rock that the castle was perched upon. Djuayne was nowhere to be seen, sent on some mission or other according to the grunts of the guardsmen when pressed by Felipe. They were at ease.

'Oh, that was another time that happened!' Felipe howled over his soup to a baroness from some far-off region. The gigantic dining hall was alight with frivolity, of laughs, music, drink and food. The King perched himself in the middle. He did enjoy moving about the table, speaking to his subjects – or rather, compatriots. He had a kindly disposition for a king and appeared to take his official position in his stride. All in all, he seemed a good king, albeit, he held counsel with the duplicitous Silque. These were Ramkus's observations as he rolled back in his comfortable chair, listening to Sophia tell him of the people who were present.

'The people clothed with purple sashes have come from a landlocked principality. They make good wine, but not much else,' Sophia recited as if she was re-enacting lessons that had been taught by a teacher, including the little asides.

Ramkus peered across the large room at the table lined across the other side. All the long tables connected at their end, making up three sides. Performers would come into the middle at times, and the chef – very proud of himself – was able to enter the little area to present the crème de la crème of the meal.

'Not that exciting, but important to know,' Sophia continued, noticing Ramkus's attention waning. His eyes traced along the other side of the three-parted table, over the King's table, then directly into Sophia's grey blue gaze. Her hair was down across her shoulders, glistening with the blaring, brightly lit candles. He nodded, smiling, pleasantly occupied by the setting. He was making his best effort to see the light of the situation, which meant drinking and eating. He was also pleased to be in Sophia's presence.

A faint burning sensation began to arise in his foot that was upon a tuffet. It began to build, till he wanted to get up.

'Ha! Got you!' Felipe arose from up in front of Ramkus in the open area in the middle. He was holding a feather, stealing a wink at Sophia. 'How are you enjoying this evening, Princess?' he quipped with charm.

Sophia gave him a curt look. 'It *was* going quite well.'

'Well, it could get a little more *interesting* a bit later. *If you know what I mean…*' Felipe gave a wink

'Monsieur Felipe, you are incorrigible,' Sophia threw her head back, 'and I shall take my leave. I'll be back in a moment, Ramkus.'

Ramkus nodded, 'I'll be here, where I can't hobble off without making people laugh and laugh.'

'Hmm, that may be quite an interesting sight to compete against,' Felipe said in consideration. He then directed his attention to Sophia, 'I'll be performing some pieces tonight, don't go too far,' Felipe imparted, raising his eyebrows.

Sophia shook her head, then looked at Ramkus, patting him on the arm as she got up to leave them.

When she had gone, Felipe slipped under the table and took her position. 'You seem to have really perked up, Felipe,' Ramkus said.

'Aye,' Felipe nodded to himself, pleasant in thought, 'I think I needed to get back to performing. It's what I do, it is what makes me happy.'

'Why must you torment the Princess with your manner, though?' Ramkus asked.

'Are you serious my boy? I do it for you!'

Ramkus stared at him, questioningly.

'Do you not see how she works for your attention when approached by another person?' He rolled his eyes, 'Looks like it is back to lessons about the *finer points of life* for you!'

'No, I get it, it's just…'

Felipe waited for Ramkus to continue to search for his answer.

'I don't know if I want to,' Ramkus finished.

'What do you mean? She is most definitely attracted to you. She wants you to show her some affection. It is simple.'

'How is it simple? This is the **Princess**! And what happens to my journey? What happens to my duty, my life? I cannot help but remind myself that I am meant to be a Guardian, Felipe. Not someone *attached* to the Empire.'

'Ah,' Felipe said reproachfully. He began to realise the magnitude of such a decision.

'This type of relationship would be permanent, something I could not escape. This is not for me, Felipe,' Ramkus explained dejectedly.

'What is to say it is permanent, Ramkus? Who is to say your journey truly is as a Guardian even? You don't even know what a girl like Sophia would want.'

Ramkus turned, facing the other side of the banquet hall table; the guests were in hysterics at something the King – who had slowly been making his way around the room, greeting everyone – had said with a beaming smile. Ramkus looked back to the bard who was also watching, mouth smiling wide.

Released from the heaviness of his meanderings, he changed the topic.

'Indeed, your mood has changed, Felipe.'

'This is not the worst place to be, my dear Ramkus. I'll let you find that out for yourself. If you'll excuse me.' Felipe got up and grabbed his guitar that had been propped up on the other side. He looked at his friend. 'Don't be so determined to dismiss one direction without even exploring the path.' Felipe turned and marched up to the King. He had been getting close to those whom he needed to; after fighting his conscience off and doing what came naturally - entertaining people and performing – he did not miss a beat in his step.

Ramkus took up his cup, and drank the rich, full-bodied red wine. He rested back and watched his friend who was all smiles as he got ready to perform.

An odd man, he thought to himself, *a wise one at times, and one who plays the fool the next.*

XXX

The heat from the waters relaxed all his muscles. Ramkus gave himself over to the calming steams and vapours of the pool. Felipe emerged in the middle, after having submerged with an elegant dive.

'Oh, is that not the greatest!' Felipe yelled to the high vaulted ceiling which held small droplets of condensation, not quite ready to fall as it was still too warm an atmosphere. Large braziers were alight at the corners of the pool; heavy intoxicating scents burning from them. They provided no smoke, but burnt with vigour. Supposedly herbs with healing properties had been thrown in, a medicament prescribed by the surgeon. It seemed more a "cleansing" tool, one which the Empire's priests would use - that little something that would help *heal* one within the faith. Still, it smelt pleasant, and relaxed Ramkus as he sat on the ledge of the pool, steadying himself into one of his "prescribed" exercises to gain strength in his withering leg. He observed the well-lit pool hall: soldiers stood at the doors, keeping guard – or watch; Ramkus could not tell. There seemed to be many hallways in these quarters, and they sounded as if they lead to other pool halls and training facilities. They were supposed to be private - for the nobility - but were seemingly seldom used, and therefore offered to the "guests" with insistence. Felipe submerged and re-emerged, his long, black, curled hair now straight and dripping, held back. He wiped the water from his eyes.

'So, how does it feel? Can you move it a bit better?'

Ramkus tried moving the leg in the waters without resistance.

'It does feel a little better,' Ramkus declared, as he started massaging it.

'Good. Do you even know exactly what they did to it?' Felipe enquired as Ramkus decided it was his time to start swimming off into the waters.

'Not really, the surgeon has not gone into too much detail during his brief visits. He seems to be purely interested in admiring his own handiwork without consultation with the *actual patient,*' Ramkus yelled back at Felipe whilst he glided through the heavenly waters on his back. 'He did tell me what he has done – in technical, medical terms - and how I am able to get it into the best shape possible with exercises. Feels like he may have cleaned up some broken or chipped bone, though,'. He began to kick with the "bad" leg, 'Now it is starting to feel good.'

'Ah,' Felipe called back, beginning to rest upon the ledge. He tried not to sprawl himself out too much, for they were swimming in the usual swimming garments of the Empire: *nothing*... It would also be a little rude to make himself *too* comfortable in front of Ramkus. 'What else has he got you doing?' Felipe yelled across the hall.

Ramkus returned to the ledge after a few moments of kicking. 'Simple exercises, then I get to do some proper training. Not exactly sure what that entails.' He rested back along the ledge once he reached it, fiddling around with the leg, making sure he knew the particulars of his body, and had survived the swim.

'Hmm. They do seem to be making an extreme effort with you. I wonder *why*?' Felipe muttered, alluding to other carnal matters.

'Why must you press the issue. Once I am able to, I am back on my way. Have they tried to get *you* to convince me otherwise?' Ramkus shot back.

'Hah! No.' Felipe sighed, 'Perhaps I have just seen so much of the world to know when a great situation has arisen.'

'But it is not mine!' Ramkus decried once more.

There was clank of footsteps, and a clink of metal as the heavily armoured Royal Guards changed over.

'Must need to swap over a lot in here, since it is so hot,' Felipe said nonchalantly, changing the topic with the first chance he could.

Ramkus shook his head. 'By the way,' he cocked his head up, 'what is the situation between you and Giselda? You seem *interested*.'

Felipe gave a reproachful, startled look. 'Nothing. There is no situation,' he scowled, submerging himself back into the waters.

XXX

'I like what I see Silque,' the King whispered to his advisor from his chair at the head of the banquet table. 'You may have really come up with something.' The King was admiring his daughter talking to the Guardian; he was intrigued by the man.

'Thank you, my liege,' Silque replied subserviently.

'I daresay we were lucky that this lad was actually attractive to her. Laying the intrigue in front of her worked a treat. I will grant you that.'

The dinner this evening was a much smaller affair. Held in a cosier dining hall, with a fire place on one end. The light was dimmer in this room than others, which allowed the faint shadows to take flight on the walls that surrounded.

'Yes, my liege. But we must not forget, it is he who we needs to... *come to his senses*,' Silque hissed.

'Well, it does appear the feelings are mutual on the *attraction* front, at least. Good we have sat them together.'

'Your majesty,' Felipe the bard was approaching, 'may I provide some entertainment before the main feast?'

The King of the Ronato family clasped his hands together with a tremendous show of glee.

'But of course! Proceed!' he roared with enthusiasm.

'Something playful, good bard?'

Felipe nodded, understanding the exact sort of music the King requested. He looked towards his companion and his new *fancy*, deep in their conversation; noting this was also the focus for the King tonight. There were others in the hall, mostly those close to the Royal family, serving some vital purposes to his majesty. Eyes looked up from their conversations, as Felipe began to play a song on the guitar with no lyrics, so that conversations could continue away without danger of complete interruption.

'I shall take you, once you are able,' Sophia said. A blue star on her chest raised up and down, sparkling in the fires prominent glow. Her eyes shimmering as she spoke to Ramkus.

'I would like that. Still, a lot more work to go through, I fear.' He knew he could easily fall for her, and to be sat next to her so often was torture at times; holding himself back. For what reason, though? What exactly was this *Guardian life* he was meant to lead. Somehow, he remained focussed, held back. He probably would have acted like this in any case, for what seemed proper royal protocol.

'Well, if you would like me to help, I could train with you.'

'Thank you, that would be great!' *What am I saying? More time with her, more time to get lost from the path that I am meant to be travelling. This is not me.* His dark voice did not even speak, giving no rebuttal, no guidance. It laughed though, it laughed mercilessly. No advice, as if it was meaningless to speak such sense.

She smiled.

'You'd better watch out, she may work you a lot harder than you think,' Giselda chimed in; she had been occupying herself with her thoughts before interjecting. She sat on the other side of Sophia, watching Felipe and the other people dining, listening to the conversation. She blushed as she forgot she was not part of this intense affair.

Ramkus chuckled, 'All the better, means I will be ready to leave sooner.'

Sophia did not say anything, nor let her face move with any emotion. It was her eyes that betrayed her, burning with a rage, with a sickness at the mention, the thought. Ramkus knew the path he was going on, *with* her.

XXX

'Don't be such a baby!' yelled Sophia as she lurched over the hobbling Guardian. He was panting, in serious pain, lifting a set of weights and placing as much of the strain on his – now named – "bad leg".

'Fine, drop them. It will do,' Sophia nodded after a moment where she watched the continued anguish on Ramkus's face. She did not think she would enjoy barking orders so much.

'Are you sure I am meant to be pushing it *this* hard? The surgeon said I was not to strain it too much,' Ramkus panted.

Sophia gave a resolute nod, hiding the fib between her teeth.

'I would also put you through some sparring training, but it would be cruel to force you to lose to a girl.'

'Which girl would I be sparring against?' Ramkus asked in confusion.

'Me of course! I wouldn't let you…' She turned away so as not to show her blushing state. Luckily Ramkus was keeling over, his back was quite strained. The bruises and welts – as well as what may have been broken bones – were not happy to exude much effort; especially after living the high life of relaxation for the last few days.

'So even the *Princess* has to learn to fight?' he exclaimed. Sophia took the question as an insult - of both not being considered apt at fighting, and the jealous conclusion that he may have potentially trained with another girl - forgetting the limited knowledge of the Empire the Guardian had.

'Of course! It would be absurd not to have been taught to fight. I was trained by some of the best fighters and weapon masters we have to offer. You think Djuayne was a painful ordeal? Just wait till you duel me!' Her eyes were smouldering; her body heaved; muscles tensed.

'How is the old rapscallion doing?' Felipe suddenly appeared from one of the passageways into the private gymnasium. He regarded the weights littered around, making quizzical glances at them and their uses. He did not see the flustered Sophia turn and walk to the wall as Ramkus stood up straight, not sure if he had really insulted Sophia or not.

'He's been put through his paces... so far,' Sophia called as she rested her back on the wall, semi squatting.

'Maybe you'd like to join us, Felipe?' Ramkus said.

'Oh no. *Not I.* I may join you for a swim in the baths after, though.'

'I think it's about time I did, actually,' Ramkus replied as he sought to get out of what was becoming a seething warzone, with Sophia's flaming anger from being indirectly insulted by the smallest aside.

'Fine, go,' Sophia said hotly.

'Thank you,' Ramkus said, averting eye contact from the tormentor. He couldn't understand how she could become so upset. He also didn't want to see what other torments she could inflict.

'Oh, this is the life!' Felipe relaxed, saying his usual catchcry, spreading out on the shallow seat in the bathing pool. The water was especially warm.

'I just don't get that girl,' Ramkus said to himself as much as he did Felipe. 'I asked about her being trained to fight, and she started going ballistic. Not to mention, she pushed me *way* too hard. As much as I have recovered, the exercises she was making me do did not seem appropriate in getting my knee back to how it was.'

'Ha, you *asked* an Empirical Princess if she was trained to fight? You may as well have asked if she was a child!' Felipe started to chuckle to himself. 'You see my dear boy, to not be trained as a Princess, or even someone of nobility in the Empire - even as a female – is merely unconscionable. Slaves don't train; those that have been conquered do not get the chance; this is the privilege, the right, the obligation to the Empire. It is part of their *being*. It completes them. Understand?'

A hearty scream which sounded feminine was heard from around the corners to the training room. The two looked at each other as they rose, grabbing their towels and peering around the corner down the hallway. They tiptoed their way down, leaving patterns of droplets etched into the small crevices of the stone slabbed floor. Peering around the corner into the room, they saw Sophia standing over Giselda who was sobbing on the ground. 'I'm sorry Giselda,' Sophia was saying, 'that damn fool has gotten me so angry!'

Felipe looked at Ramkus with large eyes held wide open large, indicating this was a situation they shouldn't be caught in. He started tip toeing away. Ramkus followed walking quietly behind.

'I really don't get the Empire,' Ramkus said as they sunk back into the baths.

'No, my boy, you don't get girls,' Felipe replied with a wink.

XXX

'Things appear to be following their apparent course, your Majesty,' Silque said in an hypnotic voice.

'Yes, indeed they are.' The King paused, frowning. 'Have you been spying, Silque?' He asked as he observed the advisor pacing back and forth in front of him. The King was lying on a chaise-lounge, reading letters, opening them with delicate incisions from a pen knife that could have been mistaken for a proper blade. The braziers in the large ornate room billowed with transparent smoke. Aromas lay heavy in the room and intoxicated those present with the air of the importance of where they were; reminding them of the necessary diplomatic functioning of the Kingdom, and where all the most important decisions would be meditated on: the King's study.

'No, your Majesty, I have heard rumblings.'

'Hah! I have too, the fool got my daughter in a red-hot state the other day! She went and beat up her handmaiden afterwards!' he chuckled, amused by the absurdity.

'I believe that was a *training mishap*, your Majesty,' Silque said slowly.

'Whatever, it shows she is aggressive and powerful, my daughter.' There was a pride in the King's voice, as he regarded a letter, and began to write one in reply. A small writing desk was to the side of chaise lounge. Quills, inks, wax, seals, and thick stately paper were held on it, as well as the letters - both opened and unopened.

'You should have a page-servant write down what you think, your Majesty,' Silque said as an aside.

'No, I like to write myself, it keeps me *centred*,' the King mused without looking up from his jottings.

'As you wish,' Silque acquiesced unemotionally.

There was a pause in conversation, as Silque stopped pacing in front of the King. The King feigned to notice until it became apparent the unease would not stop.

'Yes, Silque? What have you come for?' The King continued to write.

Silque grimaced, thinking to himself before he spoke. 'I wonder, Sire, if perhaps we should progress things between them a little more *quickly.*'

The King paused from his writing, looking up to meet Silque's gaze. 'What do you mean Silque? It is going fine. There is no need to interfere. Let it blossom as it should. I *repeat*, there is no need to get involved.' He knew fa too well the inner workings of Silque's mind.

Silque ground his teeth, 'Your Majesty, I fear that if we do not force things quickly, the Guardian may take off too soon. *And...*' Silque paused.

'Yes?' the King pushed Silque to finish cautiously.

'I fear if Djuayne gets back from his last mission, he may *involve* himself, somehow.'

The King thought for a second. He shook his head. 'No Silque, let it progress as it should, there is no need for *our* involvement. I wouldn't even guess as to what you have in mind. It is not as if he can be forced into anything emotionally or dutifully, correct? He has no allegiance to us, we have no control or hold over him. He is a guest, and we shall leave it to occur naturally.'

Dutifully, Silque considered to himself, *forcing one into a duty.*

'Yes, my Lord, of course.' Silque nodded, before turning and heading to the door, bowing before exiting. *'Force him into duty'* he said to himself.

XXX

Days passed, words were forgiven, tunes were learnt, food was eaten. And in all this time, a bond started to grow. A bond of attraction, one of desires and thoughts. The bard observed with curiosity, as he also played upon his chances to be accepted as the Court Bard. A lucky break for him, even with the small persistent thoughts in the back of his head that these people were responsible for the eradication of many of his forefathers; of capturing and enslaving his people. He thought himself

different. He sat in the small private dining room where
Ramkus and he often found themselves in the mornings, with the
chef happily preparing them meals.

He was busily playing away at his guitar when Harold the priest
wandered in.

'Harold! My dear… Priest! We have not seen you in quite a
while,' he said gleefully.

'No,' the monotone voice rang true. 'We?'

'Oh, well, *he* has been asked to go for a walk with his *fancy*…
With her Majesty,' Felipe replied a tad dejectedly.

'Oh, well, I wished to apologise to him.' Harold stood with his
hands behind himself.

'What, why?'

'For failing to pray hard enough for him. I should have prayed
harder.' His face grew in consternation. He had obviously
brooded upon this, his conscience seemed darkened.

Felipe gave a very puzzled look. 'What, you think the injuries
in the duel to him are on account of you?'

'Yes. I have been resolving myself since that day, the reason
you have not seen me.'

'Resolving?' Felipe was becoming very interested in this
theological action and thought.

'Fasting, beatings, tortures of the mind, body, and spirit,' the
priest said in his drawling voice. 'The usual sort of priest stuff.'
Felipe looked him up and down with concern.

'Hah!' Harold said in a considerably, non-exuberant, manner.
'Got you. But in all seriousness, I have been resolving to offer
my apologies for not aiding Ramkus better.'

The priest is starting to get a bit of a sense of humour, Felipe
thought with a smirk. 'I still don't see why it is your fault.'

'I could have stopped the fight once an illegal weapon was seen
to be used.'

Felipe looked in shock, 'You mean the sword Djuayne had? I
thought it was legal?'

'Yes. But seeing as we did have an opportunity to inspect the weapon once it came out. Had we done that, Ramkus may have *slipped* away, back on his journey.'

Felipe's shock turned to surprise at the unsuspected nous of the priest. *Too bad it has come too late.* 'Oh, stop worrying about it. If that happened, it would mean I wouldn't be sitting...'

Felipe knew he would sound quite selfish if he finished this comment.

'Ah, well,' Harold said. 'No, the fact of the matter is, I was secretly rooting for our champion to win. I feel ashamed to have not been impartial in such things. It shows a lack of moral pedigree,' Harold said, looking at his feet.

'That's not much of an *Empirical* thing to say,' Felipe commented, his eyes resting on the priest who was giving the impression he had been chided.

'I guess I am not worthy of being in the Empire to feel it so.'

Felipe continued to study the man, as the priest shifted his weight from one leg to the other, avoiding Felipe's heavy gaze.

'I really don't know what I am anymore. As soon as I was chosen to work in the Royal Palace - even as a lower one of the Order... Things became so stifled here.'

Felipe did not want to hear this; in fact, he did not accept that life here may not be as good as he had hoped. His mind was reverting to now considering Harold as playing some priestly mind game upon him.

'You have to deal with what you've got,' Felipe said with an insouciant air.

Felipe's words made little – if any – dent in Harold's concern that he be heard. 'It is very lonely as a priest in a kingdom that honours warriors.'

Felipe was bemused by the tune of the conversation, as if a bard should be giving life advice to a priest.

'Become a warrior priest then,' Felipe blurted out, unsure of himself as he rested back on his chair, guitar in hand, feet on the table. He laughed at such a notion in his mind, and failed to see the true cries of the person in front of him. *It would be a funny sight, though: a warrior priest*, he thought.

'With my stature? Do you think I'd be able to fight, let alone train with the likes of Djuayne? No, I'd be sent as a peasant's son would: to train in the lands of *nowhere in particular*. Not my type of thing being up to one's knees in mud and shit, as orders are barked at you.'

Felipe laughed at Harold's use of word "shit". It sounded very funny coming from the monotone voice of Harold, not to mention someone of a religious order.

'You think that funny?' Harold said in frustration.

'No, sorry. I just do not know why you seek me out. I know little of the Empire. At present, I am here because of Ramkus,' he admitted. He looked to the ceiling, 'And only the gods know for how long that will be.'

XXX

Sophia guided Ramkus by the arm. He was beginning to get some "life" back into his bad leg. Still limping, though. This new test: the stairs of the Rock. He was not looking forward to the ascent back up later, but he was excited to touch the grasses below; walking barefoot on the land, perhaps reaching the beach. He was in Sophia's hands - quite literally - now. She was still acting a touch offended and being short with him; showing him who was in control in a very stately and officious manner. Back to being on terms of formality even if she was acting very intensely towards him. It was an odd way to treat him, as they were virtually arm in arm as they walked down into the well-lit, carved out interior of the rock the castle was perched upon so proudly.

'You know, it was not us who built these stairs,' Sophia began to lecture. 'It was the first people, and even then, these people were different from those *Elven folk*. Of the sea, these ones were. I would care to guess some of the islands still have remnants of the people who carved this place out.'

Ramkus knew to keep his mouth shut from offending her majesty with any political debate, but the silence begged for a question to be asked.

They arrived at one of the alcoves where there were large cracks showing the sea below. The intricate web of staircases made sense if one kept turning left.

'Are you listening?' Sophia snapped.

'Yes, Sophia,' Ramkus said with a fright

'Your Highness!' she continued to rise in fiery temperament.

'Your Highness, I was waiting for you to continue what you were saying. Ah!' Ramkus stepped awkwardly and fell a little as Sophia became soft and caring once more, looking to aid him.

'Are you alright?' She asked sympathetically.

'Yes,' he said, knowing that such a ruse of feigning pain would warm the antipathy she was laying out.

'Please, continue what you were saying,' he said as they turned back into the central staircases of the Rock, and away from the internal carved walls.

'Whomever had built this place, we destroyed those people. We destroyed them after they fled in here. *Cowards*. We destroyed what was inside, for it was not always merely a staircase,' she continued with fire.

'Oh?' Ramkus simply replied, not wanting to get into a heated argument.

'No, it was their city. A ghastly creation. Who would live *in* a mound like this?'

This has the air of the types of stories the Empire would tell their own people, justifying a massacre to themselves, Ramkus thought. The way she spoke, it was as if she was tempting Ramkus, baiting him into disagreement. But would it lead into a trap of hers? This was indeed her families land now, where its foundations came from requiring all guilt to be disowned, and anyone who dared argue anything other than her families claim would need putting in their place.

'We built our Castle high on top, showing that we are a beacon of civilisation in what was a forsaken world,' she paused.

'Where did the Empire come from, then?' Ramkus asked innocently.

They stopped, as she regarded him with depth and understanding. 'Wherever man comes from,' she answered, continuing their descent.

'What is that supposed to mean?' he responded.

'Can *you* really talk, *Guardian*?' She said reproachfully before sighing and resigning herself to the reality of the situation; it was now no secret that the whole of the royal court – and guests – knew the man was not simply a bard, but actually the Guardian Order. 'I guess it is unfair of me to think you understood or knew much of our culture or history, as Giselda has said.' Her voice became soft as she started to glide into thought. 'We originally came from a land far South, far out to sea, one of an advanced civilisation, of all sorts of pleasures for man. A place where life was of ease; where some men could not help but be restless. These were our people. We were not content in that state, and sought to break free from the spell of complete pleasure. It was not wholesome, it was not right. We were created to inhabit and explore the whole of this world. So, we sailed far, to places such as here in Elantra, we conquered these lands because that is what we are, conquerors. Our main base – where our capital is – is far West of here, along the coast in a bay. We had to conquer that also.'

'Do you feel like a conqueror, Sophia?' Ramkus said, snapping Sophia out of her dreamlike state. She faced him once more, her face bitter contemplation: plagued with thoughts she dared not say.

'It is not easy being a princess,' she whispered, her voice trailing off with a sadness he had not heard from her before. She turned and began to walk again, slowly.

'I don't think any life is meant to be easy, Sophia,' Ramkus said as they made the final descent of the steps before coming out onto the entrance of the Rock. She smiled at him, her hair glistening in the sunshine, picking up with the light sea breeze. 'It was down there a stranger fought gallantly in the face of the Empirical Sergeant, Captain of the King's Guard, Champion of his people. One of the best fighters ever,' Sophia said with grace, alluding to the "champion" being the antagonist. Ramkus smirked as they made their way onto the lawns. None of the tents stood anymore, no signs of the festivities remained. It was merely a nicely maintained lawn. Trees were sparsely dotted about all the way down to the small beach and dock. They took their footwear off - Sophia with her sandals, Ramkus with his boots which he insisted on wearing - and let their feet sink into the heavenly earth. Sophia wandered on ahead as Ramkus surveyed the misty coast when it came into view, wishing to get into the water for a swim. He looked up the beach once he reached it; Sophia had disappeared.

A sudden panic spread through his body, he was alert. He raced up the beach in agony, his knee unable to bend. Every step a painful reminder of some surgical reparations on a deeply ingrained injury. He felt helpless, far from how he had begun; how far he had fallen. He followed the steps to where they turned into some bushes that were rustling. Suddenly, something moved.

'Hah! Got you!' Sophia jumped out at Ramkus, falling on top of him. This first reaction was to change the mood that had encompassed him - and it was only the smallest of reactionary feelings that let him hold back from engaging in whatever battle may have ensued. The tiniest of thoughts stopped him from allowing his animalistic instincts to overwhelm him. He had barely restrained himself even now. Sophia knocked him to the ground, keeping him pinned there. Her hair was lying on his face, blocking the view of anything else but her face. His emotions shot, he reclaimed himself, controlling his actions; he

stared in a complete trance into the blue grey eyes of the girl.
They were within a soft breath of each other, transfixed on one
another.

Ramkus realised after a few seconds, his knee was bent in an
awkward position, and stifling pain was shooting through his
body.

'Argh,' he grumbled, lifting Sophia off him with as much care as
he could muster.

'Oh, are you alright?' She asked with concern, realising she had
inflicted pain upon him.

He straightened out his legs quickly, breathing heavily, letting
the pain become a dull throbbing.

'Yes. *Fine*,' he said in short, sharp breaths.

'Sorry…'

He stood after a few moments, kicking his leg out. His eye took
the trail back into the gardens that Sophia had jumped out from.
Green vibrant leaves on the most remarkable plants. The
colours impressed on the viewer to take in all their glory: blue
hues, reds, purples, oranges; it seemed well tended and curated,
much like the castle. They took the path wandering within the
colourful bloom. Sophia declared such and such flowers to be
daffodils; dandelions; sunflowers; foxgloves, lavender; roses;
she went on in this way. Not too far into these gardens, a
running stream could be heard. Ramkus led on in intrigue, as
the sound became much quicker; louder; stronger. A state of
urgency overtook him; walking with purpose, and in an alert
manner once more.

'The river,' Sophia finally announced. 'It runs from the sea,
behind the castle, dividing us from the forest at large.'

'It looks like a mighty one,' Ramkus said, as he considered it
fifty yards across, flowing with seething might out to the sea. A
hardened red bridge arched over it further down towards the
castle; connecting the gardens to the forest on the other side,
seemingly *taming* it in the Empire's opinion. No obstacle was
too great for their strength.

'It connects to the river network in this region. Have you heard of how the rivers are the life blood of this place? Each branch a vein?'

'I have,' Ramkus answered, staring out in thought.

'Well,' she tried not to sound surprised, 'anyway, it's not one you would want to swim in. The water is extremely powerful, even the galleys with twenty rowers struggle against the current tidal flow. Are you listening?' she asked as Ramkus came back to attention. She smiled, content with her powers for the moment. 'Time to make the climb back up to the castle.' Ramkus grumbled at the thought.

With much effort and great pain – and in a fair amount of time – Ramkus and Sophia made it back to the top of the Rock, standing in front of the castle. He was considerably exhausted as she turned to face him, staring into him. Waiting for him to thank her, appreciate her...

'Thank you, Sophia,' he said, staring back into the beautiful smiling eyes of the girl. He moved close to her; she dared not move.

'Ah, Ramkus,' a monotone voice bellowed out from the castle entrance.

'Harold,' Ramkus said, slowly. Sophia smiled and left Ramkus to the priest's attention. Ramkus watched after her, before slowly turning to Harold. 'Harold...' Ramkus said, once more.

XXX

'Another oyster?' Sophia asked as she leant into Ramkus's view. Another banquet; another invitation to be seated next to Sophia. 'Of course,' he replied as the bard played away. A few eyes rested on the two with curious expressions. The King was always smiling when his gaze fell upon them, but never did he approach the two. In fact, no one ever tended to approach the two when they were together - save for Giselda or Felipe. The servants brought food to their plates and wine to their chalices without any heed. It was easy, comfortable, leisurely. Ramkus was soon forgetting this was not the life he had lived, previously.

XXX

Ramkus spun, placing the staff in front of him to deflect the wooden blade. He winced as his recovering knee took a little pressure. She came in with a back slash, spinning herself as he deflected once more; the blade's follow through went down as Ramkus spun back like a panther.

Calm; no aggression.

Sophia cursed at the Guardian, *how dare he be this good!* He danced as she came in for another attack, deflecting, dodging. Her aggression was becoming manifest, a hindrance to her now. He smiled as he glided past her. Her padded shirt had not been used, nor did his thin leather vest which Sophia thought he took out of arrogance, that he could take her heavy body shots with indifference. It served his purpose to be quick and agile. Onlookers, servants, and Giselda all watched the flurry of attacks and evasion of Ramkus with intrigue. Silque wandered in – at least Ramkus thought it him from the corner of his eye. Sophia threw her sword down in rage and fury, putting her hands on her hips. Ramkus stood, beginning to play around with his staff. As quick as a flash, Sophia jumped to the floor, grabbing the sword and thrusting it upwards into Ramkus's rib cage. He was not quick enough to deflect as she rested the blade on his tabard.

'Heart shot.' She smiled with glee.

XXX

They danced in unison, step in step with each other - he was a quick learner.

307

There was a desperation in her steps, in her movements, as if he was chasing her. The onlookers were now not only throwing glances, but watching them. The braziers heat and smoke gave a mad energy to the night, as did the musicians who were trying to keep up with the two dancers. Ramkus gazed searchingly into the blue grey eyes of Sophia. They were joined; their bodies closely tied; their breath, one. They flung themselves about with recklessness, not giving a care for any others.

Felipe was in deep contemplation on how to describe the scene for his next song. Theirs was the madness of the dance, bringing each other closer and closer, together.

XXX

He moved with such great ease now, his knee was not at the forefront of his mind as it once was. She darted at him, the usual deflection; he moved behind her as she threw a punch, hitting nothing but air. Turning, she thrust with her wooden sword, throwing her whole body at him, losing her step as he spun and dodged. She fell, but did not hit the floor; she was in his arms. His firm stature; probably the greatest reassurance to her. She was lost in his blue eyes as he stared at her without any intentions. She reached her arms up around his neck; to bring herself closer to him, to his gaze.

XXX

Felipe was left to his own devices in these days. Happy to wander the palace, to speak to the dignitaries. There was not as many people in the palace as before; there was to be a migration back to the regular palace in their capitol at some stage soon.

He had been invited by guests to visit them, indeed to join them for the journey to their usual residences. Still, his heart was on the invitation to be a court bard. He walked a passage he had not seen before, or had he? He did not know as it was a maze of passages and rooms. This was the private quarters after all and he ought to familiarise himself with such surrounds, *for future reference*. A smell came from one room, a smell that seemed to be fairly rancid. *What on earth could such a smell be in here*, he thought. *A privy?* he put it down to, but still wished to know for certain. Opening a door with a turn of a knob he judged the odour to come from: a non-descript one. He pushed it ajar.

'Holy shit!' he coughed, turning away.

A badly beaten naked body lay against the wall.

Felipe – covering his mouth with a handkerchief - turned back from his initial reaction to observe the body, trying to figure out if he was alive or dead. He seemed to feel he recognised the face, the blonde hair, the features - even though badly beaten - he racked his brain, squinting his eyes and hoping the person was not beyond saving.

'Are you alright?' he said, realising how pathetic his voice was. Eyelids moved, the mouth fell open slightly. Felipe walked in to see if he could help. He kept his mouth covered and rose from the awful concoction of blood, sweat, tears, and shit.

'Are you a prisoner?' Felipe asked, wondering why there was no lock on the door.

The mouth agape, trying to speak. Instead, it let out a shallow laugh.

'I am allowed to go,' the man coughed in short breaths. 'If I can,' he cleared his throat. 'They have got what they want now.' His head fell.

'Hey, hey! Stay with me,' Felipe lent down, almost fainting as he closely inspected the bloody body, beaten and bruised, left to die. The eyes looked up.

'Save yourself,' the man coughed. 'And your friend. They want him.' The man's eyes rolled back.

'Oh shit,' Felipe shuddered. 'Oh shit, oh shit,' his mind was racing. He shouldn't be caught here with this man. He was sure he had witnessed death overcome this nameless one; his warning rang in Felipe's mind.

309

How did he know I had come with a friend? What did they want with Ramkus? Why was this man treated so poorly, beaten to death?

Felipe backed out of the room as fast as his fright ridden body would let him. He looked to either side of the corridor, closing the door quickly and walking with briskness, until he heard someone coming. He turned and started down the other direction. Another passageway led down to the right of this. He went down it and waited to spy who may be coming.

Silque appeared, looking around, entering the room with the nameless man.

'Oh shit,' Felipe said to himself as he breathed heavily, deciding to get back to *safer passageways* as soon as possible.

XXX

'He is dead, your majesty,' Silque declared.

'I see.' the King was emotionless.

'I also believe it may be worth *moving things* along with the other matter with haste,' Silque added.

'Oh, why?' the King replied angrily. 'It seems to be running its course in its natural rhythm?'

'I have heard Djuayne will be back soon from his mission, sire. Things may be… *affected* by him. *If you know what I mean.* He cannot be trusted to let the Guardian – or your daughter – be without interference.'

The King sat back in his chair. He pushed the palms of his hands together and looked out the large windows towards the sky. His forefingers on his lips. 'I see,' he finally replied, 'and you have something in mind to *speed things* up then?'

'Yes, your majesty. Leave it to me.' Silque smiled with menace.

XXX

'Where is he, where is he?' Felipe muttered to himself as he scoured the halls of the palace. 'Always with that damn Princess, she is probably part of this!' He was fretting, sweating, visibly distressed. He tried to pull himself together as he passed by some guards. He could have sworn they were looking at him differently. 'Why do they want him? *Shit*, this is my fault. Who was that man, I am sure I have seen him before! Come to think of it, there was that other soldier we'd seen in Refton, watching us when we first met the King in his court...' Muttering out loud was not of his nature, he was petrified. 'They have kept an eye on us for longer than we've known!' He passed by the rooms of interconnecting halls, into the area of his own quarters. *Best I quicken up*, he thought.

As Ramkus relaxed into the warm waters, he spread half out on the bath steps, looking at the ceiling. He heard a giggle from one of the doorways. Sophia and Giselda emerged in the *men's* bathing hall. Ramkus shuddered: *Have I come to the wrong bath hall?* The two girls acted without trepidation, taking immediate notice of him on the other side of the pool, smiling at him. He looked away.

'Sorry, I did not realise I was in the wrong pool. I'll get out,' he said, looking at the wall, focussing his attention as best he could away from the sight of them.

'You're not, Ramkus,' Sophia cried out, as the girls giggled again. He tried to stop peering over in their direction. They were stripping their clothes off. He swallowed as he observed the supple body of Sophia; she was acting without a care that he was not about. She smiled as his eyes met hers. She plunged into the waters with an agile dive.

The hell are they getting up to? he thought, as Giselda glided down into the pool after Sophia. He straightened up, noting the guards at the doors were unflinching.

'You think the body is so sacred as to not be looked at by another?' Sophia yelled out as she regarded his rigid behaviour.

'No, I…' He did not know how or what to say to them as they floated above the steaming pools waters, watching him.

They moved to the end of the pool and relaxed themselves, heeding no attention to Ramkus who was confused as to what was protocol. *Why is Giselda here as well? Merely to take in what Sophia was hoping to sway with her charm?* His reaction was consistent with a Guardian, trying to remain focussed, fight against urges – at least, that is what he thought to himself.

'Ramkus,' a voice bellowed, 'I've been looking for you… Ahh!?' Felipe entered and regarded the two girls at the end of the pool. 'Your Highness. Giselda…'

'Monsieur Felipe,' the girls called out. He stared, flabbergasted. He hadn't seen girls swim naked with men in such circumstances before.

'Felipe, what are they doing?' Ramkus whispered as loudly as he could whilst Felipe approached.

'Ah…?'

'Join us Felipe,' Giselda cried from the other side of the pool. Felipe stood in contemplation. 'Ahh…' The contours of the thin, tight, fit body of Giselda. For what he could see - and all he could imagine under the water – held his attention, and had his own body in hysterics.

He looked to Ramkus who shook his head and shrugged in confusion. In that instant, Felipe was under the spell, one he had cast for himself so often; to live in that dream of freedom, expression, love. The most important things in life still stood for him, it prevailed over common sense, and self-preservation. His glinted smile belied the forgotten, sordid, state of affairs; indeed, he wanted so hard to believe he was mistaken with what he had experienced before, continuing so hard to accept any belief that it simply did not happen, to dispel any ill-thoughts he had purely conjured up himself. He removed his clothes and bathed in the waters as requested. His charming self, his debonair moustache twitching to the hum of that moment, the delightful smile coming his way. His was not entirely a desire for Giselda, it was for that feeling which made him feel whole, that fed the ego telling him he existed for the purpose to feel the motions, to experience the body. He was gliding through the water; his wet, long black hair trailing behind him as he came to Giselda, moving about her in a synchronised motion of encirclement. He was in his element; his moment. The spell had certainly been cast upon himself.

Ramkus - watching on - followed suit, timidly. Sophia came to him also. *What does this mean for me? Why do I hold myself back from what is* right*: to feel love; to give it.*
Sophia merely smiled at him, with her blonde hair draped on her shoulders. *Those eyes, they hold so much thought, knowledge, desire.* His own eyes were of a deep blue that held a comfort, a charm of intimacy in the world; steadfast, strength, power, kindness, madness. She was infatuated, embracing his neck, pulling herself to him as they met in the steamy pool. Their bodies became entwined.
'I want you,' she whispered in his ear.

XXX

'Do you remember when we first met, Felipe,' Giselda said as she stirred the sheets, turning to him. 'I know it was only a "fling" for you, but it was more for me. You have something our people don't have.'
'What is that, my dear?' Felipe stretched out, letting Giselda fall on his bare chest, staring at the brick work on the ceiling. He pulled a cup of wine from the bed side table with his free arm, sipping a bit before offering the cup to Giselda. Her body seemed highly strung, ready to bolt. He felt emasculated when he noticed how much fitter she must be, so refrained from comment: *Mine is a strength of the heart and soul,* he reaffirmed to himself.

'A Freedom. A desire to travel, to leave lands that were inherited, that requested tending. You stood for a new order: head strong, an adventurer. And you adapted to the world with such ease!' Giselda was shining a heavy spotlight of upon Felipe's life.

'It sounds like you are quite entranced with the poem of life, my dear.'

'Entranced? It became my life, my desire. How else do you think I came here? I wouldn't fit in with the others - our people in the forest. I have no *desire* to live my whole life tending to one parcel of forest! There is a headstrongness, a stubbornness to our people. You should see the ones around here, they must have some of *those from the sea's* blood mixed in; born to protect what is theirs, to fight with clenched teeth.' Giselda's impassioned cry only grew as she delved into their shared past.

'We – our colony – we were not fighters, we just had to. We did not adapt, we did not see what the conquerors brought with them. They brought their whole world here, it all came together for them!'

Felipe regarded Giselda's romantic vision of the world, weighing it up to what he had experienced.

'You were the spark, Felipe, and I have never forgotten all those years ago… *nor forgiven.*'

He smiled, remembering fondly those years when life seemed more carefree. The roads held little disturbance, there was always a bed and food at every inn. People relied not only on stories, but news of the world, in awe of the situations and world that they were told of, so far away. *Has it really changed?*

Then a thought came back to him, the one he wanted to blot out. The reason he had found himself in today's predicament. *I have to find Ramkus.*

It was to Ramkus's own quarters that Sophia had led the Guardian. Out of sight of the guards – as Sophia thought – the privacy she considered necessary; the privacy of herself with the

Guardian. As she came up against the walls when the door closed, Ramkus closed in, closely tied to her, cradling her neck. She shivered.

'No,' She surrendered. Ramkus looked into her eyes. 'No,' she repeated softly, 'I cannot.'

Ramkus crooked his head to the side, dropping his hand from the embrace. His wet, light brown hair dishevelled, dripping remorsefully. He stood back.

'I am the Princess,' Sophia cried sadly, 'I cannot do these things.'

'Yet you seek my embrace,' Ramkus answered back in a slow drawl. He looked at her, adoring her svelte body that was clung to by a thin dress, thrown on in haste to travel the halls. She bit her lip. In his mind, he withdrew. He had no reason to be here, it was not of him. Pure desires, simple desires.

Should I not be better a man than to desire? Why am I in this predicament? The questions came at him in short, sharp succession. He felt he was at odds with himself, that he had done so much wrong. In the distant reaches, there was a maniacal laugh that would have rushed through the self-imposed feelings of punishment, had it – the madness - been given the power to do so.

'It is not that I do not want to, it is that I… ah' Sophia paused. 'Royal Protocol would have me be… you understand?'

'No?'

Sophia stood proudly after a moment of acting innocent. 'Pure; that is what.' She stood to attention, regaining her composure. She hadn't been in a position like this before, and was not the type to say sorry. 'I shouldn't have been placed in this situation. This is all your fault. How dare you!' She was losing self-control.

'Mine? What the hell?' He knew such a fight was futile, the best option would be to defuse than t fight. 'Fine, I am sorry.' She stared at him, walking to the window that overlooked the mountain range in the far distance. 'Good,' she said. '… No, I am sorry… I am not in the best frame of mind. I haven't been for a while. I don't know what overcame me,' she lied. 'I need some time to regather my thoughts. We will talk later,' she said in a commanding fashion.

Ramkus bowed with deferment. Sophia nodded regally, and left with the light patter of her footsteps down the corridor.

Ramkus was left to wonder what on earth that was all about, as prying eyes - which had been gleefully watching - readied to report the whole affair.

XXX

He wandered up to the rooftop garden, the braziers alight with a vivid glow that set upon the hedge trees, making a playful mystique. *The days must be getting colder*, he thought as the sun was dimming above a transparent sky. The mountains stood forlorn in the distance, a picture that seemed to inspire thoughts that cast ones' mind far from this platitude. He smiled, knowingly. The wild winds above dropped, and next to the garden the running river could now be heard. It seemed drowned out most of the time whilst up at the peak of the Rock. He had never thought to look at it - the river - running furiously past the Rock below. It was a clean drop from the ledge he looked from, right down into its depths. Bits of wood dragged from the banks, sinking in the maelstrom, thrashing about as the waters pulled them down into the heart of the forest. Tree cover did its best to conceal the winding path, but the width of the river did allow Ramkus to trace its ways into the green wild. It looked alive.

'It is beautiful,' a soft voice said.

Ramkus looked to his side without surprise, he knew the voice, he already sensed the presence before words needed to be exchanged.

'I would love to travel past those mountains. I have always looked to them, since I started coming here with my parents...' Sophia paused. Ramkus did not dare say anything untoward. 'It is not much of a life being trapped inside, training in so many arts - *the best there is to offer*. People coming from all different lands, talking politics, of other worlds, trade. I know so much but have seen so little, I haven't even... explained myself,' her voice trailed off with the wind as it picked up again. They began walking to a pleasant spot in the garden.

'I have never really met people my age before, at least ones that have lived and aren't seemingly *inbred*,' she laughed. She was on edge. 'Those are mostly the nobles. Keeping to themselves, only bowing to each King that can keep them safe and ensure that they can keep intact what they think are *their* rights, and *their* wealth.'

'And you are not like that?' he asked wistfully.

'Me?' Hah! No, my father's line, they never chose nobles daughters. One of the reasons I have not been thrown to a noble family - nor have they tried... He also... wants me to *have a say*.'

The flames of the braziers flared up. A servant appeared up the stairs, approaching them. There had stirred no other life other than the two till then.

'Drinks, your Highness? Monsieur Ramkus?' The servant held a silver tray with some neatly adorned chalices, filled with wine. Ramkus smiled, enjoying the title of achievement for a bard as if he deserved it; Sophia hid her amusement at what she considered a *ruse* to his true nature. He reached for one of the glasses.

'No Monsieur, that one is for the Princess,' the servant stammered.

'He is right, see the additional jewellery and artwork. These are in fact my Houses silverware: reserved for only those of my house. See how the artwork matches with my bracelet?' She dangled her feminine arm in front of Ramkus, showing her wrist

which held the tightly bound, golden alloy bracelet, binding her
to the Empire.

'Ah, so it is a punishable offence for me to drink out of it,' he
stated dryly.

She smiled, 'Take a sip and see.' She leant in as he took a sip of
her drink.

'Delicious,' he winked as he grabbed the *cheaper* chalice. The
servant did not budge. 'Hmm, your chalice actually makes it
taste different too,' he commented after taken a swig from his.
She stared over the top of her *House* chalice at him, sipping the
wine as if it were a divine nectar.

The servant bowed and left them.

'Well I guess you already know about us *Guardians*,' Ramkus
picked up the conversation.

'Born of the earth; thunder; wind; water; and fire. A lightning
strike marking the crevasse from whence you rise,' Sophia
recited. 'One arisen, you are *irrepressible*.'

'Hah! I guess? I actually don't know. I just woke up in a field,'
he imparted playfully.

She looked at him with intrigue, 'These are not just legends.
Why else would you awake as men with such physical attributes
and such power? You are the great levellers, doing the work of
the Gods. The world's duties.'

'You actually know more than I do on the topic, it seems. Are
there no women Guardians?' he pressed.

She was surprised by comment. 'No, it is said you are only
men,' her voice held a certain mystique. 'I am not sure why that
is exactly,' she finished in a light, half joking manner.

They laughed. Ramkus felt the wine going to his head. He
swayed a little as if the winds were going to pick him up. There
was a euphoria and a tingle of dread passing over him like a
stream which he had no choice but the surrender to.

A dark shadow rose from the stairs and slid without effort
towards the two.

'Good to see you two this early evening. *Sophia*. *Ramkus*,' a
sly voice greeted them.

'Silque,' Sophia almost hissed back, surely not pleased by his
presence, nor his overly familiar attitude towards her. Ramkus
nodded as he tried to steady himself.

'Are we enjoying this auspicious date? One of the most
important of our year,' his voice lowered. 'One to get married
on,' his voice seemed to echo in Ramkus's ear.

Did Sophia hear that? The voice of Silque droned on in
Ramkus's mind. His head felt like a massive gong was painfully
ringing throughout. The words continued, menacingly, as a trail
of some sort of shining powder, barely visible, surrounded his
vision for a moment.

'I shall take my leave,' Ramkus caught Silque say after a dizzied
state in which Silque and Sophia exchanged some short sharp
comments. *Or had they?* Time was unfathomable right now.

'He is such a cunning serpent,' Sophia commented after Silque
was out of sight. 'I have never trusted him, ever since he joined
our services. I don't even know where he is from.' She
regarded Ramkus and gave a peculiar smile. 'And what's come
over you now?'

He had no idea as to the answer of that question. The sights of
Sophia were all that his mind could focus on, all his universe
seemed to be. Movements of his body, his mouth, they formed
cognitively but unrecognisably. His mind now flashed above
cheers and tears, the embrace of Sophia as the sky turned around
and around. Flowers blew to the wind, leaves took flight, and
conversations around him now ran on and on. The lights blared
and delighted. There were movements on his body, embraces
and purrs. He took little heed of what he did not recognise. He
did not fear, he did not know how to; lost to a world which he
may as well have come from originally. The sights and sounds
were of rushing, sensations that fitted with his world, the world
of old, his reasoning of it. Faces: Felipe; the King; Giselda;

Silque; Poncho, they seemed real and happy. Although Felipe's looked like nothing he would call overjoyed, more forlorn, holding back from saying something: *A tongue-tied bard, ha!* His mind took him even further back, to Abergrass, Kef and Rab, his quick movements in flight. The world was coming back as a burning sensation took him by the wrists. A large cauldron simmered in the centre of his view, as he looked up and swore that the sun had decided to play with him. He then held a chalice of red wine whilst more movement of colour and pageantry danced about. *Music, music!* The great leveller, he understood that, the emotions made sense, whereas little else did. But he could tell, beauty was on his right, friendship in front... In front but trying, trying to express knowledge in a manner unbecoming of his friend. He was finally relaxed in an embrace, now of warmth - maybe not of his friendship - but of a warmth and tenderness. It overwhelmed as he took flight past the moon and stars. He was back on the plane-lands, he need not understand them, only be with them. He soared, powerfully, over a dominion; of earth; of people; creatures; cities; civilisations! His understanding, his knowledge, his life, was coming back. But all the while, there was a laughing at the back of his mind: maniacal laughter.

He knew who was laughing; he knew his only "friend".

Why does he laugh so?

Chapter XIII

There was a sweet scent of fruit and roses, and a warmth which
touched his body; the touch of the sun. But there was also
another warmth, of a supple body - not his. Although not yet
coming to his senses, he embraced the entanglement of the other
body. The sound of waves droned on constantly, a reminder of
life. Birds began chirping high up on the Rock - *or have they
been all this time.* A soft female noise was raised from the other
resting body. His mind - as lucid as it was – began to sharpen
itself. His eyes opened to face Sophia, wrapped around him. He
was in a large bedroom, in her soft clasp which matched the
finesse of the sheets.
They were both naked.
What happened? He wondered, as he began to move his head
around, taking in the finely crafted tapestries, the desk and
couches in the corner, the massive fireplace, and a curtain which
seemed to conceal a changing spot with a huge wardrobe. There
were small swallows perched on the window sill which
overlooked the coastline.
The sun should not have touched me, if that's the view, he
thought. He then noticed the mirrors that stood in particular
corners of the ceiling, bringing in a brightness that would only
be matched with direct sunlight outside. Looking around, he
relaxed as he saw his staff near the end of the bed's head rest.
He was incredibly comfortable and unsure as the whether he
should wake Sophia.
How did this happen? A sound came to him, a laughter: his old
friend. *What does he know?*
Ramkus brought his face down to let his body rest back on
Sophia. But before he could settle, he let out a sudden cry: his
arm held a bracelet, intricate in design and adorned with jewels.
Sophia shot up, 'What's wrong?' Her hair was in a tangle, but
she did not show signs of drowsiness.

Ramkus brought his other wrist around, slowly feeling the metallic touch, but not wanting to believe. His other wrist also held a band, of different design, but equally as impressive.

'Oh, you'll get used to them. Look, they match!' Sophia said with enthusiasm, bringing her wrist... not to the one that marked of belonging to the Empire, but rather, the one reserved for marriage... It was a band of significant design, binding Ramkus and Sophia's in holy matrimony.

'What has happened!?' Ramkus cried out in disbelief. 'What did you do!?'

Sophia shook her head in confusion, not understanding his reaction. 'What did I do?' she said calmly, 'What do you mean? We got married, silly!' She took Ramus reaction in jest. 'You proposed to me, remember?'

'No?! What are you talking about?!' His body was writhing, in throes of anger, confusion, guilt, annoyance.

Sophia's face showed worry, 'You proposed to me at the rooftop, and because of the particular date - one of the many auspicious dates you said – we were married last night.'

Ramkus kept studying his wrist, his hands were trembling. 'No? I did not!' His whole body had begun to tremble. 'I remember the rooftop, but...' his voice quietened. He staggered for thoughts of what had happened; the time had been lost, he could not remember a thing. 'What did you do to me?' he let out hoarsely. Staring at his wrists, he was shaking violently now, almost convulsing with rage and fear at what had occurred.

'This is not what is meant to happen!' He shot up and snatched his staff.

'Ramkus, please, calm down. You're worrying me,' she said timidly.

Anger scorched across Ramkus's mind, a blackness on his thoughts. His mood: wild and dangerous.

'What did you do!' he yelled. His senses, his instincts were coming to; a panic was felt, as if he were a trapped beast.

Sophia could only watch in fear, as he stormed around, winding up, ready to lash out. The main door creaked as a guardsman peered in.

'Are you alright, Princess?' the soldier asked as Sophia, taken by surprise, gave out a shriek.

Ramkus charged at the guardsman, smashing his staff down on the man, knocking him to the ground. A second guardsman burst in after, sword unsheathed.

'The Prince?' he said, as he started to strike at Ramkus.

Ramkus wore nothing, any hit would cut flesh. But he was not *Ramkus* in this moment, he was "the *Prince*", and all methodical, planned, strategic fighting became a brutish game of power and precision, to inflict massive damage in a short amount of time. As blows from the guardsman's sword were deflected, one end of the staff got behind the guardsman's leg, tripping him, and the other end came down hard, smashing the guardsman's skull. Blood began to flow.

Sophia gave another cry, as Ramkus - or rather a demon - looked at her with a small smile of glee. She shrieked in horror.

Footsteps could be heard charging down the hallway outside as Ramkus, the *Prince*, threw himself outside to escape the incoming assault.

The hallway was palatial; which meant lots of space; which meant lots of soldiers could move throughout at pace. He backed away, looking at them as they stopped and regarded him with bemusement.

The first soldier who had been smote by Ramkus was up again, stumbled out the door. 'Get him!' he squeaked, before collapsing.

'Get the Prince!' the soldiers who had already been running with a great deal of energy now sprinted down the hallway at the naked Prince.

Ramkus turned and fled to the other direction.

He appeared to leap and bound with ease. It was a long hallway, and before he reached the end where it turned, two soldiers came around the corner, ready to attack.

Commotion was flying about the castle. Soldiers came at him with swords unsheathed. Ramkus smiled nastily, jumping to the wall and coming down with his staff at great speed, smashing one of the soldiers in the neck, breaking it. He then spun on the ground, hitting the other soldier who tried to use his sword to slice his head. Too slow, the staff cracked into the soldier's head, lifting him from the ground and into the wall.

With the two soldiers indisposed, Ramkus picked up his pace and led the charging group of men after him once more.

'What is that sound?' the King demanded to know. 'Are we under some sort of attack?'

'I shall go find out, your Majesty,' a plump page replied, bowing and moving out of the King's study hastily.

'Well, I believe things went quite well, Silque. The two should make a fine couple.' The King gave a cheeky smile, 'And not to mention some *good-looking* children.'

Silque stood in front of the King. 'Thank you, my King. You seem very, *relaxed.*'

'Well, my lineage should be preserved. Although, I have not heard from any talks about Guardians' having children?'

'I do not believe it to be a physiological problem, Sire, rather that the Guardian Orders obtrusive nature in not enjoying the normalities of *our human experience.*' Silque smiled, delighted with his summation.

'Hmm, so we have freed this Ramkus from his Order?' The King was quick to query.

'We got to him *early*,' Silque's eye twitched. As sure as he was of himself, he knew he was hedging his bets on an outcome that was extremely audacious. To change the nature of a Guardian; the nature of a man. But of course, he had used the greatest element that can make such changes possible: man's counterpart, man's love.

'Hrmph, well, we shall see how that Order takes it. I doubt they are able to say anything. I have met a few; dealt with them rather. Very *anachronistic*. Stuck in antiquity. Their ways are blindingly rigid and outdated. Probably the best thing for the boy to have come to us.' The King nodded as if giving a royal decree to his words.

'I agree, you Majesty. You have done a great thing by allowing him to join our ranks.'

'Hah! It was of his own volition. I dare not think it of my own doing. We are men, Silque. I do not want a son-in-law to be fearful of anyone, even me. He needs to stand up to the Gods if need be! If I have been good to anyone, it is that bard. Then again, I am quite fond of that one.' The King looked to the ceiling, bemused with the thought.

Silque nodded as the page sidled back in. His girth making it a struggle to catch his breath.

'Your Majesty.' *Breath* 'it's.' *Wheeze*, 'the Prince.' *Cough*.

'Spit it out! The King demanded, moving forward to the edge of his seat, ready as if to admonish the bearer of news. He did not like having his mood change so quickly.

'He's gone mad and killed some of the.' *Breath*, 'Guards!'

A silence eschewed, the humming of braziers burning was audible, as the silence stifled all other movement. The King's eyes enlarged, staring into space. He turned to Silque without emotion, regarding him with a reproachful and questioningly look. Silque's face dropped, his eyes meeting the King's.

The page let out a wheezing as his heavy breathing started again.

Ramkus knew little of where he was. His mind was afloat as his survival instincts took control. A side of him enjoyed the confrontation, inflicting damage, drawing attention to himself. He did not heed any sores or pains, and was only struggling a little due to his poorly knee; purely from a lack of muscle in the leg rather than the joint itself. He had entered into another room, seemingly used for meetings of a trade or diplomatic nature. A map of the known world lay sprawled out on the central wooden table. His mind completely amess, he jumped on the table, kicking the candles that were positioned at its edges. He waited for the assault of the soldiers. Their heavy steps marked the distance.

Wait. Wait. Now!

He jumped from the table at the double door, knocking into two unsuspecting soldiers who had darted inside. The weight of the hit pushed them back into those behind.

Ramkus smiled nastily, baring his teeth; his eyes bloodshot. He moved as quick as a panther, smacking his staff into the unprepared soldiers. He leapt back onto the table, only to jump back into the fray of the soldiers whom had regrouped, regathering their position only to be knocked down again.

He laughed maniacally, as if he had been imbued with a demonic speed and strength. He sped over the soldiers, stepping on those whom had fallen to the ground. He was out the door and into the outer cloisters again. Running down the passage, it opened up to become a balcony, overlooking the mountainous range that had held a type of hope. It seemed so distant a thought now, he was merely living in this impulsive reality where he no longer existed. No, that was not correct, what was left was this "Princc" that the guards called out to, that they charged at, that they feared. This was *their* "Prince".

There was water rushing underneath the balcony – albeit the balcony did not so much "hang out" over the river and away from the castle, as pillars still held up the roof. This open cloister-balcony ran from this mountain view, around the castle to the seaside.

A sickening thought came to him, to try and knock as many of the soldiers off this balcony as he could.

The contingent of guard soldiers approached, steadily, well-armed, in fear of the raging, demonic beast. There was almost a score of them now, some brandishing bruises from this recent battle already.

He stood there, bare of any cloth, smiling, taunting the next challenger – or all challengers at once – to come at him.

One did, raising his sword, charging. Ramkus dropped to the ground, bringing his staff up, extending as far as he could control, hitting the soldier under the chin before he could defend or evade. Ramkus spun around and smashed the soldier around the back with a heavy crack, aiming to knock him to the ledge and over. The soldier grunted, hitting the balustrade, almost toppling over the edge, but in some odd manoeuvre, was able to keep his balance and fall to the castle floor instead.

A disappointment crept into the madness of the Prince. He searched for another to attack him, willing the opponents on. The instinct for survival was bearing him not only forward, but into a deep chasm of madness. *I shouldn't want this*, a voice cut into his mind. *This is not what I am meant to be.* The crazed bloodlust was becoming unsettled. *What am I becoming?* Ramkus questioned. His exasperation and manner changed - as did his body language. The soldiers sensed this shift, rushing at him; but too late. He dashed off ahead of them once more, but with his conscience regained.

Felipe lay on his back, smiling at the ceiling in deep thought; Giselda lay on his chest, asleep. *How did it all happen?* he thought to himself. *They were only a small little number. He was looking forward to leaving, he had no desire to remain at all. Does a woman change a man that quickly?* Giselda moved, stirring the sheets, letting more visible sunlight hit their bodies from the window. She was under Felipe's chin, tickling him slightly with her hair.

He smiled at the sight of her and began to concentrate back on his riddle. He traced back through time. *They were in the pool; then he did not see him until the impending - nay the **immediate** marriage - was the take place. Very rushed, but also seemingly*

327

expected. The reasoning was always that it was due to some religious day or rather. A flimsy excuse, he surmised, at least by his account. His instinct was that this was all wrong; it did not sit well with him at all.

When he had seen Ramkus for the first time after the bathing pool, he looked all out of sorts; happy yes, but not of any deep thought or care. He had appeared to possess himself in only the briefest of moments, a clarity as to the occupation of listening to any other. Overtaken by someone else, it appeared. He could not get a word in, as all the "dignitaries" were congratulating him, filling his wine bowl.

Felipe had acted in such a way as to raise Ramkus's attention, but to no avail. All he could do was play the tunes of a wedding feast, merrily, for his friend... As well as make sure Ramkus kept his staff with him. Felipe shook his head, *truly not a Guardian if he forgot his staff,* he thought. His lack of care for his only worldly possession was another reason why he did not feel this marriage for Ramkus was of his own volition. He did not want to think such thoughts, but he set his mind on such a course. *Was this a ploy? And if so, what was the gain?*

Felipe looked down to Giselda, he did not want to believe *she* was used in any way to keep him away from minding Ramkus. Yet what had Felipe seen before his little rendezvous? What had he wished to tell Ramkus? He shuddered, a deep breath then flowed into his lungs, and his body became tense.

What good could I have done for Ramkus anyway. Keep an eye on him, that is all. How selfish have I been to let this whole situation arise; all because I wanted a life of comfort. At what cost!? A tear rolled down his cheek. *At what cost,* he questioned himself again. *What could become of Ramkus now? There is no way he can escape this fate now, he is bound to the Empire. To his wife! To the life of royalty. That was not what he wanted at all...*

Giselda moved again, snuggling herself into Felipe's shoulder. He wrapped his arm around her tighter.

It is easy enough for me to leave the situation, for I am a bard.
No one really cares what happens to me if I leave. He felt
Giselda's breathing and heartbeat. He continued along this line
of thought. *Why would Ramkus want such a life? He wouldn't,*
that is settled. So why would they?

He thought back to the fight at the mountain, in the cleft, where
a hooded stranger had attacked them. *Was that man not sent to*
try Ramkus out, perhaps? Do they want him as a fighter? How
would they know he was a Guardian, and what could he become
for them? No, that was a separate incident, not from the
Empire. That fighter was nothing of the Empire in looks or
movement. Probably the Guardian Order themselves testing
him.

A loud sound of cries and footsteps came from outside the room.
Giselda woke with a fright.

'What is that sound?' she said in an angered, frightful voice.

'I am not sure,' Felipe got up and ran to the door, not before
putting some trousers on. 'What's going on?' he yelled, once
outside. 'Some sort of drill?'

There were other "guests" wandering about, shrugging. Some
soldiers raced down the quarters.

'What is happening? Felipe asked when in earshot.

'The Prince has attacked some guards,' one of the soldiers said.
'He has gone completely mad!'

Felipe did not take the information in at first. *Who the hell is the*
Prince? He wondered. Then his heart sank.

His run had led to the inevitable destination: the rooftop garden.
There were tables out, and many chairs, as if some party had
taken place the previous night. He barely recalled - through
missing images - what the "event" had been. It had all started
here... **After the drink***!* He did not have much time to think.
His options were becoming slim - or rather, non-existent. The
soldiers started up from two sides, where the only entry and exit
to this area was by steps.

He was trapped.

Some over-zealous soldiers came at him: he deflected the shots, and countered. Taking swift strikes to suppress their advance, he was being backed to one of the open edges overlooking the forest floor.

A trapped, wild animal he must have looked. His naked, hairy chested body was dripping with sweat. His hair swished about his head. Holding his staff in a position where none dared to lunge at him; he looked to the trees as if for some last refuge. Too small, too far away. *Can I fight my way out?* The whole of the garden was swarming. He dared not try. *Could I give myself up? What would happen then?*

He despised this place, he despised these people and what they had done to him, once again having been *manipulated.* He edged backwards slowly as the soldiers advanced.

A sound came to him.

'Drop you weapon!' barked one of the soldiers in a gruff command.

It was the sound of water.

'Give yourself up!'

That sweet, sweet sound of running water.

'We will show you mercy.'

His mind came back to the calmness of the void, the water that surrounded him when he swam in the deep colds reaches of the sea all that time ago.

'Now, or we will be forced to attack!'

Ramkus stepped slowly, but surely, onto the ledge. He glanced down. 'Fuck,' he said to himself - the drop would certainly kill him.

He looked at the soldiers - they would certainly kill him.

His mind raced. *It is a straight drop at least.*

'This is your last chance!' the bark came.

Ramkus looked at them. His other mind - his survival instincts - had been suppressed. He was sure of himself. He was determined.

'Attack!' The soldiers began to scream and charge. Ramkus smiled as he stepped backwards.

The rush of air hit him as he plunged downwards.

It felt as if he was trying to take flight, hurtling further and further down. He became tense, fully aware. He held out his staff as the air began to nip at his skin. He placed the staff into the rock face, on an angle so as to provide some breaking motion whilst hurtling downward so as not to let his bare body touch the rock surface which would surely rip him apart. For as much as it did not stop the Guardian, it slowed him just enough that he did not feel he would die on impact with the river below.

As the water rushed up at him, he removed the staff, and placed it in front of him to "break" the water slightly. He entered the cold embrace with a snap. The impact felt like it had smashed him internally. Externally, he was bashed and bruised. He kept hold of his staff in some form of a miracle, as the torrent he had completely forgotten about dragged him with magnificent force, down through the forest. The sky became the view of life, as he struggled to stay afloat. It then became leaves, which seemed to want to choke him. His body dragged on rocks and snags, scrapping, cutting, and bruising him. His energy depleted, he still somehow held onto life and onto his staff.

How long he was in this maelstrom, he did not know, for the river ran with such ferocity that he did not even know how far he had been dragged along it. He slipped in and out of consciousness as the river moved left and right; and with one last effort whilst barely conscious, he kicked and swam with the last vestiges of strength to the left bank. The reeds held themselves out as if offering him a hand to grab onto, trying to help save him. He lurched up onto the grassy bank. Little streams of sunlight hit his body. He lay, giving a small chuckle before losing all consciousness.

XXX

He had heard the story; pieced it together from those that spoke in hushed tones, and those that blasted out indecencies of what they would do if they were ever in a room with the "Prince". There was much conjecture on the part of the dignitaries; of what this meant for the Empire or the Ronato Royal Court at present, or even how the other royal lineages of the Empire would take to such news. As far as Felipe could tell, this was the greatest scandal to have ever hit the Empire! The diplomats would have no hard time dealing with the Guardian, should he ever come into diplomatically arranged talks.

How would word spread? What story would be told, for the very nature of the situation perplexed even Felipe. He was sure his friend was not the monster they spoke of. His physical prowess, yes, but he'd never killed anyone before, nor acted as the well described beast when fighting.

As far as he could understand, the official line that was still top secret from the populous, ran as such: Ramkus had maliciously bewitched the Princess, taking her hand in marriage - taking her to bed - purely as an attack on the Empire. He had then murdered a helpless guard who was standing idly by, and then two more that tried to "calm" him. He then bashed a few more unsuspecting "friendly", "kind" soldiers, who pursued him to find out what had happened, desecrating many hallways and rooms before heading to the rooftop garden and committing suicide.

Felipe did not believe the "official" story, nor that Ramkus had died – neither did many of the people he had spoken to. No body had been found, and many scouting parties had indeed been sent out to find the remains... or Ramkus, whom may still be living. In fact, the parties that had been sent out were of a large host of heavily armoured men. *Imagine if Djuayne were here*, Felipe pondered. *No doubt he would lead the chase; he would want to destroy Ramkus. He'd been summoned for sure by now.*

Felipe wandered to the window of his room, picking up his guitar, he began to play sombrely without much thought.

'And what of me?' he said to himself. 'How do I get *myself* out of this situation?'

He rested with his leg up, looking out to the mountain range: full of mystery, full of stories, and it held *his* people. A low fog was rolling in over the terrain, enveloping the lushness, giving the appearance of being above a cloud. He was stunned by not having the answer to his own questions, deciding on meditation as a means to arrive upon the direction he should take. He sat cross legged upon the ground, calming himself. *There are two options: leave; or stay.* Either suggested he may find problems along the way.

As far as those whom he had been around for a while knew of him, he was the close companion of the "Prince"; but over time had seen less and less of him, as other preoccupations took precedence. Maybe Ramkus had changed in that time, but he doubted it. There had to be something more sinister at play: *How does the other man – the man who died in that room - fit in?* Felipe started thinking back. *Was that a dream?* His skin became prickly with goose-bumps. *Will that happen to me?* he pondered this, coming to notion that he may have to make a quick exit from this place. *But how to get past some many? Would the* chase *not then also be after me as some sort of accomplice? The people want blood now, no matter whose it is. Is it then best to align myself with the Empire? Under a theatrical duress? What do they think of me, those higher up? The King: who knows what he would be like after this travesty. The Princess: she would probably think rather poorly of me,* he stopped the train of thought and considered how she would recover. *And what of the Princess, now left alone by her "Prince". She will get over him; it was too quick a romance and nuptials. Maybe I would be able to get some insight from Giselda – who is at present tending to the Princess... But what if Giselda cannot be trusted either?* He was sure of her, he felt

he knew how her heart beat. The only person he did not trust in
the Court – for he could not tell where their thoughts lay – was
Silque.
'Silque' he said aloud, 'What are you… What do you want…'
Even the Priest Harold, or Poncho could be trusted to a degree;
but something else lurked within *that* man.

His meditation led him nowhere but troubled thoughts. He arose
and decided the best course of action would be to wander the
castle and see how people treated him. Hopefully he would not
bump into any others that knew him well, they *should* be
preoccupied. He may also be able to *get-on-side* with a
dignitary if he was asked to play a tune to change the heavy
feeling that had befallen the castle. No one really knew of what
to do or how to act. He walked out, stepping with a lack of deep
thought - what he felt appropriate - and guitar on his back. The
cloisters held little movement: the guard soldiers whom stood at
some passageways looked on, uneasily tense. Servants rushed
with an even more hurried step, giving looks of suspicion.
Night was falling, and the sky was clear as Felipe walked along
the border cloisters that peaked over the forests. The velvet strip
of light blue deemed the day over, and the sun began putting
itself to rest whilst the moon took the responsibility of lighting
the world. A full moon, with much light from the stars. *It will
give Ramkus as good a run out of the forest*, Felipe thought;
although, as he looked down, he saw the fog that was rolling in
from the mountains: it was incredibly thick and heavy; the type
ripe for horror tales. He shuddered at the thought, and at
realising it was indeed getting much colder. *If only I had
listened to some of the incantations of my grandmother. I'd
offer what I could for his safe passage… and mine.* A guilt was
beginning to well, all the things that he regretted were trying to
force themselves upon him at once. He dashed any hopes of that
type of help, as he left his thoughts and moved along down the
hallway. He came to the main hall that he had been his first

introduction to true palatial lifestyle. It was brimming with life - albeit of a dark and secretive type. People spoke in whispers, raised eyebrows. Although all candles were lit, along with the fire places and braziers, a darkness seemed to shroud the scene. People were smoking and drinking cautiously. Those eating only nibbled at their food. Nobody dared ease themselves on the couches or cushions.

'Who to speak to,' Felipe said to himself. He noticed he did not draw any different attention to himself: *I am not considered part of the Ramkus affair.*

There was a lack of music, so he brought the guitar from his back, and started to play softly, a slow deep, and powerful song. He played from his heart, something that he had not done for a long time. He walked the circles of people, never entering, only playing a tune that drew attention and languishing emotions. He felt he was completely alone in the magnificent hall of people; all others were statues of other worldly beings. *Maybe I can make an escape; but to where?* He stopped playing and approached the buffet table, pouring himself some wine, picking at some olives that tasted of nothingness.

'Bard!' one of the dignitaries called out to him.

Felipe turned around and realised he had become the main attraction for many of the people in the hall.

He was a little taken aback, but answered. 'Yes, kind sir?' in the direction of where the voice had come from.

The man spoke up again, clad in a rich burgundy silk suit that looked like a wall of fabric. He was non-descript otherwise, *probably a merchant*, Felipe thought.

'Bard, would you be so kind as to tell us what news is from the King?'

Taken aback once more. 'What do you mean, sir?' Felipe answered in surprise.

'Well, are you not close to the King?' the man continued.

'Not that close, where did that idea come from?' Felipe responded with bemusement.

'Are you not always at banquets, speaking and playing for the King? Are you not his personal bard?'

Felipe gave a troubled look. He realised how many of these people he did not recognise, many of whom did not eat at the table with the King, let alone speak to him or play for him almost every night. He looked to the ground and shook his head.

'I have never actually been *considered that* by the Court. I have never been *told that* by them,' Felipe looked up.

'Well, we were told you were his personal bard, in any case. I am sorry to have asked,' the man said with an air of indignation.

'No, no, it is fine. I have not heard anything,' Felipe gathered himself.

Am I indeed already part of the Court now? To leave would be very suspicious, very dangerous.

The conversation was a tad awkward now, and there was little else to say.

'Would you wish for me to play for you?' Felipe asked as a small crowd that had swarmed to overhear the conversation. He considered what he should play, deciding, even if it did insult, it was the most appropriate thing he could think of: a lament of the forests demise, but of hope as one wanders through them again: *In the old tongue of my people.*

As he sang in a tongue he doubted any could understand, he saw Giselda, standing at the outer of the throng, resting on a pillar, tired and drawn out, sad and concerned. Tears were rolling down her face. He looked back to his crowd who were seemingly lost in their own thoughts, sipping from their chalices. To his left, out of the corner of his eye, he spotted those whom he did not want to see. Both of them: Silque, accompanied by Djuayne. They stared at Felipe with disgust, and looked to be holding back a rage of abusive words. They did not utter a sound, though. They continued to follow him with their gaze, a gaze that commanded his obedience lest he end up in the same state as the dead man in the room…

The man from Kerwood! The man who turned his back on the Empire. The man whom I had seen speaking to Ramkus. They must have known of Ramkus long before he had come here!

The song ended, as a small applause was sounded. He was not expected to play on, nor would it have been appropriate.

Moving to Giselda, as if she would provide him with the answer as to what he should do.

Her face held a deep sense of hardship, the face of a life held against her will.

'What do I do?' He whispered, as if he knew she was of the same mindset, not caring for her own issues.

'They have you too, now,' Giselda sniffed, looking into space. 'Just like me.'

Felipe stared at her, 'I had nothing to do with this *situation*,' he pleaded.

'I know Felipe, trust me, I know. But you're now caught up in it. Now a political pawn who will be kept as long as you can be used. You're a friend to the most heinous man the Empire has ever wanted to chase down. They will use a person like you for their own ends, keeping you close - unless you're better to them *dead*. All you can do is play along.'

'What do you mean, Giselda?' Felipe asked, astonished.

'I don't know,' she sniffed, 'but those with ambition will use anything they can get their hands on for their own gain. They probably don't know how to proceed in this search for Ramkus – assuming he lives – but *they* will be concocting some sort of plan.' She looked away, 'It may be for future use, years from now.'

So that's what happened to you, he surmised without saying. He thought of the man in the room.

'Who are *they*?' he asked.

She nodded a little and looked behind him. He turned to see Djuayne and Silque standing, looking at him. Silque nodded at

Felipe with burning eyes, observing away; Djuayne spat, hitting a dignitary with the spittle by accident. He did not take notice as he turned away. The dignitary, however, did notice, looking at him, then cowering back to his conversation when realising it was the giant of a man, hero of the Empire.

'I should never have come here, nor brought *him* here,' Felipe said. 'He is not the monster they make him out to be. At least, not as I have known *him*.' He let the train of thought die before asking, 'How is the Princess?'

Giselda did not flinch at the question. 'Sophia is shaken up, incredibly upset, as you can imagine. She feels she is to blame. He was not himself at all, not that evening. She felt she should have known it was all wrong.'

'Ah, hmm.' Felipe went back to his train of thought, 'If anyone should be blamed for knowing something was amiss, it was me.' Upset with himself and his predicament, he took Giselda's hand and kissed it, pressing it firmly and looking into her eyes before bowing and walking out of the hall.

He wandered the hallways to the main steps outside of the castle under a brilliant clear night sky, starlight twinkling. He looked about resting on the view that took in the mountains. He watched the fog that spread upon the forest.

'I am sorry, my friend,' he said softly.

On a bank, cold, wet, bashed, bruised, cut with scars still bleeding, a barely conscious Ramkus looked up to the sky.

'I'm sorry, my friend,' he said.

Part II

The Flight to Freedom

Chapter XIV

A chill charged his limbs, striking his torso until a sharp shiver
ran through his body. He ached in agony, to the extent his only
ability to move was by shaking. His body could not awaken
without being pained, even his eyes took their time to open. He
was lying on his back, facing a ceiling of cloud. Nothing else
could be seen through this fog that lay heavily atop him. He
rocked himself over, lifting his dripping, cold body from the
ground. Oh, how he hurt! Clots of blackened blood adorned his
limbs as if gems; he felt lucky that one *sensitive* region was left
unscathed, but it was not too much of a relief, as the rest of his
body was coming up in welts, and freshly closed cuts were
opening up once more under the strains of his flexing. His hand
hit a long, smooth, slender stick: *My staff!* At least he had that.
The shroud of silence was deafening; he could barely make out
where the river was. In a muddled state, he considered plunging
back in, but quickly came back to his senses. His mind shut
away recent events, he was purely of a focus to survive; relying
on his base instinct - a different person entirely. A cunning
smile came to his purple, frozen lips, one that had been
suppressed. He knew he needed to be this person at present; to
let *him* take over. For the moment though, all he could do was
lie and wait for his blood to warm, and his strength to return.

He finally arose, shivering and stretching out his naked body as
best he could. Taking up his staff, he walked the moist earth and
headed from the river into what should be the dense forest. He
could hardly see five yards ahead in the dark fog, making out
trees and branches here and there. Tripping a few times before
using his staff as a guide on the floor in front of him. He did not
feel the cold anymore, nor much else including the pain. His
other senses were pricked, listening, watching, *feeling* as best he

could the sounds and movements of the veiled night. No light shone.

The fog seemed to cling to him as a thin fabric, wistfully trailing his body as he broke he broke through it.

He instinctively jumped towards a noise, ready to attack: it was an owl.

The slow drudge carried him forward, whilst a clouded mind dared not think.

The forest - from what he made out - was not as dense as others he had experienced. Massive trees loomed hither, shedding their limbs to cover the whole of the forest floor with shade. It seemed the forest had been walked many a time, cleared of much debris that would have stood in the way. Small bits of bark and mud slowly clung higher up his legs and arms, whilst his feet were almost completely covered by the forest floor. Often a small creek would find its way in between where he wandered. Gulches up and down, moving all in one direction. He changed his direction, following these small ravines till he found his way on to what must have been an actual path. He decided to follow it, for no other reason than it was easier to walk upon and seek his way to the mountains; he considered they would surely meander that way in any case, and therefore it was the way to go.

Movement on the sides of the path put him at the ready; shrieks of manifest horror came to his ears: in reality it was a night bird somehow able to catch its prey through the dense cloud.

'I have to figure out what I should do,' he said to himself, trying to pierce the fog and comfort himself with his voice. He needed to know he existed in a solid reality, for he looked down at his completely bare body. Apart from his chest hair, he was completely exposed and very cold.

'What if I bump into someone,' he considered.

Thud. Thud. Thud.

Sounds of something stamping the earth came from the path. He lay low on the ground, not sure of his surroundings. A dim light started to grow as if out of a deep tunnel, coming into focus, lighter still. It was the thud of a number of hooves. He tried to jump to the forest cover, but it was too late, they were upon him in no time, and they were not stopping. He dropped lower to the ground, peering up as best he could towards the oncoming lantern without drawing attention to himself.

The lantern was held aloft on a pole in front of a cavalcade of dark beasts racing side by side. He could not make out the colours, only the sounds of what appeared to be heavy armour clanking. He covered his head, readying as if they were going to bludgeon him upon discovering him. Perspiring a clammy sweat, he held himself together as best he could, tensing tightly, lying directly in the centre of the path. By pure luck the cavalcade of heavily armoured horsemen travelled either side of the path around him. They did not see the butt naked body lying in between.

It seemed the fog had hidden him, as they could not see the ground properly. Breathing a sigh of relief, he wondered what on earth these men were doing out here in this fog. Dangerous that they should use these roads at such speed. *I could have been knocked down -or worse! - if not for sheer luck.* He looked to heavens in thanks, and was met with only the sheer morose feeling of claustrophobia.

Shaking his head, he kept moving, staggering, wondering in his somewhat concussed state if he should have asked for some help. The sounds of the thuds softened quite quickly into the distance, and he was left alone, to fight and fend for himself against the frights of the night once more.

His mind took a turn: '*Clothes*, what on earth am I to use,' he muttered at his predicament. 'Some leaves? A branch?'

Looking around, he could hardly see anything resembling a green leaf or vine. He concluded that he would walk until light approached: either from the morning sunlight; or the lifting of the fog.

Continuing down the path which appeared to run straight and – hopefully – in the direction he thought headed to the mountain range.

Thud. Thud. Thud: the sound of hooves again, but not as heavy as before. They kept trampling through, this time giving Ramkus enough time to hide behind a tree. He watched as another cavalcade of eight horsemen, slowing to a canter, rode by. His delirious state of mind came back as he almost jumped out to ask for directions, when he realised the colours they wore: a deep burgundy.

He instantly hid lower, listening as the riders began to talk amongst themselves.

'He must have died. Who the hell would survive a drop like that and then survive in the forest on a night like this. Stupid to be searching at this hour when it will only be a body we are looking for. We will need better light for that!' One of the riders broke off into a dissent at the current situation.

'Just deal with it,' another rider called out.

'Yeah, it's better than sitting around as a sentry tonight. You're only whinging cause you're *afraid!*'

The banter went off into the distance as it dawned on Ramkus the cavalcades were in search of him!

He sighed, looking into the forest, resigning himself to wandering further into its dark heart.

He was not of sound mind at all.

'I wonder what time it is,' he mumbled to himself, 'the fog at least appears to be lifting.' He could now see the steam rising off his heavily punished body. He brushed off some clammy sweat and bracken. *I completely forgot, I could make a fire to keep warm! How damn stupid am I. Or maybe not, I may be spotted if I did make one. Have I even seen any rocks good enough to light a fire?* His mind stumbled over itself with thought, now preoccupied with foraging a ground that was a tad more visible, as the fog of his own mind began to lift also. His movement slowed whilst looking about for the necessary tools, for the little lift in the fog still proved difficult to combat. He found what seemed to be two decent stones, then searched behind a tree's bark to find dry strips of kindling. His body's movement was becoming staggered, as the muscles began to freeze.

'I am an idiot, this is not going to work.' He shivered as he smashed the stones together without much effect. He was quietly becoming cold to the point of hypothermia and realising his folly.

Tried as he might, the sparks failed to take. He placed them on each other and yelled into the silence, bringing his staff down on the stones, breaking them and letting of a magnificent array of light as if fire had flown from his body and through the staff. The little bit of kindling he had attempted to strike with the stones was now smoking. He breathed deeply at the great effort he had produced. The fire was left to take its own course for the moment, whilst he searched for some more wood and logs.

Once these were consumed by the creeping light, he baked in the warmth. The glow of the small fire in the fog was intense. He stared into it, as if it were speaking to him. He was transfixed in his fire worship, listening to it, concentrating on the voice that crackled from deep within.

He closed his eyes, crossed his legs, and let meditation envelop him.

*"**You see now that I am your only friend**," the voice spoke. Ramkus looked around the well-lit room. It seemed to be the same sort of dungeon that he had been in previously. And the voice that spoke in front of him: his usual devil.*
*"**Prince, that is what they called me.**" The voice was pleased*

'And so that is how you shall be remembered, dear friend,*'*
Ramkus's voice held terse bitterness, the anger of having
charged straight into this maniacal being, having him run
amok.

Shaven head, clad in heavy black leather that was adorned
with spikes and chains. There was a twisted smile, one that
relished all that may be thrown at him; the challenge to
prove his might, inflict it. The eyes were deep, dark, a void
where a small fire flashed.

"Did we not survive? How could you have been so stupid
as to have followed that bard!"

'He helped!'

"He got you in that situation, you cannot trust anyone!"

'Anyone but you?'

"Hah!" *Prince strolled slowly, deliberately, menacingly,*
around the room. A deep hole lay in the middle, filled with
coals. Ramkus kept his eye on this fiend.

'So, what do you propose?' Ramkus continued.

"We take the world!" *Prince implored.* **"Show them**
whom they must listen to: only we know the way!"

'Way to what?'

Prince laughed incredulously.

'You're a madman,' Ramkus growled through clenched
teeth.

"I am you," *Prince said. He smiled,* **"We move forward,**
always forward, each decision leads us to the next step,
whether up or down. There is always that next step."

Ramkus did not want to agree to this, but he knew it was the
advice he needed right now.

He opened his eyes to envisage the embers of the fire beaming
beyond reproach, the warmth retreating. He looked about,
noticing the lift in the fog which had risen much higher above
the ground. He could make out the trees now, the branches and
leaves, and the light of a low hanging moon enveloped the world

in a black and blue. He was sitting, facing a hill in the distance, through the forest scene. He wondered if he should rise to the higher plateau to see where he was and spy what was about. Getting up with great effort, brushing twigs and leaves off his body, baring his clammy cold flesh. He was frozen still through, unable to thaw to any sense of feeling.

I really should not leave without my clothes ever again, he grumbled in his mind, realising the fog was lifting quickly and completely. He stared at the bare top of the hill in front which looked as if it was holding the moon precariously upon its peak. What he saw put him in a great panic and led him to jump into the cover of some bushes.

There, in front of a full moon, on the exposed hillock, stood some *"being"*. Whatever *it* was, it had its cloak flapping in the wind, silhouetted by the moon.

Ramkus's body shook with fear as what seemed like two eyes, reflecting starlight, staring right at him - or for where he *may be*. The eyes appeared to watch him from hundreds of yards away! He did not trust this place. He was frightful. He felt the small pang of instinct to drop down and cower; but this was not the devil he chose.

'Over here!' he heard voices in the distance behind him.

The fire had been spotted by others!

'I am such a foo!' he said to himself, letting Prince come to him. He sneered as he took flight into the forest depths; hunted once more.

Although the fog had lifted, the branches of the trees kept much of the moonlight at bay, and indeed, his steps were heavy, inarticulate, unsure of their poetic fluidness from previous times. He sank to his knees often as he rushed to and fro, away from the figure on the hills gaze, away from all others, all things that approached with malice.

Lanterns were scouring the forest behind him. He looked to the hill when there was a break in the tree line. The figure was still there, watching. He growled, unsure of himself, lacking final direction. Disbelieving his eyes, he glanced back at the hill once more: the figure was gone…

A shiver ran through his aching, crumpling body. The sound of the men behind was growing. *I must be leaving some scent or markings*, he thought. The branches hit him, almost smashing him to the ground, but he kept moving forward and forward. Always forward. He stopped for respite for a moment, coughing, aching, cold sweat covered him. *Where the hell am I going? Am I still on course?*

The trees seemed to move in on him, encircle him, enclose him without fresh air. He began to fret over these sights. He swore he saw the trees move, that they were coming to life! After overcoming the fear, he started the lunge at the wicked branches, the trees that wished his demise. He lashed out at them, smashing them with his staff; his strength was leaving him, the sounds of the men approaching, their lanterns light reaching for him as he looked back. He was now panting, almost tripping from the inability to use his body properly. Desperation made him take flight once more, jumping further into the dark temptress. With the last vestiges of strength, willing, pushing himself through the trees that grabbed at him and surrounded him, becoming more and more entangled with his spirit. The path became so tight that it seemed the passage was all but a small, barely human sized entrance to nothingness. Still, he leapt through.

XXX

In something of a flash, he had passed by the constricted darkness of the foreboding forest, bursting through one heavily dense wall of trees and thickets, surging into an open field. The moonlight was becoming fainter, as the nights glowing orb passed over the velvet blue sky. The ceiling of fog, the heavy thicket of forest, and the clouds overhead had all been wiped as if a heavily scrawled parchment had been turned over to a blank page. The whole feeling changed dramatically, like he had been sucked into a vacuum and come out the other side where the pressure had been completely relieved. There was harmony here; soft grass easing his bare feet's pain; fresh air that not only filled the lungs but alleviated any constriction. He did not want to look back the way he had come, he was too engrossed with this otherworldly paradise that had seemingly had bestowed upon him. Sounds of insects ran across the field, humming away in the light night air, darting in the long grass that blew gently in the soft breeze. Ramkus breathed in the scents as if it was intoxicating; he relished the peaceful aroma, the gentleness of the scene.

How he had never spotted this place from the Summer Castle's summit, he'd never know. Perhaps he was only dreaming after being hit and knocked out by his pursuers. *But it is so real.* He was in an harmonious bubble, shielded from the chaos, calmed. *It must be one of those areas left by the forest people that Felipe had talked about*, he thought before looking to the wind, closing his eyes, and letting it take his mind with it.

After a few moments respite, he made out a copse of trees in this paradise as a source of running water. Still aching, weak, deranged, it was the only place he felt certain would conceal himself. He thought he saw some animals moving, feeding on something he could himself eat. He kept moving to the small arrangement of trees for some protection from anyone's sight, should pursuers wander in here; for some reason, he didn't feel they could. Still, he was drawn this way. A force of pure will pulled him there. As he wandered in, a pool, calm and inviting, lay in front. Smells of lavender, rose, other assortments of fresh flowery scent, all came from this pool, as well as a warmth. He dropped himself in without any thought, being instantly met with relaxation from a heated spring. He laughed, 'Even nature can supply a good bath!' He found a ledge and sat back, letting the heat reside in his broken, frozen body. It warmed him, gave him strength from his escape. He fell into a deep sleep: dreams of a mountain pass, of great lakes, pristine beaches, and of archaic structures he knew not what of, but it did not matter as he retired from his pained night.

The sun had awoken itself, searching the sky with the slow movement of a slumber that it did not wish to wake too suddenly from. The orange tinge of the morning, adorned with blots of pink clouds; it would have been a sight - had he witnessed it - stretching across the field heavy with white daisies sprinkled through the crisp, green grass. And if he had watched the scene, he would have also noticed the figure of a woman, dancing with the coming dawn, approaching the copse of trees where the pool of warmth was hidden; the warmth that had embraced the frozen Guardian, thawing him.

The sound of light footsteps did not wake him; then again, these footsteps were meant to be undetectable. Little did he realise he had been watched, observed, held in contemplation upon setting foot in this retreat.

A shadow cast over him, the change in the lack of heat from the streaking sun knocked him like a dull blow. He awoke, straightening and tensing himself. Bleary eyes searched around with drunken sight, he pounced at the smallest movements, up from the pool, tripping over his staff that he had laid down for the night. He tried to jump back up, but his gaze fell upon the slender silhouette in front of him, backed by the sunlight. He dared not move, unsure if others were around. The silhouette bent herself down, and came into his focus.

She was of a slightly build, and wore tight fitted clothing; two sticks protruding on her back that had a thin chain attached to metal baubles – similar to a mace, but lighter. Her face was one of inquisition, itself interesting; she seemed feline in appearance. High cheekbones underneath eyes of a light green shade that almost blended to a yellow. They held his gaze. Her rich black hair was a long with well-maintained dreadlocks at the back. She tilted her head to take in the sight, not threatening, still thoughtful.

Neither knew what to say - or who should speak first - but since the standoff was non-confrontational, Ramkus decided to stand. His mind still waking from a deep sleep, realising only after a few moments he was stark naked. He quickly cupped himself. The girl's eyes shone with an undetectable interest at the nether region.

'Empire?' She asked in an odd, exotic accent that accentuated every letter, her stance took a more defensive attitude.

'No. No?!' He quickly realised he had shown the bracelets on his wrists, 'Shit,' he muttered through gritted teeth. 'No, I had them put on against my will. I'm sorry, I didn't know this was your place,' he pleaded, trying to sound feeble and in need of help. He forgot he actually was weakened and in need help.

'I believe you,' she laughed to his surprise, 'as I do of all who can make it.' Her voice came out like something he should hold on to every word of, as if it were the vein of a deep wisdom.

'What do you mean?' he quickly responded.

'Not everyone can enter, and therefore the land belongs to everybody who can make it here. You must have some first people's blood - or have been very lucky to find the entrance,' she answered melodically.

He gave her a quizzical look.

'You look like you need help. Come with me,' she gestured.

He nodded, still unsure. 'Thank you,' he squeaked.

Her manner was peculiar: completely at ease with her surroundings, and with him.

'We shall get you some clothes. This way.' She locked herself onto his arm, walking at just the right speed to make it seem as if she graced the land whilst also making good distance to wherever they were headed.

'My name is Miiva,' she said, 'Miiva Mareva.'

350

'Ramkus,' he replied, feeling very odd about the whole affair. 'I am sorry if I did anything to offend. I have had a… painful day, yesterday.' He did not know where to begin in his explanation of his predicament. He also did not know if this woman was fan of the Empire, or not - he surmised the latter. His mind was still clouded; there was so much to take in he felt he felt overwhelmed and unable to comprehend it all.

'Well, you certainly look beaten up. You've cuts and bruises all over. You don't have to tell me your story now. I will take you to somewhere warm and get you into some clothing,'

Ramkus looked down and blushed.

They edged through the field, into a forest of tall, sparse trees which let the light stream in like beams, almost as vivid as the trees themselves. Animals made murmurs and birds chirped, unseen only for the slightest tremors of the foliage they touched. There was a positive energy, a presence of life in these parts. The trees stood straight and erect, no gnarling roots, no branches low enough to knock a rider off. They seemed spaced as if cultivated, but still in a natural formation, allowing one to see far into its depths. The smell of the air felt like it was purifying the body when inhaled, whilst the ground underneath felt almost padded.

The walk was not far and was an easy, meandering path to the summit of a hill where a cavernous rock sat at the top. The exterior edge of the cave was polished softly through the ages, as if by a ritual of circling the rock and tracing one's hand along it time and time again. They entered the cavern and were greeted by a more *homely* state. A fire was burning brightly in the centre of the hollowed core. It illuminated every inch of the chasm, with many rugs placed upon soft clay. The floor was a flattened evenly, with the centre low, rising at the edges like a bowl with polished shelves at its edges. Light streamed in through the natural window holes. Adorned along the walls were a table, bed, wooden shelves in between ones built into the walls, herbs, elixirs, other odds and ends that Ramkus did not take too much heed of. He watched Miiva search a chest of a deep mahogany colour.

'Hmm, this should do,' she walked over to Ramkus who was sitting in front of the fire, still cupping himself. 'Try this on.' She threw a purple piece of cloth at him,

He pulled it around and regarded it: 'A dress?' he said, perplexed.

'It's the only thing that will fit. Try it on,' she insisted.

'I really need to find some proper... *manly* clothing. I have a long way to travel.'

Miiva laughed, 'This is only so we can get to the village, don't worry, we will get some better suited clothes for you there. As you may already have guessed, I only own women's clothing. Most of which would not fit your *broad* shoulders. *That* dress is the biggest thing I have.

He thought for a moment before smiling: 'Thank you.'

'You should not be so quick to shun the hand that cloaks you,' she said.

Ramkus could not tell if she was being sarcastic. 'Thank you,' he said again, in a more respectful tone.

He was quite warm, and for some reason, had felt completely at ease with Miiva, as if she were an old friend. Her true nature, her core being, seemed to shine through intensely. He did not need to think for himself, simply trust in her. Whether this was due to his mental state, or an innate feeling, it did not cross his mind to question the situation any further.

'Now, these may fit you also.' She tossed some high wedged, orange suede shoes at him.

He gave a respectful look. 'Are you sure you are not making fun of me?'

She gave a hearty laugh that filled the room, the light pervading them appeared to grow with it.

'Put this on as well.' She hurled a scarf at him, 'Cover your face.'

He did as instructed, fully in her control.

'No, not over your eyes. Like this.' She came over to him, releasing his wrapping and re-doing it so as to cover his face with the scarf, aside from his vison. 'They'll think you are a visiting enchantress.'

'Enchantress?' a muffled voice came out.

'Of course. What did you think *I* was?' she said as she picked up a satchel with cord to carry over her shoulder. 'Come, let's see what we can do with you.'

The path over the other side the hill was easy travelling; ferns sprouted up, wild flowers decorated spots hither and thither. Although it could not be seen from the hill, the "village" was not far from Miiva's rock cavern. It came across as if it were a natural occurrence of the forest, as if it had grown there of its own accord. Mostly old wooden buildings, two storeys high, massive constructs that almost mirrored large seafaring boats with large patches of moss on the hulls. It was as if these ship buildings had once been floating on water, only for it to recede and position them on the earth underneath. The village had one main thoroughfare, with a dozen of these huge boat looking huts lined along it, with a few smaller, more recently built ones, in between.

One central building stood at the end. Many people moved about; people who seemed to cherish the moment, the place, the life, the community, all getting ready for the day. *It is a simple community, but one with a great history, no doubt,* Ramus drifted off in thought.

A young man whom had his eyes on the pair moved past Miiva as she guided the masked, cross-dressing Ramkus - he had found it difficult to walk in the thoroughfare in the high wedged shoes. The young man slapped Ramkus on the butt.

'Nice arse,' the young man said, before being stunned by a lightning quick punch from the shocked and offended cross-dresser.

'Serves you right!' One of the shopkeepers called out after watching the ordeal. The young man scrambled up in a daze before retreating. Ramkus stood aghast, whilst Miiva laughed with great humour.

Many wooden based wares were on display in the market stores setup within the great boathouses: musical instruments, bows, along with pots and earthenware, weapons of an odd archaic type, herbs, delicious smelling food, honey. One appeared to be a beer hall, although it was not so full at this early hour – at least not with the type folk who brave it out during the whole night, for fear of what may be waiting at home to *greet them*.

'We are early risers here,' Miiva said, noticing Ramkus's curiosity, 'but that is no excuse to drink before midday.'

She brought him to a clothing store: tunics, boots, straps, hats, all that may be necessary were on offer.

'What can I do ye for, Miiva?' the shopkeeper came over.

'Boraf! My friend here is in need of some new clothes and boots. Do you think you could suggest any?' Miiva asked matter-of-factly.

'Certainly!' The man had a monstrous, red moustache and was clothed in what appeared to be "woodland" clothes - very common with these townsfolk. He brought out a stool and placed Ramkus's high wedge sandal upon it… along with his hairy foot. The shopkeeper looked at it, realising what type of foot he had.

'Ah, you have nice, ah, hair on your feet…' his eyes started to rise up and look at the leg. Miiva let out a huge, mischievous laugh, as Ramkus's eyes darted around, seeing if anyone else was watching.

'I forgot to mention my friend was a *he*! He *misplaced* his own clothes,' She continued to laugh as Boraf looked at Miiva and Ramkus, then shrugged. Ramkus shrugged in return.

'Misplaced? I am guessing Miiva may have had some hand in it, no doubt,' Boraf reflected.

He continued to make light chatter as he suited Ramkus's feet with something more suitable and sizing his body up for some clothes.

'These ones!' Miiva said, pointing to a pair of tight light brown shorts and matching shirt without sleeves. 'And that hat!' She pointed to a peaked hat with a feather in it: an archer's hat. Ramkus thought the selection rather peculiar, a bit childish. Looking around the town though, it did seem to be the sort of fashion everyone wore, and the hat did set it altogether.

As Ramkus began to take off the dress behind a screen, Miiva's eyes peered at the top of his head, then to a jacket, which she grabbed and gave behind the curtain, taking in a small peak. 'They must not see those *markings*', she pointed to her own wrists.

Ramkus understood the predicament these bracelets put him in immediately – they already irritated him greatly to no ends.

'And here,' Miiva reached around again, this time allowing herself to look at lower region and smile. 'This will match the jacket.' She handed a heavy belt that had compartmental pockets of various sizes for holding items.

'That's a fine staff you got there, Sir. Where did you get it?' Boraf kept conversing as he waited for Ramkus to come out.

'I found it next to me,' Ramkus replied, 'I am meant to be a Guardian,' he divulged further without thinking.

There was a silence, and the hint of suspicion in the air.

'You don't *say*…' Boraf said, mulling the information.

Miiva watched with a certain intrigue when Ramkus came out for the viewing.

'Well? What do you think?' Ramkus said.

'That you really are quite a surprise,' Miiva said slowly, as she looked him up and down thinking to herself. What that thought was, Ramkus could only guess.

Chapter XV

An urgent town meeting had been called due to the arrival of the Guardian. The assembly of "notable" individuals of the town were convening around a circular table that had had its middle removed and replaced with a large fire pit in the centre, on which coals were letting off heat. Although the huge table did not touch - nor come close to any walls of the *Main House*, which was situated at the end of the thoroughfare - it seated almost thirty individuals, whilst assistants could run around delivering notes, food, or drinks. Massive wooden pillars held up the high arched roof. An old smoky smell permeated the place, similar to the taverns Ramkus had visited, but holding a more earthy, herby aroma.

A few of the old men were sitting down smoking pipes, whilst the elder women were seated in a small gathering, speaking amongst themselves. Equal representation by both. Miiva sat to Ramkus's side; he felt that, even though it was a circular table, he was still on display for all to judge. An older man moved to the spot at Ramkus's other side, not saying a word. He was of a solid stature, tall and elegantly built. He sat down and eyed Ramkus. Another lady sat next to this man; a lady of regal importance, Ramkus felt, holding an air of grace, as well as determination and power.

'So, you are the intrigue that has caused us to call an urgent conference?' the woman spoke in a tone that resembled Miiva's: every word held importance. 'My name is Mirelle,' the woman continued, 'and along with Nessek here,' she gestured to the man in between, 'we are the heads of Lencil, the forests and lands that abound here and once upon a time touched the sea.' She brushed her white-blonde hair aside as she spoke.

'You're a Guardian?' Nessek stated scornfully. 'Come here to push us out further, dispossess us of more of *our* land?' His green eyes became inflamed as he searched Ramkus. An immediate threat seemed to burst from nowhere, Ramkus was taken aback.

'Leave him!' Miiva, who was listening quietly, bit back before Ramkus could digest what was being said.

'Yes Nessek, he is young, and also seems quite beaten up,' Mirelle scolded. 'You must excuse Nessek,' she directed her conversation to Ramkus once more, 'he remembers too vividly *particular* events from long ago.'

Ramkus shook his head, feeling slightly nauseous and confused. 'I really don't know what I should say, I don't even know how I got here. I just need to get to the Guardians mountain. I am sorry if I have caused trouble by coming here. I am not even sure how that happened.' He could not come up with any reasonable pleading.

Nessek sniffed, 'We shall see.'

Most of the seats had been filled, others stood behind in the deep reddened wood hall. Light seeped in from the small windows high above.

An uneasy calm descended on the meeting, as the sparks of the fire suddenly took life in the fire pit.

'Council of Lencil, we have called you to assemble,' Nessek roared as he rose from his chair, 'to decide upon what to do with this… man, who claims he is a *Guardian*!'

'Why on earth *did* you call us here?' An elder woman called out. 'Because of your prejudices, Nessek. Stop wasting our time, we aren't at war.'

Nessek's face reddened, 'And what always happens, eh? Whenever a Guardian has appeared it has been because of some conflict with that *vermin* out there, claiming our lands and burning our forests, so as to wipe us out! And what happens when such a *diplomat*, a *Guardian* comes, huh? We end up having to give up our land to stop that damn Empire from marching right through us! What type of trade is that? Our security for *our* land, which is given time and time again, till we have nothing left!'

'Why bring this all up again?' One of the men called out.

'Because he is telling us this Guardian came to claim our land,' another yelled back.

'Even if that is so,' the first man responded, 'why call us here now? To decide whether to hold him to ransom? The Guardian has not called the assembly himself, or even spoken to the heads of Lencil, has he?'

'Indeed,' another man called out, 'why has the assembly been called? This man is free to go as he pleases. We have never held anyone against their free will. Many of the other folk come and trade with us freely.'

'Ah, look at the state of him,' an older woman in the crowd cried out, 'he looks like he has been fighting. Has it been with some of ours?'

Miiva lent towards Ramkus, 'I am sorry,' she whispered. 'I did not mean for all this to happen. I should have tried not to say anything about you being a Guardian.'

Ramkus gave a faint smile, *I thought it was* my *slip of the tongue.*

The townsfolk looked agitated and annoyed, wanting to get on with their days labour.

'He was infiltrating the village, dressed as a woman!' Nessek thundered to another question from the crowd that Ramkus did not catch.

Mirelle was sitting back, letting the man vent his frustrations, seemingly in control of letting the situation – or Nessek – get out of control.

'I saw him with Miiva, that bloody dusk enchantress was drawing him to us, as per usual.' It was a man sporting most a sizeable bump on the nose.

'I was not!' Miiva screamed, 'I was helping him. And stop attacking the ancient arts!'

'What about that spot fire you made a few months ago?' an indeterminant person cried out.

'I was trying, something,' said Miiva meekly.

'You should not attack Miiva, she despises the Empire just as much as the next person, maybe even more,' came a measured response.

Mirelle decided it time to contain the meeting, ready to steer it towards its intended purpose. All eyes rested upon her once she stood. The crowd quietened.

'Enough of this!' she growled at the chorus of voices. 'We must learn not to get so... *excited.*' She turned slowly towards Ramkus. 'I am sure we shall get some answers as to the true reason of your journeying here, and of how someone could break through the impenetrable tree wall we crafted. Please, speak, Guardian... introduce yourself.' She guided her hand out to him, motioning for his voice and spirit to rise.

Ramkus realised he had not even told the two heads of Lencil his name. He took a few moments to compose himself before standing.

'My name is Ramkus and I am sorry if I have caused offence to you people here,' he said in a purposeful, powerful voice, filling the hall. 'I am not sure what exactly I have done to offend. Breaking a tree wall?'

'You people?' someone yelled in anger.

Ramkus stopped himself, searching for what he ought surely to have in reserve as a Guardian. What was the point of being a diplomat if you could not assuage the conversation to even be accepted into the fray in the first place. He let the comment slide. *What do they want? The truth? The truth...*

'The truth is – *friends* - I am supposedly a Guardian, and I simply want to get to the Seat of the Guardians on the Guardian Mountain - or whatever it is meant to be called. At least this is what I think I am meant to seek, meant to head towards.'

Nessek scoffed but was quickly chided by Mirelle to be quiet.

'I don't know who I am,' Ramkus continued, 'what I am meant to be, but I am on a journey which has been manipulated by many different factors and people.'

Ramkus began to tell his tale, of his first awakening, of journeying with Felipe, the places he had been to, until he got to the story of the Ronato Family's Empirical Summer Palace. He spoke in distressed tones when describing the manner in which his future and position was being twisted and moulded by all there, until the fateful last few days. The speech slowed, and he brought himself to what was becoming all too apparent, all to encompassing and complete in his memory. He demeanour darkened as he recollected killing a number of men with malice, and that was capable of killing many, *many* more. If anything, Nessek began to ease himself, and after Ramkus spoke of how he eluded those chasing him in the forest, Nessek grabbed his arm, hoisting it into the air.

'A Guardian who will fight with us!' Nessek cried, before seeing Ramkus's new jacket's sleeve roll down ever so slightly, revealing the Empirical bracelet, letting it reflect and shine in the fire's light.

Nessek looked at him with a glare of indecision as to whether he may have spoken too soon.

'They forced these on me, I wasn't right in the head!' Ramkus pleaded. He was becoming distressed that all his words would hold no weight after this little revelation. He felt so weak.

Mirelle spoke once more, 'It is alright, young Guardian, we merely wish to hear your story, you are not accused of anything. However, those bracelets, they will bind you to the Empire in many peoples' minds.'

Murmurs rang around the table.

'Well, how do I get them off?' Ramkus, tired, wearing out, pleaded for his curse to be taken from him.

The crowd was silent, watching the scene play out, not sure what to believe or say until a stocky man, shorter than the others, stood up from the table. 'The only place those bracelets can be taken off is in the forge of those who dwell in the mountains. Not just any. Oh no. It'd have to be a master gem cutter, with the right tools and forge. I'd hate to even think what a master smithy would try and do without the proper apparatuses. The only one close to here is in those mountains,' he paused, pointing in the direction Ramkus was to head, 'and I dare not think what he will say if he sees the bracelets before hearing your story.'

Murmurs rose again, as Mirelle and Nessek looked to each other. Ramkus, feeling weakened by the whole episode, sank his elbows along the table.

Mirelle stood, 'That shall adjourn *this* meeting, unless there are other matters to discuss.' She sat down and looked once more at Nessek, who wore a spiteful complexion, as if he knew what may be asked of him and of what the outcome of this meeting truly was.

People rose and wandered off without much care. Although it was an abrupt end, it seemed that this was the usual occurrence when something strange found its way upon the sacred Lencil land from the protective forest. The deliberation of the people was a necessary tool to stand united.

'Miiva,' Mirelle said calmly, 'would you mind taking the young *Guardian* back to you abode. I believe he looks in need of some rest.'

'Yes, ma'am,' Miiva said, bowing as she took the slouched Ramkus by the arm. Although tired and in need of respite, his mind was running at a feverish pace. *Who do I trust? What do I need to do?* He noted that, as welcoming as Mirelle had been in treating him, he was not a *person* to her, not *Ramkus*, he was simply the "young Guardian". He knew he needed to leave.

The walk back to Miiva's cavern was slow. Ramkus's body ached. The people in the thoroughfare did not give the Guardian any more heed than any other. It seemed all that needed to be decided of him had been, by some universal thought that struck in each mind. Miiva hummed along with a smile on her face. 'So, you're an Enchantress?' Ramkus asked in a slow, drawn out sentence.

Miiva gave a smile full of heart. 'Yes,' she declared with great pride.

'What exactly does that mean?' Ramkus probed further.

'Well,' Miiva contemplated for a second, 'I protect this village and its people by using our Ancient Arts. These particular practices that are *not allowed* to be shown to anyone outside our people… and you, as a Guardian. I can otherwise craft and provide potions, herbs, things to make one better enabled, to anyone.'

Ramkus couldn't really begin to question this or delve further. The steps up the hill began, as a gentle spray of wind and droplets hit. The rich smell of the forest took effect, enlivening Ramkus a little.

'I also know much of the world, being taught from an ancient wisdom…. In any case, you need not bother yourself too much, I will look after you.' She gave a faint smile and let her eyes radiate.

Ramkus nodded without taking the cues. 'What was meant by me breaking the tree wall?' he asked.

'Oh, yes, that *is* interesting,' Miiva's eyes grew with piqued interest. 'Do you remember how you got here?' She asked before explaining the predicament. 'A long time ago, our people began crafting the forest, creating a wall of trees that would not allow anyone into Lencil and its territories, from the river or the sea side of the forest. Only those from the mountains can get in. Of course, we do have some openings, but these are very hard to find. You most know *exactly* where to look.'

'That would make sense then,' Ramkus said without emotion, thinking back. 'I remember jumping through a small hole, the last sight before the trees closed in on me in the night.'

Miiva trailed off into her own thoughts for a while as they ambled upward. The rock home atop the hill came into view, a small waft of smoke escaping the minute crevices. When they entered, Miiva immediately left Ramkus's side, grabbing a sheepskin, laying it close to the fire for him.

'You need to rest, please,' she gestured to the sheepskin.
Ramkus happily obliged, lying down, sinking into warmth and
comfort as Miiva covered him with a light blanket. He drifted
off into a deep sleep as the embers and coals crackled away.

The fire roared as Ramkus awoke; a haze seemed to lay at
the outside of the cavern, for light did not pierce through
the nooks and crannies. Night time. He looked at the fire,
surging with power and wonder. Looking about, he noticed
something wandering, pacing like a penned panther: Prince
*"**We must get out,**" Prince said without looking to Ramkus.*
*"**These people are not going to hide us without <u>wanting</u>**
something from us..."*
Ramkus sat up as Prince came to a standstill, looking at him
over the flames, straight in the eyes.
*"**I do commend you, you chose your devil well.**"*
'The alternative was really not much to consider.'
*Prince smiled out the side of his mouth, "**Aye, now you**
have inherited the world. But <u>we</u> must take it!"*
'The World, Prince? Are you trying to play a part in my
passage?'
The fire changed swiftly to a cleaner yellow colour.
*"**What do you think you are? A Guardian?**" Prince*
licked his lips, his heavy, dense leather attire started to
shine with a gleam.
*"**We are more than that, so much more.**"*
'And how do you propose to take the world?' Ramkus said
defensively.
*"**One step at a time. One step at a time... You will**
hopefully learn that I am your friend, I am your only
friend. We shall go to the greatest heights imaginable, but
it is one step at a time that we must take."*
Ramkus found this point agreeable, but still did not dare
guess the heights Prince spoke of.

A harsh wind began to lash outside, as the light in the cave dimmed.

*"**Do you see it?**" Prince spoke with a twitch in the eye, "**Do you see it, or are you blind to all that abounds you? Hah! I shall show you in time, and you will have to realise what we must do.**"*

Ramkus scrutinised Prince, who was now squatting, looking at the flames, eyes opened wide; the flames started to glow and dance in green, purple, blue, red, white, black.

*"**Make that step soon, before I face it for you. Don't forget who keeps you alive in crises.**" Without warning, Prince pounced into the flames, laughing maniacally.*

He awoke with a start. The fire was still warm, he looked around to see if Miiva – or Prince - was there. The cavern was silent, beams of light from an early moon and stars scattered into fragments on the floor.

He was alone

XXX

Hobbling out into the dark, aching, his movements were slow and stiff. He felt – aside from the body in need of repair – well rested. A rich blue was beginning to fold over the orange hue of the horizon, as piercings of the veil started to sparkle dimly. The calm of the forest laid bare its charm and feeling of seclusion and safety. Sparks seemed to rise every so often in the direction of the distant field, rising up and fizzling out before they could reach their brethren growing in the heavens. With no sign of Miiva, and the sense that he was in the surrounds of protection, he moved forth to see what these sparkling lights were.

Edging further through the sparse trees, beams of light parted the long grass as if they were making way to give carriage to the embers of spirits, lifting leaves in their wake before rising to the sky. The beams were coming from a solitary figure in the middle of this field: Miiva. She was dancing with the dusk, as a light breeze blew; the forest seemed to have gathered together to witness her. She swung with an inspired rhythm her sticks which metallic baubles were attached to, through the last vestiges of day; the baubles shot off the beams of light every so often, as if caused by a friction with the air. Ramkus gazed at her from afar, protected at the edge of the tree line. She seemed to smile as a beam shot at Ramkus who found himself darting to take cover behind a tree. It let off a whizz and sang with the wind as it passed him by, before dispersing into the ether.

The light of the day sank further away, as the dark, velvet, blue sky rested atop the setting. The field was at peace, and the show continued for only a short while longer until Miiva let the baubles sink to the ground at her sides. Her head bent back facing the night sky, panting from the whole ordeal. She smiled deeply to the world, as if sending a prayer from her mind to whatever was beyond mortal reaches. She picked herself up, invigorated with the breath of spirit, and started towards the hiding Guardian. The sky began to shine with a radiance.

'Enjoy watching the *Ancient Arts*?' Miiva called out just as she wandered within earshot of where Ramkus hid. He came out, bemused by his own behaviour.

'I did not mean to disturb you,' he replied as they began approaching each other, walking at the edge of the field. 'What was it you were doing, anyway?'

'An old, ancient custom,' she clasped her arm around Ramkus's, whilst his other arm hobbled along with his staff, slowly. 'It actually isn't an elven one, rather the arts our forefathers who had come from the sea.'

'Elven?'

'Yes, they were the original forest dwellers. We have not totally forgotten the origins of our roots. We are an ancient mixed people in Lencil.'

'Forest dwellers. *Forest crafters*? I am starting to understand the idea of the forest wall now, but the sea people?'

Miiva stood tall, looking impassioned. 'That rocky outpost that you were *held up* in by the Empire, that was our home, many lifetimes ago. The two peoples came together there, forest and sea: it was ours.' She bit her lip, 'Then the Empire happened, and we have been cut off from part of ourselves, dispossessed of our land, and reminded of such loss by being constantly in its shadow. Some – like Nessek – are forever at war with such people. Everyone - including you *Guardians* – are to blame for our situation, according to him. To be fair to Nessek, the Guardians that were here did not help the issue long ago. It may have been generations before, but we have long memories, *and long lives*.'

There was a pause in the conversation, as the gentle breeze traced the tops of the grass; the small flowers in the field tipped and prostrated themselves.

'I take it, a diplomatic situation was a little one sided?' Ramkus picked up the conversation. 'The Guardians are perceived to have failed in their duties.'

'You could put it like that. To stop war, we had to give up land. Not just us, many, many others. When the Empire arrived here, they came with the idea of conquering all, they had no concept of peace. They swept the lands, setting themselves up for complete control. Funnily enough, the only others that stood in their way were other empires of sorts. We, the first peoples, were cast aside, seen as mere pawns, nothing.' She breathed in the sweet smells of the forest. 'And that is how it has been, fighting for our place in this world.'

'And protecting your little part of it with Ancient Arts,' added Ramkus.

'Something like that,' she replied. 'They are used to calm the waters for safe passage, as well as calm the lands – or at least *our little part of it*. Performed at dusk,' She smiled.

'I take it you enjoy practicing it at dusk… *Dusk Enchantress*,'
Ramkus said in a pleasant tone.

She smiled deeply, 'It is also a good excuse to practice with
these,' she slapped one of her sticks, the bauble started bouncing
as the connecting metal chain started to jangle. 'They're called
Pois. You never know when you may have to use them.'

Enjoying the serenity, they started back towards the cavern, as
the light of the day retreated completely. When they entered,
Miiva gestured for Ramkus to make himself at home, as she
began to prepare some tea.

'Drink,' she said, offering a pleasantly flavoured drink infused
with many herbs and flowers. Ramkus felt his energy picking
up, 'I must have slept for a good few hours',' he said.

'You slept through all of yesterday,' replied Miiva.

Ramkus looked incredulous, 'A whole day?'

'Yes, I had to sleep next to you for a while last night too. You
were having fits and would not wake. I did not think you were
to perish, but there was some devil trying to take you.'

Ramkus was confused, 'What did sleeping next to me do?'

'Healing vibes,' she responded happily. 'There is much that we
can do for each other if we know how.' She flicked her long,
black dreadlocks around as she began to prepare some food at
the other end of the cavern on a small bench. She reached into a
small hole in the rock wall which held some water and a bunch
of fresh fish, selecting some silver flapping morsel of flesh.

'Why have you decided to help me?' Ramkus asked.

Miiva hummed to herself, 'Just a feeling. That I ought to.'

'A feeling?'

'An intuition that our meeting was due to a lot more than mere
chance.' She looked at him with wild eyes before turning back
to her preparation of the fish. 'You walk alone, Ramkus. I see
that, and you are not purely a Guardian. There is much more to
you. You will change this world, somehow, and I feel I must be
part of that process.'

Ramkus began to scrutinise Miiva: *Is she manipulating me like others?*

'I don't want to manipulate you,' she said.

Did she read my mind?! Ramkus had a pang of fright electrify his body.

'I just think that certain people come into our lives for a purpose in every life we live. Usually the same souls connecting over and over again.'

Ramkus gave a reproachful look, he felt she – although never looking at him – *felt* the looks he was giving. 'Every life we live?'

'Yes,' she replied, cutting into some vegetables produced from another hole in the rock cavern, 'you have heard of rebirth?'

Ramkus sifted through his empty mind, 'No.'

A flame burst out where Miiva had begun cooking on a small fire. 'Please, seat yourself at the table.' She nodded towards a table with chairs at the side of the cavern. 'All we are is energy, Ramkus. Nothing more, nothing less. We do not possess "ourselves". But we move, we live, we are born, and we die.'

'I was not born,' Ramkus said softly.

'*Yes, that old Guardian legend.* But you came to be. What were you before?'

He was stumped.

'None of us were anything but an essence, a *soul* as I expressed it just then. Many of us – us essences – dance through lives with the same other essences as we have always.' She paused for a moment, 'I believe we knew each other long ago, in other lives. That is why I did not attack you in the stream. Although I could have, easily.'

'And this is just a feeling…'

'A feeling that…. I know you.' With a breath of resignation, she brought the food over, smiling as best she could.

Although Ramkus did not completely understand what was said, he accepted Miiva's words; whether they were to bear anything on his life now, he knew not, but he was glad to be in the presence of someone he – now thinking of it – felt a connection with, of sorts.

'Eat it all, you need your energy for the trip,' she smiled, resting her elbows on the table and her head in her hands.

Ramkus gave a sideways glance as he decimated the meal, only upon finishing realising the emptiness of his stomach from days of not eating. He guzzled down a jug of water that Miiva had placed in front of him as well.

'You have a long way to go. But first, you are to attend to those *bracelets of binding*.'

'It sounds like you have decided what is to happen to me. *You've* planned my path,' Ramkus said with chagrin.

Miiva laughed as she pushed some jars filled with pickled foods in front of him. He had been fidgeting since finishing his meal.

'Not *I*. The assembly. We met again, without you. Nessek is not happy it seems. But, he has been calmed.' She ate sparingly as she watched Ramkus who was trying to pay attention. He began trying the pickled onions, herring, cucumber, carrots, sauerkraut, losing heed of what he was meant to focus on.

After he seemed to have exhausted his curiosities, she produced a block of cheese and some bread, deciding just to watch this phenomenon: the bottomless pit.

She continued to tell his decided future after a while, 'We have decided to help you get those bracelets off by sending you upstream by night cover, this way you are likely to avoid detection by the men on the river. You may think them to be *fine* people, but the Empire's eyes are spread through those towns and havens.' She shook her head as the cheese began to deplete rapidly. 'I have forgotten how much men eat.' Her warm smile suggested something more in the comment. 'Of course, you don't have to leave right away, you can recuperate here.' She raised her shoulders and moved her head to the side, gently touching her cheek as her eyes winked, lips pursing a little.

The light from the fire place let their shadows play upon the cavernous wall.

Ramkus looked surreptitiously away from his food, giving a bit of a reproachful look, then avoiding eye contact. He gulped down some more water. 'Thank you for the meal, and for looking after me. I think it best that I was on my way,' he said with an air of fear, and of sadness. He got up, forgetting his battered body. He grunted in a fit of agony.

Miiva rushed to him, helping him back to his resting spot by the fire.

As she let him down easy, she grabbed a pipe, lighting it.

'Smoke this, it will help.'

He sat up and took a puff of the pipe Miiva had presented him – not inhaling.

'Not helping,' he said.

'No, silly, inhale it like this… and hold it,' she took the pipe and breathed in, holding the *purified* air deep in her lungs before letting out a heavy breath of white plume.

He looked at the pipe, 'It's not good for the throat,' he grunted dismissively.

'Are you some sort of singer now?' Miiva said, bemused.

'No,' he sighed, taking the pipe and inhaling the smoke. It burnt the back of his throat, making him cough in disgust. He still held a bit of the smoke in, letting it out along with some of the aches he felt. He stared at the contraption, finally trying another mouthful; the smoke burnt his throat again, but he was ready for such an effect this time. Holding the breath, his body felt itself levitate. His thoughts, his worries, lost to the world that felt far below, where his mind and body should be but *he* was not.

'Good?' Miiva asked.

'Heavy,' he stared into the flame, following its fathomless energy. He tried to move with it.

'Not now, don't get too crazy on me, I don't want you falling into the fire.' Miiva came beside Ramkus, nestling up to him.

She gazed at him, bringing his heated face from the flames with her gentle touch to meet her own.

A sudden panic leapt into his sense. 'No!' he cried, 'No, Miiva, I won't...' he withdrew himself, looking away.

She continued to gaze into the silence of the man. 'You don't have to explain yourself,' she said slowly, 'I understand,' she touched his arm gently.

'Do you? Do you *really* understand? To have been manipulated and exploited by others, to be pushed into a situation, a relationship, against your will?'

Silence once more.

'This is how you got the bracelets?' Miiva murmured.

'Did you not listen to my story, or must I bleed more for you?' Ramkus said coldly, turning from her.

'No, I did not mean to hurt you. I just meant to let you speak of your emotions, not of the episode that has befallen you.' She offered the pipe as a sign of peace.

He took it without much deliberation with himself.

'Did you love her?'

'Love? I... I don't know. We were close, very close. But I was always going to be leaving. It was not for me to have been forced into a marriage. I am a Guardian!'

'So you say. That doesn't mean you can't love someone,' her gentle voice did soothe and provide comfort to Ramkus.

He sighed, 'When I set out with my friend, my teacher Monsieur Felipe, he tried to teach me of the little joys in life. It was fun, it was light hearted, there was no mention of having one's emotions completely distorted to the extent you don't feel you can trust anyone.'

'You can't trust many, that is true Ramkus, but you should be able to *feel* whom you *can* trust. It is about learning the energies of people. You're not just a Guardian, you should not lock yourself into a mindset of being a Guardian because others tell you to do so. What do you *actually* think? What do you *actually* feel?' She drew closer again.

'I don't know, I don't even know what Guardians are meant to be like, whether they can have relationships. From what I have heard, they don't tend to have any relations at all,' he shook his head and sighed, releasing much of his body's tension.

'You see, you are already different from them. Questioning what it is to be a Guardian, what they stand for. You do not stand as a Guardian, you stand for yourself. One day you may even find someone you'll trust implicitly, completely – the one you were split from in the beginning.'

Ramkus stared back into Miiva's yellow-green eyes.

'Lie down,' she commanded, as she lay next to him, enjoying the flames and the pipe... and each other's warmth. The crackle of the fire spoke of sleep.

XXX

'How are you feeling? A voice asked, waking Ramkus from his slumber: it was Mirelle.

Bleary eyed, his mind cloudy, slowly assessing his current predicament. He felt incredibly good considering his poorly state the day before.

'Remarkable the healing qualities of Guardians, and I daresay Miss Mareva's concoctions and incantations do wonders too.'

Ramkus looked around. Miiva was not in her hollowed-out cavern: *it is dawn and she must have been out practicing the* Ancient Arts.

'No doubt, Miiva has explained your next movements?' she asked calmly.

'No, not exactly, other than where I am to head to get these shackles of bondage off.' He held his bracelets out as if Mirelle had the keys to release him.

'She hasn't? *'Well,'* Mirelle continued,' the idea is to send you upstream under night fall. The Lencil River will be flowing strongly at this time, so you will avoid detection from the agents of the Empire, who will no doubt be keeping their ears pricked and eyes concentrated upon the river crossing. Once you pass the Empires town of Fallen Crest, it is an easy journey to Balago, another of our people's village. We have already sent word of your coming and need of aid. Heading inland from Balago, you will seek out Potelo, a mountain peoples' settlement. It should not be too far away. The settlement's master gem cutter should be capable of helping you with those,' Mirelle cast her gaze downward to his wrists.

'Ah, I see,' Ramkus reflected. 'It sounds *well* thought out. When is it to be that I take the river?' his eyes drew to the ground.

'Tonight, seeing as though you seem quite steady on your feet now,' she directed.

'Oh. Tonight's nightfall?' Ramkus stated, a little shocked to realise he was to pack his bags – or lack thereof – so soon.

'I just came to confirm this. Miiva has seemed a little… *aloof* with you,' Mirelle chose her words with careful thought.

He searched her eyes for her true intentions.

'She needs to remain here to help protect our people,' Mirelle continued as if forced, seemingly pressured by the returned intent gaze of the Guardian.

Ramkus looked at her in surprise. 'I did not intend to have her come with me,' he said earnestly.

Mirelle blushed, '*Well*. I am glad you know the plan. I shall see you later to send you off.'

And with that, Mirelle nodded regally, exiting the cavern with the haste of embarrassment.

Ramkus shook his head in confusion.

Miiva returned soon after. Her nose detected an odd scent but said nothing as she greeted Ramkus for the morning. Once again, she gestured to the old beaten table, serving a morning tea and breakfast meal of bread, cheese, and salad.

As Miiva cooled her tea, she looked to one of the windows. 'She has been keeping watch over me quite a bit recently, as if to make sure I do not leave the forest,' she mused.

'Who?' Ramkus said calmly.

Miiva gave a reproachful look, 'You know who I mean. She would have probably spoken to you.'

'Oh, Mirelle,' Ramkus said without emotion.

'Do you know what it feels like to be trapped by your people?' She noticed the error of her words with this audience. She stared at him with full eyes, 'Sorry, a silly question,' she blushed. 'What I meant was, I am not meant for staying put to protect the village. I am meant for adventure, to see the world, like you. Yet I am kept here. Yes, *under my own will*, but still, I feel I have no choice in the matter.'

'Sounds more like you are being forced through coercion: emotional manipulation,' Ramkus wore a stone facade as he spoke.

Miiva continued to stare at him, 'Needless to say, Mirelle will be making sure I don't *slip off* with you.'

'Yes, she said I was to go tonight,' Ramkus stated matter-of-factly.

'Tonight?! But you are not even fully healed!' She blurted out.

'I am as good as I will be.'

There was silence in the cavern, as they drank tea and grazed on the food.

'I guess she'll make the excuse that I need to make a fog fall over the forest so as to not be there to send you off.' She looked out the window into the distance, off in her thoughts. 'Too bad for her then, I'll still be the one to lead you to the river.'

Ramkus politely wolfed down the food on offer.

The morning went like a blur, with a sequence of events that followed in quick succession that chewed through the day till Ramkus was to undertake the next part of his journey. The activities of the morning began after breakfast, with the pair heading to the glade. Miiva took her bauble-chained sticks she called *pois,* and Ramkus his staff. They decided Ramkus needed to test his healed body out; what better way than for each of them to show each other some off their moves.

They danced against each other, with no blows dealt.

Miiva's movements were artistic, acrobatic, whirling the pois along the long grass, making them part for her as she flipped and span about, leaping and twirling. In battle, Ramkus could imagine she would be a formidable opponent: one that would be difficult to get a shot in on, as well as difficult to detect where a shot would come from her.

He - although a little unsteady from recent events - slowly began spinning his staff, moving in all directions with it protecting his body. He glided across the ground, the staff going so fast about him that it became transparent. Every so often, the transparent glow would stop, and a quick strike or defensive manoeuvre was shown. It felt so natural, as if walking. *No wonder the Empire wanted to use me as one of their soldiers...* he scoffed at the thought, and pushed it from his mind. The tips of the tall trees tipped and swayed with appreciation for the show, the clouds lifted in slow waves, letting the morning sky release from its colourful shades.

After breaking a sweat, they washed in the hot pool. Miiva calculated the tidal currents, cursing the stupidity of Mirelle to send Ramkus off so soon. They would need to have him in the waters by the afternoon if he was to flow beneath the river crossing at Fallen Crest before night fall had lifted. After that, Ramkus could go on foot easily undetected, as the Empire would be unlikely to search so far upstream. They rested back silently in the waters until it was time to prepare for Ramkus's journey.

Heading back without a word, the stream of trees seemed silent, no wind stirred. They ate another decent feed of fish and salad in Miiva's cavern, Miiva concentrating her attention on each motion of chopping, placing, eating. It was a tense atmosphere for Ramkus, and was only broken when they made their way out, passing through the other side of the forest to the village of ancient longboat buildings in order to collect the small boat that would carry Ramkus along the river passage. It was known as a coracle, and ancient vessel of the water loving forefather kin. It was specifically designed for one person, for stealth upon the raging river. Miiva cursed Mirelle again for making what she thought was such a blatant error. A two-person vessel would go quicker and more efficiently than a coracle. She considered it purely an attempt by Mirelle to ensure she would be unable to *fall in by accident when setting off,* and have no choice but to head off up the river with Ramkus and *onward to adventure.* To be fair, Ramkus also thought little of the tiny boat, but considered it may be the easiest way to go undetected.

The villager entrusted to create the coracle was quite chuffed with his work, his moustache bristling with delight. The two feigned being enamoured with his craftsmanship.

They walked back through the village, Ramkus carrying the coracle over his back like a tortoise shell. Curious onlookers smiled and gave a few "fare wells", but nary a conversation. Ramkus thought this could be either due to Nessek's attitude towards him as a Guardian (and Guardians in general) or because Miiva looked like she was a storming she-devil, charging towards the path without the opportunity for small-talk. She did not allow Ramkus out of her sight.

Done with the trip to the village, Miiva went straight for the path that would lead them to her cavern. There was little time to look around and smell the heavy aroma of juniper trees that began to waft about. At least the path was easy under foot, and no missteps could be made up to the small summit of the hill that overlooked the field and village.

She grabbed a rucksack and a few items once back at her abode, then led Ramkus by the hand into the forest behind the cavern. Through one of the secret pathways overgrown by great ferns, fallen trees, and rocks; pathways that could only be known by ancient knowledge secret unto the forest dwellers… and those that broke through the *wall of trees* unawares. She continued to lead him with haste, through the mangled and gnarled forest that stood to deter entry to these lands. The river was heard rushing close by, and it became sparse and green in the forest again, not too soon after.

When the river finally came into view, they slowed, and found a particular landing spot along the river that suited Miiva.
'I used to travel from here as a child,' she smiled, 'dreaming of going farther and farther until a return was not possible.' She looked longingly at Ramkus. He could not tell if it was jealousy, or something more.
'I thought we agreed the usual spot,' a third voice came out from the foliage: Mirelle. She stepped out onto the path looking sternly at Miiva, before focussing her attention on Ramkus.
'*Never the less*, I have come to fare you well, Ramkus.'
'Thank you, Mirelle,' he replied humbly.
'Well, better now than ever,' Mirelle said hastily, looking passed Miiva's trepidation.
'Mirelle, please, you can see I am not going, but may I have a moment?' Miiva said.
Mirelle had her attention piqued toward Miiva's subservience, she smiled at her in understanding. Nodding to the Guardian, she walked back a short way down the path.
Miiva waited until she was out of earshot before speaking. 'I have got some food for you in this,' she pressed a bag of victuals into Ramkus's possession which he placed into his new belt's compartments. 'And some… *lights*… for the path.' She handed another smaller bag to him. '**Remember not to fall into the waters.**'
'I shan't…' He replied in a low voice. 'Thank you, Miiva. I think you are indeed one of those people I can trust in this world.'

She produced a massive smile, a tear fell down her cheek.

The air became heavy and heated, a lethargy held both of them, their emotions heightened.

'Maybe, we will meet again,' she mumbled.

'I hope so,' he replied, not wanting to say much more.

She rushed at him. 'Please don't forget me,' she pressed a silver ring onto his right index finger, fashioned with three bars, two solid bands on the outside of a chain design in the middle. 'This should at least help.'

He laughed, as his eyes welled. 'So much jewellery for a man,' he waved his bracelets around.

They stared into each other, embracing slowly to share a small kiss.

Their heartbeats went slowly, as time slowed for just a moment.

Nothing else was left to do other than push the coracle into the river's shallows. He positioned himself to jump in, before pushing off with his staff.

'Goodbye Miiva Mareva, Dusk Enchantress,' he called out as he left her.

'Goodbye Ramkus,' she muttered, raising her hand. He did not look back.

She watched him flow slowly but steadily upstream, into the forest depths, until he was lost from sight.

She let out a heavy sigh and began to back away.

The dampness of the riverbank made her feel as if her lagging body should be drawn downwards into the rich earth.

'He seemed like a good one,' Mirelle came out of hiding.

'Damnit Mirelle!' she said in surprise. 'Why must you always hide like that.' A tear rolled down her face, then another, before she let emotions overrun her and began to cry.

'I *watch* over things because we know those Guardians cannot be fully trusted. With this one though, we can only hope those acts of kindness have some *influence* on him.'

The meaning of the words were lost in the ether, as Mirelle
consoled the girl, who could not stop herself from falling into a
heap.

'I trust him,' Miiva murmured to herself.

Chapter XVI

The water whirled and fizzed as it passed around rocks and hit
snags, creating eddies that would try grab anything floating by.
Fish leapt at times, splashing and disrupting the peaceful sound
of the wind moving through the tree branches. The bottom of
the river could not be seen, but its waters reflected much of the
world above. Sparrows fluttered and chirruped, as the oft
animal drinking at the edges startled when the strange sight
flowed by. Ramkus found himself dozing off in abounding
thoughts as if gliding, only coming back due to being haunted by
fast rushes of the river passage around bends. All was lost in the
moment.

Such green fertile woodlands, sparsely planted with trees: *Was
this the work of the forest dwellers as well?*

The sun decided to sink into the recesses of the mountains, as
Ramkus decided to eat some of the victuals Miiva had provided.
Simple supplies of cheese and bread, salted meats, a few pieces
of fruit – it seemed to be the staple diet of those around these
parts. The coracle stayed on course, not spinning about due to
the wooden staff acting as a rudder under Ramkus's armpit. He
lay back comfortably enough, only a few splashes of water
reminding him of the peril below.

After the sun had done its dash, and the moon came with muted
light, a heavy fog akin to the night of his escape began to fall
upon the land.

'*Miiva*,' Ramkus said to himself.

He watched the path succumb to the fog. A sudden dread was
contemplated, as the little bucket boat rushed and surged in
places. Ramkus was not confident of the water, jostling in his
uneasy and unnerved state. He decided to be as passive as
possible, meditate. If anything, he would be able to get some
vitality from it. He felt he needed to be as well rested as he

could for whatever trials awaited. He may also experience his
friend in the midst of his brief relief.

The rocking of the coracle did not allow him to settle; he did,
however, hear a faint voice.

*"Try the **lights** she gave us."*

Ramkus found it difficult to reconcile with Prince, but he had
made a good point. As much as Prince was of a different strain
of rationale, he knew what to do instinctively, naturally,
instantly. Prince was not there to fight him. *No*, Prince was
there to *guide* him, albeit along a different path.

*"Come on, try the **lights!**"*

Ramkus obeyed, searching into the bag that Miiva had supplied
along with the victuals. He pulled out a small cloth sack that
had been sealed with a cloth strap. Opening it, he put his hand
inside and pulled out a *light*. He tried to make out what it was: it
seemed invariably of a soft cushioning fibre, dark, a little cap on
a stem. He looked at it quizzically, trying to figure out what it
was in the twilight, and how it worked.

A mushroom? He smelt it... *A mushroom. Perhaps fluorescent
ones.* How he even knew there were fluorescent ones was
beyond him. In any case, he started to rub the one he held. No
reaction, other than the sticky residue of the mushroom coming
off on his hand as he tore apart the weak fibre of the fungi. He
pulled out another, smelling it again. An odd smell, of earth, not
fresh, but not stale either.

"Try it," Prince said to him.

You have to be kidding me, eat it you think?

"Yes, trust me."

Ramkus took the little morsel of forest flora, passively staring
into the ether of its unknown potential. He placed it on his
tongue, bringing it into his mouth. It was quite chewy, he
detected some seasoning to make its taste more palatable. *Not
bad.* He took another mushroom: no change. Another. And
another.

He sat in wait.

The waters swirled around the reeds; he could hear it, the reeds making the smallest of cuts in the vast flowing river. The reeds, the leaves floating by, the branches which hung overhead as if placed in an orchestrated frenzy of chaotic fury. His mind was awake; the fog had lifted! He could make out the shapes through the distance, the colours of darkness started to lull into grey apathy, the path was straight as it twisted. The trees on either side mirrored each other, then collapsed in to make the most oblique and contrary visions.

Out of the corner of his eye, some giant snake-like creature burrowed and rose, twisted and turned around the great legs of the forest top. It moved behind, quickly as it floated from one side to the other, always just out of view.

He leant back; the leaves and branches moved inward with all the energy of the cosmos centring on the little coracle; they radiated outward, colours, browns, yellows, greens, *light*. He looked down. The flat face of the snake creature: a whirling face with three black circles, smacked him backwards.

He rocked his coracle, spinning around, moving hither and thither to each side as a cold jet spray hit him.

The path had now become a drop that he could not control. The world spun around the coracle, becoming quicker and quicker, as it floated from the sides of the banks. Flashes formed in the forests, as if fireworks were going off in celebration of his descent: down, down, down.

Black forms came at him, and in a great effort he raised his staff underneath the coracle where he had used it as his rudder, spinning and kicking all these shapes of darkness. But more shapes came, in all colours: whites, yellows, greens, reds. It was all he could do to evade the creatures of this new dimension.

Am I going there, or are they coming in?

He couldn't concentrate, the creatures, the spots and sparks flew at an increasing speed from all directions. His little boat rocking along precariously, back and forth, taking in water.

The atmosphere was a haze of purple now, as he tried to calm himself. The branches ahead were harbouring the creatures; moving, the life had passed to them and the leaves fell in their wake sporadically, trying to latch onto the Guardian.

He caught his breath as the path seemed to level from its startling descent; the creatures ceased their attack.

His eyes gaping at the splendour of the forest, all hues, melding and mixing with each other.

He raised his staff: the gold end of it became black, and the black became gold; his name on it emblazoned now in a bursting fire at the end. He admired the miraculous visage with a manic energy. Looking down to the stream that was now not a stream, but lines that built upon lines, and stayed in such a warped manner. It all melted into itself, not changing, but becoming more and more a surreal picture.

He closed his eyes and envisaged a red and yellow pulsation. Beams of white at the corners of vision came to be focussed upon, only to disappear into nothingness.

Another attack?

He opened his eyes to the forest as it should be, but lighter.

Ah, so the light!

It was a heavenly oasis, akin to the forest and field he had been too. The blue light sung of harmony, the tress glistened, still alive, but calm and at peace with the intruder. The waters lapped gently, and the banks of the stream flowed with bristling attentiveness to each reed and exotic element that entered it. It was a sanctuary he had entered, he was sure of it; and he lay back quietly, with the *light* switched on.

A rumbling, and he was moving upward, as if the coracle were on some sort of mechanism, being pulled up a mountain stream's path.

The water is flowing upward! And quickly, ever so quickly!

The black was not white, and he felt something far behind him catching up.

That thing, that terrible lecherous snake-thing, *it is back for more!*

He readied his staff, preparing for combat. The water rushed alongside the coracle, with the coracle, but he felt he had stopped and was vulnerable from all directions. His eyes wide, moving side to side; his mouth pursed as his nostrils flared. He smiled devilishly, awaiting the huge *snake-thing* that moved from the corner of his eyes, waiting for his chance to destroy it. But then a falling sensation, as he felt he was flying and falling at the same time. The white now became a myriad of multi-coloured visions, brimming with life, with voice! Oh, how he wished to hear all of their voices, and he *could!* All at once, singing their songs, an orchestration of life.

The snake creature, it was not evil, it was the guardian of these things. It flowed into focus along and between the long-limbed statues of an era of long-awaited existence that stood beside him, bowing.

He was panting. With his staff, a beam of power, of light, hit the statues from the end of his trusty weapon, illuminating every particular place, each awakened with greater clarity and volume than the last. They sang to him now, "Come! Come with us!" as he drifted to thoughts of being one with this forest of life: he would complete the ensemble.

"Come with us, share with us!" it continued. Purple and blue hues began to form at the edges, and in the distance of his path, a great beam, one that imprinted itself on his eyes, bursting forth. Ever so small, but ever so powerful. "Save yourself, come with us," his friends called from the sides, "Be with us". He acceded to their request.

As he tried to resolve them, he fell; falling, the world split open, and blots crashed into his vision. Blinded, periodically, he rose, then fell; rose, and fell. His staff tucked under him, propelling him down the river, urging him forward, but also keeping him afloat from these falls. It was his only companion, as those statues laughed, mocking him for daring to be one with them.

He kicked and pulled himself towards the statues; oh, how he wished to make them pay for their cruelty. But he also felt peril, all over him: a sticky residue, one that wished to drag him under. In these troubled thoughts, he remembered the calmness of being under water, a feeling that he had once upon a time experienced. He relaxed himself to this predicament. Lying bent, his body spasmed, fighting against this unnatural state of acceptance. He rose above it and kicked his way to the feet of the statues. They were calm, dead. The colours now of twilight. He hit ground hard. It smelt of a damp, burnt earth. He willed himself onto a fabric, a texture that moved under him. Breathing heavily as he lay on his back, looking up. Coughing and spluttering, his body burned, argued at his falling, his failing. As he rolled over, he spied two eyes. *Is this the snake thing? The lifeblood? No… different.*

He lay motionless, watching, as this new, brazen creature lurched forward. It was angered at Ramkus's presence. It came into view to look at its prey. Ramkus watched it, regarding it as something similar to a giant praying mantis. with its front legs as sickles, which came down on him.

Is this a dream? He found himself wondering.

His instincts took over, as he raised his staff to counter the sickles that rained down a volley of attacks: *Nope, no dream.* Ramkus met the stare of the mantis creature with a mocking smile before developing into a nasty sneer. He bent over as if to bow and accede to the challenge, but he quickly brought his staff up with a snap at the creature. The following blows were quick - whether they were well delivered, he had no real idea in his still dreamlike daze. He ran on pure instinct.

The mantis moved to and fro, dancing with the Guardian.

It countered and span in a whirlwind motion, bounding for one of the statues that now threw aside its shroud to declare itself a tree.

The creature span so quickly it surprised the Guardian and made him fall backwards.

He rolled and leapt to the side as the sickle pincers came down upon where he was.

Quick as a bolt, it came back at him, but the Guardian moved to the side as it missed again. Ramkus gave a good strike, but he missed, and the mantis was back at him in the whirlwind attack again.

He edged back, deflecting the blows that came too close for call, he backed onto a tree; an idea came to him!

He leapt to the side to evade, and at the same time swept the legs of the creature. It stumbled forward, and all it could do to stop its force from falling was stick its pincers into the bough of the tree, unable to draw them out.

Ramkus laughed as he pranced, declaring himself victor.

The maniacal laughter ceased as he readied for a blow on the mantis that was making wheezing sounds. It had turned over, somehow ripping its arms from its scythe-like pincer ends! Defenceless, wheezing, but also seemingly laughing in an horrific defiance.

Ramkus swung his staff to feign a low sweep, then lifted the staff's end up to strike down upon the creature's head. The mantis quickly deflected with its scythe-less limb to change the staff's downward angle, but the strike still broke through the defence to hit the mantis's head. As seemed to be the luck of this Guardian, during the process of his finishing blow, Ramkus's staffs other end jolted back enough to smack him in the head with its follow through. It was – as per usual - his already well battered temple that took the brunt of the ricocheted blow.

He was out instantly.

XXX

He awoke, slowly, feeling as he had often felt after waking from such circumstances: awful. There was a small shudder, a kick from a mound where the heaped body of the Mantis creature lay.

'Not dead, eh?' Ramkus grumbled as he got up with as much haste as he could muster, straight into a suitable fighting position. This was slow and arduous process, and the creature did the same, slowly and sluggishly. But this was no mantis creature, it was a man - on the shortish side - not too stout, nor too lean. Black hair, straight as an arrow, and dark and deep eyes; Ramkus could not read him too well for any underlying emotion.

The man stretched out. He winced as his back cracked, but incredibly, seemed rather relaxed, considering the previous confrontation.

Ramkus had no idea what to do, whether to relax also, or stiffen: *Is the fight over?*

The man was at ease, not one care that he had a staff pressed at him from the cautious Guardian.

'Drop it, let's fight *properly*,' the man said without looking at Ramkus.

'What on earth is wrong with you,' Ramkus was cautiously listing all his pains. They urged him to lay right back down and not move a muscle.

The man looked at him over his shoulder reproachfully. He stood side on, looking deep into the forest. 'You're weak,' he said in a mocking tone, his eye was blackened and blue.

Ramkus stared at him, horrified, hearing this man who had had the living daylight beaten out of him, stand up and ask to continue the duel. *He's as mad as Prince!*

'Screw it,' Ramkus said half in agitation, half in rage: "***Indeed***." Dropping his staff and charging at the man, he was angry that his *friend* had taken this taunt deeply. *Prince wants to* punish *this insolence.*

The man hit Ramkus in the head with his fist as soon as he came into range.

Ramkus stopped, reeling from the strike.

The man moved in, but was caught off guard by Ramkus's electric speed.

He grabbed the man with unnatural haste, lifting him, bashing the mantis man against a tree, pinning him there as the tree cracked, snapping branches and breaking bark off.

The mantis man kicked at him, getting him right in the groin. Ramkus let out a groan, dropping the man and falling to the ground.

"We can't let him beat us with such a dirty hit!", Prince cried to him his head.

Ramkus jumped to his feet, grabbing the man who had thought the fight over.

Ramkus pressed a forearm against his opponent's throat, body forced against his as he began to *punish*, and *punish*, and *punish* him. With hit, after hit, after hit of his free elbow and fist.

His nostrils flared, his eyes wide, dark with contempt.

His opponent was like rubber though, taking all of the pain, laughing to himself in between his crying.

'Ok… Ok… You're… not one… of them,' the man panted.

'One of what,' coughed Ramkus as his stamina waned.

'One of the Empire.'

Ramkus grunted, the tension in the air was lifted.

He dropped his victim and backed away feeling his own agony again once the bloodlust had faded.

'*The Empire*,' Ramkus scoffed, and looked away.

The man began to speak in pants, doubled over 'I did.. not.. know…. But I need… ed… to see… how… you fought.. to tell… Last night.. you could have been… anything… You were like… possessed… demons powers.'

They sat, breathing, panting, recovering.

As the adrenaline wore off, Ramkus felt the pain from his nether region, and vomited.

The two combatants rested as if made of stone, lurching over, licking the wounds from their battle. The mantis man was the first to make an audible sound, a groan; Ramkus lifted his head.

'Not one of them.' The man was laughing and crying, the torment he had put himself through was too much to bear on a normal mental platitude, yet this man was not normal.

'Who are you?' The words were drawn out of Ramkus's throat. His mouth was dry with a web of substance, he spat it out - blood.

The man looked to him, 'My name? *Mooyne*. You?' His demeanour had changed to an affable type.

He is actually rather pleasant to talk to, it seems.

'Ramkus,' came the reply, 'not one of the Empire, not by a long shot.'

'Ha!' Mooyne shot back. 'Then perhaps you are the person they are looking for?' he guessed. Ramkus frowned deeply, with eyes going glassy. Mooyne turned his head and spat, 'Masses of troops have been scouring through these forests for someone or something, all the way from that village by the water, the one with the bridge. Fallen Crust or something. One of their spy stations, that place.'

Ramkus took note that this was the reason he was in the coracle, hidden under the mist, attempting to pass by undetected. *That particular hot spot...* 'Fallen *Crest*... Is that behind us?' he asked warily, but hoped with fervour it was the case.

'Hah, no, it is a little bit further along.'

Ramkus smacked himself in the head, gritting his teeth, 'Bloody mushrooms,' he grumbled.

Mooyne continued, 'I didn't know what you were, just some crazed man in the water, at least I thought that you were. A stupid Empirical soldier who had gotten lost. As much as I don't want to kill an innocent man, I could not risk letting myself be found.'

Ramkus sensed the trepidation, and an opening to query Mooyne's reasons for such distaste towards the Empire, as well as *his* flight from them. 'And what is your situation with them then? You're a one-man army ready to take them out one by one?'

Mooyne laughed, 'Hah! Sort of, I just love a good fight. I doubt the Empire have ever set foot in my homeland. I struggle to think how far away it is now, but I am comfortable in these surrounds, and that is enough – as long as I get a good tussle in.'

'Why did you leave your homeland?' Ramkus asked, noticing that Mooyne did speak with a definite accent. He also looked considerably distinguishable from the people he had seen in Elantra so far.

'It is in my nature.' The words were defiant, practiced, evidently a *nature of belief* that Mooyne held to be the axiom of *his* world. Mooyne nodded, 'It is who I am.'

Ramkus frowned to himself, 'I wish I knew who I was,' he said to himself.

A pause in the conversation entered, as the two looked themselves over, picking at their cuts and bruises. Dawn was beginning to break through.

Ramkus grimaced morosely, 'Damn it, I needed to get past the bridge up ahead during nightfall.'

'Eh? Fallen *Crust*...?' Mooyne replied, 'The Empire's outpost?'

'I thought it was just a town, not an outpost?' Ramkus looked back.

'Hah! No way. Those towns cluttered around this land are bastions for the Empire, their eyes and ears function there. They see who comes in and out, there is no knowledge of what is happening in these lands that does not get past them. A smart way to totally instil a mode of control, have the only towns around function as spy outposts as well as villages. No, there are no towns that are free from the influence of the Empire, save that of the first peoples who detest the conquest and stand in its way.' Mooyne looked around with a bit of annoyance that he knew these lands better than many inhabitants.

'And it is one of those *first* peoples' villages, Balago, that I am headed,' Ramkus's head sank as is his arms rose, the bracelets gleaming in the morning sun. Miiva's ring seemed to shine with a different intensity as it held the light rather than reflect it.

Mooyne's eyes rested on this intriguing sight: a man, not of the Empire, yet bearing two very striking Empirical bracelets - one of a marriage to a very senior noble woman - clad in the attire of the forest dwellers, bearing an intricately crafted elven ring, holding the staff of an ancient order that he knew only sparingly about. Mooyne did not judge: he calculated. His eyes showed no emotions or thoughts: a trait of his people - if he so wished to use it.

This man, Mooyne thought, *I feel his presence bearing on this land, on me. He will be a significant person to this continent's future, it calls him! A future I am somehow tied too…?*

Already he had assumed that there was a need to be at Ramkus's side, his new friend, his companion perhaps, along this long wild road that spread a world of incomprehensible trials and tribulations. He didn't need to ask any questions of him, he trusted Ramkus's story would be divulged at some pint when ready to be told. And even if it didn't, it mattered little to him. He surmised the whole point of the exercise was to remove the bracelets, with the way Ramkus kept tensing when he was reminded of them upon his wrists.

He stood up, 'Well, let us get something to eat and plan out how we will get you to the forest dwellers downstream.'

Ramkus looked up at his new companion, 'Indeed.'

Mooyne seemed to fly by the handle; swiftly chasing down a rabbit when the chance presented itself. Needing only one nocked arrow to let pierce through the forests tranquillity and wrench a meal. Highly impressed, Ramkus watched on as this adept hunter fled through the trees, declaring them safe passage. His sense of smell led them to small areas where a fruit tree or two bore a couple of pieces of uneaten morsels. Animals roamed these forests with careless abandon, consuming its rich delicacies. Mooyne commented that he found it odd the Empire's men were not trained to set foot in these environments;

that they had declared war on the land, decimating large swathes for their clear-cut paths.

'All the better for me,' he quipped, as Ramkus assessed Mooyne would easily take care of a good dozen of the soldiers in these surrounds before any would be able to detect him.

It felt good to be moving, to wear off the stiffness of the aches, pains, bruises, and welts that they had both inflicted upon each other. The fact Mooyne was able to move so well without too much wincing surprised the Guardian. It was almost *superhuman*.

'A steady diet, lots of exercise, and extreme conditioning,' were what Mooyne put it all down to. This was not to say Ramkus couldn't move with such capability in his considerably battered state, he just preferred not to. *I would have spent half my existence in a beaten-up condition by now*, he mused.

The forest was a set of glorious shades as it revelled in the sparseness, it was much more open than what it was like around the town of Lencil. Less undergrowth, none of the gnarled roots which caused the forest to close up. The earth crunched under Ramkus's forest boots, whilst Mooyne seemed to dispel all sound as he moved in a wolf like manner. Ramkus chuckled to himself: *Who would have thought such a man could be comparable to a wolf!*

The bracken and dead leaves made for the earthy aroma he had become accustomed to, and the taste of the water – whenever they stopped to drink - was cool and refreshing, the type one drinks greedily after a harsh amount of exercise. Mooyne was not too particular about his manners either, sharing in the delights as Ramkus did. He wore his emotions on his sleeve, not showing any tact or filter to declare himself anything other than a hardened ranger type. His clothes – a mish mash of leathers over an immaculate fabric - seemed foreign, and his features suggested he was from another continent. When pressed for more stories of himself in their general discourse, he divulged little, other than his homeland was a lifetime away, and he had no sense to dwell upon what remained. He had learnt what he needed to there, how to fashion his weapons and clothes, hunt, kill, fight, and be merry. That he had some sort of vendetta against the Empire struck Ramkus as having a solid backstory. Once more, Mooyne was not too enthused to divulge any further information on the topic.

Mooyne was quite the impressive bushman, reading the scene with a sixth sense. Ramkus acknowledged the intellect of the man, so quick on the uptake, in devising plans, in executing them. It felt as if there was little time for asking questions, but that was simply due to the manner of their travelling through the forest. As much as it seemed like a simple saunter – Ramkus happily followed the leader here – there was a method to the way they walked at different angles, getting greater vision whilst concealing themselves. It was so natural to lose oneself in this environment that Ramkus barely found himself feeling the emotional constraints of before. That is not to say he didn't open his mouth at all. He absentmindedly began rambling on, explaining where he was headed and why. Mooyne made no comments nor asked any questions. However, he was quietly pleased that his reading of the whole situation was on point. The bracelets scratched against trees at times, leaving dents in the bark which Mooyne frowned at. 'Stop leaving markings for them to find us,' he would say, knowing full well the Empire still had no chance to "read the markings". Ramkus could only shrug and traipse the forest corridor with light steps, breathing deeply and enjoying the smattering of sunlight that filtered through.

They stopped for a lunch break after a while, which only further increased Ramkus's impression of his new travelling companion by virtue of his cooking. A mixture of rabbit, some sort of green leaf, and a tuber vegetable he'd gathered. These were cooked on, near, and in a small fire they'd started. Ramkus enjoyed the texture of the rabbit, something hardy and sinewy to get his chops on. Mooyne had made sure to conceal their whereabouts off the road. They followed it, only just out of sight, so a fire would easily have brought attention.

Ramkus admired this man's bushcraft, wishing to gain as much of the knowledge as he could from him in a short amount of time. Mooyne wasn't too unwelcoming of questions on how to do things, but was still somewhat wary of the Guardian encroaching on his solitary journey.

Resting in a small clearing with tress at their back, Mooyne produced a hunting knife and started cutting into some fallen branches that were situated about.

'So, a Guardian, huh?' Mooyne preoccupied himself with his cutting, not caring for a response either way. He had heard most of Ramkus's story by now through dribs and drabs as they moved deftly through the forest. He was not swayed either way towards his fellow combatant, 'Sounds like a bit of a burden if you ask me.'

'I wouldn't know, at least not yet. It has been a burden in some respects.' Ramkus sat meditatively, watching on as Mooyne began taking his knife to the base of the tree behind, creatively cutting shapes into it. He turned around to Ramkus and grinned, producing a boot knife and tossing it at him in such a precarious manner as to catch Ramkus off guard. Had he not the superior reflexes to catch the blades handle, he would surely have ended up slicing himself. Shaking his head, he decided better than to waste the energy and dampen the mood by admonishing his new companion. 'You're are a crazy one,' he simply said, deciding it best to focus his attention elsewhere for the moment. As he regarded Mooyne's motions, he understood this was a peace offering of sorts, and that he should follow suit.

He looked to the tree at his own back, and stabbed the knife in. The bark was not deep, with the blade hitting greenish wood underneath. Considering the simplest thing to trace, he attempted a perfect circle, pulling the boot knife through ever so slowly with great precision, completely focussing his attention on the work at hand.

He smiled at his artistry upon completing it, but found it lacking. Putting the knife point to one side, he slashed through the middle horizontally, splitting the circle in two.

'Hmm,' he mumbled to himself, 'it'll do.'

He turned his attention back to Mooyne who seemed to be finishing up his own little undertaking, shaking his head and smiling with a frown.

'*Voila!*' he said, gesturing with both hands to a well cut and shaven etching of a rabbit.

Ramkus began to laugh, admiring the work. 'A crazy one indeed,' he said, as he threw the boot knife back at Mooyne, taking delight in the look of surprise that Mooyne should encounter a reflection of his actions.

Not before too long, they stood on the outskirts of the forest facing Fallen Crest. A large stone wall with many sentries surrounded the town. It was heavily lit as night began to fall. The town was distinctively different from the sprawling mass of ad hoc homes and workshops that the *ancient* towns of first dwellers were accustomed to. Instead, it was a well-planned out and constructed set of half dozen criss-crossing streets with tall buildings either side. It had been built into a rocky cleft, unnaturally steep and difficult to pass around, whilst the other side held the bridge Ramkus was to have travelled under during the previous night's "mist protection". They decided against traversing around, as this would have taken far too long. They also decided that to take to the water beneath would be too difficult, and there was no way to ensure their safety in the murky, fast running rapids.

Mooyne also had ulterior motives that he did not disclose: he was of the disposition of wanting to cause some damage to the Empire by using a new method of terror he had come across, as well as partaking in one of his favourite past times - stealthily appropriating property that did not belong to him. He really couldn't care less how they got past the town, only that he could attend to his usual bidding.

'This is worse than usual,' Mooyne commented, frowning at the heavy stench of the cured rabbit they had just eaten as a quick meal. He gritted his teeth.

'The wall looks too well guarded to get anywhere near,' Ramkus added.

'If I wasn't in this state from being bashed up by you, I could have taken all of them,' Mooyne chided in a joking manner. 'But there is always a way.'

He thought for a while as Ramkus waited for instructions, squatting on the red rocky earth of their vantage point as best he could with his damaged knee. It was the first time he had actually let himself be truly subservient in the planning of any action.

'The sentries will probably be quite alert, waiting for anything. All those soldiers prancing about these forests in recent days… *looking for you*. The sentries know these aren't the typical easy-come-easy-go-times. Some sort of diversion would be our best option.' Mooyne pulled something out of a pouch at his back. A small round object with a piece of rope hanging out. It was his new method of attack, just what he had been waiting to use. 'But how do we get it far into town,' he muttered to himself looking at Ramkus's staff, 'How good are you with that,' he said, pointing at the Guardian's tool-of-trade.

Ramkus was a touch taken aback, 'Good enough,' he said reproachfully.

Mooyne laughed, 'So you think you could hit this if I were to throw it in the air, so as to smash it over the wall and well into the town?'

'Ah,' Ramkus caught on, 'I should be able to.'

Mooyne nodded, standing with his chest protruding, hands on hips, 'Right then, let's give it a shot.' His eyes lit up with a lunacy that Ramkus had only ever seen in those who bordered on madness – he knew it only too well. 'Let's go!' he quickly lit the wick of the "ball", and tossed it in the air, stepping back with a large elongated step that looked like a dance.

Ramkus in shock, stood to attention, readying his staff, timing the falling ball that smelt of chemicals. Falling within range, he swung… *and missed*.

His eyes shrouded over in shock. He looked at Mooyne whose mouth was agape.

'Shit,' he uttered, picking up the ball and quickly throwing it in the air again. Ramkus, alert, ready, swung again, this time smashing the *parcel of fun* high into the air and over the wall. It descended onto a roof far on the other side of the town. A massive crack of thunder – or what sounded like thunder – came as soon as the ball impacted with the hard surface. It looked like fireworks for a second, as shards of brick from the roof flew about into the town. A hum of voices came about as the glow of red and orange moved about the top of the towns rooves. Shadows and cries broke out in hysteria.

'Now, quick!' Mooyne said, running to the wall with sheer recklessness. Ramkus, without question, followed, too tired to go anywhere but forward. His mind was foggy, as he tried to comprehend what he had just taken part in.

Racing down from their perch undetected, they reached the town perimeter. Mooyne frantically tried to push through a small archway door along the wall.

The voices of the town's inhabitants became screams and shouts, as if war had been declared upon them.

A fire had started, ignited from a central point and spreading with haste. Soldiers from the wall had no choice but to leave their posts.

The small archway door would not budge. Mooyne leapt straight into his contingency plan: swinging a small rope with a hook at the end, he tossed it above the wall, pulling it to make sure it was securely tightened on the ledge on that edge of the stone wall. He began to climb it. Ramkus, thinking quickly how to climb with his staff, shoved it down his back behind his large belt on an angle so as to be able to climb without fear it would fall or be an obstacle in his ascent.

They reached the top, Ramkus almost letting his staff drop when pulling it from his behind.

'Should have just tossed it up here,' Mooyne said as Ramkus stood in one piece. Ramkus frowned; it was sound, albeit late advice. They looked around the tops of the buildings. As Mooyne had predicted, the whole town had come out to watch the events transpire in the middle of the place, even the guards and the Empires men. The fire had broken out in other parts of the town. Mooyne smiled to himself as he looked over the buildings. He saw what he was after: a reinforced square brick building that stood apart from the rest of the town near the rocky cleft.

'Quick!' he beckoned Ramkus, as he grabbed the hook and began winding the rope, all whilst racing down some stairs that led down to the interior of the town. Ramkus followed like an obedient pet.

They sped to the building, it seemed far enough away from the focus of the townsfolk for the time, and further away from the guarded bridge.

Ramkus felt something was awry, but did not consider it necessary to query what Mooyne's motives were. He only wanted to be out of the Empires hands by any means possible, and didn't care if he had to hurt anymore of their soldiers. He didn't even consider the possibility that others would be caught up in the mess. Perhaps Prince was quietly instilling his way. Screams and cries, yells and grunts came from the people fighting the fire throughout the streets, yet the two did not see one soul whilst they darted through. They stopped a short distance from the reinforced square building, as Mooyne mulled what was ahead of him. He smiled with menace.

'Come on, this way!' he said after a moment's pause.

Ramkus followed Mooyne as they came beneath one of the windows of the building. Mooyne peered in, smiled as he looked around. He grabbed Ramkus's arm to lead him away again, hauling his hook attached rope through the window, smashing the glass.

'What are you doing?' Ramkus cried indignantly.

'Just help me, don't question. You want to hurt the Empire or not?'

Ramkus looked at Mooyne reproachfully. 'Why smash a window, that will do little damage!'

'It is so we can get inside,' Mooyne explained, rolling his eyes.

'Why don't we try the door,' Ramkus ran over to what seemed the front entrance. It opened.

'Oh…' Mooyne chuckled.

Ramkus entered without any fear, but was soon on alert as he heard cries from somewhere inside the building.

'What is this place? Ramkus asked.

Mooyne was busy searching the room. It had some desks, shelves of books, and a black vault.

He paid Ramkus no heed, as he jumped to the vault and began carefully fidgeting around with the locking mechanism, trying to figure how to disassemble it. He shrugged, quickly lighting one of his bombs, and running back out the entrance.

'Fucking hell!' Ramkus cried without thinking, darting outside after Mooyne as a large "boom" went off, rocking the surrounds. Smoke began to billow out. They waited a while for it to dissipate before peering in. The two staggered back when observing the destruction that had been caused. Rubble, debris, broken furniture and metal fragments all from the explosion. Mooyne gathered himself first, 'We haven't much time,' he declared as they both ran back inside.

More cries could be heard from inside. Part of the building floor had been destroyed by the force, exposing a hidden dungeon. Papers and wooden debris littered the place almost tripping Mooyne up as sprinted to the precious vault.

'I do love some good contraband!' he yelled.

Ramkus busied himself with quickly investigating who was making the commotion below.

'Come help me,' Mooyne yelled, but Ramkus too was focussed on having a look at the ready revealed basement area. People behind bars - but naturally – of which he noted two types locked in the holding cells: hardened thugs; and a large proportion of people who seemed of the forest dwelling persuasion. The hole that had been blown in the floor was above a corridor with the cells on either side. The ceilings of the cells had been made from reinforced brick to ensure no escape, quite fortuitous considering the considerable damage the blast had created.

'Please help us!' came the cries.

Ramkus looked closer, noting no actual damage had been done to anyone – that he could see, anyway.

'Free us!' some called.

The smile of the devil came upon Ramkus, realising the chaos he might invoke by letting the two types out.

'Where are the keys?' He yelled down.

'Most likely in a black box of valuables they keep up there,' came a reply.

Ramkus looked around; his friend was collecting shimmering pieces in a bag. He scanned the room quickly as he could.

'Black box, black box,' he muttered to himself in desperation. He spotted it against the wall and shot straight towards it, only to find it locked. Shaking his head, 'A key, where to get the key?' The box had been slightly damaged so that fingers could be wedged inside. He tried prying it open, without much success, getting angry. He gritted his teeth, and with a large grunt, forced it open enough for the set of cell keys to fall out.

Mooyne had finished getting whatever he required. 'Time to go,' he said with an air of distaste, '*and thanks for the help,*' he added facetiously. 'Now we are going to be at a disadvantage in getting out.'

Ramkus smiled to himself as his demon glanced back at Mooyne with confidence and derision.

'No, my friend, we haven't.'

Ramkus jumped a good few metres down below to open the gates. A dozen forest dwellers rushed the bars of their cell. They tried thanking him for what he was about to do, but his eyes were glazed over. He instead called to the other cell where the hardened thugs – most likely criminals – sat in wait.

'You boys want to go stir some *shit* up? Want a good *fight*?' he roared to them through a nasty smile.

Through the bars, he could seem the men clearer now: some large muscular nutcases, some meeker but with eyes of menace, all watching to see what he was going to do.

'I take that as a **yes**. Good, go make a mess!' he commanded with a smile. Sneering with satisfaction as he moved to the lock, opening it.

'Don't let them out,' some of the forest dwellers protested. 'They are murderers, they deserve to be locked up!'

'Quiet!' grunted one of the criminals as he rushed out through the door, grabbing a young forest dweller that was standing at the side of his cell protesting their release. He smashed him against the bars and grabbed the throat in one fell swoop, lifting the young man off the ground through the bars.

Ramkus jumped to attention, smashing the thug in the throat. He let go of the forest dweller who crashed to the floor.

'Leave it for out there,' Ramkus growled. The thug did not hear; he was completely unconscious from the hit.

Ramkus then opened the lock of the forest dwellers cell who rushed out like a swarm of bees, wary of this rogue "rescuer" who would set murderers free before them. They gave him looks of suspicion as they passed, but were still thankful for their release.

The door to freedom was being crowded by those anxiously waiting to escape - it didn't help that it was also locked. Ramkus found the key for it on the keychain he possessed, opening it for the surge of bodies to rush past his side. A stairwell led to a trap door outside the building. Ramkus followed them, slowly.

He reached the top and was somewhat surprised to see his own "leader" still waiting for him.

'This way,' Mooyne urged, as men from the dungeon started off in other directions. 'I pray that was a good decision by you.'

He gave a small chuckle, '*Kind of thing I would do… sometimes.*'

They began to run.

Turning a corner, they saw some of the townspeople marching towards the most recent explosion, intermingled were some soldiers of the Empire and sentry guards.

'Right, this way,' Mooyne moved quickly, as they took another course. Ramkus wondered whether Mooyne was muttering to himself, rather than him.

'After them. Get them!' came cries from the street they had just been down.

They caught sight of some of the forest dwellers scurrying one way.

'Follow them!' commanded Ramkus.

'You want to give the orders now?' Mooyne replied. 'Well, it is a good suggestion.'

They sprinted through the back streets, trailing the forest dwellers. Sounds of small melees started to be heard in some of the alleyways: guttural sounds, ones of death.

'Those bastards looked like menaces. You may have actually set about some real damage by letting them loose,' Mooyne jabbered. Prince smiled to himself wickedly.

They continued to run until they found the other side of the town's wall in front of them. Mooyne launched his hook, and in one fell swoop, latched it and began to climb up the side.

The forest dwellers were below, scurrying to find an exit.

'There!' they saw the two scaling the wall. 'Help us again. Please!' they cried to Mooyne as he stood atop the town wall, scoping the scene beyond, overlooking the drop.

'Damn it' he said, reluctantly giving in to their cries, leaving the rope as Ramkus and himself jumped down the other side, hitting the ground in pain.

Without giving it much thought, they dashed into the forest as best they could, not looking back at the town, or those they had saved.

XXX

The sloped nature of the forest hid the difficulty in crossing through the thickets at speed, as the steep edges were the type one could only hope not to fall and roll a great distance down to the flats below. Ramkus and Mooyne began to slow as they tired from the potential chase; they had long suspected there were no pursuers, as the forest quietened - save for the cracks and moans of the wind, and the flutter or call of birds above. The trees started to become sparse and tall; the light seeped in through their leaves to give warmth of the new day. The two had run through the night; they were weary but did not stop. Mooyne proved to be adept at travelling in the dark: an excellent tracker through the wilds. He seemed to continually wear a mischievous smile - from what Ramkus could tell.

Perhaps our activities in Fallen Crest really did delight this mad new friend, he thought. He did not contemplate his own actions of letting the murderous criminals free before they forest dwellers. They had not seen these fellow escapees since leaving their rope for them.

Ramkus thought only of the wind in his face, and the sense of freedom he had not felt since he could remember.

Resting at a little out of the way spot along the river bank where Mooyne had decided to cast fishing line out just to see if the fish were biting, they were awoken with a startle.

Some movement from a slanted rock path above. It appeared some people were sneaking into their little place of respite.

The two jumped to attention, at the ready with staff and bow.

'Please, it is those you have already spared!' came the cry.

Slowly, a dozen of the forest dwellers emerged from the slopes, down to the little safe haven.

Ramkus and Mooyne lowered their weapons.

'Really, truly, thank you. We don't wish anything from you, just to share this spot for some rest.'

'Be our guests,' Ramkus said - his irrational demon was at bay now.

Mooyne laughed, 'Hah! Our guests? It is their land!' Ramkus gave a small chuckle, for Mooyne had shown a glimpse of his true nature, and his beliefs.

'Thank you,' the leader of the group, a dark-haired man with hawkish eyes, said. He came towards them. Upon further observation, he was a little on the short side, and fairly slim, of about thirty years of age.

'Ramkus,' Ramkus greeted the leader and his group to put them at ease; Mooyne did likewise, spitting and looking around. Ramkus thought Mooyne was perhaps trying to impress some of the group with his unperturbed attitude.

'Chaisu' the leader replied, 'We were wondering what had happened to you...' his voice trailed off as his eyes caught the suns reflection glistening off the two bracelets bound to Ramkus's wrists.

Ramkus looked upon them and sighed. 'Long story, *but I am not one of them.*'

Chaisu winced, 'I could hardly have imagined you were. With the way you let those murderers out in the town, urging them to *stir up trouble and fight.*'

Ramkus flinched, withdrawing into a small depressive thought, confused by his own actions.

Chaisu noticed this change in temperament that his words had inflicted, quickly trying to remedy the situation with a person he knew little of, other than he had saved him and his men from the dungeon. 'But you *saved* us,' he said with a beaming smile, 'so we trust you.'

Ramkus returned a faint one.

'He needs them off,' Mooyne interjected. 'You wouldn't happen to know the quickest way to a mountain folk smithy?'

'You would have to go through our town, Balago, and then take the path up the crevice. The closest Mountain village of Potelo is not too far from there, we are reasonably close to them.'

'Right where we are headed,' Mooyne spat, then patted Ramkus on the back. 'First, we rest; then you lead the way, Chaisu,' Mooyne gave a cheeky smile.

Chaisu returned it, he had no choice but to.

Chaisu's group held back, worrying themselves with eating a few nuts, resting, watching with conversation with interest. Mooyne kicked a stone before sitting back down and taking up his little fishing line.

'Ha hah!' he cried a few moments after, jumping to his feet and pulling the line quickly. A trout was hoisted onto the pebbles by Mooyne's thrust; it shimmered under the morning rays.

'Looks like we shall have a little sashimi.' He pulled the fish out and immediately ripped it in two, making sure to not catch his hand on the hook. He handed half of the fish to Ramkus.

'Shouldn't we cook it?' Ramkus queried, 'or do you think a fire will alert the pursuers?' He looked about. 'In fact, how have they not followed us by the river here? He added, pointing to the flowing waters.

'This is a protected stream, the river splits off underground and comes out here. On the other side of this area, it looks like a flat cliff, so no one thinks to stop clamber up to have a look at what is around. We are in relative safety right now. Not to mention, those forest dwellers do not want this place touched. They'll make sure our tracks are hidden.'

Ramkus sighed deeply, returning to thoughts and actions he did not feel he had truly played a part in. They were evidently part of his memories and his story, though. He lay at the trunk of a tree, nibbling on the freshly caught fish. He watched the light playfully bounce off the small waves of water, lulling himself into a slumber.

*"**You see how I help you?**"*

'How do you help? The ones who were to be helped were an oversight for you! You only wanted to let out the murderers so as to wreak havoc.'

Ramkus sat at one end of a small chamber. Light poured in from a window, faintly. His other self, Prince, at the other end of a marble bench, one ankle resting atop the other leg, at ease, but his glare intense. This was the first time Ramkus had seen him so vividly: bald head, heavy features, eyes that menaced in the void of madness too long. His black leather armour held melded spikes and bulges, chains attached in spots, predominantly under the arms. He held no weapon that Ramkus could see, but he had no reason to hold one: Why should I fear Prince?

*"**We are almost free of this,**" Prince prophesised.*

'Almost,' Ramkus agreed, 'but there is still a distance to go.'

Prince stared with a nasty smile, "***We shall see what hand we are dealt.***"

So much of his existence, his story, had now been due to the actions of Prince. He stared at his self, and began to see events. Although some of the features of being a Guardian did not come as naturally to him as others seemed to, certain premonitions and knowledge were visible to him through Prince; of events that were to come. What are the

dreams of those whom only visit others' dreams? What knowledge of the world do they possess? *He queried.*
But Ramkus knew these questions could not be answered by him, for Prince would not ever explain himself. They were on a long journey, one that he had not had a moment to realise - for he had nary a moment to truly be at ease with himself.
"That will come, soon," *Prince said, clenching his teeth, looking to where the light splintered through the windows bars.*
What is Prince's purpose? *thought Ramkus,* What does he want?
"To survive."

Ramkus awoke with a shudder, the sun had hit high noon. Mooyne was also sleeping next to him. The forest dwellers were beginning to stir, 'Time to move,' Chaisu said, standing in front of the two. 'Time to leave,' he repeated his alert. Mooyne grumbled as Ramkus prodded him to wake. Chaisu had already walked off to speak with his people, discussing the path ahead; he was obviously taking charge of this assembly. Ramkus was pleased by this, but then fell into despair. Perhaps his previous actions, and Chaisu's introduction, would mean the people of Balago would not receive him as they would have, had he arrived by the little coracle boat. He was well aware of Chaisu and his men's wariness of him.
"Let them be", a voice in his head stated. **"Better to have them fear you"**. Ramkus was beginning to despise hearing these "words of wisdom". He even wondered if the actions – of Prince – were part of some plan to put himself in this precarious, untrustworthy, position. *All planned out, eh Prince? Who else would, nay, **could** think like that? Someone who cannot be trusted.* But this seemed more than a path of pure survival, to

Ramkus. *Then again, could everything have been so well planned out?*

His mind was racing, he was confusing himself, doubting himself, doubting whether he was letting things overcome him. Maybe he was still affected from the mushrooms Miiva had given him. He began to ponder upon her, as Chaisu staggered over to the two rescuers, gesturing them to join the troop.

So began the slow march to Balago, and what would play upon Ramkus constantly now: his thoughts.

Chapter XVII

The ground was constantly changing: from rocky harsh paths, to
wet earthy underbrush. The troop tried to walk on what was the
forest path, but the it followed a terrain that had a mind of its
own: running up and down, cutting here and there. The air of
the forest was calm, but heavy, until it was obliterated by the
shards of the sun, piercing through to dispense of any dampness.
It was an utter delight to Ramkus, who needed a change in
atmosphere so as to keep awake from time to time, as well as
warm his aching body through his clothes.

Mooyne seemed to be quite reserved; not so much timid, rather
at ease and accepting of the people he was travelling with. Their
ways and manner were more natural to him. He chatted with
Chaisu every so often, trying to have a chuckle. Unfortunately,
Chaisu appeared to be still fearful of these two interlopers,
unsure if he was doing the right thing by letting them join him
and his comrades.

As clear as the forest floor became underneath the canopy of
tall, green, bristled trees, the less movement there seemed to be
from any animal life. Although there was no sense of being
watched, it was evident that animals knew how to keep in
hiding.

The company stopped at certain times to rest, eat, and drink.
Their only rations were fruits and nuts picked up from the little
resting area by the river where they had joined forces. Ramkus
craved a proper meal. He had had it good in the castle that
overlooked these lands: the food was plentiful, anything
requested was always in supply. As much as he hated to admit
it, he did enjoy himself there at times when he could let down
his guard, bath in those heated waters, play music with his lost
friend. He became glum as he reminisced on his old mentor:
Felipe. What has become of my friend?

It was whilst the sun was low, and the shadow of the forest cast a dark embrace for the impending night, that the burning fires surrounding the perimeter of Balago began to loom like a hidden camp. The sound rushing of the water came back: this heavily fortified village was completely open on its south-eastern side to the great running river of Lencil, where Ramkus was to have *washed up* and entered from. An entry that was long lost to him now. *A dangerous gamble to keep that unwalled*, he judged, before noticing a few small guard towers a good few yards from the river bank.

His bracelets glistened with the light of the fires, making him feel even more of a criminal: *The sooner they are off, the better.* The troop edged towards the entrance. Mooyne commented to Ramkus that the gate that the main road led to was used only by outsiders, 'those who were *not of the forest dwelling stature.*' Mooyne sounded as if he was of an honorary cast, one that was allowed to dabble in the secrets of the first people. *I wonder if Miiva would have let him watch the* Ancient Arts.

Their passage was not to be through the main gate, but by a secluded – and guarded - secret gate. Chaisu had good reason to want support, should these two mysterious strangers not be whom they appeared.

They knocked on the door and waited for the questioning sentries.

Chaisu gestured for Ramkus and Mooyne to conceal themselves. 'Waste of time if you ask me,' Mooyne grumbled. 'We could easily scale this, or find a hole somewhere.'

'Hmm,' Ramkus replied, 'it looks rather sturdy. I don't think these people would let any holes form, *or be made.*' He had an idea that Mooyne would do something a bit drastic when irritated.

After a few minutes of twiddling their thumbs, a sentry decided to shine a torch over the ledge and see who was trying to disturb him working whilst he slept.

Chaisu and the sentry spoke in fairly hushed tones – not that the droll conversation couldn't be followed - until the sentry started to shout. 'How can we ever trust you, Chaisu? You were bloody well captured! These men may wait till the middle of the night, and slit our throats!' he boomed from above.

'Let me speak to Figal, I beg you!' pleaded Chaisu. 'These men rescued us, they are not part of the Empire.'

Ramkus – who had been scratching his long, irritating stubble - hid his wrists at the mention of the word. 'Explain that!' the sentry pointed to Ramkus – too late it seemed.

Ramkus spoke up, 'These are why I am here.' He raised his arms, letting the bracelets shimmer in the heavy burning lights that adorned the high wooden gate. 'Word should have reached you from the Lencil forests, that a man was coming upstream a day or so ago. A man who needed help taking two bracelets off...' Ramkus said loudly.

'Beats me, I heard nothing,' replied the sentry guard.

Ramkus frowned and looked to the others. He continued to speak to the sentry, 'How can two outsiders be so feared? We are outnumbered here. Do you seriously think we would be of any danger in there, especially with the fine calibre of you guards – *if you don't mind me saying.*'

The sentry guard shrugged in his post high above. By the side of Ramkus, a buzzing sound came whirring past. Ramkus could barely make out what it was, but its impact was immediate. A crash sound came from above, as the sentry began to bleed from between the eyes. Those eyes started rolling backward, as the sentry – whose face couldn't initially be made out between the light of the fires - fell forward, out of his seat and over the wall, thumping hard onto the ground a foot away from Ramkus.

Ramkus looked behind him. Everyone's mouths were agape, stunned; all but Mooyne's, who was smiling cheekily.

Ramkus stared at him, shaking his heard. Mooyne shrugged gleefully.

'You could have killed him!' Ramkus yelled. There was only silence – save for the crackle of the massive fires atop the wall.

'Look,' Mooyne gestured to the sentry.

The sentry guard arose, groggily, looking around as if in a trance, blinking and stumbling towards the gate. He began to bang on it with his fists.

'Hey! Lemme in!' he cried out.

No reply came.

'Bum,' he grumbled under his breath, before seeming to remember something. The troop approached him as he recovered a key attached to his belt. He inserted it into a lock in the gate, which opened a small porter door, barely five feet tall. The troop moved close to the door, making sure the sentry guard did not pass through without letting them get in first. He was still visibly under the effects of his fall, holding the door open for them.

'Oh, hullo!' he said to the people in a pleasant dim-witted manner, 'After you.'

'How polite of you!' replied Mooyne after he rushed through. The others followed suit.

'Are you okay?' asked Chaisu, who stopped ahead of Ramkus.

'Certainly, I'll have another!' came the reply, as the sentry stumbled backward. Chaisu guffawed,

'Come on,' he said, holding the man up and pushing him forward. He began to swing uncontrollably, but somehow, Chaisu got him to wander through as Ramkus followed brought up the rear.

Balago was well lit within its confines by the fires atop its wall, as well as its citizens own little abodes. From the outside, it looked less of a town, and more a military post to counter Fallen Crest: hastily constructed in an apparent attempt to stop recent enemy attacks. The wall itself was of a fresh, almost green, timber, but some of the huts appeared as if ancient relics, built to survive, or rather grow…

'Chiselled from the trunks of massive trees, some of these,'
Mooyne told Ramus as he stared out at the ad hoc village.
'It is nothing compared to what it was. Well, a long time ago
that is, back when it was a beautiful town on the banks of the
river, trading in many different goods. A hub for instruments in
fact. Attacked, raided, infiltrated time and time again by
conquerors. It stands merely as a trading post these days. That
wall is relatively new. I suspect heavier attacks must have
occurred in recent days.' Mooyne stood for a while before
beckoning Ramkus, 'Come.' He gestured in the direction of a
heavily decorated house, one that obviously housed a person of
title and stature.
Ramkus looked behind at Chaisu, who was helping the
concussed sentry guard, smiling dumbly and seemingly
compliant in this state. A band of guards had now come to his
aid, talking with Chaisu. He was bleeding from the hit. *Mooyne
must have struck him with one hell of a shot.*
The sentry was at least standing, trying to regain focus.
Unfortunately, the reflection of the fires on Ramkus's bracelets
seemed to be beacons to the suspicious, scrutinising eyes of the
rest of the guards who were on duty about the town, trying to
trace down all whom had gone through the wall after sundown.
He quickly hurried along to where there was less light.

The dusty streets were not entirely deserted at this late hour, as
the residents did little to hide the fact that they were of a
disposition to seek nightly entertainment. Another two dozen of
the *trunk houses* still stood, with other shacks and housing
interspersed in an odd arrangement. The decorated residence,
with well-fashioned wood and carvings etched around it, stood
in the centre of the township. The light inside giving the sense
of warmth and wisdom being present by whomever was found in
its hearth.
There did not seem to be a central tavern as was the norm.
Instead, a few of the homes and stores had lively banter and

festivities trailing out into the torchlit side streets. Ramkus was intrigued, wanting to venture inside and see what activities the residents were up to.

Mooyne watched Ramkus's interest in the town with intrigue. 'You want to join them? They'll likely cut your head off before you can get a word in. Not that they'll mean it, but they don't know you, and this town has had so many incursions in recent times. It is not unheard of for the Empire to send undercover traders in to get a sense of the place.'

Ramkus expressed disbelief with his look.

'Yep, the people are on high alert. I don't suppose you really know of what the Empire is like with the first peoples. Very underhanded to say the least,' Mooyne lectured.

'I have a sense as to how the two *sides* get along. I did come from Lencil after all,' Ramkus stated.

'That is true. But Lencil has not had to deal with the Empire's people daily as this town has. You can see how they shy away from the usual town structure, keeping to themselves rather than having some place for *unknowns* to congregate. If you're a trader, you're either camping in your wagon, or seeking lodgings at one of the homes. Even then, there are only a few that will offer it, and you are under constant guard. If they are booked out, tough luck, you are going to be out under the stars, and outside these walls.'

'*Military post.* I think I understand it, now,' Ramkus said. 'But why would the inhabitants want to stay here if it is facing such difficult circumstances?'

Mooyne laughed, 'Why does anyone stay anywhere. It is their *home*, as it *always has been*. Where are they meant to go? And why would they essentially lay down their rightful claim to the land? That is exactly what the Empire *would* want. By staying, they are fighting for their survival.'

Ramkus nodded understandingly, seeing yet another struggle against the oppressive conquerors.

'Did you ever see it before it turned into this state of perpetual suspicion?' Ramkus asked.

Mooyne gave him an odd look. 'That assumes I have been in these parts for a long time, *and that I am of an older age than I look,*' he replied.

Ramkus wondered why there was such an emphasis on the latter part of his answer, but forgot it when Mooyne continued.

'No, I didn't, I haven't been in these parts for that long a time. As I said, I have come from so far away that it'd take over a year to traverse back. But I listen, I learn, I speak to the people and see what needs to be seen.' He sighed, 'And I am getting tired, and in need of a drink. Where is that Chaisu?'

As if on cue, the sound of running came from behind: Chaisu caught up with the two intrepid adventurers.

'You cannot see our village heads, at least not at this hour. It would bring me great shame to let you past the guard wall, only for you to wander in and annoy those in charge,' Chaisu said.

His troop had dispersed, back to their family abodes, and he felt it his duty to direct the comings and goings of the visitors.

Ramkus and Mooyne, tired from the last few days' events, stood looking at each other.

Chaisu thought of what to do to keep these two in check, exhausted himself from the whole ordeal.

To hell with it, he thought: 'If you would like, you may stay with me. I haven't a very large lodging, but it is at least a place to sleep,' Chaisu smiled in a cordial manner.

The two agreed, only after Chaisu assured in the affirmative of stocking some form of alcohol – a stiff drink was the first order of call.

They wandered down the beaten path to a hut near the river at the back of the town, nestled close to where the guard wall met the water. Beyond it lay a little thicket of woods that the guard wall enclosed.

Mooyne looked at the little shack Chaisu called home, wondering how three could fit in it without feeling too much *intimacy.* 'You'd better not be playing games with us, Chaisu,' Mooyne said. Chaisu looked at him, hurt.

'Huh, only joking, you're alright. He's alright, isn't he, Ramkus?' Mooyne patted him on the back, 'But seriously, no funny business.'

Chaisu, offended, unsure of what he was doing, let them inside his humble home.

First observations were that it was of modest means: a table with four stools; small kitchen; bed in the corner. Made from tin and odd bits of lumber, constructed hastily like much of the town. What really caught the eye was the demijohns of hard liquor - or at least it certainly caught Mooyne's eye. Whatever moonshine was in it, it had the three laughing, crying, fighting, and bonding very quickly. Mooyne was indeed right, Chaisu was an alright sort.

'This stuff tastes like camel hide! What on earth is in it?' Mooyne was all talk, he had shown no distaste for the liquor so far.

'Pff,' Chaisu grunted. 'Some of the tree sap out there, potatoes, herbs, the usual.' He burped as he slammed down another shot. 'I'd like to see what you could make.'

Ramkus nodded along to the banter, as tired as he was, he needed the relaxant.

'True, too true,' Mooyne responded without much argument, 'although back where I am from, rice is used. Now that is a good drink. Not as heavy hitting as this, though' he praised, before rising from the table and inspecting Chaisu's home. His eyes began to roll as he stumbled.

'What are you doing?' Chaisu grumbled, but simply watched Mooyne as he grabbed two pots and smashed them together.

'We need some music!' Mooyne laughed.

'Agreed!' Ramkus finally chimed in, his torso rolling about as he sat. 'You got any instruments, Chaisu?'

Chaisu shook his head.

'Oh well,' Mooyne continued to smash the pots together as a child would. 'Yah yah yah.' He screamed in a drunken stupor. Ramkus held his hands to his ears, 'Too loud, shut it up Mooyne!' he growled.

Mooyne nodded along, coming over to the table and placing the pots on Chaisu and Ramkus's heads, grabbing another for himself. The two sat dumbfounded.

Mooyne started going through Chaisu's drawers without much care. 'You got anything to eat?' He looked into a drawer and pulled out some herbs, smelling them before frowning and waving it out at Chaisu.

Chaisu nodded, 'Yes, yes.'

Ramkus was reminded of his *lights*. He fumbled around with his belt compartments before finding the little bag. It still had some mushrooms in it, although they were falling apart. He threw it on the table.

'What's that?' Mooyne asked, as Chaisu collected it and inspected the contents.

'Ohh no, what on earth were you doing carrying these around for.' He pulled them out of the bag, but they began to disintegrate. 'Yuck,' he began rubbing his hands together to get the fibres off.

Mooyne went back to searching for something to sate his hunger, 'Ahh,' he said in triumph after finding some pickled vegetables in a large jar. He placed them on the table as if it were some glorious trophy to behold. The three all dug in, grabbing the carrots, cucumber, and onions with their fingers.

'Not bad, not bad,' Mooyne commented. 'Bit too much vinegar, but that's alright.

Chaisu grimaced, 'Forgot I even had them,' he said. 'Probably been there for a bit too long now.'

Ramkus poured another shot for everyone from the large demijohn. 'To Chaisu and his hospitality,' he toasted.

'No. To you two and your rescue,' Chaisu responded as they drank.

Mooyne went back to the drawers, grabbing some bigger cups, pouring out the moonshine to the brim. 'Drink!' he commanded.

'What the hell are you doing, Mooyne? Chaisu said, whilst Ramkus accepted the offering without any hesitation.

'To Chaisu and his moonshine!' Mooyne belched in toast before skolling the hard liquor.

Ramkus followed his lead far too easily, wincing as it went down. Chaisu took it to his lips, regretfully, but finished to the bottom.

'Yah yah yah!' Mooyne sang again, raising an open hand to the ceiling.

Ramkus grabbed his staff and tapped it to the rhythm.

'I think I'm going to be sick,' Chaisu began reeling before running outside with pot on his head still.

Ramkus and Mooyne frowned and moved their heads from shoulder to shoulder before laughing and following him out into the streets.

He hadn't gone far, only down to the water edge. They approached singing, "Yah yah yah," not caring to be caught by any guards. They were far enough from any other residences that they could do as they liked, it seemed.

Chaisu was taking in heavy breaths of the fresh, night air. The smell of Juniper wood wafted about, refreshing Ramkus's senses, reminding him of the path from Miiva's residence to the town in Lencil with its boat buildings.

'That is a refreshing aroma,' he remarked wistfully without thinking, resting his weight upon his staff.

Chaisu raised himself up with one last breath, focussing not to let himself fall backwards. 'I secretly supplied some better smelling wood for the wall around my area,' he tried to focus on being as sober in conversation as possible. 'Same ones I got the sap from. Glad I did, now,' he added, before starting to hiccup.

Mooyne started to flex, tensing himself as he held in his breath, going red. Ramkus took this as a challenge and squared up, tensing his muscles, making himself go red in the face too. They stared at each other with bulging eyes. For whatever it was worth, Chaisu decided to join in, clenching his fists, going purple in the face under his pot hat before hiccupping and letting out some wind.

Mooyne and Ramkus stopped immediately and began laughing. 'Dammit Chaisu, hah! Mooyne said, as they proceeded to move away from the spot.

After the exertion of energy, they sat on the slope running down to the river, breathing heavily. Mooyne could not sit still, wandering back to Chaisu's hut.

Chaisu's eyes were rolling about. Ramkus patted him on the back, 'You alright?' he asked.

Chaisu took a deep breath and exhaled, 'Is he always like this?' he replied before Mooyne quickly returned with the cups, again filled full with moonshine.

Chaisu pushed it away, 'No, please no.'

'Just hold it, you don't have to skoll.' Mooyne pressed it firmly into Chaisu's chest. He took it reluctantly.

They rested their gaze on the night sky shimmering on the river, reflecting the path to the heavens. It seemed that the river was at peace, in between the changing tide as it was beginning to head downstream. Not a wisp of wind breached the ambiance, allowing the sounds of insects to reverberate and hum with a warmth that seemed to sit upon the scene. The men sat still, watching the water.

'Look, a shooting star!' Chaisu piped up, deciding to rest back and watch the sky. The others followed suit, glimpsing at the cosmic array of constellations. The heavens seemed to spill out in a single weave of white through the dark, but colourful, canopy of existence. The sparkling orbs throbbed and pulsed with an energy, often seeming to flash different shades. As they breathed in, it felt as if the energy was directly being absorbed into their beings, waking their senses to all that was. Life was out there, and within.

'Makes you wonder why we bother living under a roof, when there is so much more out here,' Mooyne said.

No one followed up the comment right away, as the feeling was mutual, but it started Chaisu thinking. 'Privacy, I guess,' he answered the rhetorical question.

'From what?' Ramkus couldn't help asking.

Neither Chaisu nor Mooyne wanted to answer, but Mooyne decided to guess what Chaisu was hinting at, 'Privacy *with another*, I think he means. You know…'

This Ramkus understood. 'Ahh,' he replied, thinking over those he had been intimately connected to. A melancholy took form, bitter sweet as he knew that what lay behind could be countenanced by what lay ahead.

'You got someone in mind, Chaisu?' Mooyne started to get some of his cheeky energy flowing again.

They could not tell for sure, but it appeared Chaisu was blushing. 'Maybe,' he replied. 'Not that it matters in my current circumstances, nothing can come of it. I am likely to be sent out on another reconnaissance mission soon enough. Out under the stars for many nights.' He sat up and took a swig of his drink to stop any furtherance of the talk. He was getting a bit hot under the collar.

'Ha, well, that's too bad,' Mooyne let him off. 'What about you, Ramkus.'

Ramkus immediately felt the heated question, following Chaisu's lead and sipping some of the moonshine. 'Is it me or is it getting a bit hot?' he answered instead.

'You two, Ha!' Mooyne laughed. 'Well, bottoms up.' He sat up and clinked his drink with the other two, as they finished their glasses of the harsh liquid. 'Phew, that hits the spot, whoa!' Mooyne continued. 'It is getting a bit hot!' He looked over the water as the other two began to feel the effects.

A splash in the night sky's mirror cut the calm of the atmosphere as if a sharp knife had slashed a veil. 'That water looks refreshing,' Chaisu said. His eyes were rolling around, as he stumbled getting up, almost falling over. 'I wouldn't mind going for a swim.

At the suggestion of swim, Ramkus licked his lips. 'Swim' he muttered in an intoxicated state, taking it upon himself to lead the charge, throwing off his clothes and running into the slow flowing current.

'Hey, wait up!' Mooyne called out as he and Chaisu started after him. Chaisu was tripping over himself as he tried to undress whilst running into the water.

The edge of the river was quite shallow, only to waist height, which let them stand and drop as they pleased. Mooyne chased after Ramkus and jumped kicked him into the water.

'The hell?' Ramkus laughed, not caring that he actually got hurt in the attack. He jumped at Mooyne and tried get him back Whilst the two fought for dominance, Chaisu was off in his own little world, attempting to reach the moon reflected in the water. As soon as he touched it, he began to spin around in the spot, singing Mooyne's song, 'Yah yah yah,' before slipping over a snag and falling into the deeper part of the river. 'Yah yah yah,' he cried as the undercurrent got a hold of him and began to drag him down the river.

'Yah! Yah! Yah!' he now yelled in desperation, as the other two stopped their battle to focus on his cries.

'Oh, shit,' Mooyne cursed. 'Ramkus,' he called to his friend, trying to quickly coordinate a rescue, but Ramkus was already onto it. Grabbing his staff from the shore, he ran down the bank, grumbling as his feet had rocks jabbing into his uneasy steps. Mooyne was already ahead of him, and as soon as he had gotten a bit further down than Chaisu, he ran into the water. 'Toss it here, Ramkus' he yelled. As Ramkus threw the staff to him, Mooyne quickly grabbed it and smashed the staff into the water in one fell swoop. Unfortunately, it was a direct hit upon Chaisu's head, knocking him down under the water.

'Ah, you fool,' Mooyne cried out at Chaisu rather than his own inability to control the "floatation device".

Chaisu seemed to now be floating unconscious further down into the well-lit part of the town. Ramkus ran along with him until it was *his* time to attempt the rescue. 'Mooyne,' he cried out, blinded by the town's lights, not realising the staff had already been tossed to him, it knocked him in the face. He stumbled backwards, reclaiming the staff as best he could, then beginning his own endeavour to save Chaisu. Instead of smashing it down, he waded out and thrust it in front of Chaisu to stop his body from floating any further downstream. Chaisu hit the staff pushing it hard with the flow of the river, so much so that Ramkus struggled desperately to hold him in spot with his strength. Fortunately, Mooyne arrived just in time, forcing his own body against the staff and reaching out to drag Chaisu in. He hauled him to the shore, lifting his head above the water. They stumbled onto the bank, panting. Chaisu had regained some form of consciousness, coughing up water.

'Bloody hell,' Mooyne said in relief as they all fell in a heap. Ramkus was beginning to feel rather sick from the whole drastic incident.

Before they could catch their breath, a voice boomed out from a residence further up, 'Oi! What in the blazes do you think you're doing!'

They could not see where the voice was coming from, but they soon realised how far they'd travelled downstream into the more populous area of the town.

'Perverts!' another voice boomed. Startled by the accusation, they quickly decided it best to get back to Chaisu's residence, quick smart. They gathered Chaisu between them, guiding him along the rocky shore; Ramkus with staff in hand, ruing the feeling of the jagged ground underneath on his exposed feet. Mooyne looked back to make sure no one was following, 'Hopefully that wasn't a guard,' he said, acknowledging the late hour should not bring out too many onlookers.

They put Chaisu in his home, collected their belongings from outside, and decided it best to forget the whole incident.

"Yah yah yah," the nodded to each other.

XXX

They awoke all in odd positions around the odd little dwelling, heavily hungover in the bachelor pad - Mooyne's new little name Chaisu's residence. He himself was less timid now, as he did not care too much about filtering anything he said since. When he was quizzed about being in the dungeon previously, he simply stated he had been held against his will by the Empire *'simply for being'*. But now he was much more forthcoming with his role in his towns defence. At least when he was conscious and happy to mumble a few choice sentences.

With the morning came the sun, and as it hit the hut it warmed it instantly – which was a little off-putting, for the three were reminded of last night's raucousness. The sound of the river running nearby began to became louder.

'Time for you to meet the heard of the village,' grumbled Chaisu, who fell over after trying to get up. He fell back asleep, leaving his guests to fight off their saltiness without any directions as to where to go to the toilet.

They wandered outside, heading towards the town wall to relieve themselves. In so doing, they heard someone scream at them.

'You bloody vagrants! You bloody louts! No pissing on the wall!'

Looking at each other, feeling awful and sweaty under the morning sun, they looked up at the top of the wall to see whom they had offended. But there was no one there.

'A trick of the light,' Mooyne concluded, so they kept going.

'Stop!' *the voice was coming from behind.*

It was the damn sentry from the night before! He was approaching along the gravel and dirt in a filthy rage that seemed put on for effect. After he had gotten close enough to them, he recognised the two. His memory of the night before hitting him like a lightning bolt. His rage was now not only an act, it was palpable. 'Oh, you are in one bloody mess, you two are.' He held a spear out at them that he had been using as a walking crutch, as well as unsheathing a sword at his side. 'I'm taking you to the head of the village! He'll make good work out of you.'

Ramkus and Mooyne, with arms raised, pants down, looked at each other with a lack of amusement, then started to shuffle under duress.

'So be it,' Ramkus said nonchalantly.

The guard was not amused by the pair's antics. He had let them shuffle only so far before taking it as a joke at his expense. In his chagrin, he pointed his spear at them to hurry up, but this just made them begin jumping with their arms held above their heads instead of shuffling. He finally stopped them, and told them to do their pants up. Of course, Mooyne had taken it upon himself to keep his hands up whilst trying to manoeuvre his legs to drag his garment further up his legs. The guard was going red in the face before dragging Mooyne aside and pulling his pants up himself. Mooyne gave him a wink which simply infuriated the man further, having him raise a fist. Unfortunately, he couldn't get a hit in, as the little "round up" of the intruders was on full display for the inhabitants of the town. The onlookers watched in dismay at the odd scene, stopping their usual morning routine to bear witness to the odd behaviour of the guard.

The guard lowered his spear, and his head, and led the rest of the way instead of following with his spear at their backs. Their destination was clearly the decorated residence in the middle of the town.

They were shown into a corridor and told to wait on rather painful wooden seats. Feeling worse for wear, they lurched forward in the seats as if they were naughty little children awaiting some form of punishment. Feeling too sickly, all they could do was bide their time for what was to come. In their minds, having a hangover in these circumstances was clearly punishment enough.

The *interrogation* was rather more a meeting, where the village head was treated to a *surprise visit,* in which he wished to parade around and describe to the intruders how well the town walls were at keeping out *undesirables.* His name was Figal: a large man, balding, childlike features making him seem less a leader than an affable giant who would prefer to entertain children. He explained that his co-head was on a long errand – a woman who played mother to the townsfolk. As Mooyne had explained, these first people - the forest dwellers - tended to elect a male and female head of the village, whom would hold equal sway and come to agreement on particular decisions before any actions occurred in a village. Therefore, as his co-decision maker was not around, Figal was in total control.

'So, you say you were escaping to *here*? Fleeing the Empire, wanting to have those bracelets cut taken off?' the man chatted away. 'And that you were sent *our way*, from Lencil?' He laughed. 'Why should we choose to help you?'

Ramkus was not in the mood play into Figal's good graces and plead for such help.

'Because I am a Guardian - or supposed to be. It was at the behest of Mirelle. I assume you know her?' Ramkus tried not to snap, he thought the issue of who he was would have been taken care of already - let alone had his story believed and understood. Mooyne was nodding along, looking about himself, not listening to the conversation. The sentry guard walked behind as if a faithful servant, waiting on the master's every beck and call.

'Ha, Mirelle? I do know of her, but I have never *spoken* to her, nor had any communication of any sort. That is the female Village Head's role…' the man seemed to drift off in thought, then stared at Ramkus. 'And how were you to get here then?'

'I was put in a small boat and pushed off into the river,' Ramkus stated matter-of-factly.

The man's face screwed up. 'Plausible, but we cannot help you here, we have no smith to cut those bracelets off. From what I know, they don't even cut off.'

'Apparently there is a mountain dwellers village close by that may help? Potelo?' Ramkus tried to guide Figal's rational mind. The man guffawed, 'You want to go bother our neighbours too? What you may not know is that here in Balago, as well as the mountain folk village of Potelo, we do not look too favourably on… *Guardians*. We respect ancient customs, traditions, and rituals, but recent times have not shown us the best of the Guardians decisiveness. The Empire on the other hand, have been treated very… What I am saying is, I am not sure they will want to help you too much in Potelo,' Figal divulged with an air of dignity.

'I must at least try,' Ramkus continued to argue, 'I don't wish to be banished and cursed by these bracelets. I want nothing to do with the Empire. Those people have brought *me* nothing but pain.'

Figal sat for a while, contemplating. 'Where is your Guardian staff - if you are indeed a Guardian - *how can you be without it?*' he asked with interest.

'Left with our friend, Chaisu. He is minding our gear,' Mooyne chimed in.

Figal was surprised, 'Oh, really? Let us go pay Chaisu a visit then.'

With that, the Village Head and the intruders – or whatever they were considered to be – rose and walked outside. In Ramkus and Mooyne's case, stumbling and ambling, still feeling queasy. The sentry stood behind, spear at the ready as they were to be paraded down the street into the clean air. Blue skies allowed the sun to radiate with magnitude. It would have been a glorious day, if not for last night's *festivities*.

Heavy snoring was heard from Chaisu's residence; he was found under the table in disarray.

'Chaisu!' Figal yelled. 'Get up! Why did you not report these two to me!'

Chaisu woke with a startle, hitting his head on the kitchen table under which he slept, then stumbling over.

'What a disgraceful display,' Figal shook his head. 'Explain yourself. You were away for a longer period than planned!'

'Sorry sir,' Chaisu said as if a scolded child, 'I got captured. We all got captured. The mission was doomed from the start. The Empire was looking for any excuse to take it out on us. These two rescued us,' Chaisu lowered his head, 'sort of.'

'*Sort of?*' Figal continued his tirade. 'And what is with this lack of respect by not reporting to me sooner?'

'And hitting me in the head,' the sentry chimed in from behind.

'But sir, I tried but I couldn't...' A loud yell from the village drowned out Chaisu's ability to respond - which he at least was glad of.

'Sir, sir! Finally, I have found you,' a guard came charging up the dirt path to Chaisu's home. 'A number of Empirical soldiers have been spotted moving this way,' he reported.

'Shit,' Figal growled, turning his attention to the evidently more dire, pressing situation. He looked at Chaisu, 'We'll talk later.' He moved brusquely past the two *outsiders* to meet the guard. 'What could they want.'

'They are heading here at pace, sir,' the guard said in a panic. 'Will probably be at the gates in a few minutes!'

'Bloody hell. Fine, I'll come down.' Figal started walking, 'Oh, and you two, wait here,' he said, leaving the adventurers whilst the guards all trailed their master obediently.

Mooyne and Ramkus shrugged, whilst Chaisu buried his head in his hands and started to mumble to himself, 'I am not sure which is worse: the Empire approaching; Figal's diatribe; or the hangover...'

As soon as Figal was far enough down the path to the gate, Mooyne and Ramkus picked up their supplies and weapons, and followed down the dirt path, keeping a distance from any prying eyes. Most gazes were averted towards the *meeting* at the gate.

'The Empire, they'll be after you I suspect,' Mooyne spoke.

'I reckon,' Ramkus replied. He was a man of few words when under pressure - as well as when feeling poorly from being hungover. 'But how are we meant to get out of here?'

'River?' Mooyne suggested, as they both looked at the current: it was running with great force. 'May be a bit difficult.'

They sat just out of the gates view, watching the caravans readying themselves to leave this odd trading hub. As much as it was now a military outpost, it still allowed a fair bit of trade to continue. There was a large oval area where a number of caravans and make-shift shops were set up, with warehouses behind them.

Fresh produce, alcohol, armour – Ramkus noted weapons seemed to be sold under the counter as well – candles, honey, bread. The shops and caravans appeared to be the type that could come and go with ease, the shop owners and traders only staying in town for a small bit of trade with other merchants or residents, selling either wholesale or retail respectively. A number of these traders and merchants were getting ready to leave for other towns, or return back to their own patches of earth.

A fishmonger was seen slapping down his carriage, getting frustrated, whist another man with all sorts of odds and ends loaded in his shipment whilst smoking a pipe. Another, full of musical instruments of seemingly fine quality, appeared in a fairly placid mood, humming to himself.

'Wonder where they're all going,' Ramkus said aloud.

'Yeah, I wonder too,' Mooyne yawned, stretching out his limbs before coming to himself. 'Indeed, I wonder,' he stroked his chin, looking at Ramkus. He spat out the corner of his mouth before continuing. 'Perhaps to the mountains... if you catch my drift...' He nodded to himself, smiling at his thoughts. 'If you go behind that one loaded there, I'll occupy their attention and

ask where they are headed. Hop in the back if I give the signal
that they are off to Potelo.'

With those words - and before Ramkus could even utter a
response or find out what the signal was - Mooyne began
sauntering towards the caravans, *discreetly* putting his hands in
his pockets and whistling as if he had not a care in the world,
striking up a conversation with the fish monger.

There was a little chuckle, some indiscreet talk. Ramkus –
hiding behind the cargo – did not pay close attention until he
heard the word "Potelo" almost shouted by Mooyne – the signal.
He waited for a second, smelt the fish, but involuntarily retched.
Mooyne quickly ended the conversation and wandered behind
the caravan, 'What are you doing?' he scowled upon seeing
Ramkus doubled over. 'Why didn't you get in?'

'I'm sorry, I couldn't help it,' Ramkus replied, feeling uneasy
and ill, dry retching. 'It isn't easy to handle such smells when
hungover.'

'Fine, let's see about the others, but we may have wasted our
opportunity.' Mooyne saw the fishmonger coming to the back
of his cargo and gestured to Ramkus that they should walk into
an alley beside some of warehouses that surrounded the main
trading area.

Figal was seen slapping the wooden balustrade of the sentry post
above the gate, yelling outside the gates, towards what must
have been the Empire's men. He gesticulated, then slammed his
hand down once more; a large roar of pain then came, as the
Village Head had smashed a splinter into his palm. He stamped
around, becoming furious with the whole predicament.

Ramkus laughed at the sight, whilst Mooyne dragged him to the
next cart.

'What you got in here?' Mooyne was asking the cart owner.

'All sorts of goodies,' the cart owner said. 'Want me to show
you?'

'Ah, not now, that's fine. Where are you headed?' Mooyne was starting to panic, feeling the gravity of time pushing granules of sand down the hourglass.

'An odd name was muttered that Ramkus did not register. The conversation kept on for a bit, as Mooyne tried to bartering for a new hook and line for fishing – evidently trying to keep his composure in front of the rest of the merchants.

Ramkus waited patiently, hoping there would be no movement from the enormous gate. The negotiations seemed to be reasonably calm, as Figal had calmed himself from his visible tantrum. With revulsion, and a sickening panic, Ramkus watched as the gates had started to open below where the Village Head stood.

'*Shit,*' Ramkus muttered, quickly running to the next caravan with musical instruments in it. He dove in under the tarp, not caring where it was headed, only hoping to at least not be spotted by the Empire's men. The carts began to move, as Ramkus heard Mooyne – who was walking at the front of the cart with the merchant – ask where the trader was headed.

"Potelo" came the answer, as Mooyne asked for a lift which was obliged.

Ramkus could not believe his luck, letting out a tightly held breath in relief. The cart jagged along; Ramkus squished in odd positions so as not to disturb the instruments.

Apparently – according to Mooyne's audible rolling commentary - the carts were now moving past the gates of Balago, and on to their destinations. The Empire's men had been allowed into the town so long as the trading caravans were let out first.

Ramkus had no inkling if the pressure upon Figal to open the gates had come from the Empire trying to get in; or from the merchants wanting to get out. Figal was in quite a pickle: a bad look if traders were threatened in such a commercial hub, and a double bad look if the merchants and traders were held up from commencing their commercial travels.

The spokes of the caravan moved the wooden cart from side to side, falling into puddles and old tracks along the thoroughfare in the village. Ramkus braced his legs, lining himself along the base, footsteps to either side of the cart echoed, as it came to a halt. Grunts reverberated in the instruments, as the horses stopped. A hand was placed on top the tarp to remove it.

'Stop!' Figal roared from somewhere above. His volume - although muffled under the tarp - was not diminished one iota.

'We had an agreement they would be let safe passage!'

'I only wanted to see the instruments,' a voice yelled back. Mooyne was squeaking around in his seat at the front.

'They are all sold,' grunted the merchant with indignation, almost spitting at the troops.

An eternity seemed to pass.

Ramkus could not tell if it was a stare down, or if weapons had been produced on the Empire's part.

He was perspiring clammy beads of sweat, not only from being too hot under the sheet and his current physical state, but also from the pressure of being discovered.

Finally, the carts began to move again. He still had no idea exactly what was going on, but he did feel very, very lucky.

Only for a short while, however, as he began to feel queasy. The cart jostled along, making him feel sickly from all the commotion, and his hangover.

He held on to himself for dear life, lest he ruin the instruments.

XXX

After what Ramkus considered must have been the whole day, the cart stopped around mid-morning, with the merchant wishing to *go behind a tree.* Mooyne got off and stretched his legs whilst Ramkus made some movement. The heat under the tarp; the smell of the newly varnished wood; the movements of the carriage - and the effect of the hangover - were too much. He slipped out from under the tarp and vomited at the back.

Mooyne grunted, 'He's going to see that, you fool.' He gave Ramkus a reproachful look as Ramkus lay at the end of the carriage, mouth agape, looking woeful.

'Why shouldn't I be able to come out now? The threat has passed?' Ramkus asked in a weak voice.

Because we still don't know if the Empire's men **are still** roaming this path. Bloody hell, now we have to get rid of what you've just **brought up**, look away,' Mooyne seethed, as he began to relieve himself on the spot, in an effort to conceal the remnants of what Ramkus had *brought up* of last night. The smell of urine made Ramkus feel even worse. 'Why I am going to the trouble, I'll never know,' Mooyne continued to grumble.

'Oi, what in the blazes are you doing?' the merchant yelled as he saw Mooyne. Ramkus quickly hid. 'You'll make the instruments smell of piss you fool. Why would you piss there anyway?' The merchant sauntered over to confront Mooyne who was not even bothering to answer.

The merchant quickly ripped off the tarp to let the instruments breath. 'Aye?' the merchant let out a grunt. 'Who in the blazes are *you*?' he said incredulously, staring wide eyed at the ghastly sight of the stowaway. Thinking only of his cargo, and not that these two may actually be playing a ruse on him, the merchant added, 'You'd better not 'ave damaged the instruments.'

Ramkus stared wide eyed back at him with his mouth taut, then looked at the instruments. All sorts of stringed, wooden musical instruments littered the cart, well positioned not to move during such journeys - including guitars.

'I haven't damaged any, they're fine,' Ramkus answered with a grunt, realising the merchant could pose no threat to him physically. 'I am sorry for stowing away. I would have asked, but I felt too poorly, so needed to lie down right away...' he lied, *poorly*.

The merchant studied him, 'I guess I can believe that, *if it weren't for those two bracelets you 'ave on*.' He spat, 'Empire's

man? You too, 'ey?' He turned to Mooyne, studying him as
well.

'Certainly not! Do not curse at me!' Mooyne hissed, spitting as
well but with greater force.

'Nor I. In fact, I am trying to get these damn bracelets off,
hence stowing away to Potelo,' Ramkus said, sitting up,
annoyed at having to explain himself once more. He calmed
himself, reading the need to be kinder to this man. 'If it is
alright by you?'

The merchant's facial features had calmed down from his initial
shock. 'Sure, why wouldn't it?' he answered without emotion.
Ramkus - rather than be flummoxed by the simplicity of the
answer - was pleased with himself. 'Good, I'll sit in the front as
well then,' Ramkus forced the issue, unable to bare sitting in the
cart any longer. He jumped up delightedly to go up front.

'I did not mean you could come with me, I meant it is fine by
me if you get rid those bracelets,' the merchant continued.
Ramkus now *was* flummoxed.

'Quite a bit of gold on them, I bet. They'd fetch a good price
when smelted,' The merchant added.

Ramkus thought for a bit, 'Enough to buy an instrument?'

'Oh, one of those bracelets would be plenty enough.'

'That's if they are for sale,' Mooyne interjected. 'You did say
they were all sold to those soldiers.'

The merchant shook his head, 'Only to keep their grubby hands
off them.'

Mooyne shrugged, whilst Ramkus became excited by the
prospect of owning his own guitar, as well as forcing a free trip
to Potelo. 'Great, then I shall buy one of the guitars,' he said,
pointing to one at the edge of the cart in a deep cedar colour.
The merchant pondered his predicament – and whether the
amount of gold was about the right price for in fact two or three
of the instruments. 'I guess I *will* have to take you to Potelo
then. But, say you cannot get them off?'

'Let's not think about that just yet,' Ramkus muttered quickly.

Mooyne began to relieve the rest of himself a little further down from the caravan.

'Oi! Why not go further away, you'll ruin the instruments with that smell!' the merchant growled at him. Ramkus shook his head disapprovingly. *I don't want a guitar that smells like piss.*

The caravan rocked and buckled as it was drawn by the two horses. The path was fairly open on either side, leading Ramkus to think it to be a major thoroughfare used by the Empire. The merchant had introduced himself as Kret: a merchant of the finest wooden instruments this side of the Lencil river. They had relaxed into their journey and were quietly watching the road ahead.

'Could we not travel one of the scenic paths,' Ramkus suggested uneasily, 'I don't trust these roads to keep us from the Empire's eye.'

Kret thought for a while. 'I suppose you're right, actually. I didn't like the way they eyed the cart load before. There is a path somewhere up ahead we can use.'

Ramkus had his nerves calmed, and was fairly at ease when they later turned down a new path into the forest. This forest scene did not last long, as it became rocky, with trees much more sparsely placed, but they made good time on the track. They entered into areas which lay barren and bare, seemingly left behind untouched for aeons. They were when in fact unknowingly delving back through the lands they had traversed the days previous.

'*So*, those Empire men wouldn't have been after you, would they?' Kret asked with wry smile, puffing on his pipe as he did so. 'Just curious. See, apparently there have been rumblings of an attack on the main Summer Place of that Royal family. And our own village head matriarch had been contacted about a certain individual seeking help.'

Ramkus and Mooyne looked at each other, not sure what to say.

'Don't worry, I am a good friend of hers, but you are lucky it was *I* and not another merchant or traveller that you had come across. Either way, I would have obliged to help in any case. Although it still doesn't explain who you are, *sir…*' He looked to his side a Mooyne.

'Mooyne,' came the response.

'And your profession, Mooyne?' Kret enquired.

'Many… *including assassin*,' he stared at Kret, attempting to exert some form of fear into him, the type where people do not ask further questions. Ramkus began chuckling at the attempt of poor Mooyne, who wanted to just be left alone to cure the last remnants of his hangover headache.

The two were in better spirits now that their hangovers were lifting, to some degree. Kret gave them some victuals when they sat for a late lunch whist resting the horses.

The road was neither here nor there with difficulty or ease, but the ascent up into the foothills was quite great.

'Couldn't come this way in winter,' Kret began the conversation again. 'Although it can be beautiful, it is easy to bog, and icy as hell in other parts.'

They ventured till the sun loomed heavy, as if about to fall completely from the sky. Tall pines came and went, giving way to rockier areas until the trail became flat, and headed through a saddle where the pines shot straight up in a cluster.

Smoke worked its way into the olfactory sense; that rich smell that gave a sense of warmth. The smell of food soon followed, and then the sound of a village hubbub. The pine trail led out into a large oval shaped village, not of houses, but of homes built into the walls of the saddle's mountainous edge. In the middle of this oval shaped village were conical structures made of rock and clay, spiking up like monstrous teeth from the ground. Shadows of light flickered, as smoke billowed out small chimneys, and hard metal clanks and smelting sounds escaped every so often.

The sun wound down behind the peaks of the saddle, warning of an early, cool night was about to begin in the mountain's shadow. People were still going about their business, inside the dwellings and out on the flattened hollow centre of the town. The folk were sturdy, a little shorter than the norm that Ramkus had encountered, and many of the men were bearded. They looked a hardy people, with thick arms and willing smiles. They did not pay Kret or his two companions much heed other than a smile and nod of greeting.

Kret pulled up to one of the major enclaved buildings. Light was beaming out of windows on two levels, chiselled in the white stone. Its huge double doors of thick metal stood with might. As dauntingly difficult to push open, as these doors appeared, people moved them aside with ease.

'The pub,' Kret said, 'but before that, to get those off,' he pointed to Ramkus's wrists, 'you should head to the workshop over there.' With a shake of his head, Kret indicated to the largest of the conical *teeth-like* buildings which was also connected to the rocky walls of the saddle. A huge pyre of fire was fuming out of the top where a large pointed plate sat at the apex of the building. Smaller *abodes* were joined together and around this main building, giving it a look of some jagged, jewelled crown: *The prize of the village*. Ramkus stared at the structure.

'Let's go then,' Ramkus finally broke off, but Mooyne had already left the scene for the pub, and Kret to go tend to his goods.

Shrugging, he ambled over to the building, and was immediately hit by the warmth of the workshop when he approaching from ten feet away, hearing the blistering sounds of the smelter, the bangs of metal smashed into his mind. He was drawn to it, but became self-aware that the people may not take too kindly upon seeing his wrists, judging him before he would be able to plead his case. Wearing a cloak was not a good decision either, whilst in the red-hot hearth of the village.

I'll have to risk it, hope no one sees these manacles before I have my story told.

Once the sun went down, the mountains became increasingly cold, a reason – he deduced – as to why the furnaces were also quite tempting to build close to.

He readied himself for whatever it may take to get his bondage taken off.

As he entered the workshop of furnaces, the heat almost smacked him back from the steel door. None of the dozen or so of workers paid him much heed. A few furnaces were situated around the building, directly under the cones, with a massive one in the centre. It seemed the store and other rooms were built into the rock wall of the mountainside, which had many corridors going to and fro further under the mountain. The furnaces, although seemingly in one open room, had sliding, reinforced steel doors that could separate each one, should the need arise. The workers seemed to be coming to the end of their day, as a few were gathered around an older, red-greying, bearded, stocky man who looked like he had seen many a good days' work. He walked around the small group of men, who looked as if they were making offerings to him. His crouched every so often, inspecting with an inquisitive eye at the younger workers fashioned articles. He held them in all sorts of manners to fully acknowledge the craftsmanship put into the work. The sound of the fires dampened any sound Ramkus heard, creating the feeling he was sneaking up on the small group. He waited a few metres back till the old smith took an interest in him.

'What have we here?' The man boomed with a smile, 'Ah... someone from the Empire,' his smile faded.

'No, not at all,' Ramkus looked to the bracelets that had been his bondage, holding his hands up as to plead. 'I am here to have these removed.' He moved forth as the small group let a path to the man who had a foot now atop an anvil, sticking his chest, wary of this unknown soul. 'I am no man of the Empire, I was trapped by them, forced unwillingly into having these placed upon my writs.'

The man burst forth to inspect the bracelets - and Ramkus – with a reserved strength that would surprise even the most battle-hardened warrior.

'Never had a man claim that,' he declared with a raised eyebrow. 'Never seen these types of bracelets removed either. You see here fellas,' he began to speak to his younger audience, 'the Empire brands their *subjects* with bracelet, for men: one on the right for duty to their people, and marriage on the left, and the reverse for women. The greater the craftsmanship, the greater the status of the person. And of the person he is married...' He looked at Ramkus. 'So, you were married to one?' he said in a low voice, starting to speak to Ramkus in a private manner.

'It is a long story, but it was **against** my will.' He felt trepidation on whether this was going to work, and a desire not to allow what had happened in the palace to sneak back upon his mind. 'Can you remove them?'

The old man studied Ramkus's wrists, eyeing Miiva's ring for a moment too before speaking to his young students again, 'They melt these on by placing a protective seal over the skin before clamping it on permanently. The seal is only temporary. To take the bracelet off without harm is a very difficult procedure, I'd imagine. I am not sure I could do it, and if I did, you would be in substantial pain,' he spoke now to Ramkus. 'Only someone who really was not part of the Empire would go through such a torturous procedure.'

'Will you do it?' Ramkus pleaded. 'I was directed here and told only a Master Gem Cutter could carry out such a task.'

The smith moved his mouth to the side, unsure, raising his eyes ever so slightly at the mention of Master Gem Cutters being the only people capable of fulfilling the job.

'I'll give you the gold that is smelted off of one of them as payment...'

The old man seemed suggestible, he looked down again to study the work of the bracelets, putting on a small magnifying glass. 'Aye, a good piece of gold this is, and a few jewels speckled on. More than enough. But tell me: *what do you think of the Empire?*'

Ramkus clenched his teeth, not wanting to remember his experiences right now, but he had no choice but to tell the truth, dredging up the feelings he continually strove to bury. 'I despise them with a passion,' he whispered.

The old man nodded knowingly, 'Excellent! I'll buy you dinner as well if this all goes well,' he beamed. 'Just give me a few minutes to think of how to get those bloody things off. I have some idea, and I think maybe long, long ago I heard some banter about how someone else had gone through a similar procedure, after he had become too *large* for a bracelet over a very festive and drinking binge. Lost his arm… *Only kidding*,' he chuckled, patting Ramkus on the arm in a friendly manner.

Ramkus gritted his teeth down further in anticipation.

There was a growing interest from the crowd that had overheard the situation. Many suggestions as to what to do were being thrown around.

'Cut from both sides.'

'Melt one side and cut the other.'

'Cut the hand off.' This made the little crowd laugh, but put Ramkus in a panicked state. The older smith observed the bracelets for a time, lifting his gaze from them to behind, focussing on nothing but a thought, deep in contemplation on the complex task. After a minute or two, he had made up his mind. 'The safest way would be to have them melted off. We would have to apply a thin wrap underneath. I am not sure if it will be enough protection, though, but at least the wrist won't be completely exposed to the applied force or heat. We'd have to apply the thinnest but strongest fabric underneath, something that cannot break into the skin.'

He got up and found gel and some sort of fabric that bent like leather. He grabbed Ramkus's wrists with a firm grip.

'You're sure you wish to risk this? He asked earnestly.

Ramkus's temples were tense, veins bulging, nose flaring, eyes wide like he was ready for battle. '*I must,*' he conceded.

With that answer, the smith nodded. He applied the gel around the wrists as best he could. He then measured up the thin leather like fabric to go into the very tight – almost non-existent - space underneath the bracelets, making a few cuts through it before slipping it between skin and the firmly embraced bands.

'I would suggest looking away,' the smith ordered, Ramkus obliged, but not before his eyes viewed some red-hot heavy pincers being brought from the coals of the massive furnace. He had his arms placed over a barrel of water, whilst protective glasses were placed over his eyes.

'You, lad, grab the other, you have sturdy hands,' he could hear the smith barking commands. 'We shall do this together.'

Ramkus thought this the best time to close his eyes.

'Three, two,' there was no mention of one, as they had decided to do it before Ramkus had a chance to pull away from the strong grip. His body was braced by the other smiths, and a piece of leather put in his mouth as he screamed, clenching his teeth.

The pain was unbearable, as if the smouldering could have been completely enveloped over his hands.

He tried thrashing about. The excruciating pangs of agony were almost enough to make him faint, it was white hot rage that kept him hanging on for all that it was worth. The torture seemed to go on forever and ever, and he heard nothing. His head felt like it was about to explode. *I must endure! I must!*

His heart jumped into his throat, almost about to bash its way out of his body. White translucent specks spread into his vision as he was close to being overcome. His whole body tensed tremendously, muscles bulging, veins about to pop. Yet he held on with all his will against the revulsion.

Finally, he felt a bubbling sensation, as his hands were placed into the barrel of water. He dared not open his eyes, nor move a muscle. His eyes welled from rage.

It took a minute before he was calm enough to bring his focus back to the workshop and look upon the world anew, and as he did, he looked upon the barrel. It was filled with cold stones brought from within the mountain, and icy cold water. He looked up at the smithy, but dared not drop his sight down to his hands. He was shown the smouldering pieces of gold in deformed states, and now separated small jewels that had once adorned the bracelets. The smith looked at them, inspecting with a small, one eyed microscope.

'The rocks should keep the water in that barrel cold. I think you best to keep your arms in there a good while,' the smith said. Ramkus did so, not daring to move. The small group disbanded, all talking of the procedure with enthusiasm and amazement. The smith wandered about the workshop, but when he looked back to Ramkus, he regarded for the first time Ramkus's staff that he had brought into the workshop with him. It had been placed to the side.

'You're a *Guardian?!*' The smith said incredulously. His look became one of concern.

Ramkus nodded.

He paused, before continuing. 'We haven't had the best dealings with Guardians down here, I gather you know,' the smith said, sounding a little dejected.

'Well, I'm not a Guardian, just yet. I am heading to the mountain where they are perched. Please do not think me one of them. At least not how *you* think of them'

The smith nodded, then looked upon him with intrigue. 'I have not heard a Guardian say he despised the Empire before, nor that they had been forced to be one of them. Perhaps you are a new breed who may end up doing your actual job and help the people of the world,' he said with an air of rebuke, but saw the consternation it caused in Ramkus and decided to let it slide.

'Enough of that though, I think it may be time to inspect the wrists.'

He placed his apron on a hook and came over to the barrel to look.

'Hmph,' he grunted, 'They will likely scar, I am sorry about that,' Ramkus frowned at hearing this. 'It was your desire, after all.' He then produced two little bowls which he began to divide the glistening gold from and sparkling jewels with delicate tools, then further cooled them down upon some granite rocks.

'Look,' he showed Ramkus the little bundle of treasures more closely. 'Worth a fair bit this. I can smelt it down into small fragments if you wish?'

Ramkus shook his head, not desiring anymore smelting to be done this day. The barrel of water began to feel cool, and he could finally feel his hands. He decided it was time to inspect. The dripping forearms showed deep red and blue marks around where the bracelets used to be. He winced when he looked further down at the bubbling skin that look set to peel at the slightest touch. The smith came over and gently dried the arms with a towel, then produced a gel which he applied to the arms before bandaging with a light fabric.

'I would suggest trying not to use your arms too much for a while. Easy enough said than done, I know. Here,' he gave Ramkus some of the gold and jewels, tipping them into one his belt compartments and showed the rest as being pocketed for his fee. He put an arm on Ramkus's shoulder and helped him to the door.

But, before Ramkus could exit the building, a nauseous sensation overtook him, forcing him to fall to one knee.

'Easy now,' the smith patted him on the back, making sure he did not pass out.

Ramkus couldn't lift himself in such a state of weakness. It was as if he had been hit with a wave of noxious fumes, putting him out of action. The heat of the room became a ceiling above which he could not raise himself to his full height.

'Get him some water,' the smith said loudly to one of the straggling apprentices. 'And something to chew.'

The apprentice quickly gathered some water in a well-polished metal bowl, and handed the smith a good chunk of jerky meat. The smith helped Ramkus to sit with his back on a work bench, putting the bowl in front of Ramkus's mouth, lifting it for some small sips. He stared at the jerky, frowning, considering whether it was right to give him something to chew on – especially when it looked like burnt flesh. 'Why not. Have a bite on this.' He tore off a chunk of the cured, dry meat, having Ramkus slowly motion his mouth and keep him from thinking of his sickly state.

As much as the smith wanted to help Ramkus, he also did not want the Guardian to throw up in his work space – the smell really did not do well in such a heated environment.

He let the apprentice take his leave, after he stopped to see if he could offer any further help, and

noted that it may take a few moments for the Guardian to steady himself. The best thing for someone in this situation was to be reassuring and calming, talking to them in a peaceful manner. It hadn't even been that long a time since he had had to help people in circumstances which were much worse than this. He himself had still felt the effects of having to comfort those traumatised by the bastardry of conquering forces; the death and destruction of other communities that were settled not too far from here.

He sneered at the thought of what the Empire had done, even in recent times, and slowly looked at Ramkus, considering that a predicament may come to befall Potelo. His didn't want to follow that ill prophecy, but assured himself that his town would be well secured compared to others, and that the people of the town were ready for such an ill-fated strike.

Leaving the thought, he returned to remedying the sickening response the Guardian had to having his wrists almost burnt through.

'Let me tell you about the true history of bracelets on this continent,' the smith began. Before he could start off, Ramkus had fought back the effects of his malaise, rising, swallowing the jerky, breathing in the hot smouldering air.

He coughed, and breathed again. 'Maybe over a drink,' he said slowly, smiling in appreciation of the help.

'Right you are,' the smith replied with warmth.

'Well then, shall we.' He opened the door, 'Oh, and you don't want to forget this!' he grabbed Ramkus's staff for him, admiring the craftsmanship, the lightness of it, wondering what alloy had been used. He chuckled to himself, recognising and admiring the work of the gods. '*And yet the gods creations can still be touched by man,*' he said to himself.

This was an auspicious meeting indeed.

Chapter XVIII

The town seemed to revolve around two buildings: on the right, the workshops with their blistering furnaces, extending into the open town circle somewhat; and on the left, the lively tavern, cut within the mountain on the other side of the saddle. The two meandered to the door of this tavern. The smith kept an eye on Ramkus who had turned deathly pale in the cool of the saddle shadow. The sun had been reduced to the barest of light at the top of the mountains, and the town had grown freezing in temperature. When they entered through the steel double doors, the scene was jovial and infectious, with its heat and light, sounds and smells. People were boisterous, singing, dancing, drinking, and eating on long tables. Fires at the edges of the grand hall kept the place efficiently warm. There was a second level which held not only private quarters for guests, but a second bar as well. Ramkus saw Mooyne annoying some patrons, whilst Kret was in a cavernous alcove, talking business. The smith led Ramkus upstairs, where it was quieter and the tables smaller.

Ramkus was in a daze from the pain, the cold, and the last few days. It was hitting him all at once. Scenes of the castle he had hid from his mind began to crash through.

At least I have the damn bracelets off.

He dared not raise his arms too much, fearing he would tear the delicate skin that had once held him, bound him, to the Empire, and its Princess Sophia...

They sat at a round table, and the smith went to the bar to order as Ramkus stared at a candle that was offering subdued light in the middle of the table. The flickering flame bouncing up and down in rhythm. He became immersed in it, knew only of it, wanted to be one with it. He brought it closer and started to play along with its movement.

The smith came back and slapped him on the back, 'You ok me lad?'

Ramkus finally spoke, breaking from the trance, 'Sort of. For everything that has happened, I suppose.'

The smith sat back, 'Seems like you do have an interesting tale to tell then.' He pulled out a pipe and began to fill it with tobacco and other herbs, lighting it and puffing a few heavy clouds. 'We have time, if you wish to tell it, otherwise we can sit and watch the place.' He noticed Ramkus admiring the pipe, 'Want a puff?' He produced a second one and offered it.

'No. Bad for the throat,' Ramkus replied instinctively, to which the smith laughed.

The thought of performing gave Ramkus some joyous relief, then he realised he could not risk playing a guitar with his arms in such a state: *Not now at least, maybe in a few days*.

The smith reclined into his chair, contentedly puffing away, as a bar maiden brought over some ale in steel tankards, as well as some bread and cheese which the smith took to straight away. Ramkus joined, and the smith took up his tankard to cheers with Ramkus.

'To your health,' the smith added. 'What is your name, by the way?'

'Ramkus,' the Guardian answered matter-of-factly.

'Tomriel: Master Gem Cutter, or more generally, blacksmith,' the smith replied, 'it is a *pleasure* to meet you.'

'It's funny,' Ramkus began, 'but one of my first memories is in a pub, with light dancing on the walls. Beer, tavern food. Feels like a very long time ago.'

'Well, it would be,' Tomriel said.

'Ha, no, it is not that long ago…' Ramkus started to tell of his story – in heavy detail – of his fight in the night; his flight from one town to the next; of his encounters with the Empire; experiences in pubs and of the different towns, hamlets, and villages; of the different people he had meet; he relived his precious moments without concerning himself whether his audience was listening intently.

Meals of hearty stew came to the table, as more ale was brought. A few of the Tomriel's apprentices began to join the table, listening to this story, commenting with intrigue. Upon hearing the mention of Ramkus being somewhat of a troubadour, one of the apprentices remarked that a female bard had come through Potelo some time ago that matched Sigil's appearance. Ramkus was stunned for a moment before being delighted by the thought, adding to his vitality.

The crowd swelled, and were enraptured by the storytelling of the scenes in the castle, of the escape, and of the forest dwellers. When Ramkus had finished, Tomriel was in good spirits.

'Seems I made the right choice then. Sounds as if you are on our side after all,' he commented in a cheer.

Ramkus began to look at his wrists, fidgeting absent-mindedly with Miiva's ring. Tomriel looked at it more closely now that he was out from the furnaces glare, recognising the craftsmanship, noting the rare few who wear or are even considered worthy to be given them.

'That reminds me, I didn't get to tell you the story of Lirem.' Tomriel looked around at the smiles at the mere mention of the name. He then regarded Ramkus who looked at him with interest.

'No. You didn't. Which begs the question,' Ramkus said with a cheeky smile, 'Who is Lirem?'

Tomriel smiled, inclining his head, 'Defender of the People, Protector of the Land – as is his proper title. He is - or was - a legendary hero of our lands. One whom the Empire has tried to wipe the history of. An attempt on their part dispel any camaraderie and unity between the original peoples of these lands. But I am getting off topic now. Lirem: Defender of the People, Protector of the Land, our ancient hero.' Tomriel raised his left and right in front of himself with clenched fists as he declared the title once more, before pausing to recollect his thoughts and consider how best to start.

The crowd was relishing the chance to hear the tale once more, people on other tables had stopped their conversations, sitting back with their ears pricked.

Tomriel had never been the one to play story teller. It was only in recent times that he had become somewhat of the elder of Potelo, even if he wasn't truly of the usual age to be one, and the role of public speaking was still rather new to him. He stopped and folded his arms, looking down with a smile, for an old, stout man, with a hardened face, slowly made his way to the table. Tomriel knew what this meant, he was either being spared the opportunity, or being judged. The crowd motioned for the elder to come through and take a seat.

Ramkus was drifting off for a bit, suppressing another attack of nausea. It wasn't coming on as strong as before, but it was still nagging at him. His drink was the only painkiller available when his mind came around to his circumstance. 'And so, what did the hero Lirem do for the people,' he pleaded Tomriel to continue so he could forget his pains, before realising the old man was taking a seat at their table. Ramkus took in his huge frame, his massive arms that could pulverise rock. He had a grey-white moustache that seemed to envelop his face, falling down as if it were a beard. Balding on top, with greying hair at the edges that suited his presence as somewhat of the elder spokesperson of Potelo. He wore small glasses, which sat atop a reddened bulbous nose, and a large, grey, leather cloak that appeared a symbolic gown that denoted the importance of this man; his stature; his leadership.

'Ah, well.' Tomriel started off, still smiling with his arms folded, looking down with a wry smile. 'These lands have not always had the conquerors forcing themselves upon us. We have had much more archaic enemies trying to destroy us. The mountains, forests, deserts, coasts & seas have all had attempts at being defiled by monstrous beings who once traversed upon the earth. This was in our infancy; we were small tribes setting forth to build our world. There was a time when the distinction between us of the mountains, and those of the forests and seas, even the deserts, was limited to being purely of where one decided to call home. We knew no difference between ourselves, although certain people adapted better than others when it came to settling down in one environment over another. Many would point to the environment as what has nurtured us into being as we are, both physically and mentally. We were brought forth from the land, created by the land. But I am once again getting off topic...'

It did not seem to matter those listening that he was going off on a tangent with other subjects that interested him. However, the older man was watching Tomriel with keen eyes, and looked upon Ramkus with a curiosity. He did not dare to speak, and neither did Ramkus wish to question why.

'In our small tribes, as we attempted to traipse across the continent, shape it into more inhabitable surrounds, or even move into areas which catered to our growing needs and curiosity, we were ever so often faced with other beings. Terrible malevolent entities that wished to do us harm. We fought, we won, we lost, but the threat seemed to grow greater after every battle, as if there was a brooding force that was testing us and readying to throw greater and greater threats to do so.'

Ramkus sensed the older gentleman could not contain himself, his own enthusiasm in the topic at hand was such that he wanted to wade in and take over.

His whole body seemed to quiver with a rush of excitement as he started up, his voice booming over Tomriel's. 'This was a time when Deities walked the earth, and some decided to help, some decided to step away, but none took it upon themselves to truly rally to us for the cause. Deities are fickle that way. Seemingly of a different consciousness and thought, but that is a discussion for another time.' He smiled to Ramkus, 'I am sorry, this is a tale that I oft wish to tell. I am not as much use to my townspeople as I used to be, so I do what I do well, when I can. The name is Chall, I am one of the elder heads of this little town.' He looked at Tomriel whom was showing signs of relaxation, letting the discussion take its natural course, 'I beg your pardon for the intrusion, Tomriel.'

'Not at all!' Tomriel answered, 'I was just thinking that it really should be someone like yourself to tell the tale. I am not *at that level* just yet,' he winked, expressing his acknowledgement of his position within his little community. 'Or at the very least, I am simply not as good a storyteller as you.'

Chall continued where Tomriel had left off before his interjection, showing a greater passion than before for the tale, animated and vibrant in his manner: 'We began to struggle, as we moved further and further into the land, helping areas that had been fouled once again flourish with life and beauty, the movement against us grew, pushing us back to the brink. We couldn't regain our composure - and this was on so many fronts! Without anywhere to turn, small skirmishes became battles, and eventually an all-out war. Our issue was that we were disparate as peoples, still small tribes, not trusting or understanding others as much as we needed to in order to band together. As one tribe was completely wiped out, another was then under direct threat, and then another, and another. The destruction never let up, and began to consume our lives.

'What can a people to do but fight back? You could say that we were pushing into territory we should not have, but that simply was not the case. The land was a paradise before we stepped foot into it. This enemy was rampaging like a disease, spreading its evil vapours on the land. We were *made* to care for this land, we were *made* for this land. The enemy was some sort of repugnant wound that wanted nothing more than to desecrate everything. It was unnatural.'

He looked at Ramkus with an intensity, as if the memory of the generations from aeons ago was being relived in his mind.

'Two questions,' Ramkus said as Chall stopped for a breather, 'Who or what was the enemy? And... Deities?'

Chall smiled with the knowledge of one his age, 'I'll answer the second, first. There are Deities who helped shape the world. Beings who do not face death, who wield significant and special power. We cannot truly fathom their intentions, nor what type of force they wield. They just are, or were – I have my suspicions. Mortals have never been the only beings in this world. Why, even small spirits enjoy the sunshine. Sometimes you may catch one out of the corner of your eye... Inhabiting trees, or small temples placed along the highways and secluded paths. Even this mountain has a soul and a force within her.'

A number of the patrons were smiling at this little inclusion, whether they believed the suggestion or not. Tomriel was himself drifting away in his memory of the folktales he had heard as a child. He had wished so hard to believe in them when younger, blushing from the thought of his mentors when they playfully teased him, telling him not to be a naughty child lest he upset the mountain.

'As for the primordial enemy,' Chall continued, 'revenants, darkness, blights, monsters, wickedness incarnate. Manifestations of the corrupted. That which desires to destroy the light, to decimate the land, to eradicate life. All from a single source that was everything we were not. A nothingness that grew and fought against us and our innate surge towards growing a bountiful environment.'

'Yes, but what did they look like?' Ramkus couldn't help himself.

'All sorts of beastly creatures, not only one form did they take. If you are to take a sentient being and turn them, they become ravaged due to their mind being forced back to the brink of existence.'

Tomriel burst out laughing, patting Chall on the shoulder, 'He never saw them, this is a long, *long*, time ago Ramkus. We can only imagine them.'

'I can describe them!' Chall grunted defensively with a ferocity. 'I just need to *remember*.'

The crowd laughed at this interlude, still somewhat eavesdropping and not fully allowing themselves the opportunity to join.

'As bad a beast, as awful a monster you could think of, we faced them all. There was no set description, other than there was a presence of ill in those creatures,' Tomriel offered as an answer.

'Yes, well, as Tomriel suggests… In any case,' Chall decided to get back on topic, 'we were in a dreadful state, the tribes of the first peoples were all being sent to an inevitable demise. Every step forward became two back. You must remember that this war ravaged over years, and was so sinister that often any gains into the land which seemed once a paradise could be entirely wiped out all the way back to where the people had fled, often hundreds of miles back towards major bases. Several settlements were lost at once in this way. The burden of going forward was now becoming a battle of survival, not to be pushed back to the very brink of life.

'When the people felt that it was all lost, when the tendrils of the malevolent force were striking so far in each direction upon the many people that inhabited the land, that was when Lirem first appeared: The Protector of the Land, The Defender of the People.'

'Wasn't it the other way around?' Tomriel asked quickly.

'What Defender of the Land, Protector of the People?' Chall asked gruffly.

'No, Defender of the People, Protector of the Land,' Tomriel answered, 'the order of them…'

Chall focussed, furrowing his brow.

'It does not matter, does it?' Ramkus wished to have the story proceed.

The mountain dwellers all looked at him aghast. 'Does not matter?!' Chall gasped.

Everyone went silent. The sound of the flickering flame was the only sound heard.

'Well, I guess not,' Chall acceded, proceeding once more, showing no further bother. Everyone seemed to let out a sigh of relief in unison.

'Lirem came into this world, we know not how. Simply waking from the earth from what we understood.'

Hmm, Ramkus took note.

'He had no weapons, no armour. Clothed simply, yet he carried himself like a leader without any followers. For he did not require any to follow him, yet he took the cause of the people of the coast, deserts, forests, and mountains to his heart. His focus, his drive, his cause was unwavering: he was going to destroy the destructive force plaguing the land, and allow the people and nature to flourish. He was to save the people, and the land!'

Chall stopped for a moment, gathering his breath, as well as allowing a few moments to build the anticipation of the story. Tomriel nodded along, happily memorising the mannerisms of the man he had deferred to. He was lucky to once again hear the tale, knowing it may well be one of the last times he gets to hear it rather than having to tell it. *Peaceful times should never be taken for granted, there is always some sort of enemy lurking out there*, he told himself. Acknowledging that this story cemented the nameless threats that had always faced his people, and will continue to do so for as long as they themselves existed. After the few moments of respite, Chall began anew. 'And so, Lirem, our saviour, was born of the same earth that he would save. He followed no religion, served under no god – even if he were a godsend. He existed to lead us to a world where we could survive and live, nurturing the environment to create a paradise for all.'

All of sudden, Chall bent forward with urgency, as if what he was about to say was of such importance that it could only be uttered in a clear and concise whisper. He spoke in his hushed tones as loud as he could, so all others were forced to lean in but still able to grasp his words.

'What came for us was chaos incarnate, it was the *chaos bringer* himself. A being of such magnitude that the earth itself could be torn asunder. We were not fighting something we could beat, something that we could face as mere mortals. It was Lirem, who was created by the very ground he stood, that was our only hope. But he needed help to face the source of the chaos. And so, he asked the people of the four lands, whom all rallied behind him, that he lead a small army of the finest warriors from the four realms: twenty-five of our mountain folk; twenty five from the forests; twenty-five from the coast, and twenty-five from the deserts. This war party marched behind him, knowing full well that he was marching to an uncertain battle which meant *not* knowing what he was about to face, or if he was even up to the task!'

The hum of the fire, the hubbub from the patrons below rose gently as Chall stopped for another moment.

'Why did the people see him as a leader and agree to band around him to begin with?' Ramkus suddenly asked, 'Did he have some sort of ability to sway the people?'

'Hah!' Chall chuckled, 'An inquisitive one you are.' He looked around at the other faces, showing some enthusiasm at being pressed for more information. ''Tis a story after all, so I am not entirely aware of how. But from what I believe, he had a *way* with people. He could easily command to be heard, or to be followed, and people would do so. Further from this – which is what leads me to the next part of the story – he was described as being a devil in combat. The land is large, so for him to be granted such a right as to lead the best warriors from the four corners meant he had to be known by all those he was fighting for. He travelled far and wide, and was counted as having helped all tribes he came across in their own skirmishes with the enemy. It was in this way that he exhibited his exceptional

strength and will, fighting with his bare hands. Is that a
sufficient enough answer?'

'Yes,' Ramkus inclined with a half-smile.

'Good answer. Made off the top of your head, I'm guessing,'
Tomriel jested.

'Quiet you,' Chall showed Tomriel his palm. 'Now, where was
I… His Hundred Tails, right,' Chall grunted, clearing his throat.
'So, the members of his little warband were called the hundred
tails – or tales, dependent on how you interpret the idea. A
hundred different tales from a hundred different warriors, all
leading into one - which also infers the idea that they were the
tails of one Lirem.'

'Come on, old man…' Tomriel prodded.

'Yes, well. The Hundred Tails followed Lirem as he launched
into battle after battle, directly attacking the enemy, forcing
them to flee or be destroyed themselves. The people knew their
faith was being rewarded, as the malevolent forces in areas that
the people had been pushed back from were being recalled to
face the threat of Lirem's little warband. It allowed the general
populous some peace for a while.

'Lirem and his Hundred Tails seemed to fight endlessly, day
after day. There were no losses for the Hundred, and this was
put down to some sort of divine protection that had been
bestowed upon them. They all fought with the vigour of ten
men, resting and eating little as they pressed into the darkness of
an ancient, unknown Elantra. These were the untameable lands
of the core which the first peoples had not touched. It was at
this time that the furthest lands we had traversed began to pose
no threat, as the whole of the enemy force was thrust into an
horrendous situation. The chaos wrought as much cataclysmic
power as it could direct to defeating the Hundred and Lirem.

'It was on an open steppe, under the Blue Giant mountain, that
the last battle of Lirem: Defender of the People, Protector of the
Land, and his Hundred Tails would end. The final destination of
their bloody march to eliminate the threat posed to them, and the

paradise they were meant to create upon this earth. That plain is now known as the void, and is an eerie place that no one dares enter. There is still a presence of defilement from what I have heard – although it is a difficult place to get to. No roads lead there.

'What Lirem and his men did not expect was how quickly the redrawn troops from the farthest reaches would be able regroup around their own leader. It seemed that every battle they had won, day in day out was only a small fight of no consequence. Indeed, as I had said, none had died so far, and for good reason: the enemy was only slowing them with minimal casualties for itself. On this plain, there was no cover, no protection. They were to face a force of tens of thousands. There was little in the way of tactics that one hundred and one individuals could take. As much as having a mixture of spears, axes, short blades, and longswords can assist in a tactical advantage in battles where banding together can overcome a stronger force, they were so heavily outnumbered that they simply stood no chance.

'The Hundred Tails knew that this was to be their resting place, and the only chance to help their people would be to fight to the bitter end and allow Lirem that one shot of destroying the bringer of this damnation. They knew their required sacrifice, and looked upon it with nothing but determination. They watched the unruly army, and the central figurehead at its heart: a dark being that glowered with fierce hues of purple and red, enveloping the darkness as if it was merely a force to be played with. The skies swirled in torment, lighting pelting the earth with great magnitude, vibrating within the earth, and within each heart of the Hundred Tails. They *knew*.'

Chall paused for effect, as candlelight seemed to wane at the mention of this sacrifice. No one moved, resting their drinks and meals, conscious of the sacrifice of long ago, and what it meant for their lives now; how it mirrored their own conflicts of recent times.

'Why do we not band together now,' Tomriel muttered to himself. Ramkus looked to him for some elaboration, but he was too lost in his own thoughts.

Chall paid no heed, continuing the story after a while, giving a moment for people listening to break the silence with a drink before he began.

'As they stood facing their impending deaths,' Chall said with a focussed intent, 'Lirem asked them all to give him one strand of hair each. If he was to somehow return to the people, delivering the news of what had happened, he needed to bring something back of each of the Tails. After receiving from those warriors a single hair, he placed them in a small glass container held around his neck by a simple thread. Sealing it, he knew that it was not only the hairs he was sealing, but their fates.

'And so, with little fanfare, and full awareness, Lirem and his Hundred Tails leapt into the throes of battle, cutting down swathes of enemies, till one Tail was taken down, then another, and another. Each single loss seemed to stagger Lirem, the hairs he carried around his neck grew heavy on him with each death. There was no time to reclaim the wounded, as they were set upon by the hordes of destruction. By some miracle, they were still able to cut through to the central point. As they approached, step by step, cut by cut, Tail by Tail falling, they looked upon the godly beast that summoned the monstrous creations. A giant of a man, bald, with a face of violence, of cruelty. He had no name, he was simply *the Beast*, and he was awaiting the final moments whence he could smite the hopes of the light.

'As the Tails fought them off with their weapons, Lirem jumped into the depths of conflict using his whole body. With a martial combat unknown to this world, he savaged all that came at him, using all manner of kick, knees, punches, and elbows. As he defended against the enemy's weapons, he deflected with his forearms, often taking a cut or bruise. As godly as he seemed, the abrasions and wounds on his arms began to take effect, as if some poison was inherent in each cut, chiselling away at his ability. He was immensely powerful, and although his forearms took on such punishment, they did not break. Instead, they were being withered away as if a rock was taking brunt impact until it shattered.

'By the time his last Tail had fallen, the casualties of the enemy numbered in the thousands. Still, more thousands stood to face him. But this was inconsequential, as Lirem and his Tails had accomplished their plan: He was within a breath of *the Beast*. Chall stared away, lost in the picture of his imagination, whilst Tomriel was now the one at the table playing with the fire of the candle with a look of sorrow on his face.

Ramkus was nodding off to the comforting voice of Chall, almost being overcome by his own wrists' pains. He imagined how Lirem would have felt having his skin hacked away at; at the loss of his men. He himself had lost his friends along the way, but not to death. He shook himself awake at the thought of his companions, but did not wish to dwell on them. The story was well received, and he still wished to hear it to the end. He resolved his focus as Chall brought himself to face the two men at the table again.

He gave a resolute smile, and continued: 'Lirem was no chance against the Beast in such a depleted, exhausted, ravaged state. The Beast laughed at this broken man, for having the audacity to confront him. Heavily bleeding, and acknowledging that he would likely be killed, Lirem launched himself at the Beast. The Beast, although a giant, being four times the size of a normal man, was quick and nimble. His bulky frame so powerful that when he went to hit Lirem - but had his strike evaded - he ended up striking his own soldiers who were in the cross-fire, killing them with a force that made massive dents in the earth.

Lirem dodged back and forth, left and right, around and back. He would come in and strike the Beasts vital points, hitting knees and ankles, launching himself into the air to give a blow to organs or ribs. The Beast felt no pain, he could not be contained! There was little Lirem could do, as his energy dwindled. He was fortunate that none of the Beast's forces joined in. They watched in a large circle at the savage reckoning of the man named Lirem. Their own fate rested upon this battle.

'And with one step a second to slow, and a strike connecting ever so slightly, Lirem was overcome, now taking direct hits, shielding himself with his powerful forearms that had now been reduced down to the bone.

'As he awaited the final impact upon his body, the one that would drive him back into the earth from which he came, the Beast stood back, laughing with malice. "Go back to the people, tell them of your loss. Your death does not come today, for you shall see what will be wrought before your true demise!"

'Lirem stared in disbelief. He realised he stood no chance against the Beast in such a state, nor without a weapon to defeat him. Would he really be allowed to leave? The Beast's intention for Lirem to see the total end of the four peoples of the land filled him with a nausea he could not shake. But a little voice at the back of his mind told him this was how it was to be, and to take stock, for he now knew what he faced.

'And so, like a dog with its tail between its legs, Lirem was afforded safe passage through the throngs of enemy, over the dead, and into the lands of the living. The weight of those he lost weighed heavily around his neck.

'How he managed to travel back to the closest tribe, based hundreds of miles away from the conflict, nobody would know, for to make it there was a miracle in itself. His wounds were such that he should have bled to death upon the battlefield!'

As Chall began raising hands to dramatise the story, a loud bang from the ground floor below reverberated up. The sound of patrons clamouring soon followed. Those listening to the story looked below to find the long tables being rearranged, whilst two young men of around twenty years of age were staring each other down, sticking their chests out proudly.

As Ramkus observed, this did not seem the sort of scene to make people overly worried, rather, it seemed to be one that the people below were excitable over. They shouted expressive words in the two lads ears, egging them on as as they sat across from each other, bearing smiles of intense gusto.

'On my mark...' one of those close to the action yelled, as those squaring off placed their right elbows on the table, then gripped the others hand.

'Go!' the referee cried out, as a contest of strength consumed everyone's attention.

Muscles bulged, and veins started to rise from the men's arms, spreading throughout their bodies and across their foreheads. The crowd yelled and cheered them on, but neither was giving any ground.

'Not those two louts again,' Chall shook his head. 'If I know any better, this won't be a simple arm wrestle... Yep, there we go.'

As Chall was talking, one of the combatants slapped the other with incredible power across the face, enough to knock a man out. The other took exception and slapped him back with as much vigour. Tomriel shook his head, 'These idiots would definitely get killed if we let them the opportunity.'

Ramkus was bemused by the comment: *Let them the opportunity?*

The slapping continued, as the arm wrestle was now simply a means of tying the two together so they wouldn't get out of range of each other almighty slaps. They started to rise from the long bench, knocking over drinks and pushing furniture about.

The younger ones in the crowd were in hysterics, shouting and jumping around. Those of a more modest age moved back and away from the spectacle.

The innkeeper was starting to yell at them to stop, getting fired up, trying to charge through the assembled crowd.

The fighters were still all smiles as they slapped each other one too many times backwards that it started to become a wrestling match.

'Ohh… Morons!' Tomriel exclaimed, rising from his place and speeding down the stairs.

The crowd pushed the furniture further away as they encircled the two, with their clothes ripping, they were pushed back into the centre by those watching when they strayed too close to obstacles, thereby keeping it a close combat situation.

One was picked up and squeezed in an attempt to get him to submit. Instead of giving in, he smacked his bicep on the others temple, shocking him to release. He did so, only to regather himself and tackle the other into the bystanders, knocking them all back.

'Fools! Tomriel jumped into the fray, with the innkeeper finally granted passage. They quickly grabbed the young men.

Chall started laughing, '*Youth!*' he said as if in a cheer. 'Too much energy to burn.'

'How many times have we told you idiots that there is to be no fighting in the tavern!' Tomriel boomed at the two, holding one in a headlock with the innkeeper putting a full nelson on the other.

'And this goes for all of you too!' the innkeeper roared at the young crowd who had been instrumental in the instigation of the event. They all lowered their heads as if they were being told off by a teacher. 'Out, all of you!'

The crowd began rearranging the furniture back and leaving through the doors, whilst Tomriel and the innkeeper took the hot-headed ones and booted them into the street. 'Finish it out there if you must, but until then, you're not allowed in here for an hour, the lot of you!' Tomriel shouted at the door, turning his back and walking back inside. The innkeeper seemed to be mulling over what Tomriel had just said, frowning at the prospect of letting them back inside in an hour's time.

The rest of the patrons seemed to know the drill, resettling themselves on the long tables and benches without much ado.

Chall was still laughing to himself, 'It's like this every week, it seems. Especially those two. Always been inseparable. I think

461

it would be an insult should they choose to fight anyone else besides each other. And if anyone did lay a finger on either of them, they'd have to contend with the both of them.' He shook his head as if remembering something in his past.

'I imagine you have had your fair share of fights,' Ramkus said with a hint of humour.

'Ha! And you seem one to talk...' he gave a knowing wink.

'Yes, it's part of our nature to get into a few scuffles here and there. It's just part of our makeup.'

Chall stopped talking, as Tomriel finally rose from the stairs and took his seat again, letting out a large exhale, smiling.

Chall gave him a nod, before starting off on his talk once more.

'Yes, our makeup, which brings me back to the story. Where were we?'

'Lirem almost dying, but getting back to one of the settlements,' Ramkus said.

Chall looked to Tomriel to ensure he was settled from his little peacekeeping mission, before picking up where he left off.

'Right, well then. Needless to say, Lirem did not die. It was at this time the people of the four lands had, after finding the need to hold conference with each other, decided on an appropriate arena where they could meet. A secret meeting spot, in a desert, hidden behind a small, red rock mountain that the sea flowed into and sustained a small forest. An oasis for all the people. Lirem, in his half-dead state, was taken here to be given the care of the peoples' healers. The burden of the fallen kept him from rising. When he was able to, he was called in front of the leaders of the tribes to explain what had happened. He told them of the forces, of what he faced. He described the Beast. "I cannot defeat him." Lirem cried in anguish, raising his arms high, baring his arms for all to see. He showed them the small glass container, all that remained of the Hundred Tails, dropping it to the ground and leaving the leaders to discuss what more could be done.

'No doubt the Beast would swarm the land that had just been reclaimed by Lirem and his men, so they had no choice but to act fast. They had not the men to build an army, all they could do was *cut off the head*: they had to kill the Beast.

'As they debated how this could be done, they recognised their faith and trust still lay with Lirem. He was the only one who had the ability to confront the Beast. He knew the lie of the land. Perhaps he could sneak through and confront the Beast once more, in a duel one on one. But those wounds he had had inflicted upon his arms meant he was vulnerable, he needed some sort of protection.

'Our ancient forefathers knew much more of the nature of things than we do now. It could be argued that would have survived had it not been bred out of us, or had we not had such peaceful times before the Empire came. They knew ancient arts, they knew mystical crafts.'

At the mention of ancient arts, Ramkus began to smile and roll the ring around his finger.

'It was decided,' Chall kept going, 'that they would imbue as much of their ancient craft into a weapon that Lirem could use. There was a problem though: Lirem carried no weapon. The leaders of the tribes fell silent, wondering what they could give Lirem to aid him. As if it all dawned upon them at once, the leaders thought of his forearms, how they had taken such punishment. They would create arm bracers for him, ones that held properties from all four lands, the four peoples.

'The forest dwellers sourced the leather from sacred creatures in their midst. The leather was weathered and placed in the salt waters along the coast by those who lived by the sea, and then dried and tanned beneath the great sun of the deserts under the care of its people. When it came to our forefathers, the people of the tribe helped fashion the bracers in deep forges, with a fine metallic underlay from resources within the earth. In completing them, the mystics of the tribes imparted the last traces of the Hundred Tails, burning them within the fabric.

'Lirem in this time was forlorn and lost. He traversed through the last of the tribal lands, contemplating the extinguishment of its people and the land he was meant to protect. He considered himself as having failed, believing that there was no hope, no chance now. His punishment was to watch as all was lost. When he was called back to the newly consecrated, sacred meeting spot, the leaders of the villages asked him to step forward, and presented him the arm bracers. He was perplexed, taken aback. The faith he had lost in himself, that confidence, it was being given back to him by the people. When he put them on, a strength and resolve built up in him, as if he had found a well of new potential. He was told of the manner in which the bracers came to be, and at the mention of the Hundred Tails last sacrifice, he welled up and let out a shockwave. The people were blown over, as Lirem exhibited something of the supernatural.

'His expression was once again of determination, not to let down the people that still trusted in him. Not to let those he fought beside die in vain. The plan was set in motion, the last chance, the only chance. How he was to actually fight the Beast, he did not know, but there was little time to lose. He set off on his own, with the hopes of the people, and the fate of the land.'

Chall stopped himself, it was time for a breather. The top level of the tavern was silent, only those below whom did not know of the tale being told were being merry, eating and drinking at the end of their day.

Tomriel was holding one elbow whilst stroking his jawline with his other hand. There was a solemn regard for Ramkus and his situation, as well his own role in it all.

'So, the bracers,' Ramkus piped up, 'They became Defender of the People,' he raised his left arm, 'and Protector of the Land,' he raised his right.

Tomriel winked, 'Aye, right you are. It was not only a title given to Lirem, but also how the bracers came to be symbolised. Mystical relics, sacred ideas that the Empire wish to wipe out.

They adopted the idea from us, and now claim those bracelets and their significance as of their own creation.' He let out a deep sigh.

Chall took a few more breaths before starting the last part of the story. The crowd were all ears, many faces had been turned to the old man in anticipation of the finish.

'Setting off with nothing but the clothes on his back, and the newly created bracers on his arms, Lirem stalked back into the depths of bleakness once more. It was unfortunate for him that he was to go straight to the head of this body without drawing any attention to himself, for he could spare no time for the bands of enemy striding towards the people. He felt it was his responsibility to fight all that threatened, not let them be. But it let him move as quickly as he could through lands that had been claimed back by the depraved. All he could do was watch on as those dark twisted souls settled back in, beginning their battle march towards the far-reaching strongholds of the four peoples. He could not halt them in their tracks, even though he held such a magnificent power, for it was not only the hopes and faith of the people he carried, he now held their ancient craft, their mystical strength. It pulsed within him as he heard the voices of the Hundred Tails, willing him to defend the people, and protect the land.

'As for those beings that marched, they met with the forces of the four people, fighting with a new deranged sense of reckless abandon. They weren't conscious of themselves, only of their host. In the days that it took for Lirem to travel back to where the Beast set his throne, thousands more of our people perished. It was all out war on our last footing. Our only hope was that this enemy would fall away once the central figurehead was removed. And so it was that these were to become known as our darkest days, where the sky was a constant whirlwind of tormented hues, cataclysmic forces thrashing above, below, and onto the earth we were trying to protect.

'In as timely a fashion as possible, Lirem met with the Beast. It was a rude awakening for both of them. The Beast had taken up residence in an abandoned hovel which had been completely befouled. He had been moving closer to the front lines than Lirem had anticipated, and it was his aura of maleficence that pricked Lirem's attention.

'The Beast did not have much in the way of protection, but those that surrounded him were far deadlier than any other beings he had under his control. Upon sensing Lirem, wolf-like men found his whereabouts and set about attacking him. Half a dozen of these repugnant manifestations lurched at him with their jowls snapping. As they bit at him, he shoved his bracers into their mouths. Miraculously, as they clamped down, they became overcome with a revulsion, becoming jagged and decrepit, before evaporating into the ether. The bracers were indeed imbued with such properties as to remove the defilement from the land.

'Although aware the Beast was about, Lirem had only randomly stumbled upon this hovel and was startled by the wolfmen's attack, wondering how it came to be that such forceful enemies could find him. He himself began to sense an overbearing force, for the bracers began to vibrate, picking up the vibes of an impending danger. Understanding that something was amok, Lirem stealthily moved to where the bracers seemed to vibrate with a shocking aggression. He was soon face to face with the Beast.

'The Beast, looked at him with somewhat astonishment before begging to laugh at the intrusion, believing it to be hysterical that the man in front of him, the man whom he had let go, had returned. He called for his forces, wishing to now take Lirem into custody, force him to watch the rampage that they were set to make upon the four peoples of the land. Lirem was having none of it. He was here to do one thing, and one thing only. When the Beast's wolfmen did not appear, he regarded Lirem with a darkened mood, sneering: "I see then, you have chosen your fate." Lirem answered, "No, it's not *my* fate that has been chosen. It is the fate of the land, and its people who have."

'The battle was of such ferocity that people from hundreds of miles away said they saw bolts being sent into the sky from the direction Lirem had headed. As the Beast danced around with incredible prowess, blurring in Lirem's vision, he struck with the might of a mountain. Lirem raised the bracers in defence, being hurled back. Punch after punch, the mighty Beast continued to assault Lirem without letting up. But after every hit, every strike, something else happened: the Beast's fists began to burn. Little by little, small chunks of his flesh began to evaporate. Enraged, the Beast grabbed Lirem, hurling him into rocks. Lirem was barely conscious. The thrashing he was being tormented by would have dealt massive casualties to an army, yet he withstood it. He withstood it all, unable to get his own hit in, he was merely bracing against his own destruction.

'As the barrage became more and more frenetic, the Beast became tyrannical. Pained and wounded, he was something beyond a god in his anguish and anger. Strikes seemed to rain down from the heavens, as he tried to destroy this thorn that had grown in his side. Slowly, small pants of exhaustion came from the Beast, and in these small lapses, Lirem launched himself back into the fray, punching and kicking the vital areas of this gargantuan creature. It had little effect unless the bracers touched upon wounded areas.

'Lirem tried to understand how he might destroy this foe, fighting with a savage desperation and on his last legs. But it was in vain, for the Beast had grabbed Lirem and began crushing his throat, bringing him up to face him. The Beast's eyes were a smouldering red, the enlarged pupils of a crazed maniac that knew nothing but survival. With force that would have snapped the mightiest of warrior's neck, Lirem held tight, almost fading, struggling against the giant steel like hands of the Beast. The grip was like a pincer that had melted together. He was pulled all the way to the Beast's glaring eyes until he was within an arm's length. And it was with his last vestiges of strength, he punched out at those eyes, hitting them. The Beast screamed, closing them, squeezing Lirem's neck tighter. Lirem rested the bracers on the molten knuckles of the Beast, which by the reflexes of the Beast brought Lirem back closer to the monster's face. With the impending loss of his battle for survival, Lirem dealt a volley of strikes to the eyes once more, and with the force of one hundred men, pierced through the eyelids and deep within the eyeballs.

'With the pain of the strike, the Beast snapped Lirem's neck. He hollered around in agony, but he could not pull the arms from his sockets. Slowly the intensity of the pain became a rapid pulsation, as the bracers filled with ancient mystical crafts did their work, flowing into the Beast, whittling him away. Steam rose from his body, as guttural screams pervaded for miles around. His body went into death throes, and eventually evaporated into nothingness.

'The people knew something had happened. For as they fought themselves against the dark hordes for their own survival, the enemy soldiers stopped and fell over as if on cue, disintegrating into the ground. The people knew, *ohh, they knew*. Their prayers had been answered, Lirem had bested the enemy, cut off the head of their great foe.

'With great jubilation, the four peoples celebrated. Merry were the feasts and extravagant parties that were held. But the greatest one was to be saved until their hero, their champion, the Defender of the People, Protector of the Land, had returned from his battle.

'The people waited, and waited. But Lirem did not return. They were certain that he had bested the Beast, for there were no more encounters with enemies, and all traces of their existence seemed to be eradicated. Nature quickly reclaimed its rightful place, wherever the sun shone. Yet Lirem did not return. The people could not contemplate having had their champion missing in action, defeated along with his foe.

'They sent a search party for him, walking in celebratory regalia, coming to reclaim their hero, to lead Lirem back to the newly created sacred meeting spot. As they walked through the fast recovering terrain, they had no trepidation that they would face anything untoward. When they reached the original steppe that the Hundred Tails had failed, they found no sign of him. The search party was perplexed, but having no other direction or knowledge of where to find him, they returned with the news that Lirem could not be found.

'Time passed, and ancient crafts were lost, yet this story remained. It was not until many years after, a hunting party stumbled across the hovel. It reeked of a decayed stench, a terrible resonance that made each of the party sick. The took it as an ill omen caused by something unnatural and in need of purification. Due to the history of that corner of the land, and the nature of what was described, an extraordinary meeting between the four peoples was called, something that had rarely occurred since the war was won. In fact, it was only in auspicious celebratory occasions that all four met in these times. It was decided to send four mages to determine the situation. The hope would be that they could seal away any malevolent malignancy that was growing in that hovel.

'Upon reaching the spot, the four mages set down to see what was within this stagnant place. Slowly, descending into that tomb, they found nothing but two bracers, smouldering on a pile of reddened ash. *Lirem's bracers.* Using old techniques, they were able to recollect the last few passages of Lirem's life: his stumbling on that spot by accident; the fight with the Beast. In their incantations they themselves looked into the Beast's eyes, which was enough to turn even the strongest willed person mad.

'The mages set about purifying that very ground Lirem last stood, with all the ancient craft that had been passed down at their disposal. Fortunately, enough of the knowledge of the ancient techniques worked on eliminating all the defilement the Beast had spread. It was, in a way, the true last element in the destruction of the Beast. For the bracers seemed to still hold mystical properties that stopped that reddened ash in its stead, not allowing it to manifest into anything other than the remnants of a wickedness that corrupted the nature of existence. But to finally purge that being, the four people's own hands needed to fulfil their destiny. Returning to the sacred meeting spot, the story of Lirem's battle was told by the mages, finally completing the search for their saviour.

'The people lamented the loss of the hero, the Protector of the People, Defender of the Land. In a way, there was still a small sliver of hope that he would one day return, for it was under his leadership, under his image, that the people were united. Indeed, it is perhaps why we are not as aligned as we once were, for we do not all yield with our whole spirit to a man who walked as a god, facing an evil head on in order to ensure the future of the land.'

A sad lament began to echo in a hum between Tomriel's townsfolk; solemn, a deep bellow which all seemed to know, to connect to. Not a word was shared.

When it appeared to die down a little, Ramkus, impressed with the story, asked: 'What happened to the bracers then?'

Chall looked to Tomriel, both smiling. 'The bracers serve as a significant reminder of our unity, of our struggle, of our history. They represent all of us four people, as well as the sacrifice of the Hundred Tails.' Tomriel said. 'It is only fitting that a temple be constructed, one where the story of Lirem would be preserved, one where all people could see the bracers in person, for they – from what we knew – never aged or decayed.'

'Knew?' Ramkus asked.

'Aye, knew.' Chall took over again, 'No one has seen those bracers in scores of generations.'

'But why?' Ramkus pressed with intrigue.

'Because we have lost the temple! We simply cannot find it's whereabouts anymore.' Tomriel answered regretfully.

'Yes,' Chall once again began to finish Tomriel's sentence, 'when the Empire came, the people were quite accepting of them, in fact they were welcoming them into the tribes. That was, until they waged war upon us. They were already well within the land when battles began for more territory. An emergency meeting was called in secret between the four peoples, but it was hard to know who was to be trusted anymore, as many people from the Empire had become very well entrenched within those societies. No meeting was able to take place. They knew too many of our secrets, and were well aware that such a meeting had been called. They demanded we show them where the secret meeting spot was, and with their knowledge of our history and our stories, they identified Lirem as a figurehead that the four people would all band together under once more. Ultimately, they demanded to know where the bracers were kept. And, just as we had refused to show them where the sacred meeting spot was, the people refused to show them to Lirem's temple. With fears that the Empire may follow pilgrims to the temple, the leaders of the four people all agreed to prohibit anyone to go to these spots. Due to this standoff, this relinquishing of venerated places of our four peoples birth right, we have no idea where that sacred meeting spot is, nor the temple which keeps Lirem's bracers. No one has visited them for hundreds of years.'

Chall took a breath, as Tomriel butted in to finish the story *he* had begun. 'And so, by not being allowed to visit the sacred spot of the four people or the temple of Lirem, and to completely wipe the significance of the unity under Lirem, the idea of the bracers was adopted by the Empire. They decided that they would wear simple removable bracers at first, and try and force us to wear them too as signs of bondage to them. It really took off for the Empire, and they all decided to wear them, *imitating Lirem*. It was not taken to by us, as you can imagine, and since the bracers were easy enough to take off when forced upon us, we simply decided to be unlike them and not wear the empirical bonds. So, the Empire went with a different method, deciding that wearing one would signify marriage under their law, and if one did not wear it when married, they were free of any relationship... Being well planted in our lands, in our towns, they took to the women, even those that were married by our customs... *Forcibly*...' Tomriel bit his lip, his eyes began to glaze over. 'Not one of us can say we are purely of the first people now,' he said with a sneer. 'It would be very rare to find anyone who can say that of any of the four people.' He lowered his eyes, but noticed Chall about to speak again, so he started off. 'And as the bracers could not be bound to people, the Empire decided to use a more permanent measure: melting bracelets onto the skin so they cannot be taken off.' He gave an aggressive smile as he acknowledged his defiant role in all this, a breaker of the chain - so to speak.

Ramkus began to feel woozy once more at the thought of what he had endured, of what he was trying desperately to wipe from his mind at present. 'Finally, it was decreed as one of *their* ancient customs. The Empire had officially made its own people wear the bracelets as an acknowledgement of their bond to the Empire, and a second as a bond to their partner. In that way, they adopted our heritage for themselves, as an attempt to wipe the meaning of the bracers from our consciousness, from our collective history. They tried to force a wedge into that which united us with just cause, destroying the image which we held so purely, so righteously. We do not believe in wearing such shackles of bondage, so now, it is a sign of the Empire, not of us.'

Tomriel shook his head as Chall stroked his chin, nodding.

'I see,' Ramkus said without emotion, clearly about to be sick.

'Ah, you poor lad,' Chall looked at the Guardian's wrists, fully cognisant of why the story was told. 'I guess they were trying to recruit you. I'll let you have some breathing room.' Chall smiled knowingly and stood up. Tomriel stood in appreciation, as did the other people listening in to their village elder.

As he began to take his heavy steps towards to stairs, Ramkus stood. 'Thank you,' he said politely waking from his painful delirium again.

'Hah,' Chall answered, 'Not at all. We are going to need your type for what we are facing!' his eyes hinted at the Guardian staff resting against the railing overlooking the ground floor. Ramkus inclined his head before sitting back down. Taking in the last passage of the story, of what Chall's comments imparted.

A small glint in the eyes of Tomriel, which quickly glazed over, had Ramkus wondering now about the present, of what they *were facing*, of what his part would be according to Chall. 'Are you at war? he asked, suddenly regaining full awareness of his surroundings. 'It does seem that the Empire is growing rather quickly in these parts.'

'We are not so much at war or battle, but facing injustices,' Tomriel said with measure. 'It has always been the case as for as long as we have been around and they began conquering Elantra. It's not only of how they took to the first people's women… Much more has been done, and is continuing to be done. *So is the state of this here world,*' He said glumly, as if reciting a derelict mantra. 'Put down your tools somewhere, only to have *them* surface, force you to move on. Not to mention what I said before, the fact we aren't as pure bred as we once were makes it harder for us to navigate what should be the most natural terrain to us. Nevertheless, it is still our identity, it is still *who* we are. We will not join with them, we will not become *them*.' Tomriel puffed his pipe again, contemplating something with intent. His manner was much more relaxed now after the story and his views had been imparted; he was ready to share *his* view on Guardians now. 'The Guardians were meant to be peace builders, diplomats that sat in between all peoples and individuals. Not known to some, revered by others, loathed by few. We were let down in recent years by the Guardians, and our calls now go unheeded. Perhaps the old ways of the world -

ones we all parleyed by - are gone, along with the Guardians.'
He sighed, deep in memory. The Guardian felt lost in these
words about his brethren, saddened. *Chall thinks otherwise…*
Tomriel, quickly realised the dour state of political affairs he had
dragged himself and Ramkus into, started up again with a puff
of the pipe and a quick smile. 'So where are you headed now?'
Ramkus took a second to compose himself: 'To meet the other
Guardians. I know nowhere else I am meant to go. I know not
how to be. Who I am. I was merely told what I was one day,
and so I am now on this journey. I have already seen so much, I
don't know what to fathom, where to look. I have made friends,
though, and I shall not forget their generosity as I near my goal.'
Ramkus, gave his usual spiel, attempting to emphasise who he
would seek to help in this world, began to grow tired from the
effort of the day. He watched the candle once more.
'A long way you still have,' Tomriel imparted with care.
Mooyne suddenly appeared at the top of the stairs.
'One of *these* your friends?' Tomriel said, watching Ramkus
beckoning his new travelling companion over in his weakened
state.
'Yes, sort of. I think…'
Mooyne sat down on a spare chair at the table next to theirs, and
began talking. 'Looks like you have done what you needed to
do. Kret is settling down for the night, about to get himself a
room. What do you propose doing?'
'You two can stay with me, if you'd like.' Tomriel offered
courteously.
Mooyne looked to Ramkus for an answer. His expression
unreadable.
'Thank you, that is very much obliged,' Ramkus said after a
moment's pondering on what he actually thought to do –
sleeping outside in the cold was not too appealing, and he was
not sure if the small gems or smelted gold would be
overpayment for such accommodation. The gold would need to

be separated for payment of a guitar from Kret in any case. He put those thoughts aside, 'I wouldn't mind a good night's rest.' Tomriel gave him a wink, 'Say no more.' They picked up and ambled down the stairs of the tavern, as a good few of the patrons gave nods and smiles their way as they moved to the gargantuan steel doors. Tomriel then led the two outside and down the cold street of the saddle pass to a much smaller steel door in the side of the granite mountain. The night was cold and breezeless, as a cloudless sky stretched above with the moon hidden behind the mountains. It dawned on Ramkus how much he was looking forward to sleep.

The place was warm, connected to some heating source through vents.
'Heat from the furnaces is directed here,' Tomriel said, guessing at their initial glances and appreciation of the warmth. He placed his coat on a peg at the entrance and walked them to a small room down the hallway. The walls were smooth granite, and - although it was well within the depths of the mountain - felt cosy. Some windows at the front of the residence gave natural light. However, it was light that was beamed around from mirror to mirror from the initial source of the fireplace that permeated the household. It felt inviting and bright, especially with the sparse minimalistic placement of rugs and décor that did not impose any sense of being unwelcome.
'One of you can take this room,' Tomriel said, 'the other that couch in the sitting room.' He led them down to another small room that held no natural light or mirror, only candles and a fire place.
Ramkus made himself comfortable on the firm but relaxing couch, peering into the fire. Mooyne sat down next to him, looking like he was a tad drunk. Tomriel appeared again after exiting for a short while, bringing some cheese and bread, as well as some stout beer. He also tossed Ramkus a cloak.

'Here, for tonight. And for your journey... Not too far past here, you get to the velvety plateau the Empire does not control. But it is not the Empire you should worry about. It is the cold. Lows chills hit this land quick sometimes. You may be heading South-West towards warmer plains, but it'll be a while before you get there.

Ramkus realised he had not the faintest idea where he was to actually head now. It had been a mad scramble to get out of the castle, only a few days ago. *So much has happened.*

'Where exactly do we head?' Ramkus asked.

Mooyne gave him a look of surprise, 'We?' he said, breathing out as if to belch. 'Sorry my friend, but those places aren't for me, you'll be travelling on your lonesome.'

Ramkus was silent. It was the first time he felt he was actually on his own without any support waiting for him. But he flipped the thought, savouring the challenge instead.

'In answer to your question though,' Tomriel continued, 'South, South-West I believe. I am not too certain where the Guardians Seat is. Don't think anyone in town would know either. None have travelled further than fifty miles from this place, I'd say.'

Ramkus looked to Mooyne, 'south, south-west. I agree. Or maybe due west, west-north-west. I am not sure, I have never ventured there, nor ever come near it for all I know. You should get a horse, if anything. That's my only certain advice,'

Mooyne said, trying to hide his bemusement of the situation in his inebriation. For what it was worth, the two had not seemed to learn their lesson from the morning about over-consumption of alcohol.

'Aye,' Tomriel added, 'Unfortunately we don't stock any horses here. May be able to find a farmer past the plains or in a town that is selling one. Would cost you a fair bit though, even more so if you somehow sourced one from a trader round here.'

Ramkus smiled to himself, although he could use the small jewels left over from the bracelets, he preferred thinking of other more exciting and revered ways that he may make some coin instead, what Felipe had trained him for. *Not just yet, though. In a few days.* He did not dare touch his wrists.

With the food eaten, and beer drunk, Tomriel lit his pipe and stared into the embers of the fire, getting sleepier. Mooyne left for the other room as Tomriel rose to bid the two adieu, leaving Ramkus to his own devices.

He was enamoured with the cool, smooth feeling of the granite walls, which he lay his palm on, wiping the rockface with delight. Staring at the mirrors, reflecting the light from the moon. There was a heavy warmth which gave protection within these walls. It was understandable that people sought to live within such confines, as it was a bastion of security against the outside world. *I wonder how far they dug*, Ramkus thought, as the home seemed to continue further into the depths. He considered it a mystery that would unravel at some point, as he took in the scents of the rock, and the richness of the wooden furnishings that were almost certainly made by the hands of those that dwelt in the forests.

The fire began to grow weary, and Ramkus took to the couch, falling into a deep sleep as he stared wistfully beneath the roof, decorated homely in style, but unable to hide its true nature of being deep within the chasm of the mountain.

Chapter XIX

Awakening with a start, not knowing how long he had slept due
to the lack of sunlight in the room. Candles had been lit, and
reflective mirrors put in positions to let the light from outside
burst through the room. Ramkus arose and sat up. Tomriel was
sitting not too far away, reading a book. He greeted the late riser
with a gruff, but well-meaning, grunt.

'Morning,' he said. 'There's some breakfast in the kitchen.
You certainly slept well, late morning now.'

Ramkus took a seat in the kitchen that adjoined the room he had
slept in. A selection of toast, eggs, and cooked meats had been
prepared, as well as a strong dark drink.

'Coffee,' Tomriel said, 'or at least our version of it' watching
Ramkus take a sip. Mooyne followed into the kitchen.

'Thank you for your hospitality, Tomriel,' Ramkus said
obligingly, feeling overwhelmed with what he had been openly
offered.

'Don't mention it, you paid with that gold, more than enough.
Besides, don't know when I may need your help one day…
Guardian,' Tomriel gave him a wink.

Ramkus smiled to himself, remembering the night before, of
Chall's story. *Perhaps Tomriel is coming around to what Chall
was hinting at.*

Tomriel stared up at one of the mirrors that attracted the
morning light from outside. 'Looks like it'll be a nice day.' He
put the book aside as and concentrated his attention on his
guests.

'Too bad you get stuck in that workshop all day,' Mooyne said.
'I had a look last night when I went for a breather. The whole
place seems so well insulated that you'd never get any of that
fresh, mountain air, unless you ventured far outside from it.'

'Ha!' Tomriel began to laugh. 'Too right you are. But can you
imagine how nice it is in winter! We are lucky that we don't

have to venture out *at all* once the snow sets in…' he paused mid-thought. 'Well, I guess there is no reason to hide such basic information from you, but the whole town is connected with tunnels and passages. All part of our self-defences should we have any altercations.'

'So the town is essentially built like a castle?' Ramkus asked. 'You would be able to hold off against a siege?'

'You bet we would. We've a vast amount of preserved supplies, so food is not an issue, and we have connected a number of mountain springs to supply us fresh mineral water. We could stay indoors for as long as we please, and any intruders outside would be sitting around without any options. In fact, it is probably more apt to say they would be the ones surrounded, as our homes all dwell around that centre.'

'What of the workshops though?' Mooyne quickly interjected as if he had found a chink in the armour.

'Aye, don't you worry about that workshop.' Tomriel laughed with a knowledge he did not want to share.

'Yes, but what happens if they get inside? That does end up connecting to the mountain in the largest of those rooms to produce the most heat, does it not? Wouldn't they be able to get in?' Ramkus probed.

'True, they could. But don't you think we would have an extremely robust door to stop that from occurring? Just like all these doors,' Tomriel pointed to his front entrance, 'they can be made to withstand an incredible amount of pressure. We are not known as the best smiths for nothing.' Tomriel's answer seemed to satisfy the two, although there was some further interest in the whole town schematics which would go unsatisfied.

The two adventurers gorged on their breakfast meals as if they hadn't eaten for days, before freshening up in the guest bathroom. This bathroom still held granite features, and water was somehow caught and flowing from within the rock itself.

Tomriel explained that it came directly from the mountain's streams, and was directed into homes via pipes. *This whole set up is quite ingenious*, thought Ramkus as he scrubbed his face with the mountain water that flowed freely from the tap. Tomriel had proudly elaborated, before they went in, that the whole town was hooked up to these streams, as well as the furnaces of the workshop for warmth. One of the most ingenious elements of this piping network was that they were able to control how much water received, as well as combining the heat and water source to create hot water, straight from the tap!

The water cooled a febrile heat that arose in Ramkus, a symptom of the last few days efforts. He calmed himself as he energised his pained body for the day ahead.

Mooyne, not to be outdone on the knowledge front, expounded further of what he remembered from other mountain folk settlements: 'It's actually a common feature of mountain folk settlements. The passages in the mountain Tomriel mentioned that connected to every part of the town's residencies, including stores, warehouses, workshops. The whole damn town! It's not only here in Potelo, as Tomriel seems to suggest. I would love to have seen what else the smith has up his sleeve.'

Tomriel, standing by for conversation, grunted disapprovingly, as if to say he was reconsidering broaching the topic of how Potelo was built... Ramkus knew how to read Tomriel's manner: he was simply trying to protect the secrets that only those in the village were given knowledge of, and that he himself was now feeling he had done a disservice by letting on about the defences to outsiders. He still couldn't trust these two completely, he'd only just met them the day before after all. All he could do was resign himself to positive and confident thoughts, that they were friends who would help protect Potelo, should it require such assistance.

Tomriel re-tended Ramkus's wrists, applying new creams and gels, then wrapping in a new bandage.

They both inspected the wounds with intrigue whilst this was being carried out. The recovery of the skin was remarkable. Not that it had completely healed, but it looked as if it had been a week, rather than a day, since the bracelets had been smelted off. This still didn't reduce the fact that they hurt, and the new skin could still be easily broken.

'Guardian indeed. You certainly are a lucky one,' Tomriel said.

'Don't forget, being one is what got me into this mess in the first place,' Ramkus retorted. 'People trying to use me, force me to be part of their particular goals.' Ramkus could not help himself, sneering at the thought of how he was trapped by the Empire.

Tomriel regarded him with a quiet demeanour, not letting on whether he trusted the words of the man or not; whether he would be the great bringer of order and rewrite the past wrongs of the previous Guardians. *Time will tell*, Tomriel thought.

With the two content to set off, they left Tomriel's home in the mountain, stepping out onto the streets.

It was an odd parting, with no one wanting to hold up the other, feeling the sooner they got it over and done with, the better. 'I hope we meet again one day,' said Tomriel, as it drew to their farewells.

'Likewise,' nodded Ramkus, eager to get himself on the road again, but somewhat sentimental at the kindness he had been afforded. He hugged the cloak Tomriel had provided him with around his shoulders.

'Thank you,' Mooyne nodded solemnly.

Tomriel shook his head in response, smiled briefly, before starting off in the direction of his workshop whilst the others watched on.

As if he knew their gazes were still upon him, he paused and turned around, 'Forgot these, here' he jogged back over and handed some small packages of victuals.

Saluting, he moved off, leaving the two with the feeling that an atmospheric pressure had dropped.

They looked at each other nodding at their good fortune, then sauntered back to the pub where Kret had been lodging.

The fishmonger's cart from the day before was stationed outside, leaving Ramkus to wonder how *fresh* the fish were. It turned out they were to be smoked, and thereby preserved, 'Just how they are accustomed to such things up here,' remarked Mooyne.

Kret, *merchant of the finest wooden instruments this side of the Lencil River*, was studying his cargo in a small stall he had set up in the main area of the town before he saw the two coming.

'So,' he cried out to them, 'how was the *procedure*?'

'A success it seems!' Ramkus held up the bandaged wrists, wincing as he remembered he was to move them as less as possible.

'Oh, success? Looks like it was painful...' Kret surmised from what he was shown.

'How did they actually do it?' inquired Mooyne for the first time.

Ramkus hesitated, 'Not sure. My eyes were clenched shut... But I did get *this* at the end... apart from some free wrists,' he reached into his pocket and produced the melted gold from one of the bracelets.

'And I guess you spent the other one already of some goods? That cloak looks very good on you, even if it isn't new,' Kret replied gleefully, acknowledging to his surprise that the promised transaction was actually about to occur.

'I guess it did,' Ramkus responded, 'But enough of that, what do we have on offer?'

'As you can see,' Kret gestured towards the finely crafted, wooden instruments.

Mooyne looked around the main thoroughfare, intimating his impatience, that it was time to move on, and that Ramkus should choose quickly. Ramkus paid him no heed, and Mooyne did not say anything further.

'Ah, this one,' Ramkus pulled up one of the deep red cedar guitars and strummed, not daring to play more than that, lest his wounded skin break and bleed.

'Very good choice,' Kret remarked, putting on his salesman facade.

Ramkus handed the gold. 'Thank you for getting us here, also.'

'Pleasure,' he replied courteously. 'Where are you headed next, if you don't mind me asking?'

'That way,' Ramkus pointed to the road out of the saddle and into the plains. It was the first time he noticed what the road ahead looked like. A pass that seemed cut literally through the granite of the mountains.

Freedom.

'Take this, for the guitar,' Kret stared him in the eye for a moment, then handed him some fine cloth that wrapped around the guitar and made a pouch to carry on his back, the same as Felipe had done.

Felipe. Felipe...

'You'll be travelling a fair distance before you see any people again out that way. Safe travels to you, may the road treat you well,' and with that, Kret ended the sale, and his dealing with the Guardian.

'Likewise,' Ramkus smiled to Kret.

As he parted, Ramkus turned his attention to Mooyne once more.

'Sounded like piss in the wind that guitar,' Mooyne chided with a wink, then spat. 'Hope it doesn't smell like it too.'

Ramkus raised his eyebrows, ignoring the comments. 'What will you be doing now?' he said, realising what was coming. The ground underneath seemed to feel altogether too solid right now.

'Don't know, probably head back down that way we came. I don't like the plains much, doesn't suit me,' he replied curtly.

They stood for a moment as if in a shared trance. 'Well, I guess this is goodbye then.' Ramkus hesitated, not realising he was choking up. He hadn't been able to say such words to any of his other companions, and now he wasn't sure he wanted to do so anyway.

'Don't like goodbyes much, either. Prefer not to think of the idea of *parting*. We will see each other again, I'm sure of it.' Mooyne was evidently affected by the farewell too. Even though they'd joined forces only briefly, it was a strong bond they had forged.

'I wouldn't mind that, as long as we don't have to fight it out again,' Ramkus replied, pretending to hit Mooyne in the ribs.

'Hah, well, maybe we drink it out instead,' Mooyne jested, winking knowingly. The whole ordeal was awkward for both of them. Mooyne not liking goodbyes, and Ramkus not having said a goodbye of this nature before.

'Safe travels, may the path be good to you.' Mooyne looked Ramkus in the eye and grabbed his shoulder.

'May the path be good to you, too,' Ramkus embraced the hold. They turned, and walked their separate ways, not looking back as the dust trailed behind them.

The saddle pass narrowed, as the stoic mountain homes ended, creating a rocky buffer which only allowed two a breast to pass through. He breathed in heavily, the rocky mountain air refreshing the lungs, his mind clearing. *Not much of a farewell*, he thought, musing over what it meant to leave something behind. He ran his hand along the walls of the passage, it was smooth enough to press firmly without cutting any skin, but still rough enough to feel the small granules that protruded from it. He was in a much brighter mood than the day and night before, finally relieved of his bondage and lifting from the nausea that had enveloped him. He still found it a struggle to move his wrists about, not wanting to try and tear them at any point. Tomriel had told him the longer he left the bandages on, and the less pressure he put them under, the better the scars would end up looking – if he were to have any scars at all!

I really don't want to be bearing markings before I have even begun my journey as a proper Guardian, he grumbled. A large sound of a crack from behind stirred him from these contemplative thoughts. He stopped, looking back. He could see nothing but the windy circuitry of the path.

Another snap came, and then a cry.

He stood, flummoxed, unsure if this was simply the usual carrying on of the day in Potelo. His mind clear of thoughts, he couldn't bring himself to turn around and have the peace and serenity broken. He had already said his farewells and moved on. It seemed unnatural to him to go back whence he came, as he had only ever put one foot in front of the other and moved forward on his journey.

"Keep moving," that *friend* ordered. He winced at the thought of listening to *him*.

Another crack came, and a loud commotion rang through the mountain pass, echoing through the chasm.

"Move!" Prince demanded.

Ramkus scowled at himself, shaking his head, *No!*

He turned his back on his freedom, and moved with haste through the winding bends. Luckily, he had not gone far, reaching the opening back into Potelo soon enough.

As he flung out into the open, he beheld, in the centre of the town, some large figures on horseback, dressed in a dark armour. He halted himself from flying into view, quickly dashing behind a rock to observe and make sense what was occurring.

He peered out, listening to the muffled voices of the group of:

Empirical soldiers… and different from those in Balago…

Their armour was a burgundy, heavier than ones he had seen the members of the Kings Guard such as Poncho wear, deeper in colour also. They wore large helmets, adorned with feathers and horns. Their horses all black, breathing heavily under the strain of a long, difficult journey up to the saddle.

There were around a dozen in all, standing formidably, tempting anyone to approach.

Large swords sheathed at their sides, they hadn't come to parley. Chall stood facing one of them, his large pelt draping along the ground. He rested not on a cane, but a huge, ornamental, double-bladed axe: a totem of the village and its people.

Tomriel was watching from outside his workshop, pensive, standing at the ready with a huge smithy hammer. Others stood at their doorways, awaiting some sort of signal. As Ramkus looked about at the faces, he detected that this was something much worse than the usual begrudging *visit* from the Empire: this was fateful.

He regarded the soldiers closely, reading their movements, reading their mindset, trying to figure out what they were capable of.

The one speaking to Chall seemed to be staring him down now. A frown crept across his face, and he dismounted with resignation. Ramkus held himself from trying to get any closer. He sensed he was the reason these soldiers had come upon Potelo and its people.

The soldier approached Chall. He was of a monstrous size, similar to Djuayne in height, towering over the town's elder, staring him down with indignation.

Chall, for all his age and strength, held the gaze with a tempered expression. He flicked his cloak to the side, and as if the whole town had been waiting for the sign, the people fled indoors, locking themselves within their homes. All except Tomriel, who watched as Chall and the soldier stared at each other with cold indifference.

The rest of the soldiers weren't stunned by this behaviour, although they were surprised at the calculated synchronous movement. Their heads jolted around in all directions as they watched the doors fly open and shut within an instant. Some smiled with great humour, as if it were a game; others snarled with malevolent intent, placing their hands upon the hilts of their swords.

Longswords… Ramkus watched the band of soldiers closely, trying to anticipate what they were going to do. He tightened his grip on his staff, whilst stowing the guitar away behind the rock he was himself hiding.

How do I attack a group on horseback? Should I take out the one talking to Chall. He began to contemplate the need for attack, his heightened sense of danger began to make him twitch with an odd excitement. As he clenched the staff tightly, his right wrist started to chaff. Blood started seeping through the bandage.

Shit… He had completely forgotten his predicament.

'I say this to all listening, *and I know you* are *all listening*,' the soldier boomed as he stared down Chall. 'Do you really wish to face the wrath of the Burbar Regiment? We will lay waste to your town the same as we have done for decades… the same as we had done last week!' The man began to laugh, walking around in great strides. 'Even with this small force, this **shithole** can be destroyed within half an hour. And when I say destroyed, I *mean* decimated, completely smashed into the earth that you so wish to be deeply buried in.' His expression had become nasty, baring the fangs of a spiteful rage that welled within a demented spirit. The other soldiers yelled in great exaltation. Chall and Tomriel stood firm, showing no emotion, no back-step to the taunt, to the threat of their existence. Ramkus gritted his teeth in frustration and anguish.

'You are all just ants,' the soldiers voice boomed once more, 'scurrying within your own catacombs. You built well into those walls. Oh yes, we know about your towns, we have studied them… after we kill all the inhabitants of your mountain folks' towns, we *ensure* that none escape.'

Ramkus's senses were on high alert, he detected the slightest movement of Chall's footing as the soldier continued to lay down his plan to wipe Potelo from memory.

'However,' the soldier smirked as he regarded Tomriel standing tall, before setting his eyes back on Chall, 'I am feeling generous. If you can give us the two that laid waste to Fallen Crest, I will only take one of your lives, as punishment.'

'What!?' Ramkus was about to scream out and dash into combat, sparing the townsfolk of Potelo; but a hand around his mouth, and an arm thrusting him back, stopped him before he could take off. He staggered in surprise as he lay on his back looking up at a face masked in a well camouflaged cloth. The eyes were all that could be seen: Mooyne's eyes.

Mooyne held a finger to his mouth, calming the enraged Guardian.

Ramkus was lucky that the astonishment and sound he had made were drowned out by the flinging open of a number of residents' doors in protest.

'Ahh, so you have decided to come out of hiding!' The man continued his rant. 'What do you all think then? Who has been harbouring the fugitives then, hmm? Remember, if they are not here, the offer only stands if we can get information that leads to their relatively *immediate* capture.'

Tomriel was now grinning with a madness, a readiness to act of his own volition. Ramkus was of the firm view that this was the sole reason Chall had not handed over the leadership of the town to Tomriel just yet. Had Tomriel held the ornamental axe in his hands, he would have already charged the leading soldier. Ramkus saw his fire, and wanted so much to join him in his stand against the Empire. *He had come across so calm when I first met him. A hot heart burns within.*

Mooyne, still not trusting Ramkus to do the right thing, held him loosely by the shoulders. His grip, however, was also beginning to dig in to Ramkus's flesh. He was shaking in expectation, but his mind still held a clarity of what to do. He leant behind

Ramkus and whispered into his ear. 'Just wait and watch. It's best not to get involved sometimes. At least not until the perfect opportunity arises, or it is absolutely necessary. As much as you want to join their *war*, it is *theirs*. You can only act as an outsider.'

'But those soldiers want *us!* They are threatening these people because of our actions in Fallen Crest!' Ramkus remonstrated with Mooyne, trying to stand back. Mooyne still gripped him. 'Yes, and what will you do if I don't go with you? Even if I did, they **will** kill one of these people as they have already stated. They aren't leaving this town without scarring it. I doubt their offer is legitimate... This is the *Burbar Regiment*. They aren't humans, they are demons.'

The force of Mooyne's grip was adding to the build-up of anger within Ramkus. It didn't even touch his mind to go willingly in the first place. He exhaled with great force, then breathed in with his nostrils flaring, eyes open wide. '*You want to see a demon?*'

'Just wait, trust me. Have I ever led you astray?' Mooyne asked nonchalantly.

The rage within Ramkus still hadn't tipped over, he was still able to control himself. He found himself listening, baffled by the rhetorical question posed, wanting to point out the attack on Fallen Crest was, after all, Mooyne's idea.

'Watch.' Mooyne released his grip and rolled his head around, stretching his neck and shoulders in readiness for some action. Ramkus regarded the confrontation with intensity, but nothing seemed to be happening. In the distance some steam seemed to be coming from the sides of the mountain. It was a tad perplexing to see a mountain strain and sweat as if it were a human, and it held Ramkus's attention, bringing the whole scene into focus.

The sides of the mountains are steaming!? He looked at both sides, recognising the *vents* that the people of Potelo used to warm their homes were also directed to the outside.

Chall started to motion back, as Tomriel stood forward
'Time's up!' the leader of the soldiers yelled, lifting his sword,
'You,' he pointed to one of the soldiers closest to him, 'take that
one. The old man's heads mine.' He poised himself, raising his
longsword, as Chall lifted the ornamental axe in turn. Tomriel,
swung his body slightly to face the soldier who had been
summoned, lifting the huge hammer for an impending battle.
Half the dozen soldiers - as if tactfully aware of the manner in
which the town was built - stormed the workshop, knowing it
was not locked like other doors. The remaining four began to
search for traps or hidden enemies in a manner akin to wolves
on the prowl.
'Shit,' Mooyne growled, 'I didn't expect them to be so
bloodthirsty straight out,' he grimaced and spat, revising what to
do. 'We were merely a convenient excuse for them to come and
slaughter the town!'
'Shall we charge them?' replied Ramkus quickly, aware that his
current state would not lend him to being capable of fighting too
well.
Mooyne gritted his teeth with anger and desperation, watching
the two soldiers facing off against Chall and Tomriel. Their
slow movements, their callous enjoyment in having to fight
electrified him. 'Yes!' Mooyne shouted, jumping out and
running at them. He roared a battle cry as he pulled out his bow,
firing with rapid speed.
Ramkus, left in Mooyne's wake, pulled his staff tight, and
charged forth towards the skirmish. *"If it is to be, then let it
be!"* Ramkus's dark host laughed with mirth. The hideous smile
of malevolence returned once more to his face.
The soldiers in the standoff were taken by surprise at the sudden
intrusion. Mooyne's arrows barely missed his targets, as he ran
around to edges of the horse shoe shaped centre of town. The
other four soldiers heard the cries, diverting their attention to the
ensuing battle.

Tomriel and Chall, taking the opportunity, met with their oppressor's head on, using the small opening for the first strike, pushing their opponents back.

As Ramkus dashed towards the fighting, he was impressed to see the swift movements of both Chall and Tomriel with such heavy weapons. Their strikes were parried and diverted, and the counterattacks from the longswords blocked deftly with the handles and hafts.

Chall, for his age and ability, was not to be outclassed. His physical strength was awe inspiring, as he punished the Empire's soldier who had threatened him and his town. The expression of fury was as hot as the towns furnace, as if generations of his peoples' torment and rage welled up to burst forth in this one chance of retribution.

Tomriel almost mirrored the old man with his expression, dancing strike for strike with his opponent.

Ramkus slowed his approach, unable to enter the thick of the battle. He knew though, that Chall's resolve would last only so long. Before he could assess an entry to take over, a tingling sense had him stop and lean back as far as he could go. His feet slid, as he pulled himself back from a strike that came directly down in front of him, a hairsbreadth from shaving his prominent nose.

He looked to his left, and into the face of a berserk soldier, only to place his staff at an angle to deflect the longswords upcoming swing.

'You must be the Prince,' the soldier coughed up before swinging again.

'**Yes**' he replied, '**it is *I*,**' as he leaped back, holding the staff behind him with one arm facing down.

He began to circle with the soldier, their movements seemingly in a battle of grace. Observing the combatant, he noted the difference in care and *feel* from the others he had met. *Burbar Regiment, huh.* Ramkus ducked and weaved as the soldier slashed and stabbed at him with an incredible speed and strength.

It was evident how well trained they were in combat; evidently an elite battalion of soldiers. But as Ramkus caught glimpses of the look in his enemy's eye, he could tell that this soldier was not mentally stable, either. He was simply one of a crazed group that only wished to kill and destroy. There was no hesitation, no care, no regard for anything. There was only *instinct*. Ramkus reproached himself, he knew that look all too well.

As the blade came over him, he leant back, letting it carry all the way through, before spinning himself over to face the madness. It was almost a mirror, one he did not want to look into as he regained his composure, letting his own dark passenger slide back into his place. The blade came down as he pounced to the side, then back to his original spot as it came down again where he had been.

Not wanting to break the weeping, repairing skin on his wrists, there was little he could do than accept he would either have to bear the scars of his torment, or accept a fate much worse. He had held off as long as he could without placing himself in a position to have to accept the arduous nature of his weapons movement upon his forearms.

It would not last for long, as the strikes were coming closer, edging nearer to him each time his opponent moved. He continued to jump forward and back, lunge sideways, dodge, duck, weave, all without using his staff other than as a support; but it was only by a whisker that he did not need to parry and deflect.

Elsewhere, Mooyne was in his own crazed struggle, dashing about, firing arrows towards the remaining soldiers. They struggled in their frenzy to hunt him down effectively, for when Mooyne approached them, he was able to almost tie them into striking each other. One on one they might have had a chance, but they kept getting in each other's way, and neither was giving up the chase.

Tomriel was keeping up with his tormentor, blow for blow. His movement - albeit rigid - was effective enough not to budge one iota. It was his strength that appeared to force the soldier back, as he could not be contained.

Chall too was in a similar position, but tiring. The ornamental axe was not only a talisman of the village, it was a vicious tool of combat, and was all too ready to inflict the swift, decisive justice of its holder. It seemed, however, that the leader he faced was toying with him. He laughed wretchedly, strike after strike that did not hit, and every so often *tapped* Chall to know he had an opening. It was not as if Chall was giving any ground, he was still showing he could defend those areas left vulnerable for a hit.

A cry began to sound, a yell of pain: muted, but definitely of men. The combatants all seemed to register something was amiss, as the cries lifted from the forges' conical tops. Tomriel smiled with derision, knowing the folly of the soldiers thinking they had outwitted him.

Two of the soldiers who were trying to contain Mooyne angrily stepped back from the fray to quickly investigate; walking along the edges of the town that had been built into the mountain, unsure of what had happened to their comrades. As they approached the dragon's teeth structure of the forge, a rumbling began to sound, as shards of rock started to spray down onto these two investigators. An avalanche of muddy rock was rolling down the side of the mountain, falling directly above the two, smashing down upon them. As soft as the falling rocks were, the constant smattering on their helms rendered them unconscious, as they ended up submerged in the heavy substance, effectively trapping them, should they awaken.

Their leader, whilst dancing around Chall, frowned over his shoulder before turning to Chall with a sneer.

'You think you are clever, you *who come from the mud we shit on*,' he howled.

Chall was almost breathless, the vigour of the fight wearing him thin.

Ramkus, for all he could do to evade the strikes, now needed to vanquish his opponent, if he were to help the old man. He clamped his staff hard, as blood began to soak into the bandages. But before he could strike down his enemy, the leader yelped, rearing back.

He was clasping his buttock.

Mooyne had sent an arrow hurtling across the battleground, straight into the left buttock of the man facing Chall. The cries of agony seemed to shake the mountain saddle, as a serious expression appeared on his face: an expression not of madness, but of a pure rage with which someone would stake their own life.

The other men took their cues. They were ready to increase the intensity and kill, not matter how it was to be done.

Tomriel, noticing the change and sensing that Mooyne and Ramkus would rise to meet the challenge, roared: 'Do not kill them! Do *not* kill them!'

As if the words couldn't register or weren't for them, Mooyne and Ramkus went on as if they were ready to destroy the mad men of the Empire without a second thought. The soldiers though, took this as an affront that they would be taken alive, and as if their efforts couldn't be any further enraged, it simply strengthened their resolve.

Mooyne came closer into direct fighting range, pulling his kama's out, charging head on to meet his adversary. As a clean strike swung down, Mooyne showed an elegancy in his elastic movements, easily moving side on to let the strike come down, then lunging deeply under the next slash as he spun his body to face the blade, bringing the little sickle weapons to meet it and stop the next strike in its place.

As he held the blade in place with one kama, the other slid up to the hilt of the long sword, trapping the blade in place as he jumped to greet his much larger opponent, headbutting him on the nose.

Blood spurted out as the man flew back, freeing his longsword, and bring his off hand to his face.

'Fucking bastard! *You broke my nose*?!' He shouted in a muffled manner, blood dribbling down his hand. The expression on Mooyne's face was now readable, he was incited with a hatred and anger that was bestial.

Meanwhile, Ramkus still hadn't made his strike, preoccupied with keeping an eye on those around. *Everyone has gone mad*, he thought to himself, as if his own crazed state had been lifted by seeing the way everyone else was carrying on. His own blood ran down his arms and onto his staff. He flicked it at the eyes of his attacker, not letting him come within range to strike. It was the easiest way to fight for him now, as the strain of manoeuvring the weapon was costing him his ability to hold it. *If I can wear him down enough to get one good opening for a heavy strike to his head, I can take him out.*

"Not good enough, he needs to be dealt with and forgotten. We cannot leave a man to bear a grudge against us," his friend imparted. Try as he might, he still struggled not to let *him* have his say.

Ramkus dragged the staff along the ground, as the soldier lifted his blade to strike. Dashing in, Ramkus lifted the staffs extended end up into the soldier's nether region, happy that he was not the one on the receiving end. As the soldier doubled over in a convulsive fit, the blade swing kept carrying down over Ramkus. He lifted the other end of his staff quickly for a roof bloke, deflecting the errant blade to the side. In doing so, the other extended end whipped through the soldier's stance, positioning directly between the inside of his locked legs, letting Ramkus manoeuvre forward, tripping his opponent.

Ramkus, aware of the opportunity now, readied for the final blow.

"Kill him!" his dark conscience commanded. He lifted the staff high in the air, bringing it down with such force over the throat of the soldier that it would break his neck.

No!

The staff shifted ever so slightly on its last bit of trajectory, crashing into the man's sternum. An almighty cry came out, but not only from the soldier. Chall had been struck.

Ramkus quickly surveyed the scene, unable to clearly regard what had happened. Tomriel, who was closer by, was in a torrent of rage, now swinging his huge hammer with such ferocity that any single strike would have cleanly knocked off a limb or killed should it hit directly. The soldier he had faced was backing away in defence. It was unfortunate that the soldier could not take his eye off Tomriel, for a blur of movement dashed past him, crippling him such that he fell to his knees without him comprehending how.

Mooyne had run past and used his kama to slice through the soldiers achilles tendon, his opponent trying hard to keep up. Tomriel brought the hammer up in anticipation of the final blow, his breathe steaming in the cool mountain air. He swallowed, looking down at his crumbled adversary who was unable to put up any fight, other than stab at the hefty smith. Even that seemed too much effort, as his colour began to look sickened and pale.

Mooyne's oppressor was coming in to help, leaving Tomriel to decide what he should do in that split second.

Ramkus watched, panting, feeling sick himself, before somehow toppling straight over onto his side. When he looked up to where Tomriel was, the soldier was crumpled over in a pile of blood, whilst the smith took on the next foe.

Ramkus's head was pounding, and before he could understand what had happened to himself, he flipped over onto his back, only to see a longsword being brought down to charge through him. It was by the smallest of reactions that he was missed, as the sword went through just his clothes, pinning him. It was a miraculous save.

The soldier he'd thought he had immobilised was not down and out. Far from it. The armoured chest plate had protected his sternum. Ramkus cursed his folly, as he tried to stop himself from retching. *A clear hit to the temple,* again...

He couldn't get up, nor could the soldier release the sword from the earth he had heaved it into. 'You piece of shit!' the soldier screamed as he kicked the sword, then began to kick at Ramkus. For all his worth, Ramkus rolled as best he could, kicking up and out at the soldier whilst being on his side and back. The soldier struggled to get in on him, and before he knew it, Ramkus had retrieved his staff from the ground beside him, using that to keep his attacker at bay. With the twisting and turning, Ramkus finally ripped his shirt free, and released Tomriel's old cloak which remained pinned to the ground. Had he not been in such a predicament, he would have thought more of how high quality the durability of the garment was. But as it stood, he was once again with a head wound, and not in a good mood, letting the *other* take hold.

A nasty snarl crept across his face, as the soldier backed off the staff bearing Guardian. His movements became too quick for the soldier, and a cracking rip sound came, as Ramkus released a headshot using his hips to pivot the staff like a whip through his shoulders. Blood jetted out from his bandaged wrists, spraying up in a fantastic burst across both their faces.

The soldier was down, but Prince was not finished: ***"He must pay, as they all should."***

He brought the staff up once more, ready to do what he should have done previously; what Tomriel was able to do.

He nodded to himself, *Agreed.*

But before he could, the sound and feel of a lightning bolt struck the staff, shaking Ramkus from his position and thoughts.

'No killing!' someone yelled at him... Mooyne. He had fired an arrow directly into the staff. The arrow had split into two upon impact and was lying a few yards away. The staff was unharmed.

Ramkus looked at him, puzzled, then looked about.

The rest of the soldiers had been contained, the leader screaming from not one but two arrows to his arse, unable to move. The soldier that had initially been fighting Mooyne was somehow wrapped up in a rope; and the soldier Tomriel killed, was in fact lying on his side, after having been kicked over, not killed by the hit of the hammer.

Ramkus stared, mouth agape at what had occurred. Mooyne was watching him with concern, before slowly turning to aide Tomriel who was bent over with his back to Ramkus, concerned with something on the ground. As he let himself focus, he noticed that it was Chall who was on the ground.

Taking a moment for it all the settle in, he found himself panting. His vision was coming in and out of focus as it became blurred at the edges. For all the strength Ramkus could muster, an overwhelming revulsion came from his stomach, a tepid response to the beating he had once again taken. His body started to wane as he lurched back and forth holding his staff for support. It was all too much, as the urgency and desire for the blanket of dark to once again shroud his reality floated down. He crumpled to the ground, softly.

A huge cavern without a top allowed the moonlight to stream in on an angle. Overgrown vines from the foliage above filtered down in search of water at the base of the hollowed-out rock. The sky was brightly lit with stars, elegantly radiating a warmth of some deep knowledge within the cosmos. Stalactites and stalagmites surrounded the circumference, with boulders scattered about. A deep hum of the night gave the sense that one was not alone, as the insects were out in force on the sweet, humid air which remained still, but not stifling.

A grunt came from somewhere close by. **"Of course we would come here."**

Prince, *he knew.*

He sat up, trying to understand where he was.

The moonlight seemed to become lurid over a central point in the cavern, raised too perfectly for it to be the work of nature. A small platform had either been erected or cut into the chasms floor, and upon, that a solid marble bench with its ends rolled up ornately as if to place one's head for rest. It appeared to be an altar, but for what?

"It isn't real, you know. You will learn that."

He got up, ignoring Prince who was sitting idly on a boulder, his chin resting upon a raised knee. The altar could have stood as if a testament to a forgotten era, or for someone well into the future.

"Yes, you wonder to whom that belongs," *Prince continued. He sneered,* **"I will give you a hint: the person has never, and will never, exist."**

Ramkus approached the bench, running his hand along its cold, hard edge. Light illuminated his hand as if to caress it.

"Hah. The answer is: No one. No one should ever be raised in the minds of others upon death, having their all be placed high upon a platform to rot."

Ramkus looked back into the reflective eyes of Prince. They beamed with intensity.

"The only ones to be heeded; to be revered; to be followed, are those that are well and alive. No other."

He looked back at the altar, and then to the twilight.

Chapter XX

Ramkus awoke with a startle, gasping for air as if he had been
buried under a mound of dirt. In a way he had been; his eyes
quickly grasped his surroundings: he was within the mountain
once more, or rather, underneath it. There was a mixture of cold
granite and smoothed brown surfaces. Candles flickered, whilst
a warm and glowing light had been directed into the room. He
surmised he was in an infirmary, as he had been put in a cot
close to the wall with a bed side table holding various bloodied
bandages and towels. No one else seemed to be about, although
he could hear voices murmuring from somewhere.

What had happened? Searching his memory, he traced back his
last moments. *We had defeated those Burbar Regiment
soldiers, but I had taken a beating on my head again... My
wrists!* He looked down to find his arms heavily bandaged. He
remembered the blood he oozed spraying into the eyes of the
soldier he had been facing. 'Shit,' he grumbled. He knew damn
well what running into battle had once again cost him. The
wounds were now deep. He would have to wear the scars for
the remainder of his days. ***"Better than being a servant to
them, or another human being,"*** Prince consoled him in his
own macabre way. Ramkus mustered a chuckle, as he was light
headed and able to accept what had occurred.

Murmuring still continued to sift into the infirmary. It was
rather small and cosy, with its low, smoothed ceiling of rock
feeling rather humbling. He judged it to only be able to hold six
patients at its maximum occupancy.

With nothing better to do, he got up, scanning the place. His
staff had been left to his side. He grabbed it instinctively,
almost stumbling over himself in doing so. He could have
fainted, if not for being able to use the staff as a crutch.

Water, and a few pieces of soft bread, had been left out next to a
small bowl of lukewarm soup. Realising how famished he was,

he began eating as he wondered how long he had been knocked out for.

After eating the food with relish and guzzling the water, he felt ready to start some sort of celebration with the people of Potelo. He exited into a narrow corridor that resembled a perfectly constructed and proportioned mine shaft, which he noted had many similar rooms connected. The murmuring continued to grow as he moved further down the corridor until he could make out voices.

A large group of onlookers seemed to be congregated in one of the rooms. They barely noticed as he approached, wandering inside. Tomriel was busily talking to a number of people, and immediately sought out Ramkus when he spied him. He wore a face of deep consternation, painted with dust and blood.

'Ramkus, it is good to see you have awoken and are in one piece,' he said with deep concern. Ramkus raised his bandaged arms, leading Tomriel to frown at the sight, 'Yes, I am sorry that you had to get yourself involved.'

Ramkus breathed in heavily, remembering that the Burbar Regiment had been looking for him and Mooyne. He protested the notion that he had been involved in Potelo's affairs. 'No. I am sorry Tomriel, we didn't think that we would get you involved in their pursuit of us. I am really sorry.' His distress was visible.

'What are you talking about, getting involved in their pursuit? That we harboured you? Helped you? No, the Burbar Regiment does not come to simply search for individuals who may be hiding in a town. They have been rampaging up and down the mountain ranges recently, it was only a matter of time before they struck us.' He mustered a smile for the deeply anguished Guardian. 'We had been actively preparing to be attacked, in fact. How do you think we were able to end up having only four of them bearing arms, whilst the rest were incapacitated? Or that only two of us were out to face them in the streets, not the whole town. We were ready for this a long time before you two arrived on the scene.'

Ramkus nodded, still unsure of what Tomriel was implying. He became aware of the room he was in was connected to another, separated by a curtain. A nurse was coming and going from the adjacent room with blackened bandages and instruments. Herbs, water, vials of strange substances, and other equipment were being taken in. The others who were gathered seemed fixed to their spots, talking, deliberating, worrying in hushed whispers, looking at the curtain every now and again. Tomriel followed Ramkus's gaze, and immediately forced an even more comforting demeanour. He placed a hand on Ramkus's shoulder and lead him back into the corridor.

'Have you eaten?' Tomriel asked as they continued along to a large room that centred around a staircase leading upwards. The room was littered with all sorts of items that seemed to be being stockpiled for future movement elsewhere. A covered furnace seemed to glower with a brilliant orange, lighting the room with a minimal of effort. People hurried past, offering a smile to Tomriel and the Guardian.

'Ah, yes. There was some bread and soup left by the bed.' Ramkus suddenly remembered the question, shaking himself awake. 'Tomriel, where are we? Where is Mooyne? What happened to the soldiers? And,' he gulped, coming to understand what – or whom - must have been behind the curtain, '*what of, Chall...*'

Tomriel frowned, inhaling a bitter air that had him grind his teeth. He crooked his head to his shoulder, the knotted muscles making a crunching sound. 'Chall… Well, as you have guessed, is not doing well. He has life left in him still. But,' he stamped on the ground and smashed his heavy arms to his sides, 'I should have taken the role of village elder, he was in no shape to fight! I am not lying when I say we were preparing for this day.' He growled through gritted teeth. 'We had plenty of time to have me take the mantel. That stubborn arse!'

His eyes glazed over, staring at the furnace, the only thing that seemed to create as much heated anger as he.

Trying to diffuse the tension a notch, Ramkus followed up with the simpler, less emotional questions. 'So, where exactly are we?' guessing the answer already.

Tomriel grimaced, repressing the flow of anger at his own believed shortcomings. 'We are in the mountain, naturally. Yes, you are one of the very few, the very *lucky* few, to see what us mountain folk call our native, secluded home. The outside that you saw, the *village*, it is all and well, but it is not our hearth. We do use the tavern and forge, seek the sunlight. But this is where we predominantly reside and move through when the winter months lay blankets of snow. Everything is connected, all the homes and buildings connect to the mountain not only for the air, water, and warm vents as you saw in my home, but also to each other... *as Mooyne alluded to*... It is our interconnected network which *runs behind the scenes*, so to speak. Buildings such as the infirmary, are kept within these caverns. In this spot we are actually underneath the town, rather than in the walls of the mountains.'

Ramkus let him speak freely, allowing him the opportunity to clear his mind; he needed to rid himself of the corruption he was placing upon himself, should he continue to see fault in his previous choices. 'And you say you had prepared for the soldiers to come?' Ramkus followed up when there was a lull, hoping he had not overstepped the mark.

He was lucky, the question made Tomriel smile with pride for a moment. 'Yes. It was obvious we would have to face some type of assault sooner or later. The closer towns to us have all had some sort of altercation. A number being wiped out completely... The Empire - despite what their monarchs might think is happening - are wiping us out with blades. The Burbar Regiment - an awful example of where filth comes together to rot the earth – have been rampaging for a while. The only thing different about how they proceed is that they seek to have a justification to attack, so as not to incite a rebel force of combined towns and villages. That would not look good to those citizens who they happily co-exist with and give the Empire the right to be govern them. Not to say we won't be wiped out at some point, but having more people on the Empire's side, as well as occupying areas where the Empire interests lie, assists them to further expand their influence and dominion.' Ramkus started to wonder what the origins of these other "citizens" were exactly, but his thoughts were cut off once Tomriel had breathed in enough of the rich air of the rock cavern to fill his lungs, and began to speak again. 'In any case, we had set certain traps to face the impending attack. Remember how half the group went inside the forge? Well, those steel doors that separate the furnaces inside, we had our men close them upon the soldiers, trap them with one of the furnaces blasting, exuding an enormous amount of heat that not even us blacksmiths could tolerate for long. They all fainted from the effects. And the two soldiers that got stuck in an avalanche? The ones facing off against Mooyne? That avalanche was also a trap, having some of our people setup a huge mound of dirt to be held in place near a small window they could watch from, lying in wait. Once lured, the trap was sprung, and down came the dirt to incapacitate them.' Tomriel was speaking with much more positivity now. 'The best thing was we were able to keep everyone away from the fighting, our best-case scenario to not let anyone get into direct confrontation needless.'

Incapacitate. Ramkus remembered Tomriel's cry to not kill them. 'Why incapacitate and not kill?' he asked. 'Do you wish to have captives? Won't that make the Empire even more likely to reattack with a greater force and bring about the end of Potelo?'

'Hah! No, of course not,' Tomriel answered with glee. 'Too right you are that they would act as such. No, our intention was the take them alive only to embarrass them. We plan to send them off on their horses, naked and bound. The horses have been trained to head to their own secure stockades, but the soldiers will likely free themselves before that. Knowing *these* soldiers, to be sent packing, embarrassed like this – not to mention losing in battle - will be an awful blow. They can't go back and show their faces, having failed in their mission. Some will even contemplate suicide as it is such an affront to their position and person. We hope they will devise to not let anyone know what has transpired, that they were beat and let go. No, they won't go back to town and come back with a bigger force, they will consider a new plan, but just that dozen of them.

'It is the fact that this was such a small group that we are fortunate. I daresay they were acting without any direction, so only they know of this little skirmish. If they do attack again, we can hide inside and they will have no way of actually making any dent upon us. I suspect their leader recognises this and will not even attempt to come back. He'd rather forget the whole ordeal.' Tomriel appeared to truly believe his reasoning, or at least was being incredibly hopeful it would prove correct.

'So, you think you may have stopped all attacks from the Empire?' Ramkus continued.

'No, not in the slightest. We have bought time, a lot of time, but one day the Empire will come looking to either have us swear allegiance, or to expand their territory for their own people, displacing us. It is that day we now have to prepare for, one where our best chance of existence is to leave… *or declare war.*'

Ramkus considered it may be dangerous to press any further on the mention of war. A few of the townsfolk had moved here and there around the staircase room whilst the two had been speaking, often smiling at both of them in recognition of their efforts for the day. Ramkus did not want to cause offence as he weighed his thoughts. The room itself grabbed his attention, as he could not help but be filled with an appreciation for the ability to build into such thick rock and create such a space. *I*

wonder how Mooyne feels underground and not in a forest...
Mooyne!

'Where is Mooyne?' Ramkus blurted out, surprised he hadn't considered this as one of his initial lines of inquiry. 'He wasn't hurt at all?' he asked impatiently.

'He is fine. He really was the star of the show. Amazing skills he possesses, who knew!' Tomriel said with enamoured rapture. 'That is not to say you did not do well either, but I guess you were severely limited,' he looked to Ramkus's bandages and grimaced. 'Mooyne is now watching over the prisoners.'

Ramkus was a little perplexed until he realised he hadn't even considered what had happened to the soldiers. They were still to be sent off after all, *naked and bound*. Ramkus knew *all too well* how painful it was to head into the forests in such a way, bruised and exposed to the elements.

Acknowledging his inability to do anything further for Chall, Tomriel led Ramkus up the central staircase, following through more sturdily built passageways.

There was a feeling of a much greater, much larger town down in the bowls of these mountains. That hubbub, the movement of many people going about their daily duties seemed amplified from what his first impression of the town was. Many more people seemed to dwell in Potelo than the façade of the town let on.

They arrived at a "back door" to Tomriel's residence.

'I would have taken you through the forge, but the furnaces are still creating too much heat. Not that we couldn't physically go in there, but you'd be sweating through the bandages.'

They went through his home and out into the town centre, people were clearing the dirt that had fallen in the avalanche; a number of others were surveying and concentrating their attention upon assessing how the town fared, and whether a further expansion of defences was necessary.

Ramkus spied the soldiers' horses being cared for outside the tavern. They were tethered to posts and seemed happy. He was led further along to an inconspicuous door on the taverns side.

'As I am sure you can relate to, we couldn't tend to or incarcerate those soldiers in the mountain you just saw. It would risk them learning of our *true* home, and we'd be defenceless should they figure out a way to break in. We have built *facilities* above ground to keep them from guessing how far we have built, and how many of us there actually are.'

He opened the door to a well-proportioned "storehouse" which had been quickly built into a small gaol. Most of the soldiers were being kept in an area surrounded by metal bars, whilst those that had been significantly injured were separated in other parts of the storehouse on triages. They were under the guard of some of the larger mountain folk who seemed a tad bitter to have not played a part in the fight. Although, they looked to be wearing welts and bruises in any case. *It's those fools who were slapping each other around last night!*

'Took your time,' a familiar voice called from behind them. Mooyne had concealed himself at the entranceway, hidden in case some unwanted person rushed in.

All Ramkus could do was frown in amusement and laugh, as Tomriel inclined with appreciation of the "hero".

'Hah, looks like you owe me one,' Mooyne continued.

Tomriel smiled, 'We all owe you one. But don't forget, Ramkus played his part. Who is to say you could have taken on one more?'

Mooyne nodded, 'Or a full group, had your nifty traps not been prepared.'

It seemed Mooyne and Tomriel had not been afforded a chance to regroup and discuss what had transpired, other than simple directions of what to do next.

'I doubt that, had you nor Ramkus been there, it would have succeeded as it did. We are very much indebted to the both of you,' Tomriel implored.

As this was playing out, some of the soldiers had gotten up to stare with vehemence at the threes' discourse, grabbing the metal bars with strained knuckles. 'Get back!' some of the guards growled, hitting the bars with metallic batons.

'Still fight in them then,' Mooyne's eyes glowed. 'Let me,' he urged one of the guards to hand him a baton. A few of the soldiers lunged at the bars, holding the metal and shaking it to rattle the whole frame.

'Bring it on!' one of the imprisoned soldiers cried.

'You think we are defeated?' another shouted.

'Quiet!' Mooyne yelled, striking one of the prisoner's hands with the baton. In a flash, the prisoner had grabbed the baton and yanked Mooyne with it. Another grabbed Mooyne's wrist, as the metal baton was manoeuvred around Mooyne's neck in a seemingly well-trained sequence between the assailants. Mooyne was pinned with his back to the bars, the baton being pulled tighter around his throat.

Mooyne coughed and wheezed as his breathe was being depleted. The soldiers started to punch at him from behind, whilst the guards hurried in their attempt to repress the attack. Unfortunately, their efforts to stymie the assault could not be done without going into the make shift cell.

Tomriel and Ramkus gaped at the suddenness of the attack, recognising the little they could do in such a position.

Mooyne struggled to let out a cry, having his limbs pulled into the bars, and the life drained out of him.

'Let me in there,' Ramkus said viciously, clenching his hands around his staff.

Tomriel stood ready too, searching the room for another weapon.

The guards fumbled with the key, as the soldiers looked on with derisive pleasure at the chaos they were causing.

The key clicked, door swung out, the guards leapt back as the prisoners started to pour through. In their haste they failed to see what was running towards them. Charging out in a surprisingly orderly fashion, they did not witness Ramkus leap in with a raised staff, crashing down with such force that a number of the prisoners' shoulders were dislocated, along with some skulls fractured. They crumpled to the ground as the next few took a wary approach.

Two prisoners still held Mooyne, the one choking him was becoming infuriated, trying now to exact revenge and kill him. 'Give it to them!' their leader cried, face down from his sick bed, listening to the racket but unable to rise to the occasion himself due to his injured buttock.

Tomriel rushed into the cell after Ramkus had cleared the path, launching straight at the prisoners holding Mooyne. His bulk crashed them into the bars, forcing Mooyne's release.

Ramkus moved into the cell and now faced the remaining prisoners. Three more of them. Reddy faced, they were becoming berserk, their bodies contorted in a savage manner that was reminiscent of the primordial nature held deep within the depths of the unevolved. He met them with his own mastery of the dark, rampaging with swirls of his staff, launching strike after strike in all the adversaries' directions. He did not let off for a second, as his staff's reach could exploit their lack of range. His preference was to have the swings keep them at bay whilst he was in the prison cell, until he had pinned them back and was ready to explode with his full force.

'Stop!' Mooyne screamed out, halting Ramkus in his tracks before he was about to unleash. The prisoners took the opportunity to counter, but were met with a heavy force from the side. Tomriel rushed them.

'Get out of there now!' Mooyne panted through a hoarse voice. Ramkus adjusted his focus for a moment, obliging quickly by jumping out of the cell whilst grabbing Tomriel's arm and aiding his retreat.

The prisoners were too slow to respond, as the guards shut the gate on the five prisoners who were not incapacitated. The ones

Ramkus had knocked down initially had been quickly tied with rope and thrown into another cell.

The prisoners who had been recaptured hollered and screamed, beating on the bars and walls. Those in the sick beds started to smash whatever they could - if they had the strength.

Tomriel grabbed Ramkus and Mooyne by the arms, leading them in a rush outside, coughing and panting from the effort. The dirt under foot kicked up into a cloud, slowly falling down as if mirroring the situations level of emergency.

Nodding to the guards who had been roused to full attention, he slammed the door behind him. 'Too close,' Tomriel grumbled. 'Too much strength still left in the dogs.'

'And you believe they won't come back with a vengeance?' Mooyne cried out. 'We ought to put them out of their misery!'

Tomriel stared at him, red-eyed. The anger at the soldiers attempts to cause a major fracas was beginning to be redirected at Mooyne, 'I told you, we cannot afford to do that! When we face them again, *when*, it is better to only face that smaller patrol than a whole company!'

Mooyne scoffed as Ramkus watched on, grinding the gravel under him as he switched stance.

'You don't think I want to dispose of those shits? You don't think I look at them and see the faces of my fellow people being burned, hacked, murdered, raped, massacred? If it wasn't for Chall's command, Chall's teachings, I would have long past tossed their bodies atop the mountain for the elements to consume.' Tomriel's impassioned speech had overwhelmed him. He took a deep breath and looked to the sky. 'Only the Gods know how we are meant to sedate them enough to send them packing.'

Mooyne bit his lip in frustration, acknowledging the circumstances placed upon Potelo.

The three avoided each other's gaze. Ramkus felt it was his duty to calm the air.

'Shall we perhaps sit and have a pint?' he suggested with a sense of positivity. 'I think we deserve one after what we have been through.'

Tomriel winced and inclined his head. Mooyne looked at him with a passive annoyance.

'Come on Mooyne, it'll at least reduce the burn on that throat. I am surprised you're not still wheezing,' Ramkus jested.

Mooyne gave him an irate stare, coughing, 'That's because I am trying not to.' He broke into a smile, continuing to cough as he spoke, 'I think I do need one.'

'Right then, to the tavern,' Ramkus said, once more feeling the burn on his wrists. He was quickly giving up ever having them recover fully, so simply wanted to stop the burning sensation that he knew was going to come on after the recent tiff.

'Ah, no,' Tomriel put a stop to their plans. 'I need to be down there in case something happens. However, that means we can go to the Watering Hole…' He looked at them, hoping for a reaction of intrigue. Mooyne and Ramkus looked at him puzzled instead.

He let out a chuckle, 'Our *special* drinking spot. It's just a little cavern underground specifically for special occasions. Our best alcohol is found down there. Either of you ever drunk under the earth before?' He asked in a much happier tone?

'No, only under the table,' Mooyne answered.

The three sat at a large circular table in a hollowed cavern within the expansive subterranean network of Potelo. It seemed like it was built to represent a tribal hut, low-vaulted ceiling, a fire pit surrounded by a comfortable bench. It reminded Ramkus of the town hall in Lencil, and he could imagine it being used in such a manner by the central townsfolk of Potelo. Smoke wafted through a series of vents, but the smoky aroma lingered and combined with the grey-blue rock to give an air of mystery to this sacrosanct place.

Ornate stein tankards made out of what seemed like animal horn and bone were brought by one of Tomriel's forge assistants. Tomriel raised his gargantuan tankard, but it was Mooyne who spoke first, 'To the defeat of the Burbar Regiment!'

Tomriel chuckled, 'Nay. To new friends!' The three crashed each other's tankards together. 'Once again, I thank you two, for providing us with some breathing room. I know, *some* of us,' – he looked over Mooyne and Ramkus with an exaggerated head movement and winked – 'would prefer to put these soldiers out of their misery. But now we know what we are at least dealing with for a time, and it is unlikely to be any bigger than what we dealt with today, simply by virtue of those soldiers up there,' he pointed to the ceiling, 'needing to save face and not reporting to higher ups.'

'I truly hope you are right about that,' Ramkus said, 'I don't know much about the Burbar Regiment, but the Empire itself seems to have spread thickly through these parts. From all the stories you have told us, they,' he pointed to the ceiling, 'won't take this lying down.'

'True, but we have learnt a lot about how they are likely to come at us,' Tomriel answered.

'You'll need to train your men better, if you are to stand a chance. You're traps worked this time, but who is it say they will the next?' Mooyne queried with concern.

'Who's to say that we need traps. We could happily settle underground for a good while and wait it out now. This is why it is so imperative not to have a horde of Empirical soldiers, hauling explosives and engineering apparatuses, come and break through our defences. That dozen won't be able to make a dent in the walls of this mountain, and *when* they *do* return, and find nobody willing to fight them, do you think they will report back that they require certain tools and additional assistance to finish a "personal" job they'd decided not to tell their superiors about in the first place; or worse, told them they would undertake such a job, but have so far been unable to complete?'

Tomriel's reasoning seemed right, but Ramkus and Mooyne still held reservations, mulling over whether Tomriel was too naïve to consider the soldiers being *that* interested in saving face, or being condemned with insubordination for not completing their task. He was also possibly miscalculating how much of a *bold statement* they'd made down in Fallen Crest to be pursued as they have been.

'Who is to say they won't find other allies, or source explosives elsewhere?' Mooyne probed.

'Do you think anyone here really wants to deal with those arseholes? The Empire doesn't even want to have *them* counted in their regular army ranks.' Tomriel furrowed his brow and stroked his beard. 'They are the worst of the worst, sent on missions which the regular army does not dare go. As much as I *dislike* the Empire…'

'I would have thought the word *hate* more appropriate,' Mooyne interjected.

Tomriel smiled slightly, '- A strong word, but perhaps appropriate at the present time - *Hate*, the Empire, I concede that most of the damage has been done not by their regular rank and file soldiers, but those degenerate Burbars. They seek bloodshed, they want war. They are not right in the head.'

Ramkus thought back to a certain soldier he had faced that seemed to resemble these Burbars mentality.

'This is our plan, and we have to stick to it until it doesn't work, or we decide on something better,' Tomriel stated with stubbornness.

'And who decided that?' Ramkus asked.

Tomriel took a moment before answering: 'Chall.'

The air became heavy between the trio, no one wanting to strike the conversation up again. The fire burnt at a steady rhythm, and the drink did its work on calming the muscles and nerves. They all inhaled as if in sync, acknowledging the last few hours. It was Ramkus who was first to speak, regarding Tomriel and his struggle to lift from the heavy shadow of Chall, both as his successor and from the pain of the current question of Chall's mortality. 'What was *your* idea of how to proceed?' He asked simply.

Tomriel winced, looking upward. 'I guess it is no use denying I had an opinion.' He exhaled as if to exhaust all his life, 'I proposed something greater, that we band together with the other tribes and villages, create a united front and push the Empire back. This stays between us, for no word ever reached outside the private council of Potelo. It is an extreme measure, one that creates conflict, and hence why it was shut down quickly by Chall. *It is not our way*, he declared at the time. But what is our way? I think he feared failure, and I can understand it. That tale of Lirem, it still strikes at the heart of a lot of us – at least those who remember it. But to unite again under a single banner, well, we would require another hero of extraordinary ability. As much as we get on with other mountain folk and forest dwellers, we are our own tribe, our own villages, our own towns. We have become distinctly conscious of our surrounds, our need to survive, of serving only *our* people.' He drew back from his contemplations, 'Ah, but what's the point of discussing this right now. We have survived the day… at least some of us.' His mood once again forlorn.

The three continued their little session, relaxing by the warmth from the fire, and the drink. Some simple food was brought of salted meats and bread, but this did little to break the silence that had fallen upon them. Simply sharing the experience was enough.

Before too long Ramkus felt it was once again the time to pick up and carry on his journey. As if it was a shared thought, the others rose at the same time, moving out from the sacred meeting room and through the well-built cavernous town, onto the streets above ground.

They stood at attention, looking upon the *arena* which had now been cleaned, looking as it should for those who were blissfully unaware of what had taken place, it was simply a town centre. People moved about without any worry of the events that had transpired. The tavern was open, a couple of traders had come through, the furnaces were blasting. The townsfolk seemed to have accepted what had occurred was merely part of the ordinary course of living. The fact that they did not fear any repercussions impressed upon the outsiders the sense that these inhabitants had a clear faith in their leaders, and their ability to keep the little place safe.

Mooyne looked Ramkus up and down. 'Where is your guitar?' Ramkus smiled, then began to fret, raising his index finger to pause the question for the moment whilst he ran to the spot his hidden stash had hopefully stayed put. He breathed a sigh of relief upon finding his equipment was intact, and no one had seemingly touched it – nor the supplies he had been provided by Tomriel on the original departure. He pranced back towards the two showing them.

'You are considerably proficient with that staff, even with the injuries you had endured,' Tomriel reminded Ramkus of his wrists. The drink had kept him from feeling much, especially the headache that he didn't wish to acknowledge. 'Show me,' Tomriel commanded, asking for Ramkus's wrists once more. 'I would suggest we give them another clean. Then again, it may be best to leave them for now. Not too much blood seems to have come through these dressings.' He gave a half smile, 'You did us well, I am glad to call you a friend. I am certainly pleased I did not turn you away when you first came to me.'

'As am I,' Ramkus stated.

'And what about me?' Mooyne interjected.

'Ha, it was because of I that you got to have some *fun*,' Ramkus jested with eyes wide open as if he was crazed. Mooyne started beaming a smile and meeting him with the same levelled craziness.

Tomriel looked on with a confusion and trepidation, as if there was a madness he had not counted on, and that the gaol incident may have actually been manufactured for some enjoyment.

'Mooyne, your friendship is gladly welcomed. Your acts of bravery went well beyond what we could have expected. You are entitled to be treated here for what you have done. But please... Do not seek anymore fights whilst in Potelo...'

The other two looked at each other and laughed. 'I do not think that will happen,' Ramkus said. 'Mooyne may be a bit reckless, but he only intends for such actions in places where it is deserved.'

'Hah, you speak as if you know me well.' Mooyne responded.

'Don't I?' Ramkus chuckled.

In a sudden moment, it was all too palpable. The path beckoned Ramkus as if it were a shining gem he could not help but reach out for.

'Our best to Chall,' Ramkus brought everything backdown to earth.

'Yes, he seems to be too stubborn to be in a sick bed very long,' Mooyne added.

Tomriel nodded in appreciation, not sure what to say.

The three looked down, dragging their feet in the gravel.

'Well, once again,' Ramkus said, as he embraced the other two with a determined look. 'Till we meet again.'

'Till then,' Mooyne said, matching his resolute temperament.

'Let the path be good to you,' Tomriel imparted.

And with a smile and a nod, Ramkus was on his way, forward.

XXX

The path before Ramkus was well travelled. Trees were sparsely apparent, shooting out the sides of the rocky crevice at odd angles, holding on through sheer willpower and deep planted roots. The road grew narrow in part, with its rock face twisting him around corners where the sky became a mere slit in the crevices above. The air was chilly, and he pulled the cloak about him. It warded off enough of the cold; well worn, but such use had given it significant character – especially the cut that had gone through it during his fight. The clothes Miiva had bought him were not suitable for the mountains, best for warm forests, so he utilised what he had as best he could. He rolled the ring she had given him around his right index finger, rubbing the finely crafted engravings.

He gave some thought to that fascinating creature, the first he had done so after leaving her. To be fair, he had had no opportunity to during his flight from Lencil to Potelo.

His mind then drifted to the meeting with Mooyne, a weird character he was, too. On the same train of consciousness he eventually drifted to his original travelling companion: Felipe. *What has become of you, my friend. What are you doing now?* Thoughts of what he had left further behind in his wake suddenly dawned on him, and he began to contemplate, for the first time since his escape, *Sophia*. Mixed, complex emotions rose up: an admiration and desire for her fought savagely with a deep-seeded anger at her involvement in him almost being exploited by the Empire.

He almost had to stop himself from walking and concentrate for a few moments, so as to not get into a fit of rage.

Exhaling, letting go of such spiralling thoughts; there was still a hope that she was not part of such a plan, but she could not be completely exonerated either. But he could not focus on her, nor begin to break down and dissect the whole of his time in the Summer Castle and her role in it; at least not yet.

He needed something else to turn his mind to.

Everyone was behind him on this journey now, except one: Sigilund. He smiled when he realised there was a good chance he would be reacquainting himself with her, it gave a boost to this spirit.

As he lost himself deeper within his mind, he did not notice until he was walking with the sun hanging low and blurring his vision, that he had left the mountain pass, and was on what appeared a never ending plain. Small hillocks were placed in the distance, but the land itself was incredibly flat and desolate, save but a few copses of trees, and small streams cutting through the barrenness in the distance. It was a stark contrast of white rocky mountain hitting the dry grass; with a sunset of deep purples and oranges striking him with awe.

What lay behind, lay behind; he was free.

He breathed in, and took his first steps into what he felt was the beginning of his proper journey.

Chapter XXI

Ramkus did not look back. Not for a while, at least. The massive mountain behind only presented itself in all its glory and might, once its outliers and crevices became visible. He surged further forward with determination and confidence. The mountain path at his back was now but a small crack in the distance behind, laying at the base of the towering natural wonder. This vast road of separation from the forest lands that the Empire controlled and these plains was evident in the scope of the marvellous, untouched preservation of its natural state. Ramkus only noticed it as he pressed forth into the odd, barren terrain. The steady path under foot was of hard gravel; it grated with each step - the only sounds that were real. He felt he could hear the pulse of the world, or perhaps the beat of the cosmos, moving one moment further into the vacuum of time, just as he did.

The sparse hillocks – if one could call them that - were low and far away, hiding nothing; nor did the solitary trees that stood erect in stubbornness, holding no semblance of intrigue. The sky was a masterful variation of greys and charcoals, bearing no warmth, no comfort, only motion as they rolled around and around in a perpetual turmoil, angry within and of itself. The plains seemed a macabre illustration of what would be if everything on earth was destroyed, and no seeds of life could take to the soil. Dark yellow straw, speckled shades of red and brown, the clay earth, moss and granite. All colours well mixed into a purposeful nothing, other than to be one with the whole. The sight was an endless lay of miserable land that no one would entertain staying for too long.

He was certainly alone here, and it felt as if it were truly the first time he had ever been. He drew back into his first awakening moments, realising it was so. For all intents and purposes, he had never felt so alone. There had at least been signs of life when he had first *awoken*: lights from candles and smoke from the chimneys, the little township had not been too far off from the spot either. *What was the name of that place: Abergrass?* His memory began to play all the remarkable events. He mused over his dealings with people, and with himself; that dark self that did not raise its voice in this solitude. His staff plodded along as if a companion. It had always, in a sense, been as such. *The only marking that I am a "Guardian". Am I even? Do I even have to be one?* His whole journey so far was to the Guardians Seat, a place no one really knew much of, to meet whomever was there: *And be told what exactly? How I am to be? What to be?*

He stopped for a small rest, drinking some water, eating some of the victuals Tomriel had provided. It was getting late, and thoughts of who he was were weighing on him. A breeze hit, as he wrapped the cloak tight around him. Drops of rain tried to penetrate his new garment, light drizzle, but foreboding. The weak sunset had given way to storming clouds, black and grey, rolling in as if a wave had come to pave the land below. He took this as a cue to set off again. There were no trees close enough to take shelter.

He pulled the hood of the cloak over and continued along his way. It shielded him from the elements well, as vicious lightning bolts hit the plains, sending sparks flying from the earth. Thunder roared, and he found himself in a pit of despair, angry at the world, furious that he knew not what to do. He looked back and saw the true scale of the mountains he had passed through. Even the ridge itself could be said to be a mountain. It stood as if it had cast him out into this rugged land, telling him to leave and never return.

He pressed on.

The rain pelted him, and he hoped the cloth holding his guitar was water-proofed - lucky for him, it was. He knew not what to do, other than walk on and on into this inhospitable environment. It was not like it was truly inhabitable, but the lack of life lent itself to odd thoughts as to the reason why it was devoid of some sort of *life force* or *essence*. As far as his sight could see, this level plain continued along until only the sky merged with the land. He wondered whether, if he went far enough, he'd hit the wall of sky.

The darkness of a starless night had presented itself, stating the predicament of a gloomy march further on, the promise of a storm persisted on the edges of the terrain, and his mind. It seemed he had been literally thrown to the elements, cast from his bastion of co-existence. He kept moving, in a state of glumness, one step after the other, feeling sorry for himself.

As much as he was protected under the cloak, the water still came through the small openings and cut from the fight with the Burbars. He could not see far ahead now, traipsing across the wet land. Wind gusts hit the sparse long grasses and let them shimmer like fine fabric. He kept rolling Miiva's ring around his finger with his thumb, subconsciously feeling the friction create some small warmth on the metal.

If it were not such a dire environment, he may have let himself admire the scene. As it were, all he could do was press forth until the morn.

His vision obscured, his mind as thick as mud, he scanned the vast emptiness every so often. On his right, far off in front, he thought he saw something moving in the wilderness. His believed it to be his mind playing tricks, as the droplets around his eyelashes pervading his ability to see. But then, as he approached closer after a few more minutes, off in the same direction he caught the glimpse of something rustling.

Probably a bird, he thought, *but why out there?*

Marching along, he kept abreast of the developments of life out in that spot. Nothing stirred, and he reassured himself that he was the sole movement in the empty expanse. Still, a wandering mind will play its tricks, and he continued to believe he saw a faint shimmer of life come off in the wilderness.

No markings of any kind, nothing to tell where one was, or where to go, his curiosity kept pulling him back to the one landmark of potential activity.

Then, once more, he thought he saw something bob up.

The patch of intrigue was about a mile ahead of him, and if the path remained true – which it obviously would – it would be around five hundred yards from it on the right.

The rain continued at a steady pace, leaving him with little protection whether he went and investigated or not. So, with little reason not to, he made up his mind to seek the spot out once it was directly right of the path.

His eyes trained on the patch, and every so often, the barest of movement. *If it is a bird, why is it sticking around there? Some sort of burrow or nest? Food?*

His imagination began to take flight, and with it his pace.

He traversed to the point in the path where the intrigue was directly at a right angle from the path. He looked out for any type of markers he could find that would lead him back to the path once he had left it: there were none. *I guess it will be fine as long as I know which direction to head. I'll intercept the path at some point when returning.*

He set his foot upon the muddy earth of the plains, only to have it sink an inch. *This may be a bit more difficult than expected.* The earth was a bog, soaked in the rain. He tried to step solely on the spots with mounds of long grass, getting some traction, but it was still an effort to get far compared to the path.

Is this really worth the hassle? he mulled, but saw more action ahead. His desire to discover what was in front took over, and he trudged quicker to the spot.

Jumping from firm grass mound, to firm grass mound, he started to see what lay before him. Hidden without any marker, a sandstone staircase that would fit two abreast, drawn into the bowels of the land. He came closer and stared down into the pit.

Birds were flying in and out of this hole in the ground for shelter. Water flew upon the steps into the man-made chasm. Each step had a cadence which let the water run off to the walls, but where the steps should have met the wall, a small gap allowed the waters to slosh off and down to the abyss. *Hmm? Ingenious,* were his first thoughts on seeing how the rain did not completely swamp whatever was down these steps. He then started to ponder the existence of such an oddly built structure. *Doesn't look like a mountain folk build; but they are close by... What is even down there...*

He couldn't help himself, he had to see what was below. Looking about, seeing no other signs of life, he drew into the darkness. Unfortunately, his hurriedness in trying to get out of the rain led to him slipping and tumbling on his back. 'Bloody hell!' he cried, stopping himself somewhere as he extended his hands and slowed the speed against a riveted wall. His already battered body was not enjoying this. Aches and pains were at the forefront of his mind, rather than what might lie in wait below. He had slid down a good number of yards down, still able to see the surface, but whatever was below was in complete darkness.

Tentative steps drew him further down, controlling himself with his hand on one wall, staff guiding the descent of each of the steps, until he found himself making an echo on a floor. He knew he had reached the bottom when a musty old smell of antiquity came to his olfactory sense. He swung his stuff slowly around, trying to make out any objects, but struggled to do so. He moved forward until the staff met a wall, then hit some sort of huge bowl filled with a liquid. Reaching out, he found a shelf with some rocks. *Flint?* he hoped, grabbing the rocks and smashing them together. He was in luck, and with the sparks flying off, he made out what was in the bowl which he had hit: it was filled with an oil. Striking off a spark in its direction, a flame erupted from the bowl, lighting the place. Mirrors glistened, reflecting the light about, and illuminated a torch which was resting on the shelf he had drawn the flint from. Taking it in hand and lighting it in the flamed basin, he let his eyes rest on the room. Slowly adjusting, he noticed the structure was all sandstone, with moss gathering in the nooks and crannies of the walls. The rooms were not tall, it was reminiscent of a tomb. He stood gaping at the entranceway to something greater, for off to either side of this entryway were two corridors, and in front of him were small holes that would fit personal effects.

Almost as if I am meant to leave my shoes here. He grimaced, taking it all in, before realising the intricate design of the walls. Each area of the slabs had some sort of etching, suggesting the whole place was once filled with artwork, even the steps he had taken down.

The place had an air of solemnity, of reverence and significance. He moved down the left passageway in a quiet manner, respectful of the nature of the place. It looked as if these hallowed halls had been untouched for centuries; yet, they had stood the test of time. Water ran in small troughs at the edges of the walls, and it did not seem to be simply rainwater that had collected there. The sound of its movement made the place hum with tranquillity.

Weird that no animals have made their homes down here, not even the birds seem to take to the place.

The passageway made a sharp turn right, leading into a large room that had been hidden by the wall at the entry. Four columns stood erect as if holding up the ceiling, but the etchings and art that had been placed upon them seemed to the be their raison d'etre. An altar was at the far end, with more bowls of oil, and behind it, another passage. The place was already well lit, however, Ramkus felt the need to light these two braziers as well, finding flint and rock close by which he preferred to use rather than the torch. They radiated with an intensity as he set them ablaze, and understood that they were part of a separate mirror system which lit up the room behind.

He breathed deeply in this vault of intrigue, making soft steps to the room behind. A curtain must have once held it from view, and for good reason, it gleamed a reflection of awe. As he entered the room, he beheld a wall of immaculate artistry: gold-plated, jewel encrusted, the likes he couldn't have imagined. *What is this?* He pondered, taking in the sight. His eyes took a moment to adjust to the reflection of the gold-plated wall. *It seems to be a story, but of what?* His eyes were drawn to a huge, divided, circular shape, made up of two pieces, one atop the other, but separated and separate. The space in the middle was mirrored on both sides like sharp waves rising in and out of each other, ebbing and flowing. The top side was made of a vivid, red ruby; the bottom, a deep, azure blue lapis lazuli. The lines that made up the exterior were black opal. And in the centre of this shape, the image of a man. Jewels adorning his clothing, his garment a robe of greyish diamond, upon which he wore pauldrons of sparkling alloy and a huge girdle of the same metal. At his forearms, wraps which seemed to glisten with fine threads of metal.

Lirem?

The man held no weapon, as he looked upon a small globe which danced upon his outstretched hands.

What is the meaning in this? Ramkus came closer to the image of the man, trying to decipher what he held in his hands. It was encrusted with small fragments of gold resembling land and sea, almost as if it were the world he held.

The light in the small temple seemed to grow, as the lights blared with a fresh found intensity. This sanctum held an austere reverence to someone Ramkus felt was of huge significance long ago, heralded in a way he could not fathom. Why else would a whole temple be erected for such a person? He kept thinking of the story of Lirem, of the *Defender of the People, Protector of the Land*, but he could not shake the feeling this was some other hero who was of a much more profound existence.

Taking his mind from the wonder of what he was seeing, he regarded with amazement the artistic work, the symbol of two halves that fed and bled into one another when placed together. *Who would have thought something such as this would be in the middle of nowhere. And what has happened to the people who attended to the place?*

An ancient forgotten legend that he may have been the first in centuries to behold. He was filled with appreciation for what he had been bestowed, and even aside from that, the temple had kept him dry for a few moments which he was thankful for. He smiled at his small luck, deciding to examine the temple further after having some victuals. The usual staples of the mountain folk, dried fish, hardy bread, hard cheese; things that would last in difficult conditions. There were also a few pieces of dried fruit which he happily devoured, he had not realised his hunger until he had his first bite. He stared at the water flowing down the channels against the wall, daring to see if it could be drunk. To his amazement, it was a fresh mineral water that flowed, giving him a sense of some healthy property being hidden within it.

He walked slowly around the main room once more, looking for something to make sense of. The pictures etched into the columns were only partially visible now; he did well to make out anything more than a natural scene with a person or two. Nothing struck him as out of place or memorable. He wandered to the other side of the way he had come, and saw that there was unremarkably little else than a way to the exit. He sighed in an inward expression of disappointment that nothing more could be understood of the place. An extraordinary find nonetheless, he just wished he could uncover the significance. Tracing back to the room where the jewels shone with brilliance along the gold pated wall, he decided to gaze upon the piece a little longer, for who knew if he would ever come across something so astonishing as this again.

Slumping down on the ground, his head felt heavy, and the desire for sleep dragged him away from his senses.

He was in the temple still, feeling the warmth of a tropical sun.

That cannot be right, *he thought to himself,* this place was in a barren land, and sunlight couldn't reach the floor.

He was right, of course, this was not the temple he had fallen asleep in. Although of the same construct, it was above ground, and open to the elements. A heavy humid air hung about the place, and vines draped down the exterior columns, giving the sense that the earth was claiming what had been offered to it in tribute.

As with these dreams, he looked about to find his usual guide to such visions. Prince was simply leaning on a column looking out far into the distance. From his appearance, he seemed calm and content, the first time Ramkus could say he had seen him as such.

Noticing the movement towards him, Prince said in a low voice, **"Look."**

Ramkus peered out from the temple into a vast jungle that rolled below. A sea was off in the distance, and the sun glistened with an orange intensity upon it.

Prince had nothing more to say, as they looked out on the scene. Finding his curiosity getting the better of him, Ramkus returned to the temple, wanting to find something of an answer to his riddle as to who these temples had been erected to praise; what type of people offered tributes; or for any stories it told.

The temple had one large square column in the middle of it, and each side of the temple was exposed to the world, with the same cylindrical columns he had seen in the temple of the barrens. But this central, square column seemed to be the only feature. Upon each side, the circular symbol of two halves interconnected with mirroring waves, this time

smaller, linked together, completed. Each of the four sides
symbols were in different colours: red and blue; green and
yellow; purple and teal, black and white.
Prince came to stand by his side as he observed the shape,
crossing his arms. He could sense his breath, his heartbeat,
his concentration. Ramkus stood erect, matching him. No
words exchanged, they stared at what was ahead.

He came to, shaking his head clear from the cobweb of dreams.
The light had died down somewhat, leaving him to wonder if the
oil was burning up too quickly. The same image stood in front
of him, the symbol of two halves, the revered man with the
jewelled, glistening garments. He inhaled the cool, pleasant air,
and exhaled. It was a wonder that the place did not smell of
some dank mustiness as the entrance initially did, but there was
a fresh stream of water flowing, and the entrance was not
obstructed.

He rose and decided it was time that he make his move forward,
regarding the artistry of the wall one last time.

When he exited the small room, he noticed the braziers had
indeed begun to burn with lower intensity, and the mirrors
shining light from the entrance way were diminishing in their
brightness. When he turned the corner, he started to swagger
slowly up the stairs without looking back. He made out sounds
of splodges far above. *Rain, still?* The distortion of light
coming down the stairs indicated it was once more turning to
evening, albeit the shroud of clouds denied confirmation of this
fact.

The splodging sounds continued as he ascended with care, sure
not to slip once he came to the wetter steps. He looked above,
perceiving that the landing appeared to have changed, and now
opened up into a mud path. It was as if a river had run all the
way through and cleared a path. As he got closer he became
confused: the path seemed to come out not onto a flat path as
before, but a tunnelling, muddy ravine which was over two

metres tall and curling back overhead at the edges so as not to be
allow one to escape to higher ground.

What on earth? he thought, trying to rationalise the new scene.
Has the rain washed an old, well-worn path? It stretched all the
way – as far as he could tell – back to the highway he had been
travelling. This path was too large to have been washed through
by the rain, but he could not figure out was else would have
created such a change in the terrain. He traced back how he had
gotten to the temple, as small droplets began to hit him. *I
jumped on those heads of grass for stabilisation, but they didn't
sink.*

Looking up he saw the heads of the grass he had jumped across,
beginning to rise at the edges of this new path, as if they were
growing. A low moaning began, a hum that droned. He could
not contain his disbelief, for the heads of grass now rose with
lumbering bodies, mucky grass covering what would be a face,
limbs like arms and legs. Primordial humanoid entities coming
to life from the mire.

'*What the fuck*,' he said aloud, mouth agape. He stopped short,
unable to reach these menacing grass stacks, his eyes could not
believe what they saw. The creatures continued to come up
above, moving closer to the ravine.

'Shit,' he growled through his teeth with venom, knowing he
could do nothing but run. With a mad panic, and without any
hesitation, he had to take his chance that the path wasn't a trap.
He couldn't get out any other way, as the walls were like a pit.
The droning grass-beings were moving with unrhythmic jolts, as
if awakened after a long slumber and only relearning how to
move. He darted around the path, as it slanted left and right.
The creature kept coming, droning, clambering to the edges.
They were falling in the pit path, coming after him. More were
showing up ahead at its edges. They were dropping only a few
yards behind him now. He readied his staff, as more and more
came, droning, humming. The dusk air was humid, and the
sound was like an infestation of insects.

They were beginning to almost touch him now.

'Argh!' he yelled at them.

The path was rising, but they were almost descending upon him now. He felt them grab at him, their limbs of long swathe grass. He batted away, pushing them off, but their stances were secured by whatever roots they had taken in the mud. He pushed down on one of their heads as he ran through, but instead of them bobbing down, it propelled him up.

Recognising his chance, he pushed on another for leverage, as they swarmed him, jumping up and getting his knees upon another's head. They were a head shorter than he, but he wasn't taking any chances. Unable to tightly place his feet, he kicked out as best he could to get some propulsion upwards and onto the edge of the ravine. He got halfway over, seeing the grass creatures crowd around him. He latched onto their feet with his left hand, pulling himself up, and charging through them as if they were thick shrubs. He bounced off, but got through the crowd, onto the barren land, the open land, with not another soul ahead of him. He ran, looking back at the horde of entities in their solitary slow march towards him.

They were slow, unable to make up any distance. He controlled his breathing, slowed down his pace. He was bleary eyed, as light rain and bleakness pervaded his vision again.

I have to make it back to the solid highway path, he counselled himself, starting off on an angle to meet where he considered the highway to be. *They could prop up out of nowhere again. What the hell are they?* He began to look himself over as his pace became a jog. There were no marks – other than some mud – he had been spared whatever fate was to have befallen him.

He was unable shake the unease of what he had witnessed, or that he had to escape it. His mind was in a haze, trying to figure out what had transpired; what the creatures were; the significance of the temple; the ravine path that had suddenly formed. *Were their heads what I had jumped atop to get to the entrance of the temple?*

He continued a steady pace until he hit the highway path once more, the sturdy gravel calming his nerves. He looked back. Try as he might, he could not see the grass creatures anymore. In assessing the situation, it was getting quite dark, but he wanted to ensure he could put as much distance between himself and that menacing host as he could before he would undoubtedly have to rest.

The darkness was now all enveloping under a cloud filled sky, and his step was unsure as the path stretched out as a black serpent brandished with the wounds of ferocious battles. He had been unable to see the creatures for a long while, even before the night had filled the void of the expanse. As much as he wanted to keep moving, it was a pointless effort, all he could hope for now was for a few moments without any rain so he could sleep. He had limited vision to find any kindling to help start a fire, and the dampness suggested it would be an exercise in futility. Reluctantly, he fell to the ground. Eating only a meagre amount of the supplies – for he felt he could not stomach a full feed whilst still queasy from the flight away from the weird monsters. He set about huddling himself in a position of security and warmth, or at least the little that could be had. His mind was a blur, and exacerbated a fitful night where little sleep came. The only joy was the low light of the coming dawn.

If ever there was a day of pure trudging, this seemed it. Fully awakened by dawn, lucky to have been afforded a few hours of little drizzle, he got to his feet. Each step seemed to carry the weight of the world with it, and he was ever mindful not to step off the path and onto any grass. It was only around midday that he started to forget about looking over his shoulder for any signs of unwanted life. The only thing that stirred was the wind, and small birds that flew about looking for food. He stopped rarely, and when he did, only chewed a small ration.

The landscape had not changed at all, still the macabre dark colours of a melting brown, red, softened green and yellow. The clouds gathered pace, crashing into themselves in a range of greys. The wind dragged the small tussocks of grass from side to side, and the horizon split the earth from sky dramatically. The afternoon brought drizzle, turning into a heavy rain. Ramkus pulled the cloak about him, as small hail began to fall, turning into large rocks. No cover, he bowed to the onslaught, hunching over and continuing along. The cloak gave some protection, but his back was taking a beating with every hit feeling like a dull kick. When the hail stopped and gave way to rain once more, he breathed a heavy air of delight, almost keeling over and breaking into tears of thankfulness. The rain did not let up the whole afternoon, whilst he continued his solitary march through the barrenness of a forgotten land. He would not allow himself to become one with it, this was not where he would cower and fall.

After a number of hours, the heavy rain stopped. It was night once more, and the moons glare finally broke through in a brilliant radiating twilight that offered much light, allowing him to see further into the distance. He looked behind to observe how far he had come: *a good distance to cover in a day*, he judged. He came to focus on what was in front of him now: a forest that spanned all the way across the horizon, just above the tip of the land and under the night sky.
A lone tree to the side of the road was not too far off from where he was, and made for a good marker to head for and make camp. It took an inordinate amount of time to heave through the wet and windy terrain to this tree, and by the time he had arrived, he felt too tired to start a camp fire. However, with his clothes wet, and the cold setting in, he forced himself to stumble around and find kindling - or at least as long as he could be bothered to do so – and was relieved to finally start a fire from sparks of his

staff on a rock. It took a while to build up, and the heat did not penetrate till long after his body had accepted the cold.

The heavy crackling of wet wood kept him awake, until he found a comfortable position against the tree trunk, falling into a deep and troubled slumber.

It was night time, and the sea was calm. It spread out as if ice, reaching to not too distant islands which seemed to have been thrown there by the gods. They appeared to simply erect themselves out of the water without any sloping. The water was cyan, and he moved to it instinctively. The white sand crunched under his foot, moving far back into a stretch of palm trees before being lost.

To his right, a cliff far off into the distance looked as if it were lifting a spectacularly large, full moon to the heavens. No one stood in front of it, no dark interloper. Looking about, there was no one. Only he was privy to the beauty; no Prince.

He breathed in the warm air, and was moved into direct action by a small breeze. He walked into the water, once again naked to the elements, it seemed to greet him with nothing but comfort.

Above, the cosmos had opened to myriad of stars, sparkling brilliantly against not the recent simple dark night sky, but one of a purple, pink, apricot. There was as much colour as darkness, the two intermingling in a grand display of power. He knew that as much as this seemed ordered, it was a chaotic interchange that had been, since the beginning of time, playing out.

He was now wading in the water, at peace, dipping his head in and out. The water became darker as he moved further into it from the sandy bank. It was as it had been before, he was completely lost to the depths, and he was at peace.

Lying face up, he stared into the sky, thinking nothing, knowing all.
In the prehistoric reaches of the world, this land still stood.
He needed to see that it did.

Chapter XXII

Awakening to little finches singing their morning chorus, the
sun was already in the cloud filled sky, looking as if it had been
torn asunder by some great malevolent force. *Or perhaps a
benevolent force, letting that sun hit the earth so comfortingly.*
His clothes were still wet, so he refuelled the camp fire and hung
his garments around it. He found a small stream nearby which
he drank from, and splashed himself with the freezing running
water as if it were to cleanse him from the muddy residue the
land and its creatures had thrust upon him, not only physically,
but mentally.

Eating a fair quantity of his supplies, he once again had not
realised how hungry he was until he had the first mouthful of
bread. He threw some to the finches that were dancing about in
the ground. Life sprung back to him. Happily watching the
finches for a few moments, they brought with them an energy
that carried on to him; their playfulness resonated with his
chilled situation.

He was thankful.

Continuing his march, to his surprise, he made up a fair amount
of distance. The gravel road did not hold much in the way of
obstacles, for the storm water had drained off of it to the sides.
By midday the forest that stretched across the whole of the
plains was within a short run. The trees stood as if they were a
readying army, about to hold against a mighty torrent of
elemental rage and force back anything that came against them.
He stopped and ate, now running low on supplies. He moved
off in vain hope that he would find an inn or some human life,
somewhere.

By the early afternoon he met with the forest. Tall pines placed
all along in a straight line, poised now to attack the ridge behind

him, rather than stand in defence. Sounds of birds, of running streams, and animals, all brought a happier sentiment to him than the plain of the lifelessness – aside from his petrifying encounter - that he had endured. Only the elements truly reined there, and solitude was the only true way of being. In a way, he was relieved to have found evidence that he was not alone in these alien lands, even if it was only the small birds or malevolent grass creatures.

The forest path did not waver much, but the overflowing canopy of intense green drew the attention away from what was in front. He could no longer see the sky that had been a constant in his last passage. A few flecks of light smashed through in a striking fashion, but this was the only light from the heavens now. He walked through in a daze, happy. This stunned state lasted until he saw light coming from the other end: the way out.

What a sight to behold!

And with such a thought, the barren void he had ventured through was left to the recesses of his mind. He had only to move forward into the sereneness now, with the questions of the past locked deeply away within his subconscious, it would only be through an odd necessity in the future that would have him ever revisit such memories again.

Green fervent grass spread down the side of the forest that he had come out from. It spread across a vast range of rolling hills, touching upon alluring lakes that reflected the last vestiges of sun. Small households and a village could be made out. People, life, moving about against the silhouette of small snow-capped mountains miles and miles away. They were like crystal under a whimsical mixed orange, yellow, and purple sky where clouds moved as if in a painting. These mountains stretched from left to right in his view, a wall to whatever lay beyond. It did not concern Ramkus, as he released himself to the lands, dropping his shoulders and smiling. He was exhausted, but he had made it.

Ambling to an apple tree that stood atop one of the hills overlooking this picturesque setting, a scene not even the finest painter could encapsulate.

The little households that were spread about looked lively, with smoke lifting from their chimneys. He laughed, and he cried. In his own way he had made it to his freedom. Pulling an apple from the tree, he delighted in its delicious, sensuous flavour. Nothing could be sweeter right now, life was finally good! He was on the road that he was meant to be, free from the trials that lay behind. Grabbing the guitar from the cloth that hung about him, he began to play it, caress it, let the music melt into a harmony with all else that surrounded.

His scolded wrists withheld most of the playing, but he did not focus on that, rather the serenity of the music that spoke of what he saw. He was *happy*. He could sit like this, listening to cows in the distance, to the birds in the trees, to the running streams and rivers below: *For an eternity*.

In honour of the occasion, he decided to leave a mark; something that symbolised his presence, a signpost that declared he had travelled beyond the obstacles behind, putting them to rest at the recesses of his mind. He took a small knife that Tomriel had included in his supplies out of a compartment on his belt, and thought of what emblem to make. He smirked as it came to him: the *perfect circle*, which he had first tried to accomplish when moving through the forest with Mooyne.

He settled the knife into the base of the tree and let its weight drop down in a curve, then pulled up and round, completing the work. Regarding it, he thought it imperfect, and as before, struck a horizontal line through it.

At least I *know what it signifies, and where to find it*, he thought. He then considered whether he would ever get to see the little marking again. Like the circle itself, fulfilling some roundabout journey before reaching the starting point once more.

Calming his mind, he put such thoughts aside, and rested contentedly.

His dozing lasted until the sun was beginning to completely fall away and leave only a faint glow. He was startled, not by any danger, but of the absolute serenity; it was unnatural to him. The sky was a pink hue, with clouds latching on to the colour. The lands below where now a deeper green, as if the ground wished to create a relaxing bed for him in any given spot he should please. The ponds and rivers he spotted were a deep velvet, the kind of water that invited one to fall into its depths, or drink its nectar greedily. He dared not move, lest he spoil this moment: his *freedom*, his *safety*.

Contemplations were drawn to heavy load of smoke escaping from a chimney far off. The building was on a large dwelling and appeared to have a few people gathering about. As best as he could observe, it was an Inn. Smiling to himself, he considered his first true attempt to be a bard without any assistance. He was incredibly thankful at his luck of being able to learn for a time under a maestro. Although he was a novice, he had been well versed in a number of routines, protocols, and people, and felt he could satisfy a humble dwelling. He brushed himself off and made for the gravel path, all the while in a contented mood, unflappable by anything. He was one with the world, not fighting it, not running from it, not asking anything more of it.

So this must be what it is like, he mused, happy to go along with such a life.

He sauntered on.

The Inn was a homely establishment: a brightly lit, old, wooden, single-story construct where a few dozen people were seated at long tables, eating their fill, guzzling from earthenware mugs. They were plainly dressed, a farming community which was brought together by this one communal establishment; it meant much to their lives. They lived a simple life, one that Ramkus felt he had just walked for a moment.

Enquiring as to being able to perform, he was told the usual details: food, board, maybe a coin or two if he inspired more drinking. He took his spot and began to play to the crowd. The acoustics for the concert were decent enough, and he gently eased the patrons from their conversations to his guitar playing. He played simply and softly, and it was only after a time he decided to sing to them as their attention began to draw upon him. More candles were being lit, and the fire place to his side gathered momentum with the light from outside drawing to a close.

The crowd was lulled into the performance, and it went as well as he could have hoped for. The guitar played exquisitely and carried the sounds of the forest it was made from. The mood he had been in was exuding itself onto the scene.

It was perfect; he was content.

He finished up his songs and took a breather.

The audience gave rounds of applause as the barman set out some food out for him: soup, bread, cold meats, and cheese.

'Not bad at all,' the barman said, 'We've been quite fortunate as of late, a few bards have come through here. Really helps the community spirit,' he continued, wiping his hands up and down his apron.

Ramkus started on his meal, wondering if, perhaps, one of those bards was his friend Sigil. She seemed to be the only thing he knew was certainly ahead of him in this new world. 'You have a girl bard through here?' he asked.

'Oh, aye, a real pretty one, quite young too, but very mature and capable. Or maybe that's just what her people are like.' The barman focussed his attention on drawing some ale for the other customers, readying themselves for the later performance. Wine was flowing from big flagons. Ramkus was able to get a sample before setting up for his next performance, one to ease the audience in better moods.

His room was a simple lodging, and it suited him. He sunk into freshly washed sheets for the first time in quite a while, drifting off into a sleep that was once again deep, where the world became smaller than a raindrop, before vanishing into his consciousness.

He awoke late, and was served a basic meal of oats before setting off on the road once more. He had made a few coin from the night, but not nearly enough to buy a horse. It suited him to walk for a bit in any case. He gently glided along the worlds floor with as much a care of it as it were part of his being. Now and again, he would come across farmers with cattle or produce, ready to share a few words and a spare piece of fruit.
The world was at peace.

He did not make it to the next town that night, instead taking refuge under the stars. The weather was fair, and a fire was merely for heating the victuals he had bought from the previous town. *I wonder if these lands have ever faced hardships, ever been ravaged*, he pondered these sentiments only for a brief time. The pocket of the world seemed untouched from any pains. He was hopeful it would exist as such long into the future.

The next day the farms ended, but the road continued. With markers leading him around, the path headed through small plains, besides rivers and small lakes. Harmonious, although it began to wear on him a tad. That it should be this peaceful was not fulfilling the *being in him*. It almost became difficult. So much had occurred beforehand for it to be like this now. He checked his wounds as he marched along. The wrists had healed as best he could make out, leaving scars of reddened skin where the bracelets once were, *now bracelets of scars. Still, it's better than having those things on,* he thought.

As he meandered along, a sound in the distance started to float to him, from behind him. He turned around and noticed a cloud of dust from the path. Riders were approaching. They did not appear to be anyone in particular, but they charged down the highway, towards him. As they came further into view, Ramkus saw that one was a striking, long red-auburn haired creature, and she was leading a band of five or so riders in total. It was hard to make them all out as they moved with such speed. She burned into Ramkus's vision.

Before he knew it, they were upon him, not letting up. He had to jump to the side of the road, as they maliciously charged him without a care for his safety – much to his disgust!

As they rode past, he thought he caught the eye of the woman as she stood menacingly in her saddle at the helm of the party.

They looked like a band of mercenaries to him. At least they wore such attire, seemingly out of place in these lands.

Could they be bandits?

The trail of dust pervaded his vision and enveloped them as they went on. They did not even cast a look back at him.

Not bandits, they would have stopped and attacked me if they were. He picked up where he had left off, and kept moving along, staff in hand, attempting to get back to more comforting thoughts.

The next little village – more like a cluster of houses – came upon the path all of a sudden. After passing through an orchard, he came to a few cottages in a wide expanse, with a larger building of the same nature, built in the shade of some old oak trees. Tables were set outside in a pretty little scene, with flowers adorning the perimeters of a beer garden. A stage was set under one of the old oaks – or rather, a platform - and it was apparent that bards were very welcome here, for there was already some performing!

Ramkus listened, happily, but also scrutinising them in a manner Felipe seemed to have instilled in him. It was a *style* thing, as some of the tunes that Ramkus knew were played differently. The performance included a few different instruments: a lute, recorder, a small harp, and percussion instruments including a tambourine. Ramkus thought it a tad childish in part, as it seemed more background music that lulled the audience rather than a performance piece. The audience enjoyed it, though.

He approached the publican inside and asked for the usual: board, meal, a few coin. He wasn't sure if it would be accepted, but it turned out there was a need in the evening. He could not believe his luck! *This land must be wealthy indeed to be able to afford so much entertainment in such small surrounds.*
As it was afternoon, Ramkus decided to set down his things and have a walk off the beaten track at the back of the pub. Past the oaks, a huge lake lay stretching across the land, with a dilapidated jetty that dared to takes steps further into the depths. He walked cautiously upon it and watched the lakes waters. Standing there in calm reflection, he was brought to attention when he heard a shrill cry from the village.
He ran back, seeing commotion, people running, riders galloping away down the path.
He darted inside the inn. Some of the chairs had been damaged, the people inside were licking their wounds, carrying on as if something quite normal - but unpleasant - had run its usual course. All signs indicated that it had an easy and quick target for whatever *had* actually happened.
'Bloody she-devil!' the owner cried after a time.
'What happened?' asked Ramkus.
'Robbed, what do you think. Was that damn red-haired woman and her bandits. Always striking when we aren't expecting it!'
'She has done it before?' Ramkus looked perplexed. *How could people let such a thing happen more than once?*
'Every year or so, she rides around, preying on small villages. It is not as if it hits us too badly, but it is still theft. A day's taking and food.'

Ramkus started helping the owner once he had calmed down, setting the chairs back that had been knocked down by fleeing patrons. He began second guessing his luck as a bard that evening, doubtful of getting any money and wondered whether he would even be able to lift some of the spirits with a spritely performance after such an event.

The performers outside had apparently fled in the panic, and the patrons had locked themselves in their homes nearby.

Once the place had been tidied, the owner let his staff off for the rest of the afternoon in order to calm their nerves. It seemed to be a usual occurrence, spirits were dampened but not broken.

This was a way of life, bandits and marauders were as common as a wild storm - at least they were less damaging; only the purse went, not the home.

The owner sat at a table with Ramkus, mulling over what had happened, calming himself.

'We have had *offers of protection*, cities saying they'd help not just us but the surrounding villages as well. We would have to pay just as much to have soldiers situated here as had been taken from the robbery – Doomed if you do, damned if you don't. It may be more common for towns and villages close to the cities, *bigger* towns and villages, but we don't want to become a pawn of those *people*.' The owner began to weigh up his options. 'Besides, not even sure it would deter thieves.'

'So, there is no one to help you fight off bandits?' Ramkus asked.

'No. Aye, it is a lifestyle we have had to live with for a long time. That is not to say our neighbours in other villages wouldn't help out, but you saw how quick it was, and it happens to them too. Best to just move on from it, just expect it can *and will* happen.' His temper had clouded considerably, 'This is the free life, a community life, we don't want to change.'

Ramkus, playing devil's advocate, probed him on the subject of change. 'You don't think it worth the feeling of security?'

543

'Why would we?' the owner cried, 'what for!? Protection which means giving up what you are? It is not worth it. I have seen it happen in other villages in my youth. We are lucky we don't have it forced upon us by one of the empires or kingdoms that seek to control and implement themselves everywhere they go. We have neighbouring kingdoms and cities fighting each other constantly, and have done so through the millennia. Too busy instead with their own little skirmishes to bother laying claim to us'

'Aren't Guardians meant to stop that sort of thing?' Ramkus added after seeing the chance to query the man's understanding of the topic.

Unfortunately, it seemed that the public – as per the owner's understanding - knew Guardian's only as physical fighters, hired by the people as some sort of champion; not to act in a diplomatic fashion. There was much disinformation about Guardians, many legends and tales that Ramkus had overheard in his short time. At least he knew how to discern and understand the context of what was said as best he could.

The owner looked Ramkus over, and his staff. His eyes looked Ramkus up and down, 'Are you one then? A Guardian?'

'I think I am, yet to be told otherwise,' Ramkus answered.

The man's brows furrowed, 'Perhaps you could help us out, seeing as they are on the path. Maybe just teach 'em a lesson. May stop 'em for a while at least?' he said suggestively.

'Maybe,' Ramkus mused, not really sure how such a mission would be carried out.

'Funny. I thought you were a bard.'

Ramus chuckled, 'Both. Well, travelling as a bard these days. I am heading to the seat of the Guardians, for whatever training and life lessons I am meant to have there. I really don't know what to expect, or even much of the Guardians to tell you the truth.'

'Quite a long way that is.' The owner got up and started the fire. 'Not a bad plan to get there by travelling as a bard. You really need a horse if you want to make any headway, though.'
'I am aware,' Ramkus frowned. 'I need to get a lot more money before I can do that.'
The owner nodded, 'Aye, hmm, maybe if you get those bandits, you'd get the coin also. If it is ours, keep it. Payment for beating 'em up. If not, well, you don't know where it came from. And, oh, I don't think you'll be making any coin tonight I am afraid.' The owner said regretfully. 'We will feed you, and you've a room, but I doubt any will want to come here tonight.'
Ramkus nodded, understandingly.

He sat for a moment longer, before getting out his guitar and playing it absentmindedly whilst the place was quiet, save for the small crackles from the hearth. He did not think he would get to the bandits in time, as he was once again aware he was not making the quickest effort in getting to his destination.
He smiled to himself: *Then again, I am content on this road... so far.* For how long that would be, that was the question.

XXX

He wandered from little village to little village, slowly winding towards the Seat of the Guardians – at least as far as he knew he was, for no one knew for certain where it was located, just that it was far away in the direction he was heading. He got little coin for his performances, but this was fine, he was able to practice his art, living a fairly peaceful existence. However, something seemed amiss. He wanted to take part in this world, but felt he was only ever a bystander. He saw fights in pubs, but was not worth his while to get involved – mostly for the fact it was usually during his performances, and seen as a sign he was not doing his job in quelling any dark moods patrons may have. Some days it rained, and he stayed put; other days the sunshine did not let him tarry in a place too long. The path wound around small mountains which housed impressive inns, where all manner of folk descended; and it rounded villages along main river arterials where the crowds could only be described as *worldly*. And of course, shrouding the mystery of each area were forests. None were like the dense Forest Dweller types, nor of oppressive one he had survived. In fact, many had inhabitants who seemed to live ideally within the confines of the tree canopy, with the flora and fauna being the only necessary companions. There were inns along these forest paths too, and as much as he enjoyed playing in them, he longed to dance under that radiant sphere of warmth, rather than walk in the green havens.

If there was one thing that seemed to be constant in all of these travails, it was that the towns and villages *were* getting bigger, and this meant one thing: he was heading towards a major city. *If I play at a big venue there, I may be able to get enough money for a horse*, he considered.

It was only after rising upon a road with grape vines on either side, that he saw the fabled city he was searching for, the one he dared to dream would hold just the opportunity he desired. With walls over fifty yards high, and a river flowing at its edges, it stood proudly underneath the pulsating sun. Its structure was mighty and tall, with spires looking as if placed by giants, reaching into the sky; it was a feat of mankind!

Wayfarers nodded with their wide brimmed straw hats to him, carrying produce in wicker baskets on their backs. Fishing, cleaning, and bathing was being carried out in the river along the city's perimeter, as the urban sprawl was beginning to take place. Not too many homes stood outside the massive sandstone walls, with the remnants of buildings looking more like extensions of skeletal remains that had been carried to the earth outside. The closer Ramkus got, the more hustle and bustle in the streets. Carts, merchants, calls, cries, laughter, aromas of scented herbs and flowers, other smells of a repulsive nature, blood, sweat. It was the usual offering from a large inhabited settlement.

Ramkus strode over the bridge with a gleam of satisfaction, and in through a massive gate that was overseen by some tired soldiers in full clad armour. Their eyes looked over Ramkus, but did not find reason to stop and question. The city held wide streets: part dirt, part stone. However, it was the height of the buildings which was of amazement; some stood five stories high, with balconies and terraces at such great heights. *I guess they have to offer these small outdoor areas; an escape from living on top of one another for a brief moment*, he thought. He knew he certainly could not stand being in such a populated place for too long.

The architecture created a lean, long set of buildings, with archways of polished stone providing a sense of expansiveness to allow large wagons through its streets. The styles of the colourful streets offered an easily navigable city; people knew where they belonged. The muddy dirt thoroughfares matched some of the sandstone buildings, whereas paved streets had well-built structures of a chalky colour erected alongside. Some of the smaller, less inviting establishments were of bare wood. The light was not shut out by the height of the buildings, but neither was it found in abundance. The criss-crossing streets seemed to have been created not as an ad hoc construction, but something very well planned. *Must be fairly recent, possibly reconstructed after being razed.*

As with all towns and cities which held many people, the streets all led towards the main square: a place where people could meet, shop, and find the largest and most profitable pubs around. The main square was as central as Ramkus could guess, right in the heart of the city. The streets, although not entirely straight, were easy enough to steer through to find one of the fabled large pubs of the city: The Waylayers Arms. It stood alone from other buildings, next to a great oak, the only greenery that Ramkus had seen inside, aside from the flowers on people's balconies and terraces. He entered and was greeted by a throng of people all clambering around the rich-red, wooden interior. There were stairs that led up to four levels of drinking and eating areas, with the very top, fifth floor, reserved for the rooms of guests and workers. After getting through the surge, he spoke to a bar maiden who directed him to go upstairs to the owner, if he wished to get some work as a bard. Every level he went up there was entertainment. It seemed this place would be difficult to make a truly enviable amount of coin as a bard, there was so much *opposition*. And it wasn't only bards, but entertainers of all sorts: knife throwers, fire breathers, acrobats, jugglers! Still, he pushed on and was able to settle the usual lodging with an underling of the owner, albeit, his times were to be *well after* the *main* acts of the evening. He would have to work his way up through the ranks if he wanted to make large quantities of money, with so many others in competition. Ramkus felt the eyes of other performers on him when he made his way back down stairs after dropping his staff in the small room he was provided – if you could call an alcove with a bench next to a window a room. Unfortunately for a person who had lived in a castle, it was a little below his expectations. *At least it is something*, he corrected his ego.

It dawned on him how Felipe had acted when he was in *competition*, trying to posture over the opponent whilst exuding a performance with every one of his practiced movements. This battle was actually fierce, and although Ramkus had been lucky so far, he could see how certain employment from a royal court would best the travelling life.

He ate some food at a "staff" room: a selection of foodstuffs that were looking a little old. Taking some bread, he went for a walk through the city which he had learnt was called Lellel.

This was nothing like he had experienced before, he felt quite out of place. So many people, running to and fro with an air of importance. He walked into a cleaner district where there were green spaces on the streets. The architecture, dress, and people, felt of a much more pretentious nature. He was treated with disdain by those he passed, as if he were an eyesore whom did not belong. He realised it had been a while since he had shaved, and his hair was in a bit of a tangle. Upon finding a barber, he proceeded to get a good trim; his hair cut fairly short, and facial hair now all but gone. The cost put a chill down his spine, but he concluded that this is what it cost in a city of such size, and if he was to make any extra coin, he ought to invest in his appearance.

He kept walking, looking at the sights, revelling in the vibe, taking in all around him. He was a voyeur of the people. There was little entertainment on these streets, as most people appeared to be going about their daily business with a busy fervour, insisting the importance of their position meant the world revolved around their actions. The further he travelled this area of the city, the more it became sparse of people, only those either relaxing on their daily constitutional, or servants hastily carrying out their duties.

He finally came upon the reason for the change in the city: the royal court was in the vicinity. It was heavily guarded with bulky soldiers standing at attention outside sturdy, tall gates on the fenced perimeter; savage spikes adorned along the whole way. The centre of these royal grounds was taken up by a massive castle, and the buildings that stood in close proximity to it were only different in that they were notably smaller in size and lesser in decadence.

Have they ever ventured into the country side? Ramkus mused, now wondering whether it was going to really be worth staying in this city, in this situation. He already missed the easy-going travel of recent days, but he knew he had far to go. *Over mountains, through valleys, across waters, many miles in many lands I must pass, all to get to the Seat of the Guardians.* To ride on horseback would be best, even if not his preference.

Turning his back on the ostentatious parade of buildings, he noticed the few people wandering about. One, a girl in her mid-teens, caught his eye. He felt she was in some way distressed: *Perhaps that feeling of being pent up.* Her gaze caught his, noticing he was looking at her, she darted away from the seat she was sitting upon.
He took his leave.

Having walked far from the well maintained, wealthier end of city, Ramkus trotted through what must have been the derelict portion. The buildings stood at most three stories high, but most were two. The majority seemed to be of wood, small holes in walls, rooves dilapidated in parts, the people looked at him with bemusement in their grubby attire. That was not to say they weren't washed, for laundry was flapping in the wind along single clotheslines attached between buildings.
Often the eye of thuggish looking bystanders who were gathered in groups stopped his wondering thoughts; these were the types of beefy brutes who enjoyed being bandits: stealing, fighting, forcing people into uncompromising situations. They weren't the type to associate with. Yet Ramkus wandered through without much worry, it was still daylight, and what threat did he pose for the city gangs.

Heading back to the staff room for an early supper, he found the foods had been changed at this time, taking great delight in getting what was the freshest food from the pots on offer. Hot baked goods, stews, soups. After having his fill, all he could do was take another walk to settle his stomach and have another stroll around the city.

Deciding this time to venture outside of the cities walls where it would be calmer from the constant movement inside, he noticed the girl he had seen outside the royal court area. She was on the bridge that came across the river moat from the other side, looking at the waters, deep in contemplation. At this hour, there was little in the way of people crossing over either way.

The sun was beginning to fall, and people were readying themselves for the night. It was an easy feeling, watching the sun go down in the distance, not being consumed by the city and its congestion of so many people in one spot, their clambering over each other in pursuit of a *cause* that Ramkus could hardly understand.

The girl was mumbling something to herself, milling around. She sat down on the edge of the bridge… with a large rock by her side… tied with some rope… to her legs.

Before Ramkus could understand what was going to happen, she pushed the rock over the edge, and followed it. He ran to the spot she had been and dove into the waters below.

XXX

'She jumped over,' Ramkus began to retell the story, panting from the adrenaline rush, his hair still wet, 'her legs bound to the rock.'

His audience weighed his words, judging this outsider they knew nothing of.

'I leapt after her without a thought. As the current tried to drag me away, I held her. Luckily, I had landed not too far from where she had dropped. I had to swim deep, as the rock dragged her far down, and it was unfortunate I did not have a knife on me, as it would have made releasing her a lot easier.'

'And so, you untied the knot on the rock,' a nobleman stated, eyes ridiculing Ramkus with begrudging intonations.

'Yes, it was far easier to slip it off the rock than her feet. In fact, it did slip off, and she went further down the river with the

current. I followed in tow.' He breathed heavily before
exhaling the coolness still in his lungs.

The room was of no modest expense, although small and
considered an anteroom, it was adorned with landscape
paintings, wall mounts with small busts and statues. It was a
wonder how this decadence had come about - it was even more
grandiose than the Summer Castle of the Ronato family of the
Empire. Two guards stood at the door, as the richly dressed
nobleman picked apart the facts, disbelieving the story, looking
for some sort of calculated motive. Distrust hung over him.

'I followed her down, grabbing her at the first opportunity. She
did not fight. There was no struggle at all, not even a care. I
could not tell if she was conscious or not, but it seemed to me
she was still alive.' The clothes he had been provided with felt
heavy and inadequate, as his foresters attire lay drying in front
of the fireplace. The nobleman was deep in thought, not sure
what to make of the situation.

Ramkus continued, 'So I swam to the nearest shore with her. A
number of townsfolk were still out along the river at the time.
They helped drag us in, whilst one of them fetched the guards
for help.'

The nobleman squinted and pursed his lips. 'A simple, *heroic*
story then,' he said, unamused. 'And who is this *hero* then,
hmm? Where do you hail from? Why the scarred wrists?'

Ramkus shot back a dangerous glance he probably should not
have, as it would no doubt have shown a weak spot for this
inquisitor to poke at. 'That is a long story,' Ramkus said slowly,
coldly. 'It can be simply put that I am a Guardian, and I am
travelling to the Seat of the Guardians, paying my way as a
bard.' He tried to dispel any arguments one might have to such
a declaration.

Indeed, the nobleman did not know how to approach this
statement of fact. He did not know whether to believe such far-
fetched stories or not. He knew that the truth was never usually
so easily given, and that men play mind games. If there was one

thing he was certain of, though, it was that that truth - and people – always turned over when money was involved. Whether this *hero* truly was a Guardian, *or working for an enemy*, he could be won over by such means.

And yet, the stories from the peasants rang true of all this man before him had said. He was a hero and deserved thanks, *and to be sent on his way as soon as possible.* His skepticism outweighed any generosity.

'You must excuse my indiscretion in asking you these questions,' he started once more, his cloudy demeanour lifting to a conciliatory tone, 'I cannot believe my daughter would simply tie a heavily weighted rock to her feet, and jump off a bridge. I cannot *believe* she would try to drown herself. I can see no reason for this, so it is *simply* something **I will not believe**. No, *what I believe happened was*: she was kidnapped, bound, and dumped. You did not see her jump, *merely fall*. Being the good fellow that you are, you went after her. For doing such acts, you shall be rewarded. Name your price.'

Ramkus was bemused, not sure what to say.

'Come now, I do not have all day. A pouch of gold coin? A *sack*?' The nobleman opened his palms as if gesturing to the invisible reward on offer.

'Ah, I need a horse,' Ramkus stuttered.

'Alright, a horse, and a sack of coin. I wish you a good day.' The nobleman nodded with a begrudging smile that turned into a frown. He rose quickly and walked out of the room, whispering a few words into the guards' ears which they appeared to consent to.

Ramkus stared into the fire as the guards came to ease their arms a little.

'He has no idea, that man,' one of the guards said aloud. The other looked at him.

'Not so loud,' the other scolded.

'He's a right to know,' the first guard protested, 'Baron VonWilton is too preoccupied by the comings and goings of the court, plotting for and against things to happen, always with his own self at heart. Unfortunately, 'e does not see 'ow this affects 'is daughter, who is basically locked away in the 'ouse and nobleman's quarters. She's depressed just as 'er mother was. Going to follow the same route. It upsets us even. We can see it coming, but the Baron won't listen to anyone, nor would anyone try raise the topic.'

'That's more the problem, no one wants to pipe up,' the other guard finished the thought, giving up on trying to hide anything from the *hero*.

Ramkus listened, nodding understandingly.

'But what you did was a good thing. Too bad 'e thinks it may 'ave been *your* fault,' the first guard to speak continued.

'Doubt he believes your Guardian story,' the other guard chimed in on queue.

Ramkus sat up in protest to his story being a work of fiction, but thought it would do little. He went to his clothes, *dry enough*, he thought. 'Well, time I went,' he said without emotion.

'Right, follow us then.' They guards were obviously hoping to move on to other duties rather than stand guard over the Guardian.

They led Ramkus out a back way, so as not to allow him the opportunity to see the main rooms. He followed into the gardens, thinking that it was quite remarkable for something so wondrous to be hidden within a bustling city; with a number of ancient trees and grass freely growing, unperturbed by the confinement of the city. If not for the circumstances, he would have taken his time and surveyed the scene. The stables were part of this beautiful set up, and it was where he was presented with a horse.

'Yours, as you requested,' the guard leading the horse said.

'Fantastic,' Ramkus replied with enthusiasm, astounded that his singular goal in this city had already been accomplished. He admired the chestnut mare, 'No saddle?'

'Need to be a better negotiator. It'll cost you… You did get a sack of coin as well, after all. *Maybe it should be reduced to a pouch?*'

Ramkus shrugged, not knowing if the guards were actually allowed to sell a saddle, or if the price was too steep. 'Agreed,' he said, suspiciously.

The guards smiled to one another.

Secretly, he was perplexed as to how his whole situation had changed so dramatically and was susceptible to any suggestion so long as he got the horse.

He gave his thanks, as he was given the pouch of coin. The saddle was fitted to the horse, and he quickly leapt upon it, setting off for the city's streets that lay beyond the spiked fence under the moonlight.

As he marvelled at the exterior of the Manor house he had just been in, he noticed in one of the windows that the curtain was drawn back. The girl he had saved was looking out at him. He could not tell if she was happy or not - or suffice to say, happy with his actions to save her.

I don't even know her name. He stared up at her, taking stock the words of the guards, now understanding that the poor thing was a mere possession of her father, unable to live a proper, wholesome life. He sighed as he was let out of the gates by another pair of guards, hopeful that her situation would resolve itself.

Nothing more I can do.

XXX

He unsaddled the horse in the large open stable of the massive tavern and swaggered inside. He had not realised how late it was; the dying banter of the evening's customers, the glowing embers of the fire, the many half full tankards and mugs, the lack of entertainment…

I missed my performance! he suddenly realised. It mattered little, though, as he now had his horse, some money, and was content to leave the city as soon as he could. He quietly - without trying to draw any attention- went to the top floor. After walking on the creaking floorboards and waking some other performers sleeping nearby, he finally entered his small, alcove-closet room shaking his head: he wasn't sure if the death threats due to being too loud were really that warranted.

Tired, he looked around the makeshift room, musing how bare it was...

His guitar was not there!

He jumped outside in confusion, only to be greeted by one of the office workers. A small fellow with small circular glasses, stubble that could be mistaken for an attempt at a beard. His expression was rather nonchalant, but he tried to hold the presence of superiority.

'Boss'll see you in the morning,' he merely said without regards. 'He has your instrument.'

Ramkus did not know how to respond. He went back to the room, making sure all his other supplies were still intact. His most important item - his staff - was still in its spot. Evidently they must have thought the guitar was the only item of worth. Relieved by at least finding this significant crutch of his, but disgruntled none-the-less, he went to the workers canteen. As was to be expected at such an hour, it was bare, save for some stale bread and over ripened fruit, nothing that looked very appetising. He gathered what seemed halfway decent leftovers and went back to the room – making sure not to step too heavily on his return - and ate. He decided to try sleep and sleep till morning before mustering up a plan to reclaim his guitar, should he need one.

Unfortunately, he did not sleep well that night, mostly due to the uncomfortable placement of the bed next to the window. Light from street lamps somehow still poured through from below, and a poor-quality mattress that was not fit for a full-grown man's size, were always going to give him a hard time. Still, with the little sleep he had, he dreamt.

He was in the shell of a small tavern, Prince was standing with his back to him, looking at the paintings on the wall. They seemed lifeless and dull impressions of moody landscapes, with particular focus on the sky upon first inspection.

"We should just run from this place, belt up whoever opposes us, get the guitar back," *Prince said without emotion. He turned to Ramkus,* ***"This place reeks of despicable people, you know it, I know it."*** *Turning, he smiled, baring his teeth.*

Ramkus shook his head, studying the place. It was bleak, dark, no life, no warmth.

'Get out; yes. But we shall have to see what this boss *has to say. I* am *in the wrong here.'*

"The boss will cheat you!" *Prince growled.*

'I missed a show, but gained all I needed, why must I impose an aggressive manner?' Ramkus queried.

"You do not get it, do you. You must exact a <u>will</u>! A <u>desire</u>! You need to be the one in control, in forcing others to do what you want, lest you be treated like a dog." *Prince kicked his leg behind him.*

'Maybe so, but there is no need at present. The path is gentle enough, for now,' Ramkus answered.

"Hah!" *Prince hackled* ***"We shall see about that!"*** *He laughed as he turned, back to the painting. His black leather armour suggested extreme power. The spikes glistened, his stature domineering.*

Ramkus looked at the paintings again, recognising now that these were not lifeless paintings, but of immense power; chaotic elements that brought barrages of movement and forcefulness. He looked away and closed his eyes.

Awakening with the coming of dawn, the light streaked in, warming him quickly. He felt very rough; for the "bed" was far too painful to get any meaningful sleep from, no matter how hard he tried. He readied himself, wondering how long he had actually been out for, and whether he could get his guitar back already. He mulled over what had taken place the night before, smiling that he had gained a horse from the events that had unfolded.

He got his things ready, and headed to the office, remembering he may have to be quiet whilst walking on the creaking floor boards so as not to wake the other guests and workers.

However, there was already some loud quarrelling coming from the boss's office. A man's husky voice battling against the timbre of an angry, young woman's. Ramkus stood at the end of the corridor before the door. He waited for the commotion to calm down, but it did not look like it would any time soon.

The voices continued to rise, before something was smashed in the room sending Ramkus into action. He burst through the door to find a fat bearded man, standing behind a table, hands splayed as he looked to be yelling across it at a gorgeous young lady... a lady who wore blue velvet vest and trousers, and a white blouse. Her hair was blonde, eyes blue... It was Sigilund!

Ramkus looked around at the two of them, taking in the room in his alert, active state. He noticed a smashed plate close to where Sigil was seated. They looked at him with astonishment, forcing a break in their argument.

Sigil's face became stern before turning into a wicked smile. It was the type of change that happens in a split second, where one's expression of happiness in a turn of events morphs into a resoluteness of action from the knowledge that *they* now had the upper hand in their situation. Sigil had gained a trump card which this *boss* would regret.

'I have come to collect my guitar,' Ramkus broke the silence.

The man began to snarl as Sigil stood up. An obscure flare in
her manner.

'You did not show up for your performance. It'll cost you.' The
man scoffed, now smiling to himself as if an idea had crossed
his mind. His eyes darted back and forth between Sigil and
Ramkus.

Ramkus moved forward a step, looking at the two who were
both gazing at him in a way that assumed he was to be of use to
either of them. He was not certain how.

'How much?' Ramus asked.

'Give him nothing, he is a cheat!' Sigil erupted.

'A cheat, you are the swindler, you whore. Trying to cheat me
you are,' the Boss snapped back.

Sigil stood up straighter in a rage, 'Cheat, me? For putting up
with this despicable display. I did not agree to be put in a
situation like that. Those people are horrible! Give me what I
asked or you'll have to deal with,' Sigil moved to Ramkus and
leant on him.

He wanted nothing to do with this, especially after how Sigil had
used him before. *Will she do it again? And to think I was so
looking forward to seeing her again!* He wanted to speak to
Sigil alone, not be dragged into her games. Besides, he had no
idea she was to be found here in these circumstances; his
purpose was his guitar.

'Will this be enough?' He pulled away from Sigil, presenting
his pouch of coins from his belt, taking a few out.

'Let me see.' The Boss leant in, as Ramkus pulled back before
he got too close. 'I just want to make sure it's real,' the Boss
decried.

Ramkus flipped him a coin, which he tried to bend, inspecting it
closely. 'Fine, the pouch.'

'The whole pouch? You must be kidding!' Ramkus protested.

'If you want your instrument…' the Boss looked behind him and
found the guitar. 'Nice one this is.'

'Fine,' Ramkus said, not wanting the man's grubby fingers on it. He placed the pouch on the table and was handed the guitar. But before the Boss could put his fingers on the pouch, Sigil swooped in and snatched it, grabbing Ramkus's arm in the process.

'Quick!' she cried, running for the door.

'Thief!' the Boss yelled after them. 'Thieves! Everybody up! Get the thieves!' He hollered.

The two raced out of the room.

'Hope you have everything,' Sigil said quickly as they darted down the stairs.

'Have you?' Ramkus answered just as quick, wondering if she had, indeed, prepared for something like this.

'Uh-huh,' she exhaled, as she grabbed a pile of things next to the balustrade of the stairs, taking in a heavy breath, 'thought something like *this* may happen, *or worse*.'

'**Thieves!**' the Boss yelled from the top floor landing, 'Close the doors!' His command was screamed down to two bouncers at the entrance. Some sickly and sleeping patrons were moving about, wondering what the commotion was. The place stank like urine and stale beer.

They made their way to the second floor, sliding down the steps, hearing the sound of the boss thudding down after them, yelling: 'Thieves! Thieves!'

The bouncers were readying themselves to stop the two in flight. Ramkus began to prepare himself for a bit of a tussle too, as they got to the first floor. Before he could, Sigil led him through another room - a private dining room - where a handful of angry looking thugs with very menacing weapons were relaxing. Ramkus could see why she wanted to go this way, there was a window onto the side of the next building's roof, and then a jump down onto the street. The men were playing cards; they were not amused by the intrusion.

'Shit,' Sigil squealed, pulling Ramkus back and shutting the door forcefully. 'Looks like we have to go through the main door,' she said under her breath. 'I did not expect that...'

'That is planning for you,' Ramkus quipped, understanding from the look from Sigil that it was an inopportune time for such comments.

They raced to the ground floor, only to be met by the two bouncers, and another four of the weapon-carrying thug types that these types of establishments call employees. *Seemed the Boss's screaming worked,* Ramkus mused.

'Stay back,' Ramkus said, handing his guitar to Sigil, keeping his staff. He held his arm in front of her at the bottom of the stairs and stood for a second.

Waiting. Waiting. The thuggish employees began to close towards him. Some were walking brazenly, and it was those who held their guards down that were to be his initial targets. Ramkus darted at the first, jabbing the shoulder of one with his staff, before coming around with the other end to knock another thug in the head. He sprang back at the two at the door and swiped at their legs, knocking one down. The other jumped back and pressed against the wall. Ramkus then returned his attention to the four reinforcements. All eyes were now on him, as a path to the main entrance had been cleared for Sigil. She took her chance and dashed out whilst they were not noticing, instruments in hand.

As Ramkus ran towards two who hadn't been hit, he found them brazenly coming at him, in turn. He let go with some long-range staff attacks, using the length of the weapon to keep his distance until he could get in and throw and elbow under the chin of one of the thugs. Moving under the thug's arm and sliding behind him, he dragged the staff to trip the man up, letting it trail through before spinning it down and smacking it upon the adversary whilst he was falling to the ground.

He charged at the wall as the other employees began grumbling, finally realising that this bard with a staff was no ordinary fighter. Ramkus hadn't used much force to put them down, a decision he would soon regret as he leaned back, pressing against the wall for another attack on one whom was still standing. Surging forth, he found himself hurtling towards the ground, tripped by the thug he had only hit in the shoulder, seemingly recovered and ready for another shot.

He fell flat on his face, as the last one who was about to be attacked ran in and grabbed him from behind and tried to choke him.

Ramkus struggled, whilst the others began to gather around and give him a few punches.

'Oi! You bloody shits have ruined our card games. You promised us privacy!' The *guests* whose party Ramkus and Sigil had intruded upon had come out of the room, not too pleased. Angry and drunk, they began to take enjoyment in smashing the walls and furniture. One started yelling at the Boss who was watching from the second-floor landing upstairs, as the others decided they wanted some *biffo*.

The employees' attention was soon taken up trying to defend themselves from their *guests*, as they threw massive swings with their bulky tattooed arms. Sure enough, a bar brawl broke out. Mugs and tankards were flying, chairs and tables being thrown about. Instead of the lively hubbub of a pub, screams and shouts reverberated off the walls. Patrons who had been unaware of any squabbling before, awoke in a frightened panic, hiding and taking refuge before beginning to throw punches themselves. The whole place became a mad house of fighting, with blood being strewn about the place.

Ramkus found himself thrown to the ground as the attention was turned to other *pressing issues*. He gathered himself, his staff, and fled for the door.

Before he could, he was once again grabbed from behind. It was one of the bouncers who had been guarding the door. He held Ramkus, gathering him in a half nelson, choking him yet again. His throat was burning, as he had barely recovered from the earlier attempt to break his windpipe. He tried to elbow behind him, but could not, the bouncer was too big. Suddenly he heard the bouncer yell out a curse and let go. He was grabbing his buttocks, reeling in pain.

When Ramkus looked around to see what happened, Sigil stood behind the bouncer with a knife. She had just stabbed the man's buttock, deeply. *He'll struggle to ever sit again.*

'Quick!' Sigil said, not taking a moment to watch any of the fracas in the room. She sped out the doors, followed by Ramkus who was bemused by the state he had somehow left the tavern in. People were fighting and screaming on all floors now, as anything and everything was being thrown about. It looked like the place had exploded of its own volition.

'Hurry,' Sigil said, looking back inside, 'We need to get the hell out of here!'

They charged out of The Waylayers Arms, onto the city streets. The light was coming over the walls of the city, blinding to look at, but warm. Ramkus led the way, taking Sigil by the arm as she carried their things. They rushed to the stable, Ramkus saddled his horse quickly.

Sigil allowed herself to exhale, recognising her own plight during these small moments of respite and how she had reacted. She watched as the man she had once run from, whom she had stolen from, showed no ill towards her, only the desire to save them. He leapt onto the horse after attaching the instruments, then helped Sigil get on behind him.

Fighting could still be heard from the tavern, as they quickly bolted off, out of the city against the oncoming traffic which was heading for the trade markets. They did not take in any of the sights, the way the sun gave off its golden gleam to the waking city. Too focussed on their escape, they were conscious of how they were only met with indifference from the soldiers standing guard at the gate. They crossed the bridge without hassle and moved into a canter as they galloped out onto the fields: their freedom.

The city lay behind, but they dared not look. The mountains surrounding the edges of the valley were pristinely clear, reflecting that brilliant orbs light in its morning greeting of radiance. The rays stretched far over the plains, enveloping all the fertile land under a magnificent warmth.

Where Ramkus and Sigilund were to go to in this brilliant setting, only the path knew.

Everything lay in front of them.

Chapter XXIII

There was a freshness to the air; even with no wind, the stretches of plains were clear and clean of any disturbances. The land rolled on for miles, until it met golden foothills, the beginnings of the giant mountains which crept ever so gently higher and steeper. It was a massive valley, one which the path seemed to be the small, straight spine of, daring not to inch to either side lest it cause pain and wake the wrath of these watchful giants at its edges. There was the odd copse of trees, brimming with birds. Small streams following their way along, every so often gathering enough water in one place to become a pond. The plains themselves were covered in a thick swath of golden grass, and only when a cottage came into view did anything resembling the green, softer variety show itself.

It was nearing afternoon, and the two were snug in the horse saddle. Sigil was deep in thought, deep in comfort, hugging tightly to Ramkus. Her thoughts led into dreams, and she awoke herself with a jolt when almost about to fall. Ramkus kept the pace steady and calm. His mind was at peace as he continued towards what he believed was his goal, something that would fulfil him. The movement was natural, to be on the path was homely.

He was without worry, riding along happily.

It was only when a small village came into their range during the late afternoon that any real discussion came about.

'Looks like a town, Sigil. How do you feel about trying to get some work there for the evening?' Ramkus suggested in a calm demeanour.

'You don't have to ask twice,' she replied, then added, 'are you suggesting we go as a duet?'

'I think we would do quite well. Have you ever performed with another?' he raised an eyebrow.

Sigil thought for a moment, 'I don't think I have, professionally,' was her response. 'But you were well versed with that other bard. Perhaps you could lead?'

Ramkus laughed, 'I don't think it will take much work for you to get into the *swing of things*. You are more of a professional than I.'

The villagers seemed a little suspicious of the two as they entered. The few in the streets appeared to judge them until they saw the instruments and believed they were as what they declared they were: bards. They were given the usual – board and food – for an evening of entertainment. When they went to their room, they stood perplexed for a while: it was a double bed. Sigil frowned, frustrated.

'I guess they assumed we were…' Ramkus started.

'There were no other rooms available,' Sigil lashed at him.

He shrugged, as they set their things down, as she calmed herself.

'Sorry for snapping,' Sigil said, 'I just do not like the assumption a woman must be attached to a man.'

Ramkus thought for a moment, sitting on the bed, looking out the window. It was set overlooking the aspect of the ever-extending expanse they were journeying. 'You haven't found the path easy, have you,' he finally responded.

Sigil said nothing.

'It makes sense why you took that money when we first met, and from that man at the last tavern.' He kept his eyes on the view out the window.

'I took what I was due!' Sigil snapped again.

'I am not blaming you,' he turned his attention to her, 'I think you were entitled to both,' he responded without vitriol.

Sigil stared, mouth a smidgen ajar as Ramkus gazed back at her.

'No, I haven't,' she said, coming to sit beside him on the bed after regaining her composure.

'Haven't what?' Ramkus asked.

'*Haven't found the path easy*. It has been nothing but one moment of calamity after another. Robbed, shunned, thought so little of. *You* have had it easy,' she said forcefully, trying to hide the emotions that went with her experiences.

'Ha!' Ramkus could not help but burst out, shaking his head. 'I have not found it easy, not at all. But I don't wish to dwell on it at present. Just promise you won't run off again, it is a lot easier with someone to share the way with.' The inchoate sense of his attraction to Sigil was dawning upon him: she was as he, alone on the path; alone in this world. There was a desire to share this common ground with her, at least for a while.

She looked at him and nodded.

The room was quite homely: a picture on the wall above a chest of drawers, seat and desk in the corner, bed sheets nicely cleaned and feeling comfortable.

Sigil sat closer to Ramkus, resting her head on his shoulder. She began to weep, as Ramkus held his arm around her shoulder.

'One day, you'll be a star,' he whispered in her ear, 'and these experiences will simply be a memory.'

XXX

The performance was of as high a quality as anyone would have experienced and expected in a major city. Although there were moments in which the two lacked the finishing touch as a performance duo, they matched each other with care and knowledge of the music. Ramkus was a surprise talent, his ear quickly adapted, his mind focussed, his skills – although still not as honed as a true guitarist – were adequate enough to pull him through difficult passages.

The crowd – a simple, carefree folk – were pleased with the renditions. It was not much of the world that these people got to see. News was brought from travellers, merchants, and performers such as these two, but little else came their way.

Most were farmers, the odd artisan; this was the natural state of affairs for most of these sorts of places along the road.

At least these towns are there for those who live on the fringes, a stark reminder of society's ability to protect itself from turning to the wilderness. Shielding themselves from the elements, and not give up their humanity by falling all the way into the savageness man once turned its back upon. His thoughts laid bare what path one could take.

The two were applauded merrily, and treated as guests. Most of the few dozen came to tell of their enjoyment, as the bar ladies served them some of their finest ciders - on the house.

'A nice little town this is,' Ramkus remarked to Sigil. 'The simple life.'

'Not that simple,' the bar lady said as she caught Ramkus's comment, eavesdropping as she cleaned glasses to the side of them. She was a stout woman of early forties age, someone who others would think twice before insulting.

'How so?' Sigil asked.

'We not only get you nice folk coming through,' she said studying the glass in her hands, 'we get a lot of brutes too. Those on the road whom have had a fair share of bad luck in their lives, and have decided to turn rotten. Probably bad parenting.'

'Do you serve them here?' asked Ramkus.

'Hah, serve!' the woman turned to them. 'Those bandits aren't coming in here, we keep an eye out. Unfortunately, they still ravage the place, breaking things as they come through, getting angry when they aren't let in. Often stealing things - being so angry - only to cast them aside when they find out what they've stolen is worthless and of no use to them. What's a bandit going to do with a rake?' She laughed, 'Ah, but that is the way of the world.' She regarded the pair, 'You two look like you may need to disguise yourselves better out there. You don't look like you could handle yourselves in a fight.'

Both Ramkus and Sigil objected, but found themselves talking to her rear.

Ramkus pondered for a while. 'Back at that tavern, you did know how to use that knife quite well,' he said in a low voice. Sigil went red, 'I was taught to handle myself at a young age.' 'Ha, well, what I meant was, you didn't even think about it. It takes a real beating to teach one to act in moments like that.' How he knew this, he did not know. Smiling, and without noticing, he massaged his bad knee.

Sigil went silent, 'I need some air,' she said after a pause. She got up – a little tipsy – with Ramkus helping her from her stool. He thought he saw some tears run down her face, but she quickly hurried outside before he could be sure.

He sat in bewilderment as he sipped his drink, musing upon the path ahead. He had experienced his excitement for the week - his journey seemed to be nothing but excitement – and of this bard life which he was enjoying. A bit of respite from being a Guardian, and he was able to make people happy. His path was blissful for the moment, and offered time to relax - save for the confusion with his new travelling companion which dragged his mind away from such tranquillity. Funnily enough, it was only a few days that he had been alone in his existence, and although he relished the company of others, he was not in need of it. At least, that is what he meditated on, humming a tune to himself. He waited patiently, but Sigil did not return, so after finishing his drink, he headed outside. Due to the vivid lighting of the candles and fires in the tavern, he had to take a second to adjust his vision to the evening glow and calm. No clouds in the sky, the stars pierced the dark veil of the night sky. He looked around but saw no one nearby resembling her, only some of the townsfolk smoking and talking in hushed whispers. They nodded to Ramkus as he passed by in his search, continuing their conversations in the background.

In the distance, down the road, a lone tree stood, upon which a girl was leaning, seemingly seeking out the path beyond, and the world at large.

He took strides in perfect motions under the pale moonlight, grating the gravel beneath his boots, alerting the person he believed to be Sigil of his presence.

She turned slightly upon hearing the sound. She had not expected him to follow. Unguarded, she had been sobbing during a deep reflection of her life – as best as Ramkus could figure.

He stood beside her, saying nothing, looking out at the path, the stars, the plain: life.

It was only after a time that there was any movement made. The heavens let their thoughts traverse past those plains till it was time to return. It was Sigil who made that first motion.

'Let's go,' she said plainly, in a calm manner.

Ramkus nodded to her, and turned to walk back towards the light of the village pub. Nothing was said, as they entered the main hall. The patrons were still smiling at them every now and again, in good spirits as the night began to wind down. Sigil was putting on a smile as they took a seat in front of the fire place.

'Thank you,' she said to him.

Ramkus merely winked. It was odd, but he was now having some instinctive sense of how to approach people and their issues. Some needed prodding, some needed support. Perhaps this innate nature was part of the Guardian make-up. At least that was what he put this down to. Regardless, Sigil had a deep, emotional turmoil that she seemed to be running from... Or running to. And now was not the time to ask.

They sipped a smouldering hot drink which was flavoured with a small bit of alcohol. Feeling time catch them.

In need of a good sleep, they returned to their room.

They did not sleep close to each other as they had that night in Refton when they had first met. This time they slept to either side of the bed. Every now and again, Ramkus thought he heard small cry from Sigil, from whatever befell her in her dreams. He began to grow weary himself, falling once more into a deep sleep.

He was in the middle of the fields he had been travelling that day, although it seemed different; higher in altitude with the sky closer. He could see for miles around, and it seemed the plateau fell at the edges into a deep blue. Staring at him, crouched, half smiling: Prince. Clad in his heavy, black leather armour; he looked as solid as a rock. **"What do you think you are doing, strolling along the path? Stop resting, stop being weak!"** *Prince demanded.* **"We need to get to the Guardian's Seat as soon as we can!"**

'Why?' Ramkus answered, 'What is the urgency? There has been nothing but urgency and pain on this damn road. Why can I not enjoy the simple path for a while?'

Prince began to growl, **"We need to know what we are capable of! We need to assume our place. You wish to go from day to day <u>Surviving</u>? That is not <u>living</u>!"**

The wind picked up as the incandescent clouds pilfered the blue, becoming gargantuan giants that moved into masses of chaos and creation. It seemed like power of imagination made solid. They did not threaten, staying a pristine white. The sun was shining as bright as possible.

Living, *Ramkus thought,* What on earth is that? This is not a life of mere survival right now, there is no need to force anything. *He was enjoying the path for once. He began to laugh at Prince's suggestion. Prince's eyes grew wide, and a nasty smile came across his face.*

The clouds suddenly turned grey, charcoal, then black, blocking out the sun in a demonic wash. Wind howled and thunder started to pierce the land's calm. The golden grass thrashed about as rain came in sideways, hitting the earth with brute force. Every few seconds, lightning sparked convulsively all around in the distance.

The sun was gone and a mist enveloped the edges of the once pristine view of the surrounds.

"Remember," Prince stated, "Change is a certainty. Be ready, lest we need to kill again." He laughed, "I am fine with that. Are you?" He raised from his crouching position, standing at full height. Ramkus's vision was violently assaulted by a streak of lighting on the spot Prince had been. When he regained his vision, Prince was gone.

Ramkus arose with a jolt, as if the lightning that had hit Prince had splintered off and hit him also. Rain was hitting the window of the room. He got up to look; the view outside was limited severely. He looked over Sigil. She was making small frightened movements in her sleep. He got back in the bed and touched her slightly. She stirred herself into a half-awakened state of fear, moving her body to the other side, she clung to him in her frightened, half dreaming, half delirious state. She stopped shaking, and fell back into her slumber, hugging Ramkus tightly. He clenched his teeth, staring at the limited view out the window.

What is this world of survival? he questioned, as he fell into his own dreams again.

XXX

They set off on the road again. Back in the saddle, both were in deep contemplation. Ramkus was questioning what his dark-tempered friend was really after, if not only *survival* for now. He also started to brood upon Prince's ominous words, knowing full well the gravity of his situation, especially with Sigil. The girl herself was having deep troubles, and as much as he would try to help her, he knew he would not be able to. Her path lay on a different course, one that he could not lead her on, nor follow.

The plains were rising ever so slightly, heading further from where the coast was – from what Ramkus could read of the continent – ever so slowly heading North-West. He had no idea where exactly he was headed, and didn't even think to ask. At present, he was content to let the horse move along, having Sigil hug his back.

Wild flowers started to parade themselves in the fields, and the sweet scent of fruits came up from orchards in the distance. The land seemed to curve when it neared the mountains far off, as the valley began to rise itself, out from the shadows of its brethren, rising to be one of them, or even grander in scale. They stopped at a small wayward tea house, which was a novelty.

'Whatever happened to that other money we made in Refton when we first met?' Ramkus enquired. Sigil shot a reproachful look. Ramkus attempted to diffuse the situation, 'I am only asking, not telling you off for *leaving abruptly*... I was going to give that money to you anyway,' he added.

Sigil sipped her citrus flavoured tea from the fine bone china cup, looking out from the small table that was placed under a small wooden roof where wisterias and lesser notable flowers adorned the frame.

'I lost it,' she said nonchalantly.

'Lost?' Ramkus asked incredulously.

'Lost. Well, I was cheated out of it. I did not realise the currency was of no value in the kingdom or territory I was in. Hopefully this coin is good here, for when I did pass that *Currency Exchange*,' she rolled her eyes, 'I thought they were trying to rip me off. The exchange rate was horrendous. What did *you* make of that place.'

Ramkus stayed quiet, not sure what he could add or ask.

573

'Well, anyway, when I got to Lellel I ordered one of the nice rooms and a decent meal at that damn inn – as well as work. After spending the night there, I tried to pay with the coin from the *Empire's* territory - which they took - but also said I was in debt, for the coin was only going to be able to pay for half of what I owed due to it not being *their* currency.' Sigil was clenching her teeth, her fist straining on the table. 'Those shits held me for ransom! I was a slave!' She was fuming, 'But not knowing how to stand up for myself in bloody **Man's World**, I did what I was told. I paid off my debt. However, after hearing what other performers were making there, *I was the one who was owed a debt.* They used me!' She slammed her fist, 'And that was when I had the argument with the boss, and ran into you again.' She turned her gaze onto Ramkus, questioningly. 'Very good timing.'

Ramkus gave a small smile, 'Very good indeed.'

'I hope that place was torn to shreds. You know those thugs who began fighting the security, they are highly wanted criminals in these parts, and yet they are welcome into that *establishment* with open arms. That Waylayers Arm is a crime den.'

Ramkus realised this was the most they'd talked in the last few days. Sigil was finally beginning to unravel her anger, let out the tension.

He rested his arms on the table. Sigil - still seething – looked with bemusement at his scarred wrists. She questioned him with her eyes. 'What happened to you?' she asked a tad stunned.

He breathed in slowly through his nose as he looked upon them, 'A long story,' he exhaled dejectedly.

'I bet that *boar* you were with was involved in some way,' she said, realising she was not holding back for anyone. She stopped herself, tempering her mood that had gotten a little too hot.

They finished their drinks and were brought some fruits and bread, along with honey and jams. Both were transfixed on the view, happy not to be in the saddle for a time.

After a while, Ramkus spoke up, 'Where *are* you headed, Sigil?' he asked in his warmest manner.

She wiped her hands together, 'Somewhere where I can be respected. I suppose away from the cities of these wretched lands. I may try the bastion of Eredin, have you heard of it?'

'I have. It is where they have the bard-off, or festival, or concert?' he replied.

She did not look surprised in the slightest that he knew of it, instead letting her thoughts drift off. 'Yes, I suppose if there is anywhere a girl can get away from *expectations*, it's there. At least for a girl with some talent.'

Ramkus nodded. 'May learn a thing or two as well.'

Sigil gave him a weird look.

Feeling under pressure for being misunderstood, he explained hurriedly, 'They surely have some of the finest musicians and bards contend in the festivities, or even just attend. Many maestros to learn from.'

'Oh, yes,' she said and gave a laugh.' A pause came over the two, before she made to move. 'Shall we?' Ramkus thought it seemed as if she could not allow herself to relax for too long; as if something kept chasing her away from any slight piece happiness.

Sigil paid with the coin - rather than their wares - and they got back on the horse for another stretch of freedom road.

The farms were becoming more sparsely spread, as the valley concentrated its grip on merging with the plains which were now somewhat of a plateau. That night they slept under the stars, having only a small bundle of victuals brought from the tiny roadside tea house. They decided that if it was to be like this, they may have to take to visiting the small farmsteads to purchase some food, or purloin from the trees. The night was clear, the horizon a still blue, and the mass of stars seemed to light the dark night with a vivid finish. In fact, it was so well lit on the plateau that it seemed as if the stars were trying to break through a heavy set of armour to create day again.

Speaking little, they lay against a sheltered rock, eating and warming themselves by a fire they'd been able to muster enough firewood for.

'Let's play some music,' Sigil suddenly suggested to break the silence. 'We'll play a game: I play a small tune, and you match it with something different, but continuing the melody.'

Ramkus agreed, and they set off. Sigil starting with a simple tune for a few seconds, letting Ramkus take over for a few bars before it was her turn again, then Ramkus once more, and so on. They continued into the night, making sweet music, embracing each other's domain of sound, admiring each other's form. They looked into each other's eyes, and deeper: into that which each other were, naked in their expression. They were more exposed than ever, vulnerable to each other's rejection, or acceptance; that small part of oneself that only lasts a moment, a display of the small precious slither of one's being. Sigil's music became dark and complex, twisting in part, writhing to get out. Ramkus's music tried to lift, to search, to understand; it was a music of concern and quest. Every so often, a small dark patch arose from his playing, one that dropped out of the tune altogether, something attempting to break free and deride the whole "game". It ended with a sudden stop, when light started to sparkle in Sigilund's eyes.

'I learnt that on the ship when I came over,' she said. 'All of it...' her face sombre.

Ramkus came close to her, beaming with a smile as he gently touched her face, searching her eyes, searching for her. She shirked away, but he brought her to face him again.

'Don't run away,' he said softly, smiling gently.

'I'm not running away!' she yelled, and the cheerful mood was broken. 'I am **not** running away! What would you know?!

You've never had to turn your back on your family. Never had
to kill to rescue yourself because no one else would come to
your aid...' She gritted her teeth.

'Kill?' he murmured questioningly.

Sigil looked aghast, shocked with herself. She turned to stare at
the fire, thinking, not knowing what to do, petrified as if reliving
some horrid dream.

Ramkus tried to calm her, 'It's okay Sigil, it will all be okay,' he
tried to move closer to her and provide some comfort.

She watched him with pleading eyes, before seeming to snap,
becoming angry and venomous. 'Get away from me!' She
jumped up, and in a flash produced a dagger that she kept
concealed in her boot, holding it out at him. 'Don't you dare
come any closer!' she screamed at the confused Guardian as he
knelt before her.

They locked eyes for what seemed hours. Ramkus kept his
vision on hers, not letting her go, attempting to lead her by his
will, by pure human contact and sense, until she left that
defensive solitude she had cloaked herself in for far too long.
He would not let her lose herself.

The horse sensed the situation and became frightened, neighing,
drawing attention to itself as the tension rose. It fled, leaving the
two: Sigil pointing her pointed dagger, Ramkus kneeling, staring
at her.

Time stood still, the wind held, the stars dared not shimmer.
Ramkus gave in, turning to the fire, sitting cross legged, staring.
Sigil remained steadfast, resolute, determined to protect herself
from all.

From what though?

Ramkus calmed himself, sitting glumly, whilst Sigil regarded
this man who meant no harm, who created no friction, who
allowed her to be as she was.

She relented after a while, feeling the situation having been
lifted. The horse was gone, and she had nowhere to run to. She
sheathed the dagger and sat next to Ramkus.

'I'm sorry,' she whispered.

They seemed to breathe in tune with each other.

'Don't be,' Ramkus replied, 'never be sorry. I know not what you have been through. You only wish to protect yourself, to survive. There is no shame in that,' the Guardian passively imparted.

She sat, a small bit dumbfounded, and then began to rest her head on his shoulder. As he did not embrace, she took it upon herself to wrap his arm around her.

He was confused, unable to figure out how to help, other than to be there.

'We really should try to find that horse,' she said.

'It'll be back. It will get hungry soon enough,' he suggested. This was not the case, however, and the morning was spent chasing the tracks across the plateau which had a terrain of boggy water where ancient rain seemed to have found a permanent resting place. Eventually they found it and caused it to return to their fold, setting off on the road mid-morning.

Their path hedged over hills along the plateau, over and under small rises in the rough grass; it was still predominantly fields of pasture for fruits and vegetables. Small patches of forest could be seen knotting themselves here and there into the tapestry. The mountains they had once traversed the bottoms of had now become sign posts for the direction they were headed. Snow covered the tops, as swathes of pine trees cascaded down at gradual and steep degrees. They found the farmsteads few and far between, and there was no sign of any more roadside tea houses they'd come to enjoy. The last village had been days ago. With the moon already visible in a pale blue sky, and altocumulus clouds beginning to take form atop their mountain guides, the pair spotted a farmhouse a few miles off which they decided to seek respite at. As had been the case on many days, the two silently enjoyed each other's company; Sigil feeling strengthened by the night previous. She felt a new path was

being laid out before her, and she was within reach of its
summit.

Reaching the farmhouse, they were welcomed warmly by an old
farmer and his wife. These elders had grown accustomed to the
comings and goings of strangers, finding that their solitude only
lasted a few days before the next highway adventurer journeyed
upon them. Sigilund and Ramkus made sure to pay their
gratitude respectfully, providing some entertainment – even if it
was not seen to be necessary. The meal was a heavy casserole
of turkey and wild bird, with softened root vegetables. The
farmer, whilst twisting his moustache, told the pair of his
exploits out on the *moors,* as he called them.
'Lots of game' he said, 'And when the world is silent, it is as if
you were one with the cosmos. Feeling its every fragment. The
air is intoxicating with its stillness.' He talked with a certain
hint of being well educated, but preferring the quiet life.
The wife watched him with a smile as he divulged his inner
harmony with these lands. They enjoyed a peach pie, whilst the
rest of the left-over turkey and game birds were fed to the dogs
that sat on the verandah watching over the farmer's horses that
were being kept in a small pen. Ramkus's horse - which may as
well be considered Sigil's now too - was kept along with them,
revitalised to be with its kind for the short while.

Bidding the old couple a good night as the conversation began to
slow, the farmers insisted that, rather than make camp outside,
they be shown to – and urged to make use of at the couple's
behest – the converted barn which had been specifically made as
suitable accommodation for travellers. There was a number of
small beds and a bathtub. They happily, and graciously
accepted the invitation, and settled into the humble dwelling.
Sigil decided to bath in some water drawn from the well outside
the guest quarters, and warmed by the small pot stove.

'Ramkus,' she said lightly, 'look away,' as if daring him for a glance whilst she entered into the water.

Ramkus – as came naturally to him – decided against anything that would amount to a suggestion. He strode outside and peered off into the distance. The farmstead rolled down one side, granting a magnificent view of a mountain far away into the distance, on the other side of a great river that was set below the rise. There were forests on either side of the land, with the trees sparsely holding firm against the elements. The plains were not usually so easy to give way to such vegetation. The night air was crisp, with wisps of wind bringing the scents of the forests. *How far must we have climbed?* Clouds moved quickly, and the stars became great beacons for his gaze. The calmness was almost a foreboding talisman of something to come. The light of the farmhouse and the barn's candles stood against all that was unknown in this world.

When he heard Sigil get out of the bath, he waited for a moment to let her change before asking permission to have a quick wash himself.

The lukewarm water was a relief to his skin. It was one of the first times he was able to examine the cuts and bruises he'd picked up, as well as just relax without the tension of pre-empting whatever may come around the corner. His knee seemed to have completely healed from its operation, the scar becoming less visible, and the leg muscles having increased in strength considerably. His wrists were not as blemished as before, although the skin was still a different colour and marked. He finished up his bath, and retired into one of the beds. Sigil was still outside as he called out good night. She walked in wearing only a nightgown which he tried not to stare at. He caught a smile from her when she came in.

'Good night,' she said softly, before blowing out the candles and getting into one of the other beds.

As he began to doze, he felt the sheet go up.

'Sigilund,' he grunted in his almost sleeping state.

'Shh… I'm cold, do you mind if we share? I have grown accustomed to it…' She whispered.

He begrudgingly gave up a large portion of the small bed as she placed her head on his chest, hugging him tightly.

Morning broke with deep cuts of sunshine slashing through gaps in the walls. The orange ray warmed the bed, along with the two whom occupied it. Sigil, feeling the heave of Ramkus's heavy, hairy pectoral muscles, smiled to herself whilst she moved a little further onto him, feeling his manly body with its muscular sinews. He kept sleeping, or trying to, as the bed became much heated. Sigilund started moving, grinding closer to him. He held her tightly in an attempt to stop her so that he may rest for a few more seconds. It did not deter her as she moved to face him, her lips close to his.

A large crash came from outside from something breaking, startling the two into action. Ramkus jumped up and grabbed his staff. Peering outdoors for what was happening: Bandits, a handful, were smashing down the gate to the horses; some had them tethered.

Ramkus raced outside to confront them in his semi-naked, aroused state. It was too late as the horses were being led away, charging on.

'Come back and fight you cowards!' he yelled after them. One bandit shifted on their horse, twenty paces away, turning to him. Ramkus stood, stunned. In front of him was the auburn-haired bandit woman he had heard about many days ago, the one who had led the attack on the small town he had played at. The very same one that had led a band of men charging down a road almost running him down. She turned her horse around to face him, eyes beaming, looking him up and down in a salacious manner. She then looked behind him; Sigil had come out. Her eyes lowered to Ramkus again as she winked. Rearing her horse around, she sped off.

'Can't we go after them?' Sigil cried. 'The poor farmers have had their horses stolen!'

'As has ours,' Ramkus replied gruffly, gesturing to where their own horse had been kept. 'They have all been taken.' He stared through the dust cloud settling along the road.

'What on earth is all this screaming!?' the old farmer ran out. Taking a second to comprehend the aftermath, he took off his singlet, threw it to the ground, and stomped on it.

Ramkus's eyes trailed off after the auburn-haired woman as she joined her comrades, galloping into the distance.

The two left the farm quite quickly soon after, feeling an embarrassment of sorts. The farmer was in a foul mood, as his wife tried to calm him down. She offered to make them breakfast, and even apologised for the loss of their own horse. However, this only fuelled further embarrassment, as they felt partly to blame: the younger couple not having looked after the elderly one in an appropriate manner.

They bid farewell only after being forced to take provisions for the road. They made sure to leave some coins in the barn as a sorry and thank you – even if it had already been refused when offered by hand.

With their instruments on their backs, they set off once more.

The sky was a deep blue, one that the eye could easily get lost in, making for an easy state to meditate. Ramkus was unsure how to feel, walking along the path with golden fields on either side. In the end, he contended the whole ordeal was an *easy come, easy go* sort on his part, and that it was *kinder to his groin* not to be in the saddle at all, anyway. Sigil was quiet, humming to herself, admiring the scenery in all its splendour. Her whole mood had changed since her outburst in the moors nights before. She was coming into herself, letting go of something she held as a well-guarded secret; in this case it seemed an unfathomable darkness that she could not escape from. Her ascent from this dark past was not an accident now, she knew she was headed to fabled lands of Eredin, where people would treat her with respect.

'I dreamed of going there as a child,' she said aloud without realising. 'Even before I jumped on the ship and learnt to be a bard. I had always dreamed of being there.'

'Learning on a ship?' Ramkus said queryingly.

'Well, I had learnt to sing folk tunes and had handled some instruments before, but it was only after I stowed away on the ship to come to Elantra that I learnt to be a bard.'

Ramkus looked at her, puzzled. 'But you only arrived in Elantra a few months back. You learnt to be a professional in such a quick time!?' he asked incredulously.

'Did you not say you had only learnt a few months back, also?' She raised an eyebrow.

Ramkus gave a chuckle, 'Yes, but I had a constant companion to teach me. What of you?'

Sigil became quiet for a moment, 'I was lucky too. Once I was found out, the crew threatened to throw me overboard. They calmed down after some time, reducing the threat to merely leaving me at the next port. A travelling merchant, one who sold instruments – lutes, funnily enough – took pity on me and took me under her wing. I think she read me from the beginning, that I *needed* help, that I *needed* to run away. She taught me how to truly perform, after seeing I had at least learnt to play the basics - thanks to my grandfather. She gave me my lute.' Sigil smiled, 'She also told me to meet her in Eredin for the Eredin Bard Festival, show her how good I had become,' she said excitedly, beaming at the thought.

Ramkus laughed, 'When you get there, see if there is some sort of winners board. See if my old mentor is on there. I tend to believe him when he says he won the bard-off competition twice! But, well,' Ramkus drifted off into thought. He tried to force himself away from delving into the topic of losing his friend again, as Sigil looked at him with intrigue: that such a man she abhorred could have been so famous a person in her craft was beyond reason. Ramkus did not notice, continuing to come to terms with his path. 'For me, it is the Guardians Seat. Wherever that is.'

She smiled at him knowingly, as they kept walking. The day was becoming quite warm.

It was slow going now they had lost the horse, and also more of an endurance test at the greater altitude. They had climbed higher than they had realised, but their muscles and lungs felt it. After passing through a small forest, another plain was before them. A building on the side of the road could be seen, not too far off, with a board standing at the side of it.

'One of those damn currency exchanges,' Sigil exclaimed without the vex she had previously exhibited. She had actually been rather pleasant and happy this past day: *A weight has been lifted,* Ramkus thought, *she is almost where she wants to be.*

As they came closer, they noticed a number of horses in a back pen, ones that looked very, *very* familiar. They looked to each other.

'You don't suppose those bandits are hiding in there?' Ramkus asked, examining the exterior with caution.

'If they are, you think you can take them all at once? There was quite a number of them, I doubt they are going to freely hand over the horses,' Sigil replied.

Ramkus guffawed, inspecting the horses. There appeared to be only two that he did not recognise as his own or the farmers'.

'I'm not sure they are in there now, in any case. There aren't enough horses in that pen, probably out raiding another farm or village. I would have thought these currency exchanges were meant to be *safe* and *secure* to some degree. Would you have money on the premises if it were not protected?' he mulled over the idea rather than waiting for Sigil's answer.

'Well, they are. Sort of an *unwritten* code as I take it,' she responded. 'Attacking one would set the bordering nations

584

soldiers upon you. I doubt anyone wants to deal with a few bands of soldiers on their tail. Only the most heinous criminals get that sort of treatment, where neighbouring territories decide to come together to fight a common threat. You should know these types of rules, you're a Guardian after all.'

Ramkus grunted and frowned, 'I know very little of this world. Let's check this place out anyway.'

They began to tread carefully, sneaking upon the building. As they came to the windows which held pot plants on the exterior, they peered inside. A man was looking out the window with a pipe in his mouth. He spotted them straight away and gave them a queer look.

They ducked down.

'I think he saw you,' Ramkus imparted as they both grimaced, standing up and entering the premises.

The man was resting, seated at the front of his table, contentedly smoking his pipe, arms crossed as he continued to give them a funny look. He was a fairly skinny man, wearing a wide brimmed hat indoors. There were shelves along some of the walls, with one side holding a huge map with smaller, detailed ones lining around it as well other paraphernalia, such flags and titles. The shelves held books and supplies, whilst one shelf behind the man was adorned with documents, badges, stamps, and some further official looking documents were below it on a cabinet.

'Can I, *help* you?' the man inquired in a sarcastic tone.

'You mind telling us where you got those horses?' Ramkus blurted out without tact, coming directly to face the man.

The man studied Ramkus, 'Some people came through, sold them to me,' he said reservedly, '*I take it you have seen them before?*' he gave a questioning look at the aggression from Ramkus.

Ramkus smirked, 'They were stolen last night, but I suppose you realised that as you were dealing with a *certain* type of people, *ehh.*' He raised his staff a little in front of the man.

'I paid a good price, I admit,' the man replied, inching
backwards, sensing the impending threat. 'I remind you, I am a
neutral official,' he stated.

'Ramkus, don't act too hastily,' Sigil came in.

'A *fair* price?' Ramkus asked.

'Ramkus, this won't get you anywhere.' She turned to the
official, '*Sir*, how much were they purchased for?' She asked.

'I bet he knew they were the farming couple's...' Ramkus
grumbled under his breath, locking eyes with the official.

The man thought for a second, 'Look, I bought them with money
that belongs to the *Verselion Kingdom*, those horses belong to
this currency house after sale. A *Bona fide purchase, without
notice.*'

Ramkus scoffed.

'How much?' Sigil asked matter-of-factly.

'600 *plaques.*'

'In *Sarchel's* currency?' Sigil came back.

As much as Ramkus knew it was not just to pay for the return of
stolen horses, he acquiesced to the quickest possible route in
remedying the situation. He also caught on that Sigil was of this
mindset early on.

'Well, conversion is thirteen plaques to two *colleques*, so:
ninety-two, ninety-three colleques?'

'Is that *fair*? Ramkus grunted, raising the staff under the chin of
the currency exchange official. The man studied the staff, then
scrutinised Ramkus, as his mouth grew agape, lowering the pipe
so that he had to retrieve it with his hand before falling.

'A *Guardian!?*' he said with astonishment. 'You needn't
threaten me, I know full well my duty to *your* type. I must
admit, you're not acting in the *appropriate decorum*,' the man
scolded, obviously use to dealing with all types and ranks. He
also knew how to deal with difficult, angry customers, and he
recognised Ramkus as someone who wouldn't do any harm to a
person who was innocent - at least by his own judgement.

'Half that, as a token of goodwill, to a *Guardian.*' The man bowed sarcastically. Ramkus looked to Sigil; she produced the coin which the official took behind his desk, quickly counting it. 'We also expect they will be delivered back to the farmer and his wife down the road,' Ramkus ordered.

'Patience Guardian, *patience.* Unfortunately, I cannot leave this post, you can take them yourself, or I will get the most *trustworthy* person heading that way to take them,' he said as he finished counting the colleques. 'Do you also want to exchange the rest? There is not much left.'

'Some,' Sigil said nonchalantly.

'Where are you headed to? I have a few regions' currencies here. It is somewhat of a junction for a number of kingdoms and nations.'

'Whatever Eredin uses,' she said, before asking reservedly, 'Is it far?'

'A little, your best to have some plaques and a few *relks*. You know the direction, don't you?' The man raised his head from his desk, seeing the unsure face of Sigil, and the restless Guardian behind her.

'I'll show you,' the official walked up to the large map.

'We are here,' he pointed to a spot on the finely crafted document, 'so it is further north-west for you, until you are through this mountain pass; then through the *Nelve Kingdom* due west, then north.'

Ramkus was taken aback by the size of the world on the map – or rather, the continent of Elantra, to be more precise. He looked for Abergrass, his first *stop* in Elantra, transfixed. He traced the path down the coast with the sea to the East – Kerwood, Refton - until he saw where the supposedly hidden Summer Palace was: *Felipe... Sophia...* He gritted his teeth against any flood of complex emotions, then continued to survey the map. There were red jottings around where the river and forest were, indicating the disputed domain that the Empire and forest dwellers contended over... *which Miiva protects.* He twisted the ring on his finger and frowned sadly before looking up at the map again. He followed the lines of the river up to Fallen Crest, and further along to Balago; then through the mountain pass to Potelo, where Tomriel released him from his manacles and he fought against the Empires men for the last time... *with Mooyne.* Shaking his head, he looked upon the no man's land where the odd, ancient temple was decaying and the grass creatures inhabited; then ran his eyes along till he spotted the city of Lellel where Sigil and he had fled the Waylayers Arms. He finished his scan of the map, tracing the last road he had travelled: the ascent North-West to this currency exchange, which was well highlighted on the map.

'Where is the Guardian's Seat?' Ramkus asked.

The official gave a quizzical look. 'Aren't you a Guardian? Shouldn't you know?' he asked.

'It is a long story, but that is where I am headed at present. I am not trained in *cordiality*...' Ramkus hinted to his current predicament of only just finding himself in this world.

The official shrugged, 'Well, it is here.' He pointed to a spot very far to the West: inland, past a number of mountains, lakes, rivers, territories. An inordinately long stretch of journey to go. He gave a defeated look. *At least it isn't entirely on the other side of the map.* He sighed, holding his staff steadfast. Gritting his teeth, he tried to imprint the path from here to the Guardian's Seat in his mind – *It is at least a fairly direct path. It does not look like there is any territory shaded in the Empires colours.* He began to smile and nod to himself. *The path of a Guardian.*

The two bought some provisions from the small amount on offer, then set off again upon their horse. It was a sombre mood; the study of the map had concluded what neither wanted to admit: a parting; a farewell. Ramkus reflected on his previous companions also; how the friends he had made had gone their separate ways, leaving him alone in the world.

Alone. He nodded to himself as a resoluteness came from such thoughts. *The path of the Guardian, indeed.* He had learnt from these people. They all possessed such qualities that made life vibrant, and he deeply regretted that he did not journey with them all for longer than he did. But another tune took his mood: that each time he left one, another friend arose. Companions in the most peculiar of places, in the most absurd of situations. And they were all ready to lend themselves to making life *that little bit more comforting.*

He did not mind his few days of travelling alone, but still, he preferred to be amongst others; it invoked conversation, joy, and an enjoyment of the world at large. Companionship, he would miss it with Sigilund for sure, knowing someone was sharing this rocky path, even for a little while. It was for them to walk their own paths, and even though this meant an end, their journey would be cherished in memory, and the lesson learnt: to enjoy the ride.

The path went on, life went on, and he had a goal to reach after all. He had one hope though: that the Guardian's path was not a life of loneliness. Solitude - although maybe deep down he could endure and even grow from it – his life was richer from sharing with those along the way. This is what he knew, this is what he hoped for.

"We shall see," a dark voice whispered.

It was in plain sight: a signpost. Two diverging paths - the fork in the road. The bodies of both riders sagged with regret upon their acknowledgement. One road kept straight in a northern direction, climbing ever so slightly higher on a gradient; the other, to the west, falling slightly down from this altitude. The grass swayed in a gentle breeze that held no sense of warmth or cold – nothing held to this wind, it brought no sense of what was to come.

The gravel crumbled under the horse's hooves, slowly coming to a stop that they did not want.

They both got off.

'Shall we break?' She asked as Ramkus readied himself, detaching his guitar from the side and adjusting it on his back. Sigil observed his actions, 'The horse is *yours*, Ramkus,' she said as if hurt. 'I should be the one setting off to walk!' he said with a little chuckle.

He studied the horizon and was overcome. It dawned on him, the splendour that unravelled. He laughed: *It is all ahead of me! Every single bit! My journey is out there, in this beautiful world!* He watched the ever-changing sky, as a deep azure morphed into a light array of yellow and orange hues skittling toward the edges of the horizon - where he was to head to. Mountains could be made out; forests that seemed so lush and comforting; great lakes and inland seas; steppes and plains; marbled rollicking terrains; cities and towns; people. He was overcome with the thought of what was ahead, and each step was one of nourishment to his being, it brought strength. How far he had come! How much he had learnt, and so much more to be done!

'Ramkus,' Sigilund touched him.

He beamed as he turned to her: a smile of warmth and promise; one that reassured that everything was in its right place; that there would be a tomorrow to wash away the unwanted blemishes of today.

'The horse is yours, *Sigil*,' he answered. 'You'll need it more than I.'

'No goodbyes now, let's break for a while,' she held back the tears.

'It is easier this way. It is easier that we take off now.' His words carried a comforting spirit that only desired the best for her.

She understood, but still protested. 'No!' A tear rolled down her cheek as she declared softly, 'I need you.'

He smiled, 'You do not. You do not need me. All the strength you will need is within you. We have both helped each other on

the way, but we have our own paths to tread in this world, and
we must follow them.'

'I'm scared of what is out there,' she remonstrated.

'You will be a star, Sigil!' he declared. 'The world will be
shaken by you. But you must do it on your own. Your past is
now washed away: you are free!'

She began to tremble and lunged at him, her face coming to
meet his. She stared at him for a second, as they slowly
embraced. He held her head and rocked her.

'Take care, Sigilund. I will come hear you in Eredin one day,'
he whispered as she clung to him.

After a few moments, they separated. She wiped her face and
began to search out her road ahead.

'You are sure about the horse?' she asked, not looking at him.
'After all I have taken from you?

'Taken!? You have *given* me much more than you realise!' he
shot back with great admiration.

She got some of the supplies together and handed them to him,
then took the sack of plaques.

'Here,' she said, offering the last bit of money she had.

Ramkus laughed, 'But that isn't accepted currency this way.
No, I will be fine.'

They looked at each other for a moment before embracing again.
They once more searched each other's eyes. Ramkus gave a
half smile, then kissed her, as she frowned, fighting back tears.

'You are one of the only kind people in the world,' she said,
barely audible.

'I doubt that,' he replied, looking deep into her, knowing it was
simply heightened emotions. 'Until we meet again,' he said
beaming, lifting his head, smelling the wind, breathing in the
world, smiling as he turned to regard his path. He was ready.

Sigil got on the horse in a depressed state, not saying a word,
looking for him to turn to her. He did, with a huge grin, as she
returned a weak one. She moved the horse onward.

He watched her for a while, as she sped off in a reluctant posture, not attempting to peer back. He grinned to himself. It was the end of a long chapter in his journey so far, but there was much more ahead. The world was all in front of him, all the answers to his mysteries.

Touching his wrists, feeling the naked skin that had been scarred, he reflected on the flight from the Summer Palace, but he shirked the thought. *No time for reminiscing just now.*

He placed his staff a step ahead of him, put one step in front of the other, and set off for the Seat of the Guardians… and his place in the world.

Epilogue

The spread of dense jungle forest finally gave way to the base of his destination: a rocky outcrop that seemed to spring up from nowhere. The twisting path spread between a small lake and a field until it hit the first small, straight edged, stone part of the mountain. Steps had been cut into the rock, steps that stretched up high into the misty peaks. It was a narrow path, steep and dangerous, and it led to his ultimate goal: The Seat of the Guardians.

He could not stop smiling, 'Finally, finally I have made it!' he said to himself as he observed the last part of his journey with an overwhelming enthusiasm.

He was dishevelled, the clothes he had received long ago were torn and in need of replacement. He looked quite out of sorts in the last stretch of this journey, donning shorts that were surrounded by a thick belt, a short-sleeved shirt. The cloak he received from Tomriel still held true, but had been unnecessary in recent times and oft held under his arm instead of around him. He breathed heavily, sucking in the damp, fresh air, readying himself for the climb.

He had no idea what to expect, but had been ready for this moment, this *homecoming*, ever since he had first heard of it from Felipe, long ago.

He took his first step up.

How much he had had seen and learnt, and how much there was still to see and learn!

He started at a steady pace, preferring not to place his staff on the steps, rather hold it on an angle.

So many questions he had, so many ideas he wanted to share; the life that he had enjoyed, his outlook on the world. The dark humming of his *friend* began in his mind. Ramkus smiled, combating it with his own music, humming along in a pleasant mood, not letting Prince come to the fore.

After a while he reached a cleft, deciding to stop and look out at the view.

This stone mountain had seemed so ominous, it had stood out from the forests and the jungles, easy to spot from miles away as it drew all eyes towards it. Fog was rolling at its base, rising up to the altitude he had stopped as if toying with him. Ramkus watched as it quickly spread and withdrew, giving only so much visibility for a time before the view retreated and all that was observable was lost once more. One could be deceived that the fog was something that could not be broken through; it was tremendously dense at times. He waited until it fell, and finally saw in full view the lake that had stretched out below; still and peaceful, as calm as the trees that stood by its side.

It reminded Ramkus of the night in Lencil, of the place he had met Miiva. He fidgeted with the ring he had been given by her absent-mindedly. *What an enchanting girl*, he thought, laughing at the fact she was described as an *enchantress* after all. Casting that spell of fog to protect him. She trusted him from the start, finding him limp and naked, resting in that warm spring. There was something magical about that place, about Miiva. He wondered if he would ever see the place, or Miiva, again. He was overcome by a feeling in which *knew* he would.

Beginning his trek up the dangerous mountain steps after the brief pause, edging in between the crevices, back into his thoughts. Of course, Miiva was not the only girl; he had his first *experience* in Kerwood with Clara, whom had also helped him and Felipe escape.

Alas he ended up where he did not want, in the Summer Palace, at the beck and call of royalty. He felt poorly about that, for he deeply admired Sophia. She had been very good to him, but she had played a part in the Empire's game: having him drugged, making him part of the whole Empirical machinations, the rank and file of warmongering conquerors. The madness he

developed, waking beside her. He was not happy with his
actions: *But were they really my actions?*
He smiled as he remembered how he was at least able to bridge
himself back to his role, his confidence in his being, after
walking the path with Sigilund when he had chanced upon her in
Lellel. *I hope she does well.*

The narrowing steps hit a small retreat where ornamental lamp
structures made of stone set a meditative mood. They were like
miniature shrines housing tiny Gods. Gnarled trees with green
bracken stood to the side, shading some stone bench seats. Steps
were laid out in between many small, marble stones which had
been neatly tidied into a little pebble garden as if it were grass.
A small pond was at the edge, dripping with water from a stream
coming down the rock facade. He immediately felt the serenity
hit him. *Am I here?*
There was no sight of another living being.
He pressed on.

The path once again came out along the cliff face. The fog was
lifting, or rather, he was ascending out of it.
He looked up and saw it! Finally, what he had been seeking: the
Seat of the Guardians. Huge columns built into the stone face,
window slots, a balcony that could see all the lands below, large
weathered steel doors that had withstood the test of time. It was
- as he had assumed it would be - an ancient, ceremonial looking
place, built from the very earth. A fortress fit for a mystical,
sacred order; the stronghold for his kind, his ilk, his people. He
had not *felt* he was a Guardian as much as he had now, nor truly
accepted the reality either. It was always a myth that played
upon his mind; but here, in literal stone, he was at his rightful
home.
He was excited to meet the other Guardians, other people with
whom he shared the same purpose, same story, his clan. *This is
my family!* Borne of nothing, from nothing, simply awakening

from a field, he needed to share this world, this experience of life, with others whom understood the exact emotions he had gone through, who had endured similar trials and tribulations. There was little activity from the cracks and crevices; smoke did rise from inside, however. To the furthest reaches where more steps twisted around to reach he spied an open room that appeared to hold special significance. He trudged up the foreboding, dangerous steps. The path started to get wider, and the miniature lamp shrines were situated along every now and again. Crevices in the stone cliff face made to hold candles were also in abundance.

It must look remarkable when they are all alight, he thought. *How many would get to see it, though?*

He came to the first large balcony that led into the hard, solemn, mountain structure. He stopped to take it all in. Grey and foreboding, it had been weathered by the elements, making it seem smooth and archaic. Hardly any bits of moss could cling to such a surface, yet there were small reminders that life can spring in the most difficult of places.

When he turned to a wall where a few vines were hanging over a bench, he was startled to see an old man smoking a pipe. He was even more so surprised that the man did not take too much notice of him. Sitting as if a monk, his white beard draped down to his crossed legs, highlighting his bald top. To fit the monk look, he was clothed in an ancient garb.

'Hello!' Ramkus cried with excitement, unable to restrain himself tactfully.

The old man looked up, out of a daze, 'Hello,' came the simple reply, a little curt. The man inspected Ramkus up and down. 'I suppose you're here for a job, not sure we have much in the way at the moment. Didn't your village chieftain tell you?' he responded gruffly.

Ramkus was perplexed, not knowing how to respond. 'Ah, I don't have a chieftain. I am one of you: a Guardian!' he declared with pride.

'What?' the old man said, 'Don't play with me, boy. Just because you painted a stick does not make you a Guardian. We haven't had any new blood for an inordinately long time, aeons!'
'But I am!' implored Ramkus, unsure of himself, of what he'd had to believe and clutch to so as to drag himself through world without any guidance.
The old man looked him over again, scrutinising him with greater interest. He got up and looked Ramkus in the eye, then tapped Ramkus's staff with his pipe. 'May I?' he asked, gesturing to the staff. Ramkus gave it to him without hesitation. The old man read the staffs movements, touching the gold tipped ends, reading the name in the golden ruins.
'Ramkys, eh?' Still looking over Ramkus from head to tail. 'Don't believe it was *written* that we would see another Guardian for a long while. I guess we shall see, come with me.'
Ramkys? Ramkus was perplexed, madly questioning the name in his mind. *Have I been given the wrong name? Does this make a difference to me? Will I have to change one of the first things I had been given? How did I never notice it in the ruins when they were right in front of me!?... Can I read ruins?* His mind went into revolt.
The old man began to walk towards the doors, leading the confounded Ramkus through two large steel framed doors. It would take a massive effort to have to force them open, luckily, they were slightly ajar. He walked with great pace, unbecoming of his years - as far as Ramkus could guess.
Walking through the doors timidly, it took a while for Ramkus's eyes to adjust to the light inside, even with the windows above allowing light through. Braziers were alight, but with not much effect.
Slowly, Ramkus's vision adjusted. The room was a massive, stone block chamber, not much in the way of furnishings; a few chairs and tables, an odd painting on the wall, some armours and antique trinkets that all looked from foreign lands. Fireplaces on both side walls. They kept walking until they made it to a door.

'You're sure you aren't playing me? You aren't one of the townsfolk below, dressing up and pretending to be a Guardian?' the old man raised an eyebrow.

'No, and what do you mean by that? Why would anyone try and *trick* you?' Ramkus asked, incensed at such a suggestion.

'I guess that *is* what a new Guardian would say,' the old man began to chortle. 'Well, in short, as you may have experienced, some people actually treat us with a sacred *air*. A few towns quite close by see to it that we are provided with everything we require. It gives them a purpose in this world. Often, they will send up young people to work. Usually chefs or cleaners. Not much work to be done here though, really. Oh, except the building works, lots of restoration. They also bring up fresh food, daily. And a lot of stone art. You saw those lamp holders? Beautifully crafted. They – and the stone seats – were all lugged up here, rather than made on the spot. Imagine that! *The poor souls...* But I suppose it gives them some worth, feeds their pride.'

Does this old guy realise what I have been through to get here? All he seems to be doing is rambling, Ramkus thought.

'We are actually in quite a bit of debt to them, but they see this as their sole reason as a people.'

He keeps repeating his point.

'Anyway, you'll learn all of this in due course. Sit here for a minute.' The old man showed him to a wooden framed seat with leather upholstery. '*Kursa*, was it?

'Ramkus...' Ramkus replied slowly, *choosing* his name.

'Only kidding, Kursa was one of our champions for a while, in a bygone era. You'll learn this.' The old man kept talking. 'I better go search for the others. I'll be back in a short while. By the way, where have you come from?'

'You mean the place I *awoke*?' Ramkus asked.

The old man nodded.

'Abergrass,' he answered.

'Never heard of it. Was it far?' the old man said without much thought.

Ramkus was taken aback. 'Well, I thought so. It was in a remote corner of this world, at least it felt like it. In the Erevon realm of Elantra.'

'Erevon?' the old man's eyes widened. 'My poor boy, you *have* come far!' he nodded along to himself. 'Right, well, sit here and I'll be back soon.'

He opened the door and went into a room which beamed with light, which retreated as soon the doors closed, leaving Ramkus in the great chamber, alone. Candles and torches were placed about, unlit. It felt cold, unused, as if it was only for certain ceremonial occasions, still well kept in case of need for such a purpose. Parts of the walls, he noticed, were built with beautiful mosaics. He could not help himself, he got up and began to admire the art, remembering and comparing them in the back of his mind to the ancient artworks he had come across on his journey so far.

As he looked about the chamber slowly, his eyes rested upon a massive tapestry hung in the centre. Once his eyes began to focus better, the tapestry's lines settled on the fabric to form a map, not any old map, but a gargantuan one of the *world!* Much grander and larger than the ones he witnessed in currency exchanges – they had only shown Elantra, if that. The land mass was massive - at least as much as he had ever seen it portrayed. He stood, astonished. This was his world, what he was the Guardian of. He admired the colours and names, the boundaries, the seas, the continents. He looked for where he now stood, The Seat of the Guardians - finding it difficult to grasp its position, he searched for Abergrass. After a brief period of calibrating his position, he found it. It stood with a more archaic name, but that was it for sure; far, far away, long lost from his presence. He then traced his way to this spot, along the paths, the rivers, the mountains. There were massive desert lands, forests, mountains, lakes, and seas that he had never considered possible. He wondered if he would ever see these places.

It dawned on him that this was not just a large chamber, it was a great hall. The smell of many a good nights' lay dormant. There was no sound, it was as if a dark vacuum had drawn the noise completely out of the place. He wondered how, why, and when this place had been used. He smiled as he remembered the questions that were in more pressing need of being answered. The whole of his universe was about to be made clear, or so he thought. Where his place was in this world; what Guardians *do*; what exactly *his purpose* was, *his role*; where did his essence come from; what is it to be a Guardian; what is a Guardian permitted and not permitted to do. He recalled moments of his first few days, the old woman who had charged at him from the caravan, declaring he would *die by his own blood*; the hooded man atop the hill where he had. *The fight!* He was becoming overwhelmed as the old monk looking man entered the hall again.

'Ah,' he said understandingly, 'The Great Map. Very outdated. Though there are some places on there that still go by those names.'

'I have so many questions!' Ramkus blurted out, unable to contain himself anymore.

'But naturally,' the old man said. 'Firstly, I ought to introduce myself. I haven't had to do so for a very long time. I am Lento, one of the elder Guardians. One of the eldest, or oldest dependent on who you are.' His eyes started to hold a little tinge of sadness. 'I am now, somewhat, an old patron of the Seat, rarely getting much of a say against the others. You will meet them on the actual Seat.' He paused, trying to look cheerful to the newcomer. 'Time has changed much…' He stopped what he was going to say, giving an attempted happy smile instead. 'Right, well, let us see the others. They'll go through some other passages to get there. I think you may find this place a little confusing to begin with. It is a sacred and

ancient site, mind you, with many secrets, many paths – some
that we don't even know about!' He patted Ramkus on the
shoulder, 'Shall we.'

They stepped back outdoors.

Ramkus stood tall and proud, walking with pride in his stride.
He had achieved his aim, reached his goal, and was about to be
admitted into his order. This was what he was, one of them: a
Guardian. One of an ancient set of people delegated
responsibilities to look after this world, as he saw it. Their place
in the grand scheme was of importance and respect, of grandeur
and compassion. Their role was vital to all tribes, nations, clans,
and people, and the world was indebted to these mystical
individuals whom hopes of peace and harmony rested upon.

He was led further around the mountains edge to a long, exposed
ledge which seemed to be built into a cleft. It was decorated
with old ornamental stone work of a grand, but humble, design.
Well-groomed trees stood firm in the rock, baring long branches
and green bracken. They appeared venerated by those who lived
beside them, as if they were inhabited by small tree spirits. This
area must not have been as affected from the weather as the
"entrance", as moss grew in patches over some of the stone wall,
as well as off the side of the cliff. As bleak as many stone
fortresses that had withstood the ages, this one still had life.

The fog had set in again over the lands below. It felt like he
now walked in a temple that perched above the clouds, above
the world. They rose up some further steps to a level that sat on
top of the great hall. More old columns stood, seemingly
holding up the roof of the mountaintop to provide a vast open,
but undercover, courtyard.

'One of the training rooms,' Lento said.

'For what?' Ramkus asked.

Lento looked at him questioningly. 'You have lived this world,
are you saying you did not come into any physical conflict?
Hah!'

'I've had my fair share,' Ramkus said begrudgingly under his breath.

'Good, I hope you did. We need to keep ourselves sharp in our reflexes and movements, quick on our feet, just in case. Also adds a level of respect when people are dealing with men who know how to overcome others physically. Ah, but that is not what we are; it is more about *knowing but never using.*'

Ramkus gave a nod.

They passed by the training room, curling along the cliff face until it climbed another level to a "room" set on a separate peak as it split from the main mountain structure. Ramkus could see it was another "open" sort of room as before, although much smaller, and the other side of the "room" had no back wall, it over-looked the other side of the mountain.

This is the peak of the mountain, this is it, it has to be: The Seat of the Guardians.

Lento looked at him, understanding his internal query, 'Yes, this is the Seat of the Guardians – or the Guardians Seat,' he chuckled. 'Stay here.' Lento pointed at a spot where a small bench rested on a platform a few metres below, a little waiting area just before the *Seat* began.

'I'll make sure they are ready,' Lento said cordially.

'Is there some sort of ceremony?' Ramkus asked.

Lento thought for a bit, 'I cannot actually remember, it is just that those at the Seat want to be at their spots before someone enters – dependent on the situation.'

'Oh,' Ramkus said, a little unsure as to whether he did hope for some pomp and ceremony in celebration of his arrival, or even a small welcoming party.

Lento went off inside, as Ramkus looked to a large bowl to his side; it was filled with water and a goldfish. The goldfish moved slowly in the bowl's clear water, striking to another spot every so often. He looked out at the lack of view for the moment: the grey, ominous, rolling clouds threatened below. Mountain tops could be outlined far off in the surrounding lands, high above this spot, but his world enclosed around him, just as the bowl surrounded the goldfish. If there was one thing he could not endure, it was being kept stationary, being kept in one spot. He thought upon the time he spent in the Empire's Summer Palace, high above the lands; how much he despised being held there. It had built up, that restriction, until he had finally snapped, becoming that monster in the process: *Prince*. Yet his friend had remained – happily, for all he knew. He rubbed his scarred wrists and felt for the guitar tied at his back. His little relief in that world far away.

Lento came back. 'Well, all of them seem to be there, except Cegbard, but he is like that, off on his own devices. Anyway, please,' he showed him around the corner. Ramkus's heart started to race: *The moment of truth!*

As he came around, he saw four old men, spread out at a long stone table that positioned close to the other cliff edge where another split peak rose a few metres away. It was jagged, as was much of the room. A cold air swirled.

Three of the Guardians appeared to be placed around one central figure. Ramkus stared at him: he looked strong, and was of a larger build than Ramkus, clean shaven with short light hair. He judged him as a type to be bereft of words, more of action. This man was holding an expression that seemed to befit the room. He was unmoved, seeming more annoyed for some reason. His eyes, piercing, aggressive, scrutinising. Ramkus was completely focussed on this man who appeared to be the one to make the decisions here upon the Seat; or have the final word, so to speak. 'Staff!' the man demanded with a loud, gruff voice. Ramkus did not know how to feel about being commanded like that, he was petrified, he hadn't even looked at the other Guardians. He came forward, unsure of himself, looking for someone to support him. All were old, not as aggressive, but none wore expressions that could be described of bordering pleasantness. One thing that struck him, and made him feel *worthy* of being there was that all of those seated held the same styled Guardian staff as his. *The symbol of a Guardian.*

He handed the staff to the gruff leader of this ensemble, careful not to tread unawares or do anything that would be judged negatively.

'Ramkys,' the man said, twisting his mouth.

'Ramk*us*,' Ramkus replied, unable to help himself.

The man sneered at him with incredulity. He handed the staff back as Ramkus moved to his original spot. There was a profuse sense he was not welcome.

The man stood up, wearing the dark clothing Ramkus once had. They were more refined, however, than what he had been adorned with when he had first awoken. The Guardian walked around one of the others, then around the table, slowly. Arms on show, he was of a hardened muscle, weathered by the elements just as this mountain and Seat had been. The way he moved was threatening.

Disgust was worn on his face as he came to Ramkus, walking around him as he inspected the tattered clothing, the well-worn cloak, the guitar at his back. Ramkus stood as still as possible. The Guardian came around to face him; he was considerably taller than Ramkus, and it seemed as if he was not only looking down upon Ramkus figuratively.

'Welcome to the Guardians Seat…' the man paused, '*Guardian*,' he said with a scowl. 'Welcome to your… *home.*' Ramkus looked around at the faces of the other Guardians, then back to this one staring down at him with contempt.

He stood motionless, devoid of emotion.

There was nowhere to go; he had met his goal.

This was home; he was **home**.

Glossary

Territories

Abergrass   Small village of around six homesteads/buildings. Annexed to field Ramkus awoke in.

Balago   Elven village that leads through a crevice, to a mountain village. Along the major river that runs from the Summer Palace.

Capital   Capital of the Empire, upon where orders for the rest of the Empire are derived.

Elantra   The first lands (continent) Ramkus tread upon. Bordered by the mountain range to the South and South West, Pintos sea/ocean to the East.

Erevon Realm   Realm Ramkus awoke in, comprises of Abergrass, Kerwood, Refton, Summer palace of the Ronalto Empire. Borders with massive stretch of mountain.

Fallen Crest   Town along the river outside Lencil where the Empire keeps watch of those coming up and downstream. Ramkus attempted to avoid it in a coracle, but ended up attacking it with Mooyne.

Fritiland   South West of Refton, West of Summer palace. Said to be a Bard's paradise.

Isles of Montreyer   Where Sigil is from, far North East by sea from Refton. Inhabitants are warriors, sailing on massive warships, raiding whomever they please.

Kerwood   Small town in Sorbo Forest, river runs through it out to sea. Inn provides a nice fish broth, bath, big drinking hall.

Lellel	City Kingdom far from the Empire's lands. A massive city with many interior buildings being five stories high. Major pub where Ramkus met Sigilund for a second time. Baron Von Wilton and his daughter reside here.
Lencil	Forests where Miiva lives, lands that the Empire took over and placed their Summer palace upon the Rock. Mirelle and Nessek are the village heads.
Lencil River	River outside of Lencil which runs past Fallen Crest and Balago.
Muolton	Town west along Sunden Range, where Hodgerise comes from.
Oppressive Forest	Outside of Refton, past the "Conville". Oppressive, knotted and gnarled trees, difficult to get through, deep mist, claustrophobic. Ramkus goes a tad mad in it.
Potelo	Mountain Folk village near Balago. Ramkus has his bracelets cut off in the smelters here. Sits within a saddle. Main attractions being the workshop with massive furnaces, and pub/tavern, built into the mountain with two huge steel doors.
Reelo Kingdom	Kingdom far away which holds the Eredin Bard Festival.
Refton	Town far way off from Kerwood.
Relton	Town that was to the right of a fork in the road which Ramkus and Felipe hit with a troop of Kings Guards.
the Rock	Summer Castle perched is upon it, Summer Palace surrounds it. Built by first people, hollowed out, used as staircase to castle.

Sorbo Forest	First forest Ramkus entered into, large, fertile and earthy. Kerwood lies within it.
Summer Castle	Ronato Family reside there for a fair bit of the year. Along the coast, built on an ancient forest dwellers/sea peoples village in the Rock.
Sunden Mountain Range	Area in which a conflict between natives and the Empire occurred. Outpost was controlled by Solento.
Trucce	City in Vicce, where merchant's daughter in the Rose Hotel was from.
Vicce	Kingdom where a merchant's daughter in Rose Hotel was from.

People

Baron VonWilton	Baron of the city Lellel, his daughter attempts to kills herself by jumping off a bridge, Ramkus recues her and, although the Baron cannot prove anything and is still suspicious, provides Ramkus with a horse and gold.
Boraf	Shopkeeper in Miiva's town in Lencil. Red moustached, sells clothing.
Cegbard	One of the elder Guardians, mentioned by Lento but not at Ramkus's arrival.
Chaisu	Leader of a band of forest dwellers held captive in the Empire's 'Spy town' outside of Lencil, connected to the Summer Palace, connect via a bridge. Escaped and led Ramkus and Mooyne to the Elven town Balago. Dark haired, short and slim, hawkish eyes.

Chall   Village elder and head of Polento. Huge frame, large arms, balding on top with greying hair. Moustache that drops down as if a beard.

Clara Miller   Red-haired (strawberry blonde) green eyed country girl whom Ramkus met in the Kerwood pub, and slept with. Helped save them from the Empire at one stage, grew up on a farm and helps at a local mill.

Corinth   Female merchant met at the Rose Hotel playing cards.

Djuayne Antagno   Sergeant of the Empire, Captain of the King's Guard. Six foot seven, long brown hair that is well maintained, green piercing eyes, muscular, arrogant, master swordsman. Uses the Longsword in combat.

Exelda   Female merchant met at the Rose Hotel playing cards.

Felipe   Bard, plays guitar, wears black and has a sombrero. Similar to a mariachi. Lively, well poised, intent, charmer. Teacher of Ramkus in the arts of being a bard, and life in general. Ramkus's first friend.

Black-as-midnight moustache, and black curly hair, brown eyes.

Eredin Bard Festival finalist 5 times, twice winning it.

Figal   Male Head of town of Balago. A large man, balding, childlike features making him seem less a leader than an affable giant.

Fleureb   Innkeeper at Abergrass Inn.

Giselda
Close friend, confidant, training partner, of Sophia. Short cropped brown hair, small and fit, gentle features which held a hint of the first peoples.

Harold
Wears white gown with gold ribbon. Priest of the Empire who accompanies Ramkus for his duel with Djuayne.

Hodgerise
Husband of Revla. Burly man with thick black beard. Lives in a shepherds hut, travelling from Refton to Kerwood with crazed old woman.

Kerf
Second man to speak to Ramkus, outside the Abergrass Inn (with his friend Rab). Balding, pudgy red nose, portly.

Kret
Merchant whose cart of wooden instruments Ramkus stowed away in to get from Balago to Polento. Ramkus bought guitar from him. Titled: Merchant of the finest wooden instruments this side of Lencil River.

King Irving the V of the Ronato Family
Head of the Royal Ronato family, one of the great royal families of the Empire. Resides in Elantra, father of Sophia. Wears a simple golden crown, deep red fabric, leather etched with jewels, fur cloak, many beautiful rings, bracelets. Typical attire of a king. Not too stern, white trimmed beard; long whitening hair; grey blue eyes.

Lento
Oldest Guardian at the Seat of the Guardians, meets Ramkus upon his ascent up the mountain and into the Seat. Offers much wisdom, talks a fair bit. White beard, bald, smokes a pipe.

Miiva Mareva
Met in the Elven glade. An enchantress forest dweller, mixed with sea voyager. Slender, wears tight fitted clothing, has two sticks with long chains at the end and metal baubles attached which she uses for ceremony and as weapons: they're

called Pois. Feline features: high cheekbones, feline green almost yellow eyes, long black, well-maintained dreadlock hair. Protects the first peoples' forest with ancient magic. Also known as The Dusk Enchantress.

Mirelle
Female head of Lencil with Nessek, lands occupied by the Empire for their Summer Palace. Speaks like Miiva. Long white blonde hair, appears quite regal, holding grace, determination and power.

Mooyne
Odd looking shortish man, tough as nails, crazy, great fighter using kama weapons (small sickles). Met Ramkus after a fight when Ramkus was escaping in a coracle down a river from the Summer Palace of the Empire. Not from Elantra, much farther away.

Mrill
Female merchant met at the Rose Hotel playing cards.

Nessek
Male head of Lencil with Mirelle, lands occupied by the Empire for their Summer Palace. Fairly old, green eyes, elegantly built, large stature.

Pilgrim (Old Man)
Old man with wise words, met on the outskirts of Refton when Ramkus fought the hooded foe. White wispy beard, resolute, powerful, keen eyes, walks with a cane.

Poncho
Kings Guard leader for Ronalto family. Clean haircut, strong features, solid, military type. Wears a beautifully etched leather vest with gold trimmings. Very official, leads Felipe and Ramkus out of the Oppressive Forest after scaring off some bandits.

Rab First man to speak to Ramkus, outside the Abergrass Inn (with his friend Kerf). Wore a bucket hat, portly, drunk.

Revla Wife of Hodgerise. Lives in a shepherds hut, travelling from Refton to Kerwood with crazed old woman.

Sigilund (Sigil) Petite girl who Ramkus and Felipe had a "bard off" with at the Rose Hotel in Refton. Blue velvet blouse vest white blouse, blue velvet trousers, blue cap, sharp features, blonde curls down to shoulders. Plays the lute, blue eyes. From the Isles of Montreyer.

Silque Slippery advisor to the King of the Empire - Ronato family – or rather a "wormtongue" of sorts. Skinny, malevolent, conniving.

Solento Blonde-haired stranger Ramkus spoke with at Kerwood Inn. Was of a high rank, commanding an outpost in the Sunden Montain Range, before disobeying orders and fleeing. Fell for a forest dweller.

Sophia Princess of the Ronato family. Fairly tall, slim and fit, light blonde hair, grey blue eyes, falls for Ramkus.

Tilda Daughter of Yazin the doctor along the coast.

Tomriel Smith from Potelo who removes Ramkus's bracelets. Decent stout mountain folk, smokes a pipe, older, red-greying, bearded, stocky man. Teacher of other smiths.

A Master Gem Cutter

Yazin Physician/doctor found on the coast, out from Kerwood. Father of Tilda.

Peoples/Groups

Burbar Regiment   Extreme barbaric regiment of the Empire.

Empire   The Empire that inhabited Elantra, making its people succumb to the Empires will and way. Bandits forced into the wider, more desolate world to survive. Currency in use – Empirical crowns (not referred to).

Kings Guard   Soldiers of high rank that answer to the Empirical King (manner in which Empire has King's overseeing the territory rather than a true empire).

Nelve Kingdom   Mentioned on the path for Sigilund to Eredin at the currency house. Currency in use - Relks.

Ronato Family   One of the royal Empirical families. Residing in the Summer Castle at times in Elantra.

Sarchel Kingdom   Where the city of Lellel is, and Baron VonWilton resides, tavern that Sigilund and Ramkus fled. Currency in use – Colleques

Verselion Kingdom   Currency house's overarching kingdom. Currency in use – Plaques

Places

Abergrass Inn   Inn at Abergrass

Kerwood Inn   Inn at Kerwood. Serve Fish broth, has baths.

Sea Soldiers Spit   Rowdy soldier saloon in Refton

Summer Palace	Summer palace of the Ronato family in Elantra. Found outside Refton and a number of Convilles. Runs beside a mighty river, near the sea. Situated on top of an ancient first people (sea and forest hybrids) home.
The Rose Hotel	Picturesque hotel in Refton where Ramkus and Felipe performed. Has roses around its outside balcony.
Seat of the Guardians	Ramkus's destination, where the Guardians assemble and call home – as far as he considers.
The Waylayers Arms	Major pub in Lellel where Ramkus stayed and met Sigil for the second time. Fleeing after a major altercation where the place became an arena.

Miscellaneous (Songs, gods, animals, fictitious characters etc.)

Covered Assailant/ Hooded Stranger	An assailant, covered up, attacking Ramkus when resting at the rock shelter on the way from Kerwood to Refton. Also seen at the Kerwood Inn.
The Beast	A giant of a being, four times the size of a normal man, leader and source of the malevolent forces that sought to wipe the four peoples of the land in ancient times. Fought Lirem.
Bessy the Cow	Cow used as part of a ploy to thieve unsuspecting travelers along the road from Kerwood.
Conville	Convenient Village, placed outside other villages by the Empire as spy stations. Sell overpriced items.

Eredin Bard Festival	Bard Festival held in Eredin, Reelo Kingdom. Holds the Eredin Bard Competition which Felipe was a finalist five times, winning twice.
Elissandra	Mentioned in song with her lover Keilorudder.
Empirical Bracelets/Band	Bracelets attached to the wrists of people of stature (right for man, left for woman), and/or marriage (left for man, right for woman). Adorned with jewels or etchings to signify position, allegiance, etc. Burnt onto the skin via a special ceremony, almost impossible to get off unscathed.
The Great Map	A great map of the world that is displayed in the Guardian Seat's grate hall.
Keilorudder	Mentioned in song by Felipe, with his lover Elissandra.
Kursa	Mentioned as a Guardian Champion by Lento.
Lawns of Beaqueathment	Lawns below Summer Palace where Djuayne fought Ramkus. Bequeathed by the people who fought for them.
Lirem	Ancient legendary figure in Elantra who was the Defender of the people, Protector of the land.
Lirem's Hundred Tails	Lirem's hundred warriors that fought with him against the armies of the Beast. Twenty-five of each forest dwellers, mountain folk, desert people, coast people.
Old Man (Pilgrim)	Old man who had an air about him, watched Ramkus fight the covered assailant on the way from Kerwood to Refton.
Perillo Bugs	Delicate crayfish, a delicacy.

Procto   Great hero of the Empire whom there is a celebration for each year.